Etherya's Earth Volume 2

Books 4-6

By

REBECCA HEFNER

Contents

The Reluctant Savior
Copyright
Dedication
Map of Etherya's Earth
Prologue
Chapter 1
Chapter 2
Chapter 3
Chapter 4
Chapter 5
Chapter 6
Chapter 7
Chapter 8
Chapter 9
Chapter 10
Chapter 11
Chapter 12
Chapter 13
Chapter 14
Chapter 15
Chapter 16
Chapter 17
Chapter 18
Chapter 19
Chapter 20
Chapter 21
Chapter 22
Chapter 23
Chapter 24
Chapter 25
Chapter 26
Chapter 27
Chapter 28
Chapter 29
Chapter 30
Chapter 31
Epilogue
Acknowledgments

The Impassioned Choice
Copyright
Dedication
Prologue
Chapter 1
Chapter 2
Chapter 3
Chapter 4
Chapter 5
Chapter 6
Chapter 7
Chapter 8
Chapter 9
Chapter 10
Chapter 11
Chapter 12
Chapter 13
Chapter 14
Chapter 15
Chapter 16
Chapter 17
Chapter 18
Chapter 19
Chapter 20
Chapter 21
Chapter 22
Chapter 23
Chapter 24
Chapter 25
Chapter 26
Chapter 27
Chapter 28
Chapter 29
Chapter 30
Chapter 31
Chapter 32
Chapter 33
Chapter 34
Chapter 35
Chapter 36
Chapter 37
Chapter 38
Chapter 39
Epilogue
Acknowledgments

The Cryptic Prophecy
Copyright
Dedication
Map of Etherya's Earth
Chapter 1
Chapter 2
Chapter 3
Chapter 4
Chapter 5
Chapter 6
Chapter 7
Chapter 8
Chapter 9
Chapter 10
Chapter 11
Chapter 12
Chapter 13
Chapter 14
Chapter 15
Chapter 16
Chapter 17
Chapter 18
Chapter 19
Chapter 20
Chapter 21
Chapter 22
Chapter 23
Chapter 24
Chapter 25
Chapter 26
Chapter 27
Chapter 28
Chapter 29
Chapter 30
Chapter 31
Chapter 32
Chapter 33
Chapter 34
Epilogue
Bonus Scene
Acknowledgments
About the Author

This book is a work of fiction. Names, characters, places and incidents are the product of the author's imagination and are used fictitiously. Any resemblance to actual events, locales or persons, living or dead, is coincidental.

Copyright © 2019 by Rebecca Hefner. All rights reserved, including the right to reproduce, distribute or transmit in any form or by any means.

Cover Design: CDG Cover Designs, CDGCoverdesigns.com
Editor: Megan McKeever, NY Book Editors
Proofreader: Bryony Leah

Chapter 1

Evie threw back her head, laughing at whatever the man was dribbling on about. Although quite handsome and a Vampyre soldier, she was bored to tears. Immortals always seemed to do that to her: endlessly bore her out of her ever-loving mind.

There were only a few who could keep her attention. One whose attention she was trying to procure at this very moment. Surreptitiously searching the large banquet hall, she wondered if he was observing her with the hulking man. Just in case, she slid her palm over the Vampyre's broad chest, eyebrow lifting in a silent invite to ask her to dance later.

The Vampyre smiled, his fangs glowing in the soft banquet lighting. She couldn't remember his name but didn't really care. Names seemed to have meaning to everyone for some damn reason. Didn't they know the futility in that? Why the inhabitants of this awful planet thought that their lives had any significance was beyond her. What a waste of time. It would be easier if everyone realized that their existence was squalid and pointless.

Sipping her drink, she chewed the crunchy ice as her eyes darted around the room. Her brother had gotten married earlier today. The idiot was so in love with the spunky Vampyre princess that she fought not to barf in his face when he was reciting his vows.

Darkrip used to be quite evil, as she'd seen firsthand during her early years in the Deamon caves. Having their father's blood course through his veins ensured his malevolence. But he'd also had such goodness, trying to keep their father from raping and torturing her and her mother, Rina. Although he'd been unsuccessful, she appreciated his pithy efforts. Evie guessed she was happy for him. If he wanted to attach himself to one vagina for the rest of his life, good for him. Wrinkling her nose in distaste,

An Excerpt from the Forgotten Fairytale of the Soothsayers...

Once, many moons ago, when the planet was still so new, the beautiful woman sat upon the grass, inhaling the vibrant scent of nearby wildflowers. Eyes closed, her ears perked as she heard the rustling behind her. Turning her head, she saw the man step from the forest.

"Hello," she said, her voice so soft and sweet. "It is so rare that I see another. And what are you called?"

"I am Galredad," he said, his voice as deep as the nearby ocean. "I rarely see others upon this planet as well. It is quite lonely. Perhaps we could become acquainted."

"Perhaps we could." Gesturing to the grass beside her, she said, "Sit down and let's see if we can make conversation."

He sat, crossing his legs as he regarded her. "You are quite beautiful."

The woman gave a shy grin. "And you are quite handsome."

White teeth glowed from his brilliant smile. "We seem to be conversing quite well so far."

"That, we do," she said, lips fully curved as she gazed upon him. "That, we do..."

"Markdor and Calla understand that you were trying to save Rina. But yes, it is quite amazing that they were able to forgive your transgressions against them. They love their children as much as you love yours. They understand that every ounce of energy needs to be amalgamated in order to reunite the species."

Valktor nodded. "Yes. I will go to them and spend every second willing it to happen. Miranda is strong, and so are Sathan and Latimus. Although it might be futile, I still have a seed of hope, my goddess."

"As do I." Placing her hazy hands on his cheeks, she pulled him to her, giving him a soft kiss upon his brow. "Now, go."

He vanished, leaving behind the scent of his resolve to do everything in his power to restore the world beneath them to greatness. Trying not to let hopelessness choke her, Etherya contemplated the gurgling water of the fountain. Tears fell to mingle with the clear liquid.

Perhaps she cried for a small eternity; perhaps only for a moment. Once the wetness dried, she lifted her face to the galaxy above and disappeared. Keeping watch over her planet, she waited...

Gently, the goddess placed the sharp tip of the nail of her index finger over the vein pulsing in the sleeping child's neck. Closing her eyes, she extended the nail into the vein. Transferring as much of her energy as she could, she let it bleed through her finger into Evie's body. It would only make her stronger, which was desperately needed to defeat her father. Etherya knew that the Universe would be displeased with her action, since she was forbidden to help the immortals. They were supposed to live and die by their free will. But the prophecy had already been forged, and she'd lost too much to worry about upsetting the balance. The Awakening had shifted her world so severely that she wondered if it would ever piece itself back together.

Lifting her lids, she observed Evie's hair turn from raven black to her own shade of bright red. Understanding that the energy transfer was complete, she withdrew her nail. The tiny wound bled onto the babe's snowy skin but it would heal quickly enough. If only all of the sweet child's future wounds would be so small.

"I've done what I can, little Evie," she said, stroking her soft cheek.

The girl opened her eyes to stare up at Etherya with her stunning olive-green irises. It was as if her precious Valktor was looking into her soul. Inhaling a huge breath, Evie began to wail. Knowing that she must go, Etherya blew one last kiss to the crying baby.

Dematerializing, the goddess transported to the Passage. A beautiful fountain sat within the grounds, water flowing under the gorgeous blue sky. The stone structure was adorned with angels and demons, monsters and sirens, plumes of water shooting from the eerie creatures' mouths to rest in the pool below. Valktor stood by the fountain, watching the liquid circulate in its endless pattern. Floating over to his side, Etherya regarded the once-magnificent Slayer king.

"It is done."

Valktor's emerald eyes darted over her face. "And you feel that she will be the one?"

"It is unclear," Etherya said, gazing down at the translucent water. "But she has the power to kill him. Only time will tell."

"Thank you," Valktor said, his eyes welling with tears. "I'm sorry that it has come to this. It's all my fault."

"No," she said, her voice sounding so faraway. "It is mine. But that is a story I long-ago stopped sharing. Go sit with Markdor and Calla and continue to send your energy to the Earth. Your children are all so important if we are ever going to see peace again. It is imperative that you keep willing it to happen."

"We will. I'm so thankful for their forgiveness. Now that they are in the Passage, they could choose to hate me for eternity. It is a magnificent gift that I don't deserve."

Prologue

Several years after the Awakening...

The goddess Etherya materialized into the dark lair of the cave. In the murky light, she saw the child. Small and pale, the newborn baby slept upon the dirt-covered blanket. Rina had borne her in this lair, where she slept when the Dark Lord wasn't torturing her. Knowing that he was doing that right now, Etherya's broken heart beat in her airy body.

Darkrip would be with them, his father forcing him to watch the savage cruelty inflicted upon his mother. Crimeous had grown so strong. Although she wanted to save her precious children, she could not. But she would do her best to ensure that the Dark Lord would perish one day. Many centuries from now, the babe that slept before her would possess the power to end him.

Etherya sighed as she contemplated the tiny girl. A battle already raged within her. Although she was barely three weeks old, the goddess felt the struggle. She was much more evil than Darkrip and therefore extremely powerful. Crimeous's paramountcy had grown exponentially in the years since Rina had birthed Darkrip, and every extra shred of malignity was embedded in their daughter. Although Etherya could see much, Evie's future was unclear. Many centuries from now, she would be faced with a choice. Terrified, the goddess prayed to the Universe that she would choose righteousness over malevolence.

It had to be her, since her powers were so substantial. Sadly, no one else had the prepotency to kill Crimeous. Of course, Evie wouldn't realize this for many decades. Her early life would be filled with so much pain. It would be agonizing and demoralizing. Hurting for her, Etherya ran her cloudy hand over the baby's dark hair.

"I'm so sorry, my darling girl," she said, her tone filled with sadness. "Please, remember that I love you with all I am inside."

The Reluctant Savior

Etherya's Earth, Book 4

By

REBECCA HEFNER

*For those of us who are a bit broken inside...
Who learned how to build walls and soldier on...
May you one day find your Kenden, whomever he, she or they might be.*

she reminded herself of her vow to never settle down. How positively uninteresting.

Not to mention that she didn't really buy into the whole "kids and family" reverie these immortals seemed to be increasingly employing. Her half-sister Miranda was head-over-heels for the Vampyre king, the warrior Latimus had turned into a lovesick sap over his bonded mate Lila, and now, her brother was in love too. Good grief. They'd all gone mad.

Evie loved adventure. Living in the human world for the last eight centuries had afforded her lots of that. Along with handsome men, great sex, luscious wine and beautiful excursions. Why anyone would want to tie themselves to another person for eternity was beyond her.

Oh, and then there was the little tidbit that any children she spawned would have her father's villainous blood. No, thanks. She had enough shit to deal with, controlling her evil half, already. Bringing another progeny into the world would be extremely foolish.

Narrowing her lids, she regarded Arderin as she danced with her brother atop the wooden dance floor. Lord, he was terrible. Thank god the spirited beauty was leading him. Her abdomen was slightly distended in her gorgeous white gown, causing Evie to shake her head. Darkrip was a fool to procreate with her. But it was his life, so she let him be. Hopefully, the little brat wouldn't be as depraved as their father. Only time would tell.

"Did you scare Draylok away?" a baritone voice asked behind her.

Hating the shiver that ran down her spine, Evie turned to gaze upon the man she'd previously been searching for. "Was that his name? I couldn't remember. I was too busy admiring his other...attributes."

Coming to stand beside her, Kenden arched a russet-colored eyebrow. "He's known to be quite a catch. Not only is he one of our best soldiers but he's single and looking to settle down."

Evie scrunched her features. "Thanks for the warning. I'll make sure to avoid him at all costs."

His velvet laugh surrounded her. "Yes, we wouldn't want you to get emotionally involved with anyone you seduce."

"Oh, Kenden," she said, turning to face him fully. "You think you have me pegged. It's so ridiculously unbecoming. Perhaps that's why you never get laid. I think you need a nice woman to fuck this serious streak out of you. It's quite unattractive."

She was lying through her teeth, of course, as she found the Slayer commander insanely gorgeous. There was something about his mop of chestnut-brown hair, angular features and blazing white teeth between his full lips. And those eyes. They seemed to melt like milk chocolate left on a hot stove. More often than not, she found herself drowning in them.

Determined to keep the upper hand, she licked her lips, slowly and seductively.

"If you want a fuck-buddy, just ask me. I'll come looking for you once I'm done with the Vampyre soldier."

Those striking eyes narrowed. "That's the difference between you and me, Evie. I don't do fuck-buddies. I believe in monogamy and relationships and *feelings*. You use seduction as a weapon. It's off-putting and extremely unattractive to me. So, I guess we're both repulsed by each other."

"I guess so," she snapped, breaking her gaze from his to stare at the dance floor. Sipping her drink, she contemplated his lie. He was fiercely attracted to her—this, she knew to be true. As the daughter of the Dark Lord, she could read images in others' minds. Kenden had so many images of fucking her that he could probably start his own porn site.

She had no idea why he fought his desire to sleep with her, knowing that he wanted it so badly. It seemed futile to her. They obviously would do the deed one day. Two people who possessed so much pulsing energy between them were bound to. She'd learned this over her many centuries of seducing men.

Never had she had to work so hard to get a man in her bed. It infuriated the hell out of her. What a cruel joke the Universe played on her, instilling such intense yearning for a man who was determined to fight his attraction to her so vehemently.

But Evie was nothing if not resilient and she loved a challenge. She would have him in her bed and inside her deepest place one day soon. Getting the upper hand on men had become an obsession of hers. It somehow allowed her to process and move on from all the grief and pain from the rapes and violations in her youth.

The arrogant and handsome Slayer commander had another thing coming if he continued to delude himself. Determination and will were her greatest strengths.

Gathering her wits and giving him her most glorious smile, she said, "Well, now that we've established our revulsion of each other, do you want to dance?"

White teeth gleamed as his full lips curved. Chuckling, he took the drink from her hand and set it on the nearby table. Clutching her hand in his firm grip, he said, "Why not?"

With his muscular frame, he led her to the dance floor.

Kenden pulled Evie close, loving how perfectly her lithe body molded into his. Her slender, five-foot, six-inch frame fit to him like an expertly-crafted puzzle piece. Inhaling, he smelled the fruity scent of her flame-red hair. Feeling himself grow hard in his suit pants, he spun her away from him. Pulling her back in, she gave him a blazing smile. Goddamnit, she was absolutely gorgeous.

"How did you become such a good dancer?" Olive-green eyes sparkled with mischief and desire as she looked up at him.

He shrugged. "I was an aristocrat before I was a soldier. We used to have lavish parties before your mother was taken. Dancing was required learning for me."

"Hmmm..." she said, arching a perfectly-plucked brow. "Makes me wonder if your moves are as good *off* the dance floor."

Chuckling, he shook his head. "Guess you'll never know, since we've decided we repulse each other."

Those magnificent almond-shaped eyes narrowed. "We'll see."

Holding her close, he swayed with her to the human pop song. After a moment, he said, "I'm not interested, Evie. I need to be clear about that."

The heat of anger flashed through her thin frame. "The images in your mind would suggest otherwise."

"I have a lot of images in my mind. Very few of which I act upon."

"How absolutely boring," she said, perplexion in her gaze. "Don't you enjoy getting laid?"

His irises darted back and forth between hers. "I'm ready to settle down. I want a wife that I can build a home with and lots of children. You've been very clear that you don't want any of that. That you'll return to the human world after you fully commit to fighting your father and hopefully fulfill the prophecy. We don't want the same things, and I'm not willing to waste my time."

"Good god," she said, rolling her eyes. "All of you are completely insane. Whatever happened to having a good fuck and moving on? I don't know what the hell is in the water over here, but it's utterly annoying."

Kenden couldn't stop the smile that spread across his face. "Sorry to disappoint. I'm a serial monogamist. I only sleep with women that I'm in a serious relationship with."

Disbelief marred her expression. "What about when you were young? Surely, then—?"

"I've slept with nine women in my life, Evie. That's it. I'm not nearly as experienced as you. All of them were like-minded women whom I dated for no less than a decade. Some of them for several decades. As the commander, I was never able to settle down, so they eventually married and started families, but I assure you that once we defeat your father, I'm ready. The next woman I sleep with will be my wife."

Her scarlet eyebrow arched, making her look so sexy. "Is that a challenge?"

"It's just a fact. I'm not a bullshitter, Evie. You know that by now. I don't want there to be any doubt as to where I stand."

"Oh, fine," she said, scrunching her features. The faint freckles across her nose moved under the pale light. He'd always thought them so appealing. "Go on and be a damn monk for all I care." The song ended, and she stepped back. "I'm going to find the Vampyre and get laid. Some of us actually like sex." Lifting her chin, she pivoted and stalked away from him.

Kenden couldn't stop his chuckle. Man, she was something else. He wondered if he'd ever been as attracted to a woman as he was to Evie. Contemplating, he realized that was unlikely. But attraction didn't mean love or caring—this, he knew to be true. Evie was a master of seduction and used sex to manipulate men for power and control. Vowing to never succumb to her charms, he crossed the dance floor to speak to his cousin.

"Hey," he said, approaching Miranda where she stood against the wall of the ballroom. "I think I'm heading out. I want to get back to Uteria since I have to train the troops early in the morning."

Miranda regarded him, mischief swimming in her olive-green irises. "Looked like you were having fun dancing with Evie."

Kenden rolled his eyes. "Enough with the matchmaking. It's not happening. I told you that." Leaning down, he gave her a peck on the cheek. "See you in a few days."

"Hey," she said, grabbing his wrist as he began to walk away. "I love you. I realized recently that I don't say that to you as much anymore, and I need you to know. You were there for me before I had Sathan or Tordor or anyone. You'll always be such an important person in my life, Ken. I just need you to know that."

Love for his amazing cousin coursed through his muscular frame. They'd only had each other for so long. Thrilled for the wonderful life she'd built, he pulled her into his embrace.

"I love you too," he said, kissing the top of her silky hair. "You're my person, Miranda. You always will be, even though you leave me all the time to hang at this pretentious Vampyre compound."

Clutching her arms around his waist, she chuckled at his teasing. "You're my person too. But one day soon, you're going to find a new person. A woman who can challenge you and love you as much as Sathan loves me. And I'm betting with everything I have that it might just be Evie."

Laughing, he pulled back and regarded her. "If this queen thing doesn't work out, I think you need to open a courting service. You're relentless."

"Yep," she said, biting her bottom lip as her emerald irises swam with gaiety. "I'm pretty awesome at it. Just ask Latimus and Lila."

"You're awesome at anything you set your mind to. We all know that." Giving her one last soft kiss on the forehead, he squeezed her hand. "See ya later."

Heart full, Kenden walked through the darkened hallway of the castle, through the barracks warehouse and out to the train platform. Walking down the concrete stairs, he boarded the train. During the thirty-minute ride, he reflected on the night. The ceremony had been beautiful, and he was very happy for Arderin and Darkrip.

Once at Uteria, he climbed in the four-wheeler that he'd parked there earlier in the day. Hopping in, he reveled in the wind whipping his hair as he drove through the warm night under the bright moonlight. Pulling up to his four-bedroom home, he cut the vehicle's engine and trodded up the porch steps. Locking the large front door behind him, he headed upstairs to his bedroom.

He'd built the home recently, anticipating that he would settle down soon, once the army of immortals defeated Crimeous. Wanting lots of kids, he'd built four bedrooms, knowing he could expand down the road if needed. Turning on the bedside lamp, he removed his suit and set about brushing his teeth.

Naked, he slid under the soft covers, pulling them up to cover his chest. Staring at the ceiling, he couldn't stop the image of Evie's face from blazing across his mind. His feelings for her were rather complicated, and it frustrated him that she could read his inner musings. Consumed with a deep well of compassion for her, he understood that she'd been raped and tortured by her father as a child. No matter how complex his opinion of her, he firmly believed that no child should ever have to suffer such trauma.

The fact that she'd returned to the immortal world gave him hope. She insisted that she would enlist in battle with the immortal army if she could identify something she deemed worthy of her effort. Kenden admired her gumption and knew that, if they could convince her to fight, she would be a powerful ally indeed.

If they lived in another world, where they wanted the same things and had visions of similar futures, he would be honored to court her. She had Rina's blood in spades although she always tried to deny it. Evie had so many of the qualities that he admired in a woman: intelligence, humor, confidence, frankness and, of course, her undeniable beauty. For one moment, he let himself imagine the life they could build together. It would be filled with passion and desire, frustration and compromise.

She wasn't an easy person, but that suited Kenden just fine. He loved nothing more than a challenge and building a life with the fiery redhead would certainly present one. But he also wanted children, which she professed to never consider. It was too bad, really, since he wanted it all: the messy meals, playing with the tots in the meadow outside his home, the school productions and talent shows. Kenden had always craved those things and was smart enough to realize that he would never have them with Evie. Shelving his attraction to her, he forced himself to push her from his thoughts.

Reaching over, he clicked off the light. There, in the darkness, he lay in the home he'd built for his future family, knowing that one day it would come to fruition.

Closing his eyes, he smiled in contentment.

As he drifted off to sleep, he could've sworn that he was enveloped in the fragrant scent of Evie's shampoo. Giving in to the notion of holding her, he fell into his dreams.

"So," the woman said in her lilting voice, "How did you come to be on this planet? I was so sure I knew of all the creatures the Universe instilled here."

The man absently picked at the flowers beside him with his long, tapered fingers. "I was born in the Elven world, not too far distant when one walks through the ether."

"How lovely," she said, giving him a wistful smile. "Is it a beautiful place?"

"More beautiful than anything I've ever seen," he said, his expression becoming one of longing.

"Oh, please, do tell me about it. I love hearing of far-off lands."

"Well," he said, grinning, "where do I begin? There are so many stories to tell…"

Chapter 2

When the faint light of dawn slid through the curtains of her cabin, Evie awoke. Stretching, she yawned and ran her legs over the soft sheets. Recalling the previous evening, she scrunched her face. She'd been set to bone the Vampyre and wake up in his bed. That is, until she'd danced with Kenden, alleviating the desire to have any man's hands on her but his. Bastard.

Sighing, she lifted from the bed to get ready for the day. Once dressed in her expensive, tailored, forest-green khakis with silky drawstrings at the ankles, a white V-neck sweater and Valentino Garavani sandals, she headed to the main castle to find Miranda.

Evie absolutely loved luxurious and high-priced clothing. Not only was it a powerful tool in seducing men, but she wore it like a suit of armor. Men were visual creatures, easily led by a confident and well-dressed woman. They were quite content to focus on her beauty and glamour. Her attire was a potent armament that ensured men wouldn't think to look deeper inside, at the girl who had been tortured and defiled so many centuries ago. No, that girl was long-dead, and she'd be damned if anyone dredged her up. Ever.

She decided to walk to the castle instead of dematerializing. It was a warm morning with a soft breeze, as most were on Etherya's Earth. The immortal world exhibited a temperate climate with few rainy days. While some might thrive in that environment, Evie sometimes missed the unpredictability of the weather in the human world.

Feeling her lips curve, she reminisced about the large beads of rain that would fall during the powerful afternoon thunderstorms under the darkened clouds in Western North Carolina. The drops always reminded her of tears being cast down to Earth by an angry god screaming in the sky, with claps of thunder and bolts of lightning.

She also missed the snow. There was a wholesome purity in the white powder that reminded her that things could be clean and pristine. A welcome acknowledgement that the dark part inside her detested but still somehow craved. Skiing in the mountains of Japan and Colorado had been one of her favorite pastimes.

And, oh, how she had loved the hot, humid nights along the Amalfi Coast of Italy. The breeze of the immortal world always swept away what little humidity existed. Although many detested the sticky air, Evie always loved the sheen of sweat that formed on her skin as she sat under the stars in the dense blanket of heat.

They all called to her, these comforts of the place she'd built her life in for so many centuries. She wouldn't go so far as to call the human world "home," for she'd never really had one of those, but it certainly was the closest she'd ever come to one. Longing for the familiar enveloped her as she trudged along the open meadow.

As her sandals crunched the grass, she noticed Kenden's pretty house off in the distance. It was only about a five-minute walk from her cabin, and she found herself wondering if he was training the troops. He'd been extremely focused on preparing them to fight her father, and she admired his tenacity. Score another one for Mr. Perfect.

With an inward eye-roll, she continued to the castle near Uteria's town square. Nodding hello to Sadie as she passed her in the foyer, Evie headed to her sister's royal office chamber. The door was slightly ajar, and Evie could see her sitting in the high, leather-backed chair behind the mahogany desk, feeding Tordor from her breast.

"You're here early," Evie said, pushing the door open and approaching the desk.

"Yup," Miranda said, gesturing for Evie to sit in one of the chairs across from her. "Sathan is training with Latimus and the troops at Astaria today, so I figured I'd come home early and get started on some paperwork. My favorite."

Evie chuckled, knowing Miranda detested the administrative portion of the queen's duties. "So, Sathan will be fighting with the soldiers?"

Miranda nodded, her expression filled with vague worry and frustration. "I've tried to talk him out of it, but he's determined. And although everyone says I'm stubborn as hell, my caveman husband is about as pliant as a rock when he's made up his mind."

Studying her, Evie shook her foot atop her crossed legs. It was an absent habit that she employed when she was contemplating. "Will you be fighting as well?"

Exhaling a breath, she shook her head. "Sathan and I discussed it and we need to make sure one of us holds down the fort. I wish I could though. I want to beat the shit out of that maniac. If not for what he did to Lila, then for what he did to our first child." Gently, she feathered her fingers over Tordor's soft black hair. "Isn't that right, little man? We're gonna kick that bastard's ass for hurting our family."

Something akin to guilt speared through Evie and she brushed it away. "I was as responsible as my father. You should hate me as well."

Inhaling a breath, Miranda's green eyes bore into her. Good god. It was if her mother was staring her down. "As we've discussed, although your actions spurred the battle earlier than we anticipated, I blame your father for our baby's death."

Evie gazed at her, struggling to tamp down the self-loathing that always reared its head when she thought of the child who had perished. "I don't deserve your forgiveness."

Her sister's expression softened a bit, filled with the compassion that she possessed so much of, and that Evie rarely merited.

"You know, you're going to have to try harder to convince me you're a bad person, Evie," Miranda said. "You claim to be so evil but you're one of the most candid and straightforward people I've ever met. Not really qualities that wicked people possess."

Evie arched a brow. "Then, I'll make a more fervent attempt. Because I'm a conniving bitch."

Throwing back her head, Miranda laughed. One of the loud, throaty laughs she was known for. "We'll see. Regardless, I know you would've acted differently if you'd known I was pregnant."

Tordor chose that moment to detach from his mother's breast and spit up all over her chest.

"Well, shit," Miranda said, wiping the gunk off with the towel that sat draped across her shoulder. "Just when I think having kids is awesome, the bugger pukes all over me." Pulling up her shirt to cover her breast, she began to burp her son. Hitting one of the buttons on the phone that sat on her desk, she said, "Dahlia? I'm ready for you to come get Tordor."

"Sure thing," the nanny's voice chimed over the intercom.

The sweet girl came into the room and swooped up the child, cooing to him as she departed.

"She's good with him," Evie said of the straw-blond caretaker. "But very young."

"Yes," Miranda said, standing to stretch. "Aron knows her family and trusts her immensely. She's twenty and hasn't gone through her change yet."

"When did you go through your change?" Evie asked, annoyed that she was curious. She was coming to like her sister very much. It made it hard to keep the distance that she so often imposed on people.

"When I was twenty-six. You?"

"Twenty-eight," Evie said. "At least, I think so. The years all ran together in the caves."

Sympathy permeated her sister's expression, causing Evie to straighten her spine. She didn't have time for emotion. How absolutely illogical.

"I've come to inform you that I've discerned something I want badly enough to fight with you all. I would like to meet with you, Sathan and Kenden to discuss it."

"Okay," Miranda said with a nod. Lowering into the chair, she rested her forearms on the desk. "If it's within our power, we'll do it. We need you, Evie."

"I know," she said, hating how her heart quickened at the words. "It's a strange feeling, since no one really ever has."

"I'm so sorry," she said, slowly shaking her head. "My father was cold to me but he still loved me and did the best he could. You deserved better. I promise, now that I've found you, we're family for life. I'm never letting you believe you don't deserve to be loved, sis."

"Sweet but unwarranted. Nevertheless, let's see how you feel after I name my price. I have a suspicion you might think otherwise, but who knows?"

Miranda grinned. "We'll see. On another note, how are your sessions going with Darkrip?"

"Good," Evie said with a tilt of her head. "He's picking up on the human dark magic very quickly. Although I haven't committed to fighting my father yet, I don't mind helping Darkrip learn. Wielding black magic is quite enjoyable and it's nice to have a reason to use it again."

"Thank you," she said, her gaze full of determination. "I appreciate you dedicating the time to train our brother. I've become close with him and I hope that you and I can do the same. I want to get to know you, Evie."

How could one possess such genuineness? Evie had no idea. Her sister was a damn saint. Rina must've passed all those genes on to her and Darkrip, leaving none behind for Evie's wasted entrance into this pissant excuse for a world.

"We all want a lot of things, but they rarely happen." Standing, Evie narrowed her eyes. "When can I expect to meet with the three of you?"

"Tomorrow at lunch should be good, here in my office. If that doesn't work, I'll text you, but I think it should be fine for Ken and Sathan. Thanks for coming to a decision. We're excited that you're part of our team."

With a caustic glare, Evie pivoted. "For now," she said, strolling from the room and closing the door behind her, the sound a soft, ominous click.

Aron smiled and lowered the hand that had been lifted in a wave goodbye to the nice Vampyre couple. The newly married pair—or *bonded*, he should say, since that was what Vampyres called it—were lovely. Content, he began to put away the folding chairs.

Today, he'd held an orientation for the fifty Vampyres that were moving to Uteria next week. As Miranda and Sathan continued to unite the species, it was imperative that members of both tribes inhabited all six of the immortal compounds.

Aron had volunteered to orient the new Uterians during the last combined council meeting. Descended from one of the oldest bloodlines of Slayer aristocrats, his ancestors had lived long before the Awakening. He considered it his duty to bring peace to Etherya's children and was honored to help in some small way.

If he was honest, it also allowed him to support Miranda. Their queen was a magnificent ruler. Strong, steadfast and immensely intelligent.

Oh, and there was one more thing. Aron was completely, mindlessly in love with her.

Sighing, he continued to fold and stack the chairs. The meeting had been held in the ballroom of Uteria's main castle, and he took his time restocking the chairs in the wide closet near the entrance. Once finished, he headed out of the compound's large mahogany doors into the mid-afternoon sunlight.

The sounds of Uteria's main square whizzed by him as he walked. Dogs barked, children squealed as they played, birds cawed as they flew above. The place he'd always called home was buzzing with its always-present energy, causing his lips to curve into a grin as he walked.

Finally, he arrived at the gallery and entered. Moira was standing to the left, showing a painting that sat affixed to the wall to one of their regular patrons. Knowing Moira, the man wouldn't leave without the canvas boxed and paid for. She was a phenomenal salesperson, and Aron was thrilled that she seemed to thrive at the gallery.

Heading to stand behind the sales counter, he absently leafed through the mail as he heard her answering questions in the otherwise quiet gallery. Although she had no knowledge of fine art before her stint at the store, she'd learned quickly. Impressed by her ability to retain such dense and intricate information, he listened.

"Absolutely, sir," she said confidently. "It reminds me of a Dali as well. I know he's your favorite surrealist. Unfortunately, I can only offer you a ten-percent discount, good through close of business today. We have an event this weekend, and I'm sure it will sell at full price once our patrons see how exquisite it is."

The man's features drew together. "I'll only purchase today for a twenty-percent discount, Moira. We discussed this."

"That was before we received an additional thirty RSVP's for this weekend's engagement. I never consented to twenty-percent, although I do appreciate the effort, sir."

"Stop calling me 'sir,'" he said, giving her a light-hearted glare. "You make me feel like a washed-up old snob." Eyes narrowed, teeming with deliberation, he studied her. "Ten percent and dinner with me at Maltese's," he said, referencing the fancy Italian restaurant that adorned Uteria's town square.

Out of the corner of his eye, Aron saw Moira's sly grin. It wasn't the first time a customer had tried to negotiate a date with her. To his knowledge, she'd never accepted.

"I'm flattered, Tobias," she said, "but it's ten-percent flat today. Or I'll sell it on Saturday so fast you won't remember it was here."

Tobias shook his head, his tawny brown hair staying perfectly in place, coiffed like a proper aristocrat. "Fine. But can you at least personally deliver it? I'd love your opinion as to where to hang it at my home."

"Sadly, no. It's against our insurance policy for me to touch a painting once it's left the store. If it sustains damage, I can't prove that I didn't cause it. It's too much of a risk. Let me get this boxed up for you. Aron can ring you up," she said, jerking her head toward the front counter. "Excuse me."

Lifting her thin arms, she proceeded to grasp the piece and abscond with it to the back warehouse.

"Your girl is wily, Aron," Tobias said, approaching him at the counter. "Sometimes, I think you just hired her to swindle me out of my money."

Aron breathed a laugh. "That, she is, although she's anything but my girl. In my mind, she'll always belong to Diabolos. May the goddess have peace on his soul."

Tobias arched a chestnut brow. "Still loyal to Etherya after all these centuries? I thought you'd long given up on that."

"I'm loyal to many things that I think are just and true. That's why it was so easy for me to support Miranda becoming queen. The blood of Valktor runs strong through her."

"That, it does," Tobias agreed.

Aron completed the transaction with his old friend, and they chatted as Moira boxed the painting in the back room. Once finished, she appeared, a broad smile dominating her pretty face.

"You're all set, sir," she said. Her tone dared him to scold her for using the formal address. "I look forward to seeing you again soon."

"As do I, my dear," he said with a nod. Clutching the artwork, he retreated from the store.

Aron couldn't stop his chuckle as Moira's azure eyes swam with elation. "Son of a bitch, that felt *amazing*." Stretching out her arms, she twirled around, head tilted back, graceful as a ballerina. Coming to a stop, she trained her gaze on him. "He still thought he could get twenty percent out of me. Some people never learn."

"You're ruthless, Moira," Aron said, winking at her. "Hiring you was the best thing Preston and I ever did."

Red splotches appeared on her cheeks, showing her embarrassment at his compliment. Blond hair fell in a wave from behind her neck and shoulders as she contemplated him. "You know, Preston didn't want to hire me at all. He thought a laborer's daughter would be too stupid to understand fine art. I only have this position because of you. I'm so thankful you stood up for me."

"Of course, I stood up for you, angel," he said, employing the nickname he'd called her since childhood. "You're the wife of my best friend. It's my duty to protect you and look out for you. It's an honor that I take very seriously."

Ocean-blue irises darted between his own as she regarded him in silence.

"What?" he asked.

"Nothing," she said, dismissively waving her hand. "It's just...Diabolos has been in the Passage for seven centuries. I know it's hard for you to acknowledge that sometimes, since you two were so close, but he's gone, Aron. I'm not his wife anymore. I'm not anyone's wife."

"I know," he said, the ache of his friend's passing gnawing his gut as it usually did. "I just miss him. He was a good man. I want to do right by him and by you."

Those huge doe eyes brimmed with emotions he couldn't decipher. Chalking it up to her grief over losing Diabolos, he tried to lighten the moment. "That was a good one about the insurance policy. Did you make that up on the fly?"

"You bet your ass I did," she said, lifting a brow. "Tobias is sweet, but I'm not in the market for a husband. I find that I like my independence just fine."

"That's good to hear. But one day, you'll want to have children, no?"

Laying her pale hand on the counter, she looked to the ceiling. "I'm not sure. Maybe. It's not something I've spent a lot of time thinking about."

"Well, if and when you do decide to marry again, he'll be a lucky man. You're one in a million, Moira."

"Thanks," she said, her tone soft and sweet. "You've always been so kind and supportive of me. All those centuries ago, when Diabolos proposed to me and his parents threatened to disown him, you came to my defense. They only reconsidered because of you."

Aron thought back to those days, so long ago. Moira was the daughter of his family's housekeeper, Celia. Widowed when her soldier husband was killed in the War of the Species, Celia and Moira had moved into Aron's family's large estate. Being one of the oldest aristocratic dynasties, Moira used to tease him that his house was bigger than Uteria's castle. She hadn't been far off. The home was massive.

Diabolos and his wealthy family were Aron's neighbors. Less than a year apart in age, the three of them used to play as children in the grassy meadows that surrounded their homes. His friend would always watch Moira with an intense gleam in his eye and profess his desire to own her one day. Aron had always thought that quite strange, as one couldn't own another person, but he figured that his friend just meant to marry Moira when they grew into adulthood.

As she evolved into womanhood, Moira matured into her beauty. Aron spent many wistful nights as a young man imagining his hands upon her soft, pale skin. But he was a polite man, perhaps too much so, and Diabolos had always been so ardent in his pursuit of her. As soon as she went through her immortal change in her mid-twenties, he'd asked for her hand in marriage.

Aron could still remember the burn, deep inside his chest, when he'd learned of their engagement. Knowing that he'd never caress her silky skin, he'd wished them well, sincere in his desire for their happiness. He'd become quite an expert in that over the centuries—wishing women he pined for bliss with other men. It was rather unfulfilling. Perhaps, for once in his life, he could actually fall for a woman who wasn't in love with someone else. It would be a major improvement on the sad state of his romantic existence thus far. Giving himself a mental shake, he disengaged from the dreary thoughts.

"I wanted you to be happy, Moira," he said, smiling down at her. She was at least six inches shorter than his six-foot frame. "I'll always fight to make that happen. Diabolos was distraught when you disappeared. We had no idea that you thought he was abducted and murdered, nor that you fled to Restia to hide from the war. He wanted to find you so badly."

"I'll bet he did," she murmured, her nostrils flaring. "Well, I'm safe now. And truly happy for the first time in centuries. I'm so glad we reconnected."

"Me too. You're a great plus-one for all these weddings we seem to have lately. I had no idea you were such a fantastic dancer."

White teeth toyed with her bottom lip. Aron found the act quite charming. "I used to hide and watch you and Diabolos take your dance lessons. Then, I'd practice in my room at night. Guess it paid off."

"Sneaky little thing, weren't you?" he asked.

"You don't know the half of it." Running her hand through her hair, she surveyed the room. "I think Tobias was the last customer we're going to have today. Want me to close up?"

"Sure," Aron said, heading to the cash register to total it for the day. "Why don't you square everything away, and I'll walk you home?"

"You don't have to do that. My apartment's on the other side of town from your castle."

"Stop teasing me, wench," he said, winking at her again. He hoped the nickname or the gesture didn't piss her off. They had an easy rapport, and he felt so comfortable around her. "You know I'd lose my gentleman card if I didn't walk you home. Let me just tally this up."

"Okay," she said, placing her hands in the pockets of her black slacks. "Give me a few minutes to clean up in the back."

His gaze cemented to her backside as she sauntered to the warehouse, the sway of her hips mesmerizing. Mentally scolding himself, he remembered that she was his dead best friend's wife. That made her extremely off-limits. Aron was a stickler for morality and decorum and would never disrespect his friend's memory by making a pass at his wife. Shaking the image of her slim waist and curvy body from his mind, he set about balancing the day's transactions.

A few minutes later, they locked up and began an unhurried walk down the main street toward Moira's one-bedroom apartment. Aron knew the landlord and had helped her secure the lease. The man had been hesitant to rent to her, knowing that she had no assets, so Aron had secretly given him a generous security deposit on Moira's behalf. Knowing how proud she was, he didn't want her to see it as charity.

When they were children, she would always stare wistfully at the sky and tell him of her intentions to make a better life than her mother had. She was embarrassed to be the child of a servant and was determined to rise above her station. Aron had always assured her that she was his equal and capable of doing anything she set her mind to. Being born a servant didn't make one less than, just as being an aristocrat didn't make one extraordinary. He firmly believed that one must strive to the highest morals and ethics at all times. In his opinion, that was what dictated one's worth. Moira had those qualities in spades. He was intensely proud of how she'd rebuilt her life after returning to Uteria.

Arriving at the front door of her building, she turned to face him. The sun had fallen behind the far-off mountains, and her face glowed in the dim light of dusk. Tilting her head back, she licked her pink lips. Aron felt himself grow thick and hard in his expensive tailored trousers.

"Good night, angel," he said.

"Good night," she said, her lips glistening with the saliva that her tongue had lathered there. "Thanks for walking me home."

"You're welcome." Placing a brotherly kiss on the soft skin of her forehead, he rotated and walked toward the large mansion he solely inhabited. His parents had passed centuries ago, leaving the large compound to him, the solitary heir. Willing his body to relax, he inhaled deep breaths filled with the scents of impending nightfall.

A nd so he told her, the magnificent woman beside him, about the lush world of the Elves. Tall trees, with leaves of evergreen at the crest, covered expansive forests. Below the hulking redwoods and oaks, there were rolling hills dotted with flowers of every color and size.

The Elves were a simple people, building homes with nary a space between them so they could become close with their neighbors. Many raised livestock behind their small homes, cultivating the pigs and cows to be so fattened that the meat was never short of succulent.

"I can still taste the meat from my neighbor's bounty," Galredad said, closing his eyes. "I have never had food like it in centuries."

"So, you must've been here a long time."

"Yes," he said, his gaze turning sad and lowering to the ground. "I left my world behind when it was destroyed..."

Chapter 3

Kenden entered his cousin's office chamber the next day starving for lunch. A spread of sandwiches and wraps sat on the long conference table, and he thanked the gods. Grabbing a sandwich, he began adorning it with mustard and mayonnaise.

"Hey," Miranda said, entering. "Aren't you going to wait for us?"

Kenden smiled at her as Sathan entered behind her. "Sorry. I'm famished. I've been training the troops since seven a.m. Do you mind?" he asked, lifting the food in anticipation.

"It's fine," she said, coming to look over the spread. "Do you want anything?" she asked her husband.

"No food for me," Sathan said. "I've never really developed a taste for it like Arderin has. Although, since she's pregnant with a Slayer-Deamon, that might be increasing her appetite."

"How's she feeling?" Kenden asked.

"Good," Sathan said, sitting at the large table. "Her morning sickness has abated quite a bit, and she seems happy now that she's bonded with Darkrip."

"That's great," Kenden said, swallowing the large bite. "I'm really happy for them."

"Me too," Miranda said, sitting at the head of the table. "I love that Darkrip fell for my husband's sister. It's a family affair all around."

Kenden chuckled. "Yep, it's awesome." Finishing the sandwich, he deposited the paper plate and napkin in the trash. Coming to sit at Miranda's left, he asked, "Have you heard from Evie? She said noon, right?"

Miranda nodded. "She should be here soon. I wonder what her price will be for fighting with us. She says I might not like it."

"No use in speculating," Kenden said. "Evie plays it close to the vest. Guess we'll find out soon enough."

No sooner did the words leave his mouth than she breezed into the room.

"Well, hello," she said, the ever-present mischievous grin on her full lips. "I see everyone's here."

"Hey, Evie," Miranda said, gesturing to the chair beside Sathan. "Have a seat."

"Thanks, but I'll stand." Sauntering to the chair at the other end of the long table, she regarded them. With lean fingers, she clutched the top of the leather chair in front of her.

"I realize you all are busy, so I'll cut to the chase. I've finally decided on something I want badly enough to fight with you. If the request is granted and fulfilled, I will be ready to train for our cause immediately afterward. If not, I'll return to the human world. Those are my terms. Understood?"

"Yes," Miranda said. "What is it? We'll do everything we can to accommodate."

The corners of Evie's lips curved, her green eyes simmering. Strolling to the window, she fingered the thin white curtains and looked out over the meadow.

"There have been very few things I haven't been able to secure in the past eight centuries. I'm an extremely resilient and confident person and can usually manipulate those around me with ease." Turning, she regarded them.

"However, there is something that I haven't been able to procure, and I'm tired of wasting time with futile attempts. Therefore, I find myself forced to take action."

Approaching Kenden, she stood beside him, her irises searching his. "I want the Slayer commander in my bed. Three nights together, and I will consider the demand satisfied. That is my stipulation."

Kenden felt his eyebrows draw together as he gaped up at her. "Excuse me but what?"

"You heard me," she said, scowling down at him.

Surprise coursed through Kenden, compounded with flashes of anger. "You want to sleep with me? *That's* your demand?"

"Don't look so shocked," she said, waving a dismissive hand. "It's obvious we both want what I'm asking for. You're too much of a prude and a saint to act on it, so I'm forcing your hand. Three nights in your bed, and we're done. It's nothing."

Exasperated, Kenden looked at Miranda. "Am I taking crazy pills here?"

"Wow, Evie," Miranda said, her olive-green eyes wide. Kenden found himself pissed that they were also filled with amusement. "That's a very interesting request. I don't...um...well, Ken? What do you think?"

"What do I think?" he asked, incensed. Standing, he stared down at Evie. "Are you fucking insane?"

"Good grief," Evie said, rolling her eyes. "It's not as if you're a quivering virgin. We're both consenting adults here. It might be nice for you to actually get boned for once in your life."

Fury, strong and true, filled every fiber of his core. "You've got a lot of nerve, Evie. And let me tell you something about consent. It requires two people."

"Don't tell me about consent, you arrogant prick," she said through clenched teeth. "I know more about that word that you'll ever begin to fathom." Placing her hands in her pockets, she slowly began pacing around the table as she talked. "To me, this request is simple. Kenden and I both want what I'm proposing, but he's determined not to act on it. I'm simply expediting something that, in my opinion, is bound to happen."

Lifting her arms, she gently ran her hands over the smooth fabric of the leather chair that sat at the opposite end of the table from Miranda. "I imagine you all think I should be embarrassed, asking for something that you consider salacious. But I assure you," she said, her tone becoming pensive, "I lost the ability to feel embarrassment centuries ago. Perhaps the first time my father raped me. Perhaps the first time multiple Deamon soldiers held me down and did the same. Who knows?" she asked.

Gazing at the floor, she lifted her hands to rub her upper arms. Kenden thought the gesture so tragic, as if she was attempting to soothe herself from the transgressions she spoke of. Through his anger, he felt a wave of empathy. Although she was infuriating half the time, no one deserved to be violated in the way she had.

"There has to be another way, Evie," he said, ensuring his tone was calm and understanding. "This request is about control. I won't let you have it, and you want to take it from me. Let's think of something else you want. I'll do everything I can to make it happen."

Those almond-shaped eyes narrowed, her irises shooting daggers at him. "I've made my decision. It's futile to argue with me. I'll give you a week to decide. After that, I'm gone."

"This is ridiculous," he said, shaking his head. "There has to be something else—"

"No," she snapped. "I won't let you make me second-guess myself." Walking around the table, she came to stand in front of the office door. "One week. I would suggest you contemplate quickly. I find myself missing the human world." Arching her eyebrow, she made eye contact with each of them. Giving a nod, she opened the door and strolled through, closing it behind her.

Miranda blew out a breath, the air fanning the hair above her forehead. "Holy shit," she said, stunned.

"This is absurd," Kenden said, running a hand through the brown hair at his temple. "Is she for real?"

"It would seem so," Sathan said, eyeing him, his expression weary.

"Who knew you were so irresistible, Ken?" Miranda asked, mirth swimming in her eyes.

"You do *not* get to make a joke of this," he said, pointing at her. "This is not funny!"

Unable to control her laughter, she covered her mouth with her hands, shoulders quaking.

"Goddamnit, Miranda!" Kenden said, exasperated.

"Okay, okay," Sathan said, training a scolding glare on his wife. "I know it seems funny, but Ken is obviously upset." Addressing Kenden, he asked, "What can we do to help while you consider her demand?"

"I can lend you some erotic novels from my bookshelf so that you can study up," Miranda said, doubling over with laughter in her chair as she snorted.

Kenden scowled and regarded Sathan. "She does know that I'm not laughing, right?" he muttered to the Vampyre king.

"Oh, don't be such a stick in the mud," Miranda said, wiping tears from her eyes. "It's obvious you want to bone her. Just do it already. If that's all she needs to fight with us, it seems like a small ask to me."

"Well, it's not you who has to fulfill her request. This is absolutely ridiculous. I don't have time for this crap." Stalking around the table, he looked down at his cousin. "Don't tell anyone about this, you hear me?"

"Yes," Miranda said, struggling to contain her giggles, mock innocence all over her flawless face. "Although it might be hard, since you're so...*alluring*." Laughter burst from her throat as she doubled over again.

"She's exasperating when she's caught in one of these giggle-fests," Sathan said, standing to address Kenden. "Believe me, I know. I usually have to mentally restrain myself from strangling her."

"Hey!" Miranda said through her snickers.

"Let me know what you need, Ken," Sathan said, his demeanor much more serious than his wife's. "If this is something you won't contemplate, we need to know right away so we can strategize on how to tell Evie."

Sighing, Kenden rubbed his forehead with his fingers. "Let me just think for a bit. She dropped a damn bomb on me. God, she's infuriating."

Sathan lifted an eyebrow. "That, she is. Take some time but let me know what I can do. We need to move this along."

Kenden nodded. "I'm going to head back and finish up the afternoon training session. I'll be in touch." Sparing one last glare at Miranda, he stalked from the room.

As he headed to the training field, fury and indignation threatened to choke him. Who in the hell did Evie think she was, demanding something like that of him? Sex was a tool for her, used to manipulate men to her will. And she'd found a way to use it against him, even though he'd sworn she never would. If he wasn't so damn pissed, he'd actually be impressed. She'd gotten one over on him.

Kenden had always prided himself on his ability to strategize and see every angle of a situation. The fact that she'd been able to spring a surprise demand of this magnitude vexed him. He'd underestimated her. Vowing it would never happen again, he brainstormed his next move as he plodded under the afternoon sun.

Evie stalked from the royal office chamber, blood coursing through her supple frame. Nerves threatened to choke her, but she held firm. Confident that she hadn't relayed any of the insecurity she was inwardly experiencing, she headed down the stairs to Sadie's infirmary.

The Slayer physician was applying some sort of serum to her forearm. As her thin fingers massaged her scarred skin, Evie realized it must be some of the burn-healing salve that Arderin and Nolan had created for her.

"Hello, Sadie," she said softly, not wanting to startle her.

"Oh," she said, lifting her head. "I didn't see you, Evie. Can I help you with something?"

"I need you to do a physical on me," Evie said, "but I can come back."

"It's fine," Sadie said, screwing the top back on the tube of salve and setting it on the counter. "Have a seat on the table."

Evie arranged herself on the bed, the white paper crunching underneath her.

"So, why do you need a physical?" Sadie asked.

"I'm anticipating taking a new lover. Although I've always used protection in the past, I don't wish to do so with him. So, I want you to check me out, make sure I'm healthy and complete a full STD-screening panel. I also had an IUD implanted a year ago and it should be good for another four years, but I'd like you to confirm that."

"Okay," Sadie said, her eyes widening a bit. "It's refreshing to speak to someone so candid. I'll be happy to help. Let me just start a chart for you."

Evie regarded her as she pulled out a yellow folder, used a hole-puncher at the top and placed some blank papers inside.

"In the human world, physicians mostly use electronic records now."

"I know," Sadie said, giving her a shy smile. "But Nolan and I are the only physicians in this world, and we both prefer paper. I guess we're dinosaurs." Pulling a gown from the cabinet under the counter, she handed it to Evie. "Go ahead and fully disrobe, the opening of the gown in front. I'll be back in a few minutes."

The Slayer left and returned a few minutes later, after Evie had shed her clothes. Fingering the gown, her legs hanging off the table, she answered

Sadie's questions as she sat in front of her on the rolling stool. Medical history, sexual history, history of illnesses.

"Have you ever been a victim of sexual assault?" Sadie asked.

Evie couldn't control the laugh that escaped in a puff from her throat. "Yes. Repeatedly, for the first few decades of my life."

The Slayer's eyebrows drew together, her face a mask of compassion. "I'm so sorry."

Evie shrugged. "Water under the bridge. I got over it centuries ago."

Pretty hazel eyes studied her, making Evie uncomfortable. "I'm glad to hear it. Just so you know, I'm well-versed in human psychology. I would be happy to schedule a session with you if you want to talk."

Evie's lips formed a frigid smile. "Thanks, but I don't really think of those times anymore. I saw multiple psychologists and therapists when I lived in the human world. In the end, one has to get over these things on their own."

Sadie blinked a few times. "Okay. Well, just know that I'm here if you change your mind. Ken most likely put my number in your phone when he programmed it."

Evie nodded. The examination continued, Sadie performing a gynecologic exam and then drawing blood to run the various tests. Afterward, she placed the chart on the counter and faced Evie.

"You're all set. I should have the test results by Thursday morning. Nolan and I will be running a health screening in the main square on Thursday, but I'll take a break and meet you here in the infirmary to give you the results. Want to meet me here at noon on Thursday?"

"Sure," Evie said. "I don't mean to pry, but I can read images in others' minds. Is it too presumptuous of me to inform you that I see the thoughts you have about Nolan?"

The unburnt side of Sadie's face flushed. "Probably. But maybe I shouldn't squander the opportunity to pick your brain. No one's ever been attracted to me before. It's a bit scary. I don't know the first thing about sex or love or any of that stuff."

Evie gave a throaty laugh. "You don't need to, honey. Believe me, I've seen the images in his mind too. They were quite overwhelming when he was dancing with you at Darkrip's wedding. He wants to bend you over and do all sorts of scandalous things to your pretty little body. Mark my words."

Sadie bit her lip. "I'm anything but pretty, but thanks for the pep talk. You're so confident. I wish I was."

She slid from the table, holding the robe closed. "It took me a long time to become so. When I was young, I was a doormat. Useless and broken. You'll get there. I think Nolan is the perfect person to help you on your journey. He's quite handsome."

The Slayer grinned. "He is. I'm flattered that he's interested."

Evie lifted her brow. "Oh, he's more than interested, sweetheart. Trust me."

Sadie chuckled, her multicolored irises roving over Evie's face. "You're pretty cool, Evie. I think you might not want people to know it, but you are."

"Don't tell anyone. The last thing I need is more friends. Miranda already wants to inscribe matching BFF tattoos on our foreheads."

"Well, Miranda's awesome too, and when she's determined, she usually accomplishes her goal."

"Yes," Evie said, "it's quite irritating. Are we done here?"

"Yup," Sadie said with a nod. "I'll let you get dressed and I'll see you here on Thursday."

"Great, thanks."

Before closing the door behind her, Sadie pivoted. "You deserve people who care about you, Evie. I'm sorry you don't believe that. I hope you'll change your mind one day." With one last soft smile, she closed the door behind her.

Alone, Evie donned her clothes, considering the Slayer's words and hating that she wished they were true.

"Oh, I'm so sorry, my friend," the woman said, wracked with sorrow as she lifted her hands to her cheeks. "How did your world die?"

Galredad sighed. "There was a great flood, one that washed away all that existed. And then, a great fire that burned every trace of my realm to the ground. It's all gone," he said, wrapping his arms around his knees, "as if it never existed in the first place. And now, I feel so lonely."

"What a terrible story," she said, gently caressing his arm. "I have never heard its equal."

"Oh, you will," he said, his tone ominous, "for I have learned that the Universe always lies in wait, calculating the perfect time to destroy one's happiness..."

Chapter 4

Three days later, Kenden stood outside his home chopping wood for the fireplace. He'd built one so that he could indulge his love of relaxing by a warm fire each evening after he trained the troops. Lately, he'd been exhausted from the grueling sessions and was thrilled to have the day off.

Under the glowing orb of the afternoon sun, he plunged the axe through the log that sat upon the stump, splintering it in half. Picking up one of the halved pieces, he placed it upright and proceeded to divide it again.

It was grunt work, mindless and draining. It cleared his head so that he couldn't focus on Evie or her ridiculous demand. Or on the fact he'd been avoiding her like a damn coward. Gritting his teeth, he thrust the axe into a new stalk of wood.

Kenden wouldn't even begin to delude himself that her request was about anything other than manipulation and control. Although he knew she desired him, that was most likely an afterthought for her. No, Evie thrived on power and dominance, on being able to dictate her own terms, and anyone who was unlucky enough to be stuck in her path was doomed.

Breathing a bitter laugh, he took a break to run his forearm over his face, wiping away the sweat. It ran down his neck, onto his chest, bare above his gray sweatpants. Sighing, he set the axe down to lift the water bottle and consume several continuous gulps.

She materialized in front of him as if he'd willed her there. Lowering the bottle, he swallowed. "Hello, Evie."

"Well, hello," she said, her voice sultry and sure. "And what do we have here? My god, you're a fucking Adonis, aren't you? Who knew you had a perfectly chiseled six-pack?"

Rolling his eyes, he threw the empty container on the ground. "What do you want? I'm busy."

White teeth threatened to blind him as she smiled. Approaching him, her irises wandered over his sweat-covered chest, unabashed and slow. "I can't wait to lick every single crevice of you, sweetheart."

He clenched his teeth, forcing himself to remain calm. Staring down at her, he struggled to keep the anger from his voice. "I'm not sleeping with you, Evie."

Full red lips pursed as she made a *tsk, tsk, tsk* with her gorgeous mouth. "Now, Kenden, let's not be hasty. I think you've avoided me long enough. I never pegged you for a wuss." Lifting her hand, she slid the pads of her fingers over his pecs.

"Stop it," he said, grabbing her wrist. Holding it in a vice-like grip, he pulled her closer. "I won't deny that I want you, but not like this. I told you, I don't do casual sex."

"You're literally the only man who has ever said those words to me." Yanking her wrist from his grasp, her eyes narrowed. "Fine. Then name your terms. Perhaps I'm willing to negotiate."

"Name my terms," he said, his tone flat.

"Come on," she said, lifting her arms, sounding exasperated. "You just admitted you want me. Begrudgingly, but we both know I can read the images in your mind. So, tell me. What will it take for you to grant my request?"

Inhaling a deep breath, he pondered. "I would want to court you, like I would any woman I make love to."

"It's called 'dating' in the human world."

"Fine," he said, annoyed at her correction. "I'd want to date you. Get to know you. The thought of sleeping with someone I don't know anything about isn't appealing to me. I like to have a connection with women I'm intimate with."

Laughter bounded from her throat. "My god, you really are a boy scout. It's absolutely unbecoming."

"Then, leave me the fuck alone," he said, incensed by her. "If it's that off-putting to you."

Compressing her lips, she regarded him. As the silence stretched between them, he felt himself growing more uncomfortable. She looked so sure and confident in her expensive clothing. Next to her, in his sweat-soaked pants, he felt like a scrub.

"I don't have time for this," he muttered, lowering to pick up the empty bottle. When he attempted to breeze past her, she grabbed his forearm.

"Wait," she said, her voice quiet. "Let me think for a damn minute."

Heart pounding at her touch, he stared down at her. She was several inches shorter than his six-foot, two-inch frame but her eyes threatened to suck the air out of his lungs. They were so wide, so deep, that he felt he might drown in them if he didn't escape.

"It's never been this difficult for me before," she said, blinking as she held his gaze. "Men mostly want to fuck me and move on. I don't understand your reluctance to do the same."

Compassion swamped him, although it was unwelcome, causing him to think of the first time he'd spoken to her in the hotel in France. She'd sworn that there was no one she'd ever loved; no one who'd loved her. Empathy pulsed in his gut. What a lonely existence she must lead. How did one live so long without affection?

"I can't speak for anyone else but myself. I want more than just a good fuck, Evie. It's something I've come to expect and feel that I deserve." Unable to stop himself, he lifted his hand to palm her cheek. Rubbing the pad of his thumb over her soft skin, the tiny freckles across her nose seemed to glisten in the sunlight. "Maybe you deserve the same. You won't know until you try."

Expelling a long breath, her irises darted back and forth between his. They were filled with curiosity and deliberation and, if he had to guess, a slight bit of fear. Steeling herself, she straightened her spine. Wrenching from his touch, she distanced herself several feet.

"So, if I let you date me, you'll sleep with me afterward?"

Mulling her question, he stared into her grass-green eyes.

"Yes," he said finally, giving her a firm nod. "Three dates followed by three nights together. If you agree to those terms, I'll concede."

Red lips curved into a sexy smile. As she stood before him, he reveled in her splendor. Inwardly admitting that he'd never met a woman more beautiful, he waited.

"Fine," she said, smirking. "I agree." Holding out her hand, a manila folder materialized onto her palm. Closing the distance between them, she slapped it onto his chest. "For you to look over. I had Sadie perform a physical on me, and we met earlier today to discuss the results. I'm clean. I don't want to use protection with you, so I'd urge you to get tested if you have any doubt as to whether you're clean too."

Good god. She was the most straightforward person he'd ever known. "I'm clean. I get tested regularly and haven't been with anyone in several decades."

The perfect features of her face scrunched. "How absolutely dreadful. Thank goodness I've come along to remedy that."

His nostrils flared. "And if you get pregnant?"

She shrugged. "I have an IUD. Won't happen. Get ready, big boy. We're going to have some fun together." She waggled her scarlet eyebrows.

Against his will, he chuckled. "Good lord, Evie. You're something else."

"You bet your goddamn ass I am," she said with a nod. "So, when's our first *date*?" she asked, making quotation marks in the air with her fingers.

He couldn't stop his grin. "Saturday. I'll be done training the troops at five. I'll pick you up at your cabin at six-thirty. Wear something pretty."

"Oh, were you under the impression that you could boss me around now that I've negotiated with you? Don't delude yourself, Kenden. I'm in control here. You'd do well to remember that. Ta-ta for now." With a puff of air, she vanished.

Shaking his head, he muttered to himself, frustrated. Flipping through the folder, he read her results. Clean as a whistle. Well, damn. Craving a shower and a bit of peace, he headed inside to contemplate what in the ever-loving hell had just happened.

Nolan watched Sadie address the couple that stood inside their booth at Uteria's main square. The afternoon sun flirted with the distant mountaintops, foreshadowing an end to the pretty day. Thanking Sadie, the couple walked away, hand-in-hand.

"They're trying to get pregnant," Sadie said, smiling up at him. Her gorgeous, multicolored hazel eyes were magnificent in the sun's dying rays. "I hope it takes. She had trouble with her first husband, who was abducted in the raids centuries ago. Hopefully, this time will be easier for her."

"Hope so," he said, his lips curving into a grin. Such was her way, always wishing others happiness and hope. He'd never met a person more caring and selfless than Sadie.

"Should we break this down?" she asked, gesturing around the booth. "I think we're about done here."

"Sure," he said with a nod. They chatted as they worked, disassembling the various medical equipment and tent components. Nolan made sure he did the bulk of the heavy lifting. Not only because she was so slight but because a proper gentleman would never let a lady do manual labor when he was perfectly capable of doing that himself. His dear mother had ingrained that in him centuries ago.

"Well," she said, fisting her hands on her jean-clad hips, under her white lab coat. "I think we did it. Ken said he'd send some soldiers over in four-wheelers to transport everything back to the infirmary."

Nolan nodded. "I was thinking about grabbing a bite before I head back to Astaria. You hungry?"

A flush crossed the unburnt half of her face, causing his blood to pound through his body. Smiling shyly, she said, "I could eat."

"Come on then," he said, extending his hand. Clutching her unburnt one, he threaded his fingers though hers, squeezing tightly. Leisurely, they strolled through town, coming to a stop in front of one of the Irish pubs.

They sat at the bar, Sadie wriggling her nose at the bartender's offer of a free shot with an appetizer. "Just a beer for me," she said.

"Same," Nolan said, also ordering them some wings and fries.

They chatted, catching up on everything and nothing. Nolan reveled in her genuine laugh and twinkling eyes. It had been like this ever since he'd kissed her that first time. Unable to control the fall, he knew he was tumbling into love with her.

It was quite amazing for someone such as him, who'd been alone and so very unhappy, stuck in a world that wasn't his. Long ago, he'd accepted that was his lot in life. A penance for the mistake he'd made when he discovered the immortal world. And then, out of nowhere, she had appeared. Those tiny hands, that soft smile, even the portions of her that were so badly burned—they all beckoned to him. Causing him to want to wrap himself around her and never let go.

Unable to control his need to touch her, he lifted a finger, tracing it softly over her cheek. "Your skin is healing nicely here."

Her throat bobbled as she swallowed and her tone was just raspy enough to cause him to harden beneath his dress pants. "Yes. The serum is awesome. I can't believe you and Arderin created it for me. It's the most amazing thing anyone's ever done for me."

"We were happy to. You do so much for others. It's nice to have it reciprocated for once, I would imagine."

"It is," she said, nodding against his finger. "Thank you, Nolan."

"You're welcome, sweetie." With one last caress of her smooth skin, he pulled his finger away. Missing that slight contact, he studied her from his barstool. "So, I heard about Evie's ultimatum to Kenden. Sathan told me and swore me to secrecy. Wow. Didn't see that coming."

Sadie tweaked her bottom lip with her teeth. "Seriously. Miranda did the same with me. She and I had a good laugh, but now, I feel bad. I mean, he shouldn't be placed in the position of being with her if he doesn't want to."

Nolan arched a chestnut brow. "I've observed the heat between those two, and if I had to guess, I'd say that it won't be a hardship for him. He's extremely attracted to her."

"Well, she's gorgeous," she said with a shrug, "so it makes sense. We're surrounded by a lot of breathtaking women in this world. It makes me wonder what the rest of us mere underlings are supposed to do."

Their food came, and they arranged their plates, scooping up various pieces and squirting out ketchup. After swallowing, Nolan said, "You're one of the gorgeous ones too, you know? To me, at least."

He could see the pulse pounding in her neck as she gazed at him, her irises full with emotion. "You're the only one who's ever thought so."

"Good," he said, munching on a fry. "It increases my chances of winning you over."

She smiled as she nibbled. "And what happens then?"

Lathering a wing in ranch dressing, he took a bite, contemplating. Finally, his pupils latched on to hers. "Are you open to marrying a human? I think it's time I asked you that. Because I want to continue spending time with you, Sadie, and if that happens, I think that might be where we end up."

Her lids blinked up and down several times as she studied him. "I've never thought about it. I never thought anyone would want to marry me, so it seemed a moot point to waste time contemplating it."

"Hmmm..." he said, finishing the wing and setting the bone on the plate. "Well, maybe you should reassess."

Biting her lip, the flesh squeezed around her teeth. Nolan had to gnaw the inside of his mouth to contain his groan. The action was so sexy.

"Maybe I should," she said, reaching down to grab a wing and dip it in blue cheese. "But not until I complete the regimen with the serum. I wouldn't want to walk down the aisle with anyone looking like I do now."

Anger, swift and true, gripped him as she spoke. It always welled in him when she disparaged herself like that. "I told you, I don't want to hear you say things like that. It's beneath you."

Inhaling deeply, she finished the bite and wiped her hands on the white napkin. "I know. It's just hard. No one sees me like you do."

"I would argue that many do. Starting with Miranda, Arderin, Lila. You're shortchanging yourself."

She scrutinized him, remaining silent as she sipped her beer.

"There's something else you should think about," he said softly. "I can't give you children. Although we know that different species can mate to produce children, especially the purer their blood, a human would never be able to procreate with an immortal. For someone as nurturing as you, it's something to consider."

Her forehead furrowed as she contemplated. "I've never thought of having kids either. It never even seemed a remote possibility. But in my fantasies, I have them. I think I'd be a pretty good mom."

Nolan reached out to tuck a strand of her silky brown hair back between her ear and red ballcap. "You'd be fantastic."

"Thanks," she said, her lids lowering in embarrassment.

"Well, I think that's enough serious talk for today. What do you say? Let's finish up here, and then, I'll walk you to the castle."

After another round of beers, he paid the tab, shoving the bills back at her when she laid them on the counter. Together, they meandered back through town, to the long concrete stairs that led to the main castle's enormous mahogany front doors.

"The health screening went well today. We should do another one soon."

"Okay," she said, nodding. "Thanks for dinner and for walking me home."

"You're welcome." Several soldiers trudged by them, pounding up the steps, and Nolan figured they were heading inside to meet with Miranda or Kenden. Feeling that the moment had passed, he lifted her hand, placing a gentle kiss on the inside of her wrist. "Sweet dreams, Sadie."

Releasing her soft skin, he began to retreat, stopping short when she called his name.

"Yes?" he asked, pivoting.

Her eyes seemed huge as they glowed in the dim moonlight. "Aren't you going to kiss me goodbye?"

The groan escaped his lips before he could stop it. With firm steps, he plodded toward her, pulling her into his arms and cementing his lips to hers. Reveling in her tiny mewls, he plundered her mouth. Pulling off her cap, he tossed it to the ground, moaning as his tongue battled with hers.

"Well, damn," a female voice said beside them. "I'm just in time for the show."

Sadie gasped and pulled back, her face flaming. "Miranda—we were just…"

"Oh, honey, I know what you were doing. Believe me. Good stuff, guys." Miranda winked at Nolan. "It's about time someone made out with our girl."

Nolan chuckled, bending over to grab Sadie's cap and hand it to her. "It was all her fault. I was ready to head to the train, but she couldn't resist me."

"Nolan!" Sadie said, swatting his arm. "I swear, Miranda, I didn't mean to—"

"Mean to, what?" she asked. "Get some action? Why in the hell not? It's awesome. I'm heading in to meet with some of the soldiers. Sorry I interrupted. See ya!" Black hair swaying, she jogged up the stairs.

"Busted," Sadie said, looking up at him with mirth in her brilliant eyes. "Too bad. It was getting good."

He laughed. "Sure was, sweetie." Cupping her cheek, he ran the pad of his thumb over her lips. "See you soon."

"See you soon," she said, her voice gravelly.

With one last peck to her soft lips, he headed for the train, smiling under the moonlight the entire way.

O n Friday, Kenden headed to Astaria to train the troops. Latimus needed the day off for a parent-teacher conference at Jack's school, and he had no problem covering. Working with the Vampyre commander had become seamless, and they formed an immensely talented team. Kenden had never met a man more dedicated to his troops, nor more skilled in battle. Latimus possessed a general's mind and the physicality of ten men. Together, they led an intensely powerful combined army.

Several hours in to the training, Sathan approached him where he stood on the hill, observing the soldiers perform their drills. The Vampyre king's large body blocked the rays of the sun as he situated beside him.

"It's so beautiful today," Sathan said, lifting his face to the sky, eyes closed. Inhaling a deep breath, he shook his head. "I'm so thankful to Etherya. It's been so long since we've seen the sun."

"Indeed," Kenden said, nodding his head. "I'm thrilled for your people."

"*Our* people," Sathan said, training his black irises on him. "You are as much responsible for lifting the curse as anyone. We truly appreciate everything you've done, Ken. I know Latimus feels the same."

"Happy to do it. We've lived with war and hate for a thousand years. It's time for it to end."

Sathan ran a hand through his thick hair, as he often did when he was pondering something. "Yes, it is. Our final step is to defeat Crimeous. Where do you stand with Evie's proposal? If you won't do it, I understand, but we need to make a decision and strategize how to move forward."

Kicking the ground with the toe of his boot, he said, "I agreed. She came to see me yesterday. We compromised on an...*arrangement* of sorts."

"Really?" A raven-black eyebrow arched. "That's good to hear. I figured the cunning Slayer commander would figure out a way to regain the upper hand."

"She pulled a fast one on me," he said, scowling down at the sparring field. "She's so damn smart. And uses the fact that people underestimate her to manipulate everything around her. I should've anticipated it."

"Then, she seems a worthy opponent for you," Sathan said, his full lips curving into a grin. "For you are the most cunning person I've ever met."

Evie's flawless face flashed through Kenden's mind, reminding him not only of her cleverness but her incomparable beauty. "Perhaps. I'm pissed as hell, but I also recognize that her intelligence and shrewdness will come in handy when we fight her father."

"Let's hope so."

They stood in silence, thick arms crossed, watching the troops.

"Did Miranda send you to speak to me?"

"Yes," Sathan said. "She thinks you're still mad at her."

The corner of his lips curved. "I'm not, but it's fun to see her squirm. I think I'll let her sweat for a while."

Sathan chuckled. "You know she'll give you a few days, minimum, and then come looking for you."

"Can't wait," Kenden said.

"And you're okay with the terms you set with Evie?"

Nostrils flared as he clenched his jaw. "Yes. It's so bizarre, but now that I've had a chance to process it, I see a lot of things clearly. Evie's never had one person who loved her. I think Miranda and Darkrip want to, but she's so closed off, they don't stand a chance. Maybe this will open something inside her. Break down some of the walls she's built to protect herself. Who knows?"

"It doesn't hurt that she's absolutely stunning," Sathan said. "I mean, I love my wife and she'll always be the most beautiful woman in the universe, but Evie's got something. I know she pushed you into it but I can't imagine it will be a chore to sleep with her."

"I was lying to myself and to her that I didn't want it to happen. With anyone else, that wouldn't have mattered, but she can read the images in my mind, so I was fucked." Rubbing his hands over his face, he blew out a breath through puffed cheeks. "It's done now. Might as well make the best of it."

"Truer words, my friend," Sathan said. "Well, don't hesitate to call upon me if you need. It's imperative that we remain in communication while you're, um, getting to know her better."

"Yeah," Kenden said absently. "Thanks. And tell Miranda not to bother me while I'm courting Evie. She's meddlesome, and I don't want her involved in my business."

"My bonded? Meddlesome?" he asked with mock indignation. "Never."

"Right," he said, laughing.

With a tip of his head, Sathan trudged back down the hill toward the main castle at Astaria. Knowing the troops needed a break, Kenden trod down to see what Glarys had prepared for lunch.

"You must not believe that!" the woman cried. "The Universe is powerful and filled with so much goodness. You must have faith, my friend."

Galredad scoffed. "Faith. I have no use for faith anymore. I have lost everything."

"Renewal is a constant theme of our Universe. Although you have lost so much, you must believe in rebirth. Perhaps that is why you were put in my path today. Perchance we were meant to meet."

That caused the man to smile, if only a little. "Perhaps we were…"

Chapter 5

On Saturday, Kenden finished training the soldiers and headed home to shower. As he got ready for the evening, he decided he needed to dress the part to knock Evie's socks off. She always dressed impeccably, making his usual tactical gear look cold and boring. Throwing on slacks, loafers, a buttoned-down, collared shirt, suit jacket and tie, he couldn't tamp down the swell of nerves in his gut. Annoyed, he contemplated why.

Being a man who enjoyed monogamy and intimacy, he hadn't been with a woman in many decades. Although that might seem foreign to another man, Kenden had been so consumed with protecting his people that he'd barely noticed the years fly by. His previous lover, Katia, had been a lovely woman with straw-blond hair and a kind smile. Their couplings had been sweet and slow, scheduled around army trainings and Vampyre raids. Eventually, she'd expressed her desire to start a family. Not foreseeing an end to the War of the Species, they had ended their relationship, Kenden wishing her well.

Never had he felt one-tenth the desire for her that he felt for Evie. In fact, all his former lovers paled in comparison to the intense longing he felt for her. Knowing that, he reluctantly questioned himself. With so much time passing since his last lover, would he be able to please the red-headed temptress? Lord knew she was innately more experienced than him. She'd probably had lovers with moves Kenden had never fathomed.

Shaking his head, as he walked along the grassy field that separated his home from her cabin, he vowed to stop doubting himself. The woman had gone out of her way to corner him into sleeping with her. Hell, it was the stipulation she'd dictated for fighting her evil father and hopefully fulfilling the prophecy. She must want him badly.

Anticipation coursed through him while he imagined caressing her silky skin. Would he be able to love her body without developing feelings for her as well? Not wanting to examine the answer, he continued to her cabin, his soft shoes swishing along the grass.

When he arrived at the wooden steps that led to the front door, it swung open slowly. Filling the doorframe, her slender body was draped in a long, formfitting black dress that showed every minute curve. The flare of her hips; the globes of her perfect breasts, which he knew she'd received via a human plastic surgeon; the paleness of her thigh and knee that were on show through the slit. By the goddess, she was magnificent. Struggling to breathe, he watched her descend the stairs ever so slowly in her red-bottom stilettos.

Eye-level with him, as she stood on the lowest step, her full, red lips curved into a seductive smile. "I can see you like my outfit."

Kenden's throat bobbled as he swallowed. "There's never been any doubt as to your beauty, Evie." Grasping her hand, he lifted the back of it to his mouth. "You look stunning," he said, brushing a kiss against her smooth skin.

"Thank you," she said, dropping her hand. He took solace in the fact that her slender neck pulsed when she swallowed. Although trying to conceal it, she wasn't as unaffected by him as she pretended.

"Ready?"

She nodded. "I can't walk across the grass in these heels, so I'll have to transport us. Where to?"

"The main square at Restia. I made reservations at the expensive steakhouse. Figured I should spend some of the money I inherited but never seem to use."

Her throaty laugh made his dick swell in his pants. Good god, they'd only just begun, and he was hard as an untried teenager.

"Let's get on with it then," she said. Sliding her arms around his neck, she leaned in to him. "I need to hold you close during the transfer."

Nodding, he pulled her against him. "Your brother has transported me before."

One perfectly-plucked scarlet eyebrow arched. "But were you pushing *that* into his hip?" she asked, rubbing against his erection.

Mentally restraining his groan, and telling himself not to rise to her taunting, he clutched her against him. Unashamed, he grinded into her. "I'm only a man, Evie. You know I want you. The fact that I'm aroused shouldn't be a shock."

"Hmmm..." she said, threading the fingers of one hand through the thick hair at the back of his head. "We could just jump to the good part now. If you're so inclined."

"No way," he said, feeling the corner of his lips curve. "You might just happen to think our date is the best part. And then, you'd feel so empty for skipping ahead."

"Boring," she said, rolling her eyes. "But part of the deal, so fine. To Restia we go." Clutching him close, she closed her lids. With a *whoosh*, they were flying, hurtling through time and space, and then, in a moment, they were at Restia.

The town square on the satellite Slayer compound was smaller than Uteria's. Being that Restia was roughly half the size, it made sense. The compound was quaint, possessing a charm that Kenden always felt drawn to. Extending his arm to Evie, she threaded hers through, and he led her to the restaurant.

The cobblestones of the sidewalk felt warm below them as the sun set in the distance. Glancing down, her hair seemed afire in the balmy air. Several passersby nodded their heads at Kenden, and he reciprocated in kind.

"Everyone seems to know you, Commander," she said, grinning up at him.

"Yes. I come here quite often. My mother was from Restia. She moved to Uteria when she married my father."

"How scandalous," Evie said. "Knowing what I do about immortals and their aristocratic bloodlines, I can't imagine your rich father's family was happy about him marrying someone from Restia."

"Uncle Marsias used to tell me that my grandfather hated the idea at first, but I think eventually, my lovely mother won him over. Penethia. That was her name. But my father called her Penny. '*My sweet Penny*,' he used to say. He was head over heels for her."

"Well, well. That makes even my cold, unromantic heart tingle. And what happened to them?"

"They both died in the Awakening. My father, Brenden, always attended the blood-banking festivals. Being brother to King Marsias, Father always tried to help him with the royal duties even though he was the younger son. They were each other's only siblings and were very close. When Valktor slaughtered Calla and Markdor, my parents were nearby. In retaliation, several Vampyre soldiers struck them down. From what I've been told, the bloodshed that day was unimaginable."

Evie sighed. "I'm sorry," she said, gazing up at him. "Everyone always says that dear ol' Grandpa was a good man, but I always questioned the truth of that sentiment. How could it be so if he murdered the Vampyre royals?"

"Miranda saw your grandfather when she was in the Passage. His actions were a twisted attempt to save your mother. Valktor would've done anything for Rina. His love for her was some of the purest I've ever seen."

She wrinkled her nose. "Well, he might have tried to find a different way. What an absolute fool, believing that my father would free Mother. He should've known she was doomed."

"We have the luxury of hindsight now, but who's to say what we would do in the moment, when a choice of that magnitude is forced upon us?"

"Perhaps," she said with a shrug. "No matter. What's done is done. And now, once I collect my...*stipulation* from you, maybe I can finally rid the world of the bastard."

"All our hopes, pinned on your shoulders," Kenden said jovially, trying to lighten the mood. "Hope it's not too overwhelming."

"Not a fucking chance," she said, straightening her spine. "I can't wait to murder that asshole."

Her confidence was bold and extremely attractive to him. "Can't wait to see the day."

They arrived at the thick oak doors of the restaurant. Pulling one open for her, she sauntered inside. Kenden couldn't help but notice the appreciative glances of each of the male staff members as the host led them to the table. From the bartender to the servers to the damn busboys, not one man passed up the opportunity to drink in her beauty. Feeling possessive—and pissed that he was—he shuffled them to the table with a firm hand on her lower back and pulled out her chair a bit roughly.

"Don't worry, darling," she said, patting his cheek. The placating gesture incensed him, and he clenched his teeth to stop himself from telling her to go to hell. "You have to get used to it if you're going to date me. I've spent a hundred lifetimes learning how to make men salivate when I walk by. Just remember, you asked for this."

"Sit down," he commanded, his tone low and firm.

"Oh, Ken. Don't be a stick in the mud—"

"Sit."

Throwing her head back, she gave a silky laugh. The pale skin of her throat glowed, and he wanted to rip every man's eyes out for gawking at her. Sparing him a wink, she sat in the cushy chair, letting him push it in behind her. She was lucky he didn't push her through the damn table. Infuriating woman.

Sitting across from her, they perused the menu, ordering a fancy bottle of red and two steaks. The candle in between them emitted a soft glow on the white tablecloth as they toasted to defeating Crimeous. Watching her full lips caress the glass and imbibe the red liquid made all sorts of things happen inside his trousers. How would those plushy lips feel around his cock? Uncomfortable, he shifted in his seat.

"There, there," she said, her voice so seductive. "We'll get to that part soon enough."

"Stop reading my thoughts," he snapped, taking a sip of wine. "It's obtrusive and beneath you."

"Is it?" she asked. "You don't know what's beneath me, honey. It ain't much."

Unable to help himself, he laughed. Realizing he needed to relax if he was going to enjoy this at all, he forced himself to calm down and breathe. Several minutes later, they were making easy conversation, as if they'd know each other for centuries.

"No!" she said, snickering behind her wine glass. "And you actually broke her nose?"

"Well, what was I supposed to do?" he asked, shrugging innocently. "Miranda told me not to coddle her, and she kept leaving her face unprotected. Eventually, I had to force her to learn."

"Good god, you're a beast," Evie said, shaking her head. "Remind me never to train with you."

Chuckling, he smiled. "We'll get there eventually. I'll need you to do some sessions with the troops, so they learn to trust you. But for now, how are your lessons going with Darkrip?"

"Good," she said with a nod. "He picks up human dark magic like he was made to wield it. It took me several decades to get to the level of proficiency that he's at after several weeks. It's absolutely annoying."

"Well, I'm glad he has a knack for it. We need you both to be as strong as possible to beat Crimeous. What about the joint force-field that you two need to generate to prevent your father from dematerializing? Now that we've come to an agreement, will you start working on that?"

Setting down her wine glass, Evie's features drew together. "Yes. He and I actually began working on it yesterday, now that you've conceded to my terms," she said, her gaze unwavering. "I'll continue to work with him as long as our arrangement is satisfied."

Twirling the wine glass by the stem, she continued, "To be honest, it was a disaster. Conjoining our abilities was much more difficult than I'd anticipated. Our combined powers have a different energy field than our powers alone. It's as if I have a different kind of…I don't know…DNA or something that he doesn't possess. It's quite strange."

Kenden studied her, thinking back to all the old soothsayer gossip he'd gathered over the centuries. One of the oldest tales prophesized that Etherya had injected one of Crimeous's children with her own blood. Contemplating, he wondered if the story could even begin to be factual. Etherya was always so sure to stay apart from her people, knowing the Universe would be displeased if she interfered in their free will.

"It can't be true," Evie said, reading the images in his mind. "No one with Etherya's blood could've suffered the way I did in my youth."

Compassion slammed his solar plexus, and he reached out to cover her hand where it sat atop the table.

"Don't," she said, pulling it away and placing it on her lap. "That was centuries ago. I don't want your pity."

"I don't pity you—"

"Yes, you do. I don't blame you. You're a very empathetic person. But it's a waste of your energy. Use it to defeat my father instead."

Noting her impassive expression, he relented.

Their steaks arrived: hers a filet, his a ribeye. Delving in, they caught up on stories of the past and wishes for days ahead in a world where her father no longer existed. Feeling so comfortable with her, the dinner seemed to fly by, and Kenden found his heart pounding in anticipation of the evening's conclusion.

Once he paid the check, she finished the last of her wine and eyed him seductively. "So, are we done here? Ready for the main course?"

Breathing a laugh, he stood and extended his hand. "Not yet. We're going to walk along the river. It's really pretty. C'mon."

She gave him a droll look from her chair. "While I appreciate this whole seduction track you're on, let me remind you that I'm a sure thing. We are clear on that, yes?"

"Stop being difficult," he said, shaking his hand at her. "The night is young and it's warm tonight. Walk with me."

Standing, she fit her hand into his, latching onto him with her gaze. "If I'm not careful, you might just seduce me into enjoying being courted."

"How terrible," he teased, leading her through the restaurant and outside into the gorgeous night.

Hand-in-hand, they strolled along the stone sidewalk, beyond the bridge that overlooked the river. Under the pale light of the stars, they meandered down the paved walkway that ran parallel to the water.

"It's very serene," she said, closing her eyes and inhaling a deep breath. "Much like the rivers that run through Colorado. I always enjoyed walking along them."

"Tell me about your favorite places in the human world."

Mischief entered her eyes as she arched a brow. "So you can come looking for me in case I defect?"

"So I can get to know you better," he said, tugging on her hand. "Come on. It won't hurt to let yourself get personal just a tiny fraction. Will it?"

"Nothing hurts until you agree to let it," she muttered, making his heart squeeze.

"Tell me about Japan," he said, unrelenting. "It seems like you love it there."

"I do," she said, her tone wistful. "It's just so beautiful, filled with a history of war and harmony, religion and meditation. There's this gorgeous city by the sea. The cliffs have always called to me. Sunsets filled with colors that you never knew existed..."

As she spoke, he found himself entranced by her. By her smile. By her scent. By the longing in her voice as she spoke so reverently about the places she treasured. While they strolled, he listened, engrossed in every fiber of her. An immeasurable time later, they stood back at the bridge, side-to-side, observing the clear water flow beneath.

"It seems like you really enjoyed Italy," he said, gazing down at her as his forearms rested on the railing of the bridge. "Francesco spoke so fondly of you when I met him."

Her features drew together slightly as she absently stared ahead, her face becoming a mask of what he could only discern as remorse. "Yes. He was a wonderful man. Perhaps the one man who understood me above all others in my long, endless life."

Her slender body seemed to pulse beside him, the energy filled with numerous emotions. Understanding washed over him as he watched her silent struggle.

"You killed him," he said softly. "Once you figured out that he told me where to find you."

"Yes," she whispered, her gaze never leaving the gently gurgling river.

"And you regret it."

Inhaling deeply, her eyelids narrowed. "Perhaps. Or maybe not. I'm quite torn about it, which is strange for me. I've never regretted killing, especially men. But I find that things are changing inside me faster than they have in centuries. It's foreign and extremely frustrating."

"I've killed many in my day too. Soldiers have the burdensome task of killing many to save others. It's something that I've struggled with, as many soldiers have."

"Ah, but I'm not a soldier," she said, still staring ahead. "So, what excuse do I have? Except that I'm an evil bitch who revels in the deaths of my victims."

Kenden considered. "From the few statements you've made to me on the subject, men have often tried to harm you. So, in a way, you were your own soldier. Killing them to save yourself."

She shrugged. "And the others? I've killed many, mostly in my youth, for fun and for sport. Don't exonerate me, Ken. It's futile."

"Your brother has embraced his Slayer side for centuries," Kenden said, his tone encouraging. "It's possible that you could do the same."

"And where's the fun in that? I'm just fine, thank you."

Tilting his head to look at the water, he let the silence envelop them, unsure of what to say.

"Does it make it less evil if he was sick?" she asked, her voice scratchy.

"What?" he asked, feeling his brows draw together.

"Francesco. He was riddled with cancer. I could smell it on him, sure as if I saw the tumors myself. They were growing in multiple organs of his body. When I feel regret, I tell myself that I saved him months of suffering with chemo and tubes, nurses and hospitals. He had a granddaughter. An American. I observed her over a decade ago, when she was visiting him in Italy. They sat outside at a café, and I watched them from afar, remembering our time together. She was in her early twenties then, but a little spitfire. She would've never let him die gracefully. She would've tried everything to extend his life, surely causing him to suffer. So, does it make me less evil that I saved him from all that when I snapped his neck?"

"I'm not sure," Kenden said, sliding his hand over hers where it hung over the rail. Threading their fingers together, he squeezed. "But I think it definitely makes you less evil that you're asking the question. So, there's that." Smiling, he bumped her shoulder with his.

"Good god," she said, shaking her head at him. "You're so fucking perfect. How do you do it? Any other man would've told me to go fuck myself. But here you are, courting me so that you can do your duty and save your people. You're a goddamned fairytale prince, Ken."

Feeling his grin widen, he drew her to him, aligning the front of his body with hers. "I'm just a man who wants happiness for those I love. That includes my people. It's easy to fight for them because I care."

Disengaging her hand from his, she slid her palms up his chest and over his neck, causing him to shiver. Landing on his face, she cupped his cheeks. "Well, hot damn," she said, lifting on her toes. "I've never kissed a boy scout. Show me how good it can be."

Slowly moving toward her, he nudged her nose with his. "Don't trivialize this, Evie," he said, exulted at how she shuddered in his arms. "No labels here. Just you and me."

"How positively dull—"

Her words ended in a gasp as he dragged her into him. Snaking an arm around her waist, he fisted the other in her thick red hair. Groaning, he thrust his tongue into her mouth, his heart slamming in his chest when hers jutted back against it. Sliding over her wet tongue, he plundered her, needing to explore the desire that burned for her so intensely.

Thin fingers slid through his hair, scratching his scalp as she drove her tongue through his lips. Melding her body against his, she licked him and then slid her lips over his tongue, back and forth, spurring him to imagine the same motion over his engorged shaft. Growling, he bit her bottom lip and then gently sucked it through his teeth, giving as good as he got, needing her to know that he'd suck her tiny little nub in just that way once they were anywhere close to a bed.

"Oh, god," she groaned, opening wide to slather her tongue over his again. "Take me home and fuck me. Now."

Lifting his head, he studied her as he panted. Olive-green eyes, filled with lust, stared back at him. Cheeks reddened, lips swollen, she looked like a disheveled goddess.

"I can't promise that I can just fuck you, Evie," he said, clutching her hair with his fist. "I'm not very good at doing this without developing feelings. I'm not really wired that way."

"Fine," she said, breathless. "Have all the feelings you want. I don't care right now. Let's go home."

Irises darting back and forth between hers, he contemplated. Knowing he was lost, he drew her in. "Okay," he said, lowering his forehead to hers. "Your place, or mine?"

As her lips curved, she closed her lids and transported them to her cabin.

"So, did all Elves share your traits?" the woman asked, lightly touching his pointed ears with her fingertips.

"Yes," he said, nodding. "We all have tapered ears and thin bodies. I thought us a lovely species."

"How wonderful," she said, giving him a poignant smile. After some time, she stood, wiping the grass away from her white dress.

"I must leave for now, but I wish to see you again. Will you come to this place tomorrow?"

The man stood and gently grasped her thin wrists. "My lady, I would come to this place for a thousand eternities if it meant that I could look upon your face."

Feeling her cheeks grow warm, the woman nodded. "Until tomorrow then..."

Chapter 6

Once beside her bed, Evie cemented her lips to Kenden's, drawing his tongue into her mouth for another deep kiss. Wanting him inside her as quickly as possible, she dematerialized her dress, thongs and heels, causing them to land in a heap on the floor beside the bathroom.

"Whoa," Kenden said, straightening and looking extremely uncomfortable. "Can we slow down a second?"

Something akin to embarrassment flushed through Evie, causing every inch of her exposed skin to feel hot and itchy as they stood by the bed. Reminding herself that it was impossible for her to feel something that ridiculous, she refused to back down.

"Why?" she said, lifting her arms, palms up, as she stood naked in front of him.

"There's no reason we have to rush," he said, disengaging to walk to her closet. Rummaging around, he found a silky robe. Stalking toward her, he draped it over her shoulders, holding one side up so she could snake an arm through.

Shooting him an annoyed glare, she donned the robe and watched in disbelief as he knotted the belt. "Well, I think this is the first time I've had a man put my clothes back *on* before having sex."

Blowing out a breath through puffed cheeks, he regarded her. The brown centers of his eyes were blazing with desire but also with concern. And that made her extremely uncomfortable.

"I'm not like other men," he said, his gaze firm. "Maybe one day, you'll realize that. For now, I want to get to know your body. Slowly, so that I can figure out how to make you feel good."

Evie was slammed with the insane urge to cry. Tears formed in her eyes against her will, and she struggled to keep her chin from quivering. She'd been with so many men, all of them eager and randy. Not one of them had ever taken the time to stop and assess what she might need. And why would they? Long ago, she'd learned that sex was an exchange; her body traded for the moments where her partners were drunk with arousal. Those were her instants of control, where she knew she had the upper hand. Nothing in her world had ever surpassed that feeling.

Until now. Right at this moment, when this handsome-as-sin man with care in his eyes was pleading with her to let him pleasure her. The world had gone mad.

Fear surged through her, threatening to choke her. Struggling to breathe, she stared up at him. No way in hell was she letting him have control. If she slowed down and let him spend time figuring out all the ways to please her with those broad hands, she would never regain her sanity. Terrified to let someone open her up that way, she crossed her arms over her chest. Willing the tears not to fall, she clutched on to the anger that always lived inside.

"What difference does it make if we go fast or slow? We're here to fuck, aren't we?"

"We're here to love each other," he said. His expression was impassive and impossible to read, making her feel as if she was drowning.

"No," she said, shaking her head. "I don't acknowledge that word. Use it again and you'll see how evil I really am."

"Evie—"

"I mean it," she said through gritted teeth. "Now, let's do this, or let's not, but I'm not turning this into some Hallmark movie love scene. I want sex, and you agreed to my terms. Or are you reneging?"

His angular features contorted with fury. "You're determined to control every aspect of this, but it's not happening, Evie. There are two of us here. Or do you not care if I enjoy it?"

She scoffed. "As if a man wouldn't enjoy sex. You're out of your mind."

"I don't enjoy it unless I know my partner is receiving pleasure. That's what turns me on the most."

"Good god," she said, slapping her palm to her forehead. "He's a fucking saint."

"Hey," he said, grabbing her wrist at her forehead and tugging her toward the long mirror that stood beside the dresser in the bedroom. Bringing her to stand in front of him, he locked on to her eyes in the reflection. As his gaze bore into hers, he removed his suit jacket, tossing it on the floor. Unbuttoning his shirt at the wrists, he rolled the sleeves halfway up his arms.

Raising his hands to gently rub her upper arms, he rested his chin on her shoulder, never breaking eye contact. "I know this is hard for you," he said, his voice a deep rumble beside her ear. Hating the goosebumps that rose on her flesh, she refused to look away. "You learned so long ago that men would hurt you if you trusted them."

Opening her mouth to argue, he shifted his hand over it. When she tried to lift her arms to pull it away, he held them down with his thick arm across her waist.

Shaking his hand from her mouth with a violent twist of her head, she warned, "Many men have restrained me like this. Most paid with their lives. You have two seconds to let me go."

His grip gentled but he didn't release her. "I understand," he said, his voice so soothing. "But you're going to have to learn to trust someone eventually, Evie."

"Says who?"

"I say," he said, the dominant words making her shudder. She'd never let a man come close to dominating her. Yet, for some reason, she stood still in his arms. "I want you to trust me. Just for tonight, I want you to let go and let me take care of you. Can you do that for me? I promise, I won't hurt you. It's a vow I take very seriously."

Goddamnit, those fucking tears were back, jeopardizing the thin veil of control she had on her emotions. Opening her lips to tell him to fuck off, she closed them immediately, unable to form the words. Pressing them together, she fought like hell not to cry.

Kenden's thick chest expanded against her back as he inhaled a long breath. Dropping his hands, he embraced her waist with both arms, the thickness of his tan forearms seeming to glow against the purple robe. Seeing his strong arms crossed above her midsection sent a wet rush of desire to her core.

"Yes," he whispered, soft lips brushing her ear as he gazed at her reflection. "That's good. Relax. I've got you."

"I can't," she warbled, one thick tear sliding down her cheek. Mortified, she tried to lift her hand to wipe it away, only to find it encased in his hold.

"You're so damn beautiful right now," he said, kissing a path to the tear and sipping it from her face. "My god, Evie. You deserve to be cherished. Let me love you."

Tilting her head, she stared into his eyes, cursing the emotions that swirled within. He just gazed into her, those chocolate irises so warm and open.

"I can't."

"Yes, you can." Softly, he stroked her bare forearm with his thick fingers. The action was so mesmerizing, so soothing.

Gazing up at him, she realized she had already lost. Petrified, she eased further into him. Swallowing thickly, she nodded. "Okay," she whispered.

Exhaling a breath, he rested his forehead on hers. "Thank the goddess. Am I going to have to fight you this hard every time we make love?"

Something escaped her throat, feeling foreign, and she realized it was laughter. How strange, to laugh when being held by a man who was about to have sex with her. Searching her brain, she wondered if that had ever happened before. Not that she could recall, but she rather liked it. It was quite uncomfortable but also familiar in a strange way.

"I can't vouch for anything past tonight, but for now, I'll relent. Do your worst, Commander. I won't fight it."

Grinning, he touched his lips to hers. It was a sweet kiss, filled with hope and anticipation. Gesturing to the mirror with his head, he said, "Watch me while I touch you."

The directive was so sexy that she almost groaned. Turning to face the mirror, she waited. Ever so slowly, he unlatched his arms from her waist. Running his palms over the silk that covered her abdomen, he slid them over her chest, grazing her breasts. Eyes locked onto hers, his hands roved back down. Caressing, his fingertips grazed up her back until they landed in between her shoulders. With the pads of his thumbs, he began massaging her neck.

The muscles there were so tense, filled with the strain of always having to hold her head high, for if one wasn't aware, they couldn't sense danger. She'd learned that lesson centuries ago.

Unconscious of making the decision, she closed her eyes. Lolling back, her head rested on his shoulder as he massaged away the stiffness.

"You're so tense," he said, his thumbs working magic on her neck.

"Mmmm..." she replied, unable to form any other words. Forget her powers. His fingers were more adept at rendering her motionless than any freezing spell she'd ever placed on another.

"That's it," he soothed. Warmth from his stomach seeped into her back, making her want to melt in a puddle to the floor. "See how good it feels to let go?"

"It's been so long," she said, not realizing she'd said the words aloud until he grumbled in her ear.

"I know, baby," he said, pressing a kiss to her temple.

"I hate that endearment," she mumbled.

"Okay, baby," he said, teasing her.

"Screw you."

The rumble of his deep chuckle vibrated through her. Giving her neck one last squeeze, he threaded his arms under hers, sliding his hands around to the "V" that comprised the opening of her robe. Lifting her lids, she searched the reflection. Brown eyes unwavering, he slowly pulled the fabric apart.

Cold air rushed against her bare breasts, causing her nipples to pebble. Beginning to pant, she watched the mirror with rapt anticipation. The purple fabric sat open, baring her chest and stomach, the silky belt still holding the lower half closed.

His broad hand rubbed her stomach, causing the muscles underneath to quiver. Sliding his hands up, he cupped her breasts, testing the fullness.

"Ken," she whispered, wishing she wasn't trembling beneath him.

"So perfect," he rasped, warm breath heating her ear.

"Touch me," she pleaded.

"Do you want me to tug on those hard little nipples?"

"You know I do."

Lowering a hand, he picked up one of the ends of the tie to the robe. Lifting it, he brought it to one of the straining nubs, gently feathering the soft fabric over it.

Tilting her head back onto his shoulder, she strained toward the material.

"That's it, sweetheart. Reach for it. Does that feel good?"

"Yes," she moaned, looking up at him. "Stop teasing me."

"Look back at the mirror," he said, so confident and sure. "I'll stop teasing when you stop trying to tell me what to do."

"Bastard," she said, following his directive. Body throbbing, she let the feeling take her as he swished the soft fabric over one nipple, then the other. Back and forth, over and over, she thought she might burst with anticipation.

Finally, he lowered the fabric. Skimming the pads of his fingers up her sides, he slid them over to her nipples, latching on with his forefinger and thumb. Watching her in the reflection, breathing hard into the crevice of her ear, he squeezed.

"You're trying to kill me," she moaned, barely recognizing the woman in the mirror with swollen lips and flushed skin.

"I'm trying to please you," he said, tugging the nubs between his fingers in a lazy rhythm. Each tug sent a jolt of moisture between her thighs. "I want so much for you to enjoy being touched."

"I'm enjoying it, believe me," she said, breathing a laugh. "Get on with it. I'm ready to have you inside me."

"Not on your life, sweetheart. We're just getting started."

Groaning, she relaxed into him, letting him tug and play with her nipples. Eventually, he ceased the maddening pulls, skating his hands down to the belt of the robe. Untying the knot, he spread the fabric.

"Red," he said, tracing the tiny strip of hair atop her mound with his index finger.

"Mmm hmm..."

"I was curious."

"I bet you were."

Chuckling, he slid his hands lower. Gripping the inside of her thighs, he spread them slightly. Watching his hand slide toward her core was the sexiest thing she'd ever seen.

With one finger, he traced the lips of her opening. Unashamed, she purred, straining toward him for more.

"I'm barely touching you, and you're soaking my finger. God, Evie. It's so hot."

"I know," she said, panting. "Please, Ken. Make me come."

White teeth glowed as he smiled at her. Goddamnit, his smile was so gorgeous. "Yes, ma'am." Closing his teeth on the rim of her ear, he inserted his middle finger inside her.

Evie cursed, curving her hips to impale him further. Straining up into her, he crooked his finger back and forth. "Where's your spot, baby? Is it there? Or maybe there?"

"Everywhere," she rasped. Writhing in his arms, she jutted into his hand. "More."

Chuckling against her ear, he inserted another finger. Moving them within her, he brought his other hand to toy with her clit. As his thick fingers stretched her, gyrating inside, he rubbed the engorged nub with the pad of his fingers.

"Does that feel good, sweetheart?"

"Yessss...don't stop. Oh, god."

Opening her eyes, she locked onto his beautiful, coffee-colored irises.

"I've seen you like this in my dreams. It's so much better than I imagined. Take my fingers and come for me. I want to feel you gush all over me."

High-pitched mewls escaped her, spurred on by his steamy words. "I'm so close."

"Yes, you are. I can feel your tight little walls choking my fingers." Increasing the pace of both hands, his fingers frenzied on her clit, he demanded, "Come. Now. I've got you."

Flinging her head back, she exploded, every cell in her body shooting bursts of energy to her core. Collapsing in his arms, he held her somehow, still stimulating her as she convulsed. Throbbing and quaking, she gave up control, letting him support her, too raw to care. Even though her legs seemed to be comprised of jelly, she eventually began to feel the floor underneath her feet. Sinking into Kenden's warmth, she reveled in his embrace.

Mustering the energy to lift her lids, she found those arresting eyes in the reflection. They were sated but somehow still filled with hunger. She realized he was happy that she'd found her release first. Something that rarely happened with the men she fucked.

Pulling his hand from her, he brought his fingers to his mouth. Eyes never leaving hers, he closed his lips over his index finger, sliding it out slowly so he could drink her taste from it. Once finished, he lowered his third finger, rubbing it on her lower lip, spreading her essence over the plushy flesh. Parting her lips, he stuck the finger inside, growling when she closed around it. Backing it out slowly, she sipped herself from him.

Placing those fingers on her cheek, he turned her face toward his. Merging his lips to hers, his tongue pushed inside, searching. Making a suggestive noise in the back of his throat, he lapped every inch of her mouth.

"Kissing you while I taste the deepest part of you in your mouth is so sexy," he said against her lips.

"Everything about you is sexy," she said, too replete to come up with something clever. Usually, she was a master at finding the right words to gain the upper hand during sex, but tonight, she was spent. Completely.

"I'm glad you think so. I'm at a huge disadvantage since I can't read your thoughts."

Amused, she nipped at his bottom lip. "I think it's pretty obvious I want you. I mean, I staked the future of two species on it."

His low-toned chuckle washed over her, enveloping her expended frame with its warmth. Walls down, she inwardly admitted how good it felt.

"I'm glad. How about I get out of these clothes so I can accomplish my mission?"

She grinned. "Do you want me to dematerialize them?"

He shook his head. "I want you to undress me. Slowly. Like I'm the first man you've ever undressed and the last man you ever will." Rotating her to face him, he cupped her cheeks. "Got it?"

"Yes, sir, Commander," she said, arching a brow. Excited to see those abs again, she set about following his order.

∞

Kenden's blood coursed through his body, thanks to the pounding organ in his chest, as Evie unlaced his tie with her thin fingers. Tossing the silky cloth to the floor, she slowly unbuttoned his shirt. Opening the fabric, she pushed it from his shoulders.

"Good grief," she breathed, raking her red nails over his pecs and stomach. "Your abs are fucking delectable."

"A nice side-effect of my occupation."

"Mmmm..." she murmured, the pads of her fingers brushing over the tiny brown hairs on his chest.

Dropping her hands, she unbuckled his belt, pulling it from the loops and throwing it on the floor. After freeing the button and lowering the zipper, she inserted her hand inside. Grabbing his length, she set him free.

"I love seeing your hand around my cock," he said, his voice seeming to come from far away. Lowering his forehead to rest on hers, he groaned when she began tugging the length, back and forth.

"You're very well-endowed, Commander." Those full lips formed a seductive smile.

"Thank god. I need every advantage with you."

Fusing his lips to hers, he drew her to him, needing to envelop her mouth with his. Shooting high-pitched mewls down the back of his throat, he felt a *whoosh* and realized she'd dematerialized the rest of his attire.

"Sorry, but I've had enough of slow and steady. I need you to fuck me."

Unable to control his growl, he bent his knees and palmed her ass. Lifting her, he rotated and gently threw her on the bed. Tiny giggles escaped her as she bounced, the globes of her breasts moving in tandem with her gorgeous body.

"You look so damn adorable right now," he said, smiling down at her.

"Get over here, you infuriating man." Arms outstretched, she beckoned to him.

Sliding over her, he aligned his body with hers. Balancing his weight on one arm, he reached down with the other to grab her behind the knee. Lifting her leg, he pushed it toward her shoulder. Straightening his arm, palm flat on the mattress, he anchored her thin leg so that she was open to him.

Touching the head of his cock to her slick center, he watched her. Those lips were open, short breaths escaping, eyes heavy-lidded and filled with arousal.

Every muscle of his taut body was on fire as he began to push inside her. Like the sweetest, wettest glove, the plushy walls of her core sucked him inside.

"Yes. Stretch me open," she pleaded below him. "You can go faster."

"No," he said through gritted teeth. Locked on to her magnificent irises, he continued jutting forward, inch by inch. "I want you to *feel* me, sweetheart. Every single bit."

Tossing her head back, her hips undulated to meet him. The action was filled with frustration and desire. Her sultry moans drove him wild as he eased himself into her.

Skin coated with sweat, he finally reached the hilt, cock pulsing as it rested fully inside her warmth. "Look at me," he commanded.

Latching her pupils on to his, she waited.

He withdrew completely and then thrust into her, hard and sure.

"Yessss..."

Increasing the pace, he began fucking her in earnest, making sure to impale her fully each time. Red flushes of fire burned her fair skin, making her look so exquisite in the dim light of the bedside lamp. His shaft was a frayed mass of nerves, the pleasure so intense that he wondered if he'd ever felt anything that compared. Deciding it impossible, he drew her other leg up, anchoring it on his straightened arm. She was fully exposed to him, her legs bent and resting on his arms as her knees stretched toward her shoulders.

Needing to make it good for her, he hammered inside, hitting the spot that sat deep within. Feeling her tense around him, he knew she was close. Fusing his lips to hers, he sucked in her scream before she threw her head back and began to convulse around him.

Wave upon wave of pleasure doused him as her drenched walls milked him. Unable to hold on any longer, he threaded his fingers in her hair, buried his face in her neck and shot into her. Jets pulsed out of him as she throbbed beneath him, both of them finding their release as they shouted words of desire and passion.

Inhaling the fragrant scent of her skin, Kenden held her, loving how their bodies seemed to quake together in the aftermath. Lifting a shaking hand, she caressed his thick hair, causing him to shudder inside her spent body.

They lay like that for minutes, maybe hours, sated and sanguine. Every so often, she would trail her fingertips down his broad back, and his would tangle in her hair. It was lazy, almost gluttonous, and Kenden didn't give a damn.

"I should clean us up and head home but I'm about to fall asleep," he murmured into her shoulder.

"Let's stay here and say fuck it. I feel too good to move."

Chuckling, he pressed a soft kiss on her velvety skin. With strong arms, he repositioned their heads to the pillows, pulling the covers over their bodies. Nuzzling into her, wedged to her side as his thick arm drew her close, he fell into darkness, thanking every god above that she was sated.

And so it went, for centuries in the timeframe of some worlds. The two friends would meet, sating each other's loneliness, as they spoke of days gone by and futures ahead. They formed a strong bond. One of friendship and gaiety.

The woman knew that the man had grown to love her, in the way that a man loves a woman, and her heart hurt at the realization. For, although she loved the man as a dear friend, she did not possess the ability to love romantically. It was something the Universe had not instilled in her when it had conceived her in the moment of creation.

Slowly, her heart began to fill with dread, knowing she would have to eventually tell the man that she could never love him as he loved her...

Chapter 7

Sunlight burned Evie's eyes as she forced them open. Refusing to capitulate to the bright rays, she stared ahead. Kenden snored softly behind her, his arm wrenched around her waist. Warm breath heated the back of her neck as he respired into her, and she realized something extremely important.

She was *pissed*.

Mentally screaming every curse word in her extensive repertoire, she gritted her teeth. The sound of her molars grinding together could probably be heard at the main castle. What in the ever-loving hell had she been thinking?

First, she'd let her guard down, telling Kenden her deepest thoughts as if she was a teenage girl dying to join the popular clique. In a moment of weakness, she'd discussed Francesco's death with him. Stupid and careless.

Then, she'd let him take her home and gain the upper hand. Those strong hands had torn down the seemingly impenetrable walls she'd built long ago. Scoffing, she shook her head into the pillow. Impenetrable her ass.

Next, she'd cried. As in, tears down her cheeks, throat swollen, ugly-cried. Mother of all gods. What otherworldly spirit had invaded her body last night? That was the only explanation that was even remotely possible. She hadn't cried in centuries. Well, for the most part, she begrudgingly admitted, thinking of Francesco again.

And finally, she'd let him stay over. In her bed. Evie usually preferred to stay at her lovers' residences. It allowed her the freedom to disappear whenever the hell she pleased. But no, Kenden had stayed. Cuddling with her like they were high school sweethearts. At one point, he'd woken her, his impressive shaft pressed against her back, and she'd slithered into him. Biting her neck with those perfect teeth, he'd impaled her from behind, giving her another round of exquisite sex. Bastard.

Now, she was lying here in Mr. Perfect's embrace, wondering how in god's name she was going to extricate her body from his.

"If you want to get up, go ahead," he mumbled behind her. The deep timbre of his voice sent all sorts of tingles through her body. "I have to get up soon anyway to train the troops."

"Fine," she said, shrugging off his arm and rising. She absolutely did not miss the heat from his broad body. Nope. Not one bit. Shrugging on her robe, she headed to the kitchen to make coffee. It was early, and Evie didn't do mornings. Not well, anyway, and definitely not cordially.

As the coffee brewed, she inhaled the smell, attempting to calm her jitters. He would leave soon enough. She'd see him out and get back to putting up those defenses that she was so damn proud of. And why shouldn't she be? They'd protected her for ages. This situation with Kenden was temporary. She'd do well to remember that before she fell down the rabbit hole of acting like a complete romantic moron.

"I smell coffee," he said, strolling into the kitchen looking like a bronzed Adonis. Shirt unbuttoned, slacks and loafers on, jacket and tie thrown over his arm. He certainly wasn't worried about making a walk of shame home.

"Yep. I only made enough for myself. Sorry." Pouring some into a ceramic mug, she added creamer from the fridge and came to stand by the small island in the middle of the cramped kitchen. Leaning her hip on it, she smiled sweetly. "Get home safely."

Eyes narrowed as he gave her a knowing grin. "I think there's enough left in the pot for me to have a cup before I go."

"Nope," she said, blinking rapidly. "Too bad. See ya around. Hope the training goes well."

He stood for a moment, a few feet from her, contemplating. Throwing his jacket and tie on the nearby two-seater table, he stalked to the cabinet, pulled down a mug and poured himself a cup from the coffee maker.

Telling herself not to rise to the bait, Evie gave him her most saccharine smile. "Oh, I guess there was enough. Good to know since I didn't offer you any."

Kenden took a sip, chestnut irises observing her over the rim of the mug. Slowly approaching, he set the cup down and faced her, reclining against the island with his hip. There, they stood, mirroring each other as they leaned on the counter, deciding the next move in the game they were suddenly playing.

"So, that's it, huh?" he asked, one eyebrow arched. "We had fun together, and now, you're so anxious for me to leave that you're physically restraining yourself from pushing me out the door?"

"You can stay as long as you want," she said, her tone ever so polite. "I just thought you had stuff to do today. And so do I. I have a session with Darkrip and I need to get ready."

Reaching for the mug, he leisurely swallowed another swig of coffee, amusement pulsing in his eyes. "Your session with Darkrip isn't until ten. It's seven-fifteen."

Of course, the kingdom's commander would know everyone on the compound's schedule. Evie found it infuriating. That, compounded by the fact he was silently laughing at her, made her want to punch him square in his handsome face.

"Well, you're invading my privacy," she snapped. "I should've transported us to your house last night. I'm not sure what sort of temporary insanity made me choose the cabin, but you need to leave. I don't do morning-after bagels and banter, Commander. So, drink up and get the hell out of my house."

Setting the mug on the island, he reached over and attempted to grasp her wrists. Pulling them away, she scowled at him. "Don't touch me."

Gazing down at her, he closed the distance between them until their combined energy seemed to sizzle. Refusing to back down, she lifted her chin, glowering up at him.

"I'm sorry you feel uncomfortable about what happened between us last night, but that's the only apology I'm going to make." Goose bumps washed over her flesh from his silky baritone. "I won't apologize for asking you to open yourself up to me, Evie. It was so beautiful to see you that way, and I wish that you would let yourself be with someone who demands that of you. You deserve to be with a partner who pushes you to be your best self and to be trusting and vulnerable. It's time for you to have that."

What an arrogant bastard he was. Fuming, Evie slammed her mug down on the counter. "Don't tell me what I want or need, you son of a bitch. You don't know the first thing about me. I don't want a partner and I sure as hell don't want to be vulnerable. Now, get the fuck out of my house."

Kenden sighed, long and slow, and shook his head as he regarded her. "Let's talk when I can be assured you won't rip my eyeballs out with your fingernails. I'll text you later." Sauntering over to the table, he picked up his coat and tie. He looked so gorgeous, staring at her as he was framed by the sunlight from the nearby windows. Evie considered that the only reason she didn't hurl the nearby mug right into his attractive face. After all, it would be a tragedy to break that perfect, angular nose.

"Thank you for a lovely evening," he said softly. And then, he was gone.

Evie stood by the counter as the minutes ticked away, each stroke of the second hand another instant to ponder what the hell had happened last night and the grave mistakes she'd made. When the undrunk coffee was cold and her pounding heart had returned to normal, she placed the cups in the sink and headed to shower, hoping to wash it all away.

∞

Darkrip watched his sister fail miserably at generating the combined force-field they were working on. Facing each other in the open meadow near her cabin, she stood across from him, frustration lining her expression. From his outstretched hands extended a perfect, solid but almost invisible barrier. From hers, the energy was frazzled and sparking. Realizing they were wasting their time, he dropped his hands, the fuzzy barrier vanishing into thin air.

"What the fuck?" Evie yelled, fisting her hands at her sides so that the hazy plasma around her also disintegrated. "I was getting there. Why did you stop?"

His pupils darted around her face. "You're frazzled. Your mind is somewhere else. It's futile for us to continue."

Almond-shaped eyes narrowed. "Screw you. I'll get it. Let's try again." She lifted her hands and began to generate the block of energy again. Darkrip remained still, eyeing her.

Exhaling a furious breath, she fisted her hands on her hips. "If we don't get this, we're as good as dead. The bastard will chew us up and spit us out. Is that what you want? What will happen to your Vampyre and the little brat she's carrying?"

"I understand the consequences of not generating the force-field effectively," he said, keeping his tone calm. "However, I don't want to waste time practicing with you when you're obviously torn up about fucking Ken last night. Or do you want to deny it?"

Her features drew together, the freckles darkening under the red flash of anger on her skin. "That's none of your business. Stop reading my thoughts."

Lifting his fingers to his chin, Darkrip stroked, looking to the blue sky as he contemplated. "I could use this opportunity to ridicule you as you did me when I fell for Arderin. How positively amusing," he murmured.

"I'm not *falling* for anyone," she spat, thrusting her chin out. "I don't work that way. I didn't think you did either, but the snarky princess must have a golden vagina or something. It's absolutely ridiculous."

Trying to control his mirth, he watched her stomp around the grass, mumbling to herself. "He's a good match for you. I can see these things. Ask Miranda. I knew the night she met Sathan that it was only a matter of time."

Evie crossed her arms over her chest. "Ken's a fucking boy scout who wouldn't last a hot minute with someone as evil as me. Just because you turned into a damn choir boy doesn't mean I will. Let it go. I'm going to grab some water inside. Give me five."

As Darkrip watched her stalk to the cabin, he realized he needed to have a talk with Kenden once the bargain he'd struck with Evie was completed. The Slayer commander was wise but it was important he knew how much he affected Evie. It was imperative that she was one-hundred percent focused when they fought their father. Otherwise, the future of the immortals was doomed.

Sauntering back outside, she thrust a bottle of water at him. "Drink up. I'm ready. I'm actually enjoying the challenge and determined to get this. We'll work on the force-field for another hour, and then, I want to go over the black magic freezing spell."

Deciding not to push her—for now—he took a swig of the water, cherishing it under the midday sun. Sated, they got to work.

After the hour spent on the combined barrier, Evie formed a hexagram in the grass with sticks she'd gathered from the nearby forest. Closing their eyes, they called upon the forces of dark magic and voodoo from the human world. Together, they took turns casting freezing spells upon each other. Since Crimeous was so powerful, they weren't able to immobilize him as they could others. With the human magic, they hoped to enhance their abilities enough to halt him in place, so they could surround him with the force-field that would alleviate his powers. Only then could Evie thrust the Blade of Pestilence into his gristly body, hopefully ridding him from the planet.

As the bright orb above began its daily descent toward the far-off mountains, they sat down on the crunchy grass to assess their progress.

"We're there with the human magic but we have more work to do on the force-field," he said, picking at the grass near his thigh.

"Yes," she said, nodding. "I don't know why I'm having such a hard time with it. I'm used to being excessively more powerful than you."

Darkrip chuckled. "Maybe you're losing your touch now that you're a big softie for the Commander."

Evie rolled her eyes. "Enough. Sex is just another function to me, like breathing or eating. Feelings and emotions have absolutely nothing to do with it. Once we defeat Father, I'm heading back to the human world."

"Well, Arderin and I would love that. I'll be raising the baby while she's completing her medical training and would love for our daughter to get to know her Aunt Evie."

She snorted. "Don't get too excited. I'm okay with kids for a while but then they annoy the ever-loving shit out of me." Glancing over, she pondered. "But maybe I'll like your kid. We'll see. Hope she looks like Arderin. You're an ugly son of a bitch."

His laughter echoed across the open field. "I can always count on you to knock my arrogance down a few notches, sis."

After a moment, he asked, "Would it be so terrible to try something new? To consider attempting a serious relationship with a man? I'm not saying run away and elope tomorrow, but perhaps something more than sex? I can tell you, from my own experience, opening yourself up that way creates so many new possibilities that I never even fathomed. Arderin was brave enough to love me even with all the terrible things I've done in the past. It's such a gift. I want you to have that, Evie."

"No one will ever love me," she said, drawing her knees up to her chest and embracing them with her thin arms. "I learned that long ago. Even Mother wasn't capable."

Darkrip sighed. "Mother was quite deranged once you were old enough to remember her. He'd tortured every last fraction of spirit from her. But I assure you, she loved you. When you were a baby, she was obsessed with making sure he never hurt you."

Evie scoffed. "Well, she did a piss-poor job."

"Yes. As did I. We both let you down." Straightening his spine, he placed his hand on her shoulder. "But it doesn't mean that we didn't love you." Struggling with feelings that were still so new to him, he said, "I love you now, Evie. I hope you understand that."

Shaking off his hand, she gazed at him, chin resting on her knees. "It's not possible. I'm rotten inside."

Darkrip couldn't control his smile. "Are you really? Is it that bad? I think there's a lot of good in you."

She gave a *harrumph*. "You're delusional."

"Look at you, training to fight with us. Risking your life to save two species. That's pretty amazing. Why are you doing it?"

Her expression was wistful as she stared across the grassy meadow. "I don't know."

"Come on. There must be some reason why you came back. You hate the immortal world, and yet you're jeopardizing your future to fight with us."

Exhaling a breath, her eyelids narrowed. "I guess I'd become complacent with the humans. I'd never really spent any time in the immortal world, outside of the Deamon caves, and I was intrigued. The thought of killing father captivated me, and I was curious to meet Miranda."

"That's a good start," he said, nodding. "But I think you need to identify exactly what you're fighting for. Having clear goals and objectives will help you when things get tough. And I'm sure they will. Father must know you're here."

"I wonder about that as I sit outside my cabin at night sometimes," she said. Straightening her legs, she crossed them at the ankles and rested on outstretched arms behind her back. "He hasn't approached me yet. I don't think he understands the extent of my powers. When he finds out, who knows what he'll do?"

"That's exactly why you need specific goals. To remind you of what you're fighting for. He'll play dirty, and you need to remain true to the cause."

"The cause," she said with a joyless laugh. "Saving tribes of people who want nothing to do with me."

"I want something to do with you," he said, placing his hand over hers. "Miranda does too. And I'm pretty sure Kenden is dead-set on making whatever arrangement you have with him more permanent."

"Not after this morning," she said, her tone wry. "I was an absolute bitch to him."

"Not to be an ass, but he's probably used to that from you, Evie."

Chuckling, she locked her green gaze onto his. "You may be right."

Releasing her hand, Darkrip stood and brushed off his pants. "I have to get home. I told Arderin I'd cook tonight. She's craving food now that she's pregnant."

Evie stood and closed the distance between them. Gently, she brushed some stray grass off his shirt, the absent gesture so caring that he wondered if she even knew how natural it was for her. "You're a domesticated idiot. Mister cook-the-meals and stay-at-home dad. My god, I never thought I'd see the day."

He spiked a brow. "Me neither. Believe me." Placing a kiss on her forehead, he said, "See ya." With a *whoosh*, he dematerialized home to his beloved wife.

Moira watched Aron as he directed the delivery men around the park. The council had voted to build an extensive new playground in Uteria's lush main square, and of course, Aron had volunteered to run point. Panting, she lifted the metal container to her lips, chugging the cold water.

She'd come out here for her daily run. It was a great way to start the day before she had to head to the gallery. Smiling, she thought of Tobias. Last week, she'd made a rather large sale to him. That, combined with the amazing show they'd had this past weekend, had led to the highest week of sales since she'd started. Setting an intention that this one would be even better, she stretched against the wide oak tree that stood tall beside her.

Aron must've sensed her watching him from across the park because he lifted his hand in a wave to her. Waving back, she told her stupid heart to stop pounding. He was just about the most adorable man she'd ever met.

Wrinkling her nose, Moira realized it was ridiculous to think a man adorable. Most women wanted someone sexy and hot. Like her bastard ex-husband. He'd been as handsome and charming as a human movie star—until the first time he'd hit her. Narrowing her eyes, she contemplated the memories as she stretched.

The beatings had started out small. A backhand across the cheek here, a forceful shake from his vice-like grip on her upper arms there. Always needing to parade her around as the beauty on his arm, he would become consumed with fury when her face bruised. Much of her stipend, controlled by Diabolos and deposited into her account monthly, was spent buying makeup to cover up the welts. She'd learned very quickly that if she didn't conceal them well, he would beat her more violently when they returned home.

Aron had been around during those decades, never fathoming that his best friend, whom he idolized, could hurt his wife. She'd wanted so many times to run to him, to tell him how terrible Diabolos was. Sadly, Moira never gained the courage, choosing to live with her fear.

She'd known Aron all her life. As a high-born aristocrat, he could've disregarded her, the daughter of their housekeeper. But he'd always accepted her, all those centuries ago, telling her that she was worthy. If only she'd had the guts to believe him.

When Diabolos proposed to her, she saw it as a way out. An opportunity to ascend to a higher station. Never did she think it would instead transport her to a life of so much pain and violence. In the fantasies of her youth, she had often imagined marrying Aron. With his handsome face and kind demeanor, he too could've elevated her position in society. But Aron was quite rigid in his beliefs about bloodlines and heirs. Although he claimed to see her as an equal, she knew he would choose to settle down with a high-born aristocratic woman one day. Diabolos, on the other hand? He'd hated their stuffy, expensive world. His jealousy of Aron had always been clear to Moira, as his bloodline didn't extend nearly as far back. But Aron hadn't seemed to notice, always brushing off her husband's jabs with his affable humor and affection.

The tipping point had come the night of the great feast, over eight centuries ago. King Marsias had gathered all the aristocrats together at the main castle for a grand dinner, hoping to get them to pledge extra money to fund the War of the Species. Diabolos had insisted she wear a low-cut, formfitting dress to show off her beauty and her breasts. He felt that he owned her, sure as the watch or the cufflinks upon his wrist, and he wanted his possession to be paraded for all to see.

The dinner had been quite boring, and she'd struck up a conversation with a nice man seated to her left at the elongated dinner table. Long ago, she'd forgotten his name, but he possessed kind eyes and a quick wit.

Moira thoroughly enjoyed their conversation and found herself laughing quite often during dinner.

When the dessert arrived, and the man excused himself to the restroom, she turned to look at her husband. Forcefully, her heart plummeted in her chest. A mask of rage, the likes of which she had never seen, covered his angular features. Fear clasped around her throat, and she dreaded returning home.

She'd said good night to Aron, pleading with him through her eyes. He'd just smiled and given her a peck on the cheek, wishing her and Diabolos a good evening. Her husband's thick body pulsed with fury as he escorted her home in silence, their footsteps ominous on the cold stone sidewalk. Once inside, she'd turned to him, anxious to explain that she'd felt nothing for the man who sat beside her at dinner.

Before she could utter a word, the back of his hand splintered her face. Reeling from the blow, she plodded into the large adjoining dining room and collapsed on the mahogany table. Falling onto it with the top of her body, she felt him behind her, pulling up her dress.

She'd never know where the rush of adrenaline came from that night. Lord knows, she'd let him beat her so many times before. But there, lying across the table, her face throbbing with pain as he pulled at the silky fabric, something snapped in her. With a feral growl, she forced her head back, smacking him in the nose. Cursing, he fell back, holding his hand to his bleeding face.

"You bitch!" he cried, grabbing a chunk of her hair and pulling her to him. Undeterred, she kneed him in the balls, wrenching from his grasp to run away. She made it about half the length of the long table when he seized her again. Fisting her hair in his large hand, he slammed her face into the table. With a mighty roar, he lifted her head again and banged it into the thick wooden chair beside her.

Stars flooded her vision, and she knew that she was dying. Collapsing on the floor, she lifted her hand to her hairline, above her neck, realizing she was gushing blood. Diabolos stood above her, fists clenched at his sides as he prepared to murder her with one last blow.

From so far away, a knock sounded. Was it the Passage? Requesting her to come over to the other side? Surely, she wouldn't hurt so much one she was there. Voices spoke from the front door, Moira only discerning every other sentence.

'Vampyres raiding tonight...stay inside if you can...they're all over the damn compound...'

Grasping on to every last ounce of strength, she rose on wobbly legs. Through the kitchen and out the back door she trudged, until she heard the screams of battle. Desperate to reach them, she slogged until she saw a Vampyre soldier.

His eyebrows drew together as he approached her. "Are you hurt? Our soldiers are under orders not to harm women." Moira found his deep voice so comforting.

"Not from raid..." she sputtered. "Husband hit me. Please, help. He'll kill me."

The Vampyre's almost translucent blue eyes roved over her. "Okay. I've got you."

The large man lifted her, carrying her to one of the metal-barred carriages that the troops used to transport Slayers to Astaria. Sitting her inside, he'd given one of the men orders to clean and address her wounds.

An eternity later, another Vampyre entered the carriage, this one even larger than the one who'd transported her, if possible. "What do we have, Takel?" he asked.

"I carried her here after I found her like this. She says someone beat her."

The massive Vampyre lifted her chin, carefully observing her face. "What is your name?"

"Moira," she rasped.

Ice-blue eyes darted over her injuries. "We can't take you with us, Moira. I'm sorry. You need to go home."

"Please," she begged, knowing this was the one opportunity to save her life. "He'll kill me. Take me with you. I'll perform whatever labor you need. I'll feed your people from my own vein. Whatever it takes."

After a moment of contemplation, his broad arms enfolded her, lifting her and cradling her to his chest. He carried her to a different carriage, this one with a royal crest. Black horses were attached to the front, ready to pull their cargo back to Astaria.

Stepping inside, he lay her across the cushioned seat. With concern in his eyes, he regarded her. "Our king has banned the abduction of women and children. You know this, yes?"

She nodded, praying with everything inside that he would defy the decree.

"I'm reluctant to help you, but you remind me of someone that I...care about very much. I think she would want me to help you."

"Please," she said, tears beginning to fall down her cheeks.

Inhaling a large breath, he nodded. "Okay. Don't move. I'll be back within the hour."

True to his word, the hulking Vampyre had returned and transported her to Astaria. Only later did she learn that he was Latimus, brother to King Sathan and commander of the vast Vampyre army. Thankful for his protection, he'd given her a cabin to stay in on the outskirts of Astaria.

Weeks later, after she'd healed, he'd come to her. With sadness and pain in his blue irises, he'd explained that there was someone he loved and whom he could never have. Understanding washed over Moira as she realized *this* was the woman she reminded him of. Wanting to comfort him, she'd offered herself to him, wanting to soothe the man who'd saved her life.

And so it had gone for centuries. Latimus would come to her when his craving for Lila became too much to bear. He had other women who lived in the cabins, women he had also saved. Moira thought him so kind and often wondered if Lila knew his true feelings. Surely, she couldn't love another over someone as decent as Latimus.

Centuries later, Lila broke the betrothal. Latimus came to her, explaining that he still couldn't have the woman who'd been promised to his brother, but urging her and the other women to return to the Slayer compounds. Moira realized that he couldn't fathom being with anyone else in a world where Lila was free. It was heartbreaking and touching and, after placing a sweet kiss goodbye on his broad lips, she had headed back to the compound she'd called home, all those centuries ago.

First, she'd gone to Aron. She didn't know why he was the one whom she felt comfortable approaching. Perhaps because she trusted that he would protect her from Diabolos once he realized she was alive. With shaking hands, she'd knocked on his door, reveling in the joy on his handsome face when he'd first seen her. Scooping her up in a huge embrace, he told her of Diabolos' passing several centuries ago in a riding accident. He'd had a swift fall and cleanly broken his neck. Bastard. Moira silently wished he'd suffered more.

Afraid to tell Aron where she'd been, she lied to him, telling him that she'd been abducted the night of the raid and escaped, fleeing to live at Restia. She told him that she'd thought Diabolos dead and saw no reason to return to Uteria.

Somehow, Aron bought the flimsy story. Biting her lip, Moira realized it was because he was such a genuine person, always seeing the best in others. It was probably a foreign concept to him that she wouldn't be truthful.

At night, when she lay in the darkness, guilt consumed her for lying to him. But fear of his condemnation as well as a slight bit of shame held her back from imparting the truth. Aron was a traditionalist, believing in the old-school rules for women. He'd told her many times in his youth that he wished to marry a virgin and felt that women should save their virginity for their husbands. She didn't blame him for the views, which she considered stuffy and outdated. He was a product of his upbringing and eternities-old teachings. But she feared what he would think of her, knowing she had traded her body for her safety. Terrified he would hate her and judge her a whore, she decided to stick with the lies.

And now, over a year later, she was also stuck in infatuation. With him. The benevolent aristocrat who'd done so much to help her piece her life back together. Observing him with the laborers as they lined up the various wooden slats and metal bars that would become the playground, she noticed how kind he was to them. Many aristocrats would look down their nose at laborers, but not Aron. Sighing, she reveled in his graciousness.

Longing permeated his attractive features as Miranda approached. Giving him a broad smile, the queen gestured around the future playground, most likely asking him for a progress update. Aron's firm body was slightly tense as he spoke to her, kind and jovial. Love for her seemed to wash off his strong frame in waves. Moira wondered how no one else saw it. He was mad for her.

Moira knew that Aron had proposed to Miranda, only to be shot down when she fell for the Vampyre king. How that must have hurt her proud friend. Rubbing her hand over her heart, she let herself imagine for one moment that he was on his knee in front of her, lifting his mother's ring, asking her to be his wife. How magnificent that would be.

Shaking her head, she mentally scolded herself for living in a damn fairy tale. Not only would Aron never think to marry someone with a servant's bloodline but he was determined to place her on a pedestal as Diabolos' wife. Aron's code of honor would never let him even think of touching his friend's wife, even if he was dead. Frustrated, Moira clenched her jaw.

Done with her stretching, she chugged the contents of her metal canister and decided to head home. She needed to shower and prepare for work. And, if she was honest, she could no longer watch the man she pined for stare at the woman he loved in the way he could never love her.

The woman waited, hoping against hope that the man would release his affection toward her. Sadly, it wasn't meant to be. Knowing she must be gentle but honest, she regarded him under the setting sun.

"I am sorry, my dear Galredad," she said.

"For what?" he asked.

"I have felt your fondness for me and have let it progress too far. I am not like the others of this planet and cannot feel romantic love. I beg you to understand that I care so much for you, in the way that I can, and hope we can remain friends."

The man's face turned cold, causing the woman to shiver...

Chapter 8

Evie's phone buzzed promptly at seven p.m. Monday evening. Glancing toward the device, as she sat at the tiny kitchen table eating a microwave dinner that tasted like cardboard, she scowled.

Kenden: Is it safe to contact you? I want to call but want to make sure you won't reach through the phone and dislodge my testicles.

Oh, so he thought he was funny? Jerk. Picking up the phone, she typed.

Evie: I can't guarantee the safety of your balls. Ever. But you can call me if you want. I'll answer.

Seconds later, the phone buzzed, and she lifted it to her ear. "Hello, Commander," she said, trying to keep her tone light.

"Hello, Evie," he said. Goddamnit, his voice was like warm, melted butter. Maybe she should mentally squeeze his testicles after all. Then, he wouldn't be able to talk in that silken baritone and make her gush in her damn thong. "What are you doing?"

Evie grimaced. "Eating a really shitty dinner. You?"

"Same. I wish I'd learned to cook, but Jana is so great that I always let her cook for me," he said, referencing the main castle's housekeeper.

"I'm actually a pretty good cook."

"No shit," he said, his smile seeming to travel over the phone. "When did you learn?"

"I learned a lot of useless crap over eight centuries in the human world, believe me. I took at least twenty French cooking courses when I lived in Paris."

"Hot damn. I need to see this in action."

Evie chuckled in spite of herself. "Well, maybe I'll cook for you on one of our *dates*." Silence stretched, making her uncomfortable. "I mean, if you still want to continue with the bargain. I was a pretty big bitch to you yesterday morning."

He was quiet, and Evie could almost hear the wheels of his mind churning. "Do I have an out? You were pretty clear in your ultimatum."

A crack shot down her heart that he actually wanted out of their agreement. Self-hate coursed through her, reminding her that this was just one more example of how far decent people would go to escape from her if she gave them a choice. Determined to retain the upper hand, she said, "Sorry, but the deal's still on. Two more dates, or I go back to the human world. I know it's not what you want, but I hold all the cards."

Kenden sighed, sending the sad sound through the phone. "It's not what I want at all—"

"Well, too fucking bad," she snapped, annoyed at him, especially since she'd let herself be so vulnerable with him the other night. "Because it's two more nights of fucking or nothing. Take it or leave it."

"Are you done?" he asked angrily.

She didn't respond.

"What I was trying to say, before someone rudely interrupted me, is that this arrangement is not what I want at all. I'd rather just date you, without there having to be some bargain or timeline."

"Huh," she said, feeling her eyebrows draw together. "Interesting, since you were pretty clear at my brother's wedding that you weren't interested in fucking me."

"That hasn't changed, Evie. I'm not interested just fucking you, as I think I've told you numerous times now. Since that was all you seemed to want, I wasn't interested in pursuing anything further. Now that we've established that we can actually have a good time together, I find myself wanting to spend what extra time I have with you."

Her heart dropped to her stomach, landing in an anxious pit as she absorbed his words. Why in the hell did she react to him this way? Many other men had bestowed beautiful words upon her. None of them had even phased her. But this man, with his sincerity and honesty, threatened to give her a damn heart attack.

"That sounds very serious, Commander, and serious is not on the agenda for me. I assure you, if you give me two more dates, your sentence will be served."

"Fine," he said, sounding resigned and annoyed. "I'm really swamped with the troops, so I'd like to stick to Saturdays if that's okay with you. We can have our second date this Saturday and the last one the following Saturday. Sound good?"

"Sure," she said, trying to sound more nonchalant than she was. "What is it this Saturday? More romantic strolls by the river?"

"I have the day off, so I was thinking we could hang during the day if that works for you. There's a great hiking trail that I'd love to show you. If you like that sort of thing."

"Well, it's your lucky day because I actually love hiking. As I told you, I spent some time in Colorado. The hiking there is fantastic."

"Great," he said. "I'll pick you up at ten a.m. on Saturday. Sound good?"

"I'll be ready. I'll make sure to wear my tightest sports bra so you can ogle my tits and then pretend that you didn't."

His chuckle almost made her squirm. "Now that I've been inside you, I think I can stop pretending. You have gorgeous breasts, Evie, and you damn well know it. If I don't see you on the compound, I'll see you on Saturday. Sweet dreams."

With a click, the phone went dead. As she watched the light of the device fade, she imagined she'd be having very sweet dreams this evening. Of a tall, sweaty man throwing her over a rock by a secluded hiking trail and banging her mindless. Sweet indeed.

※

Kenden entered Miranda's royal office chamber on Tuesday afternoon. The day's training had gone well, and he needed to speak to his cousin about a few things before heading home.

Miranda was sitting at her desk, holding a small square object in her hand. As he sat down in one of the chairs across from the mahogany desk, she gave him a sad smile.

"I found this in the drawer when I returned from Astaria the first time. It's a picture of Mother. Father must've kept it here and looked at it when his longing for her became too much to bear."

"He loved her so much," Kenden said. "Perhaps to his detriment."

Miranda nodded. Sighing, she placed the picture back in the drawer, closing it softly. Lifting her magnificent olive irises to his, they seemed to glisten as they shined with tears. "I can't tell if you're pissed at me or just pretending you are, but I'm ready to grovel."

Kenden breathed a laugh. "Now, that's something I'm dying to see," he said, arching a brow.

Her chin quivered, only slightly, and he felt a tiny crack down his heart. She was the person he'd loved most in the world for so very long. Although he enjoyed teasing her, he certainly didn't want to cause her any pain. Kenden opened his mouth to tell her he'd forgiven her days ago.

"Okay," she said, straightening her spine and lifting her chin before he could speak. "What do I have to do to secure your forgiveness? Public humiliation? A fancy bottle of red? Or…oh—I could chop wood for your fireplace for a month. Am I getting warm?"

Kenden felt his lips curve. "Actually, I really like chopping wood. There's something cathartic about manual labor."

She gave him one of her blazing smiles. "No one would guess you're an aristocrat if they didn't already know it, Ken. You're just a good ol' fashioned guy's guy."

He chuckled. "Yeah, as you always remind me, I'm quite boring."

Love for him swept over her features, causing his heart to swell. "Boring and stable and unfaltering. Thank god. I don't think I would've survived without you. You're my other half, Ken. I need you." Her throat bobbed as she swallowed thickly. "I'm so sorry. I didn't mean to make fun of the situation with Evie. I really hope you can forgive me. I was just shocked, honestly, and you know I react to tense situations with humor. Please, don't be mad at me."

His eyes narrowed as he debated making her squirm just a bit more. "What kind of public humiliation did you have in mind?"

"Ken," she said, her tone pleading.

Shaking his head, he sat up and reached across the desk. Placing his hand in hers, they laced their fingers. "I forgave you days ago, Randi," he said, genuinely smiling. "I was just shocked and a bit embarrassed, but you know I love teasing you. I could never be mad at you." He squeezed her hand. "But I reserve the right to use the 'public humiliation' card whenever I see fit. One use only, to be fair."

Miranda exhaled a laugh. "Okay," she said, relief evident in her flawless features. "I accept. Those are pretty easy terms. You're losing your edge."

"Never," he said, winking and sitting back in his chair.

"Thank you," she said, running a hand through her hair as she sat back and swiveled in the large chair. "So, what do you need? I know you didn't just search me out to ensure my future humiliation."

"We need to manufacture a hundred more long-range walkies and seven hundred more TECs. I want to make sure we're armed with extras when we attack Crimeous."

"Sure thing. I'll work with Sathan to approve the budget for the laborers on the outer compounds. Just submit a purchase order for me so I can keep track. This war is expensive, especially with the new weapons. I'll be happy when we kill that bastard and can use the funds for the betterment of our kingdom. The new playground's coming along, and we need more improvements like that."

"Agreed," Kenden said.

Miranda gnawed her bottom lip. "So, how are things going with Evie?"

Kenden shot her an acerbic look. "Miranda—"

"I'm just asking a simple question," she interrupted, lifting her hands in the air, palms up, and shrugging.

"No, you're nosy as hell and trying to snoop in my business."

"Of course, I'm nosy," she said, scrunching her features. "Have you freaking met me?"

Laughing in spite of himself, Kenden rubbed his forehead with his fingers. "It's going fine. She's a very complicated woman, and I'm trying my best to understand her."

Miranda studied him, her lips forming a smile. "Well, you're the most patient, understanding person I know, so she's in good hands. I know you're not thrilled with this situation, but I think she's good for you in a lot of ways."

"Is that so?" he asked, lifting a sardonic brow.

"Yes," she said with a confident nod. "It's been a long time since someone has had the voracity to challenge you, Ken. I think she's a worthy opponent for you. I also think that you're very attracted to her and that you're the perfect person to help her recognize the goodness she has within."

"She's convinced she's rotten inside. It's quite sad," he said softly, rubbing his palms together as he contemplated the scarlet-haired beauty who seemed to consume his every thought lately.

"Well, she's no Mother Teresa, that's for sure, but she's my mother's daughter. I have faith that she'll choose the light. The longer she's here, surrounded by people who are determined to make that happen, the better. Although I know you weren't enamored with the circumstances that led to you courting her, I think you two could have something really great together."

"She swears her time in the immortal world is temporary."

"I swore I wanted to kill Sathan with the Blade," Miranda said with a slight shrug. "Things change. Plus, it doesn't hurt for you to get boned, Ken. It's been a while. She was right about that."

"Okay," Kenden said, standing and running his hand over his hair. "I'm definitely *not* going to sit here and discuss my sex life with you. Let's leave it at the fact that I'm enjoying my time with her and feel a deep well of compassion due to the violence she experienced when she was young. I want to help her understand that not everything that involves emotion involves pain. If I can accomplish that while courting her, then I'll consider it a win."

Affection filled Miranda's features as she stood and walked around the desk. Sliding her arms around Kenden's waist, she laid her head on his broad chest. "You're the best man I know, Ken. She's so lucky to be with you. If anyone can find her goodness, it's you. I love you so much."

"I love you too," he said, embracing her and kissing her on her silky head.

Disengaging, she looked up at him. "I can still find us some really fancy wine, if you like? It's almost dinner time. Jana said she's making halibut and fresh veggies."

"Well, hot damn," he said. "It's my lucky day. Only an idiot would pass on that."

Arm-in-arm, they strolled to the kitchen to devour the sweet housekeeper's delicious food.

On Wednesday, Evie dematerialized to the spot where Miranda had texted her. She didn't appreciate being dictated to but figured her sister wouldn't bother unless it was important. Glancing around, she noticed the open meadow under the midday sky. Not a trace of civilization could be seen.

With a *whoosh*, Darkrip materialized, Miranda in his arms.

"Guess you were summoned too," Evie muttered to her brother.

Miranda shot her a glare. "I *asked* you both to meet me here so that I can discuss something important with you."

"Fine," Evie said with a shrug. "What do you need?"

Inhaling a deep breath, Miranda's green irises traveled back and forth between theirs.

"Sathan and I have decided to build another compound here. It will be a joint compound, consisting of Slayers and Vampyres."

"That's great," Darkrip said. "It's nice to see the kingdom growing."

"Yes, it is," Miranda said with a nod. "We also anticipate needing to house Deamons here, after we defeat Crimeous."

Evie's eyebrows drew together. "For what purpose?"

"There will be many women from his harem who have no place to go. We also suspect that several of his men will surrender in exchange for their lives. Although they need to be held accountable for their actions, we wish to start anew. If a Deamon truly wants to atone and is willing to pay his debt to society, we want to offer him a home. Others who won't concede will be placed in the prison that we'll build on the outskirts of the new compound."

"Wow," Darkrip said, his tone cautious. "That's assuming a lot, Miranda. Deamons have been crafted by my father to be extremely malicious. I appreciate your compassion, but we need to make sure it's warranted."

"I understand," she said. "Believe me, we didn't come to this decision lightly. But we've discussed this with many on the council, and Lila has studied human societies extensively. The countries that rehabilitate their prisoners most effectively have the lowest reincarceration rates. Most of those offenders go on to contribute greatly to society. Plus, it's the humane thing to do. We've made our decision."

"Okay," Evie said, crossing her arms over her chest. "So, what does this have to do with us?"

Miranda's features softened. "You both are children of Valktor. You share his blood as much as I do. I was raised to be the Slayer Queen but I don't want to deny you your destiny. I would like to offer you the opportunity to co-govern the new compound. Being the descendants of our grandfather, and half-Deamon, you both would garner a respect from the Deamon inhabitants that Sathan and I never could."

Evie and Darkrip stared at their sister, both a bit stunned.

"Look," Miranda said, lifting her arms at her sides. "I know this is a shock. But we have to think of the livelihood of the kingdom down the road. We can't let the Deamons continue to live in the caves. Ken and Latimus will destroy them all once we win the war. They'll need leaders. You two are the most capable in my eyes. You're both my family, and I want us to build the future of our world together."

"It's a really nice offer," Darkrip said, taking her hand. "I would love to help you, but I made a promise to Arderin, and I have to see that through. Once she's done with her medical training in the human world, I'd be happy to consider this. But for now, I have to decline."

"Fair enough," Miranda said, squeezing his hand. "What about you, Evie?" she asked, pinning her with her green gaze.

"Um, yeah," Evie said, rubbing the back of her neck. "I thought I'd been pretty clear that I'm heading back to the human world after this. No offense, but I hate it here. And I definitely don't want to add Governor to my list of titles. Mean, angry bitch suits me just fine."

Miranda breathed a laugh. "Well, I wouldn't call you mean, exactly..."

They all chuckled.

Miranda grabbed Evie's hand as well. "I understand your reluctance to stay here. You've never had a home or a purpose. That's something I'm trying to remedy. You're a very confident and powerful person, Evie. I think you'd make an excellent leader. I won't push you, but I don't want you to answer now. Think on it. We have time until the battle. Can you at least do that for me?"

"Miranda—"

"I gave you a home, my forgiveness and my best intention to make you my family," Miranda interrupted. "All I'm asking is for you to consider this."

"Fine," Evie said, pulling her hand away. "I'll consider, since you've been so cordial, but don't get your hopes up. I don't see myself staying here."

"Even if the Commander wins you over?" Darkrip asked, arching a brow.

"Screw you," Evie said, scowling at him.

"Hey, it could happen," Miranda said. "Look at Darkrip. He's a lovesick pansy over Arderin."

Darkrip rolled his eyes. "Says the woman who gets googly-eyed when her husband so much as walks into a room."

"Don't make fun of me," she said, swatting him. "My husband is hot. I can't help it."

They all laughed, and Evie realized she was enjoying the moment. Maybe this whole sibling thing wasn't half-bad. Or maybe she was turning into a sentimental prick, living so close to all this lovey-dovey bullshit. Christ.

"C'mon," Miranda said, pivoting and beckoning them with her arm. "I want to show you guys where we plan to build."

For the next several hours, Evie followed her sister around, unwillingly affected by her enthusiasm for the future. Silently wishing she could feel the same.

"**W**hy do you tell me things that aren't true?" the man asked with anger. "I see your cheeks warm from my words and your heart beat fast from my touch."

"I only have the capacity to love those from my womb. It has always been so," the woman said. "But I do feel so warm from your words, and my heart does beat fast, because I consider you such a wonderful friend."

The man's face became a mask of rage. "I do not want a friend," he yelled, his deep voice booming across the field. "I want to love you, as a man loves a woman, and I will settle for no less."

The woman sighed. "Then, I am sorry to say that we cannot see each other anymore. Goodbye, my dear Galredad. I hope you find peace in this world." Turning, she began to walk away.

But not before the man grabbed her arm, halting her retreat...

Chapter 9

On Saturday, Kenden threw on his athletic shorts, t-shirt and sneakers and headed outside to wait for Evie to appear. He'd offered to pick her up at her cabin, but she'd vehemently refused, allowing her to have one more instance of control. Sighing, he sat in one of the wooden rocking chairs on the porch of his house. The sky was a beautiful blue and the day was warm, perfect for a hike. A breeze seemed to ruffle the grass in front of the porch, and suddenly, she appeared.

Like a mermaid rising from the ocean, she was a vision to him. Red hair pulled into a bouncy ponytail behind her flawless face. Black yoga pants hugging her hips and thighs, stopping at her calves. She wore only a black sports bra, her breasts spilling from the top like she promised. The pale swath of skin that comprised her stomach seemed to call to him. Gray sneakers completed her ensemble.

Rising ever so slowly, he ambled down the porch stairs toward her, not stopping until only inches separated them. Pleasure coursed through him when she had to lift her chin to maintain eye contact. At least he had a physical advantage over her, if nothing else.

"Well, I did promise you I'd wear something that showcased my tits," she said, grinning up at him.

"You sure did," he said, allowing his eyes to rove over her. Lifting his finger, he gently traced her collarbone. "Hope you wore sunscreen. Wouldn't want them to burn before I get my hands on them later."

"Lathered and ready," she said. God, he loved the challenge in her voice.

"Then, let's go," he said, extending his hand to her.

Grabbing it, she drew him close. "Where to? I'll transport us."

"Nope," he said, motioning his head toward the four-wheeler. "I'm driving. Hop in. You'll have to throw your leg over the side because the door is welded shut."

She lifted a scarlet brow. "Not the red-carpet welcome I've come to expect from you."

"Shut up and get in the car," he said, playfully biting at her lips.

She nipped right back and then seemed to bounce to the passenger side. Once in, he revved the engine. "It's mostly dirt roads, so things are gonna get bumpy. Hold on."

Kenden drove them along the wall, past the massive doors that led outside the compound, to the open field east of the River Thayne. Riding in silence, he studied her, that silky ponytail blowing in the breeze. Eyes closed, she was magnificent as she inhaled the fresh air. Eventually, they came to the foothills of the nearby mountain range, rolling and gentle above.

"Made it," he said, anchoring his arm on the door and jumping from the four-wheeler. Coming around, he offered her his hand. "Need help?"

"Not on your life, Commander," she said, using her arms to hoist herself out. Landing on her feet, she brushed her hands over her thighs. "Where to?"

"You're going to let me lead? I'm shocked."

"You know the trail," Evie said, holding her hands up, palms facing forward. "I defer to you. Tonight, when we're in bed, I might not be so nice. I'd take advantage while you can."

Chuckling, Kenden reached into the back to grab their supplies. Once his belt was loaded with two knives and a Glock, and they both had water, they began their trudge along the path.

The trail was gorgeous, dotted with various trees and bushes with leaves of green and brown. Dirt and rocks lined the way as their sneaker-clad feet navigated the terrain. A small river gurgled nearby, every so often intersecting with the path. The incline grew steeper as they went, Kenden always reaching back and offering her a hand. Of course, Evie never took it, but a gentleman always offered anyway.

"So, are you always armed?" she asked, making conversation as they trekked.

"Yes," he said, grunting as he climbed over a particularly large rock. "It's been imbedded in me forever. Part of my training."

"Who trained you?" she asked. "After the Awakening?"

"I was distraught that I wasn't at the blood-banking," he said, resignation burning in his chest. "There was a terrible flu circulating around the compound, and I caught it. I was twenty at the time and usually went with my parents but was too sick to go that year. I'll never forgive myself that I wasn't there to save them."

"It wasn't your fault," she said, her tone compassionate. "If you'd been there, you probably would've died."

"Maybe," he said, shrugging as they strolled down a relatively straight part of the trail. "But I still feel responsible."

"I think you feel responsible for a lot of things," she said, those green eyes so deep as she stared up at him. "You can't be everyone's savior, Ken."

"Well, I wish I could've been theirs," he said, sighing. "Regardless, I realized quickly that we needed an army. After the Vampyre's first raid, we were decimated. I'd studied human warfare in school and loved it. All the cunning and strategy, I had a knack for it. Marsias realized it and commissioned me Commander. From there, I set about studying everything I could about warfare and battle. I drafted our strongest men and formed a competent army. So, I guess you could say, I was self-trained. And that consumed my life for ten centuries."

"It's very noble," she said, lifting her bottle to take a sip.

"Want to sit for a minute?" he asked, noticing that she was slightly panting.

"Sure," she said, lowering to a nearby rock. "You're showing me up. I feel inadequate."

Laughing, he took a swig of water as he sat atop a stone on the opposite side of the trail. "Don't worry. I won't tell anyone you couldn't keep up with me."

"Jerk," she teased, smiling at him. His heart slammed at those beautiful teeth and full lips.

"You've protected your people for all these years," she said, shaking her head in wonder. "It's very admirable. I know I like to chide you, but I respect that immensely. I've rarely known a person as selfless as you, Ken. It's amazing that you let me within fifty feet of your humble perfection."

Sorrow choked him, knowing that she saw herself this way. Although she had many flaws, she was the product of so much hurt and violence. It clawed at him, knowing that he'd protected so many but hadn't protected her. It would've been impossible, as he hadn't known of her existence, but his need to save her still scraped at him.

"I'm sorry you had to suffer for all those decades in the caves. I wish—"

"Wishes are for old women at fountains and kids waiting for the tooth fairy," Evie interrupted. "I don't talk about my past with anyone."

Annoyance rushed through him. At her, for being so closed-off. At himself, for caring that she was. They sat in silence, sipping the water, breathing in the air. Suddenly, she stood.

"Do you hear that?" she asked, her head darting to various points behind them.

"Yes," he said softly, standing to assess the situation. "It could be an animal."

"Not likely," she muttered, her jaw clenching. "We need to—"

Before she could finish, the cries of battle overwhelmed them. Deamons, at least thirty strong from Kenden's assessment, swarmed from the trees that surrounded them. Dragging her toward him, he did his best to shield her.

"Give me a break," she said, wrenching her wrist from his grip and glaring up at him in anger. "I'm not one of your meek Slayer women." Pulling a knife from his belt, she turned to face the oncoming soldiers.

The Deamons attacked, strong and sure, circling them as they held various weapons. Guns, eight-shooters, swords—all were on deck for the ambush. Suddenly, the weapons disappeared from the Deamons' grips, and Kenden knew Evie had dematerialized them. Drawing his gun in one hand and a knife in the other, Kenden got to work.

He shot two of the creatures dead between the eyes, turning to plunge the blade into the side of another. Looking over his shoulder, he saw Evie as she fought. By the goddess, she was a machine. Lifting her hand, she drew one of the Deamons toward her with her mind, clutched his throat and gutted him with the knife. The contents of his abdomen spilled onto the ground, and she picked up one of the intestines. Using it like a lasso, she swung it around another soldier's neck, drawing him close and plunging the knife into his genitals. Good god.

"He raped one of the harem women last night," Evie said, daring him to judge her as she looked over her shoulder. "I saw the image in his mind. I'll cut off every one of these bastard's balls who dares to rape a woman. Fucking watch me."

A grunt sounded at Kenden's side, and he resumed fighting, realizing he'd have time to process what an effective and lethal warrior she was later. Together, they fought, determined and solid, until only two Deamons were left.

"Let's knock them unconscious and take them back to Uteria for questioning," Kenden said. "They might be able to give us intel on how much your father knows about your presence here."

"Fuck that," she said, facing him as she held the Deamons frozen with her outstretched hand, palm up. "I'm going to murder these assholes."

"No," Kenden said, trying to keep his voice calm. "We need information, Evie. Sometimes, that's more valuable than death."

"But not as fulfilling. Give me your gun."

"No," he said, clutching the weapon.

Evie's features contorted into something raw and angry. It would've cowered most men. Instead, Kenden stood firm, understanding that she was dangling on a precipice between reason and madness.

"Give me the fucking gun," she said through clenched teeth. "I won't ask again."

"No," he repeated, determined to stand his ground. Wanting so badly for her to choose pragmatism over heated rage.

Those stunning eyes narrowed, and she lifted her other hand, facing Kenden. Suddenly, any feeling that he had below his neck vanished. She'd frozen him, sure as if she'd turned him to stone.

"You're going to learn very quickly that I don't like being defied, Commander," she said, her nostrils flaring. Walking over to his motionless body, she picked up the gun, which had fallen to the ground from his limp hand. The two Deamon soldiers still stood behind her, unable to move. "Now, watch me gut these bastards like the slimy little assholes they are. Then, you can release any notions you have about me being '*good inside*.'" She made quotation marks with her fingers, difficult since she held his Glock in one hand. "And then, you can tell sweet Miranda how I dismembered these soldiers and ensure she stops looking at me through rose-colored glasses as well."

Turning, she sauntered toward the immobile Deamons. Lifting the gun, she ran the nozzle over one of the soldier's cheeks as he shivered with terror.

"Scared little thing, aren't you?" she asked, running the barrel of the gun down his neck. "Were you scared when my father tied up several of the harem women last night and let you and your friend here violate them? Hmmm?"

The Deamon sniveled, baring his teeth to her. "Crimeous will kill you, bitch!" he screamed.

Evie pistol-whipped him, causing his head to fly sideways. "Now, now. I'd shut the fuck up real quick if you want to keep at least one of your balls attached before I murder you. Capisce?"

"Evie, you don't need to torture them," Kenden said, frustrated that he couldn't move a muscle. "If you're going to kill them, do it humanely."

"Humane. Such a nice word. Were these two *humane* when they violated their victims?" she asked, pointing back and forth between the prisoners with the gun. Giving a *tsk, tsk, tsk* with her tongue, she said, "I think not. So, let's dole out the same treatment they gave those women, shall we?"

Kenden proceeded to watch her, his stomach rolling. She cut off the pants of both men, throwing them to the ground. Baring their genitals, she lifted the gun and shot one of them directly in the right testicle. The Deamon wailed in pain, his eyes seeming to pop from his head. Looking to the other man, she dropped the gun and picked up the knife. Extending his flaccid shaft in her hand, she sliced it off with the blade. Never had he heard a man squeal with so much agony.

Kenden had seen the spoils of war. Blood and gore didn't faze him. It hadn't in centuries. But seeing the woman he'd held in his arms only days ago, whom he was coming to cherish and care for, torture these men shifted something inside him. It was dark and dirty, and he wished like hell they'd never been attacked.

"I can read the images in your mind," she said softly, her tone so sad. She still faced the Deamons, now almost unconscious from their maiming. "I know. It's awful. *I'm* awful. I wish I wasn't this way."

He almost missed the gleam from the tear that fell from her face as she stood with her back to him. Almost. It glimmered with the moisture of her despair and the promise that somewhere, deep inside, she still had the ability to feel remorse for her actions.

"You need to kill them, Evie," he said, his throat raw from emotion. "You've tortured them enough."

She scoffed, causing the strands of her ponytail to bob. "It's never enough. That's what you'll never understand about me, Ken." The droop of her shoulders was heartbreaking. "I always need more. I thrive on the violence. On the pain. It's a terrible curse."

Walking toward the soldier on the right, she plunged the knife into his neck. Circling him, she cut a long trail until his entire neck was gaping open. Pushing his head back, it hung, almost swinging from the still-connected spinal cord. Approaching the other soldier, she grabbed his chin. "Tell me you're sorry. For all the women you raped."

"Never," he said, spittle flying from between his teeth.

Lifting the gun from the ground, she returned to clutch his chin. Sticking the barrel in his mouth, she maneuvered it back and forth, causing the man to groan in pain. "Say it, asshole."

He garbled something unintelligible due to the object in his mouth, but it wasn't what Evie wanted to hear. Cocking the gun, her eyes grew wide as she watched the Deamon tremble. Confident as Kenden had ever seen her, she pulled the trigger. The man's brains spattered to the rocks beyond and everywhere in between.

Pivoting, Evie came to stand before him. Icy, heavy dread began to pulse through Kenden's unmoving body. Never had he seen anything like the sight before him. Evie—gorgeous, flawless Evie—blood-stained and pulsing with rage. Bits of Deamon spatter marred the white expanse of her stomach above the yoga pants, and she still held the gun in her hand.

But none of that made his blood run cold. With what he'd seen in his life, it never could.

No, what rocked him to his core was the look in her olive-green eyes.

Pleasure, pure and limitless, to the depths he'd never seen, glowed in the striking orbs.

As he silently beckoned to her with his eyes, she dropped the gun to the ground, following suit and crumpling to sit on the dirt. Wide, emerald orbs stared up at him as she hugged her knees to her chest.

"I need a moment," she said, her knuckles white as she squeezed her arms around her.

"Okay," Kenden said, his voice scratchy.

As she lowered her forehead to her knees, he watched her tremble violently, wondering the entire time if it was from pleasure or remorse.

Evie heaved a ragged sigh into her knees, knowing she needed to stand the hell up. Resolved, she inhaled a deep breath and lifted to her feet. Refusing to meet Ken's eyes, she flicked her hand, giving him control of his muscles.

"Evie—"

"Please, don't touch me," she said, staring at the dead bodies that surrounded them. "I'm not trying to be a bitch. I just can't have anyone touch me right now."

"Okay," he said, his voice so steady and composed. His firm calmness usually rankled her, but she was too raw to muster up the irritation. "We need to clean up the bodies. I'm going to call Darkrip so he can transport some soldiers here."

Evie barely heard the conversation he had with her brother, too entranced by the corpses of her father's soldiers. She'd placed a shield on her thoughts, ensuring Crimeous wouldn't read them, but his spies were vast. It was only a matter of time before he began tracking her. She thought she'd be scared. Maybe curious. Pissed for sure. She never anticipated feeling the emptiness inside at the discovery that her father knew of her presence in the immortal world. After so many centuries of being fueled by burning rage, it was disconcerting to feel numb.

Her brother appeared, the Slayer soldier Larkin along with him. Darkrip dematerialized again and again, bringing ten Slayer soldiers to the site of the battle.

"We'll get this cleaned up," Darkrip said, patting Kenden on the shoulder. "You two should go back to the compound," he said, gesturing with his head toward Evie.

"I'm fine," she said, although her tone was lifeless. "I can help if you want."

"We've got it," Larkin said. "I'll drive the four-wheeler back. You guys should update Miranda and Sathan. They're at Astaria."

Kenden approached her cautiously. She knew it wasn't because he was afraid but because he somehow understood how dazed she felt. "Can you transport us to Astaria? After that, we'll go home and shower."

Evie nodded, too exhausted to reply. Kenden's firm arms embraced her, clutching her tight. Grasping her hands behind his neck, she transported them to Astaria.

Once in Sathan's office chamber, Miranda rushed to her. "Evie, are you okay? Darkrip updated us."

"Don't," Evie said, holding up a hand. "I can't be touched by anyone but Ken right now. Please."

"Okay." Miranda nodded, backing away. Evie and Kenden stood by the conference table, Miranda and Sathan in front of his mahogany desk. "Can you tell us what happened?"

Kenden recounted the story while Evie rubbed her upper arms, irritation softly pounding through her veins. She'd let the evil take over, unable to stop herself from torturing the bastards. Kenden's chocolate irises had regarded her, filled with disgust and horror. Self-loathing threatened to drown her as she lifted her gaze to Sathan's.

"I'm happy to hear that you defeated them so handily," Sathan said. "Darkrip told me you were a competent warrior and that you've trained with humans over the centuries."

"Yes," Evie said, holding his gaze, pushing away the shame and self-revulsion. "I trained with the samurai of Japan, the armies of Alexander the Great, Attila the Hun and William Wallace. Most didn't welcome women in their ranks, but with my powers, they all thought I was a witch. That made me a potent ally."

"Daughters of Rina know how to kick ass," Miranda said. "I don't doubt you're awesome, Evie."

"I enjoyed it," Evie said, lifting her chin to stare at her sister. "Every single slaughter. Every single death. It's not a hardship for me to kill others. Ken wanted me to kill the Deamons humanely. I'm not capable. You all need to know that."

"She could see images in their minds of them raping Deamon harem women," Kenden said.

"Don't make excuses for me," she snapped. "I keep trying to tell you all how horrible I am. I don't know how to make you believe me."

"Let's table this discussion for another day," Miranda said, shooting a look at Kenden. "You both are covered in Deamon blood and need to wash off the attack. Evie, are you able to transport back to Uteria?"

"Yes," she whispered with a nod.

"Good. You're tough, so I have no doubt you'll be fine. Guys, can you give us a minute?"

Sathan pecked his wife on the cheek and left the room, Kenden following behind as he closed the door with a click.

"Thank you for killing them all," Miranda said. "I fucking hate Deamons. Ken is very pragmatic about war, but I would've done the same. Any man who rapes a woman deserves to get his dick cut off a hundred times. If that makes you evil, then I am too."

"And yet, you want to rehabilitate them," Evie said, confused.

Miranda exhaled a large breath. "There's what I want and what I know is right. Sathan and Ken are good for me. They calm me down so I don't act impulsively. I hate to tell you, sis, but it's a trait of our bloodline. We can't control our impulses sometimes. Perhaps yours is magnified, because of your father's blood, but I'm not going to judge you for having the same affliction I have."

"You people are all so damn forgiving," Evie said. "It's absolutely maddening."

Miranda chuckled. "It's all part of my masterplan to win you over. Don't look now, but I think it's working."

Evie felt the corners of her lips turn up. "Maybe."

After a moment, Evie said, "I cried. In front of Ken. I never cry," she said, shaking her head slowly. "I feel remorse now, every time I kill, even if the victims deserve it. I feel like I've lost my grip on everything I knew. Everything I believed. What the hell is happening to me? I feel like the Earth is crumbling under my feet, and I have no idea how to control it."

Miranda perched on the side of the conference room table with her hip. "Control is a big thing for you. I get it. You've had to grab on to it with an iron fist for so long. If you're going to lose it, Ken is the right person to catch you. He's amazing."

"I know," Evie said, glancing at the floor. "Why does he put up with me? I have nothing to offer him but pain and spite."

"Ken's always been a bit of a savior," Miranda said with a smile. "He has a built-in sense of compassion that drives him to protect those he loves. But he's not without his flaws. He's rigid and set in his ways. If he spends one more hour in that shed of his, he might literally die of boredom. You bring passion into his life, and it's something he sorely needs. Don't sell yourself short, Evie. I think you both have a lot to offer each other if you'd open yourself to him."

"My feelings for him are so different than any other man. It's terrifying."

"Good," Miranda said. "Then, there's hope." Standing, she inched closer to Evie, careful to leave some space between them. "Don't pull away from him today. Let him support you. You're masterful at thriving on your own, but that isolation can fuel your anger. Let it go and let him help you."

"I need the anger," Evie said. "It's the only way I know how to survive."

"Then, perhaps it's time you learn a different way."

Evie studied her sister, speaking words so wise. Not knowing what else to say, she turned to open the door and transport back to Uteria.

"**P**lease, my love," Galredad said, his voice pleading. "I have lost everything. I need your love. Without it, I might as well have perished along with the others."

"I'm so very sorry," she said, cupping his cheek. "But this must be goodbye."

The woman attempted to turn but was restrained yet again. There, under the blazing sun, his face began to contort into a mask of fury and vehemence so dark and sinister that the woman experienced something akin to fear.

"Release your grip," she commanded.

"No," was his firm reply...

Chapter 10

Kenden released Evie as soon as she transported them to his bedroom, acknowledging that they both needed space. Traversing to the mahogany dresser, he turned, leaning his lower back against it as he regarded her.

She stood before him, a war-ravaged beauty, uncertainty swimming in her limitless orbs.

"I need to go back to my cabin and shower," she said softly. He'd rarely seen her so unsure, and it moved something inside his chest.

Exhaling a huge breath, he held up his hand, palm forward. "I'm just trying to process this, Evie. Watching you torture those Deamons was…difficult for me."

"I told you I was evil—"

"Wait," he said, slicing his hand through the air. "This isn't going to turn into a discussion about your Deamon side. I accept that part of you. But what I need to know is if you can embrace your Slayer side. Otherwise, this will never work. And I don't mean you and me," he said, straightening his spine as he stood tall. "I mean you against your father."

Slowly, he began closing the distance between them. When he reached her, he lifted her chin with his fingers. "I want so badly to believe you'll choose the goodness, Evie. But I need you to believe it too."

Her pupils darted back and forth between his. "I'm not sure I can make that promise," she said, her expression so genuine it almost broke his heart. "My evil half has always been my greatest soldier. After so many centuries, it's difficult to push it away."

Sighing, he cupped her cheek. Small splats of Deamon blood marred the smooth skin. "We both need to wash off the battle. Let's do that first." Stepping back, he held out his hand. "Come on," he said, gesturing with his head to the bathroom.

"I should shower at my cabin," she said, rubbing her upper arms with her thin fingers. "I think that might be best. I can't imagine you'd want to be in my presence right now anyway."

"Evie," he said, shaking his head ever so slowly as he regarded her. "I'm a soldier. I've seen the worst displays of torture and death. I'm not repulsed by your actions, although they were gruesome. I'm...disheartened, I guess. I wanted so badly for you to choose rationality over anger. The battle within you is going to be so much harder for you to fight than any skirmish against your father."

"I know," she said. "It's just so hard to side with righteousness when the fury consumes me. No one's ever been there to care that I chose another way."

"I care," he said, his voice almost a growl. "And I need you to trust me on that. I'll support you if you choose the goodness. Always."

"I don't trust anyone."

"That ends today," he said, extending his hand to her again. "Let's wash off the battle."

Green irises searched his, and he thought she might dematerialize away. "I don't understand how you could still want to touch me."

Swallowing thickly, he spoke the truth. "I've never desired anyone as much as you, Evie. I think you could destroy the whole damn planet, and I'd still want you. But I'd rather you just take a shower with me. Let's comfort each other and let the planet survive another day. Come on," he said, shaking his hand. He gave her a gentle smile, wanting to assure her that he supported her, even through her complexity and doubt.

After a small eternity, she placed her hand in his. "Okay," she whispered.

Gripping her tight, he led her to the large master bathroom. Silently, they undressed. Kenden picked up her clothes and threw them in the hamper against the wall. "I'll get them cleaned. Jana is mad for me. She'll do it if I ask her."

That spurred a slight curve of her gorgeous lips. "Should I be jealous?"

"Definitely. I have a thing for housekeepers born centuries before the Awakening."

She smiled then, a bit broken but pure, and he realized that everything might just be okay. Naked, he drew her into the shower, starting the spray so that it sluiced over their battle-rough bodies. Nudging her under the nozzle, he made sure her hair was doused. Grasping the nearby shampoo bottle, he poured a coin-sized amount in his hand and began washing the thick scarlet strands.

With his broad fingers, he massaged her scalp, pulling her back into his body. His erection had appeared the second she'd lost her clothes but that didn't matter right now. What mattered was Evie. It was imperative that she understood that he wouldn't condemn her, even if she made mistakes. He didn't need perfection, he just needed her to strive to be the best version of herself.

Her head lolled back, resting at the juncture of his chest and shoulder. "It feels so good," she moaned, arching toward his fingers as he worked.

"We need to get some of your shampoo for my shower. The scent always drives me crazy. This one won't do it justice."

"Mmmm..." she said. Her gloss-free lips were pink, he noticed as he stared down at her. She always wore lipstick, and he'd rarely seen her without. Lids closed, her face was a mask of pleasure. Knowing that he was giving it to her did all sorts of things to his insides.

"Let me rinse you," he murmured. Pressing her toward the spray, he helped her clean the suds from her hair. With the cloth that hung on the nearby rack, he proceeded to wash her body. Once finished, she repeated his actions, running the cloth over his straining body. Finished, she threw the rag on the tile floor of the shower.

"I think we need to do something about this," she said, grasping his straining length.

"Not right now," he said, kissing her forehead.

Leading her from the shower, onto the plushy mat, he grabbed a towel and dried her off. Wrapping the towel around her, she covered herself while he toweled off. Clutching the cloth where it intersected her breasts, he pulled it away and threw it to the floor. Lowering, he picked her up as if she was made of feathers.

He lay her on the bed, gently urging her to lie on her stomach. "From behind?" she asked with that sultry voice. "I'm quickly realizing that's how you like it best, Commander."

Chuckling, he felt his muscles release at her teasing. They were easing back into their saucy banter; into the place where they were comfortable. Thanking all the gods, he pulled a pillow to each side of her head so she could rest her face in between. "I do like it that way. But for now, I want you to relax."

Straddling her lower back, he began to massage her shoulders with his broad hands.

"*Ohmygod*," she breathed, the words rushing out together. "That's it. You're perfect. I give up."

"Shut up, Evie," he said, smiling as she unwound in his hands. "Let me make you feel good."

Reaching over to his bedside table, he squirted some lotion on his hands. Rubbing them together to warm the liquid, he placed his palms on her lower back. Moving up to her shoulders and back down again, she writhed beneath him.

"Do me a favor and go lower, hmmm?"

Kenden breathed a laugh. "Not yet, sweetheart. You need to release some tension. You're tight as hell."

"Getting attacked by my father's thugs will do that to you."

Feeling his brows draw together, he remained silent, loathing that she'd been spawned by such a terrible creature. He spent several minutes on her back and then shifted to sit on his knees beside her. Intense and thorough, he massaged the backs of her thighs and her calves, eventually coming to rest on the globes of her perfect ass.

Thick fingers maneuvered the tissues there, causing her to purr into the pillows. After thoroughly loosening the straining tension from her cheeks, he parted her thighs. Lowering his hand, he rubbed her wet slit with his middle finger.

Teasing, tantalizing, he rimmed her opening until she began to squirm. Clutching the pillow underneath her head, she looked over her shoulder, slightly resting on her side.

"Please," she begged, undulating her hips toward him.

"Okay, baby," he murmured, inching the finger through her taut opening. "There you are. So wet and snug. Squeeze my finger, sweetheart."

She did, the constriction of her walls causing his erection to harden to the point of pain. If he didn't bury himself into her soon, he might die from unspent arousal.

"I know you want to be inside me," she rasped. "Your hands aren't enough. I need you."

The words tore something inside him, ripping open the cage that held the beast of his desire. Lowering beside her, he aligned her back with his front. Lifting her leg, he slid it over his hip, opening her.

"Is this what you want?" he growled, sliding the head of his cock over her dripping core.

"Yes," she hissed, pleading at him with those gorgeous eyes over her shoulder. "Please—"

She barely finished the word as he impaled her, causing her body to bow back against him. "Too much?" he asked, concerned that he was hurting her.

"Never enough," she said, dropping her forehead to the bed and pushing into him. "Goddamnit, fuck me."

Gritting his teeth, Kenden hammered into her, unable to control the jut of his hips. Her essence slid all over his straining shaft, driving him insane with lust. Grasping her thigh, he moved against her, the primal urge to bury himself deep inside drowning out any other voice in his head.

"I love being with you like this," he growled into her shoulder, biting the skin there. "Fucking you hard, feeling you squeeze my cock. Oh, god, Evie. It's so good."

"I know," she said, reaching up to grasp his hair. The tiny pinpricks of pain from the tugging only urged him on. Sliding his arm around, he found her little nub, nestled below the strip of red hair, with the pads of his fingers. Wanting to make her feel something close to the bliss he was experiencing, he began rubbing in concentric circles while he pounded her from behind.

"Ken," she cried, almost making him come from that sultry voice.

"I'm right here, baby. I've got you."

Her fingers tightened in his hair, magnifying the pleasure to a point so intense, he felt something burst inside. "Come," he commanded, his lips on her ear. "I want to feel your pussy choke me until I can't breathe."

Snapping her head back, she tensed. With a loud wail, she began convulsing in his arms, the shaking so severe that he had to hold her in place with his thick arm. The feeling of her walls constricting his shaft was too much, and he let go, spurting into her, releasing every bit of arousal into her warmth.

Kenden's hips jerked uncontrollably for what seemed like hours, causing him to collapse behind her once the last pulses died down. "Good god, woman," he said, kissing her neck as he held her close. Reveling in her shiver at the touch of his lips, he grinned. "Sex with you is unbelievable. I've never experienced anything like it."

"Mmmm..." she said, lids closed as she stretched against him like a cat sitting in a sunny windowsill. "It's because of our chemistry. It's off the charts. New for me too. Never been like this."

The fragmented sentences meant she was close to drifting off. No wonder, after the rush of adrenaline they'd both experienced earlier. Compounded by some pretty amazing sex.

Detaching from her, he lifted from the bed as she groaned.

"No. Just a few more minutes. I promise, I eventually hate cuddling. But come back for now."

He leaned down and kissed her by the fiery hair at her temple. "Be right back. Let me get something to clean us up."

Locating the washcloth they'd used earlier, he brought it out, facing her as he lifted her leg and wiped the evidence of their loving. She watched him through slitted eyes, looking content and sated. Depositing the cloth in the hamper, he fell back into bed, hauling her to sprawl across his chest.

"You're hairy," she mumbled, running her fingers through his chest hair.

"Mmm hmm. I never understood why men shaved their chests. Weird, if you ask me." Gently, he traced the pad of his finger over the top of her ear. "They're not pointed like Darkrip's," he said.

"No," she murmured into his pecs. "I had them surgically altered decades ago. Wanted all traces of that bastard erased from my memory."

He held her, skimming his palm over her thick, damp hair. Tightening his arm, he silently acknowledged the strength she'd shown by leaving her terrible past behind to forge a new life in a world that wasn't hers. It was quite remarkable.

"I love your body," she said, her fingers feeling so good as they caressed him. "You're insanely hot."

Chuckling, he kissed the top of her head. "You're the most gorgeous woman I've ever seen, Evie. It's unsettling. I feel inadequate next to your beauty and all those fancy clothes."

"They're just a shield," she said softly as her muscles relaxed into his. "So people don't hurt me."

"I know, baby," he said, running his fingers through her hair. "I wish people hadn't hurt you. I want to protect you so they can't anymore."

"I protect myself. Always have." The words were a bit warbled due to her lips being pressed into his skin. He stroked her, hating how lonely her life had been to this point. Vowing to make sure it never was again.

"You can't be my savior, Ken," she said, her palm coming to rest over his chest. "I'm beyond saving. I'm sorry. I wish I could be the woman you see when you look at me."

"I want you to be exactly who you are," he said, feeling her shudder. Maybe at the baritone of his voice, maybe at his words. "That's enough for me. One day, you'll figure that out."

"Don't count on it," she murmured. And then, she drifted into slumber.

Evie awoke with a start, the unfamiliar surroundings causing her heart to pound.

"I'm here," Kenden's deep voice said behind her. Pulling her close with his arm, he snuggled into her side. "You're safe."

There, in the darkness, terror threatened to squeeze every last breath from her straining lungs. He looked so peaceful, already falling back asleep as his face rested on the pillow. Moonlight strayed in from the uncovered window, highlighting his angular features. She'd been fucking him for less than two weeks and was already becoming addicted. Goddamnit.

It was everything she detested. Monogamy. Intimacy. Need. Every word made her shrink further inside herself. As he softly snored next to her, she had the insane desire to strangle him. Not because she wanted to cause him harm but because she wanted to save herself. From him and his beautiful words and his understanding demeanor. No, she couldn't let herself fall for that. In her mind, every outcome of their relationship ended in disaster.

He'd choke on his disappointment. Of whom she couldn't be. Whom she'd never become. She was a demented bitch but she couldn't let that happen to Kenden. He was too good, too noble.

One more date, next week. She'd cherish that time with him since it would be their last. Then, she'd set about defeating her father and getting on with her damn life. There was no future here for her.

Hearing her stomach grumble, she dematerialized to Kenden's downstairs kitchen. Searching the fridge and pantry, she didn't find much, but with her cooking skills, she found enough to throw something together.

Twenty minutes later, he strolled into the kitchen. "Something smells good," he said, walking to the island that sat in the middle of the large room.

"I told you I could cook. Although, you have all the trimmings of a proclaimed bachelor. I could barely find anything to work with but I managed."

Handing him a plate with a steaming omelet, she motioned to the island with her head. "Sit down and eat. It's nine o'clock. We fell asleep for a while."

Kenden sat at the counter, slicing off a large chunk of the omelet with his fork. Shoving it in his mouth, he chewed. "Mmmm..." he said appreciatively. "This is damn good. You're hired. Move in with me and cook. I can pay you in massages."

Laughing, Evie scooped her own omelet from the pan onto a plate. Sitting next to him on the stool, she took a bite. "That's a hefty price to place on one's massages. Sure you're worth it?"

"You tell me," he said, brown eyes sparkling with mirth.

"Hmmm..." she said, chewing. After swallowing, she said, "I guess you're okay."

"Pfft," he said, flicking his hand. "You're insane, woman. I'm fucking awesome. Don't even go there."

They settled into conversation, easy and comfortable. Once the omelets were finished and the dishes put away, Kenden poured them a glass of wine. Sitting on his couch in the darkened living room, they fell into silence.

"Are you having regrets?" she asked softly.

His eyebrows drew together. "About what?"

She rubbed the rim of her glass with the pad of her finger. "Let's see. That you're stuck in a bargain with an evil Deamon? One who revels in torturing and maiming others? I can't believe you still fucked me. Someone as faultless as you shouldn't want to touch anyone as wretched as me."

Inhaling a deep breath, he grasped her wine glass and set them both on the coffee table. Gently grabbing her wrists, he pulled her toward him. Facing her, he stared down into her eyes.

"If you think I don't understand for one second how merciless you can be, you've underestimated me. What you did to those Deamons is child's play for you. I can bet you've tortured others in your past much more vehemently."

"I have," she said, giving a slight nod. "Doesn't that sicken you? To know that you've been inside someone so evil?"

Chestnut irises darted back and forth as he rubbed her wrists with the pads of his thumbs. Evie found the gesture so soothing.

"I've told you this before, in ways that might not have been clear, so let me say it now so that there's no doubt. You have your father's blood. It's malevolent and awful, and I'm sorry that it runs through you. Not because it's a part of you but because it calls you to listen to your worst impulses. That makes it dangerous.

"You've done an amazing job at piecing your life together on your own. I can't imagine how difficult that was. Even though you dismiss your mother's half, it burns so brightly in you. Rina was magnificent. A shining star in our little world. Your brilliance puts hers to shame. Your biggest flaw, at this point in your life, is not allowing yourself to make better choices. Choosing to side with your Deamon half instead of your Slayer half. I see the struggle in you. And the fact that you struggle is all I need. It means there's hope, and I can work with hope. It blazed in me for a thousand years during the War of the Species, and eventually, the tribes reunited. I have enough patience to wait for you, Evie. You're worth it."

She shook her head, the gesture slow and resigned, and whispered, "I'm sorry."

"Why?" he asked, his forehead furrowing.

"Because I'm going to let you down. So fucking hard. It's going to devastate you. I wish I could save you from it."

His gorgeous lips curved as he arched a brow. "I know you're powerful, but even you can't see the future, Evie."

"Sadly, on this, I can." Reaching toward him, she cupped his cheeks. "You deserve a nice woman who will give you lots of babies and a happy home. I truly hope you find her one day." Drawing him toward her, she placed a soft kiss on his lips.

"Don't," he murmured against her. "Don't leave. I want to hold you."

"I'm always going to leave. You're smart enough to know that."

Giving him one last kiss, she dematerialized to the place she felt most comfortable. Her small cabin. Alone and numb.

The woman struck him, hard upon the face, and Galredad gritted his teeth. Fueled by all of the loss and loneliness inside, he threw her body to the ground, climbing on top to ravage her. For in his twisted mind, if he could only show her his love, she would understand.

She struggled beneath him, enhancing his rage, until he felt himself become something rather ugly and squalid. Forgetting himself, his only objective became to hurt her, so she would see how terrible it felt...

Chapter 11

Nolan whistled as he trekked toward the main castle at Uteria. He'd decided to surprise Sadie, securing a reservation at the fancy restaurant that sat in the main square. Clutching the bouquet of flowers in his hand, he noticed how tight his grip was. Similar to the clench of nerves deep in his abdomen.

Being a meticulous person, he had the night planned out, from the first moment he approached her until the end. He was going to ask her to move in with him at Astaria. Knowing that this was the next natural step for them, his heart pulsed blood through his body. If all went well, he'd escort his tiny Slayer home after dinner and finally hold her in his arms as they planned their future.

Nolan knew Sadie was a virgin. He certainly didn't want to rush her. But their increasingly heated kisses had been driving him wild. If she wasn't ready for intercourse, he could at least nibble her small breasts and kiss her deepest place until she writhed under him. Imagining how pretty she'd look when she obtained her release caused his throbbing shaft to twitch in his pants. He'd never wanted a woman as much.

Truth be told, he wasn't that experienced either. He'd only been with a handful of women before he came through the ether. The strict world of Georgian England where he lived during his youth didn't promote promiscuity. It was quite similar to the societies of the immortals in that way. Bloodlines and virgin brides were cherished.

Nolan hadn't been with a woman in over three hundred years. Something that had led to intense loneliness and despair while being trapped in the immortal world. Until sweet Sadie blazed into his sphere. A beautiful savior with a kind smile and generous heart. She'd plucked him from the abyss of lonesomeness and pieced him back into a semblance of a man. Thanking every god that existed, he trekked forward.

Entering the large doors of the castle, he shuffled downstairs toward her infirmary. Approaching the exam rooms, he heard her speaking to someone.

"Everything looks great, Sagtikos. Your vitals are good and your heart is healthy. No marathons for you, but otherwise, you're going to lead a perfectly normal life."

"Thank you, Sadie," a male voice said. Nolan heard a rustling and assumed he was sliding off the exam table. Not wanting to interrupt their appointment, he leaned back against the wall. "I was worried when you caught the heart murmur, especially as an adult. Glad to know my ticker's going to make it."

She laughed. Always so sweet, so soft. "Yep. You're good. Don't go using that heart to break others, okay? I saw you walking with Ariel in the park the other day. She's quite a catch."

Silence echoed for a few moments.

"What if I don't want Ariel?" the man asked. "We've known each other forever, Sadie, but something's changed in you. It's absolutely stunning."

Sadie cleared her throat. "It's my burns. Nolan and Arderin made a salve for me so that my skin would heal. It's amazing, and my cheek is almost completely clear."

"And your arm," the man said, his voice low and almost seductive. Was he touching Sadie? Nolan clenched his teeth, debating if he should intervene.

"Yes," she said, a bit of annoyance in her tone. "Eventually, my entire right side will be healed. I'll look normal again."

The room was quiet. "And then what? Surely, you'll want to marry and have a family."

"I hope so, yes."

"With the human doctor with the fancy accent? He can't give you children, Sadie."

"Not biologically, no. But we have a fully-functioning sperm bank right here. If we choose that route, I could always get inseminated. There are plenty of couples who can't have kids naturally and always find a way."

Nolan heard shuffling again and realized his heart was pounding. He knew he shouldn't be listening to their conversation but he was tethered to the wall by curiosity.

"I could give you children. So could other Slayer men. It would be foolish to tie yourself to a human. I hope you've thought of this. Don't you want to at least play the field a bit before you settle down with the first man who's ever courted you?"

"I...don't know," she said, her tone hesitant. "I've never thought about being with anyone else. Nolan's the only man who's ever been attracted to me."

"I'm attracted to you, Sadie. Others will be too. Don't place yourself in a box before you see what's out there. That's all I'm saying."

Nolan's breath caught in his throat. Uncertainty, strong and true, coursed through his veins. Not wanting to call attention to himself, he surreptitiously headed back up the stairs, out of the castle and into the afternoon sunlight. Under the blue sky, he stood, running his hand through his thick brown hair. The scent of the flowers surrounded him, still held in the grip of his other hand.

Thrumming with doubt, as the birds sang above, he replayed the overheard conversation in his head.

What if she wanted to date other men? Once she was fully healed, surely others would want to court her. Since he was pretty sure he was in love with her, he hadn't even considered that she might want to play the field. Cursing himself for moving too quickly, he rubbed his fingers over his forehead in frustration.

Always extremely thorough, Nolan had analyzed their situation methodically, concluding that it was time they cohabitate. Now, he recognized that they both needed more time to decide what was best. He felt compelled to take a step back and deliberate. Asking her to commit to him so soon after her skin was healing was unfair, especially since he couldn't give her children.

"Hey, Nolan," a voice said behind him. "Whatcha doing at the castle?"

"Hi, Moira," he said, straightening to his full height. "Nice to see you again. I, um, was just leaving."

"Beautiful flowers," she said, gesturing with her head. "For someone special?" White teeth glowed from her pretty smile.

"Uh, not really. Here," he said, thrusting them at her. "Please, take them. I don't want them to go to waste."

"Oh, I couldn't—"

"I insist," he said, all but shoving the flowers into her hands. "Now, if you'll excuse me, I have to get back to Astaria. Have a good evening."

Breaking into a full-on speed-walk, Nolan headed to the train station and boarded the next train bound for Astaria. Sitting in the car as it chugged along, worry crept in. Had he overreacted? He was usually so calm and steadfast at giving others relationship advice but realized quickly, as the train approached Astaria, that it wasn't so easy when it was your own heart in the balance.

※

Sadie gritted her teeth, becoming more frustrated by the minute at her conversation with Sagtikos. What an ass, questioning her life decisions. Where the heck had he been when she'd been burnt to a crisp these past centuries? Nowhere. No, the only man who'd ever even thought to look her way when she was ugly and scarred was Nolan. That gift of acceptance was worth so much more to her than having his biological child.

Knowing that Sagtikos would never understand, she shook her head. "Look, we've been friends a long time, but this really isn't your business. I love Nolan, human or not, just as he cared for me when no one else could. So, I really wish you'd stop discussing something that doesn't concern you. In the future, it would probably be best if you saw him for your checkups."

"Sadie—"

"No," she said, shaking off his arm. "Your appointment is complete. Please, leave the gown on the table. I'll see you around the compound, Sagtikos." Giving him a nod, she closed the door firmly behind her.

Frustrated that the checkup with her friend had taken such a turn, Sadie headed up the stairs, looking for Kenden. He was like a brother to her, always so kind and warm. Wanting his advice, she roamed around the castle, entering the large foyer by the front door.

"Hey, Sadie," Moira said, seeming to bounce inside. The woman was quite attractive with her deep blue eyes and thick blond hair. "How's it going?"

"Just great," Sadie said a bit sarcastically. "Gorgeous flowers. Who gave them to you? A suitor?"

Moira laughed. "I wish. No, I saw Nolan leaving here just a minute ago. He kind of just shoved them at me. But I guess I'll take them home and put them in water. It's been about a million centuries since a man gave me flowers. I should probably take advantage of it."

How strange. Nolan had been at Uteria and not told her? And he'd given Moira flowers? Why? Dread filled Sadie as she looked at the stunning Slayer. Was Nolan attracted to her? Sadie had always assumed they were exclusively dating but she'd never asked him. Good lord, she'd never dated anyone until now. In their modern world, was it appropriate to date more than one woman at once? Hurt constricted her throat and tears welled in her eyes.

"Well, they're beautiful," Sadie said. "Enjoy them. I have to, um, head outside for a bit. See you later."

Sadie jogged toward the front door, holding her ballcap to her head so it didn't fly off in the breeze. Reaching the park that sat in the middle of Uteria's main square, she held her palms to her cheeks. There, under the old oak tree, she cursed herself a fool as she somehow managed to hold the tears inside.

Moira headed toward Miranda's royal office chamber, not understanding what vibe she was putting off that was causing people to bolt from her presence today. Did she forget to put on deodorant? Looking around the darkened hallway, she quickly sniffed under her arm. Nope. Shower fresh. Deciding that maybe everyone was just a bit insane, she knocked on Miranda's door.

"Come in."

Easing the door open, Moira stepped inside, closing it behind her.

"Did you bring me flowers?" Miranda teased. "You'll have to give notes to my husband. He's been slacking lately."

"Oh, um, I kind of seemed to pick them up on my way here. I'll just leave them on the table while we speak." Setting the bouquet down on the conference table, Moira nervously rubbed her wet palms over her jean-clad thighs.

"Have a seat," Miranda said, waving toward the chairs in front of her mahogany desk. "I was so excited to hear that you wanted to meet with me. Any friend of Aron's is a friend of mine."

"Thank you, Queen Miranda," Moira said, curtsying. "I really appreciate your time."

Miranda's face contorted with distain. Standing, she walked over and placed her hand on Moira's shoulder. "Um, yeah. A few things. One," she said, holding up a finger, "don't ever curtsy to me again. Are we in the fourth century? Good god. And two," she said, holding up two fingers, "it's just Miranda. I can stand the whole *Queen* thing". She made quotation marks with her fingers. Drawing Moira toward her desk by gently tugging her arm, she gestured for her to sit.

"Sorry," Moira said. "I hope I didn't offend you."

Miranda threw back her head and laughed, hearty and bold. "Good lord, no. I'm just a woman who speaks her mind. And I hear you are too," she said, arching a raven-black brow. "Lila told me about your conversation in the gallery when you first met. You're a straight shooter, Moira. I freaking love that."

Relaxing a bit, Moira sat back in her chair. "I needed her to know. That Latimus always loved her. I would've wanted someone to tell me. I know it made her uncomfortable but felt it vital that she understood."

The queen smiled. "That's pretty awesome. Not many women would go out of their way to ensure a man from their past had happiness with his current lover."

"Why not?" Moira said with a shrug. "We're all women just trying to do our best in this world. We need to support each other and lift one another up. It's the only way to be our best selves and find happiness."

Grinning, Miranda sat back in her chair, swiveling absently. "Damn. I like you. Okay, so, let me have it. What do you need? I know it must be important if you asked for one-on-one time with your *queen*." She snickered and rolled her eyes, mocking herself. It was extremely endearing to Moira.

"Aron's birthday is on Thursday. I know this isn't giving you much notice since it's Monday, but I'd like to do something special for him. He's done so much to help me since I've returned. He's very...*fond* of you, so I thought that maybe we could plan a surprise for him. He's super-involved with the playground, and it's almost finished, so I was thinking we could have the unveiling on Thursday and throw him a surprise party. Is that lame?" she asked, feeling like a bit of a dolt in front of the queen.

Miranda shook her head, causing Moira to imagine puffs of steam exiting her ears as the wheels spun in her mind. "No. It's not lame at all. It's fucking brilliant. Aron is a damn saint. He'll only be happy if his birthday is celebrated while he's helping others. Let's throw him a surprise party, and I'll declare it a holiday. A kingdom-wide day of service. We'll name it in honor of Aron and officially open the playground. People can volunteer to clean up the park, do community service, whatever," she said, waving her hand. "Aron and his do-gooder heart will get a kick out of that."

Moira could feel herself beaming. "He would love that. Thank you, Miranda. It's more than I could've even asked."

"Of course," she said with a nod. "Aron was instrumental in cementing my appointment as queen. I most likely wouldn't be here without his support. It's well-deserved."

"You're so kind," Moira said, shaking her head. "I can see why he loves you." Realizing her slipup, she inhaled a sharp breath. "I mean, um, I, uh—"

"You can stop the foot-in-mouth routine," Miranda said, shooting her a droll look. "I'm an expert at it, believe me."

"Sorry," Moira said, rubbing the back of her neck. "Shit. I shouldn't have said that. Aaaaaand now I went and cursed in front of the queen. Crap."

Miranda giggled, her gorgeous green eyes filled with amusement. "Oh, honey, if no one cursed in front of me, I'd never have one damn conversation." They chuckled for a moment, and then, the queen's features softened. "He doesn't, you know."

"Excuse me?"

"Love me," Miranda said. "I know it seems that way, and maybe in his mind he thinks he does. But he loves a version of me that doesn't exist. One that's regal and perfect. Believe me, that sure as hell isn't me. Ask my husband. He'll happily tell you what a pain in the ass I am." Leaning forward, she rested her forearms on the desk. "If you ask me, he might just love you. I've never seen Aron so relaxed and carefree around anyone else. It's awesome for a guy as rigid as he is. It says something about his true feelings for you that he's able to let his guard down."

"Yeah," Moira said, rubbing her palms together between her knees. "I don't think so. He doesn't really see me that way. I was married to his best friend who died centuries ago. I think he just has this sense of protective loyalty toward me. I'd never be equal to him. I'm a servant's daughter. Not one drop of aristocratic blood in me."

Miranda's eyes narrowed. "Do you think that would truly matter to a man as good as Aron? In the end? I don't think it would."

Feeling uncomfortable, Moira shrugged. "I've thought about it a lot. There are a lot of circumstances that will only allow us to be friends. And that's okay. He's been a godsend to me ever since I returned to Uteria. I'm thankful for the friendship we share."

Miranda studied her. "Does he know where you were for the last eight centuries?"

Moira swallowed. Hard. "No," she whispered.

"Ah ha," Miranda said slowly. "I see."

"I'm pretty sure it was wrong to lie to him but I'm also pretty sure he would've thrown me out on my ass if he knew I'd...*given* myself to someone and not tried to work it out with my husband."

The queen chewed her lip. "Lila told me about the scar on your neck. Did your husband give that to you?"

Moira nodded, looking at the floor.

"So, what in the hell was there to work out? I'd have gotten as far away as possible too."

Inhaling a huge breath, she sighed. "It's not that simple."

"It usually never is." Standing, Miranda came to sit in the chair opposite her. Grabbing her hands, she bore her gaze into Moira's. "Let's throw Aron an awesome party and make a goddamn national holiday in his name. What do you say? Fuck all this heavy shit. It'll work out, Moira. I promise." She shook her hands and gave that brilliant smile.

"I say, hell yes," Moira said, beaming back.

And with that, the Aron, Son of Jakal, Kingdom-Wide Day of Service was born.

Regaining her wits, the woman pushed the man away. Summoning the strength of the heavens, she drew a lightning bolt from the sky and shot it into his body. His skin burned, becoming wrinkled and shriveled.

Closing her eyes, the woman called upon the force of the sun. As Galredad lay sprawled on the grass, the bright orb began to singe away his skin.

"Why do you hurt me so?" he cried, struggling to survive the pain.

"I do not wish to," she said, hovering above him as a lone tear ran down her cheek. "But you have become someone quite awful."

Swamped with sadness, the woman vanished...

Chapter 12

On Thursday, Evie took extra time to get ready, wanting to fortify the shield comprised of her expensive clothing and flawless features. She hadn't spoken to Kenden since leaving his house, showing her cowardice. It was appalling. Evie never showed fear and certainly not to men. She should've stayed and let him rock her world another time or two, showing him their connection was only sexual. Instead, he'd dug into her soul, as if he'd taken a damn course on how to swirl her into an emotional wreck.

Not on her fucking life. Evie had no idea when her existence had turned into a bad version of a "very special episode of Oprah" but she was over it. Eyeing her reflection in the mirror, she lifted her chin with resolve. No more crying. No more *intimacy*. Good god. She'd be cordial to Kenden today, at Aron's ceremony, and fuck him on Saturday. After that, they would become soldiers in the same war. Acquaintances who would work together to defeat her father before she returned to the human world. No other option existed.

Anticipating the day, she observed her scowl in the reflection. Miranda had texted her, indicating that she expected Evie to attend. She was getting pretty tired of dear ol' sis dictating orders to her. She'd have a talk with the queen about that as well. Evie didn't follow orders, no matter whose bloodline ran through them.

Slowly scrutinizing her face in the mirror, Evie reveled in her beauty. She'd never been vain. That was for women who craved the attention of men. Instead, she was practical. Her beauty was innate, just as a tree had bark or a bird could fly. It held no value to her, but she understood its importance in controlling her circumstances. Women reluctantly venerated her for it; men salivated over it. And for that, she was grateful she'd inherited her mother's features.

Narrowing her eyes, she ran soft fingers over her hair. The red tresses were an anomaly. As far as she knew, Rina nor Valktor had any trace of the coloring. Perhaps it was inherited from her wretched father. He'd told her once that the scarlet tresses were the same blazing red as Etherya's. As if she'd believe any lies that escaped the monster's reedy lips.

Inhaling deep with resolve, she approached the closet and donned a white cardigan. In the long mirror affixed to the closet door, it looked angelic over the green V-neck, sleeveless silk blouse and dark, thin-legged designer jeans. Slipping on bejeweled sandals, she closed her lids and dematerialized to the playground at Uteria's main square.

Sensations of buzzing sounds and children's amused shrieks greeted her as her feet were tickled by the green grass. There must've been a thousand people milling around the rectangular park, with its thick oak trees, and the nearby town square. The playground was mostly finished. Monkey bars, swings, see-saws—all were currently occupied by energy-filled munchkins under the puffy clouds and warm sunbeams. Picnic tables dotted the perimeter of the dirt-covered swath that comprised the playground.

Evie spotted Darkrip and Arderin sitting with Lila, Latimus and Heden at one of the wooden tables. Miranda sat on a blanket nearby, rubbing Tordor's black hair as he sat beside her. His tiny lips sucked a pacifier as he took in the surroundings, and Evie's heart skipped a beat. Had she ever been as innocent as the little bugger? The chances were slim to none.

Sathan stood behind Miranda, bulky arms crossed in his favorite stance, while Kenden stood beside him. They chatted cordially as Evie reaffirmed her intention to remain emotionless.

"Hello, Evie," a warm voice said from behind.

"Hello, Aron," she said, pasting on a smile. "Looks like we have you to thank for this day of family bliss and perfection."

He chuckled and rubbed the back of his neck, looking slightly embarrassed. "Miranda got some bug in her ear and decided to make a spectacle. I'm always happy to give a speech here and there, but we should be focusing on the kids. I don't mind being the center of attention but it's certainly not something I crave."

"How interesting. I thrive on it," she said, arching a brow.

"I don't mind sharing the spotlight. Never have."

Evie shrugged. "Seems to me, that might push you to the back of the line where it's dark and no one can see you. Maybe it's time you learned to shove up front."

An unreadable emotion passed over his features. "Maybe."

"Aron?" Moira called as she approached. "I think they're ready for you." Gazing at Evie, she said, "I didn't mean to interrupt though. If you want to wait a few minutes..."

"It's fine," Aron said, nodding. "Let's do it."

Evie watched them grin at each other, reading the images in their minds. Their desire for each other was palpable. But there was a man between them, one who was long gone, as well as Moira's lies. Interesting. It moved something in her, watching these almost-lovers who were too afraid to act on their feelings. Strange, since nothing had incited fascination in her for quite a while.

"After the ceremony winds down, perhaps you could give me a tour of your house, Aron?" Evie said. "Miranda told me that it's featured on the walking tours of Uteria and was built long before the Awakening. And maybe Moira can come along, since she lived there after her father died."

Aron's eyebrows lifted. "I'd be happy to."

"I... Sure, I can come along. My mother was the housekeeper, so she showed me all the secret passageways."

"Great," Evie said. "Maybe after sunset."

Miranda called Aron's name from her now-standing perch beside the blanket, and he headed in her direction, Evie and Moira falling into step behind him.

"You knew I grew up in Aron's house because you can read my thoughts," Moira said beside her as they strolled.

"Yes," Evie said.

"Great," she muttered.

Evie chuckled. "I won't tell him about your time at Astaria, if that's what you're worried about. But take it from me, he wants to sleep with you."

Moira's blue eyes grew wide as she lifted her head. "He's in love with someone else."

"Believe me, sweetheart," Evie said, "this ain't about love. That man wants to bone you until your pretty little head shatters the headboard. You can believe me or not, but it's true."

The Slayer chewed her lower lip. "I was so sure he didn't see me that way."

"Oh, he sees you in a *lot* of ways. Now, I learned a long time ago that I get into trouble when I spread others' thoughts around, so I'll end this conversation here. Take the info and do with it what you will."

"I, um, yeah. Will do. Thanks, Evie."

They came to stand at the front of the crowd, where Miranda had tied a red ribbon from the jungle gym to the monkey bars. Lifting a pair of scissors fashioned for a giant, the queen gave a speech extolling Aron's virtues as he beamed by her side. Evie thought him a handsome man. Short brown hair, mahogany-colored eyes, small but well-proportioned features. He was slight and probably around six feet tall, but that would mean Moira, who was a few inches shorter than her, would fit like a glove in his arms.

Nice, thick lips would be perfect for kissing. He could use them on Moira's mouth...or somewhere more exciting. He'd be tentative at first, but spitfire little Moira would unwind him until he let go and ravaged her. How very exciting.

"He's in love with Miranda," a baritone said softly in her ear. "So, don't get any ideas."

"Well, well, if it isn't the arrogant Slayer commander," she said, looking up into Kenden's melted chocolate irises. "You just know everything, don't you? How awful it must be to deal with us mere minions." She batted her eyelashes, hoping to draw his ire.

Instead, he stayed calm, mired in his always unflappable demeanor. God, she hated him for it.

"I'd be careful throwing accusations of arrogance around," he challenged. "Pot and kettle and all that."

"Arrogance is for fools," she snapped, furious at her pounding heart. "A wasted emotion for people who require adoration. I don't need anyone to think I'm right or intelligent."

"Because you already are?" he taunted.

"Because I wasn't born with the ability to care. About anything. Including what others think about me. It's a powerful trait and one I'm damn proud of."

His gorgeous features softened, filling with the compassion that comprised so much of his nature. "I think you have the ability to care about a lot of things, Evie."

"Then you're a bigger moron than I thought," she said, focusing back on the ceremony.

Miranda handed Aron the gigantic scissors, and he cut the ribbon. The crowd erupted in voracious cheers as they smiled and waved. Everyone began to disperse, and Evie felt Kenden's hand on her upper back.

"Can we talk for a minute?"

"I need to speak to Miranda," she said, turning to face him so that she could pull away from his touch.

"Okay," he said, his eyes darting between hers. "Afterward?"

"Aron's going to give me a tour of his house, and then, I'm heading home."

Kenden sighed and ran a hand through his hair. "You haven't answered any of my texts this week, nor my voicemails. So, are we done here? Do you even want to see me on Saturday?"

Agony swept through her, unwanted and vicious, imagining that last Saturday's grizzly battle would be their last time together. Although she wanted to create space between them, she couldn't let that be the end. Whatever it was that existed between them deserved better. Something they could remember fondly, centuries in the future, when they thought back upon their time with each other. Even her emotionless soul desired that last solemn memory.

"I don't want last Saturday to be the end. If you're willing, I'd like to see our agreement through."

Every muscle in her throat constricted as he studied her, silent and contemplative. God. Fucking. Damn it. The prick of tears began to spark behind her eyes. Willing them away with every cell of her father's malevolent blood, she vowed that she wouldn't let him see her vulnerability.

He remained quiet for so long that she was sure he would say no. Wanting to stave off the rejection, she opened her mouth to tell him that she would release him from their bargain. Although she hated capitulating to him, it was better than having him wring her soul out like a dirty rag.

"I'd like to see it through too," he said, before she could speak.

She closed her mouth. Something so vivid and genuine swam in his deep brown eyes. "Fine," she said, crossing her arms over her chest.

"And after that?" he asked, his tone almost pleading, as if he already knew the answer but wanted to sway her toward a different outcome.

"After that, I'll train with your army. As your comrade and your soldier. I don't renege on my deals, Ken. I promised you I'd fight if you met my ultimatum. After that, I'll become your best warrior. That's all that can be between us. You know deep down, it's true. Smart generals know when to retreat in a losing battle."

He sighed, sad and long. "That, they do." His dejected tone almost broke her unfeeling heart. Encircling her wrist, he drew her hand to his full, sexy lips. "I'll pick you up at your cabin at five," he said, gliding a kiss over her palm. "I have something that I want to show you. I'll drive us there in the four-wheeler. After that, maybe you can show me how to cook in the kitchen I never use? You can text me what ingredients to have on hand. Is that okay?"

Unable to help herself, Evie slid her palm over the soft, clean-shaven skin of his lower jaw. Cupping his cheek, she grinned. "It sounds fucking perfect."

"Great," he said, pecking her hand once more before she dropped it to her side.

"What's up, lovebirds?" Miranda chimed, walking toward them with Tordor on her hip. "Thanks for coming, Evie. It was a nice ceremony, right?"

"Yes," Evie said with a nod. "But I need to have a chat with you about your nasty little habit of thinking you can tell me where to be all the time. It's become rather intolerable."

"Whoa," Kenden said, shooting them both a look. "I think that's my cue to leave. I'll be over there with Latimus. If we see fists being thrown, we're butting in." Giving Evie an endearing wink that absolutely did *not* make her insides melt, he stalked away.

Miranda shifted Tordor to her other hip. "You're really gonna have it out with me while I've got this little monster strapped to my hip? Low blow, sis. Seriously."

"I'm not joking, Miranda," Evie said, attempting to tamp down her anger. "I know you like to joke when things are tense, but I'm not one of your subjects. I don't answer to anyone. Are we clear?"

Miranda stared at her, heat clouding her eyes. She was pissed. Evie thrived on it, as she always thrived on anger.

"Who are you really mad at, Evie?" Miranda asked. "Me? Or yourself, for actually showing up when I ask you? It seems to me, this might be the first time in your life that people care about you enough to want you around. Perhaps that scares the shit out of you."

"One thing I hate more than entitled immortal royals is people who try to psychoanalyze me," Evie said, taking a half-step closer, shortening the distance. "Poor, pitiful Evie, who was raped by her evil father. We just need to love her, and she'll be fine. Well, fuck you, Miranda. Take your self-help books and herbal ginger tea and shove them up your servant-wiped ass. You'll never come close to understanding anything about me but you'd better stop thinking you can boss me around. I'm here by choice and I can leave just as easily."

"Then fucking leave!" Miranda yelled, fury flashing in her grass-green eyes. "You have some nerve calling me entitled, Evie. You waltz in here, after you did everything in your power to almost get me killed and tear my kingdom apart. I hope you're not the one to kill Crimeous because then, I can put a sword in my hand and fight you like I've wanted to every damn time you treat me like shit. Family means something to me, but you shove it back in my face like it's poisonous. If you hate it so much, then go. We'll find another way to kill Crimeous. I'm done putting up with your crap."

Evie opened her mouth to unleash every curse word in her extensive repertoire on her sister, but Lila and Arderin rushed to their sides before she could speak.

"You two are making a scene," Lila scolded in her saccharine voice. Taking Tordor from Miranda's arms, she balanced him on her voluptuous, jean-clad hip. "It's beneath both of you. If you want to argue, do it in private."

"Um, yeah, I'm all for that," Arderin said, standing opposite of Lila so that they formed a haphazard square. "I'll bring the popcorn. It'll be better than Kandi and Phaedra's feud."

The three other women stilled to give Arderin a confused glare.

"Real Housewives of Atlanta?" Arderin asked, lifting her hands and staring at them like they were daft. "Forget it. The point is, I'd like to see you two throw down, but not here. Our people deserve better from their leaders."

Lila gave her a huge smile. "That's so diplomatic, Arderin. Sathan would be so proud of you."

"Obviously," she said, rolling her eyes and winking at Lila.

It broke the tension a bit, and Evie warily regarded Miranda.

"I'm sorry," Miranda breathed, rubbing her fingers over her forehead. "That was uncalled for. Evie, I apologize for *summoning* you or whatever," she said, making quotation marks with her fingers. "I just really want you to be part of this family and I want you to be at every function. Not because I want to boss you around but because I want to spend time with you. I hope you can accept my apology."

Well, shit. Evie studied them, the three stunning women before her. Arderin to her left, with an air of innocence but also a streak of mischief. It was easy to see why Darkrip was wild for her. Miranda across from Evie, their mother's eyes in her striking face, filled with sorrow and remorse. Lila to her right, probably the most beautiful woman she'd ever met, balancing the baby on her hip as if she'd been born with him attached. Never had Evie met a female more destined to be a mother. Too bad her asshole father had maimed her.

God, Crimeous was an abhorrent creature. Evie should've been directing her anger at him, not at the sister who'd welcomed her into her compound with open arms even after Evie's treacherous deeds when she'd lost her child. Unused to regret and guilt, she wanted to melt into the ground. She was no better than her father. A soulless creature who caused everyone pain. Self-loathing threatened to drown her.

"Hey," Miranda said, reaching over to grab Evie's hand. "It's okay. I get passionate. I've cursed Sathan out so much worse."

"True story," Arderin mumbled.

"Please, don't dematerialize," Miranda pleaded. "Stay here and enjoy the day with us. Hang with the three of us. We're super-fun, I promise. Arderin will tell you all about the Kardashians, and Lila can show you what it's like to be perfect."

Lila swatted Miranda on her arm, snickering. "Stop it. I'm only half-perfect."

They chuckled as Evie observed them. The three of them emanated the energy and ease that only close friends shared. Never having close girlfriends, she'd always wondered what that felt like.

"C'mon," Arderin said, threading her arm through Evie's. "Let's share secrets about my husband. I need dirt." Tugging on her arm, Evie let her lead the way to one of the picnic tables. They sat for hours, Evie eventually relaxing as the three of them regaled her with stories from their marriages with their beloved but flawed men.

At one point, Arderin and Lila went to get them a round of beers, leaving her alone with Miranda at the table.

"I don't really feel remorse often, but I'd like to tell you that I'm sorry, Miranda. I misjudged you. I appreciate you asking me to be here today."

"Thank you," Miranda said, covering her hand where it rested atop the wooden table. "And that's all we need to say."

The ladies returned with the beers, and they drank while the setting sun sparked a glow upon their backs. If Evie had been someone even remotely normal, she might have thought it one of the most enjoyable afternoons of her life.

※

After the sun set, Moira walked with Aron and Evie along the cobblestone sidewalk to his house. As they strolled, Moira's heart thudded from the information Evie had given her. Was Aron truly attracted to her? Would he be able to push aside his love for Miranda, and his loyalty to Diabolos, to be with her?

The questions swirled as they entered his large mansion. Together, she and Aron showed Evie the twenty-bedroom abode. From the expansive kitchen to the recently upgraded private movie theater to the spacious master bedroom. Aron was a proud man, and she could sense his pleasure at showing Evie his home.

The estate was immaculately kept by the live-in housekeeper that Aron had hired several centuries ago. Moira had been distraught to learn that her mother had died while she'd been at Astaria. When she'd returned to Uteria, Aron had led her to his back yard, where he'd erected a beautiful headstone for her. Moira visited it often, Aron always allowing her free rein of his home. The gesture of building a memorial for her servant mother was just another example of Aron's kind heart. As they stood in his master chamber, by the large bed, she couldn't focus on their conversation. Longing for him had consumed her, spurred on by Evie's confirmation that he desired her.

"Well, this has been lovely, but look at the time," Evie said, lifting her arm to look at her watch. Except her arm was bare. Locking her stunning green gaze on Moira, she said, "It's time for Cinderella to leave the ball. See you both later." Shooting Moira a subtle wink from her almond-shaped eyes, she vanished.

"That was strange," Aron said, his expression puzzled. "I hope she liked the tour."

"She seemed to," Moira said, her voice sounding like it was trapped in a tunnel a thousand miles away.

"Well, should we head downstairs?" he asked, offering his hand to her.

Moira remained frozen, every cell in her body quivering as she stood by his sizeable bed. Mustering courage from some deep well within, she moved toward him until her body brushed his. Tilting her head back, she stared deep into his gentle brown eyes.

Lifting her hands, she slid them over his clean-shaven cheeks, ever so slowly.

His brows drew together. "Moira?"

Her pupils darted back and forth between his, her throat threatening to cut off every ounce of air. "I want you, Aron," she said, hating the gravel in her voice.

A puff of breath escaped his full lips as he straightened his spine, elevating his height a fraction to look down into her. "Moira—"

"I don't want to live with regrets," she said, cutting off his protest. "I've learned the hard way that life is so precious. Every day we waste is one we'll never get back. I don't want to live like that anymore."

He smiled at her and grabbed her wrists as her hands framed his face. "You're just lonely and tired, angel. The goddess knows, this can be a lonely world. Let's go downstairs and have a drink. We can chat as long as you want."

"No," she said, vowing to stand her ground. Pulling her hands from his face, they formed fists at her sides. "This isn't about loneliness and it isn't about finding a warm body to be with. It's about us, Aron. I trust you more than anyone in the world. I desire you more than any man. It's time I acted on it." Grasping the bottom of her silky, sleeveless blouse, she drew it over her head and tossed it to the ground.

Aron's eyes widened, soaking in the image of her flat stomach and pert breasts, held up by her light-blue lace bra.

Shaking his head, he said, "Diabolos—"

"Diabolos is dead," she said, lifting her chin. "I won't let you use him as a wedge between us anymore."

Inching toward him, she clutched his hands. Lifting them, she settled them around her waist. Reflexively, he dragged her closer. Encouraged, she slid her palms up the fabric of his polo shirt, over his chest, clutching them behind his neck. The bare skin of her upper body bracketed his, and heat seemed to emanate from his toned frame.

"Moira," he whispered, lowering his forehead to rest on hers. Indecision swam in his eyes, so close to hers.

"I don't care if you imagine I'm Miranda. You can call me by her name. Whatever you need to do to be with me."

His features drew together, his expression a mask of confusion. "Why in the hell would I imagine I'm with any other woman when I have you in my arms?" he asked. The growl in his tone sent shivers up her spine. With firm hands, he caressed the soft skin of her back, causing her to purr against him.

Lifting to her toes, she gently touched her lips to his. He stood so very still, panting at the light contact. And then, he snapped. Raggedly moaning her name, he drew her to him with an arm around the waist. Plunging the other into her hair, he opened his mouth over hers.

Moira almost cried at his capitulation, thrusting her fingers into his short brown hair to pull him into her. Their tongues warred as he unclasped her bra, throwing it to the floor. With shaking fingers, she grabbed the hem of his shirt, yanking it from his body.

Unable to contain her moan, as her nipples felt the scratch of the tiny hairs on his chest, she pressed into him, needing more.

"I need these off," she said, maintaining contact with his mouth as she unbuttoned his slacks and began pushing them down his hips. With a frustrated grunt, he pulled them off along with his boxer-briefs. Cementing his lips to hers and bending at the knees, he picked her up and carried her to the bed.

Her back upon the soft covers, he snapped open her jeans, unzipped the metal and slithered them down her legs. Moira noticed his hands shaking as he slid off her sandals, her jeans and thong following shortly after.

Naked, he leaned over her, his gorgeous body in between her open legs. Smiling down at her, he shrugged. "I haven't done this in a really long time," he said. "I'm shaking like a damn virgin."

"It's so cute," she said, palming his face as he loomed above her.

"I don't want to be cute," he said, nipping her lips. "Good god woman, do you want me to lose my erection? I want to be hot and sexy and whatever else you women salivate over."

Moira laughed. "You're so hot." Running her fingers over his toned abs, she grinned up at him while she still held his cheek. "I promise."

Staring into her, his lips curved, and he touched the head of his shaft to her center. Exhaling a breath, he shook his head. "You're so wet," he whispered.

"Only for you," she said, drawing his head down for a kiss. "Please, Aron," she murmured against his mouth.

"I should get a condom," he said.

"I'm on the pill and just saw Sadie recently. Everything's fine. I trust you."

His deep brown eyes, filled with so much emotion, skated back and forth between hers. Lowering his hand, the pads of his fingers pulled at the lips of her core, causing her to mewl. Holding her open, he began jutting into her, panting as he held her gaze.

"Your eyes are so blue right now," he said, his hips pushing him further and further into her. "You feel so good. Oh, god."

With his full length inside her, she threw her head back on the bed, closing her eyes with ecstasy. Relaxing, so that she could open to him more, she groaned as he began to pound her.

Into her he slid, drawing out and plunging in again, in an endless rhythm that threatened to drown her in pleasure. Unable to see him, with her head thrown back on the bed, she felt his palm cover hers as it rested face-up beside her head. Intimate and possessive, he entwined his fingers with hers, clutching her hand as he loved her.

Tears stung her eyes as she trained her gaze upon him. His coffee-colored irises stared into her with such reverence, she thought her heart might burst. Lifting her legs, she surrounded him with them, crossing her ankles across his back. It created a new angle, and he took advantage, hitting a spot with his shaft that drove her wild.

"I'm so close," she cried, locked onto him.

"Me too," he said, clutching her hand even harder as he hammered her. "God, Moira, I'm so deep. Fuck, it feels amazing."

Seeing his thin grip on control shattered something inside her, and her body bowed, convulsing as the orgasm overtook her. He shouted above her, calling her name as he began shooting into her. Together, they crashed, clutching each other close as they fell back to Earth. Shaken and sated, Moira reveled in the weight of his warm body as it stretched over her.

Lifting his head, he gazed into her. With soft fingertips, he stroked her cheek. "Well, I certainly didn't expect *that* on the house tour."

Laughter burst from her throat. She loved how relaxed he was, his handsome face so sweet as he grinned at her. "You mean you don't bone every one of the patrons who tours your home?"

Chuckling, he pecked her on the lips. "No, but it might increase the popularity of the excursion."

She snickered, shaking her head at him. Concern flooded her as his expression grew serious.

"What is it?" she asked.

"Just making sure you're okay that we didn't use protection."

"Yes," she whispered, brushing the pads of her fingers along his strong jaw. "I promise, I just had a physical. Everything was clear."

"Okay," he said, stroking her hair. "I haven't been checked in a few decades, but my last physical was clean, and I haven't been with a woman in over a century. So, I guess I should thank you for breaking my streak."

"You're certainly welcome," she said, absently caressing his shoulder. "I've wanted you like that for so long."

He grinned. "I had no idea. I'm kind of an idiot when it comes to romance." Moira loved the way his fingers threaded through her tresses. "I guess it's been a while for you too. Unless you were with someone at Restia?"

Her stomach dropped to her knees so rapidly that she wondered how the organ didn't shoot from her body altogether. Was this the opportunity to tell him where she'd been? In the aftermath of their lovemaking?

Deciding it would ruin the moment, she tamped down the self-revulsion that threatened to strangle her as she lied to him. "Nope," she said, her voice soft. "I wasn't with anyone at Restia."

Smiling, he kissed her lips and pulled her to stand. After cleaning themselves up in his marble bathroom, he tugged her toward the bed. "Will you stay here tonight?"

Moira studied him, chewing her bottom lip. By the goddess, she wanted to. So badly. But self-loathing at her continued deception led to doubt that was quickly eating her from the inside out.

"Please?" he asked, squeezing her hand.

He looked so adorable, naked longing on his face beside the turned-down bed. Knowing she didn't deserve to be held in his strong arms, she followed him into bed. When he spooned her close, cementing his front to her back in the darkness, she waited until his breathing slowed. Once it was even and steady, she allowed the silent tears to run down her cheeks, wondering how long it would take him to discover her lies.

∞

Sadie observed Nolan as he chatted with Sathan under the moonlight. The day was winding down, and he'd be heading back to Astaria soon. She wanted to speak to him, to ask him why he'd been distant lately, but shyness held her back. And a strong dose of fear. What if he'd decided their courtship was over? Best-case scenario? It might break the heart that she'd so tentatively allowed open. Worst? It would completely destroy her.

"You should just go talk to him, you know?" Kenden said, placing a supportive hand on her upper back as he approached. "He's mad for you."

"Yeah," she said, maneuvering her lip with her teeth as she stared absently at Nolan. "He's pulled away a bit lately. I don't know if it's something I did...or said." Blowing out a frustrated breath, she shook her head. "Maybe he wants to be with someone else."

"Doubtful," Kenden said, his hand so soothing as it caressed her through her sweatshirt. He'd always been like a brother, and she loved him immensely. "Although, I'm certainly no expert at love. The woman I'm courting wants to rip my organs from my body half the time. Not an ideal recipe for happily ever after."

Sadie snorted as she giggled. "That's a nice visual."

Kenden smiled. "I'll go distract Sathan so you can corner him. Come on." With a gentle push on her back, they began walking across the park.

"Sathan, before you and Miranda head home, I need to speak to you about next week's trainings," Kenden said.

"Sure," the king nodded. Excusing himself, he departed with Kenden, leaving Sadie alone with Nolan.

"Hi," she said, beaming up at him, determined to put on a brave face. "I feel like I haven't talked to you in a few days. You usually text me so many medical articles I stay up reading way past my bedtime."

"Sorry," he said, grinning sheepishly. "I've been helping Lila run the pop-up clinics for the Slayers that recently moved to Lynia and Naria, and this week has been crazy."

"I can help if you need me to. My schedule's not super-booked next week."

"That wasn't an attempt to guilt you into helping me," he said, winking. The gesture made her insides swirl. "But if you have free time next week, maybe we should have a chat. Do you want to grab drinks? Maybe on Wednesday?"

Little bugs of anxiety swam through her gut at his words. "We can chat now. What did you want to talk about?"

Looking uncomfortable, he ran a hand through his hair. "I, um, I don't know if this is the right place—"

"You're pulling away from me, Nolan," she said, willing away the angry tears she felt forming behind her eyes. "If you want to see other people, just tell me."

He cleared his throat, his Adam's apple bobbing as he swallowed. "I feel like we might have moved too fast, Sadie. That's all. I don't want to deny you anything. You're going to be so beautiful once your skin has healed—"

Pain coursed through her. "As opposed to now?"

His eyes narrowed. "Cheap shot, Sadie. You know I think you're stunning. I always have."

Then, why was he giving other women flowers? She wanted to scream the question at him but knew that if she did, the tears would flow, and she'd look like a moron. "If you think we moved too fast, then I don't want to bother you. I think it's best we take some time apart. You can communicate with me through text or email regarding our shared patients."

"Sadie, I'm trying to do what's best for you," he said, reaching for her arm.

"No!" She slapped his hand away. "I can't do this. I hope you find what you need, Nolan. Good night."

Unable to stomach anymore humiliation, she all but fled to her room at the castle. Once there, she climbed into bed, wishing her clinical skills were extensive enough to piece together her shattered heart.

The man crawled from the meadow to the protection of the forest, away from the murderous sun. Drowning in the loathing and despair from the loss of yet another person he loved, Galredad devolved into a malevolent creature comprised of hate and pain. Needing shelter, he slithered to the caves, knowing they could protect him from the traitorous star above.

Once inside, he seethed, plotting his revenge. For a small eternity, he waited, wanting nothing more than to destroy the woman whom he'd trusted after all others were lost to him. Vowing to never concede in his quest for vengeance, centuries upon centuries passed...

Chapter 13

On Saturday, Kenden showered after training the troops and dressed in jeans, sneakers and a polo shirt. He'd told Evie to dress casually but knowing her, she'd still be draped in designer clothing. Hopping in the four-wheeler, he began the short trek to her cabin.

Once outside, she opened the door and walked down the three wooden steps carrying a small bag. As predicted, she wore designer jeans, a red, silky, sleeveless blouse and fancy-looking sandals. He jogged around to open her door, and she flung the satchel in the back of the vehicle.

"Not that I'll need pajamas," she said, so sexy as she arched an eyebrow. "But I brought some toiletries so I can at least brush my teeth. I plan to spend every second of our last night together rocking your world, Commander."

"So, you're staying all night?" he asked, brushing his lips against hers as she stood beside the vehicle door he held open for her. "Even if I want to cuddle with you and smother you with feelings?"

Throwing her head back, she laughed, the skin of her pale neck calling to him. "There won't be much time for cuddling, but sure, I'll let you smother me in between." Sitting on the leather seat, he closed the door behind her, situated himself behind the wheel, and they were off.

They chatted companionably as he drove, their voices loud over the whipping wind from the open-air four-wheeler. Ten minutes in, they approached the River Thayne, and he cut the engine. Exiting the vehicle, he came around to lead her out.

"*This* is where you wanted to bring me?" she asked, annoyance in her voice.

"Yes," he said, shaking his outstretched hand at her. "Come on."

With a sardonic roll of her gorgeous green eyes, she departed the four-wheeler, grasping his hand. The sun had just set behind the far-off mountains, and dusk surrounded them in its inky glow. Buzzing insects chirped, invisible along the riverbank, as he escorted her to the large tree.

"Isn't bringing me to Mommy's gravesite a little cliché?"

Kenden sighed, the sound flowing around them sure as the gurgling river nearby. "I wanted you to have a part of her. To see the place where Miranda and I remembered her. I thought it might help you connect with her spirit. It runs so deeply through you."

Evie scoffed. "I'm not really in the mood for a 'you have good inside you' speech right now," she said, making quotation marks with her fingers in the air.

"This isn't about that," he said, reminding himself to stay calm. Evie liked to push people's buttons in tense situations, and he refused to rise to the bait. Grasping her hand, he lifted it to the tree, holding her palm to the jagged bark. Covering her hand with his, he gazed into her eyes, still so vivid in the dimness of the rising moonlight.

"This is about your heritage. Your blood. Rina and Valktor. It's a proud lineage for an amazing woman."

"I'm not amazing, Ken," she said, those eyes muddled with confusion. "I don't understand why you insist on seeing something that isn't there."

Lowering her hand from the tree, she turned to face the river. The hunch of her shoulders showed a dejection that he was sure she'd hide from anyone else. Hope surged through him that she'd let him see even that fraction of her vulnerability.

"She always called me Miranda," Evie said softly.

"Rina?" he asked.

"Yes," she said, giving a slight nod. The red strands of her hair glowed as fireflies flamed around her. Kenden found the image stunning, her outline illuminated as he gave her space.

"I was ten when he first raped me." Thin fingers appeared over the backs of her upper arms as she rubbed them. "Rina was insane at that point. A shell of whomever she'd been before he tortured it out of her. He was angry that she didn't fight back. He threatened to punish her by hurting me. I don't think she understood. I didn't blame her for that."

Dropping her arms, she straightened her spine, staring off into the distance. Kenden wanted so badly to hold her but felt she needed space. Inching closer, he made sure not to touch her as her back still faced him.

"That first time was so confusing for me. Crimeous had always been a background figure. Mother raised me and kept me away from him for the first few years of my life. I guess I owe her for that at least." Lifting her chin, she continued. "He tore off the ragged clothes I was wearing and began hurting me, making sure she saw everything. Darkrip was eighteen. He tried to save me, but Father froze him in place. I'll never forget his eyes. There was so much hatred in them for the bastard."

Finally, she turned. Inhaling a large breath, she shrugged. "And so it went. For a small eternity in my mind. Every time he violated me, Rina would beg him not to hurt Miranda. She was too far gone to comprehend that it was her other daughter being victimized. I should've understood. But instead, I was furious. I interpreted that as proof she didn't love me as she'd loved Miranda and never would."

Kenden, usually so calm and composed, was assailed by warring emotions. Compassion that his beautiful Evie had endured such appalling trauma when she was only a child. Heartbreak that she would take Rina's mischaracterization of her as Miranda as evidence that she didn't love her. But most of all, rage at Crimeous for hurting her so badly. He'd never wanted to murder the bastard more. Vowing to crush every bone in his body, he regarded the stunning woman who stood before him on the soft green grass.

"I understand why you would interpret it that way," he said, locking on to her gaze. "But I knew Rina. There wasn't one impure bone in her body. It would've been impossible for her not to love her child."

"I know that now," Evie said, sounding detached from the words. "I've seen the best therapists the human world has to offer. But it doesn't really mean anything. I never knew her. Her spirit was crushed by the time I had any ability to understand the world."

Reaching into the pocket of his jeans, he pulled out a locket. Balancing it on his outstretched palm, he asked, "Do you know what this is?"

She shook her head.

"I found it when we were looking for Darkrip and Arderin. It's from the lair where Crimeous held Rina hostage." Opening the necklace, a lock of red hair sat inside. "The hair is yours. I'm certain of it."

Tentatively, she lifted a finger, tracing the pad over the soft strand. "It looks like my color."

Kenden nodded. "She did the same for Miranda. Before she was taken. She would cut locks of her hair and keep them in little trinkets like this. I think she did the same for you."

Even the threat of darkness couldn't disguise the moisture in Evie's eyes. "It's a nice story."

"And a true one," he said, lifting her hand to place the locket into her palm. Closing her fingers around it, he held them tight. "I know it with every fiber of my being."

Olive-green irises darted back and forth between his. "I don't know what you want me to do with this."

The corners of his lips turned up. "There's my Evie. Thinking everyone has an agenda. I don't want you do anything with it. Except keep it as a symbol of a mother who loved you very much."

"No one loves me," she whispered. "I'm an abomination."

He gave a breathy laugh. "That terrible, huh?"

"Yup," she said, her lips forming a gorgeous smile.

"I don't think so. You're all bluster and no bite. I've got you figured out, Evie."

She arched a scarlet brow. "Letting you think you understand me might just be right where I want you. Have you considered that?"

"Stop trying to outmaneuver me, woman," he said, drawing her close as he still held her hand. "Haven't you figured out by now, I'm extremely patient and always ensure I get the last move?"

Clutching the locket in her hand, she slid her arms around his neck. "The last move is unforeseeable when you're immortal, my friend." Lifting to her toes, she pressed her lips to his.

Kenden pressed back, needing her to know how wrong she was. How could she think herself unlovable when he was tumbling down the chasm of that very emotion with her more and more each day? Never had he met a more infuriating, frustrating, passionate woman. It was everything he thought he'd never crave and the embodiment of all he now yearned for. She'd pulled him into her abyss, and, Etherya help him, he never wanted to escape.

Thick fingers clutched her silky red hair as his tongue sild over hers. Lost in her, he milked her lips, her tongue, her gorgeous mouth. Like a starved man in search of his last meal, he consumed her, reveling in the tiny purrs that filled him.

Panting, he rested his forehead on hers. Lifting her lids, she stared into him. "I'm determined to be in your life, Evie. You've pushed everyone away so far, but I'm not like the others. You're not pulling one over on me. Get used to that now."

"I'm smarter than you are, Ken," she said, grinning up at him. "I know you've rarely met someone who is. It must drive you crazy."

"It does. Crazy with admiration at how you continue to outfox me. I've never met a more capable opponent. It's so fucking attractive."

"Goddamnit," she said, stealing a kiss from his lips. "I need to fuck you."

"Not yet," he said, gently snipping her bottom lip with his teeth. "I want to sit here with you and let you absorb the energy of this place. You deserve to feel her love for you. I think you'll feel it best here."

"Why are you always telling me to wait to bone you?" she teased. "It could give a girl a complex."

"I don't think there's any swaying your confidence, sweetheart." Giving her one last peck, he pulled her toward the tree. Sitting down, with his back against the thick oak, he held his hand up to her. Grasping it, she sat, enveloped in his embrace.

Surrounded by the symphony of the crickets, he held her, humbled that she'd given him the gift of telling him about her past. Even though it was a small snippet, it was a start. To a forged trust and a tentative tether. A thin, shared understanding that would always connect them.

"Did you erect the headstone for Rina?" she asked, gesturing with her head toward the tiny marble monument beside the tree.

"Miranda and Sathan placed it for their child. The one who died when she fought Crimeous."

Evie stiffened. Wanting to soothe her, he tightened his arms around her.

"How can Miranda still speak to me?" she asked, her tone laced with sadness. "Or Sathan? My actions killed their child. I'm the embodiment of my father. It's revolting."

"Miranda has always had a great capacity for love and forgiveness. It's what makes her such a strong leader. She understands your motivations came from the place inside where you hold your anger and pain."

"Then, she's a fool. I'm capable of so much worse. You all have no idea."

"Capability doesn't mean anything without intent. And you'll never convince me that you wanted to hurt their child. You don't have it in you, Evie."

She opened her mouth to refute him, and he turned her face, his fingers lining her chin. "Don't even try to argue with me on that."

"I was so consumed by anger when you found me. Sometimes, I wonder if I would've made the same choices even if I'd known she was pregnant. What do you say to that?"

"I say that it's really easy to speak in hypotheticals. There's no way you would've hurt their baby."

Her pupils scurried over his face, contemplating. "You're scaring the shit out of me," she said, her voice raspy.

"Because you think I'm wrong?" he asked, his brow furrowing.

"Because I'm terrified you might be right." Cupping his cheek, she shook her head. "I don't know how to live in a world where I'm not evil, Ken. I think it might break me."

The words were so genuine, so raw, that he felt his own heart crumble at her admission. "Then it's a good thing you found someone who's really good at piecing shit back together."

Body pulsing, he stared into her glassy eyes.

"What if all the pieces are too shattered?"

"Then, I'll spend an eternity gluing them until they fit just right. Maybe even better than before."

The lone tear blazed a trail down her flawless cheek. "I've cried more in front of you than I've cried in a thousand years," she whispered.

Capturing the wetness with his lips, he settled them over hers. "I'm honored that you let me see you cry," he said against her mouth. "I want you to give me everything, Evie."

"I can't," she breathed, the words exiting violently from her throat. "But I can give you tonight." Molding her lips to his, she gave him a sweet kiss. "Let's go home."

Lifting them to their feet, he granted her request.

※

Once home, Kenden kicked off his sneakers at the back door and opened the large refrigerator to pull out the ingredients that Evie had instructed him to have available. Evie interrupted him, closing the refrigerator door. Gazing up at him, she gently threaded her fingers through his.

Leading him to the darkened living room, she urged him to sit on the brown leather couch. Green irises swam with emotion as she straddled him, sliding her arms over his shoulders. Full, red lips enveloped his as his broad hands cupped the straining globes of her ass through her tight jeans. The kiss started sweetly but quickly evolved into a warring of tongues and a straining of bodies. Slender fingers pulled his shirt over his head, and she settled back into him, thrusting inside his mouth as she writhed on top of his thighs.

He divested her shirt and almost tore away her bra. Inhaling at the sight of her gorgeous breasts, he palmed them, caressing them slightly. With slitted eyes, she inched toward him, bringing the reddened, pebbled nipple to rest on his lips. Staring up at her, he closed his mouth around the tiny nub.

Her lithe body bowed, fingers clutching his hair as she drew him closer. His tongue teased the sensitive spot, lathering it as he growled against her skin. Sensing she needed more, he closed his teeth around the turgid point.

"Yessss," she hissed, gyrating above him while he loved her. Kissing a trail to her other breast, he gave it equal and fervent attention. Lust racked his muscular frame as his cock pulsed inside his jeans, longing to plunge into her warmth.

Lifting his chin with the pads of her fingers, she latched her mouth to his again. With a stir of air, their clothes were instantly dematerialized, reforming on the floor by the fireplace. Her lips blazed a path over his cheek until they rested on his ear. Warm breath flooded the cavity, causing him to shiver.

"Get ready, Commander. I'm going to show you how sweet surrender can be."

A shudder wracked his body, and he pulled her dripping core over his shaft. "I can't wait to be inside you," he whispered.

Her throaty laugh almost made him shoot his load right there. God, she was the sexiest woman he'd ever touched.

"No fucking way, baby," she said, using the endearment she proclaimed to detest. "Now, be a good boy and clutch my hair. I don't care if you pull it. I like the pain."

Trailing pecs down his neck, over the brown hairs on his chest and down his quivering abdomen, she fell to her knees in front of him. Arching a brow, her lips quirked into a smile. "This hardwood's got to go." Grabbing a pillow from the end of the couch, she tossed it to the floor and situated her knees on top, in between his open legs. "Much better."

Kenden's breath was labored as she grasped his straining length in her hand. "You're hard as a rock," she said.

"Fuck yes," he whispered, threading his hands through her gorgeous hair. "I'm wild for you, Evie." Tugging the strands, careful not to pull too hard, he urged her toward his pulsing phallus.

"Is this what you want?" she asked, swiping her tongue over the sensitive head. Kenden thought his eyes might pop out of their sockets. Never had he been so aroused. Clenching her hair tighter, her olive eyes lit with pleasure. "You're figuring me out, aren't you? Pull even harder, and I'll suck you dry."

Being a smart man, he knew when to listen. Grasping the exquisite red tresses, he jutted his hips toward her face, resting his cock on her lips. Her resulting smile was *everything*. Grass-green irises fastened upon his, she opened her mouth and slid over him.

He couldn't control the undulation of his hips as she consumed him. Every cell in his iron shaft burned with pleasure as her wet mouth created silky pressure on his straining skin. Seeing her like this, on her knees, naked before him, dredged up every possessive instinct inside. So much of her life was spent with defenses held firm and high. The vulnerability she showed as she purred around him was heartbreakingly beautiful. By the goddess, he wanted her like this for eternity. To come home to her, tired and spent, and have her love him.

Telling himself to check the feelings that she so often chided him for, he forced himself to be in the moment. When his balls begin to tingle, he drew her head away.

"Let me get you off," she said, confusion in her eyes as she stared up at him with wet, swollen lips.

"I want to be inside you when I come."

Those lips formed a pout, and he chuckled. Reaching for her, he lifted her under the knees as she wrapped her arms around his neck. Carrying her to the end of the couch, he slid her down his body.

Turning her to face the sofa, he placed his palm on her back and gently urged her to lie on her stomach over the large, leather-covered arm of the couch. Wriggling her perfect ass at him as it lay bare and exposed, she giggled. "From behind again? You're dirty, Commander."

Leaning over her, he covered her body with his. "You like it. Don't deny it, sweetheart," he whispered in her ear. Reveling in her shiver, he traced his lips down her spine until he came to the small of her back. Running the tips of his fingers over the juncture of her lower back and buttocks, he caressed lower, to palm the cheeks. Spreading them open, he kneeled and began kissing the flesh.

She moaned, the sound muffled by the smooth leather of the sofa, driving him mad with arousal. Holding the lips of her sex open, he tongued her there, swiping up every drop of her wetness. Finding the nub at the top of her slit with his finger, he circled it as he impaled her with his tongue.

She cried his name, pushing herself onto his face; into his finger. Unable to wait any longer, he stood behind her. Spreading her legs, he slid the head of his shaft over her wet, sensitive flesh.

Grunting with desire, he thrust into her. Once, twice...until he was at the hilt. The dripping walls of her center clutched him, clouding his vision as she lifted her hips to meet him. Shoving into her, over and over, his broad hands grasped her hips. Needing more, he threaded his arms under her thighs, separating her feet from the floor. Holding her lower body suspended, he pummeled her as she moaned from the couch.

Wracked from the ministrations from her mouth, and now, her tight channel, he knew he wouldn't last long. Reaching underneath, he stimulated her clit as he jackknifed into her.

"Oh god," she called from below, sounding as if she was drowning from the ringing in his ears.

"I'm almost there," he gritted out, the sounds of their bodies slapping together driving him mad with desire. "Let go, baby. Come with me."

By some miracle of the goddess, Evie actually listened to him for once. Her body grew limp as a strained spaghetti noodle, opening to him even more as he pounded her. Reveling in her responsiveness, he clenched his teeth and let himself explode.

Shouting her name, he collapsed over her, spasming as he shot every last drop into her. Their bodies convulsed so violently that they fell to the couch in a heap, Kenden somehow managing to stay inside her as he cuddled her close atop the soft leather of the sofa.

Breathless and panting, he surrounded her, unable to let her go in the intimate moment. And maybe forever. Burying his face in her hair, he closed his eyes and let his muscles shake away the remnants of their lovemaking.

There in the darkness, holding her close, he admitted the truth. If he couldn't figure out how to make her stay, it might just destroy him.

Evie slid into consciousness, sure as she slid the skin of her legs over Kenden's soft sheets. Eyes closed, she smiled as he nibbled her neck.

"You taste so good," he murmured, his deep voice causing her to melt against him more. Remembering last night's intimate dinner, the succulent flavor still lingered. The luscious chicken cordon bleu had been perfect. Along with the zesty spread of vegetables, drizzled in olive oil and sprinkled with herbs, and finished with a dash of lemon juice. She'd paired that with a light green baby kale salad topped with fried bacon and goat cheese. Damn, but she was a good cook.

Kenden's face had been a mask of pleasure as they ate at the expansive island in the middle of the kitchen. He'd opened a vintage red, and they'd laughed as they recounted stories from their past. Sated and relaxed from lovemaking, it had damn near been perfect.

Afterward, he'd led her upstairs, into the bathroom, where they brushed their teeth in his dual sinks. Evie had washed away her makeup, usually so careful not to let anyone see her without that shield. Kenden had cupped her moisturized, flushed cheeks, vowing to count every freckle across her nose. She'd always hated her freckles, thinking them ugly, but when he brushed his lips against them, it had liquefied something inside her deadened heart.

He'd carried her to the bed, gently laying her over the sheets, her hair fanning on the pillow. Not from the back again. Not last night. No, he'd slithered over her, aligning his body with hers as he stared into her. Urging her eyes to remain open, he'd loved her as he clutched her hands beside her head on the pillow. Never had Evie experienced something so intimate. To say it terrified her would be an understatement. It *consumed* her, stealing her breath, forcing her to face the fact that Kenden had burrowed not only into her heart but into her blackened soul. And that was something she must remedy, for he deserved so much better than her rotten, malevolent core.

Knowing it was time, she yearned for one more moment. Allowing herself that, she pushed her back into his front, the warmth of his body enveloping her. And then, already hating every piece of herself, she began to draw away.

Sitting on the edge of the bed, she pulled the silky robe she'd packed onto her shoulders. Standing, she tied it at the waist and headed to the bathroom to dress. Once yesterday's clothes were donned, she leaned against the bathroom counter and gazed at her own eyes in the mirror.

It's what's best for him, she silently told herself, knowing it was true. Better that they make a clean break now than let whatever the hell was between them evolve into something even messier. They had no future, and although it was fun to pretend, she had a job to do, and it was time she got around to accomplishing it.

Inhaling a huge breath, she gave her reflection one last nod of confidence and opened the bathroom door. Kenden had slipped on sweatpants that hung low, under his six-pack. The muscles that led toward the waistband formed a "V," causing her mouth to water. *No, Evie!* she mentally scolded. Another round of fabulous sex would just make this harder. After packing her small satchel, she came to stand before him as he waited in between the mahogany dresser and expansive bed. Head tilted back, she locked on to his gaze.

"Well," she said, determined to keep her tone light. "It's been amazing, Commander. You certainly know how to honor an agreement."

His expression was impassive, his brown irises slowly perusing her face. Leaning his hip on the dresser, he crossed his arms over his broad chest. "What are you trying to prove, Evie?"

"Nothing," she said with a shrug. "I named my terms, and you met them. I'll be on the sparring field at eight a.m. sharp Monday morning, ready to train with the troops. It should be fun. I haven't fought with an army in centuries. I'll be rusty but I have quick muscle memory. It will come back in a snap, trust me."

"I have no doubt about your skills as a warrior," he said, his voice so low. "But your skills as a person fucking suck sometimes."

She arched a brow. "Well, don't protect my fragile heart. Give it to me. I think you're looking for a fight here."

"I'm looking for you to care!" he said, the heat in his tone rising as his nostrils flared. "For you to give a shit about me and what we have together. How can you walk away so callously?"

"It's just sex, Ken," she said, lifting her hands in frustration. "I told you that from the beginning—"

"Fuck you, Evie," he interrupted, straightening away from the dresser. "That's bullshit, and you know it. You're a goddamn coward. It's so beneath you, it makes me sick."

"Oh, sweetheart," she said with a biting laugh. "You can't begin to fathom what's beneath me. You look at me with those chocolate-as-sin eyes, dripping with sincerity, and think your goodness can wash my evil away. It doesn't work like that, Ken. I won't taint you with my nature. I'm giving you a gift. One you should thank me for. If I didn't give a damn, I'd use you until you shriveled and throw you out with the trash."

He shook his head. So slow, so sad. The disappointment in his chestnut irises threatened to choke her. "You're lying to yourself if you think we're done here. You know it, and I know it. And I didn't peg you for a person who thrives on dishonesty."

"I don't really give a shit who you pegged me for, you pompous ass. We had a good time together, and let's remember it like adults. We have a war to win, and that won't ever happen if we delude ourselves into thinking this was more than fucking. Get over it, Ken. I already am."

"Liar," he said, inching closer to her. Snaking his hand behind her neck, she gasped as he pulled her face within a hairsbreadth of his. "Stop being a coward—"

Her hand shot to his throat, cutting off his words as he leered down at her. Rage clouded his eyes, his strong jaw clenched. "Don't ever grab me without my consent again. I'll fucking murder you." His pulse was strong under her palm as she held him, also freezing him with her mind. "Thanks for the good fucks and the scenic field trips. Now, leave me the hell alone unless we're training. Got it?" Not waiting for an answer, she brushed a kiss, gentle and brief, on his full lips. Knowing that she needed to let him breathe, she closed her eyes and dematerialized to her cabin.

Once there, she wandered around the tiny space, shaken and restless. Stepping out onto the grass under the bright morning sun, she lay down upon the cushy ground. She'd lain like this so many times, on her back, with men above her. Never, in the long span of her wretched life had any of them meant anything. Never until Kenden.

Under the clouds, she could almost see him above her. Staring into her as he loved her. Whispering words that could never be true. Unwilling to acknowledge her tears, she let them fall, soaking the ground below. And when she was done, she walked back inside, determined to ensure he stayed at arm's length. Using the anger and pain that always existed within, she proceeded to rebuild every wall he'd torn down with his firm hands and tender heart.

The man devolved into an evil monster, forgetting his time in the Elven world and even his wonderful memories with the woman. All that consumed him were feelings of hate and retribution.

Plotting his revenge, he studied the dark forces of the Universe, becoming immensely strong and potent. He developed powers that were unthinkable for other immortals upon the planet...

Chapter 14

True to her word, Evie materialized to the sparring field at Uteria at eight o'clock on Monday morning. The sun was bright in the sky as hundreds of soldiers milled about the turf. Comprised of Vampyres and Slayers, the combined immortal army was vast.

"Good morning, Evie," Latimus said, giving her a nod. "We're excited to have you train with us."

"As am I," she said. "Let's kick that bastard's ass."

Kenden absently listened to their conversation, watching the men stretch in the distance. How a woman who was about to train for battle could look so sexy was something he'd never understand. Scarlet hair was pulled into a thick bun atop her head. Black leggings stopped at her calves above gray Saucony sneakers. A tight black tank top bracketed her perfect breasts.

After their argument Sunday morning, he'd been a wreck. He'd shuffled around the house, trying not to smell her perfume in every corner. Sadly, the effort had been futile. She lingered in all the places they'd touched and every room where she'd given him her gorgeous smile. Today, the smile was gone, replaced by an expression of resolve and fortitude.

"Hello, Commander," she said, chin lifted proudly.

"Good morning," he said, hating her. Loving her. Not knowing what the difference was anymore. "Ready to meet the men?"

Her grin almost buckled his knees. "You bet your perfect ass, I am. Let's go."

Kenden and Latimus walked her toward the open field. Addressing the soldiers, Kenden explained that Evie was the newest member of their team and was to be accepted immediately. Informing the men that they were to treat her as an equal and spar with her using their full effort, the soldiers cheered and saluted in approval.

"You're not trying to get me killed, are you?" she asked, gazing up at him.

"You'd be pissed if I told them to go easy on you," Kenden said.

"So fucking true. Hand me a sword." Thrusting out her hand, Latimus stepped forward and armed her with the weapon she requested. Waggling her eyebrows, she said, "Let's have some fun, boys. Hmmm?" Pivoting to face the troops, she sauntered toward the first group of men, ready to train.

"Damn," Latimus said, rubbing the back of his neck. "She's something else."

"Tell me about it," Kenden muttered.

"Are you guys okay?"

"Not even close," Kenden said, staring abstractedly at the field.

"Is this going to fuck up your head?"

"No," he said, staring at the ground as he kicked it with his army boot. "There's too much on the line to lose it now. I'm straight. You have my word."

Latimus patted him on the back. "Never doubted you, man. Come on. Let's get down there and prepare to kill that asshole."

The two commanders strolled down the hill, onto the meadow, and dispersed to work with different bands of men. For hours, they practiced and sparred, Evie fighting along with them. She never showed one sign of fatigue, impressing him as the soldiers towered over her slight frame. Although she was slender, she was mighty. She had the power to kill them all with a flick of her wrist. It would be a huge advantage when they fought the Deamons, and for that, Kenden was grateful.

He'd agreed to her ridiculous ultimatum with the understanding that having her powers available alongside his soldiers would be invaluable. At least, that's what he told himself. Otherwise, he would have to admit that he'd accepted her terms for other reasons. Ones that had to do with emotions and feelings. All the things that threatened to drown him, and repulsed her. Pushing those thoughts away, he focused on his army.

After lunch, Darkrip materialized for the afternoon session, his morning comprised of a visit to see Nolan with Arderin.

"How's your wife doing, man?" Kenden asked him.

"Great," Darkrip said, beaming with pride. "She's five and a half months now, and the bump is so damn cute. I'm a fucking wreck, but she's a rock. We're having a little girl. It's unbelievable."

"Miranda told me," Kenden said, his lips curving. Who would've thought that the man he met so recently, who professed to be evil, would've turned into such a caring bonded mate and father? Love really was miraculous. Would Evie be able to make the same transformation? The question filled him with doubt, but he still clung to hope. Only time would tell if she could transform that intensely. It was a huge gamble but one that Kenden felt was important.

Reprimanding his drifting thoughts, he focused back on Darkrip. "I'm really happy for you guys. Arderin certainly seems to keep you on your toes."

"She's infuriating. Stubborn woman," he muttered, shaking his head. "I'm obsessed with her. I'll never understand why she loves me but I'm so fucking honored."

Kenden smiled, crossing his arms over his chest as they observed the soldiers returning to the field from lunch.

"Enough about that though," Darkrip said. "I vomit in my mouth when I hear myself talk about her." Patting Kenden on the shoulder, he asked, "What's going on with you and Evie?"

Kenden sighed. "Our agreement has been honored. She's going to train with us and attack when we're ready."

"Right," Darkrip said, his tone flat. "I think you and I need to talk. How about tomorrow? At the pub in Uteria's main square after training?"

"Sure," Kenden said, wanting so badly to know the parts of Evie that she kept closely hidden. Darkrip would be able to shed some light, if small, and that comforted him somehow. "Seven p.m. I'll meet you there."

Darkrip gave a nod and one more pat of solidarity on the shoulder. Plodding down to the sparring turf, he joined Evie's group of men. For the next several hours, they proceeded to practice forming the joint force-field as soldiers fought to disarm them. They needed the experience if they were going to surround Crimeous while his Deamon soldiers battled to protect him.

Watching from the hill, Kenden couldn't help but admire what a strong warrior Evie was. He knew she'd fought with many human armies over the centuries, and it showed. She was deft with a sword and most likely with other weapons. Those skills combined with her powers made her almost invincible.

Increasingly liking their chances against the Dark Lord, he trekked down the hill to implement some afternoon drills.

∞

Kenden walked into the quaint Irish pub promptly at seven o'clock on Wednesday. Darkrip's broad shoulders were hunched over the bar as he lifted a pint to his mouth.

"You started without me?" Kenden teased, sliding onto the stool beside him

"Sorry," Darkrip said, smiling. "I got here early and was ready for a beer."

The mustached bartender appeared, and Kenden ordered an IPA. Lifting it, he clinked his glass with Darkrip's. "To your wife and child. Congrats, man."

"Thanks," Darkrip said, grinning as he sipped. "Weird. Still so fucking weird," he said, setting down the glass. "I'm going to be a father. Good lord, I hope I do a good job. I'm terrified."

Kenden felt the corner of his lips curve. "You've got this. You're going to do great. And if you suck, Arderin will pick up your slack."

Darkrip chuckled. "Thank god."

They caught up on life, chatting cordially. Kenden hadn't spent much time with Miranda's brother but he found that he liked him immensely. His transformation to living by his Slayer half was commendable, and he was quite curious as to how he made the choice.

"It was my mother," Darkrip said, his elbow resting on the lip of the bar. "She appeared to me centuries ago and asked for my word. I gave it to her and vowed to honor it. It was the only thing that kept me going for so long."

"You loved her very much," Kenden said.

"Yes," he said with a nod. "My love for her was strong enough to motivate me into action. Sadly, Evie didn't experience the same connection with her. I wish she'd known Mother when she was still cognizant. She loved her so much, even though Evie won't let herself believe it."

"She told me the same thing," Kenden said, taking a sip of his beer. "She's convinced that she only loved you and Miranda."

Darkrip's brows drew together. "I can't believe she told you about Mother. She rarely opens up about the past."

"I know. She told me about the first time your father violated her too. It was a huge step for her to tell me. I was surprised but extremely honored that she trusted me enough to talk about it."

"Wow," Darkrip said, shaking his head. "She cares for you more than I thought if she spoke to you about the past. That's usually extremely off-limits."

Kenden sighed. "I think she cares for me, but who knows? She's built so many walls that every time I tear one down, I'm met with a hundred more. It's so damn frustrating."

Green irises probed his own. "Why do you care about her so much? Not to be an ass, but she can be a huge bitch sometimes."

Kenden laughed. "So true. It started out as attraction. When I first saw her in France, I was floored. I mean, socked-in-the-chest, unable to breathe, floored. She's the most stunningly beautiful woman I've ever seen." Rubbing the glass with the pad of his thumb, he stared absently at the liquid inside. "But then, I began to realize how broken she was. How much she'd been violated and how torturous it must've been. She told me she'd never had anyone who cared for her, nor had she cared for anyone else. It moved something in me. I felt empathy to depths that I'd never felt before. I found myself wanting so badly to show her that someone could care for her."

"That's admirable. It reminds me of Arderin. She cared for my blackened soul even though I didn't deserve it and probably never will. It's hard for creatures like me and Evie to understand how you guys can feel sympathy toward us."

Kenden's brow furrowed. "I've always been this way. Miranda says I have a savior complex. She's right, although I'd never admit it to her," he said, grinning.

"Evie doesn't need saving," Darkrip said, understanding in his olive eyes. "She needs an equal. Someone who will challenge her and bring out her goodness, against her will if needed. I think you're the right person to do that. I hope you won't give up on her. She's beginning to change, although it's hard for her to accept. I think a lot of that has to do with her feelings for you."

"She swears she doesn't have any feelings for me at all," he muttered.

Darkrip scoffed. "Uh, yeah, I can read the images in her mind. She's quite preoccupied with you. It's very interesting. I don't think she has any idea how to handle it. It throws her off-balance, and that's just what she needs. Being uncomfortable will help her push through and become the person she's meant to be. She reminds me so much of Mother. I think she would want me to help Evie live by her Slayer side."

"Your mother was remarkable," Kenden said. "I loved her very much. She always challenged Uncle Marsias, that was for sure. He was insanely devoted to her."

"I wish I could've known her when she lived here," Darkrip said, swallowing thickly. "But I can at least honor her by helping Evie. I wanted to talk to you, so that you understand how deeply scarred she is. Her anger and pain are so imbedded in her psyche that you're going to have to battle to pull the goodness out of her. It won't be easy, but I'm hoping that you can care for her enough to help her. I think you might be the only person who can."

Kenden blinked, looking at the stained wood of the bar. "I care for her. Very deeply. It's frustrating, since she's determined not to care for me back, but it's there, and I'm too much of a straight-shooter to deny it."

"Good," he said, giving a nod of his raven-black head. "I want to tell you a bit about what she experienced in the caves and some details that I think will help you. I don't want to violate her privacy but I think that having a better understanding of her will help your cause."

"Okay."

Inhaling a deep breath, Darkrip began to tell him bits and pieces from Evie's two centuries in the Deamon caves. Compassion, deep and true, swelled in Kenden's heart as he learned of the numerous violations and brutalizations she'd experienced. It was a miracle that she'd even survived. The fact she'd gone on to piece together a successful life in the human world was astounding. Admiration for her coursed through his veins.

"That's good," Darkrip said, patting his shoulder. "The feelings you're having. Remember those when she pushes you away." Standing, Darkrip threw some bills on the counter. "I've told you all I can without infringing on her privacy more than I already have. The rest is up to you. I want so badly for her to find happiness with you. I think that will solidify her reason to fight with us."

Chugging the last of his beer, Kenden stood and shook his hand. "Thank you. I appreciate everything you've told me and promise I'll do my best to take care of her. Even though she's determined to push me away."

Darkrip smiled. "Man, you and Arderin are two peas in a pod. It's amazing. Evie and I are very lucky. Now, speaking of my wife, I need to get home and cook her dinner. I've figured out that the better the food tastes, the more she wants to thank me later, if you catch my drift."

Chuckling, Kenden nodded. "Loud and clear. Thanks, Darkrip."

"Anytime." Closing his lids, the Slayer-Deamon disappeared.

Sitting back down, Kenden ordered another drink and allowed himself to absorb the information that Evie's brother had given him.

Eventually, the wicked creature began to grow an army. Vast and sinister, they would help him in his efforts to destroy every fragment of the immortal world. For agony had become his existence and he would not rest until every other being in the realm felt his unassuageable anguish...

Archived in the hidden files by King Valktor, never to be released again. This decree recorded on the first day of the ninth month of the thirty-seventh year of the fourteenth century after Creation.

Archivists note: The King has become quite insistent that we do not tell this story to our children. It is imperative that our world-balance is kept in order and that none surmise the true origin of the creatures that dwell in the caves. Ergo, this will be the last entry shared.

Chapter 15

By the week's end, Evie's body was tired and battered. It felt magnificent. She'd always loved fighting in battle, and Kenden's soldiers held nothing back. As the training finished up, she studied the handsome commander. He was collecting the SSWs from the remaining soldiers, compiling them into a four-wheeler. Once they'd all been loaded, he jumped inside and revved the engine. Dusk had fallen, and she watched his hair whip in the dim light as he drove away.

Left alone on the sparring field, she rubbed her upper arms. A chill ran down her spine as she found herself wondering what Kenden was doing for the weekend. Where was he headed? To spend time with Sadie perhaps? She knew he had a close relationship with the Slayer physician.

Deciding she'd like to find out, she transported to the main square and perched on the stone wall. It gave her a nice view of the castle and she'd be able to see Kenden when he returned from the barracks to eat dinner.

Twenty minutes later, he appeared, sauntering from the barracks behind the castle. Approaching the massive wooden doors that led inside the large mansion, Evie admired his confident swagger. God, she hated how handsome he was. It was extremely unfair.

Suddenly, his broad lips curved into a smile, the whites of his teeth almost blinding under the just-risen moon. Was he smiling at her? Feeling her heartbeat quicken, she lifted her hand to wave. And then dropped it just as quickly.

A perky little blond jaunted up to him, her wavy hair bouncing behind her. Kenden enfolded her in his strong arms, causing Evie a moment of panic. Who in the hell was this woman, and why did Kenden feel the need to touch her?

Releasing her, he grinned down at her as they spoke. He appeared so relaxed in her presence, his hands now resting on his waist as the woman gestured with her arms while speaking. Evie imagined cutting them off and shoving them down her throat.

Narrowing her eyes, she entered Kenden's head, reading his mind. *Katia.* The name appeared to her, dragged from his thoughts, along with several images of Kenden entwined with her perfect little body. Goddamnit. Jealousy snaked its way through every cell of Evie's frame, almost choking her with its viciousness. How dare the little bitch smile up at her man like that, with that innocent face and come-hither expression. Visions of murder flashed through Evie's brain, and she struggled to tamp them down.

Kenden was anything but *her* man. She'd do well to remember that. Fury bubbled inside as she watched them, almost drowning her in its grip. Knowing that she needed to calm down, she closed her eyes and transported back to her cabin. To be alone, like she wanted. Yes, she wanted to be alone and untethered and solitary. Reminding herself of that repeatedly, she began to cook dinner as she stewed in her anger.

The stir-fry she whipped up was unappealing, probably due to the insane jealousy sweeping through her veins, and she only ate a small portion. Once the leftovers were stowed and the kitchen cleaned, Evie pulled on her silken pajamas and prepared for bed. As she rubbed the fancy night cream into her freshly-washed cheeks, she couldn't shake the rage of her jealous resentment. Staring at her reflection, she wondered if she'd ever felt the emotion. Unable to recall anything remotely close, she admitted that this was her first experience with the green-eyed monster. It was rather annoying and stirred up every ounce of virulence that dwelled within.

In that moment, she made the decision to confront Kenden. Tomorrow, she would search him out at his shed. She knew he liked to spend his weekend mornings there when he wasn't training the troops. There were things that needed to be said, especially after the disastrous way they'd ended their sexual relationship. Evie hated loose ends and vowed to tie up every dangling, complicated one with the alluring commander.

Feeling her eyelids narrow, she realized she'd probably be unable to contain the fury of her jealousy. It was so potent as it coursed through her body. Deciding that he was strong enough to take it, she pledged not to sugarcoat her words. After all, Kenden seemed unfazed by her vitriolic moods, something that impressed Evie, knowing how they'd cowered so many before him. Feeling her lips curve, she admitted that his calm demeanor in her worst moments was extremely attractive. Rarely had someone been able to handle her fits of wrath.

Rubbing the soft bedsheet with her palm, she imagined, for one moment, that he was there beside her. Holding her after one of their bouts of passion. Forming a fist, she pounded the mattress, giving a *harrumph* as she turned on her side. Letting the emotions war within, she closed her eyes, wondering if nightmares would haunt her sleep, as they so often did.

※

The next morning, Kenden was holed up in his shed studying blueprints of the Deamon caves. The tiny shack was his absolute favorite place on the planet. A thoughtful and curious student of war, he loved studying maps of the terrain where future battles would occur. It only heightened his chances of success, and that was greatly needed against someone as powerful as Crimeous.

Kenden smelled her before she appeared at the door of the shed. The fragrance of her perfume was all-consuming. Clenching his teeth, he vowed to remain calm. Curiosity had him wondering why she'd decided to approach him. They'd spent the week barely communicating.

He'd helped Evie train with the troops and then left her alone. Needing to thoroughly prepare before confronting her, if they were going to have any chance at a relationship or a future, he'd decided to give her some distance. Hell, maybe she'd miss him a fraction of the amount he missed her. Doubtful, but a guy could hope. Regardless, she was after something. Evie always was. He was determined to retain the upper hand here, in his shed. The one place he'd sought solace for a thousand years.

Slender body silhouetted by the morning sunlight, she lifted her arms, placing her palms flat on each side of the shed doorframe. It was the pose of a Greek goddess, stone-like and magnificent. Wanting to appear nonplussed, he lowered his eyes back to the map he'd been studying.

"I'd give you the line about 'all work and no play' but I think that might be futile with you, Mr. Serious." Her voice was sultry, the come-hither tone causing him to stiffen in his faded jeans.

"It's imperative that I know every inch of the Deamon caves where we plan to attack," he said, striving to keep his voice even. "Although you profess not to care about anyone but yourself, I'd like to prevent as many of our soldiers' deaths as possible."

"Ah, yes," she said, sauntering into the shed. "The noble commander. How tedious it must be to be so exceptional all the time." With her slender arm, she closed the door, the soft click making an ominous sound.

Kenden stared at her from the stool where he sat, behind the wooden table. Upon it rested the map, the paper spread under his forearms. "I'm right in the middle of this, Evie, and not quite sure why you're here. I met the terms of your demand, and you've made it very clear that our relationship only exists on the battlefield. Unless I'm missing something."

Ignoring him, she walked slowly around the small cabin. Weapons lined the wooden walls, collected by him over the centuries. Always an inquisitive scholar of war, he'd studied as many weapons as he could—human, Vampyre, Deamon and Slayer—so that he could strategize effectively.

Her white slacks and blue silk, sleeveless blouse somehow seemed too pristine for his shed. Although clean, it was sparse. It was no place for her expensive tailored clothes and much more suited to his jeans, t-shirt and sneakers.

In curiosity, her thin fingers tinkered with one of the metal weapons. "A musket," she mused, her voice quiet.

"Yes," he said, setting down the pencil he'd been using to make notes on the map. "From eighteenth century America."

She nodded. "I used one of these to shoot a man who got a bit too friendly a few centuries ago. It felt magnificent in my hands."

Kenden felt his eyes narrow. "I imagine you've used quite a few armaments on many men who've tried to take the upper hand."

The corner of her gorgeous lips turned up. "You imagine correctly." Turning to face him, those olive-green eyes bore into his. "Men have a nasty habit of thinking they can have control with a pretty woman. I consider it a duty and a privilege to prove them wrong."

Compassion coursed through him as he remembered the stories that Darkrip told him the other evening. Crimeous had repeatedly raped her for years. Once Rina perished, he'd thrown Evie to his Deamon soldiers, letting them violate her for decades until she'd realized her true power. And then, as Darkrip had recounted, she'd made each and every soldier who'd violated her pay. First, with torture. Ultimately, with their lives.

"Your pity is wasted on me," she said, inching closer to the table. Resting her palms flat on top, she leaned forward, gazing into him. "I'm just fine and I don't need the superhero routine. You play the knight in shining armor well, but I'm no damsel in distress."

Slowly, he stood, placing his palms flat on top of the drawings. Closing in, he brought his face within inches of hers, their bodies separated by the two-foot-wide table. "I'd never mistake you for someone who wanted or needed anyone, Evie. Let's be clear about that."

Her perfect scarlet brow arched. "Good." Tilting her face toward his, she brushed her lips across his mouth. Fuck. He wanted her so badly.

"No," he said, his tone gruff. "We want different things, Evie. I can't just have sex with you and move on. I'm sorry, but I can't."

Rolling her eyes, she straightened her spine. Crossing her arms over her perfect breasts, she regarded him. "You're hard as a rock right now. It's futile for you to deny it."

"I won't deny it," he said, keeping his voice steady. "But I won't be another man who just fucks you. You deserve better, and so do I. So, we do it my way, or we don't do it at all."

"*Your* way," she said, scoffing as she shook her head. "Candles and late-nineties R&B? Or warm baths and massages? Am I close?"

Gritting his teeth at her sarcasm, Kenden felt the anger well in his gut. Striding around the table, he grasped her upper arms and drew her to him. She crashed into his body, and he threaded his fingers through her soft hair. Tilting her head back, he latched on to her with his eyes.

"With *emotion*," he said, hating that she'd gotten a rise out of him. "With caring and feeling. That's how I want to make love to you. Otherwise, leave me the hell alone."

Desire flashed in her eyes. With her thin hand, she palmed his length where it threatened to burst behind the fly of his jeans. "But you're so ready—"

"No," he said, pulling her hand away. Inhaling, he took a step back, creating distance. "Not like this."

"Like what?" she asked, her chiding tone infuriating him. "Like *Katia*?" she asked, the woman's name spouted with vitriol from her lips. "Should I let you smother me in tender kisses and whisper words of love?"

"I did love her," he said, shrugging. "Like I've loved every woman I've been intimate with. I told you that."

"Did you fuck her last night?" Evie asked.

"That's none of your business."

"You'll never feel one ounce of desire for her like you feel for me," she said, lifting her hand to caress his cheek. "Admit it."

He grabbed her wrist, prompting anger to flash in her eyes.

"Let go of me."

Furious, he squeezed harder. Those almond-shaped eyes widened, filled with rage.

"Let. Me. Go." The words were mangled through clenched teeth.

Heart pounding, he held fast onto her wrist. Lifting her other hand, she crashed the palm into his cheek. Growling, he latched onto that arm as well. Yanking her around, he rotated her so that her back slammed against the wooden wall of the shed.

Arousal quickly replaced the fury in her green irises.

"Yessss," she hissed, disengaging her wrists from his grasp and sliding her palms down his abdomen. Deftly, her fingers attempted to unzip his pants. "Take me hard, against the wall."

He stilled her hands with his own. Lifting her arms above her head, he held them prisoner, with one hand around her crossed wrists. "You'd like that, wouldn't you?"

"Yes," she said, panting.

Realization coursed through him. "You want me to hurt you," he said, sadness swamping him.

"God, yes," she said, a pleading tone in her voice. "Pain feels so good to me. You have no idea."

Staring down at her, he felt the animal inside him roar. He'd always kept it restrained. Hidden. Vowing to be cool and collected. What would it feel like to free the beast of his lust for this complicated woman? Many in his life had told him he was too controlled; too unspontaneous. Capitulating to the arousal pulsing within, he clamped his jaw with resolve.

Using his free hand, Kenden yanked her shirt out of her waistband. Releasing her wrists, he grabbed onto the collar with both fists and ripped it down the middle. Throwing the tattered silk to the floor, he unbuttoned her pants. After lowering the zipper, he inserted his hands in between her hips and the lacy material of her thong. Pushing them to the ground, he growled, "Step out."

She nudged out of her sandals and kicked the pants away. "I could've just dematerialized my clothes—"

Standing to his full height, he stuck his fingers in her hair and pulled her head back. "Shut up," he said, lowering his mouth to hers.

Inhaling her gasp, he thrust his tongue into her mouth, slathering it over hers. Blood coursed through his muscled frame as he gyrated his hips against her body, clad only in her silky pink bra.

"You want me to make you feel pain?" he asked, biting her lower lip and then sliding his tongue over it to wash away the sting.

"Yes," she whimpered. "It always feels so good."

"Of course, it does," he said, tilting his head to devour her mouth from a different angle. The tiny responding mewls that escaped her throat drove him mad. Disengaging from her, he gazed into her as they panted. "If someone hurts you while loving you, it makes it easier for you to dismiss them when it's over."

Anger flashed in her stunning eyes. "Don't psychoanalyze me, you son of a bitch."

"It's true," he said, reaching down to unbutton his jeans and lower the fly. Pushing them and his boxer briefs to his knees, he bent down. After grabbing the luscious globes of her ass, he picked her up. Instinctively, her legs wrapped around his waist.

Holding her, he aligned himself with her dripping core. Locking his eyes onto hers, he thrust her back against the wall, simultaneously thrusting his turgid cock into her wetness. Caught up in his burning arousal for her, he'd forgotten that two nails protruded from the wall behind her. A weapon had once hung there that had recently been taken down for polishing.

Her body stiffened as the nails impaled her back. Those magnificent emerald irises filled with pleasure-pain as she opened her mouth wide and gasped.

Cursing, he started to pull her away, hoping to save her from the pain.

"No!" she cried, clutching him tighter. "It doesn't hurt. Please. Like this."

Hesitating, he studied her, as the lush walls of her center still surrounded him.

"Please, Ken."

The soft cry shattered something inside him. Capitulating, he began sliding within her.

"Darkrip told me that you feel pleasure from pain," he said, slowly pulling his shaft out of her wet channel and then inserting it fully again. "So, I'll give it to you, Evie, even though it kills me." Grunting, he increased the speed of his strokes, the plushy folds of her core choking his cock.

Her head lolled back as she moaned, consumed by passion. "Faster," she commanded, clutching her arms behind his neck.

Using his hands, he moved her slender hips up and down in a mindless rhythm. His balls slapped against her as he hammered into her flushed body. Knowing that the barbs that protruded from the wall were lodged in the frail skin of her back made him want to retch, but she plodded on, seeming enthralled by the multiple sensations. Not even beginning to understand how something that painful could cause pleasure, he tried not to let his self-revulsion at hurting her choke him.

"It feels amazing," she said, lifting her head to lock her gaze on to his. Threading her fingers through his hair, on both sides of his head, she held on for dear life as he jackknifed into her.

"I hate hurting you," he said through gritted teeth. "Can't you see that, Evie? I don't want to be another man who hurts you."

Emotion entered her eyes, so vibrant and true. Sure that she'd never intended for him to see it, he realized how vulnerable she was at this moment. How raw.

"Don't you understand?" he pleaded, bringing one hand up to cup her cheek. "I want to love you. I don't want to cause you pain."

"No," she said, shaking her head violently, forcing his hand away. "No one loves me. Just fuck me. Oh, god." Tilting her head back, her body went limp. Unable to deny himself the pleasure of being inside her, he continued, his body at war with his mind. Groaning, he slid both hands further under her, lifting her up and down on his thick cock.

Continuing to pound her, he lowered his head, burying his face in her neck. Sweat poured from him as he inhaled the sweet scent of her skin. Kissing a path up her neck, he placed his lips on her ear. "This is more than fucking. You can try to deny it but you know it's true."

She moaned, shaking her head against the wall, her fire-red hair creating a blaze against the wood. "There's nothing more than fucking. There never will be for me."

"Goddamnit," Kenden said, moving his face so that his forehead rested on hers. "Look at me."

Opening her lids, she complied. "Do you not *feel* this?" he asked, needing her to understand how special the energy was between them. By the goddess, he'd never felt anything as consuming as what he felt with her.

"It feels so good," she said. His heart threatened to shatter when wetness entered her eyes. "It always feels so good with you."

"Let yourself feel it, baby," he said, rubbing the skin of his forehead against hers as he loved her. "It could be like this forever."

"No," she said, her voice strangled. "I don't want that."

Snarling at her, he bared his teeth. "Liar."

Pulling him to her, with her fingers still clutched in his hair, she kissed him. Jabbing her tongue in his mouth, she drew his out to war with hers. Figuring that she was trying to silence him, he let her.

Battling with her tongue, he moved her upon him, fucking her as if it were the last time he'd ever do the deed. Hell, it was so good, maybe it would be. The tip of his shaft threatened to explode as he connected with the spot deep inside her that he knew would send her over the edge. Tiny purrs escaped from her, into his mouth, and he growled in approval. The muscles of his thighs and calves quivered as he felt his balls begin to tingle.

Unlatching from him, she threw her head back and wailed, calling his name in the dim light of the shack. Convulsing around him, he felt the rush of moisture from her climax wash over the straining nerve-endings of his shaft. Cursing, he began to come, holding on to her for dear life as he jetted his release into her. Burying his face in the juncture of her neck and shoulder, he spurted into her for what seemed to be a small lifetime. Eventually, his cock slowed its pulsing, relaxing and softening in her sweet, luscious warmth. Sated, he clutched her close, needing to inhale her scent.

Evie trembled as he held her, her supple body wrapped around his, her gorgeous hair falling over his shoulder. Her quivering shook him to his core. He loved nothing more than to see her vulnerable and open.

The drops of their loving slowly began to drip down his upper thighs, drawing him slowly back to Earth. Lifting his head, he brought his hand up to caress her cheek.

"Are you okay?" he asked, his voice scratchy.

She nodded, those magnificent eyes filled with so many emotions that he had no idea how to differentiate.

"Let's get you cleaned up," he said, rubbing the pad of his thumb over her swollen lower lip.

She didn't speak. Instead, she just watched him, her expression wary. Still inside her, he separated her from the wall. She hissed a breath through her teeth as the soft skin of her back disengaged from the nails.

Hating that he'd hurt her, he stared down into her eyes.

"I'm okay," she said. "Like I told you, pain hurts for me but it also courses pleasure through my body. I'm fine."

Gazing into her, he questioned the truth of her statement. She didn't look fine. She looked shaken...and guileless...and beautiful.

Nudging off his sneakers, he used his feet to pull off his jeans and underwear. Tossing them on the floor by kicking them, he turned away from the wall. Holding her tight, he carried her to the tiny cot he kept in the shed. He'd sometimes slept there, before he'd built his house, on nights he was too tired to walk back to the main castle. It rested against the wall, opposite the door, behind the wooden table.

Sliding out of her, he set her on her feet. Reaching for the box of tissues on the small table at the head of the cot, he grabbed several and lowered in front of her. Crouching down, he gently rubbed away the evidence of their loving from her thighs.

"Lie down on the cot, on your stomach."

She arched a brow. "Are you going to take me from behind? I thought you might need at least a few minutes of recovery time."

From his kneeling position, he shot her a glare. "I'm going to clean the wounds on your back. Lie down, Evie. And take off your bra."

"Wow," she said, reaching behind to unclasp the garment. "I'm pretty sure that's the most unromantic way any man has ordered me to remove my bra." Pulling it off her breasts, she threw it on the floor.

Kenden slowly stood, running the tip of his nose up her stomach and between her breasts, until he came to his full height. "Don't throw your other lovers in my face. I don't like it." Gently, he nipped at her lips.

"Well, look who's possessive." The always-present glint of mischief was in her eyes as she chided him, but they were also still bursting with unnamed feelings. She was rattled, even though she was trying to hide it.

"Right now, I'm the only one sharing your bed. It's going to stay that way until we both decide that we're ready to move on. Got it?"

She breathed a laugh. "I dictate the terms of who shares my bed."

"Oh, I know it," he said, rubbing his lips against hers. "But you came here looking for me, sweetheart, so I'm in charge of this negotiation. Now, lie the hell down."

"God, you're so sexy when you boss me around," she said, giving him a sultry smile. "Fine. Stitch me up if you must." With a dramatic sigh, she lowered onto the cot, crossing her arms underneath her head as she watched him mill about the shed.

After wiping his release from his shaft with the tissues, Kenden stalked over and grabbed his boxer-briefs, shrugging them on. Locating the first-aid kit, which he kept in the file cabinet by the front door, he walked to her and sat down on the hard floor. Opening the kit, he pulled out the travel-sized bottle of alcohol, cotton swabs and bandages.

Two quarter-sized lacerations marred her flawless skin, one inside each of her shoulder blades. Wetting a cotton ball with alcohol, he held it over one of the wounds. "This will probably hurt."

"Good," she said, the word slightly garbled as her cheek rested on her arm.

Lowering the soft swab to her skin, his heart clenched at the rasp of her indrawn breath when it connected with the wound.

"You okay?" he asked softly.

She nodded, her eyes seeming to glow in the soft light that emanated from the lightbulb hanging from the ceiling in the middle of the shed.

Kenden commenced cleaning the lacerations, ensuring they wouldn't be infected, and then covered them with two large bandages. Putting everything back in the first-aid kit, he closed it and pushed it aside. Lifting his broad hand, he stroked her silky, scarlet hair as she gazed at him.

Silence pervaded the room but instead of being stifling, it was welcome. There, in the dim light, he caressed her while she watched him, her lids growing heavy. Content to just observe her breathe, he reveled in her beauty. Never had he met a woman more exquisite.

Letting her fall into sleep, he sat by her side as long as his body allowed. Then, exhausted by their lovemaking, he let himself fall as well.

Chapter 16

Evie gasped a breath, coming into consciousness as her eyes darted around the small space. Then, she remembered. She was in Kenden's shed, recovering from what was probably the most intense sexual experience of her life. Letting her pupils settle on him, her heart constricted in her chest as she rested on her stomach.

There on the dirty floor he lay, snoring softly as he slept. Aching to touch him, she slid her fingers into his hair. Gently, she soothed him, waiting for him to rouse. Those lids opened slowly, and he regarded her with his always-sexy deep brown eyes.

"Why are you sleeping on the floor?" she asked, a slight teasing in her tone.

He shrugged. "I didn't want you to wake up somewhere unfamiliar. I wanted to be here, so you'd see me when you awoke."

Emotion clawed at her throat, threatening to close it as she reeled from his words. He was such a good man. One who deserved a woman who would give him everything he desired. Something pulsed inside her as she stared at him, her fingers never ceasing their ministrations on his thick hair. Terrified that it was love, she pushed it away. She'd never felt anything remotely close to that emotion and vowed she never would.

"Thank you," she whispered, humbled by him. "I like seeing you when I wake up. It's the first time that's ever happened to me."

"I like it too," he said, reaching up to caress her cheek with the pads of his fingers. "It could happen every morning if you moved in with me. I have so much space, and I'm sure you're tired of living in that tiny cabin."

The hand in his hair froze. "Ken..." she said softly, struggling to find the right words to deny his ridiculous request.

"Don't say you don't want to. I've always appreciated how straightforward you are, sweetheart. It's beneath you to lie about this."

Inhaling a deep breath, she felt her irises darting over his face. "I'm a nightmare, Ken. A goddamn nightmare. You don't want to live with me."

His thick lips curved into a smile. "Um, I'm pretty sure I just indicated that I do."

Sliding her hand from his hair to his cheek, she cupped his face. "I'm a monster in the morning. Bitchy as hell until I've had several cups of coffee. I use too much hot water and leave a huge clump of hair behind each time I shower."

He chuckled, the sound so deep it sent shivers through her body. "Well, I'm pretty handy. If you clog the drain, I'll snake it."

Fear lodged in her gut as she tried to think of more excuses. Better excuses. There were so many, weren't there?

"I know you're scared, baby," he said, his thumb so soothing as it caressed her cheek. "I am too. I've never felt about anyone the way I feel about you."

"I don't want your feelings, Ken. I've tried to tell you that."

"I know," he said, looking like a sad puppy. "But they exist, and I'm a straight-shooter. It's one of the many things we have in common."

Evie scoffed. "We don't have anything in common."

His eyebrow arched as he grinned. "Wanna bet? We're both competent soldiers, enthralled by war. We thrive on honesty and candidness and both love a good steak. You cook a mean chicken cordon bleu, and I'm a whiz at washing the dishes. I think we have to live together just to streamline efficiencies. We'd have the most proficient house on the compound."

She laughed in spite of herself. "A compelling argument, but wasted. I can't move in with you. I don't want that level of commitment."

"I don't need any level of commitment from you, Evie. I just want you. Let's keep it simple and not define it. Having you in my home will mean you can sleep with me anytime you damn well please. That has to be somewhat enticing, no?" His smile was so adorable that her heart threatened to burst in her chest.

"If I was going to be enticed by anything, it would be unlimited access to your gorgeous cock. It's fucking magnificent."

He breathed a laugh. "Then, move in with me. No timeframe, no restrictions. Just you and me and unlimited sex."

Evie was thoroughly enjoying their banter. He was so captivatingly charming.

"I can't," she whispered.

Sitting up, he slid his arms around her and pulled her off the cot to straddle his lap. She wrapped her legs around him, loving the feel of his erection on her naked core through his boxer briefs.

"Yes, you can." Gently, he nibbled her lower lip. "Move in with me."

"No," she said, shaking her head as her arms surrounded his neck.

Reaching down, he pulled himself through the hole of his underwear. Lifting her by the globe of her butt with his other hand, he positioned the head of his shaft at the delicate skin of her deepest place. Ever so softly, he rubbed the sensitive tip against the wet lips of her core.

"Move in with me," he said, his voice gravelly.

"No," she said, almost moaning from the sweet contact.

Slowly, he began to nudge himself into her. Clutching onto his hair, she bit her lip to contain her groan. The soft skin of his straining cock felt so good as it stretched her. Eventually, he reached the hilt. Touching his forehead to hers, he jutted back and forth, stimulating the spot that brought her so much pleasure.

"Move in with me," he repeated, his gaze locked onto hers.

"Oh, god," she wailed, gyrating her hips to magnify the contact. "You're not playing fair."

"I never cheat but I always make sure the odds are in my favor." Nudging his nose with hers, he drove into her channel in short bursts that felt amazing. "Move in with me, and I'll make you scream."

"What if you end up hating me?" The question was wrenched from her pleasure-drenched body, too aroused to care how vulnerable it made her.

"Won't happen," he said, his tone confident. "Say yes, sweetheart. You can do it."

Purring with desire, she placed her lips against his, her lissome frame shuddering. "I'll stay with you this weekend. It's all I can give right now. Now, fuck me like you mean it."

"I love the way you compromise," he said, gently biting her plushy lower lip. Pushing her back to the floor, he began hammering into her, honoring his word to make her scream. It felt so good, she damn near forgot to be terrified that she'd been handled. Even if there were concessions, he'd gotten her to capitulate. And damn, if that wasn't hot as hell. Loving his brain almost as much as his cock, she let Kenden bone her into senselessness.

They spent the weekend together, Evie cooking dinner on Saturday and Sunday. Both afternoons, while preparing the food, she stared out the window, watching Kenden chop wood that would be used for their evening fire. Muscles, tanned and bulging, stretched under the buttery sunlight, causing Evie intense pangs of longing in her gut.

Every so often, he would lift the metal container to his mouth and drink, his thick throat bobbing as he swallowed. Wiping his lips with the back of his arm, he smiled at her through the window and gave a wave. Annoyed that she was even considering waving back, she would scowl each time and curse him in her head. How dare he look at her with those gorgeous eyes and tan, sweaty skin? Bastard.

At night, after dinner, they sat by the fire. Kenden rubbed her feet while they chatted about life and war and the upcoming battle they faced. It was all too surreal for Evie. She'd lived alone for so long, never needing companionship, and was terrified that this display of domestic bliss was going to gestate into something more. It couldn't happen. Their time together was limited. It had to be.

Good grief, he'd want her to have a hundred babies. Impossible, since they'd have her father's blood. She knew that Kenden understood this, somewhere deep inside. That their situation was all too temporary. But he seemed to carry on, not willing to acknowledge their lack of a future.

At night he pulled her close, clutching her to him after they loved each other. Never being a cuddler, she let him hold her anyway. Where was the harm in that? He was so patient and kind to her, she could at least let him smother her with his strong body. The warmth from his solid frame would wash over her as they drifted, causing Evie to take a mental snapshot. Although never a sentimental fool, she did want to remember their time together when she returned to the human world. She would recall these moments, when they were sated and content, so fondly.

Monday came, and a new week of training along with it. Evie fought tirelessly with the troops, returning to her cabin on Monday evening. Rubbing her upper arms as she stood beside the lonely bed, she admitted that she missed him. It was unwelcome and rather annoying.

By mid-week, she was struck with a yearning so intense she could actually feel it throbbing in her stomach. Brushing her teeth under the florescent light of the small bathroom, clad in her silky robe, she ached for him. Unable to stop herself, she transported to his house.

Kenden didn't seem fazed as she appeared from thin air. His eyes met hers in the reflection as he slid the brush over his teeth. Leaning over to rinse, he deposited the toothbrush in the nearby cup and rested his palms beside the sink. "Hello, Evie," he said, his irises locked on hers in the mirror.

Unable to form words, she slowly approached. Placing her palms on his back, she caressed his straining muscles. Sliding her arms around his waist, she rested her forehead between his shoulder blades. There, they stood, breathless, motionless, in the white marble bathroom.

Eventually, Kenden turned, picking her up and carrying her to the four-post bed. Discarding her robe and his underwear, he loomed above her, magnificent and striking. Entering her, inch by inch, his melted-chocolate eyes communicated emotions that she craved against her will. Afterward, he pulled her limp body to his side, surrounding her with his corded arms.

"For someone who doesn't want to live with me, you sure show up here a lot," he murmured into her hair.

Evie didn't answer. How could she? Instead, she ran her hand through the thick hairs on his chest, loving how they tickled her palm. Nestling into his side, she gave way to her dreams.

Chapter 17

Thursday, alone in her cabin after the day's training, Evie looked at the text from Miranda, expecting to feel another wave of anger at her beckoning.

Miranda: We're having a joint Slayer-Vampyre BBQ tonight so the species can mingle. Hope you'll come. NOT summoning you. Just really want you there so we can hang.

Inhaling a deep breath, Evie searched her feelings. Not only was she not incensed, but she almost felt a sense of elation that her headstrong sister seemed determined to spend time with her. The joy at the text was ridiculous, but what did she expect with the shit show her life had recently become? She'd turned into an emotional sap, craving Kenden's company and crying like a teenage girl in line for a Shawn Mendes concert. It was so absolutely frustrating that Evie gave up trying to push it away. At this point, she was too tired to fight the insane sentiments. Giving in to them, she prepped to head to the barbeque.

Throwing on jeans, so she could sit in the green grass if needed, a loose tank and sandals, she materialized to the playground at Uteria's main square. Right away, she saw Jack's red hair swishing as he jumped around the monkey bars, daring the other kids to traverse them as quickly as he did. Feeling her lips twitch, she admitted that she liked the little tyke. Lila and Latimus's adopted son had a competitive spirit that was admirable, especially for a kid who'd been through what he had.

Kenden approached her, handing her a red solo cup. "It's beer from the keg. We don't really get too fancy during these barbeques."

"Who needs fancy?" she asked, taking a sip. "It tastes fine to me. I've always loved a good beer."

"Be still, my beating heart," he said, sipping from his own cup. "You're adding to the tally of things we have in common. Careful."

Chuckling, she beamed up at him. "I guess there are worse people I could share similarities with." Glancing around, Evie noticed members of the royal family lounging around the picnic tables under a large redwood. "I need to grab some food. I'm starving."

"Come on," he said, offering his hand to her.

Evie hesitated, staring at his broad hand.

"The whole compound knows we're sleeping together. I think it's okay if you hold my hand."

Scowling up at him, she grabbed his hand and interlaced their fingers. The challenge in his voice had rankled her, which she was sure was his intended consequence.

Tugging her gently, Kenden led her to where the royal family was sitting. Arderin, so beautiful with the flush of her pregnancy, was in the middle of stealing Darkrip's fork and eating the large bite of meat he'd procured on top.

"Good grief, woman," Darkrip said, shooting her a light-hearted glare. "You don't even need food. Why do you insist on eating mine all the time?"

"Because it drives you nuts," was her good-natured reply as she waggled her eyebrows.

"You'll pay for that later," he murmured into her ear.

"God, I hope so," she said, fangs squishing her bottom lip as she gave him a come-hither smile.

Evie set her cup on the table and headed to the line of grills to get some food. Scooping some on top of the thick paper plate, she noticed Sathan cooking behind one of the large metal grills.

"Didn't know Vampyres knew how to barbeque," Evie said to him.

He grabbed a piece of grilled chicken with large metal tongs and deposited it on her plate. "Miranda says it makes me more approachable to our people, doing everyday tasks like grilling. Let me know what you think. I hope it's not too dry."

"I'm sure it's fine," she said, continuing down the line to spoon some macaroni salad onto her plate. Pondering, she admitted that she was thankful for the Vampyre king's cordiality toward her. They certainly hadn't gotten off to the best start, and Evie assumed that he was making his best effort to tolerate her due to Miranda's urging and the fact he needed her to possibly fulfill the prophecy. Inwardly, she hoped she was the descendant of Valktor to kill her father. It would be a great service to both species and would perhaps exonerate Evie from the disastrous decisions she'd made when Kenden first found her, if only slightly.

Heading back to the table, she sat across from her brother and Arderin, Miranda to her right.

"How's my husband doing up there?" Miranda asked, surreptitiously glancing over her shoulder. "He's not thrilled that I made him cook, but I'm the boss." She flicked her glossy hair over her shoulder as she grinned.

"Pretty well," Evie said, cutting into the chicken with her plastic fork and knife. Ingesting a bite, she chewed. "It's quite tasty. Don't think it will kill me, maybe to your husband's chagrin."

"No way," Miranda said, squeezing her wrist. "We're happy to have you here, Evie. All of us."

"Thank you," she said softly, humbled by her sister's acceptance.

Kenden sat down to Evie's left, his plate heaving with food.

"Careful, or you'll lose those abs you're so proud of," Evie teased.

"Not on your life, sweetheart," he said, grinning. "I need them to tempt you when you want run away from me."

Stuffing a huge bite of food into his mouth, situated atop the plastic fork, he chewed. The muscles in his jaw, sinewed and corded, strained as his mouth worked. For the love of all the gods, Evie was marveling at his jaw muscles. This really had to stop. She'd gone fucking insane.

"Okay," Miranda said, standing and tossing her plate in the nearby trash can. "I'm gonna go mingle. Anybody want to come with?"

"Yep," Arderin said, bouncing up from the table. "I need to roam around. This baby's having a dance-off in my stomach."

Darkrip's face clouded with concern. "Do you need to see Sadie?" he asked from his perch on the picnic bench.

"No," Arderin said, bending to give him a peck on the lips. "She's just cantankerous like her dad, being all cooped up in there. Can't wait to meet her. She's going to be a handful."

"Don't I know it," Darkrip muttered. "I'm terrified."

Arderin laughed, the sound melodious and sweet. "Don't worry, I'll save you. Thank the goddess you bonded with someone who's tough."

"Tough as nails," he said, squeezing her hand. "I'll finish up and come find you guys. Love you."

"Love you," she whispered, giving him an absent kiss on the forehead before walking away with Miranda.

Evie smiled, finding that she was truly happy for her brother. How amazing. It had been so long since she'd felt happiness for others. It was foreign yet somehow welcome. Kenden's knee brushed hers under the table, and she stared up at him, realizing he'd bumped her intentionally. Love, deep and true, glowed in his gorgeous eyes. Starting into them, Evie could only form one thought: *Holy shit, I am so fucked.*

As the three of them were finishing the last of the scrumptious food, Lila sauntered over to sit beside Evie, Jack at her side. Her face glowed as she gave a gorgeous smile, although it was a bit hesitant and shy.

"Hi, Evie," she said in her melodic tone. "I hope you don't mind, but I have a favor to ask you."

"Shoot," Evie said, her gaze traveling to Jack, who was beaming up at her, his crooked teeth somehow adorable between his tiny red lips.

"Jack is enthralled by the samurai he learned about in school. It's become a bit of an obsession. Latimus told me that you trained with the samurai in Japan for many decades. I was wondering if you could tell him a bit about your experience."

Evie eyed the little scamp, unable not to smile back. Something about his red hair and freckled face called to her.

"Better yet, why don't I show you?" Standing, Evie rubbed her palms over her thighs. "Got a sword lying around anywhere?"

Pleasure burst in Jack's wide brown eyes. "Yes!" he said, nodding furiously. "Give me a sec, okay?"

"Okay," Evie said, chuckling as he ran toward the playground. Thirty seconds later, he returned triumphant, two toy swords in hand.

"Come on," she said, motioning him toward the open grass a few feet away from the picnic table. Facing him, she grabbed the base of one of the plastic swords. With the respect that one would employ when addressing a master samurai, Evie began showing Jack different stances, lunges and methods she'd learned in her extensive training. Once she'd explained the basics, she began sparring with him.

The plastic blades clanked and shuddered as they fought, the boy determined to best her. Brow furrowed, he jousted and grunted as she skated around his weapon, dodging his jabs.

"Whoa, there," she said, leaning over to rest on her knees. "You're playing dirty. You almost stabbed me in the liver."

His eyes grew round as saucers. "Are you okay? I'm sorry. I didn't mean—"

Evie sliced her sword through the air, cutting off his words as she knocked his weapon to the ground. "First lesson of warfare, kid. Don't get distracted."

Jack stared up at her, his chin trembling slightly. *Shit.* Of course, she'd scared the crap out of the little bugger. Evie had always been terrible with kids. Yet another reason why she'd never let Kenden tie himself to her. No way would she deny the certain future 'Dad of the Year' the opportunity to have children. It would be the height of selfishness to taint his offspring with her father's awful blood.

Leaning down, she reached toward Jack, hoping to soothe him by ruffling his thick hair, the color so like her own. "I'm sorry, Jack—"

Bending down, he grabbed his sword from the grass and thrust the point into her midsection. Not too hard to hurt her, but enough to spur a large exhale from her shocked body. The rascal had taken advantage of her lowered position to regain the upper hand. To say she was impressed would be an understatement.

"I surrender," she said, laughing as she held up her hands and dropped her weapon. "You're a smart one, aren't you?" Arching a brow, she reveled in his huge smile.

"Did you think I was gonna cry?" he asked, excitement in his tone. "I wanted to trick you, so you'd underestimate me. Latimus always says that having your opponent underestimate you is the best way to gain the advantage."

"He's absolutely right," she said. "You're a pretty awesome warrior, Jack. I assume you want to be a soldier one day?"

"Yep," he said, eagerness evident in his nod. "Latimus says I can join the army when I'm eighteen, and I'm going to work my way up to be his second-in-command one day."

"Well, he'd better watch out, or you might usurp him and become the commander yourself. You're pretty sly."

"What does 'you-syrup' mean?" he asked, his brow furrowing.

Evie snickered. "It means you'll take the position of commander from him against his will, because your skills will be better."

"Oh," he said, shaking his head. "I wouldn't do that. He's awesome. I wouldn't take anything from him. I don't mind sharing."

"What a sweet boy you are," she said, reverently stroking his head. Had she ever had the ability to be so open and loving? It moved something in her as she stared into his deep brown eyes. "Well, then, maybe you can be co-commanders. How's that?"

"Perfect," he said, grinning from ear-to-ear.

"Okay, sweetheart," Lila said, seeming to float over toward them. "It's getting late, and we need to say our goodbyes. I think Aunt Evie has shown you enough for today. What do you say?"

"Thank you, Aunt Evie," he said, the tone of his voice so sincere.

"Just 'Evie' is fine, kid," she said, shooting Lila a good-natured glare. "And you're welcome. We'll train again one day soon, okay?"

"Okay," he shouted, rushing toward her and throwing his arms around her waist. Feeling extremely uncomfortable but also a bit overwhelmed by her affection toward him, she hugged him back. Sparing a glance toward Kenden, still sitting at the picnic table with Darkrip, she could see he was transfixed by the scene. Great. Just what she needed. The noble Slayer commander bombarded with images of her loving interactions with a child. Good lord. Stiffening, she pulled away from Jack.

Unable to bring herself to sit beside Kenden, she walked toward Latimus, who was standing under the large elm tree several feet away. Making up some unnecessary question to ask him about the next morning's training, she cowered to her fear, too afraid to face the only man who, in ten long centuries, made her crave things deep inside that could never become reality.

Chapter 18

Darkrip heard the shrieks as soon as he stood up to throw his empty plate in the trash. Off in the distance, they pierced the night, ominous and shrill. Deamons rushed toward the park, what seemed like hundreds of the beady-eyed creatures, and his brain locked on to her name: *Arderin*.

Turning, he searched for her in the distance, throat choked by fear. She carried their babe, so powerful inside her womb, and it made her a prime target for Crimeous. The Dark Lord vowed that he would abduct the child and raise it to be evil; an undefeatable warrior in his army due to the offspring's combined bloodline from her powerful grandparents. Determined to never let that happen, Darkrip closed his eyes, locating Arderin on the outskirts of the main square with Miranda.

Transporting to them, he pulled her slender body close.

"I'm taking you to Astaria," he growled. "Hold on."

Clutching his beloved wife, he conveyed to the main castle at the Vampyre compound. Releasing her, he observed her ice-blue irises, filled with fear. Not for herself, but for those she left behind.

"Stay here," he said, kissing her on her pink lips. "I'm going back to help them."

Astaria had an impenetrable wall built by Etherya. One that Crimeous had never succeeded in breaking through. His bonded would be protected while he fought with the others at Uteria.

"Please, be safe," she whispered, tears swimming in her eyes.

"I will, princess. I'll be back before you know it." With one last brush of his lips to her cheek, he materialized back to Uteria.

The battle was raging now. Clashes of swords sounded in tandem with pops from machine guns and discharges from TECs. Darkrip spotted Kenden, surrounded by Deamons, fighting each one off with an SSW. Evie stood to his side, wielding her powers to disintegrate their weapons and help the powerful Slayer commander.

Latimus was yards away, working in tandem with Larkin, battling the creatures with a knife in one hand and a Glock in the other.

"Hey!" Miranda yelled, running up to Darkrip, Tordor on her hip. "Materialize a sword for me, will ya? Then, I need you to transport Tordor, Lila and Jack to Astaria. After that, come back here and help me kick these bastards' asses."

Darkrip smiled, reading the excitement at getting to fight again coursing through his half-sister's veins. Miranda was a competent warrior and had laid down her weapons since becoming a mother. Sensing she needed the tussle, he grabbed Tordor from her and envisioned a sword, which promptly appeared in her hands.

Sathan appeared beside her, breathless, with a knife drawn from his belt.

"You need to go to Astaria, Miranda," he said in his deep baritone. "We can't lose you."

Grabbing his t-shirt by the neck, Miranda yanked him to her. "No offense, but no fucking way. I'm tired of letting everyone else fight these assholes." She placed a firm kiss on his lips. "Are you gonna fight with me, or not? Because I seem to remember we make a pretty great team."

Sathan snarled, Darkrip sensing that he was both frustrated and extremely aroused by his wife's question. "Get Tordor to Astaria," the Vampyre said, his eyes never leaving Miranda's. "And give me a sword too. I want to slaughter these bastards."

Darkrip complied, the object appearing in Sathan's hand, and then closed his lids to transport Tordor to Astaria. Handing the toddler to Arderin, he returned to Uteria to look for Lila and Jack.

Miranda and Sathan were sparring with a group of Deamons to his left, Latimus and Larkin still fighting off in the distance. Evie and Kenden seemed to be holding their own as numerous Slayer and Vampyre soldiers battled across the expansive field of the park.

"Jack!" Darkrip called, unable to locate the boy anywhere in the main square. Several of the soldiers were herding people toward the back of the castle, hoping to shield them from the skirmish.

Suddenly, he saw Lila's blond hair flash as she ran toward the playground. Jack squatted behind the see-saw, hiding from the fighting. Closing his eyes, Darkrip transported to him.

"Jack!" Lila cried, crouching beside her son.

"Let me transport him to Astaria," Darkrip said. "Then, I'll come back and get you."

"Okay." She nodded, fear latent in her lavender irises.

Darkrip grabbed the child, closing his eyes to transport them. Unable to dematerialize, his heart filled with dread.

Crimeous appeared atop the dirt-covered ground, cackling as he sauntered toward them. His long robe was black, one of the many colors he draped himself in when he chose to leave the caves. Hate for his father consumed Darkrip, and he knew the bastard had rendered him powerless.

"Well, well," the Dark Lord said in his malevolent tone. "How gallant you are, son. After all those centuries of killing alongside me, you still pretend to be good. It will never be your true nature. You know that as well as I do."

Darkrip handed Jack to Lila and pushed them behind him. "You just can't leave us the hell alone, can you, old man?" Lifting his hands, he formed fists. "If I have to, I'll fight you hand-to-hand, without my powers. I won't let you hurt the people I love."

Crimeous threw back his head, the escaping laugh awful and wicked. "Love. What a wretched word spawned from your worthless mouth. You'll never be one of them," he said, gesturing to the nearby battle with his head. "Come back with me and train. It's only a matter of time before everyone you profess to care for is dead. Don't you understand, son?"

"Don't call me son," Darkrip said through clenched teeth. "Now, fight me if you want but leave the boy and the woman out of it."

Scoffing, Crimeous lifted his hand and sliced it through the air. Darkrip felt his body flying and he landed with a thud several feet away on the dirt. Lila clutched Jack tight, turning away to shield him with her body.

"Now, now," the Dark Lord chided, approaching them slowly. "It's okay, my beauty. I still imagine raping you in front of Latimus. I never even thought of doing it in front of your child. How magnificent."

Lila sat Jack down and turned to face Crimeous while the boy clutched her waist from behind. Pulling a knife from her belt, she lifted it in anticipation. Darkrip thought the action so brave for someone raised as an aristocrat, far away from war. He desperately wanted to help her, but his father had frozen him to stone.

When Crimeous was within inches of her, Lila jabbed with the knife, and his father swerved easily. "I'm glad to see that Latimus has armed you. A smart yet futile attempt to save you. What a waste of time, but I admire the effort."

Grabbing Lila's thick flaxen hair in his fist, he violently tossed her to the ground. Jack stood immobile, cowering in front of the Dark Lord. Chin quivering and brown eyes wide, Darkrip felt agony at his inability to help the boy.

"Now, now," Crimeous said, lifting Jack's chin with his reedy fingers. "Which way do I want to kill you? Hmmm..."

"You're really tough when you're hurting kids, asshole!" a voice shouted from the edge of the playground. Thanking every god that existed, Darkrip saw Evie jogging toward Jack. Latimus was behind her, SSW drawn, and he began striking Crimeous with the always-lit blade. As his father wailed, Evie disappeared with Jack in her arms, only to return a moment later to grab Lila from the nearby ground and evaporate again. With a *whoosh*, Evie reappeared, an SSW materializing in her hand. The glowing blade emerged from the Solar Simulator Weapon, casting an ominous luminosity under the now-darkened sky. Teeth gritted, she began attacking the Dark Lord alongside Latimus.

His father fought back, a sword in his hand, and Darkrip realized it must've been fashioned from poisoned steel. Not only would it decimate a Vampyre's self-healing body but the metal was strong enough to withstand the solar power of the SSW. The three of them fought, metal clashing against blade, in a circling dance of determination and skill.

Suddenly, Evie stood tall and lifted her hand, palm facing out. Both Latimus's and Crimeous's weapons disappeared. She spoke softly, her face illuminated by the yellow light of the SSW, still extended in her hand.

"It's time you and I had a talk," Evie said to Crimeous, holding the weapon firm. "Latimus, step away. This is between us."

Latimus's ice-blue irises darted between Evie and the Dark Lord. Giving her a nod, he backed away several feet. Still close, lest she need him if Crimeous conjured another weapon in his hand.

Clutching the hilt of her weapon with both hands, Evie retracted the glowing ember of the SSW and threw the armament on the ground. "Hello, Father."

"Hello, Evie," he said, his expression pensive and thoughtful. "How interesting. Darkrip's thoughts indicated that your powers were greater than his, but I see I've underestimated you. I can't interfere with them at all."

"Your knowledge of human dark magic is vast but it will never equal mine. I've studied it for centuries, never really comprehending why I was so enthralled by it. Now, I understand that it was because I'm meant to kill you."

Crimeous chuckled, the sound quiet. "Is that so?"

"You can't escape the prophecy, Father. It will be me or one of Miranda or Darkrip's children. You know that as well as I. You're living on borrowed time already."

"Etherya is a liar, and her prophecy is nothing more than a fairy tale. I believe in it no more than I believe these people truly accept you. You're rotten inside, child. An abhorrent manifestation of me. They tolerate you because they desperately want to rid the world of me. Once they realize you haven't the voracity to kill me, they'll cast you out like the abomination you are." He stretched out his hand, the wrist thin and pale under the sleeve of the robe. "Join me, Evie. Together, we could rule the Universe. Our combined powers would be unstoppable. You're nothing to these immortals."

"That's not true," Kenden's baritone voice called from beside Latimus. The words were laced with determination and a hint of fear. Darkrip wasn't sure if he was scared that Evie would be hurt or afraid that she would defect with his father. Or perhaps both.

"Evie is loved by every member of our family, and we honor her presence here," Kenden continued. "Your hateful words have no place here." Training his gaze on Evie, Kenden said, "The Blade is in Miranda's office."

Nodding, Evie closed her eyes. A moment later, the Blade of Pestilence appeared in her hand. Motionless, she stared at Crimeous.

"I see your struggle, child," the Dark Lord said as he stood before her. "So many emotions war within you. Your hate for me is nothing compared to your hate for yourself. You will never be able to choose the light. Killing me would be futile, for a happy existence can never be the destiny for someone like you, riddled with my blood. You take hope from Darkrip but know that you won't be able to choose the same path. Come," he said, shaking his hand. "Accompany me back to the caves, and we will combine our powers to kill every last immortal."

Evie's leaf-green eyes studied their father, blazing under the light of the full moon. Darkrip could feel her struggle, the war within magnified on her flawless face. Nostrils flared as she panted, contemplating his words. Darkrip had felt the same recently, when he'd let his father's feelings of viciousness and supremacy course through him. They were glorious, and his body pounded with terror that Evie would choose to align with him.

"We love you, Evie," Darkrip gritted from his frozen spot on the dirt. "Don't listen to the bastard. Strike him!"

The words must've snapped something within her because her chin lifted with resolve. Raising the Blade, she swung it forcefully, attempting to slice Crimeous through the neck. The Deamon screamed, rotating to materialize a sword in his hand. One-on-one, they fought, metal clashing, neither one seeming to tire. Pulling back, Crimeous held up his hand, stopping the scuffle.

"You are a competent warrior, child," he said, breathless.

"Stop calling me that," she said, jaw clenched.

"I see that I might not be able to best you hand-to-hand. Therefore, why don't I do some damage where it will hurt you the most?"

Her eyebrows drew together as she warily regarded him, hands clutched around the handle of the Blade. "What the hell does that mean?"

Throwing the sword to the ground, Crimeous materialized a knife in his hand. Quick as lightning, he rotated, throwing the knife across the ten-foot space that separated him from Kenden.

In a flash, Evie evaporated, appearing in front of Kenden to take the blow. Her gasp could be heard across the expanse of the park as the dagger entered her throat.

"No!" Kenden screamed, clutching her to his body as she collapsed on the ground. Latimus drew the SSW from Kenden's belt and charged Crimeous, Larkin and several other soldiers close behind. Within seconds of being battered by multiple solar weapons, the Dark Lord wailed and threw back his head, disappearing into thin air.

Darkrip regained movement thanks to his father's maiming and rushed to Evie's side as Kenden rocked her in his arms.

"She's bleeding out!" Kenden yelled, holding his hand across the massive injury as blood spurted around the still-inserted knife.

"Let me transport her to Sadie's infirmary."

"I'll meet you there," the Slayer physician said from above them. Darkrip knew she'd been in attendance at the picnic. "And then, can you transport to Astaria and bring Nolan and Arderin to help me? I'm going to need every hand to save her."

"Yes," Darkrip said, drawing Evie close. She was unconscious, her head lolling to the side as crimson rivulets gushed from her neck. Closing his eyes, he conveyed her to the pristine white bed of the clinic, praying for dear life to Etherya that she survived.

Chapter 19

Nolan was with Arderin, Lila, Jack and Tordor when Darkrip materialized in the sitting room. He'd been in the infirmary when Arderin had called to tell him of the attack. Unable to face Sadie, due to the absolute mess he'd created, he'd decided to forego the barbeque. Upon hearing that Uteria was raided, he headed upstairs to console the others as they waited.

"Evie's badly hurt," Darkrip said. "Sadie needs both of you. I'll take Nolan first and then Arderin."

"Okay," Nolan said, rising from the couch. "Is the battle over?"

"Yes," Darkrip said. "They're defeated for now, and Crimeous has returned to the caves. Come on."

The Slayer-Deamon whisked Nolan to one of the sterile ORs of Sadie's infirmary. Seconds later, he appeared with Arderin.

Sadie was already leaning over Evie, compressing blood-soaked gauze pads to her neck.

"Approximate five-inch laceration of the neck," she said, her speckled eyes focused and solid. "I need you to hold pressure so I can seal the edges and begin suturing. She's struggling to breathe on her own, and we'll need to insert a tube once I've closed the lesion."

Jumping into action, Nolan donned two plastic gloves from the box affixed to the wall and applied pressure. Arderin worked with deft movements behind them, loading supplies onto a sterile tray and wheeling it over. For minutes, they worked furiously, unable to control the bleeding.

Kenden ran into the room, breathless. "What can I do?" he asked, his tone distraught.

"Get Sathan in here now. I have an idea. Hurry! We must act quickly." Sadie said.

Kenden ran from the room as Nolan held his fingers to the spurting arteries and veins on Evie's throat. Unwilling to imagine the worst, Nolan clung to hope as the woman he loved stood across from him, small hands furious in their movements, proving once again how magnificent she was.

Several hours later, Nolan was exhausted. Arderin, tired from being on her pregnancy-swollen feet, had returned to Astaria with Darkrip. Evie's prognosis was fair, thanks to Sadie's quick thinking. A miracle, considering how severe her injury was.

Miranda and Kenden were chatting by Evie's bedside. The queen looked pensive, the Slayer commander distressed. Judging by Kenden's reaction as they treated Evie, it was obvious to Nolan that he was in love with her. He hoped like hell that the woman who'd saved so many this night would be able to recover enough to accept it.

"I don't want you to have to go to Astaria tonight," Miranda said, placing her hand on Nolan's shoulder. "We need you here anyway, in case her condition worsens. I asked Jana to prepare the room next to Sadie's for you. You should have everything you need up there. Toothbrush, change of clothes. If you need anything, just call Jana from the phone in the room. Sadie, you can walk him up, right? I think we all need to get some rest."

"I'm staying here," Kenden said. "I don't want her to wake up alone. You all go to bed." Approaching Nolan, he held out his hand. "Thank you for saving her, Doc. I'll never be able to repay you."

"We don't do this to be repaid," Nolan said, shaking his hand. "I'll say a prayer for her."

Nodding, Kenden drew Sadie into his embrace and whispered words of thanks into the shell of her ear. Disengaging, she came to stand before him, staring up at Nolan with her stunning eyes. The vibrancy of the hues took his breath away.

"Come on," Sadie said in her soft voice. "I'll show you to your room."

Nolan followed behind her, up the large carpeted staircase, until they were walking down the darkened hallway. Silence, thick and heavy, surrounded them as their feet padded on the hallway floor.

"Here you go," she said, turning to face him where they stood in front of the bedroom door. "Mine's next door. If you need anything." Shifting her gaze down, she kicked the rug with the toe of her sneaker. "See ya in the morning."

Frozen, he watched her walk to the next door on the right. Turning the knob, she entered, closing the door behind her with a gentle click.

Sighing, Nolan entered the chamber. Removing his clothes, he pulled the t-shirt over his head, noticing how large it was. It must've been

Sathan's, brought to his room by Jana when she prepared everything. Throwing on the black shorts, also a few sizes too big, he walked into the sparse bathroom to brush his teeth.

The mundane action seemed wrong. Hell, everything seemed wrong. Sadie was only feet away, but inside, he felt they were worlds apart. How had he messed everything up so terribly? He'd only wanted to give her space. To give her time to think of all she would be sacrificing if she settled for a life with him. Instead, he'd made her doubt herself all over again, causing him to want to murder himself. Nolan had worked so hard to pull Sadie from her shell of self-doubt. To make her realize how beautiful and remarkable she was. Frustrated at his stupidity, he ran his hands over his face.

Exhausted from the night's events, he slid under the covers, aching for her as she slept only feet away. Physically so close, but light-years away from where they'd been. Where he wanted to be. Sighing into the pillow, Nolan cascaded into a fitful slumber, filled with nightmares of his beloved Sadie marrying another. One who could give her everything he couldn't.

Chapter 20

Evie swam into awareness, feeling as if her legs were weighted down by a thousand anvils. Unable to inhale, she clutched at her throat, pulling the vices that strangled her there. Someone restrained her wrists, drawing them away, and she fought like hell to kill whoever was harming her.

"You're safe," a voice called through the plasma in her brain. A familiar voice, one that she trusted. "It's okay, baby. I've got you. Please, stop struggling."

Her lids were glued shut, and she wished she could get the damn things to separate. Finally, by some miracle of Etherya, she was able to open them. Kenden loomed above her, concern dripping in his stunning brown irises.

"You're safe," he whispered, still holding her wrists. Gently, he lowered them to her sides. Cupping her cheeks, his eyes welled with tears. "I'm here, Evie. Always. I promise, you're okay. You're not going to be able to talk, so I need you to calm down and focus on breathing. Sadie took out your breathing tube a few hours ago, but if you reopen the wound, she'll have to insert it again." Calmly, his hand stroked her face, so soothing as her heart pounded within.

"That's it," he said, smiling at her with those perfect white teeth. "I'm here."

Unable to wrangle her warring emotions, a tear slipped down her cheek. Catching it with the pad of his thumb, Kenden rubbed the wetness over her skin.

"I know, baby," he said, his tone filled with understanding. "It's awful. You must feel so helpless. I know you hate that more than anything. I promise, I won't let anyone hurt you. Now, close your eyes and get some rest." The metal legs of the chair made a scraping sound as he pulled it toward the bed and sat down. "I'm not leaving until you're well enough to tell me to go to hell," he said, his wobbly smile so endearing. "It's three a.m. and everyone's sleeping. I promise, you're okay. Close your eyes, and I'll be here when you wake up."

She blinked up at him, hating that she clutched onto his words. Inwardly admitting that she didn't want him to leave, she pleaded to him with her gaze.

"Trust me," he said, stroking her cheek. "I promise, I won't leave. Not even to go to the bathroom. I'll find a bucket if I have to."

A laugh lodged in Evie's chest, unable to exit her throat due to the massive gash in her neck.

"See how funny I am?" he asked, his other hand fingering through the hair at her temple. "One more reason to move in with me. I'll make you laugh for eternity. You have to tell Miranda though. She always says she's funnier than me. No way in hell."

Evie thought the conversation so ridiculous but understood what he was doing. If she focused on his musings, she might just forget that her father had maimed her and she was vulnerable in the infirmary. How bad was her injury? Would she regain the ability to speak?

Unable to keep her eyes open, she closed them as the questions whirled in her head, and Kenden dribbled on above her with his low-toned voice. Eventually, she conceded in her battle against unconsciousness.

The next time Evie awoke, she was able to clear her throat. Kenden sat beside her reading a book. Knowing him, it was a detailed history of some long-ago human war. Lifting his gaze to her, he smiled.

"You're awake." Setting the book on the floor, he scooted to the edge of the chair and clutched her hand. "How are you feeling?"

She tried to speak but found it impossible. Pain coursed through her body as well as the accompanying pleasure. The sensations were hellish, causing her skin to prickle. She felt like someone had rammed a truck into her body and left her muscles to disintegrate into jelly. Helplessness swamped her as she stared at him.

"Sadie said you might not be able to talk for a while. That bastard's knife hit you right in the middle of the throat. But she swears that with enough time, you'll be able to speak again." His brown irises darted over her face. "Are you thirsty?"

Realizing that she was, Evie nodded. Releasing her hand, he walked to the counter and poured some water in a plastic cup. Sitting by her side again, he lifted it to her lips. Not wanting to appear like a dying invalid, she took the water and sat up against the pillows. She might not be able to speak but she'd be damned if she couldn't hold a freaking cup to her mouth. It was extremely difficult to swallow, but she was determined. Regarding him, she sipped, wishing she could ask him the questions that were swirling within.

"You've been in and out for about two and a half days," he said. "It's almost noon on Sunday. You were amazing, Evie," he said, admiration strewn across his handsome face. "You fought him like a champ. And then, you jumped in and saved me. It was so brave. Thank you."

Evie recalled the battle and the jolt of terror she'd experienced when her father had thrown the knife directly at Kenden's heart. There'd been no other choice in her mind. She'd acted without thinking. Narrowing her eyes, she pondered that sentiment. Never had there been anyone in her life whom she'd put before herself. It was disconcerting and made her extremely uncomfortable.

"Okay," Kenden said, taking the empty container from her hands. Her throat felt raw where she had swallowed the water. "Let me have the cup before you crush it. I take it you're not thrilled that your first reaction was to save me. Sorry, sweetheart, but I think we've crossed the 'no feelings' line. It's time to admit that you're crazy about me." His lips were so full as he teased her, curved into a sexy smile. Nostrils flaring, she imagined throttling him.

"That's good," he said, winking. "You're getting your snark back. I think it's one of the things I love most about you." Her stupid heart slammed at his words. "What other questions can I answer for you?" he asked, sitting back in the chair. "Everyone is fine. You were so smart to transport Jack and Lila to Astaria—thoroughly debunking your theory that you only care for yourself, by the way," he said, lifting his finger in the air.

Evie scowled.

Kenden chuckled, shaking his head as he grinned at her. "Man, I am so going to pay for this later, aren't I?"

Unable to control the twitch of her lips, Evie gave a subtle nod.

"Worth it if it makes you smile, baby," he said, scooching forward again and cupping her cheek with his broad hand. "I thought I lost you," he almost whispered. "It tore apart something inside of me that I don't want to put back together. I'll need to explore that with you when you're ready."

Evie's breath caught, and she struggled not to pant as he stared into her.

"For now, you need to rest. I've been here for days watching over you but I'm pretty sure I stink and need to shower. Miranda offered to come hang with you when you were awake enough. I'm going to send her down." Standing, he stretched, the corded muscles of his arms making her mouth water. Pulling his phone from his belt, he shot off a text, most likely to Miranda. Replacing his phone, he contemplated her.

"Sathan gave you a blood transfusion. Being the purest-bred Vampyre, his self-healing abilities are off the charts. Sadie performed the transfusion just in time. Any later, and it wouldn't have worked. It helped save your life, and Sadie says you'll heal quickly. I know you think that Sathan doesn't care for you, but you need to know that. You're part of our family now, Evie. Prophecy or not. When you're ready, we're going to discuss that too. Your father tried to plant some pretty absurd bullshit in your head, and I'm not letting that seed grow one fucking bit. Do you understand me?"

Evie just stared at him, unable to nod. Didn't he realize that Crimeous was right? She was rotten, down to her very core. No one in this inane world needed her or cared for her. How could they? They couldn't understand the evil that churned within. Hell, she barely comprehended it herself.

"Don't go there," he said, lowering his face to within inches of hers. "It's beneath you." Placing a kiss on her forehead, he gave her jaw one last caress.

Miranda plodded into the infirmary, a huge beam strewn across her face. "Hey, sis! Thank god you're okay." Striding to the bed, she held Evie's hand. "You saved a bunch of people, including Lila and Jack. I can't even begin to thank you."

"Told you," Kenden said to Evie, squeezing her upper arm as Miranda clutched her hand. "I'll be back in about an hour," he said to Miranda.

"Take your time," she said, drawing the chair forward to sit down. "I'm sure Evie's already tired of your savior complex, right?" she joked, arching an eyebrow.

A breathy laugh escaped Evie's throat, and she nodded against the soft pillow.

"See? She's over you. Get the hell out of here. We'll see you in a bit. I'm going to regale my darling sister here with stories from your youth and how awkward you were when you used to address the troops." Looking at Evie, she said, "He was as nervous as a virgin on prom night. Our fearless commander hasn't always been so confident, believe me." Her tone was filled with mischief.

"Can you please not tell the most beautiful woman I've ever seen stories that will make her never want to kiss me again? I've grown to like kissing her very much." With one last wink at Evie and a peck to Miranda's forehead, he exited the infirmary.

As Miranda began chatting away, Evie watched the door, blood coursing through her frame at his words. She found herself unable to let go of the image of his broad back as he left the room, or the hope that he would return to her soon. Tamping down the fear of needing him so fiercely, Evie let her sister talk her to sleep.

Chapter 21

On Monday, Aron headed to the playground to assess the damage. The recent battle had wreaked carnage on the play area, the surrounding park and the main square. Frustrated at the frequent attacks by Crimeous, he rubbed his fingers across his forehead. The park was lined with downed trees, discarded swords and triggered TECs. Remnants of the scuffle also marred the main square where many vendors' tents had been damaged.

The playground, which had been enveloped in an atmosphere of hope and peace during the coronation in Aron's name, was now decimated. The see-saw lay tilted off its axis. The monkey bars and carousel were scattered in pieces across the dirty, grassy ground. Vowing to never let the bastard dissuade him, Aron began forming a plan to resurrect the entire main square.

Sensing someone behind him, he turned his head to see Lila floating toward him, coming to a stop at his side.

"Crimeous just keeps destroying everything we build," she said in her soft voice. "I want so badly for Evie to be the one who murders him."

Aron studied her pensive expression as she observed the wreckage. He'd never heard Lila speak so frankly about death but the bastard had rendered her barren. She must want him annihilated more than anyone.

"We'll defeat him," he said, grabbing the woman's hand, whom he'd come to admire considerably as he'd gotten to know her during their shared council meetings. Squeezing, she smiled, acknowledging his comforting gesture. The action contorted her face into something more glorious than it already was, if that was possible. Lila was an extremely stunning woman.

Releasing his hand, she sighed. "I rode the train with Latimus today, so I could help you start the clean-up and restoration while he trains the troops. Miranda said she's assembled a team of fifty volunteers who will be here shortly."

"Yes," Aron said with a nod. "We'll rebuild, stronger and better than before. We always do. Moira will be here soon. We closed the gallery today so that she and Preston could help."

"Wonderful," Lila said, her perfect pink lips curving as she observed him with her lavender gaze. "She's such a nice woman. Although we got off to a bit of an...*uncomfortable* start, I like her immensely."

Aron's eyebrows drew together. "Why would you get off to an uncomfortable start?" he asked, wondering why there was a slight ringing of alarm in his head.

Her eyes grew wide, filling with anxiety. "I, um...you two are together now, right? I was sure that Miranda told me you were."

"Yes," he said, annoyed for some reason.

"Okay, I, uh..." She chewed her bottom lip. "I just assumed that she would've told you about her time with Latimus. She's very direct."

Aron felt his heart plummet to his chest, wondering what in the hell the Vampyre was talking about. When did Moira spend any time with Latimus? He'd been with Lila pretty much since Aron had known him, and Moira had been at Restia for the past eight hundred years. Hadn't she?

"What time with Latimus?" he asked, his tone filled with warning and a bit of anger.

"Oh, dear," Lila said, bringing her hands to her burning cheeks. "I thought she told you, knowing that you were together. Latimus and I tell each other everything. I—" She shook her head, sorrow blazing in her purple irises. "I'm so sorry, Aron. It wasn't my place to tell you. I...I don't know what to say."

Rage coursed through Aron's toned frame, seething within as he thought of the last weeks he'd spent with Moira. She'd been staying at his house every night, sharing the intimacies of a monogamous relationship. Dinner, lounges on the porch, reading by the firelight on rainy nights. Sexual encounters that would make a young buck blush. Moira was a firecracker in bed, pushing the limits of his desire and opening him to experiences that he'd never had. But she'd had them all, hadn't she? Looking at Lila's flushed face, the extent of Moira's fabrications began to wash over him. How could he have been so blind? And why would she lie to him so extensively?

"Aron," Lila said, clutching his forearm. "You don't know the whole story. She was with Latimus for reasons that were very important. I don't want to betray her trust any further, but you need to talk to her with an open mind. Please. She deserves that."

He yanked his arm away, angry that she knew secrets he'd never even fathomed. How many others knew? Miranda? Sathan? The entire compound? He felt like the biggest fool who'd ever walked the Earth. What a massive mistake he'd made to trust Moira.

"Don't tell me that a woman who lied repeatedly to my face deserves *anything*," he spat. "I can't believe you all kept her secrets and enabled her deceit!"

"It wasn't like that, Aron." Lila's magnificent eyes welled with tears. "It was devastating for me too, when I found out about their history, but now that I know why she left Uteria, I understand. You need to give her the benefit of the doubt."

"Don't talk to me about her time at Uteria. She was married to the best man I know. The fact that she would attempt to leave him tells me all I need to know about her character." Feeling his nostrils flare, he inhaled a deep breath, attempting to control his anger. "I'll ask you to never speak about this to anyone. This is between me and Moira, and I won't have everyone in the kingdom gossiping about my personal business."

"I won't," she said, swallowing thickly. "I'm so sorry, Aron."

Moira chose that moment to bounce up to them, filled with the vibrant energy that she always seemed to possess.

"Hi, guys. I'm ready to start the clean-up. Where do you want me?"

Aron and Lila stared at her, immobile, and the realization that something was terribly wrong seemed to wash across her face.

"Aron?" she called softly.

"How could you?" he gritted, hating how gorgeous she looked under the morning sunlight. Ocean-blue eyes glowed as she gazed up at him, slowly filling with dread.

Heaving in a deep breath, she shook her head. "This isn't the place. We have a job to do. Let's discuss this tonight, when we can talk in private."

"Tell me one thing," he said, the words laced with fury. "Did you, or did you not lie to me about where you've been for the past eight hundred years?"

Moira's irises darted between his, then looked to Lila. Moving her pupils to lock back on his, Aron sensed her defeat and eventual capitulation. "Yes," she said, straightening her spine. "I lied to you. I was with Latimus for the past eight hundred years at Astaria. He kept me safe, and I gave myself to him. Being angry at me won't change it, and we have work to do. So, you can sit there and stew, or you can help me rebuild the playground for the kids. What's it going to be?"

Well, he admired her gumption if nothing else. Although she'd been the transgressor, she was daring him to shelve it so they could work toward a common goal. Appreciating her ability to compartmentalize, he caved in.

"Fine," he snapped, wishing to all the gods that Lila hadn't arrived early that morning. Then, they could go back to where everything was normal.

Where Moira was the woman he'd fallen head over heels for. The one he wanted to ask to marry him and build a life with.

But no. That life was shattered now. Moira was a liar. A schemer who'd betrayed his best friend and manipulated everyone around her. If his veins weren't coursing with loathing, he might just admire how brilliantly she'd pulled it off.

"We'll clear the park and help our people. But know that I won't tolerate being deceived, Moira. It's the manifestation of everything I detest. You're not welcome at my home anymore. I'll have a courier send over any of your things that are there. And you're fired from the gallery. I don't trust you with the money anymore. Lord knows how much you could've stolen, right from under our noses. You're never to set foot in there again. Are we clear?"

"Aron," Lila said, her soft voice pleading as she grabbed his forearm. "I don't think you understand—"

"It's fine," Moira interrupted. He expected some fight out of her, since she was always so strong and determined, but she seemed utterly defeated. "I'm just a servant's daughter after all. And a whore. You're right not to trust me. I won't bother you again."

Aron couldn't understand why he felt an overwhelming sense of compassion for her in that moment. He should hate her with his entire soul for the deception she'd executed. Instead, he felt the insane urge to comfort her. Pushing it away, he made sure his voice was gruff.

"Good. I never want to speak to you again. Stay the hell out of my way." Needing to distance himself from her crushed expression and the smell of her shiny hair, he went to join the group of volunteers that had gathered in the middle of the park.

Moira watched Aron walk away, willing the tears to stay inside her rapidly-filling eyes. After all, this was bound to happen and no less than she deserved. She'd known, somewhere deep inside, that he would hate her when he discovered her lies. Oh, how badly it hurt to have him affirm how he really saw her. A lowly servant who would steal from his gallery and portray herself as a whore to the world.

"Moira," Lila said, dragging her from her thoughts. "I'm so very sorry. I thought you'd told him. I don't know what to say. What can I do to fix this?"

"Nothing," Moira said, swiping a tear from her cheek. Vowing that would be the last one that fell, she lifted her chin defiantly. "He's right. I'm beneath him. I always have been."

"That's not even close to true," she said, empathy in her stunning irises. "You're such a wonderful person, Moira, and I've come to consider you a friend. Something I thought impossible when I first met you, considering your history with my bonded, but it happened anyway. Mostly because you're really amazing."

"Thank you, Lila," Moira said, feeling her throat close up. "I really like you too. And I don't blame you for telling Aron. I should have. I just knew that he would react exactly as he did. So, I guess it sucks to be right sometimes," she finished with a sad shrug.

"He's angry now but that will pass. You need to tell him about your husband, Moira. It's obvious he doesn't know."

Moira sighed. "He'll never believe me, especially now. He idolized Diabolos."

"You need to give him the benefit of the doubt, as much as he needs to do the same to you. Your assumptions about each other will destroy you. Believe me, I'm an expert in disastrous assumptions. They kept me and Latimus apart for a thousand years."

"But you guys always loved each other," Moira said. "Aron could never love a servant's daughter, not for the long haul. He wants an aristocratic wife. He used to talk about it when we were young."

Lila's blond eyebrows drew together. "I've never once heard him say that. And believe me, if you love someone, that stuff just doesn't matter. Latimus gave up having biological children to be with me. He didn't see it as a sacrifice at all, even though his bloodline is the purest on the planet. You need to have faith in his love for you, Moira."

"Sadly, I think I've destroyed any emotion he might have started to feel for me." Holding up a hand, she prevented Lila from answering. "What's done is done. Let's get to cleaning this playground up, huh? I find that I feel better when I have a dirty task to complete."

"Okay," Lila said, enfolding her hand. "Please, call me if you need to talk. I'm so sorry that I spilled your secret. I feel terrible."

"It's okay," Moira said, unable to be upset with the woman before her, who was always filled with such genuineness. Together, they strolled to remedy the destruction Crimeous had rendered.

Chapter 22

Nolan scribbled in Evie's chart while Sadie spoke soft words to her. She wanted Evie to stay one more night in the infirmary to monitor her vitals and would release her in the morning barring any further complications.

"I know you're tough, Evie," Sadie said, squeezing her hand as she lay in the hospital bed, "but your body has been through significant trauma. It's going to be hard to eat for several days, and I recommend soup and soft food. Otherwise, it will be difficult to swallow. I'm prescribing bed rest for a few days at Ken's house. I'd suggest you follow it. He's already sworn that if you try to go back to your cabin, he'll just drag you back to his house."

Evie scowled and wrote something on the pad that they'd given her to communicate. Sadie glanced at it and breathed a laugh.

"Yes, he's a caveman sometimes. But he wants to take care of you. Let him, okay? He's not so bad most of the time. I promise," she said, giving Evie a wink.

Evie nodded, and Nolan noticed the faint curve of her lips.

Sadie approached him and stared at him with her gorgeous, prismatic irises. "I'm heading to bed. You can file the chart before you go back to Astaria. Thanks so much for staying here over the past few days. Good night." Her warbled grin almost splintered his heart. Padding across the floor in her sneakers, she exited the room.

Nolan sighed and finished the notes. Filing away the manila folder, he turned to tell Evie goodbye.

"I'm glad you're okay, Evie," he said, smiling as he regarded her. "If you need anything, please, let me know. I'm only a phone call away."

He turned to leave but was stalled by her firm grip around his wrist. Tilting his head, he looked into her olive eyes. She seemed to be trying to speak, although he knew she hadn't quite regained the ability to talk.

Frustration surrounded her as she gripped the pen in her hand. Jotting something on the pad, she lifted it to him.

She loves you.

Nolan exhaled a ragged breath and shook his head. "I can't give her children. I don't want to make her an outsider or deny her the opportunity to marry one of her own. I'm...torn," he said, running his hand over his face. "I just want to do what's best for her."

Evie's pupils darted between his. Lifting the pad, she scribbled again.

You're enough for her. I know it's hard to believe. Maybe if you can do it, I can too.

"Maybe," he said, his heart welling with compassion for her. She probably felt like as much of an interloper in the immortal world as he often did.

"Thank you, Evie," he said, squeezing her wrist. "Get better soon. We're all rooting for you." With one last nod of his head, he left her to heal.

Upon exiting the infirmary, Nolan couldn't stop the pounding of his heart. Drawn by an invisible force, he quietly climbed the carpeted stairs that led to Sadie's room. Knocking softly on the door, he heard her voice, garbled through the wooden door. Did she say, "Come in?" Unsure, he slowly creaked open the hinges.

She was topless, standing in front of her dresser mirror, her feet bare below the cuff of her jeans. Left arm slung awkwardly behind her back, she was attempting to rub the burn-healing salve on her right side, near her shoulder blade. When she saw him in the reflection, she yelped.

Lifting her t-shirt from the dresser, she covered her breasts. Nolan had caught only a glimpse—one so supple and perfect, the other almost non-existent due to the charring. "I said, 'Don't come in!'" she yelled, her expression furious.

Knowing he was invading her privacy but powerless to do anything to the contrary, he closed the door and ambled toward her.

"Please, don't," she said, eyes locked on his in the mirror. "I don't want you to see me this way."

Pain slammed through his body at her solemn words. How could she still believe, after all this time, that he saw her as anything but gorgeous? The one woman who epitomized beauty above all others, inside and out.

Inhaling a deep breath, he laid his hands atop her bare shoulders, hating her resulting flinch.

"You can't reach your back on your own," he said, the pads of his fingers rubbing her soft skin, ever so gently. "Why didn't you ask me or Arderin for help? We could've been helping you to apply the serum this whole time."

Her chin quivered in the reflection, sending a crack so wide down Nolan's heart that he thought it might break in two. "I didn't want to bother you guys."

"Sadie," he whispered, rubbing her shoulders in earnest now, reveling in being able to touch her, if only that small bit. "Don't you know, I would do anything for you? All you have to do is ask."

Blazing irises darted between his. "I don't know anything anymore. I'm terrible at this. I wish you'd never kissed me."

Nolan felt little pangs in his eyes and realized they were filling with tears. How strange. He hadn't had the urge to cry in centuries, not since he'd realized that he could never return home. But his emotions for the woman before him were complicated, turning his stomach into a mass of knots.

"Kissing you was the only thing I've done right in three hundred years," he said, his voice gravelly. Reaching down to the dresser, he picked up the tube that held the formula. Squirting some of the clear gel on his index and middle finger, he began to massage it into the skin beside her shoulder blade.

She stood so still, her head dropping forward as his ministrations continued. Nolan worked for several minutes, covering every inch of her upper back with the healing salve. When he was finished, he pulled a tissue from the box beside the mirror, wiping it from his hands.

"See?" he asked, unable to read her since her eyes were still downcast. "That wasn't so hard. I'd be happy to help you apply the formula anytime." Grasping her thin upper arm, he turned her toward him. Placing his fingers under her chin, he tilted her head so that she was forced to meet his gaze.

"I'd do anything for you, Sadie," he said, the words laced with sadness. "It's not fair to you. I want you so badly that I would deny you a full life. One where you could marry a Slayer and have his children. I'm such a selfish bastard that I'd even do that. And you deserve so much better."

Breath exited her throat in choppy pants as an expression of extreme confusion crossed her face. Shaking her head, she asked, "What in the hell are you talking about?"

Expelling air through his puffed lips, he lifted his hand to cup her unburnt cheek. Sliding the pad of his thumb over her bottom lip, he said, "I heard you talking with your patient a few weeks ago. I shouldn't have been listening but I couldn't stop myself. You deserve to be courted by a plethora of men who will shower you with flowers and gifts. But I find myself wanting to claim you, to beg you to choose me, to never let another man love you. I should care enough for you to let you experience everything you're worthy of."

Her forehead furrowed as tears glistened in her eyes. Angry at himself for making her upset, he dropped his hand. "I'm heading back to Astaria.

I just...I don't know...I needed to see you. To talk to you." Dejected, he began to turn away.

"Wait!" she called, grabbing his forearm. "Look at me, Nolan."

Lifting his irises to hers, he noticed her fist held a death grip on the t-shirt that she still had across her breasts. He would've teased her for being nervous if the situation hadn't been so tense. Chest rising and falling with anxious breaths, she slowly lowered the shirt back to the dresser.

Standing before him was the most magnificent image he'd ever beheld. His beautiful Sadie, one perky breast on her left side, a maze of scarred tissue where the other should be. Although she'd been using the serum, the skin wasn't fully healed. Her chest had experienced extreme damage and would need several months of consistent application of the formula to mend. The mass of her breast had been charred off in the flames, all those centuries ago. Knowing how hard it must be to show him such vulnerability, he yearned to touch her. To show her with his body how magnificent she was. Inching toward her, as if pulled by an invisible tether, he slowly lifted his hand. Cupping the globe of her breast, he tested the weight in his palm.

Her gasp unleashed something inside him, causing him to want more. Lifting his thumb, he swept the pad over the pebbled nipple, the skin there so smooth and taut. Bringing his index finger to the tiny nubbin, he squeezed the sensitive point.

Sadie gave a little mewl, the sound so sexy in the quiet room. Need, swift and true, clenched inside him. Sliding his hands down her sides, he palmed her jean-clad bottom, lifting her and carrying her to the bed. Laying her across the purple comforter, he placed his forehead against hers as he sprawled over her.

"Is this okay?" he asked, not wanting to push her if she wasn't ready.

The bob of her throat was so cute as she swallowed, obviously anxious at what was surely her first sexual encounter. "Yes," she whispered, her brown hair sliding across the bed as she nodded.

"You know, I'm not very experienced either," he said, hoping to put her at ease. "I was in my early twenties when I came through the ether, and my experiences were short and clumsy. I hope I'm able to please you. I can recite every bone and muscle in the body but strictly for surgical purposes. And I'm pretty sure you'd rather I kiss your sensitive spots than perform a procedure on them."

Sadie snickered, breaking the tension a bit. "Yeah, I'd rather you kiss them. I don't know a lot either, but what you were doing to my breast felt pretty good." She bit her lip, the innocent action remarkably adorable.

"Like this?" he asked, slipping his hand down to cup the small globe again. With his fingers, he pinched the nub, causing her hips to buck against him.

"Yes," she whispered.

"Or maybe like this?" he murmured, trailing a line of kisses to the pale curve, prodding the ruddy tip with his nose. Opening his lips, he pressed them over her sensitive nipple, drawing it back in between them as he sucked.

"Oh, yes," she said, writhing beneath him. "It feels so good."

Sliding his hands under her, he lifted her lithe torso to his mouth, lathering her nipple with his tongue. Wanting so badly to satisfy her, he tuned in to her breathless reactions. Seeming to like when he sucked her deep, he closed around her again, pulling her entire areola into his mouth as the tip of his tongue flicked the pebbly nub.

She cried his name as he loved her, making his muscles shake with desire and lust. Wanting her to understand that every part of her body was beautiful, he traversed his lips across to where her other breast would be, kissing the flat center.

"Oh, Nolan," she said, threading her fingers through his hair. Her eyes shined as she stared into him. "You don't have to kiss me there."

"Yes, I do," he murmured, placing butterfly pecks all over her burnt skin. "Every part of you is desirable to me, sweetheart. I wish you could understand." Swiping his tongue over the mangled tissue of her nonexistent breast, he felt her shake with arousal.

Moving the palm of his hand to the snap of her jeans, he hesitated. "Can I take these off? If you're not ready, I understand. I don't want to do anything you don't want to do."

Reaching down, she ran the tips of her fingers over his jaw, the gesture so loving. "I've been ready since you kissed me. How could you not know that? I think that if you don't take my pants off, I might just die right here."

Chuckling, he placed a kiss on her flat abdomen. "I think Arderin's dramatic temperament is rubbing off on you."

Her resounding laugh was like a beautiful aria. Standing to his full height, he undid her jeans and slid them and her panties off her legs. Always the observant physician, he ran his hand over her right thigh. "You're healing nicely here."

Slender shoulders shrugged atop the comforter. "I can reach my thigh way better than my back."

"Well, I'm applying to be your back-salve applicator from now on," he said, waggling his eyebrows. "If it leads to getting to see you like this, I'm so in."

White teeth flashed as she smiled shyly at him. Placing his palms on her thighs above her knees, he skimmed them up the silky flesh until his thumbs brushed the lips of her sex. Small whimpers escaped her throat as he lightly feathered her there.

Sliding the pads of his thumbs over the swollen flesh, he realized how wet she was. The moisture gleamed in the pale light of the dresser lamp, beckoning to him. Rimming her opening with the tip of his index finger, he gently began nudging it inside her.

"Nolan," she pleaded, squirming on the soft bed. "Please. I want you inside me."

"Are you sure?" he asked, slowly moving his finger in and out of her tight channel. "I can kiss you here first, to get you ready."

"Um, I think I'm ready," she said, almost giggling. "I mean, I want you to kiss me there, but we can do that next time, right? I'm ready to give myself to you." Locking on to him with her kaleidoscopic eyes, fresh with shades of newly-turned autumn, her lips curved into a heartbreaking smile. "I love you, Nolan."

Every single cell in his pounding heart shattered. It was the most wondrous moment of his life, hearing those words from her stunning lips in her sweet voice. Oh, how he wanted to say it back, but his throat had closed up, and he was having a terrible time breathing. Letting instinct take over, he pulled the shirt over his head and discarded his dress pants and underwear.

Gliding his body over hers, he palmed the back of her head as he pushed her thigh open with his other hand. Grasping his straining shaft, he aligned the engorged head with her slick opening. Gazing into her, he began sliding in, the pressure on his straining shaft giving him immeasurable pleasure.

"I love you too," he whispered, the words torn from his chest as he jutted into her. "More than I ever thought possible. You're everything, Sadie," he said, groaning as the wet tissues of her tight channel choked him. Lowering his forehead to hers, he gritted his teeth. "*Everything.*"

Throwing her head back, she opened to him, the gesture such a gift as she gave him her innocence. Body relaxed, she bestowed her trust upon him, knowing he would do his best not to hurt her. Tightening his fingers in her hair, he struggled to retain his composure, wanting so badly to give her pleasure.

"I love you," she whispered against his lips, the words giving him permission to fully claim her. "I love—"

The fragment ended in a gasp as he sheathed himself completely, claiming her for what he hoped was forever. Clutching her close, he branded her with his body, the thrill at being the first to hold her like this overwhelming. Wanting to ease her pain, he placed his finger on the nub below her triangle of hair, rubbing it in concentric circles as his shaft slid through her wetness. Having been alone for so long, Nolan reveled in the beauty of making love; the pounding heartbeat of the amazing woman below him; the almost unbearable pleasure at loving someone more than himself.

Sensing she was close, he increased the pressure on her clit and lowered his mouth to suck her succulent nipple into his mouth. Drowning in the multiple sensations, her slender body bowed under him. Lids closing with desire, her mouth opened, and she screamed his name, consumed with her orgasm.

Feeling the drenched tissues of her core spasm against him was Nolan's undoing. Threading his arms under her, he pushed his hips into her once, twice...and then exploded into the most intense climax of his long life. The jets of his release pulsed into her, marking her as his, consuming him. *Mine*, his brain echoed, as his hips bucked against her. Replete, he collapsed, hoping he wasn't squashing her. He just couldn't find the energy to move. It was as if his body had lost all muscle control.

The realization that Sadie was shaking violently brought him to his senses. Worried for her, he lifted his head and cupped her cheek. "Sadie?" he asked, concerned. "Are you okay, sweetheart?"

Opening her mouth and expelling a large exhale, her lids blinked open. "Am I okay?" she repeated, an expression of wonder spread across her pretty features. "You just told me you loved me and gave me the first orgasm of my life. Uh, yeah, I think I'm going to be fine."

Chuckling, he shifted to place a kiss on her lips. "I do, Sadie. So much. I wish I could give you everything you deserve."

"Nolan," she said, threading her fingers through his hair, the action so soothing. "I don't need to have your biological children. Of course, I wish I could, but it's certainly not a deal-breaker for me. If you're open to me getting inseminated, I think that's what I'd like to do. In the future, I mean."

"I would be thrilled at that, sweetie," he said, resting his head on his hand as his elbow perched on the bed. "To see your body grow full with our children." His hand ran over her smooth stomach. "But I want you to be sure. It's still a huge sacrifice."

"It's not a sacrifice at all," she said, her hair fanning out on the bed as she shook her head. "You should have told me you eavesdropped on us," she said, scrunching her features as she shot him a playful glare. "You must've missed the end, where I told Sagtikos to go screw himself."

Laughing, he nipped at her lips. "Did you now?"

"Yep," she said, her smile so endearing. "I told him that I loved you, and he needed to stop meddling in my business."

"I should've had more faith in you. I'd brought you flowers and was going to ask you to move in with me. When I heard your conversation, I freaked out."

"That's why Moira had your flowers!" she said, realization crossing her face. "I saw her in the castle, and she said you gave them to her. I thought you were trying to court both of us."

"Seriously?" he asked. "I can barely court one woman, much less two. You're giving me way too much credit."

"Man, we were such idiots. I thought you didn't want me anymore. It broke my heart."

Crushed by her admission, he wanted to strangle himself. "I'm so sorry. I was trying to give you space while your skin healed. I didn't want to tie you to me and deny you the opportunity to find someone who could give you children."

Her lips twitched. "Can we make a pact to communicate better? Because the last few weeks have sucked. I was a wreck."

"Yes, let's do that. This has been a huge wake-up call for me. I'm always so great at giving relationship advice to everyone else but realized recently that I'm terrible at giving it to myself. Good grief. I created a mess."

"Well, thank god you busted into my room tonight," she said, entwining her arms around his neck. "And now, I'm not a virgin anymore. Holy crap."

"No, you certainly are not," he said, rubbing his nose against hers. "That was amazing, Sadie. I've never felt anything like it. I can't wait to make love to you for eternity."

A huge red splotch appeared on her unburnt cheek. "Neither can I. That was awesome, Nolan."

Basking in the glow of their coupling, they lounged for a while before prepping for bed. Nolan didn't return to Astaria that evening, preferring to hold the woman he loved in his arms as he slept upon her smooth sheets.

Chapter 23

Sadie released Evie from the infirmary early Wednesday morning. Sathan's blood had contributed to her quick healing, and Evie found herself grateful to yet another person in the immortal world. How absolutely annoying. She was becoming more and more ingratiated to the people whom she swore she didn't need. It was enough to drive her insane.

Kenden insisted on driving her to his house even though her ability to materialize was uncompromised by her injury. Once he'd carried her inside and laid her on the couch, he covered her with a fluffy blanket, tucking the corners around her.

"This is ridiculous," she muttered, scowling at him. "I'm perfectly fine." The impact of the words was weak, however, considering the scratchiness of her voice. It would still be several more days before she could speak without a rasp.

Sitting beside her, Kenden grinned as he rubbed her hair with his fingers. It absolutely did *not* feel amazing, being soothed by him. Nope. No way.

"I'm wondering if this is the first time in your life that people have gone out of their way to help you," he said in his always-calm tone. "I can't imagine how foreign it must feel."

"It feels fine," she snapped, hating every single person who'd helped her. It wouldn't matter when she returned to the land of humans. Once that happened, she'd be able to retain her footing and live in an environment she understood. Thank god. She couldn't wait for that day.

The human world certainly wasn't perfect, but it was the only place where she'd felt a sense of peace. Humans were messy creatures, extremely flawed and capable of making great mistakes. Something about that comforted Evie and pulled at her during some of the loneliest moments she'd experienced since returning to the land of Slayers and Vampyres. In the mortal world, she wasn't overwhelmed by self-doubt and fear. Although they existed, she could temper them so much easier in that environment. For some reason, now that she was back in the land of her origin, the unrest crowded her, and she often questioned herself. For someone so sure, it was disconcerting. Being in the land of humans would restore her to solid ground, even if it was isolated and solitary.

A slow burn of anxiety began to glow in her gut as she imagined living on her own, alone in the human world. Letting the images form, she imagined leaving those whom she'd come to know. Of not hearing Miranda's throaty laugh as she approached the castle at Uteria. Not seeing Jack as he grew into the competent warrior he was sure to become. Denying herself the luxury of being held in Kenden's strong arms.

Pushing the musings away, she cursed herself. Her brain was probably just on overload from her injury. Clutching the darkness within, her eyes narrowed.

"You all just need me to fulfill the prophecy," she said, unwilling to discuss everyone's sudden desire to help her any further. "Once I do that, or once I fail, you all will get over it. Believe me. You're better off without me."

His handsome features seemed overcome with sadness. "I hope that's just the drugs talking, because I don't want to have to argue with you when you're recovering."

"I'm not on any drugs," she said sullenly.

"Because you're so strong," he said. Adoration swam in his eyes, and she hated that he was placating her when she needed him to understand how futile it was to care about her. It was an absolute waste of his time. He needed to be out training the troops, not helping her heal.

"I don't want you here," she said. "I'm going to transport back to my cabin. I can't distract you, especially now that my father has attacked. We need to be as strong as possible to defeat him."

"We will be," he said, stroking her face. "Latimus is training the soldiers today. Let me be here for you. I don't want to play games, Evie. It's not who we are. Don't denigrate us to that. I want to help you recover, and you like having me around. Stop being a coward and admit it."

"I don't—"

"Stop," he said, placing two fingers over her lips. "You can pull off that crap with every other man you've been with but not me. We care about each other, Evie. And a lot more that I'm ready to say, but you're not ready to hear, so I'll keep my damn mouth shut. But you need to stop fighting me. I need you to just accept that we're in each other's lives. For now, and if I have anything to say about it, forever. I'm just as stubborn as you are. You don't want to get into a battle of wills with me, especially not when you're injured. It won't be pretty for you."

Evie scowled, hating how her heart thumped at his words. "Fine," she said, too exhausted to argue. She'd barely regained the ability to speak and still felt like someone had run over her with a snowplow. "But I'm *not* moving in with you," she said. "I'm just staying here so you won't drive me crazy. I know you'll never give up if I try to head back to my cabin."

"You're right. I'd just come over and drag you back here. I'm not letting you go, Evie. Maybe one day, if I say that enough, you'll start to believe me."

In spite of herself, she breathed a laugh. He was infuriatingly persistent. "Maybe one day, I will."

"Now, what do you want for dinner? Our lovely Jana has stocked my fridge with soup. Tomato, broccoli and cheddar, or chicken and wild rice. What will it be?"

"Tomato. I can help you cook it—"

"No way," he said, standing and shaking his head. "I know I'm an idiot in the kitchen but even I know how to use a microwave. Give me a few." Leaning down, he kissed her forehead before heading to the adjoining kitchen.

They ate in companionable silence, Evie struggling to swallow when she ingested heftier spoonfuls. Once finished, Kenden made sure soft music was emanating from the surround system speakers he'd installed upon building the house. As the classical symphony soothed her to sleep, he went outside to chop wood and work in the yard.

That evening, he led her upstairs, relenting when she told him she'd dismember him if he tried to carry her. Clutching her hand, they prepared for bed and climbed under the silken covers. Evie slid her palm to his shaft, becoming frustrated when he pulled it away and cuddled her firmly into his side.

"I don't want to open your stitches. Let's wait until you get them out on Friday," he said, placing a peck atop her red hair as her cheek rested on his chest. "We need you, Evie. It's important that you heal properly. It's okay if we just hold each other until we fall asleep."

"I don't see any reason to sleep with someone if there's no sex involved. What a waste of a perfectly good opportunity to get some action."

Kenden breathed a laugh. "You're a pain in the ass, Evie. Let me hold you. I promise, it won't be as bad as you think."

"We'll see," she said, throwing her thigh over his and spreading her fingers wide over his pecs. Moments later, his breathing began to even out, and she felt him drift into slumber. Wide awake, the tips of her fingers made lazy circles through the prickly hairs on his chest.

There was no denying that his words bothered her. *We need you, Evie.* Yes, they needed her badly. To fulfill the prophecy and save the immortal realm. But was that all? Would they ever truly need her? Just Evie, in all her fallible complexity and simmering darkness. Doubtful.

There were only two possibilities. If she killed Crimeous, they'd respect her for a while, sure. But how many years or decades would it take to forget? For the viciousness of her anger and the truth of her heritage to remind them all how terrible she truly was?

And what if she wasn't the savior? What if that burden fell to Tordor or the child Arderin was now carrying in her womb? Would they cast her back into the human world once they understood that Crimeous's child would always taint the pristine atmosphere of the land they called home?

Kenden cared for her. Hell, he most likely loved her. The descendant of Valktor who would save them all. But if she failed, if Crimeous survived, how could he stay with her? Knowing the children he so vehemently craved would have the blood of the monster they sought so doggedly to destroy?

Evie couldn't let him make that choice. Perhaps her one last act of kindness could be extricating herself from him and pushing him into the arms of Katia or someone like her. Someone who shared his desire to build a home and a family. Yes, she thought, feeling herself begin to drift. There were ways to care for someone. Sadly, the best way for her to care for Kenden would be to ensure their separation, no matter how much it hurt.

Returning from her Saturday afternoon walk, Evie shrugged off her sweater and caught her reflection in the mirror that hung by the coat closet. Fingering the reddened scar on her neck, she contemplated. Sadie had removed the stitches yesterday, the tiny pricks of the scissors along her skin thrilling. The pleasure from the small stings reminded her how much power she wielded inside her nearly-healed body.

Kenden was cataloguing the weapons with the troops, preparing the ones that would be used in their upcoming trainings. Feeling restless, Evie stepped back outside, leaving her arms bare.

Approaching Kenden's stump where he split the logs used for the fireplace, she spotted the squirrel. It sat atop the weathered stub, furiously munching an acorn from a nearby tree. Focusing on the animal, she narrowed her eyes.

The freezing spell took hold immediately. The squirrel pondered her, his beady pupils locked on to hers. Did it comprehend the supremacy she held? That she could squash his furry body with barely a thought?

Closing her lids, she tilted her face to the sky, keeping the animal immobile. Inhaling, she finally let the true strength of the evil she'd felt from Crimeous during their battle at the playground saturate her bones. Clenching her teeth, she fisted her hands, imagining crushing the necks of Vampyre and Slayer soldiers, faceless and weak. This is what would happen if she joined her father in his quest to defeat his enemies. She'd murder so many, and the extreme pleasure she would feel would be beyond compare. By the goddess, she could feel it now. It was exalting.

Her phone vibrated in her back jean pocket, pulling her from her thoughts. Scowling, she released her hold on the squirrel and watched it scurry away. Lifting the phone, she spoke.

"Hello," she said, her voice quiet even though she'd mostly regained the ability to speak normally.

"Hey," Kenden's warm voice replied. It was so serene against the raging emotions coursing through her body. "I'm almost done here. Miranda wants to know if you'd like to have dinner at the castle."

Evie deliberated, kicking the grass with the toe of her sandal. Her sister could read her well. Would she suspect the direction that Evie's thoughts had strayed since her injury? Not wanting to find out, Evie cleared her throat.

"I'm good, but you should stay. She loves spending time with you. I'm tired anyway and will probably go to bed early. I want to be ready to fight again next week."

Silence stretched, causing Evie's pulse to quicken. Kenden had become so adept at understanding her moods. Did he suspect her musings? What would that mean for the fledgling trust they'd begun to develop?

"Okay," he said, the word crackling through the device. "But please, don't go to your cabin. I'll be home in a few hours. I want to be with you tonight."

Hating how her heart slammed at his words, she lightened her tone. "Only if you promise to fuck me. Otherwise, I've reached my cuddling limit."

The reverent timbre of his chuckle enveloped her, causing her to shiver. "I'm going to make you feel so good, sweetheart. You'll be begging me to give you a break."

"Deal," she said, her lips curving. "See ya in a bit."

"See ya," he said.

Disconnecting, she noticed the little acorn-eating bugger was back, perched on the stump, taunting her. Tamping down the desire to snap its neck, she realized it reminded her of Kenden. Too trusting of her nearness; too open to her presence. Lifting her hand, she drew the squirrel toward her with her mind.

Clutching the fuzzy body in her hand, she gazed into its eyes. "Careful, little rodent. Trusting souls are always the first to be tempered by evil witches." The animal wriggled in her grasp, its claws scratching the skin of her hand, causing her to bleed in several places. Reveling in the pain of each one of the welts, she eventually threw the creature to the ground and watched it run away. Hopefully for good this time. Because next time, she might not be so nice.

Heading inside, she found Kenden's first-aid kit and cleaned the wounds, deciding she would tell him she hurt it cooking. Yes, he would believe that. For he was just as trusting as the tiny squirrel.

Chapter 24

On Monday morning Miranda called a combined council meeting. The members sat around the large table in her royal chambers, the mood somber.

"Thank you all for coming," Miranda said from her perch at the head of the table. "I've asked Evie to join us so that we can discuss next steps. It's time for us to plan the final assault on Crimeous. First of all, I'd like to thank Evie for stepping in and saving our asses during the last attack. We're all grateful to you and hope you're feeling better."

Evie regarded them from the leather seat at the opposite end of the table. Extremely uncomfortable with the unwanted gratitude, she gave a curt nod. "Good to go. I'm ready to form a battle plan and fight with you all."

Kenden's gaze was filled with concern as he sat to her right. "If you need more time, we can give it to you. I don't want you to reopen your wound." He covered her hand with his.

Drawing it away, Evie narrowed her eyes. "I'm fine," she said, trying to keep herself from snapping. Nothing would be accomplished if she let the always-boiling anger inside get the best of her. "I'm ready to attack the bastard."

Heden stood, holding a TEC in his hands. "I've revamped the TEC so that it has a bunch of new features." Maneuvering the weapon in his hand, he showcased the differences as he spoke. "The blade it deploys is now an inch longer and releases a half a second quicker. It won't seem like much, but in a battle where every moment counts, it can save lives."

"Sweet," Miranda said, lifting one of the prototypes that Heden had brought with him from the table. "And you worked on adding a solar component?"

"Yup," Heden said, nodding as he rotated his wrist and pointed at the now-deployed blade. "Each edge of the updated TEC is now embedded with the solar components of the SSW. They're not as potent as the SSWs, since they're smaller, but they should be able to maim Crimeous now. I'm hoping that they can paralyze him long enough for Evie and Darkrip to generate the barrier they need to surround him."

Darkrip spoke from his seat between Kenden and Lila. "Evie and I have had an extremely difficult time generating the combined force-field. I think that we need to spend the mornings working on that. In the afternoon sessions, we can spar with the troops and have them try to disable and disarm us. If we can't figure out how to immobilize Crimeous and stop him from interfering with my powers, then Evie won't be able to strike him down."

"Agreed," Latimus said in his deep baritone. "I think we need three solid months to form a perfectly executed battle plan. We'll alternate training weeks at Uteria and Astaria, so the soldiers can see their wives on alternative weeks. The visiting soldiers can bunk at each compound. Sound good?" he asked, training his ice-blue irises on Kenden.

"Absolutely," Kenden said with a nod. "Three months is a perfect time-frame. It will also give soldiers time to get their affairs in order. Although we're going to try our best to lose as few as possible, there will be casualties." Settling his forearms on the desk, he leaned forward to make eye contact with each of the council members. "You all should do the same. This will be the biggest attack we've ever staged upon Crimeous. His army has grown exceptionally large. If we fail, there is a possibility that he will find a way to overtake the compounds and begin systematically murdering our people. He'll start with aristocrats and work his way down. I don't want to be morbid, but we have to be realistic about what's ahead."

"No fucking way," Miranda said, her hands forming fists at her sides. "I appreciate your attempt at foresight, Ken, but there's no way in hell that bastard is going to beat us. You all can prepare if you want, but I'll never allow that thought to enter my mind. It's just not happening."

Sathan stood and placed his arm across Miranda's shoulders, drawing her in to his side. "Well, you all heard my wife. I've learned not to argue with her when she's dead-set on something." Miranda scrunched her features at him, causing him to give her a good-natured peck on the lips.

"Seriously, guys," Heden said, relaxing back into the leather chair. "I have no desire to be the last of the Vampyre royals. Ruling would force me to get married and produce an heir, and I have other priorities. There are so many new compounds of hot women that I haven't had the opportunity to, um, spend time with."

"Could we possibly have one meeting where you don't turn everything into a joke?" Latimus grumbled.

"Honestly, I'm kind of digging the comic relief," Miranda said, smiling at Heden. "Let's all remember that this is what we're fighting for. The ability to live our lives the way we choose, unaffected by evil and war. Even if Heden's jokes are terrible, I'd sure miss hearing them." She winked at Heden, causing him to wink back as he smacked his gum between his teeth.

"The plan is set," Sathan said. "Three months of extensive training followed by a well-planned attack. Let's get started. Latimus, I'll meet you at the battlefield after Miranda and I finish the budget," he said, motioning toward her desk with his head.

With that, the meeting came to an end. The members dispersed, and Evie followed her brother, Latimus and Larkin to the Uterian sparring field, Kenden at her side.

"I don't want you to fight yet if you're not ready," he said, taking her hand as they walked. Evie resisted the urge to pull it away. His concern was choking, and she did her best to remain nonchalant.

"I'm fine," she said, smiling up at him with false confidence. "Let's do this."

They made it to the meadow, Evie grabbing a sword and proceeding to spar with a group of soldiers. The exertion of physical energy was exactly what she needed and she reveled in it under the bright morning sun.

And so it went, the days of training and preparation turning into weeks. Evie fought like a champ, working with her brother on the combined force-field in the mornings and sparring with the troops in the afternoons. The mindless scuffling was soothing to her somehow, considering how restless she'd grown at Uteria.

Although she hadn't yet given up her cabin, she found herself staying with Kenden most nights. It was just easier since she could transport them from Astaria the weeks that they trained there. Once home, they fell into a seamless rhythm. She would cook, always something succulent and amazing. Kenden would clean the pots and pans, load the plates in the dishwasher, and they would share a glass of wine by the fire.

It was comfortable. Familiar. Easy. And that scared the living hell out of Evie.

Some nights, she would need space. Kenden seemed to sense that and would stay out of her way. She would walk under the stars to the wooden swing-bench her handy man had built. It sat under a large oak tree, and Evie would sip her wine as she soaked up the silence.

Her father's words had rankled her. As the weeks passed, she couldn't seem to get them out of her head. They burrowed inside, threatening to drown her in self-doubt. Increasingly becoming convinced that she wasn't the savior, she contemplated what this would mean. It would be a huge letdown and leave her without a clear path forward. Would anyone even tolerate her presence if she failed?

And then, there were the feelings of viciousness and supremacy she'd felt when she let her father's true essence run through her veins. They were so appealing; so utterly magnificent. They embodied true authority, the likes of which she'd never known. If she did choose to join Crimeous and let him combine his wicked powers with hers, they would be unstoppable. The indomitable strength she would have was unimaginable. No one would dismiss her then, would they?

"Whatcha thinking about, out here all alone?" Kenden's deep voice asked behind her.

"Nothing," she said, noting how the swing creaked as he sat beside her. Stretching his broad arm across her shoulders, they wafted back and forth under the gorgeous night sky, filled with numerous twinkling stars.

"I can't give you a life as exciting as the one you had in the human world," he said, grasping her hand atop her thigh as her other one clutched her glass. "I know it's hard to imagine what we could build together, but it could be exciting in its own way. You could govern the new compound, and I'd transition the troops from combat to a law-enforcement body. Your father would be gone, and we'd be free to make a life together. Make a family together. If you're open to that."

Evie inhaled a deep breath, the resulting sigh sad and slow. "I don't want those things, Ken." She stared at the moon-glistened grass, unable to meet his gaze.

"Not even with me? You seem to like spending time with me. I can't get you to leave my house most of the time." He bumped his shoulder against hers, acknowledging his teasing.

Tilting her head back, she closed her eyes, breathing in the fragrant air of the immortal world's balmy evening. "If it was going to be with anyone, it would be with you. But I'm too restless. Too unpredictable. Your children would have my father's wretched blood. It's unthinkable."

He didn't answer. The warmth of his hand seeped into hers as they rocked back and forth. Eventually, he spoke.

"I don't mind if they have his blood. It's something I've thought about a lot. If it means I get to build a life with you, then I accept it. It won't be easy, raising children with your powers, but it will be worth it. You're worth it, Evie."

Unable to comprehend how he could make such a sacrifice, she turned her head, locking on to his eyes. "No, I'm not."

His gorgeous smile was immediate. "Yes, you are."

"God, you're infuriating," she said, shaking her head. "Why do you love me, Ken?"

The time for skirting around the truth was over. She knew it as well as he did. He loved her, sure as the day was long. A fact that stunned the hell out of Evie.

Lifting their joined hands to his mouth, he kissed the back of hers. "We just fit, Evie. In every damn way. I'm a steady war commander who possesses a deep well of compassion with a hefty side of savior-complex. I lived for so long without passion and spontaneity, telling myself I didn't need them, but that wasn't true. You're the first person who's ever gained the upper hand on me. Every smart general understands the importance of aligning with someone who sees their vulnerabilities. It only makes them stronger. *You* make me stronger," he said, squeezing her hand.

"You're a frustratingly complex woman who needs to be challenged and loved by someone who's not afraid of you. It's time you had a partner who sees past your beauty to the remarkable woman inside. I can't imagine two people who need each other more than we do. It's meant to be."

"I won't be able to make you happy," she said softly. "And I won't consider having children. I would be a terrible mother."

"I've seen you with Tordor and Jack. You're a natural, sweetheart."

"Jack is pretty damn awesome," she said, feeling her lips curve. "That kid would challenge my father to a fight if he thought he had a chance to win. I admire his spirit."

"See?" Kenden asked, lacing his fingers with hers. "We could have a bunch of little Jacks, running around and driving us nuts. I'd love that."

"Good grief," she said, chuckling in spite of herself. "You're living in a fantasy world."

His arm tightened around her shoulders, drawing her close. "Don't knock it till you try it. I won't make you decide anything now. Let's focus on defeating your father. But, as I've stated to you before, I'm not like the other men you've been with. I'm stubborn and I'm not letting you run away from me. You can try, but it's not happening."

"I'm pretty good at hiding," she said, resting her head against his shoulder. He felt so solid, so sure. "If I don't want to be found, you won't find me. Believe me."

"We'll see, sweetheart," he said, placing a kiss on her hair. "We'll see."

There, under the moon, they swung slowly. Evie thought about telling him how far her mind had been wandering lately, relishing the evil she could possess if she united with her father. Then, she dismissed the notion. She would never align with the bastard who had harmed her so violently, all those centuries ago. Her hate for the vile creature was so much greater than her lust for ultimate supremacy. Wasn't it?

Hoping with all her might that it was, she relaxed into Kenden's body under the darkened sky.

Chapter 25

Aron awaited Max at the small table in the coffee shop. Looking at his watch, he hoped the man arrived soon. He'd requested to meet here early, and Aron had a council meeting to get to.

Maximillian breezed through the door, the tiny bell ringing behind him. Giving Aron a wave, he sauntered to the counter to order a coffee and then approached the table. Sitting down across from Aron, he pulled an envelope out of his pants pocket.

"Great to see you, Max," Aron said cordially. "You look well. How's the new baby?"

"Wonderful," the man said, eyes shining as he sipped the coffee that the barista brought over. "She's a handful though. Now that we have three kids, I've decided my wife has formed a master plan to drive me insane. She's already talking about having a fourth. I don't know where she thinks we'll fit another one." Amusement sparkled in his eyes.

"You come from a long line of aristocrats who own half the real estate in Uteria's main square," Aron said, sitting back in his chair and crossing his arms. "I'm sure you'll find some space."

"Well, you know what they say, 'Happy wife, happy life.' I don't really have a choice."

Aron chuckled. "You love Bonita to pieces and you're a great father. Another child will be a welcome addition."

"And what about you?" Max asked. "You haven't married after all these centuries. The only woman you've shown interest in is the queen, and unfortunately, she's taken."

"Yes," Aron said, frustrated yet again at what a disaster his love life was. "Maybe I'll become a monk."

"Don't be silly," Max said, waving his hand. "You're going to be a great father. What about Moira? You two were spending so much time together. I was sure you were going to court her. She's quite beautiful."

"Yes, she is," Aron said solemnly. Moira's face blazed through his mind, causing the resulting pain that he always felt when he thought of her betrayal. "But she will always belong to Diabolos."

"Well, it's too bad," Max said, pushing the envelope across the table to him. "Now that she's leaving Uteria, you've most likely lost your shot anyway."

"What do you mean?" Aron asked, picking up the envelope and opening it to observe a check.

"That's your security deposit. The lease on her apartment is up, and she's moving to Restia. She didn't tell you?"

"No," Aron said, hurt slicing through him that she would leave without telling him. But what did he expect? He'd reacted so angrily and told her never to speak to him again. She was only following his directive.

"She still doesn't know that you gave me the deposit," he said, stirring his coffee. "You were clear that you didn't want me to tell her. It was a nice thing to do for someone in her position."

"And what position is that?" Aron asked, not liking the tone of his aristocratic friend's voice.

"You know," Max said, shrugging. "A poor servant's daughter. Although she married Diabolos, she'll never be one of us."

"One of us," Aron said, his voice flat.

"An aristocrat with a proud lineage. We're the true bloodline of the Slayers, Aron. You know this. Moira's a very nice woman but she'll never rise to our status."

Blood boiled inside Aron's veins as he listened to the man across from him, whom he considered a friend. He absolutely detested the classism that existed in their kingdom and had always done his best to squash it. How dare he speak of Moira that way? Aron had never known a woman kinder and humbler, or more fun and full of life. Aching for her, he realized how much he missed her. By the goddess, he had dismissed her without a thought, not even giving her the opportunity to explain. Someone as guileless as Moira must've had a reason to lie to him so vehemently, no?

Standing, the legs of Aron's chair made an abrupt scraping noise on the tiled floor. "I don't appreciate you speaking of Moira or anyone with a laborer's bloodline that way. You know that type of prejudice is everything I abhor. Do better, Max. You sound like an ass. Thanks for the check." Giving him a nod, he exited the restaurant.

Walking under the bright morning sun, Aron allowed himself to contemplate all the scenarios as to why Moira would deceive him. Unable to come up with anything, he jogged up the stairs to the main castle at Uteria. Entering Miranda's royal office chamber, he sat down for the combined council meeting.

The attack on Crimeous was two weeks away. Latimus and Kenden had been training the troops extensively for two and a half months. They were prepared and ready. Evie and Darkrip updated everyone on their progress with the combined force-field. Although it wasn't perfect, they felt they had progressed enough to generate a barrier strong enough to immobilize the Dark Lord while Evie struck him. Evie explained that Sadie and Nolan had tested her blood, and there was indeed a different DNA imprint than Darkrip's preventing the shield from being seamless. It was a mystery to them, as the two siblings should've shared the same DNA.

Resigned to the battle, Evie still appeared confident that she would succeed. Aron hoped so, as he was ready to rid the world of the evil Deamon. He craved peace so badly and wanted to help Miranda build their kingdom to the preeminence it should have as one of Etherya's species' domains.

When the meeting was over, Miranda asked Aron to hang back so she could speak with him privately. Once everyone had exited the room, she sat on the edge of her mahogany desk, her leg swinging over the side. Aron stood a few feet from her, his back to the open window. A soft breeze blew against his neck as he waited for her to speak.

The queen's almond-shaped green eyes studied him as she seemed to struggle with what to say. Straightening her spine, she inhaled a deep breath.

"What the hell are you doing, Aron?" she finally asked.

"Excuse me?" he asked, confused by her slightly angry tone.

"With Moira," she said, looking quite disappointed in him. "What are you trying to prove? Yes, she lied to you. And yes, it was a huge deception. But have you ever asked her why? Or do you expect everyone to be perfect like you? Believe me, none of us have a shot. I'm sorry to tell you that." She lifted her arms and shrugged.

Sighing, Aron turned to the window, looking out over the green meadow behind the castle. "I'm nowhere near perfect, Miranda. You know that. I never claimed to be."

"Well, you're pretty damn close. Unfortunately, the rest of us fuck up. A lot. Moira should've told you where she was for the past eight hundred years. I'm not exonerating her for that. But you didn't even give her the benefit of the doubt. It's so unlike you. I don't understand why."

"I should've never touched her," he said, his hands resting in his pockets. "I always felt quite guilty about it. She was my best friend's wife. I coveted her even though I shouldn't have, and now, I've betrayed him so viciously for a woman who blatantly deceived me."

"I didn't know Diabolos well," Miranda said. "I hated those royal fundraising dinners my father threw and rarely attended them. But I do remember the reputation he had. It was as a vain man who liked to show off his money and possessions."

"As does every aristocrat in our kingdom," Aron said, turning to face her. "They're all pretentious assholes. If I didn't speak to those who flaunted their worth, I wouldn't have any friends at all."

Miranda smiled. "That's probably true. But you seem to hold him on a pedestal. I know you grew up with him, but have you ever considered the possibility that he wasn't as good a man as you thought?"

Aron felt his brow furrow. "Why would I ever consider that possibility?"

Miranda drew in a deep breath, rubbing her upper arm. "When you were with Moira, did you ever happen to see a scar by her hairline, above her neck?"

"No," he said, searching his brain to see if he recalled such a thing.

Miranda nodded and gnawed her bottom lip. "I don't want to betray Moira's trust but I think you need to ask her to show you her scar."

Aron's heart started to pound in his chest. "And why would I do that?"

Standing, Miranda approached him and clutched his hands. "You're a very intelligent man, Aron. I think that if you search really hard, you're going to find the answer. I don't think you'll like it but I think that somewhere, in a place you don't want to acknowledge, you know the truth."

Realization flooded Aron as he stared down at the queen. Flashes of memories from all his centuries on Earth.

The night when Moira had worn the large hat to one of their formal balls, commenting that Diabolos liked how she looked in it. She'd worn it the entire night, covering her forehead and temples.

The hot summer days where she'd worn long sleeved sweaters when they'd gone walking by the river. Aron had always chided her for not dressing appropriately for the climate.

The times when she'd winced when sitting down at the large dining room table where the three of them had dinner. She would laugh in her always affable way and tell the latest story of how her clumsiness had led to her obtaining a rather large bruise on her leg.

They were covers. All of them. Shields and stories to hide her wounds. A wave of nausea consumed Aron as the awareness set in. Diabolos, the man he'd trusted most in the world, had beaten his wife.

"It sucks," Miranda said, squeezing his hands. "To realize that someone we trust is a terrible person. I went through it when I discovered Sathan's letters to my father, buried in his desk for so many centuries. It's heartbreaking. And a good reminder that things aren't always what they seem."

Lifting a hand to his temple, Aron rubbed his forehead with the pads of his fingers. "How could I have not seen it?"

Releasing him, she perched back on the side of the desk. "Sometimes, we aren't ready to see things that are painful. But at least now, you know the truth. She ran away to escape her husband, Aron. Latimus protected her. I think they found comfort in each other during a time that they both severely needed it. I can't fault her for saving herself. Can you?"

"Damn it!" he said, running his hand through his hair. "I feel like such a fool. This whole mess has been awful and extremely embarrassing. You'd think I would've gotten smarter after you rejected me cold."

Laughing, she stood, looking at him with such admiration. "I care for you so much, Aron. I always have. But we were never quite right for each other. I know you realize that now. Sathan is my match in every way. Just as Moira is yours. It's so clear to me. I don't understand why you would throw that away. If Sathan lied to me, I would be pissed for sure and I'd give him hell about it. But I'd also give him the benefit of the doubt because I love him so damn much."

"I need to do the same," Aron said, looking dejectedly at the floor. "God, I'm such an idiot."

"Well, there's still time if you hurry. She's moving to Restia today. I tried to talk her out of it, but she's convinced she has nothing to stay here for. If I were you, I'd hurry up and change her mind."

"Thank you, Miranda," he said, pulling her in for a hug.

"You're welcome," she said, placing a kiss on his cheek. "Now, go get your woman."

Not needing any further urging, Aron fled the room.

Moira's eyebrows drew together at the knock on the door. Were the movers here already? They weren't supposed to come for another hour. Lila and Miranda had insisted on hiring professional movers for her trek to Restia, although Moira didn't want their charity. Eventually, she'd realized that arguing with the two women was futile and she'd let them hire the men. Walking over to the door, she pulled it open.

"I still have a few boxes to pack, but you can start on those—"

Her hand stilled in mid-gesture as she realized who was at the door. "Aron?"

His expression was impassive, his face too handsome for words. Mentally cursing her pounding heart, she stepped back to let him in. "Why are you here?"

His eyes darted around the room as he entered, over her half-packed boxes in the small, one-bedroom unit. Locking on to her with his gaze, he studied her.

"You're moving," he said, his tone unreadable.

"Yes," she said, nodding. "I can't afford the rent here anymore, now that I don't have the job at the gallery, and there's a restaurant that will hire me as a server at Restia."

His demeanor seemed to turn sad, along with an air of frustration. Of course, he was frustrated with her. She'd repeatedly lied to him and deceived him terribly. Understanding that she deserved no less than his vitriol, she closed the door and came to stand before him.

Staring down at her, he slowly crossed his arms over his chest. Brown irises darted back and forth between hers. The silence seemed to stretch forever, until Moira thought she might go mad.

Finally, he spoke. "Why didn't you tell me?" he asked, his voice so deep and slightly morose.

Inhaling a large breath, Moira struggled to find the courage to speak. "I thought you'd think I was a whore—" she said quietly.

"Not about your time with Latimus," he interrupted, anger flashing in his eyes. "Although, you should've told me about that too."

"I should have," she said, swallowing thickly.

"Why didn't you tell me about Diabolos?"

Moira fought to catch her breath as tears welled in her eyes. Fighting to hold them in, she clutched onto the lie she'd told for so long. Shame that she'd let her husband beat her for all those years coursed through her body, spurring the deception. "There was nothing to tell."

"No!" Aron yelled, causing her to flinch as she stared up at him. "No more lies, Moira. I'm so fucking sick of them." Uncrossing his arms, he reached for her, sliding his hands to cup her cheeks. Craving his touch for so many weeks, she couldn't stop the tears from falling. They glided over his hands, wetting them as he stared down at her. "Why?" he whispered.

"Because I didn't think you would believe me!" she cried, the words ripped from her throat. "He was your friend, wealthy and revered. I was no one."

Aron shook his head, appearing so disappointed as he stared into her. "You foolish woman. I swear to the goddess, you might just drive me into the nuthouse."

Moira was extremely uncomfortable and so shocked from his presence that a short laugh escaped her, breaking the intensity if only slightly. "You were right to be upset with me. I don't know what to say."

"I should've known when you didn't put up a fight. You *never* miss an opportunity to fight and scrape, Moira. But you let me dismiss you so easily. So fervently. I should've fucking known."

Her brow furrowed. "I don't think I've ever heard you use that word. I'm not sure what's happening right now."

"Well, I'm pissed. That happens when the woman you're crazy about spins a web of lies to protect someone who's been dead for seven centuries. I don't understand what's going on in that brain of yours."

"I didn't want to ruin your image of him," she said, pleading with him to understand. "He was your dearest friend."

"Who *beat* you," he said, clutching her face. "All those times, when you told me how clumsy you'd been. He did that to you, didn't he?"

"Yes," she whispered, closing her lids as the tears fell.

"And this," he said, sliding his hand to lift her hair. Aron sucked in a breath as he traced his fingertip down her long and ugly scar, adjacent to her hairline. "My god, Moira. How did you even survive?"

"Barely," she said, opening her eyes to look at him. "The night he gave me this scar was the night I left. I ran straight into the raid and found Latimus and never looked back. I'm so sorry, Aron. I just...I didn't know what to do."

Lowering his forehead to hers, his eyes seemed to glisten with their own unspent tears. "My god. All those years. All this time. I should've never let him have you. I should've fought for you and married you when we were young. I was trying to give you what you wanted, but Evie's right. It's time I stepped to the front of the damn line. To hell with being courteous and polite. I'm done with that."

"You couldn't have married a servant's daughter," she said, shaking her head against his.

"Says who? Some old curmudgeon who wrote a soothsayer manual a hundred centuries ago? Give me a break, Moira."

"But you always said you wanted a virgin with a pristine bloodline."

"I can't help how I was raised, Moira. I'm sure I said those things in my youth, when I was inexperienced and stupid. But you of all people should know that I don't see bloodlines when I look at people. How can you not have faith in me on that at least?"

"I should've had faith in you," she said, palming his cheeks as she drowned in remorse. "I should've told you about Diabolos and my time at Astaria and believed that you wanted me for me. But it's too late. I messed everything up."

"Did you?" he asked, his lips curving. "Are we that far gone?"

"How can you want me now? My deception was unforgivable."

"I'm so pissed, angel. At myself and at you and at this whole situation. But there's one thing I'm very clear about. I'm bone-deep in love with you. So deep that if I lose you, I don't know how I'll go on in this lonely-as-hell world. So, yes, we have a lot to figure out, but I need you to stop doubting that I want you. I've always wanted you, somewhere inside. It just took me a few centuries to figure it out."

"Aron," she breathed, aligning her body with his. "I'm not good enough for you."

"Shut up, Moira," he said, dropping his arms to clutch her around the waist. Drawing her in to his body, he placed his lips over hers.

Sinking her fingers into his hair, she moaned, lifting to her toes to meet his questing tongue. Sliding over each other, they devoured the taste of their love and desire. Moira had missed him dreadfully, and her body trembled as he kissed her so passionately.

After a small eternity, he lifted his head. "I'm pretty terrible at this romance thing and already have a complex. So, if you love me back, could you do me a favor and tell me? Because I'm really bad at getting women to say it back to—"

"I love you, you daft man," she interrupted, the waves of her laughter surrounding them. "I love you so much it hurts."

"No more hurt," he said, rubbing her nose with his. "No more pain, angel. We've had enough. I want to make you happy."

"I want to make you happy too. I promise, I'll try. I don't know if I can but I'll do everything in my power to be someone you deserve. No more lies. I promise. I'm so sorry, Aron."

"No more apologies either," he said, brushing the pad of his thumb over her lip. "Today, we're starting fresh. The past is behind us. I want to build something new with you. Are you ready for that?"

"I'm so ready," she said, her mouth almost hurting from the width of her smile. "I want to give you babies and laughter and love and whatever else I can. I want to give you everything, Aron."

"All I need is you," he said, giving her a sweet kiss. "But babies will be nice too. Making them won't be half bad either."

Moira giggled, feeling so giddy as he held her. "Oh, yeah. Making them will be awesome. Can't freaking wait."

Bending his knees, he lifted her by her butt as she squealed and wrapped her legs around his waist. "When will the movers be here?" he asked.

Moira glanced at the watch on her arm. "Forty minutes."

"Plenty of time to start baby-making," he said, carrying her to the bed. "And then, we'll have them transport your stuff to my house."

"I don't have any sheets on the bed," she said, as he threw her down gently.

Sprawling over her, he laced his fingers through hers, one on each side of her head.

"Then, we'll have to be sure not to make a mess."

Cutting off her snickers, he cemented his mouth to hers. And proceeded to show her how much fun two people could have on a sheetless mattress.

Chapter 26

Evie sat at the dressing table in her tiny cabin, applying makeup for the day's attack. One might find it strange that she would paint her face for battle, but her beauty had always been an armament for her. It gave her confidence, and the goddess knew, she needed it in spades for the feat that lay before her. For if all went well, she would kill her father today.

It was still pre-dawn, the sun not due to appear over the horizon for a half hour yet. The plan was for the troops to gather upon the sparring field at Uteria, seven hundred soldiers strong. They would load into the various hummers and tanks and head to the Deamon caves. Once inside, they would attack her father, not resting until he was dead.

Finished with her makeup, Evie stood and sheathed the Blade in the holster between her shoulder blades. The weapon felt firm upon her back, and she lifted her chin with resolve. Staring into her mother's eyes in the reflection, she vowed to be successful.

Closing her lids, she materialized to the field. Kenden jogged up to her, a huge smile on his face. "You look absolutely gorgeous," he said, admiration in his eyes as he ran the tips of his fingers over her cheek. "If they ever do a *Soldier's Weekly* magazine, you'll be the cover model for sure."

Arching a brow, she gave in to his teasing. "As I always say, it's okay to die but never okay to die ugly."

He was so achingly attractive as he grinned down at her, the curve of his lips wistful. "You're not dying today, baby," he said, lifting her chin with his fingers. "Count on it." Lowering to brush a kiss over her lips, he whispered against them, "I missed you last night."

"I needed to clear my head," she said, drawing back to stare up at him. "And besides, I'm sure you're tired of me invading your house at every turn."

"Never," he said, winking. Her damn heart almost melted at the gesture.

"You guys ready?" Latimus asked, approaching them.

"Yes," they responded, voices firm with resolve.

Miranda and Arderin stood off to the side, clutching their husbands to them as if it was the last time they'd ever see them. Evie hoped to god it wasn't.

"What is Arderin doing here?" Evie asked. "She should be at Astaria. I'm sure my father knows we're coming."

"Darkrip said she was adamant about sending him off in person. And then, he mumbled something about it being futile to argue with her." Kenden said. "We immortal men seem to find ourselves entangled with a lot of hardheaded women."

"Damn straight," Evie said with a nod.

Miranda and Arderin released their husbands, and Sathan and Darkrip began to trudge across the field to join the troops.

A jolt of lightning bolted from the gray sky, still darkened as the sun lingered below the horizon. Fire flashed, and the grass began to burn around them. Soldiers lifted their weapons, ready to take on their surprise assailants, but none could be seen. The usual war cries of the Deamons were missing.

As if in slow motion, Evie turned her head to search for Arderin. Knowing how much her father coveted the babe growing in her womb, fear slammed Evie's chest. Sure enough, Crimeous had appeared behind her, clutching him to her as he held a knife to her throat.

Darkrip screamed, his body overcome with rage and fear, and began to run toward her. The Dark Lord must've impeded his ability to dematerialize. It was the only reason he'd be approaching them on foot. Suddenly, her brother stopped short, falling to the ground, frozen.

"Call the physicians!" Crimeous yelled, his voice deep and reedy as he held the dagger to Arderin's throat. "The burned one and the human. I want the baby extricated from her body. If you do as I ask, I'll consider letting her live."

Evie slowly began approaching Crimeous across the meadow. She somehow felt it smarter to approach him slowly, rather than materialize in front of him. Any sudden movements might cause him to slash Arderin's throat. The Dark Lord seemed quite deranged as he held her, possibly from the knowledge that the vast immortal army would soon be executing an intensely skilled attack on his domain. Kenden grabbed her forearm, dragging her back a step. Staring up at him, she shook her head.

"Let me go, Ken. I have to help her. You know that."

Terror and concern swam in his coffee-colored eyes. Eventually, he released her arm. Resuming her approach, she came to stand two feet in front of her father, admiring how Arderin struggled against him although her efforts were futile.

"Let her go, Father," Evie said, trying like hell to keep her voice calm. "She's barely nine months pregnant. The child will be much more powerful if you let it gestate fully. Being a Vampyre, she needs at least two more months for it to be close to full-term."

"No!" he screamed. "She will bear the spawn now, and I will incubate it in the caves. You know nothing of my plans, you hateful child."

Drawing the Blade of Pestilence from her back, Evie clutched it with both hands. "Maybe I'll just kill you now, and the Vampyre and her spawn along with you. We certainly could use less creatures with your vile blood roaming the Earth. There's no dispute about that."

"No, Evie!" Darkrip yelled behind her. "Please, don't hurt her." Annoyed at his interference, Evie turned to give him a furious glare. Waving her hand in the air, she denigrated his ability to speak.

"That's enough intrusion from the peanut gallery," she said, making sure everyone on the field could hear. "This is between me and my father. If any of you tries to interfere again, I'll murder you. Don't test me." Sending one last determined glare across the meadow, she rotated to face her father again.

Tilting her head, she observed the creature as he clutched Arderin to his chest. Never had she seen him so unhinged; so disjointed. It was a rare crack in his usually unflappable armor, and Evie seized the opportunity to change course.

"Take me instead," she said, throwing the Blade to the ground and stretching her hand out to him. "I'm the one you want. Combining your powers with mine will make you undefeatable. We could work together to destroy Etherya's tribes in a matter of days. The babe in her belly will take decades to become that strong." Shaking her hand, she lifted her chin. "Take. Me."

"Don't do this, Evie!" Kenden yelled behind her, his voice seeming so far away. "Don't align with him. I see your struggle, but it's not you. There's another way."

Clenching her teeth, she turned to face him. His eyes pleaded with her as he stood across the meadow. "I told you *not* to interfere," she said. Jerking her head, she froze him to stone, watching him crumble to the ground. "It was inevitable that I would join him, Ken. You always knew this, somewhere deep inside. I'm sorry."

She gazed into him, willing away every scrap of emotion she'd ever felt for the kind and stubborn commander. Kenden just stared back at her from the springy grass, his eyes shining with moisture and love and silent pleas for her to make a different choice. Sighing, Evie turned back to her father.

"Well?" she asked, shrugging. "What's it going to be? The Blade is on the ground, and I'm willing to unite our abilities. The sun will rise soon and burn you to death, so you must decide quickly. Let her go, and you can have it all, Father. Are you strong enough to make the right choice?" She lifted her arm again, hand outstretched.

Crimeous's dark, beady pupils darted between hers. For one moment, Evie was sure that he'd deny her request and kill Arderin anyway. And then, with a flash of movement, he pushed Arderin to the ground. Grabbing Evie's hand, he closed his lids, dematerializing them to the main lair at the Deamon caves. Kenden's screams echoed in her head as she vanished into thin air.

Once in the lair, Evie looked around, documenting the surroundings. It wasn't so different from the space he'd held her and Rina captive, violently torturing them all those centuries ago. Light burned from torches along the rock walls. A desk sat atop a rock slab, the stone twenty feet wide and ten feet long. A bookshelf held jars with liquid in them, severed body parts floating within. Curious, Evie approached them and touched one of the jars with her finger, the glass cold and squalid.

"It's a trophy case of sorts," her father said behind her, causing her to shiver.

"How exquisite," she said, tracing the jar with the pad of her finger.

"Why did you decide to join me, child?" he asked, genuine curiosity in his gravelly voice.

Pivoting, she stared at him. This creature who had so vehemently hurt her so long ago. She thought she'd feel rage at being in his presence; instead, she just felt numb. Not a drop of emotion filled her, not even the constant wrath and anger that had churned inside her for her entire squalid existence.

"I don't know," she said, shrugging. "I think I'm curious about the evil you possess. I'd never felt the extent of it until you attacked Uteria. Mother's blood prevents me from experiencing the malevolence that deeply."

Crimeous gave a slow nod. "You've only just begun. There are so many facets to my evil. They're magnificent."

"What can I do to enhance your blood in my system more than Mother's? Surely, you have some idea."

"I could bank my blood and transfuse you. Over time, it will temper Rina's blood until there are only traces of it left. You'll become extremely powerful."

Evie nodded. "Let's start today. The immortal army will still attack, especially now that I've defected. It's imperative we work quickly."

"I have a makeshift infirmary set up where I perform the cloning of my soldiers. We can perform the first infusion today."

"Fine. But I need to get one thing straight. You were able to hurt me when I was a child because I didn't realize the scope of my capabilities. I'm not that person anymore. I'm sure you realize the extent of my abilities. You can't disable them like you can Darkrip's. Be wary, Father. I didn't fight back when I was young because I didn't know how. That's not the case anymore. Are we clear?"

"No one will attempt to lay a hand on you, child," the Dark Lord said. "I will make sure that every last Deamon receives the order."

"Good. Tell them that I'm your right-hand. We can't have any confusion on that. I need them to follow my orders if we're going to fight together."

"It will be done," Crimeous said.

"Excellent," Evie said, straightening to her full height. "Now, show me this infirmary."

Kenden regained his ability to move shortly after he watched Evie disappear with Crimeous. Screaming at the top of his lungs for her to stay, she dematerialized away. Anguish, so vibrant and true, coursed through his muscular frame. Sitting up on the soft grass, he pulled his knees to his chest, resting his elbows atop them, and thrust his fingers into his thick hair. Cradling himself, he rocked back and forth, trying to understand why his beloved Evie would make such a choice.

"Ken," Miranda called softly, her thin hand resting on his shoulder.

"No!" he cried, the magnitude of the pain he was experiencing unlike anything he'd ever felt, even when his parents died all those centuries ago.

Expelling a large breath, Miranda sat on the ground, encircling him with her arms. Together, they rocked, contemplating the huge loss that had just occurred.

Latimus wrangled the men in the background, telling them to take an hour's break before returning to the field to train. The battle would be postponed, all their plans destroyed, now that Evie had defected.

Defeated, Kenden raised his head to look at his cousin. "How could she join with him, Miranda? I don't understand."

"She saved Arderin. Maybe she saw it as the only way to accomplish that. I don't know."

Giving a ragged sigh, he ran his hand through his hair. "I need to think. I can't do it here. I need to go to my shed." Standing, he pulled Miranda up beside him by her outstretched hand.

"Can you train the troops on your own today?" Kenden asked Latimus as he approached them.

"Yes," Latimus said, concern in his expression. "But if you need me, I'm here."

"Thanks," Kenden said. "I just need some time alone to process this. Give me a few hours. I'll come find you after lunch."

Dejected, he hopped into a nearby four-wheeler and drove to his shed. It had always been the place where he could think clearly. The one point of solace where his fastidious mind could brainstorm a solution to any problem. And boy, did he need a solution now.

Entering the shack, he closed the door behind him and switched on the lightbulb that hung overhead. Walking to the wall, he gently touched the nails that protruded from the wood. He'd hurt Evie with them although he hadn't meant to. Remembering the passion that they shared in the small space threatened to rip his heart open.

Walking over to the table, he sat on the stool. The maps of the Deamon caves were spread out before him, and he slid his palm over them. Studying them, he visualized where Evie was now. Pointing to a certain spot with his finger, he trained all his energy on that one point. It was Crimeous's main lair, the one he'd been using after Kenden and Latimus destroyed so many others when they were looking for Arderin and Dark-rip. Evie was there now—of that, he had no doubt. Rubbing the map with his fingers, he felt tears well in his eyes. Wanting so badly to see her and ask why she'd chosen her Father over them, he concentrated on the spot.

Slowly, as if in a vision, the tip of his finger seemed to warm. Feeling his eyebrows draw together, Kenden resumed stroking the paper, amazed that it continued to grow hot under his touch. After a moment, the site began to shoot sparks, and then, a small piece burst into flames. Unable to believe the spontaneous combustion, Kenden grabbed a nearby water bottle, dousing the fire.

"It is a sign, my child," an airy voice said.

Lifting his head, Kenden regarded Etherya. Unsure what to do, he observed her with wide eyes. The Slayers had disowned the goddess after the Awakening, and he hadn't worshipped her in centuries. Was he supposed to bow? Or kneel?

"It is okay, son," Etherya said, floating toward him as long, red curls stretched behind. "You do not need to address me in any certain way. Goddess is fine."

"Hello, Goddess," he said, giving a reverent nod. "I'm a bit shocked at your presence."

Black irises studied him as she hovered in front of his body. "You lost your faith in me, child, but I never wavered in my faith for you. Your protection of your people is honorable. I am so proud of you."

"Thank you," he said, swallowing deeply. Always a straight-shooter, he asked the question burning in his mind. "Why did she defect, Goddess?"

"These things are always unclear. She has been struggling with her desire to align with him since he attacked Uteria months ago. She wanted to tell you but was afraid. Evie has much fear when it comes to you."

"Why?" he asked. "When I love her so much? She knows this to be true, I have no doubt."

Etherya sighed. "There is a difference between what one knows and what one believes, deep within. She is consumed by fear that your love for her is conditional."

"Upon what?"

"Many things," Etherya said. "Whether she is the one to fulfill the prophecy. Whether you'll love her once you realize how evil she is inside. Whether that malevolence will destroy all that she loves, especially any children she would have with you. Her terror fuels her doubt; her doubt fuels her self-hatred. Eventually, it will destroy her."

"I won't let that happen," Kenden said, so firm in his belief of Evie's goodness. It had always been there, located under all the internal armor she'd built. He wouldn't give up until he extricated it fully and succeeded in his efforts to help her live by it.

"That is good, Commander," Etherya said. "Your faith in her makes her strong. Things are not always as they seem. She sent you a message. One of fire, through the map." The goddess gestured to the table with her fiery head. "You need to be smart enough to listen."

Creating distance between them, the goddess began to float away. "I have already angered the Universe enough. You must discern this on your own. But you are on the right path. Stay true in your belief of her. It is warranted."

"Wait," Kenden said. Slowly, he approached the goddess. Lifting one of her long strands of hair, he ran his thumb over the silken lock. "It's the same color as Evie's," he said, his tone contemplative. "I would know it anywhere after all the times I've held her. You infused her with your blood. When?"

Etherya seemed to smile, although he couldn't be sure. "Very good, Commander. You are cunning, indeed. You will do well with my Evie. She has so much of my magnificent Valktor in her. Help her use it to make the right choice. To destroy Crimeous, once and for all. Do not wait. The time to attack is near. I will be watching over you all." Lifting her airy hand, she pulled the curl from his fingers. With nary a sound, she vanished.

Shaking his head as if it was all a dream, Kenden glanced at the table. The map sat atop, a hole burned where he had touched it earlier. It was the sign he needed. Grabbing onto hope that Evie could still be turned back to their side, he ran into the morning sunlight to tell Miranda of his encounter with the goddess.

Chapter 27

Three weeks later, the immortal army was ready to attack again. They'd needed the time to prepare an assault that wasn't centered around Evie. The new strategy was to charge forward with their massive militia, Darkrip carrying the Blade upon his back. Once he, Kenden and Latimus isolated Crimeous and Evie, they would do their best to sway her back to their side. If she turned, Darkrip would generate the force-field with her and hand her the Blade to strike down the Dark Lord.

If she didn't make the choice to reenlist with them...well, Kenden wasn't sure he would survive. All his love for the glorious beauty was entangled in the belief that she had goodness inside; that she would choose her Slayer half when everything was on the line. If she didn't, their world would be plunged into chaos. The immortal army would never be able to defeat the father-daughter powerhouse. His people would suffer, centuries upon centuries of war, until they would most likely be exterminated.

Kenden stood atop the hill that crested over the sparring field at Uteria, the just-risen sun shining upon him as his hair blew in the breeze. Arms crossed over his broad chest, he observed the soldiers. They were ready. All his centuries of training had come down to this one battle. Clenching his jaw, he hoped like hell they would succeed.

"The men are prepared," Latimus's baritone voice chimed as he came to stand beside him. "We won't fail."

"We can't fail," Kenden said, gaze trained on the troops. "It's time for our people to live in a world without war."

They stood silent, bodies firm, arms crossed, as they observed the massive army they'd built.

"How's Adelyn?" Kenden asked, tilting his head toward Latimus.

The hulking Vampyre, known for being so brooding and curt, broke into a beaming smile. "Amazing. When Lila brought her home a few weeks ago, I was a bit shocked. But we'd been discussing adopting an infant for a while. She's the most adorable thing I've ever seen. I'm already in love with her."

"That's great, man," Kenden said, patting him on the back. "I'm so happy for you guys."

"Yeah," he said, his grin comprising the width of his face. "It's unbelievable. I never thought I'd have anything like this. Lila is the most incredible person on the planet. I'm a lucky bastard."

"She's pretty awesome," Kenden said with a nod.

Latimus blinked down at him. "I'm sorry about Evie, Ken. I really am. I hope we can turn her."

"We can," he said, so confident that Evie still possessed righteousness within. "I won't contemplate anything else. She's going to join us today and murder that bastard. I feel it with everything I have."

"Okay, then," Latimus said. "Let's get to it. I'll lead the troops attacking from overhead in the Hummer, and you'll lead the ground troops with the tanks."

"Ten-four," he said.

"Once we hear you charging, we'll detonate the explosives and enter from above. He'll know we're coming, but we're equipped. I've never seen the men so determined."

"Me neither," Kenden said. "Let's go."

Knowing that all the words had been said, they plodded down the hill to meet their army. Wrangling the troops, they bounded into their armored vehicles and led them to battle.

Evie milled around the quiet cave, situated down a long hallway from Crimeous's main lair. The troops were on their way to attack. Evie could see this, as she knew her father could, and she prepared by donning her war clothes. Black yoga pants, sneakers and a thin turtleneck. She'd placed a spell upon them, so if she was struck, the blades or bullets would bounce off. The high neck was so that she didn't get her throat sliced open again. It had been rather uncomfortable, and she'd like not to repeat the experience, if possible.

Sighing, she gathered her thick hair in a ponytail, securing it so that it bobbed behind her head. Ready as she'd ever be, she transported to the main lair to join her father.

"You are ready for battle," Crimeous said, his pointed teeth glistening with saliva from the nearby torchlight. "It will not be easy. Latimus and Kenden have built a strong army."

Evie shrugged. "Nothing will ever be as strong as our combined powers. You know this, as I do. We'll decimate them. There's no other option."

Her father's pleasure at her words coursed through her. Now that she'd been banking his blood for several weeks, she could read his thoughts so well. He was mad with power, drunk with vengeance and starving for destruction. It was a potent combination of extreme maliciousness that Evie had never experienced. It made her both nauseous and exulted. A dangerous amalgamation indeed.

From high atop the rock slab, she pivoted to observe Crimeous's Deamon soldiers. They were a mighty force but not as strong as the immortal army. Many were evil, as wicked as her father. But some carried flashes of emotion and surges of conscience, causing Evie to remember her sister's wish to allow those who genuinely wanted to repent a chance at reformation. If, by some small chance, Crimeous was defeated, it would be those soldiers who benefitted from her sister's wise benevolence.

Closing her eyes, she sensed their approach. Waves upon waves of Vampyre and Slayer soldiers, charging to destroy the most spiteful creature who'd ever walked Etherya's Earth.

"Are you ready, child?" her father asked behind her.

Gritting her teeth at the term he insisted on calling her, she nodded, not bothering to turn around. "I'm ready. Let's kick some ass."

"Good. They're here."

Straightening her spine, Evie readied for the attack.

Chapter 28

Kenden marched the troops through the mouth of the cave, feeling confident as five hundred strong paraded behind him. Latimus would lead two hundred more through the holes that he blew open in the ground above, and together, they'd set about decimating the Dark Lord.

"I'll materialize to the top of the slab when I see an opening," Darkrip said beside him. "My father and Evie will be up there, letting the soldiers below take the brunt of the battle. Once you see me ascend, it's imperative you climb up and join me. We have no chance of swaying her without you. You're the only person still capable of turning her."

"I'll be there," Kenden said, observing the light from the lair begin to shine in the darkened cave. "May the gods be with you."

"I think we might need more help than even they can give, but what's the hell in asking?" Darkrip said. Gritting his teeth, he began to jog forward. Kenden yelled, "Charge!" and the cries of war erupted behind him. Resolved, he trudged into battle.

Metal clattered and shots sounded as the Deamons retaliated. Every clank that Kenden encountered as his sword struck against another enthralled him. Pulling a TEC from the arsenal around his waist, he attached it to a Deamon's head and detonated it. The slimy creature collapsed to his death on the squalid ground.

For minutes, they fought, hand-to-hand, sword against sword, fist against TEC. Some of the soldiers had guns, but Kenden never once felt the spray of bullets. Was it too much to hope that Evie was disintegrating them from her perch atop the slab, secretly helping their cause?

Pulling his thoughts back to the battle, Kenden clenched his jaw as he proceeded to destroy several more Deamons. Latimus was fighting off to his far right, his soldiers engaged and determined as Sathan fought by his side.

Approaching the slab, Kenden spied Evie. She fought the few Vampyre and Slayer soldiers who crested the stone, pushing them off as their weapons vanished to thin air. She wasn't killing them, and suddenly, he knew.

She'd defected to deceive her father. This entire time, she'd been on their side. He remembered her olive orbs, latched on to him before she disappeared. He'd been too consumed by fear to read the message in them: *Trust me*.

Filled with more love for her than he'd ever envisioned, he blazed a path toward the slab, striking Deamons along the way. Darkrip materialized to the top and began fighting his father with the Blade of Pestilence. Evie watched them from feet away, frozen, unsure whom to help.

Crimeous's sword, forged from poisoned steel, clashed against the Blade as father and son fought. Sheathing his sword in the carrier upon his back, Kenden scaled the large rock. Finding his footing on the surface, he drew a TEC from his belt. Approaching Crimeous, he saw an opening and attached it to his head, deploying it immediately.

The Dark Lord wailed in pain, dropping his sword as he clutched his forehead. Thanks to Heden's improvements, it was capable of harming Crimeous, but Kenden knew they only had moments before he recovered.

"Form the force-field!" Kenden yelled. Evie jolted at his voice, her wide eyes locking on to his. "You can do this, Evie," he said, his voice calm amidst the terrible clanking below. "I believe in you. I always have. I know you didn't betray us."

"I've been banking his blood, Ken," she said, swallowing thickly. "It's changed something in me. I did it to read his thoughts. To gain an advantage. But I think it's turned me into something even more sinister." Her gaze fell to her father struggling beside her and then landed on Darkrip. "I don't know if I can end him. My body is craving more of his blood. More of his evil. It's...*glorious*," she almost whispered, closing her eyes and tilting her face toward the heavens.

"I don't care how much of his blood you infuse," Kenden said, slowly closing the distance between them. "You will always be Rina's daughter and you will always have goodness inside." Reaching her, he placed his fingers under her chin. When she opened them, his eyes bore into her. "I love you, Evie. No matter how much of him is inside you. It's time for you to fulfill your destiny and kill him." Thrusting his hand toward Darkrip, he accepted the weapon that the Slayer-Deamon handed him. Wrapping her hand around the handle of the Blade of Pestilence, he clutched it with his own. "I believe in you."

"How sweet," Crimeous chided, recovering from the blow from the TEC and giving a malicious cackle. Picking up the poison-tipped sword beside him, he lifted it for battle. With a vicious cry, he swung his arms behind his head and attacked Kenden.

Quick to react, Kenden pulled an SSW from his belt and extended the glowing blade. The armaments clashed against each other as they fought, a battle of good and evil exemplified in the squalid lair.

Darkrip extended both hands, a cloudy plasma forming around them and extending out from his body. Latching his gaze on to Evie's, he implored her. "Form the barrier with me, Evie," he said, his deep voice rock-solid. "You can do it."

She stood for so long, a century might have passed. Forests might have grown over, civilizations might have fallen, worlds might have been destroyed. For what seemed like forever, she contemplated her brother. Ever so slowly, she sheathed the Blade in the holster upon her back. Extending her hands, the murky substance appeared. Stretching from her thin arms, it joined with Darkrip's ether. Unfortunately, after several seconds, it fizzled out.

"Fuck!" Darkrip cursed, grabbing the SSW from his belt and extending the shining ember. Crimeous gave a low chortle, pulling another weapon from the sheath on his back. The sword's blade was lined with tiny spikes dripping with poison, ready to kill any immortal with only a glance against the skin.

"The force-field won't work if you're torn, Evie!" Darkrip shouted, grunting as he battled his father. "You have to be all-in. Otherwise, we have to drag him outside and try to burn him in the sun."

Sathan crested the stone, screaming as he charged Crimeous with his SSW. "You fucking bastard!" he screamed. "You killed our child. I'll murder you!"

As they scuffled, Kenden grabbed Evie's shoulders. "Evie!" he screamed, terrified at the dazed look in her eyes. "You're too strong for this," he said, shaking her with his firm grip. "Don't choose the evil. It's not who you are anymore."

Those leaf-green orbs lifted to his, swimming with uncertainty. "I can't—"

Her words were interrupted by the sound of bullets whizzing around them. Ducking, Kenden pulled her toward him, hoping to shield her.

Disengaging from him, she lifted the Blade of Pestilence from her back, gritting her teeth as she fought the assailant: a Deamon soldier with a Glock in his hand.

Throngs of Deamon warriors began to swarm atop the slab. Lifting his SSW, Kenden attempted to hold them off. Blinded by rage against the hateful creatures, he fought tirelessly. Out of the corner of his eye, he spotted Sathan and Darkrip sparring with Crimeous. Realizing that Latimus was still leading the troops below, unless he'd been injured by an eight-shooter, he swung his weapon. There was no second chance this time. His future and that of his people depended upon his success.

Evie fought off several Deamons and pushed quite a few more Slayers and Vampyres from the elevated stone. Turning to face him, she yelled, "I'm ready! I'm not going to die today. Isolate Crimeous and stun him with a TEC. I'll form the barrier with Darkrip!"

Nodding, Kenden rushed toward the Dark Lord, waiting for an opening in between Sathan and Darkrip's blows. When he spotted one, he pounced, deploying the TEC on the pasty skin of Crimeous's forehead.

Kenden stood back as Evie jogged over. She and Darkrip extended their arms, and Kenden observed the cloudy plasma encircle the Dark Lord. Terror slowly marred Crimeous's hideous, wrinkled face as he halted, immobilized and unmoving, realizing the strength of his offsprings' combined energy.

"I'll hold the force-field, Evie," Darkrip said. "I've got it. Take the Blade and strike him."

"He's the only one on this wretched planet as evil as I am," she said, her voice so ragged it shifted something in Kenden's soul. "Once he's gone, I'll be the worst amongst us. How can I live with that?"

"I'm here, Evie," Darkrip said, his tone soothing in the dirty cave. "I have those same fears, but they're not real. Mother gave us everything we'll ever need, deep inside. You know this somewhere within but you need to have the courage to believe it. I have faith in you, and so does Ken. So do Miranda and Arderin and every single person you've drawn under your spell. You're a part of us now, and even though you're pretty damn powerful, you'll never change that."

A tear slid down her cheek, gleaming in the torchlight as she wavered.

"We can't hold him frozen forever, Evie," Darkrip said, his arms quivering with the strength he was expending to generate the barrier.

Lifting her gorgeous irises to Kenden, she asked, "How did you know I didn't defect?"

He smiled, so sure that she was going to make the right choice. "Because you love me too. And that will always outweigh any choice your Deamon side wants to make. It's so beautiful, Evie, and I'm so honored to have it."

Her nostrils flared, chin lifting slightly. Reaching behind her head, she drew the Blade from the sheath. Clutching the hilt, she swung her arms behind her head.

"Goodbye, Father," she said through clenched teeth.

Kenden waited, anxious to see her slice the Blade through his neck.

Arms held high, she stood still. So very still.

And that's when Kenden realized. Crimeous had rendered her immobile. The bastard had figured out how to manipulate her powers as he had Darkrip's. Lifting his SSW, Kenden screamed toward Darkrip and Sathan, "He's frozen her! Hold the force-field as long as you can, Darkrip!"

The laugh that enveloped the cave was so malevolent it made the hairs on Kenden's arms stand to attention. Stepping through the energy barrier that Darkrip so tenuously held, Crimeous flitted his hand through the air, effectively dispelling it.

"Did you really think it would be that easy?" Crimeous asked. "Did you truly think I wouldn't anticipate that she would choose you?" Kenden lost control of his limbs as the disgusting creature approached him, the clattering sounds of war below dulled by the ringing in his ears. Sathan and Darkrip were immobilized to his right. Staring into irises so evil, above the Dark Lord's thin nose and reedy lips, Kenden felt the loss overwhelm him. They were going to die here, in this squalid cave, at the hands of this wicked creature. He'd never get to hug Miranda again, or kiss Sadie on her beautifully imperfect cheek, or hold his gorgeous Evie in his arms.

Shrouded in despair, he stood motionless, except for the pounding of his nearly-broken heart.

Crimeous seemed to glide toward Evie as they all watched, held stationary by his immense power. Surrounding her neck with his gray hand, his thin fingers squeezed.

"Good," he said, watching her struggle to breathe. "I remember when you used to squirm like this, all those centuries ago. Perhaps I'll take you once more, to show you how stupid it was to defy me. Here, in front of the man who professes to love you. How splendid." Extending his nail, he ran it down her body, neck to abdomen, slicing the fabric of her turtleneck. Pulling the cloth from her body, he tossed it on the ground. Grabbing the Blade, he threw it to lie upon her tattered shirt. Pulling her arms to her side, he regarded her, venomous energy seeming to emanate from his lean body.

Bile rose in Kenden's throat as the monster traced the pale skin of Evie's stomach below her black sports bra. How had it come to this? He'd wanted so badly to protect her, and now, she would perish after reliving her worst memories, once more, before them all.

"There, there," Crimeous said, scratching her abdomen with his nails, filed into sharp points. "It won't be so bad. I think it will hurt the Slayer commander more than you. We'll see."

Evie's eyes darted toward the Blade, causing Kenden to notice the trembling of her fingers. How was that possible if she was immobile?

"Come closer," she said, her voice garbled. "Before you rape me, I need to tell you something."

Leaning down, his forehead almost touched hers. "What is it, child?"

Her jaw clenched so tightly that Kenden thought it might smash. "I hate it when you call me that," she said through gritted teeth.

"Then, what shall I call you, child? I'll give you that last concession before I torture and murder you."

"How about, 'Your worst fucking nightmare?'" she spat.

Opening her fingers, the Blade of Pestilence shot from the floor, straight into her palm. With a mighty yell, she thrust it into his abdomen. Crimeous cried in agony, falling backward a few steps.

"Burn in hell, you fucking asshole!"

Lifting her arms, she swished the Blade through the air, chopping off his head with one strike.

The Dark Lord's skull fell to the dirty floor, his body collapsing behind it. Heaving air through her lungs, Evie dropped the Blade to the ground, seeming shocked that she'd bested him.

"How did you regain your powers?" Kenden asked, rushing over to her.

"I'd placed a spell on my clothes. When the Blade landed on top of my shirt, I was able to pull enough energy from the magic it held to regain my abilities. Is his head reattaching?" she asked, an expression of worry overtaking her face.

Kenden, Evie, Sathan and Darkrip loomed over the severed body, watching to see if the parts congealed back together. Although Crimeous's head had been separated, his lips were still moving slightly, as if he was trying to speak. The remaining sounds of war ceased below, the troops understanding that something of great significance was occurring on the slab.

Suddenly, an enormous flash of light appeared. The goddess Etherya materialized in front of them, collapsing on her knees beside Crimeous's skull. So very gently, she picked up the cranium, placing it in her lap and stroking the gray, smooth skin at the temple.

"Etherya," the grisly whisper sounded from the barely-alive severed head. "What happened? I haven't seen you in so long."

"My beautiful Galredad," she cried, cloudy tears falling onto his face. "You lost your way so very long ago. It filled me with so much anguish. But now, you will be released from this world and can find some peace in that."

"The Passage?" he asked, blood spurting from his mouth.

"No, my friend. You have hurt too many for that. You will suffer in the Land of Lost Souls. But eternity is long, and perhaps the Universe will allow you to repent. One never understands the workings of the fickle Universe, even one as omnipotent as me. Know that I will think of you often and go knowing that you left two magnificent children behind. It is time, Galredad. Close your eyes." Lifting her cloudy hand, she gently closed his lids as the last breath exited his lips.

"All this time," Kenden said, barely able to believe the sight in front of him. "You've had a history with him all this time."

"Yes," the goddess said. Cradling Crimeous's head, she gradually set it upon the dirty ground and rose. "It is a long chronicle that you need not be bothered with. It is imperative you destroy his body, so that no others clone it." Floating over to Evie, she cupped her cheek. "Well done, my child. When I infused you with my blood, so long ago, I had hoped this would be the result. You are too brave to let your self-loathing destroy you. Please, don't let that happen. Your grandfather, mother and I love you very much." Placing a kiss to Evie's forehead, Etherya disappeared.

Kenden watched a stunned Evie lift her gaze to his, a question in them.

"I'd already figured it out," he said. "She came to see me when you defected. Her hair is identical to yours."

Evie inhaled a huge breath. "Holy shit."

"Holy shit is right," Darkrip muttered, stunned as well, as he stood beside them.

"We need to dispose of his body in the Purges of Methesda," Evie said, chin lifting with resolve. "Darkrip, you can transport the body, and I'll transport the head."

"Yes," Darkrip nodded. "Let's do it now. Ken, you'll clean up the blood? We have to make sure not one drop is left, lest someone finds it and clones it."

"Latimus, Larkin and I will take care of it," Kenden said. Strutting to Evie's side, he pulled her into his strong arms. Lowering his lips to hers, he devoured her mouth, so grateful that she was alive and unharmed.

After ending the kiss, he placed his forehead upon hers. "Wow. You just saved the world of immortals, Evie. I'm a bit in awe."

She shook her head against his, her almond eyes wide and stunned. "I've never been more overwhelmed. Maybe I'll enjoy it once we dispose of the body. I was so sure we were defeated."

"That bastard didn't stand a chance against you. You're so fucking amazing. Thank you for saving our people."

"*Your* people," she said.

"*Ours*," he corrected, placing a soft peck on her lips. "You'll realize that one day." Drawing back, he assessed her stomach and collarbone, the skin blemished with abrasions around her black sports bra. "Are you hurt anywhere?"

"No," she said, shaking her head. "Only minor scratches. I'm fine. We need to destroy the body. Come on, Darkrip. Let's do this."

She and Darkrip proceeded to pull the various parts of Crimeous's limp body close. Before they could dematerialize, a sound came from below. They pivoted to face the soldiers, whose fighting had ceased minutes ago.

Deamon soldiers, at least three hundred strong, simultaneously took a knee. Planting their weapons on the ground, they all trained their gazes upon Evie.

"Hail, Queen Evangeline," they said in unison.

If the situation hadn't been so tense, Kenden would've laughed at her stunned expression. Lifting her gaze to his, she gave a reluctant shrug. "I told my father to tell them I was in command. I thought that if we won, it would come in handy. Didn't really think that one through."

A large Deamon soldier crested the slab, coming to kneel in front of Evie as she held Crimeous's head in her arms.

"Stand, soldier," she said.

Rising, he saluted her. "I am Rekalb, captain of your father's ground troops. We had orders from our leader to accept you as Commander if he was to perish. My men and I pledge our loyalty to you. Several soldiers who only would serve your father ran from the caves when you defeated him. They will need to be reined in. For now, those of us that remain are your humble servants."

"Thank you," Evie said. Although Kenden knew she was floored, she retained her ever-present confidence and grace. She would make such a magnificent leader, he thought as he observed her. "We are going to dispose of my father's body. I would like you to help the immortals clean up the battlefield. Then, we will work with my sister to find you lodgings. I am grateful for your loyalty and do not accept it lightly."

"Yes, ma'am," Rekalb said, saluting her again. "It will be done."

Giving him a nod, she looked at Kenden. Those beautiful lips curved into a heart-wrenching smile. Then, she closed her lids and dematerialized, her brother close behind her.

Allowing himself to accept that Crimeous was finally gone, Kenden got to work spearheading the clean-up.

Chapter 29

Evie appeared at the top of the cliffs above the Purges of Methesda, her brother emerging shortly thereafter. Silent, they watched the boiling lava below, clutching parts of their father's body.

"It's time," Darkrip said, after they'd had their moment of reflection.

Nodding, Evie inhaled a deep breath and plunged her father's head into the molten plasma below.

Feeling his nostrils flare, Darkrip followed suit, flinging his father's lifeless body into the blazing ash.

Placing his arm over his sister's slender shoulders, he pulled her close. Together, they stood, watching the Dark Lord's corpus disintegrate into nothingness.

"All that death and destruction from one vile creature," she said.

"Yes," he replied, resting the side of his head against hers. "I feel the worst for Mother. She endured so much violence from him. Followed only by you. You two experienced the brunt of his viciousness."

"That's over now," she said, sliding her arm around his waist. "We have a chance at a life without his presence in the world. You're going to have a baby and be a father. How remarkable."

"Remarkable and strange as hell," he muttered, causing her to chuckle. "And you'll build a life with Ken, maybe even have a few rug rats of your own."

She stiffened against him. "That's not my path. It seemed so easy for you, but it's not for me. I wasn't lying about banking his blood. I did it to gain an advantage but it courses though me so much stronger now. I can't saddle Ken with someone so much like Father. It wouldn't be fair to someone as good and decent as he is."

Turning her with his arm, Darkrip placed both hands on her shoulders. "First of all, making the choice to be with Arderin wasn't easy for me at all.

I struggled with it terribly and hurt her very much. I still don't understand how in the hell she loves me, but she does, and I'm enormously grateful for that.

"Second," he said, squeezing her shoulders tight, needing her to listen, "Father is dead. Any traces of his evil are gone along with him. You have a chance to make a choice. To be with the man you love and who loves you back with all his heart. Don't waste it. There's good inside you, Evie, just as there is inside of me. Whether we want to believe it or not, it's there."

"I don't believe it," she whispered.

"Well, I'm pretty sure Ken does. So does Miranda, and I sure as hell do—so, sorry, sis, but you're outvoted. You're a good person, whether you want to believe it or not."

"I've done so many terrible things in my past," she said, her gaze falling to the ground.

"As have I," he said, lifting it back by placing his fingers under her chin. "They're awful, and I feel extreme guilt over them and probably always will. But every religion on the damn planet preaches atonement and forgiveness. I'm going to do everything in my power to atone for my sins for the rest of my days and hope that the Universe forgives me. I choose to live by Mother's blood and know that has to mean something. You can do the same. After all, you've always been more powerful than me, so if I can do it, then you definitely can do it." He smiled, thrilled that she grinned back at him.

"It won't be easy," she said.

"Nope," he said, shaking his head. "Never said it would be. But it will be worth it. Give Ken a chance, Evie. Give happiness a chance."

"I have absolutely no idea how to be happy."

"Well, maybe it's time you figure it out," he said, placing a sweet kiss on her forehead. "And you just saved an entire kingdom full of people. I mean, wow, there's got to be some good karma in that, right?"

Laughing, she nodded. "I studied Buddhism quite a bit in the human world and I have to say, there is a lot of karma in saving two species."

"Three species, actually. Isn't that right, *Queen Evie*?" He couldn't control his snicker.

"How insane was that?" she asked, looking genuinely perplexed. "Miranda's great at the queen stuff, but I'm not cut out for it at all."

"I would beg to differ, but my wife has taught me never to argue with a woman dead set in her opinion." Evie breathed a laugh. "But you should think about Miranda's offer to govern the new compound. I think you'd be great at it."

"Right," she said, rolling her eyes. "I'm not a leader, Darkrip. I've been hiding in the human world for centuries."

"Well, maybe it's time you came into the light. You're pretty magnificent, Evie."

Placing her palms on his cheeks, her eyebrows drew together. "Damn. I think I love you. Like, from the bottom of my heart, genuinely love you. It's so strange."

He smiled, exhilarated to hear the words from her. "I felt the same when I realized I loved Miranda. And Arderin. And you," he said, shrugging. "It's really fucking weird but also quite amazing."

"It is," she said hesitantly, shaking her head. "So damn weird. Holy shit."

Breathing a laugh, he drew her in for a hug. Drawing back, he looked into her eyes, blazing before him as brightly as Rina's had all those centuries ago. "Come on. I need to get home. Someone's got to cook for my wife."

Snorting, Evie patted his shoulder. "You're a sap, bro. It's so absurd."

"Shut up."

Joining hands, they grinned at each other. Closing their lids, they materialized back to Uteria to find their family.

Miranda enveloped Evie in the most smothering embrace of her long life when she and Darkrip appeared in front of the castle at Uteria. Noticing that her brother was being enveloped in a fervent hug of his own by his sassy Vampyre, Evie let the joy overtake her and hugged her sister back.

Hordes of people stood along the road that led to the castle, Slayer and Vampyre alike. Cheers and whistles sounded as Evie regarded them, drawing back from Miranda to absorb the enormous waves of positive energy. As someone who'd so often lived in shadows and solace, it was strange to be the object of mass adulation, but Evie figured she'd dammed well earned it.

"Holy crap, Evie!" Miranda said, grabbing her hands. "You did it! It's unbelievable. I'm floored. You saved every single one of our people. I don't know how I'll ever begin to repay you."

"I'm still a bit shocked myself," Evie said, unable not to smile back. "It will be so freeing to live in a world without him."

"Yes, it will," she said, squeezing her. "Ken, Larkin and a few of the troops are hanging back to make sure they clean and disinfect every drop of his blood from the lair. In the meantime, we need to ensure that the Deamon soldiers who want to repent are housed in the abandoned hospital. We stationed the Vampyre troops there when they first came to Uteria, and it's the perfect place for them until we build quarters for them at the new compound."

"I'll be happy to help you with that," Evie said.

"Thanks, *Queen Evie*," Miranda said, holding her hand over her mouth as she snickered. "Whether you like it or not, you're a royal now, sis."

Evie scrunched her nose. "How do you deal with it? It's so formal."

"Oh, I don't let anyone call me that. Except my husband, when we're in the bedroom and we're roleplaying…" Waving her hand, she bit her lip, looking guilty. "Shit, he'd kill me if I kept talking, so I'd better shut up now."

Evie arched a brow. "Really?" she asked. "Our buttoned-up Vampyre king?"

"You have no idea," Miranda said, threading her arm through Evie's as they began to walk toward the hospital, located several hundred yards behind the castle. "He's an absolute tiger in bed."

The crowd had calmed a bit, although the vibrant energy remained. There would be a celebration to rival all others in the main square of each immortal compound tonight. Of that, Evie was sure.

Darkrip appeared in their path, clutching Sathan. Evie realized he must've transported to the cave to grab the king. Miranda launched herself at her bonded mate, wrapping her legs around his waist as she devoured his mouth.

"It's so gross," Arderin said, coming to stand beside her. "Like, get a room already."

"I could say the same about you and Darkrip," Evie teased.

"Sweetie, you don't want to know what we'd do if we got a room. Believe me."

Chuckling, Evie accompanied them to the abandoned hospital. The Deamon troops arrived, led by Latimus, and they proceeded to help them get acclimated. Miranda decided to station soldiers around the perimeter. Although the Deamons professed loyalty to Evie, and all expressed their desire to align with the immortals, it would take time to build trust. In the meantime, extra laborers would be dispatched to build the new compound. Not needing to focus on manufacturing weapons anymore, their entire workforce would be dedicated to creating the new establishment.

After a long day, Evie returned to her cabin. Entering the small shower, she washed away the battle. Running her fingertips over the scratches on her abdomen, left there by Crimeous's pointed nails, she realized they were the last scars her father would ever bestow upon her. Physical or mental. Unable to cope with the gravity of that thought, she let the tears well in her eyes. Then, she stuck her face under the spray and let them fall away. They would be the last she'd ever shed as a result of the vile creature. Inhaling a deep breath, she turned the knob and dried off, dressing herself in jeans and a loose, comfy sweater.

Once finished, she felt restless and poured a glass of wine. Knowing others were surely celebrating brought a smile to her lips but she didn't feel like joining the revelry. Instead, she grasped the wine bottle and headed outside. Sitting on the green grass, she sipped from her glass as the sun began to dip below the horizon.

As if she'd conjured him into existence, the man of her dreams appeared atop the far-off hill. Noticing he'd showered and was dressed in fresh clothes, he must have stopped home first to rinse away the grime of war.

Approaching her, he blocked the low-hanging orb at his back as he smiled. "You bring a glass for me?"

Closing her eyes, she materialized one in her hand. "That's the great thing about dating Crimeous's daughter. You won't have to ask him for her hand in marriage, and she can make a wine glass appear on a whim."

Laughing, he sat beside her as she poured him a glass. Taking it from her, he took a swallow. "Best damn glass of wine I've ever had. Damn, but victory is sweet."

"A thousand years," she said, so comfortable with him as she leaned into his muscular frame, the wine glass hanging from her fingers as her arm dangled over her knees. "He kidnapped Mother a thousand years ago, initiating so much hate and destruction, and now, it's over."

"Thank the goddess," he said.

"So, you're an Etherya worshipper again?" she asked, arching a brow.

He shrugged. "She's growing on me. Especially now that I know she infused you. Loving her is like loving a small piece of you."

Evie nipped his shoulder. "That's sweet."

Placing his arm around her, he held her close. "I'd be content to sit here with you like this forever, Evie. I hope you know that."

Feeling her lips curve, she rested her head on his shoulder. "Then, let's do that. I don't want to discuss serious things right now. Let's just enjoy each other's company and a nice glass of wine."

"Sounds perfect."

They finished the bottle, slow and languid, until the sky had long turned dark. Clutching each other's hands, they walked inside her tiny cabin. Divesting their clothes, they loved each other, ardently and passionately, whispering words that were still too new to say vociferously. Once their war-ravaged bodies were spent and sated, they fell asleep, wrapped in each other's embrace.

Chapter 30

Miranda awoke with a start. Something was wrong. She'd always listened to her gut and did so now with anxious concern. Throwing off the covers, she disentangled herself from her husband's thick body and rose to dress.

"What is it, sweetheart?" Sathan called from the bed.

"Something's going on, but I think it's fine."

Her bonded sat up, a vein pulsing in his neck. "What do you need me to do?"

"Nothing," she said, kissing him on his broad lips. "I'm heading downstairs. Evie's down there. She needs me. Give me ten minutes. If I'm not back by then, come find us. Okay?"

"Miranda, I'm not letting you walk into danger—"

"She won't hurt me, but she's in intense pain. I feel it. It's so strange." She ran her hand through her hair. "I'll be fine. Ten minutes. Love you."

Leaving her confused husband on their rumpled sheets, she hurried down the stairs.

Throwing open the massive wooden doors to the castle, she saw her sister standing outside. The faint glow of pre-dawn flamed off in the distance, and Miranda came to stand before her.

"Evie?"

"I'm leaving," she said, swallowing thickly. "I have to. I need to think and I can't do it in the immortal world."

Miranda felt her heart crumble. "Ken will be devastated."

Evie sighed. "I know. But it's what I have to do. I came back here to defeat my father and I'm not sure what comes next. The human world is where I feel comfortable, and I need to go there."

Miranda rubbed her hands over her thighs, covered in the yoga pants she'd thrown on. "He'll come looking for you."

"Maybe," she said, lifting her hands to rub her upper arms. "But he won't find me. I'm untraceable when I don't want to be located."

"Ken's the best tracker I know. You might have met your match, Evie."

She breathed a laugh. "Perhaps. Regardless, it's what I need to do." Extending her arm, she clutched Miranda's hand. "Thank you for your offer to govern the compound. It's extremely generous, but I wouldn't even know how to go about leading people."

"You'd be fine," Miranda said, feeling her lips form a wide smile. "I'm no expert either but I seem to do okay."

"You're great at it, Miranda." Looking at their joined hands, she seemed to hesitate, and Miranda wondered if she was fighting tears. Lifting her head, her green eyes seemed to glow. "I can't give him what he wants or what he needs. I want so badly to be the person who can but I can't, Miranda. I transfused my father's blood when I stayed in the caves, and it's warped something inside of me. I feel the struggle between his evil and her goodness," she said, referencing Rina. "It's consuming me. I can't do anything until I figure out how to remedy it."

"Okay," Miranda said, understanding how difficult the battle within her must be. "But I need to say something, and I want you to listen. Daughters of Rina are extremely hardheaded but you *need* to hear me on this."

Grinning, Evie nodded. "Okay,"

"You are always welcome here. Always. Your struggle only means that you have so much good inside you that it's battling to break through. I have faith that you will defeat the darkness that comprises your father's blood and emerge more victorious than ever. When that day comes, know that you'll have a home here. The offer to govern the new compound is always on the table, even if it takes you several centuries to accept it. Do you understand me, Evie?"

"Yes," she said, the word gravelly and filled with emotion. "I've never understood what it's like to have family, but your acceptance of me is humbling. Thank you."

"You're welcome." Drawing her close, they shared a hug. "Please, be careful out there," she whispered into the shell of her ear.

"I will."

Sathan's voice called from behind. "Miranda? Are you okay?"

"Goodbye," Evie garbled, tears glistening in her eyes.

"Goodbye."

And then, she was gone. Vanished into thin air, as if she'd never existed. Miranda felt Sathan's warmth behind her, drawing her into his front, as her heart splintered.

"She'll be back, little Slayer," he said, kissing her silky hair. "Don't worry."

"I know," Miranda said, emotion clogging her throat. "But will it be soon enough to repair Ken's heart?"

Sighing, he clutched her close. "Only time will tell, sweetheart."

Turning in his arms, she slid her hand over his face. "Carry me inside and make me forget for a minute, will ya?"

Chuckling, he fused his lips to hers. "I am the queen's humble servant and will do my best to follow her command," he mumbled against her mouth.

"God, yes. We're gonna play that game. Take me upstairs. We have at least half an hour before Tordor wakes up. An hour if we're lucky."

His deep laugh reverberated through her body, shooting daggers of desire to every limb. Loving how he swung her into his broad arms, she buried her face in his neck, anticipating every sexy thing her husband was about to do to her. Squealing as he carried her up the stairs, he silenced her with his mouth, surrounding the hallway in silence so they didn't wake their son.

Kenden awoke, alone in her small cabin, already understanding that she was gone. As he'd held her last night, he'd felt the struggle within. In between their bouts of passion, she'd lain in his arms, explaining why she'd infused Crimeous's blood. Not only had it given her the ability to read his thoughts, which she couldn't do through the shield he'd erected, but it also made him trust that she'd defected.

He understood why she did it. The action was warranted and so very smart. Yet another cunning move by the remarkably astute woman he loved with his entire heart. Placing his hands beneath his head on the pillow, he realized he wasn't even angry. He'd known, somewhere deep inside, that she would leave. She needed to process the sweeping changes that had comprised her life recently. Killing her father. Her slow but steady evolution toward choosing to live by her Slayer half. Her acceptance of her love for him, Miranda, Darkrip and others. It must be intensely overwhelming for someone who'd thrived in solitude, needing no one for centuries.

Aching for her, he lifted from the bed, resolute to let her stew for a bit before finding her. And, oh, he would find her. Of that, he had no doubt. Walking into the small kitchen, he noticed that the coffee pot was on and half-full of steaming coffee. Plodding toward it, he pulled a mug from the cabinet above. Pouring himself a cup, he lifted it to his lips, sipping the warm liquid.

Lifting the note she'd left beside the pot, he read her sweeping scrawl:

Ken,
I'm sure you're not even surprised that I left, for you knew I had to. Hell, you probably know me better than I know myself at this point. It's a hard

thing, when you realize that someone understands your fears, doubts and insecurities better than you do. It makes me want to curl up into a ball and forget that I ever met you. Or held you. Or let you look at me with those sexy-as-sin eyes.

But I can't forget, as much as I want to, so I'm going to remember. I'm off in search of answers and will do my best to recall our time together fondly. I don't think it will be hard, considering that I feel more for you than I've ever felt for anyone. It's annoying and disconcerting and makes me hate you, just a little bit.

You can try to find me but, as we've already discussed, it will be a waste of your time. I want you to be happy, Ken. Marry a woman who can give you babies and love; who isn't filled with evil and memories of past atrocities, both received and committed. I deceived myself that I was good enough to be touched by you for as long as I could. You will do a disservice to yourself if you continue the same deception.

If I ever do see you again, perhaps centuries down the road, know that I will embrace you and feel true joy at the family you've built. I only want you to be happy, and this is why I can't stay.

I made coffee for you to soften the blow. At least we overcame the hurdle of me being able to share the coffee pot. You changed so much in me, Ken, and for that, I will always love you.

Be happy,
Evie

Kenden finished the letter, smiling as he sipped his coffee. Man, the woman was head over heels for him. How magnificent. But she had another thing coming if she thought for one second that he was letting her go.

Pondering how much time he would give her before he started looking, he leaned on the counter. He'd give it a few weeks, to let Evie roam the human world and to help Miranda transition the kingdoms to a realm without Crimeous.

And then, when everything was in place, he'd travel to the land of humans to claim his woman. He didn't care if it took him days, years or centuries. He'd locate her and drag her back with him, kicking and screaming if he had to. Chuckling at the image, he finished his coffee.

Making sure all the lights were off in the cabin, he shut the door behind him and headed home to start the day.

Chapter 31

Miranda stood at the wall of ether, hugging Darkrip tight. Unable to stop the tears pouring down her face, she disengaged from him and clutched Arderin close.

"We're going to be fine, Miranda," Arderin said, running her hand over her glossy hair. "I'll only be gone a few years and I think I can finish medical school pretty quickly. We'll come back to visit as much as we can. I promise."

"I can't believe I'm gonna miss this little munchkin growing up," Miranda said, kissing the forehead of the baby girl Arderin held in her arms. Straightening, she swiped at the wetness on her cheeks. "I wanted to be there to help you."

"I've read every baby book imaginable," Darkrip said, hugging Arderin to his side. "My wife has been diligently quizzing me on what I've retained, and I'm pretty sure I can keep the little monster alive."

Arderin punched his upper arm, scrunching her face at his teasing. "Don't call our daughter a monster."

Chuckling, Darkrip pecked her pink lips. "The cutest monster I've ever seen."

Arderin beamed up at him, joy evident in the tiny new family.

"I've already had Sarah Lowenstein make some calls," Sadie said, Nolan's arms around her waist as he stood behind her. "The OB-GYNs and pediatricians at UCLA are top notch. If there are any emergencies, they'll take care of Callie as if she was their own. I see no reason why they would even begin to suspect that she's not human. But her self-healing abilities should keep her healthy."

"Okay," Miranda said, leaning back into Sathan. "Are you going to survive this, darling?" she asked, rubbing his face with her palm.

"I'm not thrilled but I trust Darkrip to take care of them," he muttered.

"Thanks, Sathan," Darkrip said. "You have my word."

"Okay, little one," Latimus said, "we already said our goodbyes to you yesterday. I'm sure Lila's a mess right now because she already misses you so much, and I need to get back to her and the kids. Be safe over there."

"I will, old man," she teased, ice-blue eyes twinkling in the sunlight.

Heden gave her one last firm hug and then shook Darkrip's hand. Telling Arderin not to be a pain in the ass, they all laughed when she stuck her tongue out at her younger brother.

Then, they waved, watching as Darkrip, Arderin and Callie entered the ether and disappeared. Sighing, Miranda turned to look at Kenden, who'd been quite somber during the exchange. As the others headed to the four-wheelers, she placed her hand on his chest.

"Whoa, there. Someone's awfully quiet today. You okay?"

"Yeah," Kenden said, his lips forming a half-hearted smile. "I just miss her, Randi. Two more weeks, and then, I'm heading to find her. We need to finish the transition of the soldiers to law-enforcement as much as we can before I leave. I don't want to saddle Latimus with all the work."

"Always such a boy scout," Miranda said, linking her arm with his as they sauntered toward the vehicles.

"Evie called me that. You two must've been sharing notes."

She laughed, the sound wafting along the gentle breeze. "Maybe we were. Regardless, I've got your back. As we discussed, a quarter of the troops will remain combat ready. You and Latimus have already done a great job destroying the Deamon caves and rounding up the Deamons that need to be imprisoned. The remaining troops will be transitioned to law-enforcement, security and construction for the new compound at double their army salary, if they so choose. Not to toot my own horn, but I'm pretty awesome at this 'ruler' thing." She made quotation marks in the air with two of her fingers.

"You're remarkable," he said, placing a kiss atop her head. "You always have been."

"But you've found another person," she said, beaming up at him. "I'm so glad, Ken. I've always wanted so badly for you to find someone who would challenge you and love you and drag you from that ridiculous shed."

"Hey," he said, his eyebrows drawing together. "My shed is awesome."

She snorted. "Not even close, buddy."

Reveling in their closeness, he helped his cousin into one of the four-wheelers. True to his word, Kenden fulfilled his duties for another two weeks. And then, he traveled through the ether to locate the other half of his heart.

Kenden walked along the pebbly trail, the rocks crunching under his feet. Eventually, he came to a parting of the trees and stepped onto the stony shore. The beaches in this region of Italy were all made of tiny rocks. So different from many of the sand-splotched coastlines he'd visited recently, trying to find her.

Eventually, he'd located this small island. Only accessible by boat, it had a steep hill in the center lined with green bushes and was rarely visited by humans. It had taken several months for him to track her down but he'd anticipated that before beginning his search. Kenden was nothing if not patient and he'd systematically and methodically tracked her every movement until he'd found her here, in this place of such tranquil beauty.

She stood tall and solemn as she watched the sun tangle with the horizon. Hands thrust in the back pockets of her designer jeans, she wore a loose t-shirt and sneakers. Red hair blazing down her shoulders, she looked comfortable and peaceful. It made him happy, since he wanted peace for his beautiful Evie more than anything.

She knew he was there. Of that, he had no doubt. Evie was powerful and could see many things. Needing to touch her, he slowly approached her lithe body, sliding his hands around her waist. Clutching them across her abdomen, he waited, resting his chin on her shoulder.

She relaxed into him, causing Kenden to thank every god in the heavens. For he was holding her again, something that always drove his system into overload. Blood coursing through his veins, he inhaled her scent, closing his eyes as he exhaled. Love for her, so vibrant and true, pervaded every cell in his muscular body.

There, they stood, watching the gorgeous sunset as it dipped below the darkened ocean. Somewhere along the way, she brought her hands to rest on his forearms. Locked in the gentle embrace, they marveled at the dying embers of the bright orb.

Once the sun set, he buried his face in her hair, nuzzling the side of her neck with his nose. She shivered, the small movement giving him hope that she'd missed him at least half as much as he'd pined for her. The sensation of having her in his arms again was overwhelming.

"I missed you by two days in New Zealand," he said, loving the tiny bumps that rose up on her neck at hearing his voice. "By one day in Japan, and by only hours in North Carolina. When you said you were good at hiding, you weren't kidding, sweetheart."

Her lips twitched, eyes closed as she burrowed into his nestling. He placed a soft kiss on the sensitive skin of her neck and swore he felt her tremble in his embrace.

"Well, you found me," she said, her tone sultry and oh-so-sexy. Kenden felt himself harden in his jeans and clutched her closer. "Now, what are you going to do with me?"

Breathing in the smell of her shampoo, he grasped her closer, unable to imagine ever letting her go again. "I'm thinking I'd like to marry you, make you happy and raise a lot of babies with you."

He'd expected that would start the debate. About futures they couldn't share and things they didn't want. Instead, she tensed but only slightly. Perhaps they were making progress after all.

"If you truly don't want to have children, I won't push you, Evie. I believe that a woman should always have the ability to choose whether motherhood is something she wants or not." Drawing back, he gently spun her so that he could look into her stunning green eyes. "But if you're open to it, I'd love to have babies with you. Ones with red hair and blazing tempers and, yes, with your father's blood. I don't enter into decisions like this lightly. You're my person, Evie. Miranda will always hold such a special place in my heart, but you're the one. I love you, with everything I am and everything I aspire to be."

Those magnificent eyes filled with tears, brimming over until they began to silently slide down her cheeks. Cupping her face, he swept them away with the pads of his thumbs. "Don't cry, baby. This is a good thing. I want to build a life with you."

Evie stared into him, not bothering to hide her tears or the trembling of her chin. He was so honored that she would open herself like that to him, knowing how terribly she detested vulnerability.

Lifting her hand, she palmed his cheek. Running her thumb over his bottom lip, she gave a warbled smile through the emotions that were raging across her face. "I'm terrified," she whispered.

"I know," he said against her thumb, pulsing at her reverent admission. "So am I. I have no idea how to give you a life as exciting and fulfilling as the one you could have here. I'm so scared I'll bore you to death. I'm used to hanging in a dirty old shed for fun. Not exactly fast-paced excitement."

Her smile was blindingly vivid as she chuckled. "Excitement's overrated anyway."

"Yeah?" he asked, grinning back at her.

"Yeah," she said, smoothing her palm over his clean-shaven cheek. "You're so worried that you can't give me an exciting life when all I think about is how miserable I'm going to make you if I let you convince me to marry you."

"That bad, huh?" he teased. "I've seen you in the mornings, and it's no picnic, but I think I can handle it. I also have a pretty good eye for knowing when you need your space. I'll let you have it, Evie. I don't want to smother you. I just want to love you. Forever, if you'll let me."

She breathed a disbelieving laugh. "When you say things like that to me, my heart shatters. What in the hell did I do to deserve you?"

"You suffered so much pain and hurt for so long. It made you undeniably strong, but there's a place, deep inside you, that needs to be loved.

All this time, you thought you were unlovable. It's not true, sweetheart, and I'm going to prove that to you. Every damn day, until you believe me."

"I can't promise that I'll want to have kids, Ken," she said, her irises darting back and forth between his. "I might eventually but I don't want to lie to you. I know you want them so badly."

"I do, but I want you more," he said, needing her to understand how profoundly he loved her. He would sacrifice having children to be with her. Although it was an incredibly tough decision, he knew he'd never come close to loving another woman as much as he loved Evie. "And if that's your decision, I'll accept it. But I hope that one day, once you finally acknowledge how much I love you, you'll change your mind. Because I think you and I would slay parenting together."

The corner of her full lips curved. "We'd kick ass."

Chuckling, he pulled her close and rested his forehead upon hers. "We sure would. We're unstoppable together, Evie."

Staring into him, she sucked in a huge breath. Olive-green eyes swam with fear and contemplation as she regarded him. Finally, when he felt he would die if she didn't speak, she opened her mouth and tore his heart apart.

"I love you too," she whispered.

Breath, slow and steady, departed his lungs in an enormous exhale. "Good grief, woman. Everything with you is a damn struggle. It took you long enough."

"Get ready, big boy," she said, waggling her eyebrows against his brow. "If we're going to do this, it's probably going to be a bumpy ride."

"I wouldn't have it any other way," he said, sliding his arms down her sides to pull her into his body. "I love you so damn much." Lowering his lips to hers, he opened her mouth with them, sliding his tongue inside. Groaning, he twined his fingers in her hair as she tangled her tongue with his. The taste of her, so sweet and sultry, after such a long drought brought him endless pleasure.

There, under the starlit sky and half-risen moon, they devoured each other. Lifting his head, Kenden panted softly as he gazed down at her.

"Ready to go?"

Separating from her quivering body, he stretched his arm across the small distance between them. Opening his hand, he waited.

Evie stared at his exposed palm, the debate at whether to take it warring across her flawless face. Kenden stood firm, willing to wait for centuries if it meant she would place her hand in his at the end.

When they finally left the island, it was together, hand-in-hand, taking the first steps into their shared eternity.

Epilogue

Five years later...

The members of the secret society gathered around the wooden table. Hidden deep within one of the few caves the immortals hadn't located, each participant took their seat. The light from the lone candle in the middle of the table cast a pallid glow upon each of their faces.

"Thank you all for coming," the leader said in his baritone voice. "I have called you all together because we share a common goal: ultimate defeat of the immortal royals and all who are loyal to them. They have grown bold in their arrogance and careless with their heritage. They procreate with children of Crimeous, denigrating the pristine bloodlines that the Universe intended. My aim is only to restore the preeminence of the immortals to the glory they once had. Do you all concur?"

"Aye," came the hushed replies.

"Very well. Please, introduce yourselves. We all must understand each other's strengths and weaknesses if we are to succeed."

"My name is Vadik," one of the men said. "I was Crimeous's second-in-command, behind Rekalb. It is appalling that so many Deamons pledged loyalty to the red-haired usurper. I will stop at nothing to murder her and restore the Deamons to their true dominance, as children of Crimeous. I will always worship Crimeous as Lord. I know you do not share that belief," he said to the leader, "but I am willing to align with you to destroy the Vampyres and the Slayers. I am prepared to overlook our differences to accomplish our common goal."

"Welcome, Vadik," the leader said. "I appreciate your candor and understand the terms of your alliance. I believe that together, we can both accomplish our objectives."

"My name is Sofia," a woman said. Easing the hood of her sweatshirt off her head, black, springy curls bounced in its wake. "The red-haired bitch killed my grandfather, Francesco. I'm sure of it. I've spent the last few years tracking her. Her bastard brother broke into a lab in Houston several years ago, and that led me toward finding the ether. Once I came through, I began studying your world. Since I'm in between realms, I'll do my best to attend these meetings but I'm not always on this side."

Lifting her black cloth backpack to the table, she dumped out several devices. Sliding one across the table to each of the society members, she said, "I'm a competent hacker and have programmed these phones so they can send texts through the ether. If you need me, use these to contact me. And I suggest using them for all of our shared communications moving forward. I've installed spyware and security protection on all of them. The only person in the immortal world even close to being as skilled a hacker as I am is the youngest Vampyre sibling, and he's still leagues behind me. Regardless, I would urge caution."

"Thank you, Sofia," the leader said. "We are honored to have you on our team."

"I am Ananda," another woman said.

"And I am Diabolos," the man beside her said. "As you already know, Vadik was able to transfuse our corpses with Crimeous's blood and bring us back to life. My wife and best friend have betrayed me, and he is extremely loyal to the Slayer queen. I want nothing more than to ensure their demise."

"And the Vampyre royal family has always treated me with extreme disrespect," Ananda said. "The king banished me from the royal compound, and his younger brother put his filthy hands all over my niece, ensuring her degradation. It is a disgrace to her dear parents, and I won't stand for it."

"The Vampyre royals are garbage," a nasty, slightly higher-pitched voice chimed. "Although my husband Camron has forgiven them for causing us extreme embarrassment in public many times over, I do not share his sympathetic heart. My name is Melania, daughter of Falkon and Marika, and I won't stop until I see the bastard Latimus, his tramp bonded mate and his entire family murdered." The woman gave a nod, her silky black hair shining by the light of the flame.

"Understood," the leader said. "You all are valuable members of our society, and I'm pleased that Vadik was able to bring Diabolos and Ananda back."

Heads tilted in agreement.

Straightening his spine, long and firm to accommodate his six-foot, seven-inch height, the leader spoke. "I am Bakari, middle child of King Markdor and Queen Calla, born in between the Warrior and the Princess."

Making eye contact with everyone in the room, he let the admission float between them to have the fullest impact. "My mother and father were told that I perished when I was a babe. As you can all see, I am alive and well. The story of where I've been for a thousand years is best left for another time. Rest assured, I have a deep understanding of both this world and the human world. Over the centuries, some humans became aware of my presence, spurring the creation of the character we now know as Count Dracula. However, they are still too stupid to fathom that our world exists."

"Hey," Sofia muttered.

"Present company excluded," Bakari said with a bend of his head.

"So why do you want to fight?" Vadik asked. "You weren't loyal to Crimeous."

"No," Bakari said, "but I see the future so clearly. The immortals will rise to their full power again, now that Crimeous is gone. The royals of both species are filled with notions of democracy and freedom." His tone was laced with vitriol. "That is not what Etherya intended when she created my parents and Valktor. She wanted imminent rulers who would enforce stability and lawfulness upon her people. As a child of Markdor and Calla, I cannot stand by and watch my siblings ruin the immortal world. Therefore, I will fight to defeat them and rule the kingdom in their place, ensuring that true order is established."

"And will you be able to kill your own family?" Sofia asked.

"The Vampyre sovereigns mean nothing to me. I will systematically decimate each one of them and any subjects who pledge loyalty to them, one by one if I have to. I am something close to a god in the human world and I wish to be so here. I assure you, I know what is best for my people. My arrogance might be offensive to you, but it fuels my desire to fight."

"Fair enough," Sofia said. "We need to be smart but we need to work quickly. Some of us here aren't immortal. That bitch killed my grandfather when I was thirty-one, and I'm almost thirty-eight now. Time's ticking for me. Unfortunately, Crimeous's blood has no effect on a human body, so if I die, you can't bring me back. If you want my help, I would urge you all to get serious."

"Agreed," Bakari said. "Let's plan to meet again in three months' time. By then, we all will have had time to sufficiently brainstorm. After combining the best of our ideas, we will prepare to implement the plan to ensure the ruin of the immortal monarchs and their families. Every last one."

Eyes met, expressing acknowledgement, as they cemented their allegiance to each other.

Upon exiting the cave, they destroyed it, vowing to leave no trace behind.

Evie sat at the vanity in her bedroom, smoothing cream onto her just-washed face. Her husband entered the room, looking tired yet gorgeous as always. Sauntering toward her, he bent to kiss her hair.

"Hey, baby. How was your day?"

"Good," she said, rubbing the lotion into her hands. "Aron and I did the orientation for the new Vampyres that are moving over from Valeria. It will be nice to get some aristocratic blood on Takelia," she said, referencing the compound that was reverently named after the strong Vampyre warrior who'd perished in one of their battles. "We have a lot of laborers and prisoners but having some stuffy aristocrats to annoy is always so much fun." Her eyes sparkled in the reflection.

"There's my wife," he said, removing his shirt. The muscles in his abs seemed to ripple, causing Evie to clench her thighs together. Good lord, but her husband was *hot*. "Always looking for mischief."

"And I always seem to find it," she said, smiling at him in the mirror. "How was your day?"

"Good," Kenden said, pulling off his pants one leg at a time. "The police force on each compound is great, but the recruits at Lynia need a bit more training. We'll get there. Now that Latimus has three kids, I find myself covering more than ever."

"You should tell him if it's too much."

"You know I don't mind," he said, coming to stand behind her. Placing his hands on her shoulders, he gently began massaging them.

Studying his chocolate irises in the reflection, she sensed his anxiousness.

"What?" she asked, although she could read the images in his mind. *Shit.* She should've known by now that the powerful Slayer commander knew everyone's schedule down to the last detail.

"I was going to tell you," she said, her lips forming a pout.

"Is that so?" he asked, lifting his brows. "Because imagine my surprise when Sadie bounced up to me today, pregnant as a jaybird, and asked me if I was coming with you to the appointment tomorrow."

"Why would you come with me to a GYN appointment?" she snapped, trying to tamp down the temper that still seemed to violently flare even though she tried her best to live by her Slayer half.

"Um, maybe to accompany you to Uteria to see Miranda and Sadie? You know I don't get there as much anymore. Now that we live on Takelia, and Sadie and Nolan have taken our old house, I always look for opportunities to spend time there."

"And maybe visit your shed?" she asked, arching a scarlet brow.

"Quiet about my shed, woman," he said, scrunching his face at her. "It was my only love until you came along."

Chuckling, she regarded his reflection. Rising, she turned to face him and slide her arms around his neck.

"Oh, no, sweetheart," he said, those perfect white teeth flashing. "You're not seducing me into letting this go."

"Letting what go?" she asked innocently, moving her palm down his body until it clutched his hardened shaft.

"Evie," he said, a warning in his tone.

Closing her lids, she dematerialized his underwear. As he stood magnificently naked before her, she dropped to her knees. Opening her mouth, she placed the engorged head of his cock over her lips and drew him deep inside.

"You're not off the hook," he growled, thrusting his fingers into her thick hair. Groaning up at him, she purred.

He jutted his hips into her until he was screaming her name. Popping from her wet mouth, he lifted her to the bed and impaled her body, naked beneath her robe. Together, they rode each other, clutching sweaty skin, until they collapsed in a heap of spent desire.

"My god, woman," he said into the soft comforter, his face buried beside her head. "If you want to kill me before I can interrogate you, fine. I surrender. You're an animal."

Giving a sated chuckle, she ran her nails over his back, causing him to shiver. "You don't need to interrogate me. Just trust your wife. I do think that was required in our vows, no?"

Lifting his head, he gazed into her, placing a soft kiss on her lips. "I do trust you," he said, running his fingers through the hair at her temple. "But I had to beg you to marry me for four years. When you finally relented, I asked you to consider having kids, and you said you were open. I thought you might be going to see Sadie to possibly discuss that tomorrow. And if you are, I'm sad that you wouldn't tell me."

Inhaling a deep breath, she studied him. This beautiful man whom she was so lucky to call hers. He always challenged her to be her best self, and perhaps, in this instance, she hadn't been as forthright as she could've been.

"I'm sorry," she whispered, lifting her hand to rub his cheek with the pads of her fingers. "I was going to discuss possibly removing my IUD during the appointment tomorrow." Kenden's eyes lit with pleasure. "*Possibly*," she cautioned. "And this is exactly why I didn't tell you. You get all revved up about things and move too fast. I mean, for god's sake, you asked me to move in with you when we'd only been fucking for a month."

"But you wanted to," he said, nipping at her lips. "Admit it."

"Beside the point," she said, standing her ground. "I knew that if I told you I was considering getting pregnant, you'd have me knocked-up and on bed rest within the week."

He chortled, the sound bursting from his throat. "Is it that bad?"

"Terrible," she teased. "I can't keep up with you."

"I know I push you, baby," he said, rubbing the tip of her nose with his. "It's because I love you so damn much. You have no idea how often I think about the children we could have. The girls would have red hair and tiny freckles, and the boys would be so strong. We'd raise them to be good men, worthy of loving a woman as resilient and beautiful as their mother one day."

Evie felt the prick of tears behind her eyes. Not surprising, since the man had always possessed the ability to tear down every wall she'd erected. "Goddamnit," she whispered. "Why do you have to say stuff like that? It reminds me of how amazing you are and how I'll never deserve you."

"You deserve it all, sweetheart," he said, kissing her again. "But if you're not ready, I won't push."

"Right," she said, rolling her eyes.

"I won't," he said, his grin wide. "But you'll decide to have babies with me one day. I know it. Until then, we can just keep having mind-blowing sex. I'm one-hundred percent okay with that."

Lips twitching, she caressed his hair. "I'm going to tell her to remove the IUD."

She'd never seen him smile so broadly. "Are you sure?"

"I'm sure," she said, the words warbled since her throat seemed to be closing up.

"You're so incredible," he said softly, nuzzling into her. "I'm so in love with you, Evie. Thank you for everything you've given me. I know it's not easy for you."

"Are you seriously thanking me right now?" she asked, not comprehending how he couldn't see that she was the lucky one. Grasping his face between her hands, she spoke words so genuine and true. "You saved me, Ken. Don't you understand? You challenged me to become the person that I never even fathomed I could be. You saved my life in so many ways. I love you with my entire soul."

Lowering his lips to hers, he moaned as their tongues warred and mated. Their life together wasn't easy and would never be perfect but it was *theirs*. Something they'd built concurrently that they both so reverently cherished. Although she knew there were unseen threats looming on the horizon, Evie held fast to hope. She'd learned that after tranquility, there was always more hardship. It was the yin to the yang of life. Living for eternity, they were sure to experience as many peaks as they would valleys.

But with Kenden as her partner, she knew she would always choose light over darkness. Though she may be tempted, his love, so steadfast and sure, would always direct her to make the right choice. There was comfort in that, along with the reassurance that she'd do everything in her power to make him happy. Snuggling into her husband, she enjoyed the bliss of the moment, understanding how precious it truly was.

Acknowledgments

Finishing this book was bittersweet. Although I'm not done with the series, I knew that I would take a break after Book 4 to evaluate the next steps on this awesome, winding and sometimes scary journey of being an author. Tears streamed down my face as I wrote the letter from Evie to Kenden and I hope that you all feel as emotionally connected to these characters as I do! Thanks to each and every one of you for taking time out of your busy lives to read these books.

Several friends whom I've yet to mention have been extremely supportive and I'd like to shout them out.

Thanks to Eva for loving the series and saying that it should be made into a Netflix show. I can only hope, sister! Thanks to Liz and Sharan for sending me pictures of my books as they lounged on the beach. To Kristen for snapping a pic from a plane. To Nikki for the pic of her reading in FL. To Judy for texting me from a plane while she was crying reading TES & wondering if the guy next to her thought she was nuts...haha! To Tara for showing me the pic of her reading TEoH at jury duty. That one was great!

Thanks to Tara in CT (yes, I know two awesome Tara B.'s ☺) for leaving a review even though it's not always easy. Reviews are so important to authors and I appreciate everyone who takes the time to leave one.

Thanks to Colleen and Misty, my OGs who read and reviewed these books. Thanks to Susan for loving steamy books like I do, even though we grew up in BM...hee hee! BM book signing, here we come!

Thanks to the book bloggers who've taken a chance on me over the past few months: Rose, Karen Jo, Bonnie, SP and so many others. You'll never know how thrilled I am when you message me that you like my books. It's absolutely amazing!

Thanks to the awesome people I've meet through the #WritingCommunity on Twitter. Special shout out to amazing author Sarah Bailey who also writes steamy novels. Our discussions about our mothers reading our books are hilarious!

Thanks to Megan McKeever for the wonderful editing, as always. I feel so lucky to have found you!

Wishing you all a wonderful summer and remember that even through our flaws and mistakes, we all still have so much to give. If Kenden can love Evie for who she is inside, then we all can love ourselves too! Be kind to yourself and to others. Share your wisdom. Laugh freely and choose positivity over all. Hoping you find your Zen until we meet again!

The Impassioned Choice

Etherya's Earth, Book 5

By

Rebecca Hefner

This book is a work of fiction. Names, characters, places and incidents are the product of the author's imagination and are used fictitiously. Any resemblance to actual events, locales or persons, living or dead, is coincidental.

Copyright © 2020 by Rebecca Hefner. All rights reserved, including the right to reproduce, distribute or transmit in any form or by any means.

Cover Design: Author CD Gorri
Editor: Megan McKeever
Proofreader: Bryony Leah

Oh, Heden, how I love you—and I know everyone else does too. I'm so happy to finally give you the spotlight you deserve. Thanks for always making us laugh and for being such a sexy, warm-hearted geek.

Prologue

A few years before the Awakening...

Queen Calla groaned upon the bed, her shrill wail reminiscent of the screech owls that howled from the tall trees surrounding Astaria's castle. Clutching his bonded's hand, King Markdor whispered soothing words into the shell of her ear.

Her chapped lips formed an almost silent plea as she stared at him with her ice-blue eyes. "Why?"

"I don't know, sweetheart," Markdor said, touching his lips to her forehead. "The pain will be gone soon. I promise."

Vampyres, with their self-healing abilities, usually had seamless births, and the queen's struggles caused alarm to everyone in the anxiety-laden chamber.

"Here, my queen," one of the Slayera soothsayers said, approaching Calla and placing a fresh cloth upon her forehead. "This will help."

Several hours into the birth, Markdor had sent soldiers racing to the Slayera compound of Uteria in search of help. Slayera were prone to injury and did not possess self-healing abilities, and they had standard birth practices to alleviate a woman's suffering. The soldiers had returned with two midwives and two Slayera soothsayers, anxious to help their sister tribe's royals.

So far, their efforts were in vain.

Calla's battered body arched upon the bed. A scream tore from her throat by the fist of severe agony. One of the Slayera midwives yelled, "Push!" and a raven-haired baby began to crown. Markdor observed, stunned, as the child exited his bonded's body, blue veins stark under his pallid skin.

The midwife wrapped the child in a blanket, and one of the soothsayers rushed his body to the next room. Calla relaxed upon the bed, unaware of the commotion next door as her broken body attempted to recover.

"Where's my baby?" she called, lifting weak arms. "I need to hold him."

"He's with the caretakers, darling," Markdor soothed, swiping the wet strands of dark hair from her sweat-soaked temple.

"Please. He needs me. Bring him to me, Markdor."

With a sense of foreboding, Markdor reluctantly left the queen's side. In his heart, he knew. Every step toward the adjoining room was a step closer to learning of his child's death. Entering the room, he observed the flurry of activity as the midwives tried to resuscitate the baby.

Several agonizing minutes later, Markdor held up his hand. "Enough," he commanded softly. "We must let him go." Gently, he gathered the child in his arms and transported him to Calla. His wife held the newborn's small face to her breast, overcome with tears.

"Bakari," she whispered, pink lips against her baby's dark hair. "I will always love you."

Eventually, one of the soothsayers took Bakari from Calla's embrace, promising Markdor to prepare his body for the proper farewell to the Passage the young prince deserved. Once downstairs in the dark reaches of the castle, the Slayer soothsayers addressed the Vampyre archivists that had gathered around Bakari's body.

"He has the mark of the hidden prophecy," the eldest soothsayer said, his tone solemn and wary. With shaking hands, the man exposed the child's inner thigh where a deep pentagram was branded. A five-pointed star within a circle, the symbol elicited fear in the wise men.

"No one knows of the hidden prophecy," one of the Vampyre archivists said. "We chose to omit it from the manuals. Should we inform the king and queen?"

"No," the soothsayer said. "I will dispose of the body and rid it from this world. It is an abomination. We will prepare a coffin for the royals and let them believe the baby is inside. It is the only way."

"Treason," the youngest soothsayer whispered.

"Necessary," the eldest soothsayer replied. Wrapping the child in a blanket, he placed him in a wooden box.

Once all plans were cemented, the eldest soothsayer rode his horse, fast as the wind, to the ether at the edge of the immortal realm. Clutching the box to his treacherous body, he waded through the thick substance to the human world.

The soothsayer buried the child in a shallow grave at the base of an ancient oak tree. Beleaguered by guilt, he said a prayer to Etherya over the solemn site before reentering the immortal world. Upon returning to the soothsayer chambers at Uteria, he reached for a blank scroll and began to write:

Addition to the Hidden Prophecy of the Vampyre Offspring
Be it known that a prince was born to King Markdor and Queen Calla, third in line to the throne behind Prince Sathan and Prince Latimus. Prince Bakari bore the symbol of the hidden prophecy, which states that a marked child, born to a Vampyre royal, will bring death and destruction to Etherya's creatures. The child perished at birth and was transported to the human world, where he was buried with care. Through these actions, the realm is relieved of the burden of this prophecy.

Peace be to all of Etherya's creatures.

When the ink was dry, the soothsayer rolled the scroll tight and removed the loose stones in the wall. Crawling through the small, dark tunnel, he emerged on the other side into a cold, dry chamber. With finality, he deposited the scroll amongst the other secret prophecies and recordings.

Making sure to secure the rocks tightly back in the wall, the man exhaled a breath and let go of his nefarious deeds, for he knew soothsayers and archivists must only share the truths that would help Etherya's people. It was a sacred responsibility, of which few could comprehend the gravity. Secure in that belief, he returned to his life, the events pushed to the dark recesses of his memory.

Several days later, Markdor held Calla, grief emanating from her exhausted body.

"I don't know how to tell Sathan and Latimus about Bakari," she mumbled into Markdor's chest.

"We have time, sweetheart. We'll tell them when they're older."

"Okay," she whispered.

Only a few years later, the death of Markdor and Calla's third child would be lost to history when King Valktor struck down the Vampyre royals during the Awakening. All energy was dedicated to the War of the Species and the emerging threat of Crimeous. Bakari's presence in their world was a forgotten fairy tale, one that ceased to be told after several centuries. There were many other dark forces that took precedence in Etherya's realm.

Which is why no one in the immortal realm was aware that shortly after Bakari's burial, a woman found his shallow grave. She dug up the child and discovered the mark on his leg. Using powers that were enigmatic and potent, the woman brought the child to life.

But that is a story for another book...

Chapter 1

Six years after the immortals defeated Crimeous...

Sofia Morelli stood atop the old stone bridge, watching the river flow beneath. A narrow boat approached, slicing through the water, two men inside working in tandem to circulate the oars. Through the water they rotated, again and again, in a synchronized dance of skill and speed.

Neither of the men noticed her as they passed under the bridge, and that suited Sofia just fine. She'd learned long ago that being inconspicuous held great value. It was one of her more polished skills, helping her navigate through life on a journey with one singular purpose: to avenge her murdered grandfather.

She'd learned other skills along the way. Skills that made her invaluable in the Secret Society's quest to eradicate the immortals from the planet she called home. Before she exhaled her dying breath, she was determined to succeed.

The large man approached, his movements sure but unhurried. As she stared at the sunlit water glistening from the fresh morning sun, she waited.

"Everything is in place?" he asked, his baritone voice latent with assumed authority and the hint of arrogance that always slightly nagged her.

"Yes," Sofia said, nodding to the water. "Surveillance is embedded at all seven compounds including Takelia, although it wasn't easy. The red-haired bitch sees everything, and since that compound is new, it's extremely technologically secure."

"It's imperative that we're able to access the servers at all compounds. If you need more time—"

"I don't," Sofia said, turning to face him and sliding the hood of her sweatshirt to rest on her shoulders. Dark, springy curls bounced in its wake, falling just past her shoulder blades. Lifting her chin, she spoke with confidence. "I told you, I'm the most competent hacker you're going to find, human or immortal. The youngest Vampyre royal thinks he understands tech, but he has no idea. I'll run circles around him before he even understands what hit him. It's pretty late in the game for you to start doubting me, Bakari."

"I don't doubt you, Sofia," he said, his tone sincere. "We only have the element of surprise once. It's imperative we take advantage of it. The immortals are most powerful when they band together. We saw this when they defeated Crimeous. It's best for us to attack them separately, as they navigate their lives, before they become aware of us."

"And once they're aware?" she asked, arching a raven-dark brow.

"Then it will be all-out war," he said, solemn. "So, let's seize the opportunity of their ineptitude while we can."

"Agreed," she said, blinking up at him as she nodded.

"Once you gather the intel we need, we will contact the others to strategize our attack. You'll supply us with their schedules, daily routines and information regarding where we are likely to do the most damage."

Sofia's heart squeezed as it always did when she thought about the children of the immortal royals. Although she hated the red-haired Slayer-Deamon, the children of the immortal sovereigns were innocent. Bakari was intent on killing them as well—a part of his plan she vehemently disagreed with.

"The children aren't responsible for the sins of their parents," she said, knowing her argument would fall on deaf ears but determined to try. "Tordor is only seven, and Adelyn is barely six years old. Jack isn't even seventeen yet. Your sister has a young daughter and is pregnant. You really wish to kill her? Perhaps she can be turned."

"We've discussed this, Sofia," he said, his tone resigned. "Although Arderin lives in the human world and is less of a threat than the others, she chose to bond and procreate with a child of Crimeous. It's disgraceful. Etherya did not place us upon the Earth to denigrate bloodlines. There is an order to the world, and I will see it restored. This means innocents will perish. You must get over your childish wish to save those you deem worthy. Calinda and the spawn Arderin carries in her belly have Crimeous's malicious blood, the self-healing strength of my parents, and the power bestowed upon Valktor as Etherya's own child, created from her womb. They are abominations."

Sofia sighed, her strict Catholic upbringing precluding her from wanting to contemplate murdering a child, no matter how great the possibility of its future evil machinations. "It goes against everything I was taught."

"And what about your grandfather's murder?" he asked, a slight hint of anger lacing the words. "Did you forget that he was gutted in his own home and left for dead?"

Rage flared inside her, as it always did when she thought of the death of her beloved grandfather Francesco. Evie had squashed his light with her blood-soaked hands, and Sofia would ensure she paid for it...a thousand times over, until she begged for mercy.

"No," she snapped, feeling her nostrils flare. "I'll never forget. She destroyed the one person I had left in the world. There are consequences for that."

"Good," he said with a tilt of his head. "Clutch onto your hate. Use it to tamp down your feelings of mercy. They have no place in this mission."

"I will." Resolved, she pulled the folded papers from the large pouch in her sweatshirt, situated above her abdomen. "Here is the report on the human woman you asked me to investigate." When Bakari reached for the folder, Sofia held it back. "Tread lightly. She only *appears* human. I'm convinced she's something else entirely. Her blood runs thick with the secrets of her Native American and Creole ancestors. Tales of her presence have circulated through the parish where she lives for centuries, although she appears to only be in her thirties. If you go to Louisiana to surveil her, be careful."

"Thank you," he said, grasping the sheets and placing them into the black bag that sat upon his broad shoulder. "And where will you be over the next few months as you gather the intel we need?"

"I have a place here in Florence, but I also keep my flat in New York. Both are equipped with everything I need, but I believe Italy is where I'm supposed to be right now." Closing her eyes, she lifted her face to the blue sky. "I feel him here, as if he were by my side." Slowly, she exhaled a reverent breath.

"You will avenge him, Sofia." Bakari cupped her upper arm in a show of support. "We all will have our revenge. Stay firm in that knowledge. Call me when you have enough to move forward."

"I will."

With one last nod of ascent, the massive Vampyre drew his coat closed and turned, his loafered feet quiet against the stone walkway of the bridge.

Once he was out of sight, Sofia pivoted back toward the river, resting her forearms against the rocky surface of the bridge wall. Lacing her fingers, she prayed to God, asking for His help in avenging her grandfather, and asking His forgiveness for the carnage that would result from her quest to accomplish that goal.

Chapter 2

Two months later...

Heden sat in front of the menagerie of screens that lined his desk in the tech room. Absently clicking the mouse with his index finger, he studied the traffic analysis. He'd run the report this morning to ensure all of the compounds' servers were communicating effectively. Scanning the data, his eyes narrowed.

Nothing seemed out of the ordinary, but Heden had the distinct feeling something was awry. Scrolling through, he read the information that had been transmitted—mostly schedules of activities on the various compounds. Security trainings held by Kenden and Latimus, council meetings held by Sathan and Miranda, open health clinics run by Sadie and Nolan. All of it was very...*normal*.

And yet Heden felt the tiny hairs on the back of his neck prickle. Rubbing his bearded chin, his fastidious brain clicked into overdrive. He'd let his goatee grow into a beard a few years ago, wanting a change, although he kept it trim and groomed, noting the ladies seemed to appreciate his "manscaping." Directing the tiny arrow around the screen, he opened the task manager and catalogued the usage. The computer was running several tasks: Bluetooth applications, the webcam app he'd recently installed, a cybersecurity program, antivirus... The list went on and on. All seemed to be using the appropriate amount of CPU and memory.

Heden's finger froze above the scroll wheel of the mouse when the arrow stopped over a program he'd never seen and certainly hadn't installed: **SSHost.exe**. The program was using slightly more CPU and memory than the other programs, but nothing out of the ordinary. Opening his browser, Heden performed a search, which returned results for several other software constructs but nothing titled **SSHost.exe**.

Not recognizing it, he highlighted the program and ended the task. It disappeared from the screen but not from Heden's busy brain.

Leaning back in the desk chair, he sucked in a large breath, staring at the ceiling as he threaded his hands behind his head. Heden knew Evie had installed some updates at Takelia recently. The Slayer-Deamon was more tech-savvy than the rest of the royal family due to her time spent in the human world, so perhaps she'd instituted something to help with cybersecurity there.

A slight bit of alarm gnawed at his gut. Deciding he wanted to speak to Evie himself, he grabbed his phone to shoot her a text.

Heden: Hey, Evie. I want to check out the computer systems at Takelia. You around tomorrow?

Three dots appeared, blinking as she responded.

Evie: Sure. One p.m. is good. Or you can attend the fundraising lunch Miranda's forcing on me. It's like death and torture rolled into one, but worse.

Heden breathed a laugh. The daughter of the Dark Lord Crimeous and Miranda's mother, Princess Rina, definitely had a biting sense of humor. Heden loved her for it, as he thought his two older brothers quite stuffy and serious. It was refreshing to have someone else with a sense of humor in their extended family.

Heden: Sounds fun, but I'll be painting my toenails. And washing my hair. And something else I haven't made up yet. See you at one p.m. at the main house at Takelia.

Evie: Yup. Bring a defibrillator to shock me awake from the boredom. See ya tomorrow.

Heden closed out the remaining programs and pulled up the open port checker application. It would run silently in the background while he headed to pick up Tordor from school. Sathan and Miranda were both occupied at Uteria, and Tordor attended the elementary school on the Vampyre compound of Astaria. Since Heden lived on the compound, he'd offered to pick up his nephew and hang with him until his parents returned that evening.

Tordor's schedule was also comprised of many weekend outings and activities with children at other immortal compounds. Miranda and Sathan wanted to ensure that as the first Slayer-Vampyre hybrid, the prince was immersed in all facets of the kingdom. The immortal king and queen wanted their son to represent a new era for their realm, where they shared one world and the compounds were united.

Unable to shake his unrest, Heden's mind churned as he traveled the paved walkway from Astaria's main castle where he resided and maintained his precious tech room. The school was several blocks away, giving him time to ponder as the afternoon sun wafted over his skin. By the goddess, the heat from the rays felt amazing. Now that Vampyres had been able to tolerate sunlight for several years, living in the daylight had become normal again, but Heden remembered darker days. Times when their world had been plagued by the War of the Species and the maliciousness of Crimeous. There had been so much destruction; so much death. The peace that enveloped their world now was blissful and serene. *And possibly dangerous*, a voice in his mind whispered.

Heden stared at the sidewalk, his sneakered feet soft on the concrete. Had they been existing under a false blanket of complacency? Were there still unforeseen threats to their world? Someone who wanted to hack their technology and attack them from within?

Wracking his brain, he tried to think of a possible enemy. Darkrip and Evie had burned Crimeous's body in the Purges of Methesda. The Dark Lord would never grace their world again. Perhaps one of his followers who was left behind? Latimus and Kenden appeared confident they had captured all of the Deamons loyal to Crimeous in the months following his death. Was it possible they had miscalculated?

His thoughts were interrupted by his nephew, who waved at him as he trailed over.

"Hi, Uncle Heden."

"Hey, buddy. How was school?"

"Fine," Tordor said, shrugging.

"Just fine?"

The kid stared up at him, squinting from the sun. Not wanting him to burn his eyes, Heden squatted down.

"Did you send her the note?"

"Yeah," Tordor said, clutching the straps of his backpack as he kicked the ground. "I saw her read it by the cubby, but she didn't say anything to me afterward."

Heden gave the boy a tender smile. "Well, you're a pretty intimidating suitor. The prince of our little realm. She might be scared to tell you she likes you back."

"Maybe," Tordor said, studying Heden with his forest-green irises, the same color as Miranda's. "Or she might like someone else."

"No way, buddy," Heden said, ruffling Tordor's thick black hair, a mirror image of his father's. "You just have to woo her. Women want to be pursued. One day, I'll tell you about your Uncle Latimus and how I helped him win over your Aunt Lila. They owe it all to me." He winked conspiratorially.

"You've already told me, Uncle Heden. Like, a thousand times. You tell the same stories over and over. I think you need to get some new ones."

"Out of the mouths of babes," Heden muttered, standing and placing his hand on Tordor's shoulder. "Thanks for reminding me how boring my life is."

"You're not boring. Just old."

Heden threw his head back, laughter bellowing from deep within. "That I am, kid."

Although his nephew was young, he spoke the truth. Heden had been living the same life for centuries now. Sometimes, he would study his siblings, all immersed in their loving families, and marvel at how much they'd changed. Sathan, Latimus, and Arderin were all parents now, with responsibilities beyond anything Heden had ever comprehended. They'd built something unbreakable and poignant with mates who were their equals and whom they loved with their entire souls.

Heden loved his siblings dearly, but lately, he'd begun to feel like a third wheel. On the nights he shared family dinners with Sathan or Latimus at their homes, he would sometimes sense they were ready for him to leave so they could begin their nightly rituals, in which he wasn't included. He would take the train back to Astaria, observe the empty seat beside him and wonder if there would ever come a time in his life when he would perform those rituals. Would there be a mate and children who needed him to give them a bath, read them a bedtime story, and hold them in his arms as they fell asleep? Or was he destined to be the perpetual outsider, always welcome in his siblings' lives but never truly belonging?

Realizing Tordor's comments had stirred up the errant thoughts, Heden tamped them down, wanting to focus on spending time with the tyke. They walked back to the castle, chatting along the way in the warm, breezy day.

Heden had a soft spot for Tordor, as he did all his nieces and nephews, but a lot rested on the shoulders of the little heir. He was the symbol of their combined kingdom. Heden was no parenting expert, and Miranda and Sathan did a great job with their son, but that was a lot of pressure for a seven-year-old. Heden felt it important the prince just got to be a kid once in a while.

"Let's have a mud fight outside the barracks. Yesterday's rain left an awesome puddle of sludge we can wrestle in."

Tordor seemed hesitant as they entered the large doors to the main house. "I don't know. Mom was really upset last time we mud-wrestled. She yelled for, like, a really long time."

"She doesn't scare me," Heden said, already anticipating how furious Miranda would be when she discovered them both covered in mud. Last time they'd taken advantage of the thick, wet dirt, they had trudged it all over the expensive carpets. Their sweet housekeeper Glarys almost had a heart attack, and Heden had offered to clean every last drop. Then, he'd hired the cleaning company run by old man Withers and his three stunning daughters. They'd giggled as they cleaned, Heden helping while he ogled their luscious backsides. It certainly hadn't seemed like punishment. He'd gotten to know them *very* well that day.

"C'mon, kid," he said, pulling off his shirt and tossing it on the tile of the foyer. "Race ya."

Tordor hesitated, gaze darting around the room, and then threw down his backpack and yanked off his shirt too. Their laughter echoed down the hallway as they ran toward the barracks.

"Heden! I swear to god, you're freaking dead, you hear me?" Miranda's voice boomed throughout the castle, magnified by the acoustics of the foyer. "If my son is covered in so much as one *speck* of dirt, I'll strangle you myself!"

"Chill, Miranda," Heden said, strolling into the room as if he had all the time in the world and wasn't being stared down by an angry-as-hell woman. Rubbing the towel against his wet hair, he felt some drops land on the top of the clean t-shirt he'd just donned. "Tordor's in the bath and he's fine. We were wrestling. You know, something kids do? He can't save the kingdom if he doesn't learn to have a little fun."

Miranda's nostrils flared as she fisted her hands on her hips. Man, she was spitting mad. Heden waited for puffs of smoke to exit her ears.

"The hallway is covered in dirt."

"Is it?" He gave her his best expression of shock. "My goodness. It did rain yesterday..." Heden rubbed his chin and looked to the ceiling.

"I swear, you have the maturity of a ten-year-old." Reddened cheeks sat under her silky black bob, swishing as she crossed her arms over her chest. "He needs to be doing his homework."

"He will, Miranda," Heden said, grasping her forearm and pulling her into his firm embrace. "And how much homework can a first grader have anyway? Please, don't be mad at me." He pursed his lips and blinked rapidly, his face a mask of contrition.

"Damn it, you're hopeless," she said, breathing a laugh as she palmed his face. "Why can't I stay mad at you?"

"Because you love me to pieces. When are you leaving my idiot brother so I can properly court you and have you as my own?"

Miranda squeezed him, chuckling as she shook her head and detached from his embrace. "You couldn't handle me, buddy. Believe me."

Heden smiled as Sathan entered the room. "Thanks, bro. My son is behind on his homework, and my wife is livid. You're a real team player."

"I do what I can," Heden said, shrugging at his oldest brother. "I'll get the carpets cleaned, I promise. Tell Glarys I'll hire the cleaners again."

"I think we all know why you want to hire old man Withers' daughters again," Sathan muttered, placing his arm around Miranda's shoulders.

"I mean, if they find me irresistible, who am I to argue?"

Miranda gave one of her throaty laughs. "You're too much, Heden. Maybe you could actually settle down with one of them and stop the revolving door of endless women you seem to surround yourself with."

"I am not a one-woman man, Miranda. You should know that by now. Unless you leave Sathan, of course."

"I'm going to rip his throat out," Sathan growled to Miranda.

"Okay, boys. Enough. I've got to get my dirty kid clean, finished with homework and fed within the next two hours." She shot Heden a good-natured glare.

"Well, have fun with that. I'm out. See you old farts later." Heden snapped Sathan with his towel, causing his brother to charge him, and ran like hell from the foyer.

Once in his basement room, he finished toweling off his thick black hair and threw the cloth in the hamper. After toying around on his laptop for a while, he prepped for bed and relaxed into the soft sheets.

Placing his hands under his head, he stared at the darkened ceiling, recalling the program that had been running on the server. He hoped like hell it was something Evie had installed. Sighing, he rolled over. He'd know soon enough.

As he drifted off, Heden contemplated his earlier conversation with Miranda. She was always trying to get him to settle down and find a woman he could make a commitment to. The problem was, he'd never once met a woman who even came close to stoking that sentiment in him. His brothers' mates were amazing, both of them perfect matches for his strong, willful siblings. Heden couldn't begin to imagine finding a woman who came close to the magnificence of Miranda and Lila.

Having a reputation as a notorious flirt, Heden had always reveled in the attention he got from women. It was something that came easily to him, and he'd never lacked companionship. No, that was very easy to find.

What he had lacked all these centuries was *connection*. The sizzling spark of energy he observed between his brothers and their mates. The passion Miranda and Lila employed when challenging their husbands to be the best versions of themselves. The heat of their arguments, and the blazing desire when they forgave each other. Those feelings were so foreign to Heden.

It was as if it was all too...*easy* somehow. He couldn't recall a female who had turned him down once he'd truly set his sights on her. They would usually feign disinterest at first, in an attempt to appear coy, but he read people well. Once he gained their acquiescence and consent, Heden never felt guilty about not making a commitment. He was always sure to be completely honest with every woman he pursued that he was only looking for short-term fun. Perhaps some felt they could change his mind, but he knew that was unlikely. Heden enjoyed his freedom and the ease of his life.

Didn't he?

Gnawing on his bottom lip, he rotated onto his back, unable to sleep. Was the companionship enough without having the connection? It had been for so many centuries. What if he was ready for something more?

Deciding he needed to get laid, he huffed a breath and told himself to go to sleep. He'd hire the Withers girls tomorrow. Hanging with them would make him feel better. Perhaps if he convinced himself of that, it would stop feeling like a lie deep in his gut.

Chapter 3

The next day, Heden hopped on one of the trains that connected the seven compounds of the immortal realm and headed to Takelia. The new community had a more modern feel than the other compounds since it was built over the last few years. As he exited the train to the main town's square, he felt anxious under the early afternoon sun, ready to prove yesterday's unknown computer program was a benign anomaly that was probably mistakenly installed by Evie.

Children's laughter surrounded him as he bent to catch the ball that rolled to a stop by his sneakered feet. Picking it up, he threw it back to the kids.

"Thanks, mister," one of the girls called, the dark space between her two missing front teeth endearing.

"Sure thing, kid." A small waft of longing rushed over his skin, so slight he barely felt it. But it was there, gently coaxing him. Heden would love to have a few rugrats one day... *Many centuries down the road*, he reminded himself.

Two or three centuries at least.

Or maybe sooner...

The longing was replaced by a rush of anxiety.

Or...maybe some people were just destined to remain untethered and have lots sexy shenanigans along the way.

"Not you too," a sultry voice said behind him. "My husband has kids on the brain twenty-four-seven, and now I find you staring at the little beasts with stars in your eyes. They're not that cute. Believe me."

Chuckling, Heden tore his eyes from the children and turned to face Evie, enveloping her in a warm embrace. "Nah, they're little heathens. My bachelor card is firmly intact."

"Right," Evie muttered, studying him with her olive-green gaze. "You, my friend, are full of shit. Or did you forget I can read the thoughts flying through that ridiculously intelligent brain of yours?"

"Eh, I was just thinking about the future," he said, drawing back and shrugging. "The *very* distant future."

"Well, thank god," she said, linking her arm with his as they paced toward the castle on the corner of the main square. "You were my only holdout on the lovey-dovey shit. Let's keep it that way."

"*I'm* not the one who married Kenden," Heden said, ascending the marble stairs and grasping the golden handle attached to one of the large mahogany doors that led inside the mansion. "You knew what you were in for with that man. He's the poster child for commitment."

"I know," she sighed, lifting her hands in a defeated gesture. "I tried to fight it, but he's just so damn sexy, I was doomed from the start. It's extremely annoying. I still haven't forgiven myself for falling for him like a lovesick teenager." She waggled her auburn eyebrows. "But he's so good in bed. I mean, last night, we were trying this new thing—"

"Okay," Heden said, breathing an awkward laugh. "I think we're crossing the TMI line here."

She scrunched her features at him. "*Boring.* I thought you'd be one of the immortals who understood great sex. Oh well," she said flippantly, flicking her hair over her shoulder and entering the castle.

"How was the fundraising lunch with Miranda?"

"Fine," she said, rolling her eyes slightly. "She's so good at getting the old geezers to fork over their dough. It's not really my forte but, as governor of Takelia, I have to attend. I think I might have dozed off a time or two."

Heden chuckled. "The money will go to good use. Miranda and Sathan are dead set on creating a utopia for the realm. They won't stop until every subject is fat and happy."

"Seriously. My half-sister is a saint. I think she got all of our mother's good genes. And maybe Darkrip got a few, but he's still a bit salty."

"Arderin keeps him in check. He's so smitten with her. Our last visit was great. Your brother sure can chug a beer." Heden smiled as he recalled how he'd dragged Darkrip to a bar in the suburbs of Los Angeles, where Arderin was finishing up her medical residency training, and informed the Slayer-Deamon he needed a night off from playing "Mr. Mom." That comment hadn't gone over so well, and Darkrip had sullenly accompanied him to the establishment filled with a live DJ and blaring human music.

After a few beers, his sister's husband had loosened up and actually had some fun. Unfortunately, they'd lost track of time. Arderin was waiting for them at two a.m., hands fisted on her hips, shooting daggers from her ice-blue irises when they returned home. She'd seemed fine the next morning, so Heden assumed Darkrip had made it up to her with lots of apologies...and some other things he *definitely* didn't want to imagine in any context about his sister.

"What are you smiling about?" Evie asked.

"Just remembering the visit. Do you have any plans to go see them?"

"No, but I probably should before Ken knocks me up." Her full red lips formed a gorgeous smile. Although she professed that children annoyed her, her desire to add to their family was palpable. "I haven't been in the human world for a while and do miss it."

Evie had spent the last eight centuries of her life in the human realm, until she'd come back to the immortal world and fulfilled the prophecy by killing her father. Heden thought it an extremely brave decision and was thrilled she'd found love. Judging by the small snippets Miranda had told him, she'd had an extremely violent and painful start to her life. He was so happy she'd found a reason to stay in the immortal world.

Evie was an excellent governor and revered by the Deamons that now inhabited Takelia. The new compound was their most progressive yet, housing Deamons, Slayers and Vampyres. It was a beacon of hope for the future of an amalgamated immortal kingdom. There had been some concern the Deamons wouldn't be able to rehabilitate, but for the most part, they seamlessly blended into society. The ones that hadn't repented were now housed in the prison outside Takelia's walls, built by Latimus and Kenden to ensure they were kept away from the peaceful inhabitants of their world.

"Have a seat," she said, entering the tech room and motioning toward the chair in front of the plethora of screens.

Heden complied, marveling at the expansive room. He'd designed it with care, and since the compound was new, it had every gadget imaginable. Giddy with excitement at being surrounded by all of his hand-selected toys, he sat at the chair in front of several large monitors and began typing on the keyboard.

"So, what did you want to inspect?" Evie asked, leaning over his shoulder to observe the screen.

"You installed some updates recently, right?" he asked, fingers moving furiously over the keyboard.

"Yes. The antivirus needed updating, and I bought the new malware I ran by you last week. I installed that yesterday."

"Good," Heden said, lost in the various windows he'd pulled up on the monitor. Opening the task manager, he catalogued the programs that were running. Sure as day, about halfway down, it appeared: **SSHost.exe**.

"Is that something we should be worried about?" Evie asked, noticing he was hovering the arrow over the program.

"I'm not sure." Heden studied the CPU and memory used, noting it was identical to what appeared on his system yesterday. Nothing seemed out of the ordinary or alarming. "When you were in the human world, did you ever hear of a program called **SSHost.exe**?"

Her eyes narrowed as she looked toward the ceiling. "Not that I can recall. Usually, a host program indicates another server or VPN. Or spyware, but that would be impossible, right? No one in our world can really write spyware code other than you."

"Yes," Heden said, the burn in his gut now a full-on blaze of anxiety. "No one in *our* world."

Evie blinked down at him, confused. "A human? But why? They don't even know we exist."

Heden leaned back in the chair, threading his fingers together behind his head. "I don't know. Arderin and Darkrip are there. Perhaps someone figured out they're not human and tracked them to the ether the last time they visited us. But still, I don't understand what they would gain from spying on our servers. They really only house basic, mundane information."

Evie pulled up a chair and sat. "Well, if I wanted to hurt someone, I'd study their movements and learn their habits. Are Miranda and Sathan's schedules kept on the servers?"

"Yes. As well as yours and all the governors of the compounds. It was always easier that way, so everyone can sync their activities on their smart watches."

Evie expelled a breath through puffed cheeks. "Son of a bitch. The most likely conclusion is that someone is surveilling us."

Heden nodded. "I've got to get this program off all our computers, stat. Then, we need to have a council meeting."

"Agreed. It's probably best you don't put the council meeting on the system-wide calendar. Having us all in one room is an opportunity for whoever is surveilling us. Better yet, I'd suggest a video conference from multiple locations, just to be safe."

"Good point. Thanks, Evie. Give me a few minutes to clean this up, delete the program, and do a basic check on everything else."

"Will do." Standing, she squeezed his shoulder. "Great job picking up on this. You're pretty smart for a Vampyre."

"I do what I can," he said, winking at her.

"I'll be in my office if you need me."

Once she exited, Heden turned to the screen, determined to rid the computers of every last trace of the bug. Then, he called the governors of each compound and logged in to their computers to remove the **SSHost.exe** from their respective servers. Wanting to get back to the tech room at Astaria, which he considered "home base," he boarded the train and spent the entire ride wondering who in the hell was watching them and what they could possibly want.

Chapter 4

Sofia propped her tablet on the desk in the tiny one-bedroom apartment she kept in Florence. Late-day drops of light filtered in through the white curtains that blew in the breeze from the open window. Double-clicking on the secure app, she opened the program and stared back at herself.

Spirals of black hair fell behind her shoulders, and her almost translucent green-blue eyes were filled with determination. They were a perfect blend of her parents' eyes—the green from her father, and the blue from her mother and grandfather Francesco.

She best remembered her parents' coloring from the photographs that adorned the withered albums her grandfather gifted her when she turned ten. Days earlier, her parents had died in a car accident in her native New York City, forcing her to leave the only home she'd ever known. He'd sat with her on the brown leather couch in his Italian cottage, holding her as she cried, heartbroken.

After her parents' death, Francesco had raised her and made efforts to keep their memories alive, reminding her of their love for each other. True love, which he assured her was precious and rare.

The idea was foreign to Sofia. What the hell was romantic love anyway? She'd always been awkward around boys, and then around men, never understanding why so many people made such a big deal about dating and sex. When she'd lost her virginity while in college in Pennsylvania, she'd done it to rid herself of yet another stigma: shy, unwanted virgin.

For some reason, Sofia just hadn't fit in anywhere. Perhaps it was losing her parents at such a young age and being raised in a rural Italian town by her much older grandfather. Never having kids to play with, she'd always gravitated toward tinkering with things that could occupy her busy mind...and that she could enjoy on her own. Being alone had never been a struggle for Sofia. She'd never felt lonely or craved the company of others. Instead, she found peace in it and mostly preferred spending her time that way. The one exception was her grandfather Francesco, whom she loved with her entire heart.

Sofia had made many mistakes in her twenties regarding Francesco. Now, she lived with the agony of his loss, and the weight of her regret was unbearable. Originally, she'd planned to attend college in Italy, wanting to stay close to her grandfather. But Francesco had been firm, urging her to go to America and experience college life there.

"I don't want to leave you, Grandfather," she'd said, grasping his wrists as he stood before her. "You need me here. I won't leave you all alone."

His blue eyes had sparkled with his ever-constant love for her. "I won't let you put your life on hold for me, Sof. I'll change the locks and throw away the key if I have to. You're going to America, and that's final."

Although she'd fought for months, eventually, she caved and attended college in Pennsylvania. After graduating, she moved to New York to attend the sommelier training course at the New York International Culinary Center. Much to her surprise, she loved the city. The hustle and bustle were the perfect speed for her fastidious mind, and New York was an easy place to function alone. It wasn't strange to go to a coffee shop, dinner or a movie on your own. Sofia thrived there, but in the back of her mind, she also felt quite guilty.

She'd left Francesco alone, in the twilight of his life, living in a remote Italian village. Many times, she'd offered to move back, but he insisted she stay in New York and not waste her life on a man who'd already lived his own.

"I'm thinking about moving home with you, Grandfather," she said one day as they spoke on the phone.

"I won't even hear of it, darling girl," Francesco said. "You are enjoying your life in New York and can come and visit me once things calm down at your fancy restaurant. Italy will always be here."

"But *you* won't always be here," she whispered fervently.

"None of us will, my dear. Time is more precious for you now than it is for me. You're in your thirties now, and I know you crave children of your own."

"I do, but I have time."

His sigh echoed through the phone. "Time is the one thing we all have until we realize it's gone. You'll understand this more as you age. You've done so well, crafting a career from everything I taught you about the vines. I'm so excited to see what you will become, Sofia."

Against her better judgement, Sofia decided she would stay in New York, but she did request some time off work and purchased a ticket to Italy. Sadly, one day before she was set to depart, she received the call informing her of Francesco's death.

Shock had pervaded her bones, followed quickly by grief, and she'd collapsed to the floor to drown in unending tears. Even though she'd known she shouldn't leave her grandfather, she'd done so anyway, and he had died alone, without anyone to comfort him. Self-revulsion swamped her as she blamed herself for abandoning him when he needed her most. She knew then, in that moment, she'd never forgive herself.

Francesco had always been the one constant in her life. The one person who loved her unconditionally, even though she was a bit withdrawn and awkward. When she'd received the call that he'd suffered a heart attack in his home, fallen and broken his neck, it didn't compute in her logical brain. Francesco was extremely healthy, ate well, and stayed in rather good shape for someone in his late eighties.

Sofia smiled when she remembered the tales he would recount from his "skirt-chasing days," as he liked to call them. Women seemed to find him irresistible, a fact he reveled in. There were always two he spoke of most frequently: her grandmother Maria, and a red-haired woman named Evie.

Evie had met him in his very early twenties, and they'd had a passionate love affair. A faraway look would enter his eyes as he smiled and told tales of their fiery courtship. But his stories were also laced with cryptic musings about how she seemed more than human. How she never seemed to age and had the power to cripple a man with a stare. Sofia had attributed those comments to her grandfather's dramatic temperament, which was quite rampant.

He'd told the story of how Evie had eventually left, ensuring him she wasn't the one he wanted to bestow his love upon. In the aftermath, his shattered heart longed for companionship, and he met Maria. Her family had purchased several acres of land adjoining his estate, and the rest was history. He'd taken one look at the raven-haired beauty and declared her his future wife.

Maria declined his advances for months, fearing he was still in love with Evie, but eventually, he proved to her his intentions were true. They married a few years later and became pregnant with Sofia's mother, Lorena, in a short time.

Sadly, Maria died during childbirth. With yet another broken heart, Francesco raised Lorena, deciding to never marry again. Although he dated many women, his Maria was the only woman who had secured his heart. Eventually, Lorena married Sofia's father, an American, and her grandfather spent his remaining days on the land he'd cultivated with his wife.

Upon learning of her grandfather's death, Sofia had flown from New York to Italy to arrange his funeral. She'd gone to identify the body in the hospital, holding back tears as she kissed his cold hand in the staid room. When she entered his small cottage atop the Italian hillside, a waft of cold air had enveloped her, and she'd felt a deep sense of foreboding. Telling herself it was just sadness that this was where he'd taken his last breaths, she set about cleaning the cottage.

As she tidied up the living room, she noticed something gleaming on the wooden tabletop, under the lamp. Grasping it with her fingers, she lifted it high, examining it in the light of the setting sun that filtered through the living room window. It was a long crimson hair. Sofia scrutinized it for hours, wondering who had visited her grandfather at his home. Were they there when he died? Worse, did they have something to do with his death?

Unable to push the suspicion away, she'd headed to the local police department the next morning, demanding to see the police report and autopsy. Her grandfather had broken his neck, which the police assured her was from hitting his head as he fell to the ground after his heart attack. Yet the break seemed to be clean and precise, as if controlled by something...or someone.

The report had also shown Francesco had cancer in several of his organs. Again, this was a shock to Sofia since she'd assumed him relatively healthy, and she railed against the fact she'd left him alone and unknowingly sick.

After the funeral, Sofia hired a private forensic investigator to study the break in Francesco's neck as well as the red hair she'd found. She could still remember the man giving her the results in his office in Rome.

"The break was definitely intentional and done by another person," the investigator told her. "I'm one hundred percent sure."

"Why wouldn't the police investigate this as a homicide?" Sofia asked, crushed by the news.

The man sighed. "The police forces in these small rural towns aren't equipped for large investigations, Sofia. Your grandfather was almost ninety years old and had cancer, according to the autopsy. Their explanation of what happened was plausible, given the circumstances."

"So, because someone's old and has cancer, it's okay to murder them?"

"Of course not. But I don't think there was any malice in the local authorities' actions. That's all I'm saying."

"And what about the hair?"

The investigator flipped through the file, turning it and showing it to her. "That one is a bit more complicated."

"Complicated how?" Sofia asked, looking over the report, which appeared as an unintelligible jumble of words and symbols to her.

"The hair has DNA, but it's not...*human*. It's a sequence of polynucleotides, but not anything remotely close to ours."

"That's not..." Sofia struggled to comprehend his words. "How is that possible?"

"The simplest answer is that it's not. I had the lab test it three times. The results came back the same. We seem to have a mystery on our hands, unless you know of a completely human-like species that exists separate and unknown to us."

"That's impossible."

"It is," he said with a nod. "The only explanation I can surmise is that the hair's structure has been compromised in some way. I'm sorry I can't help you more. I'll take a reduced rate to compensate for the lack of intelligible knowledge from the hair sequencing."

"Thank you," she said, standing. "Can I take this file? And the hair?"

"They're all yours," he said, ensuring she left with both.

Later that evening, in Francesco's living room, Sofia stood over the wooden table where she'd found the auburn tress. Lifting her hands, she mimicked snapping someone's neck. As she performed the action, a few strands of hair became dislodged from her scalp, one of them landing on the table. It was all the proof she needed. Her grandfather had been murdered. But by whom?

She stayed up all night, studying the hair through the plastic bag that encased it. As she pondered, her grandfather's voice filtered through her mind.

Evie was my first love, Sofia. She was such a beauty. She never seemed to age...

My Evie was a complicated woman, Sofia. She could silence a man with only a stare...

She had a mean streak as deep as her fiery red hair...

Tracing the plastic-laden tress with the pads of her fingers, Sofia accepted the truth. This woman, whom her grandfather had loved so very long ago, had murdered him.

Armed with that knowledge, Sofia began a quest to avenge her beloved grandfather. First, she had to track down the red-haired bitch. Difficult, since she was quite elusive and never stayed in one place for long.

Sofia embarked down a painstaking path of tracing Evie's steps from when she'd dated Francesco all those years ago in Italy. Since he inhabited a small town, Sofia was eventually able to speak to others who remembered her, and she discerned Evie had moved to France after she parted with Francesco.

Armed with the woman's description and the vast resources of the Internet, she tirelessly tracked her until she discovered her, living in Paris. She seemed to live a solitary life, mostly enjoying one-night stands with handsome men but otherwise untethered. Oh, and there was one other thing... The woman appeared to be in her late-twenties. Impossible, since Francesco had told her he and Evie were roughly the same age.

Sofia tracked her for a while, building up the confidence and fortitude to confront her. She also bought a gun, deciding if Evie confessed to the crime, she might have the urge to kill her. It went against her religious beliefs, but her grandfather deserved justice, and Sofia was determined he would get it. She believed that was the only way his soul could truly rest in peace. And perhaps it was the only way she could forgive herself for leaving him.

On the day that Sofia planned to confront her, she noticed Evie walking out of her condo building, inconspicuous in jeans, a t-shirt and a cap. The stunning woman walked to the nearby park, Sofia following a safe distance behind. Glancing around, Evie straightened her shoulders and headed into a densely wooded area that surrounded the park. Hiding behind a bush, Sofia observed the woman hold her palm up, facing out. Closing her eyes, a thick, clear plasma seemed to form in front of Evie's body. And then, she walked through the ether and disappeared.

"What the hell?" Sofia whispered, running to the spot where the woman had vanished. But her effort was futile—the ether had evaporated. Sofia rubbed her eyes, wondering if she was completely insane but also convinced she'd just experienced something magical...and dark...and not of this world.

Vowing to learn everything she could about the mysterious portal of dense plasma, Sofia began an exhaustive search. It was imperative to observe another creature travel through the barrier. Burying herself in online classes, she taught herself how to code and became an extremely proficient hacker. She'd inherited more than enough to live on from her parents' insurance policy, bestowed in a trust when she turned twenty-one, and her grandfather's estate, which had appreciated nicely over the decades. It meant she could dedicate all her time to exacting vengeance for Francesco.

With her newly cemented programming skills, she installed spyware that would alert her to any surveillance videos pinged as "unexplainable." There were many false alarms, people who thought they saw ghosts or spirits, but eventually, she hit the jackpot. Two people she now knew to be Arderin and Darkrip had broken into a lab in Houston. The dark-haired man seemed to freeze the security guard that discovered him just by holding up a hand. After they'd run outside, he placed his arms around the woman. The video from across the alley was grainy, but Sofia saw what she needed: the couple had vanished into thin air.

Sofia had taken the next flight to Houston, searching every hotel for a man with a short buzz cut and a woman with long, curly black hair, until she discovered where they were staying. Several days later, they left the hotel and headed to the nearby park. Away from the prying eyes of other passersby, she observed Darkrip hold his palm to the air, generate the ether and walk through with Arderin.

Collapsing forward, Sofia gripped her knees with both hands as she panted. Holy shit. This wasn't an anomaly. There was another world that coexisted with theirs.

For years, Sofia tried and failed to replicate what she had seen, finding it impossible to recreate the dense plasma. She kept an apartment in New York City, where she used the vast resources at the public library to research every historical account of other creatures that might exist in their world. Since her grandfather's estate was large, she decided to sell it, choosing to maintain a small flat in Florence instead. With her American and European homes set, she fell down the rabbit hole of searching for an answer.

Sofia became even more comfortable in her solitude, choosing not to date or socialize. After all, what would she say to someone she met on Bumble? *Hi, I'm Sofia. My life is consumed with avenging my dead grandfather by finding an alternate world full of otherworldly creatures and ensuring the demise of an ageless witch he dated over sixty years ago.* Good god, they'd think her insane.

Of course, her self-imposed isolation was detrimental to the other main goal she aspired to achieve. Having lost Francesco, Sofia desperately longed to have a biological child—or children, if possible. With her only living relative gone, she ached to have another being to connect with in the world. Someone who shared her DNA, whose face she could look upon and see reminders of her grandfather and parents. Along with her need for revenge, the desire to have a child grew and curled in her gut with each passing year.

Realizing she most likely needed to attain vengeance before she could blaze the trail of becoming a mother, she continued to research the enigmatic ether, determined to solve the mystery of how to traverse it. One day, as she stood in the French park where she'd seen Evie disappear into thin air, Sofia felt the tiny hairs on the back of her neck stand up. Surreptitiously sliding her hand across her hip, she reached for her gun.

"Would you like to know how they generate the ether?" a deep voice called behind her, causing her to pivot and gasp.

"Who are you?" Sofia asked the man, who was over a foot taller than her, with broad shoulders and raven-black, slick hair. Her fingers tensed on the handle of her weapon.

"You don't need to shoot me, Sofia. Besides, unless you use an eight-shooter, I'll self-heal in moments."

"Who. Are. You?" she repeated through gritted teeth.

"I'm someone who can give you the answers you seek. But only if you want to find them. My help is not offered as an act of generosity. It will require payment on your part."

Sofia studied the brooding man, his energy intense and pulsing. "What type of payment?"

His thick lips twitched. "I'm looking to start a war and I need soldiers. If you commit to supporting my cause, I will help you in return."

"What cause?"

"There are changes happening in the world beyond the ether. Changes detrimental to the ways of life that have existed for millennia. There was a powerful dark enemy whom I hoped would exterminate everyone in the immortal world, but sadly, they defeated him. They now rush to create a utopia that blurs the balance mandated by Etherya. I cannot allow that to happen. I must save them from themselves."

"Etherya?" Sofia asked.

"The goddess who created the realm beyond the ether."

Sofia had been raised a devout Catholic by Francesco, taught to believe there was only one true God. But with what she'd seen over the past few years, she couldn't dismiss any slice of knowledge. Even something that contradicted her faith.

"Will it require bloodshed?"

"Yes," he said, unwavering.

Sofia considered his words, curiosity from the small snippets of information he'd already imparted causing her facile mind to churn. "Will it lead to me killing the red-haired bitch who murdered my grandfather?"

He grinned and arched his dark brow. "Absolutely."

Chewing on her lip, Sofia contemplated his proposition.

"I have several other soldiers to recruit. During that time, I will teach you how to generate the ether, and you can study the world of the immortals. All will become clear to you eventually. Who I am, and how I'm connected to the leaders of Etherya's realm. All you have to do is join me, Sofia."

Sofia closed her eyes, inhaling deeply as emotion swirled within. Intertwining her fingers, she silently prayed to the Lord above, asking his forgiveness for her next words. Then, opening her eyes, she extended her hand.

"Deal."

She watched Bakari shake her hand, their pact filling her with equal parts dread and anticipation. She would finally be able to set things right and allow her grandfather's soul to rest in peace. *But at what cost?*

Yanking herself from the memories, Sofia saw the members of the Secret Society log on to the call, one by one. Once their faces were all visible in the miniature windows onscreen, Bakari spoke.

"Thank you all for joining the call. It is a blessing Sofia has armed us with tablets that are able to communicate between the human and immortal worlds. We all appreciate your efforts, Sofia."

She nodded as the group murmured their thanks.

Bakari continued. "Sofia has logged the schedules of the immortal royals, and everyone has been sent their tasks. Let's go around the group and confirm. We'll start with Diabolos."

"Thank you," the Slayer aristocrat said. His chestnut hair was coiffed and refined. Sofia thought him passably attractive but also an arrogant douche. He had a chip on his shoulder about his wife marrying his best friend after he'd perished. He was only alive now because of the drops of Crimeous's blood their society had cloned. It held many sacred powers, including resuscitating centuries-dead immortals.

"Miranda, Sathan, Aron and Tordor will be at Uteria's castle at the specified time. I will plant the explosive and have the eight-shooter loaded. I will enter the dining room as they're eating dinner and shoot Sathan first, since he will most likely recover from the explosion. Then, I will head into the hallway before the explosive detonates. Everyone will rush to Sathan to assess his wounds, and that is where they will die. I will exit through the servant's door to the vehicle outside."

"And do you still wish to kill your wife?" Bakari asked.

"Absolutely. She has a private showing at the gallery that evening, which is why Aron will be free to join the royals for dinner. I'll approach her as she leaves through the back door of the gallery. That bitch will die screaming my name. But not before I have some fun with her."

Sofia shivered, sickened by the man's evil plans. The woman he'd been married to was far from a royal and only related to an aristocrat by marriage. If only there was some way she could steer Diabolos away from hurting her...

"Thank you, Diabolos," Bakari said, ripping her from her musings. "Melania, please detail us of your strategy."

"Everything at Valeria is set," the woman said, her tone cold and calculating. "My husband Camron will be at Naria and will be unharmed. As you know, that was a term of my alliance."

"Understood," Bakari said.

"Latimus, Lila and their two young children will be picking up Jack from his private school at Valeria and heading to his uncle Sam's house to have dinner. As the governor's wife, I will approach all of the surrounding houses and inform the Vampyres we are having an impromptu surprise banquet at the main house. This will rid the area of any witnesses. I will arrange for their transport to Valeria's main house, allowing Vadik to complete his mission."

"I will set off an explosion outside the house, causing Latimus to exit. I will shoot him with the eight-shooter first and then proceed to kill the rest of them," Vadik's deep voice stated. "All will be dead within seconds. Of that, I am sure."

"I appreciate your willingness to take out so many of our enemies, Vadik. Ananda?"

"I know the main castle at Astaria well, as I frequented it often before the king banished me," the withered lady said, her tone filled with rage. Sofia noted she must've gone through her immortal change late in life, her body locked in its wrinkled shell. "Heden will be downstairs in the tech room. I will murder him with the eight-shooter before he detects my presence, and I will escape unnoticed."

"Excellent," Bakari said. "I will set several explosives around the main dining room at Takelia. Evie, Kenden and Larkin are all confirmed to have dinner there. I will also be armed in case she attempts to transport. She will perish, along with the others." Sofia could almost feel his gaze through the monitor.

"That just leaves me," Sofia said, huffing out a breath, trying not to let the gravity of their deeds dampen her resolve. "I will approach Darkrip and Arderin's house in L.A. once they sit down to dinner with Calinda. I will shoot Arderin first with the eight-shooter. Darkrip will be so distraught, especially since she's pregnant, that I should be able to kill him directly afterward."

"Then we all have our orders," Bakari said. "We strike one week from today, early evening. Are there any last-minute details we need to discuss?"

"What if we fail?" Melania asked. "I can't be outed as a conspirator. I'm the governor's wife after all."

Sofia wrinkled her nose at the entitled woman. She was quite nasty and extremely unlikeable. Someone she never would've spoken to if she hadn't been dragged into this life of vengeance and retribution.

"The meeting point is still the same," Bakari said, referencing the hidden cave located in the uncharted woods near the Purges of Methesda. "Whether you fail or succeed, the plan is to meet there after the attacks. I expect everyone to be there."

"Aye," they all concurred in unison.

"Very well. You all are free to go. Sofia, please hang back so we can speak privately."

The other members disconnected, and Sofia waited for the Vampyre to speak.

"I see the indecision and compassion in your eyes, Sofia," Bakari said. "It worries me. Will you be able to kill my pregnant sister? If not, I can send you to Takelia instead."

"I think you're physically better matched to take on Kenden and Larkin. I can do it. Darkrip is evil and must be vanquished."

"Very well," Bakari said, his body language emitting a wariness that relayed his doubt about her ability to complete her mission. "We're counting on you. Don't let us down."

"I won't," she said, ready to be done with the annoying lecture. "I'm available on my cell if you need me." With that, she closed the cover over her tablet, ending the transmission. She was pretty sure the arrogant Vampyre wasn't thrilled about being rudely cut off, but she was over him. In fact, she was over all of it. What in the hell had she gotten herself into?

After brushing her teeth, she threw on an old tank and shorts and slipped into bed. Closing her eyes, the faces of the children that would perish by their actions began drifting across her mind. Unable to stop her tears, Sofia buried her face in the pillow and cried herself to sleep.

Chapter 5

At Astaria, Heden was hosting a teleconference of his own from the tech room.

"Can everyone hear me?" he asked, checking to make sure his computer's microphone was at maximum volume.

"Loud and clear," Miranda said, sitting beside Sathan in the conference room at Uteria.

"Good. I'm sorry to schedule this meeting so late, but Evie and I discovered something earlier today that can't wait." Heden brought everyone up to speed, informing them of the surveillance program and its subsequent removal from the servers as well as the threat he foresaw. Once all the updates had been shared, he said, "The only conclusion I can surmise is that someone from the human world is spying on us."

"Wow," Miranda said, exhaling a puff of breath that fluttered her dark hair. "That's intense. Thanks for all the information, Heden, and for getting the program off the servers. Why would anyone from the human world want to spy on us?"

"We don't know," Evie said, Kenden at her side. "I can only deduce it's someone who figured out Arderin and Darkrip aren't one of their own."

"Could it be one of their governments? The Americans, Chinese or Russians?" Latimus asked.

"It's possible," Heden said. "I just don't know. At this point, I'm going to have to go to the human world to investigate."

"Oh, Heden," Lila said from her seat beside Latimus. "What if something happens to you? Lattie," she said, clutching her bonded's muscular forearm, "you should go with him."

"Do you want me to accompany you?" Latimus asked, placing his arm around Lila's shoulders in an absent, soothing gesture.

"As much as I'd love to spend twenty-four-seven with your ugly mug, I think I should go alone." Heden's lips curved as Latimus scowled.

"You're such a dick."

"From you, that's a compliment," Heden said, smiling as he chomped the gum he'd thrown in his mouth earlier. "Don't worry, buttercup," he said, addressing Lila. "I'll be safe. It will be easier for me to track down whoever installed the surveillance program on my own. Working solo means I can work quickly and efficiently. Also, I need to warn Darkrip and Arderin."

"Is there a way to create a device that can breach the ether?" Sathan asked, worried. "I don't want Arderin there without a way to contact us any longer. This cements the need to have the ability to communicate directly with her."

"I've just never dedicated any time to developing equipment that can communicate through the ether since our world is so separate. But I think I could figure it out if I tinkered long enough. I can make that a priority as soon as I get home from tracking down our spy."

"Good," Sathan said. "We need to keep her safe since she's pregnant."

"I know, Sathan," Heden said, reminded of how protective his oldest brother was of their sister. "Darkrip will keep her safe until I can figure something out. I don't want anything to happen to her either. She's my favorite sister."

It was a recurring joke he and Latimus used to drive Arderin crazy, since she was their only sister.

"I'm going to leave in the morning," Heden said. "I've already packed and have enough Slayer blood to last over a week. I'm going to leave our schedules in the system as they were. It will appear that I'm still here, and you all are still partaking in your daily activities that are on the books. It's a great opportunity to identify a threat if they were indeed looking to strike. Although I removed the **SSHost.exe** program from our servers, I'm not confident we're completely free of spyware. Remember that as you communicate."

"We'll stay sharp, Heden, and wish you luck on your journey," Miranda said. "Promise us you'll stay safe."

"I will, Miranda," he said, giving her a reassuring grin. "If I discover anything of note, I'll come back through the ether and contact you all immediately."

"We love you," Lila said in her sweet voice.

"I love you all too, even my man bun-toting brother," Heden said. That elicited a chuckle from everyone but Latimus, whose eyes narrowed with good-natured distain. "Chop that thing off while I'm gone, will ya, bro?"

"Lay off my bonded," Lila said, pecking Latimus on his cheek. "His man bun is sexy."

Latimus finally smiled and stole a kiss from her pink lips. "Do you want me to drive you to the ether in the morning?"

"That would be great, Latimus. I take it all back. You're a specimen of true masculinity, and don't let anyone tell you otherwise."

"Call me if you need me to come over," Evie said. "I'm extremely familiar with all facets of the human world and can be there in a snap. Safe travels, Heden." She and Kenden gave a wave and closed her laptop, ending the call.

"Bye, Heden," Miranda and Sathan called in unison.

A few seconds later, the transmission ended.

Heden spent the next few hours shoring up his kingdom-wide responsibilities as the tech guru of their world. After a few hours of fitful sleep, he rose with the sun and hopped in the four-wheeler with Latimus. Armed with his supplies, he waded through the thick wall of ether and entered the human world.

Chapter 6

Sofia sat in her rented car, parked across the street from Arderin and Darkrip's home in the suburbs of L.A. It was in an unassuming cul-de-sac surrounded by other homes of similar structure and size. None of their neighbors would suspect the truth: they were living in the presence of immortal beings posing as humans so Arderin could finish her medical residency.

Lifting her binoculars, Sofia studied the family in the soft morning light under the blue sky. Darkrip was sitting with Callie at the table while Arderin scrambled eggs at the stove. Grasping the pan's handle, she swiveled, scooping a fluffy pile onto her daughter's plate and then her husband's. He grabbed her wrist as she began to turn away and drew her down for a kiss. After giving him a peck, she placed the pan in the sink and opened the refrigerator. Pulling out a clear jug filled with red liquid, she poured some for Callie, then for herself, and sat down to join them.

Sofia observed, understanding now, after years of studying the immortals, that the hybrid children of Vampyres and Slayers needed both food and Slayer blood as sustenance. The combination in equal parts kept their young hearts beating.

Callie was a beauty, a mirror image of Arderin. She had a precocious nature, which made it challenging for her parents to control her remarkable powers. As the granddaughter of Crimeous, the Dark Lord's blood ran true in her veins, as it did her father's. It was a compelling reason to dispel her from the Earth.

And yet as Sofia watched them complete the mundane task of eating breakfast together, little bugs of anxiety crawled in her stomach. Through the large bay window, Arderin reached over and grabbed the fork out of Darkrip's hand, devouring the eggs he'd stacked upon it. In retaliation, he picked up a speck of egg from his plate and threw it at her. It landed on her face, causing Callie to break into a fit of giggles.

It was all so normal. All so right. How in the world was she going to murder these people who loved each other so much? Reaching for her bag in the passenger seat, she pulled out her phone and began scrolling through pictures of her grandfather. Every time she had doubts, Sofia reminded herself that she was doing this for him. So his soul could rest.

Her thumb froze over the screen, her favorite picture of Francesco smiling back at her, blue eyes sparkling. Would he truly want her to murder these immortals? Knowing the answer deep in her soul, she whispered a curse, clicked the phone off and threw it on the seat.

Sofia had been so wracked with guilt after Francesco's death and so desperate for knowledge about the immortal world, she'd latched onto Bakari's offer without truly familiarizing herself with those she aligned against. She realized now that was a terrible misstep. If she'd taken the time to study how the immortals interacted, beyond just tracking their movements and habits, she would've observed flawed but righteous people, all of whom strived to act with morality and decency. They loved their families and children with the same ferocity she loved Francesco. Even Evie, whom she would always hate with a passion, had seemed to turn over a new leaf and saved so many immortals when she defeated Crimeous.

Refocusing on the house, Sofia emitted a soft gasp. Lifting the binoculars, she honed in on the front porch. A thick, emulsified band of air appeared beside the house. As if in a dream, she watched a body emerge. Tall and broad, the man exited the ether, a black bag strapped across his shoulders and back. The plasma disappeared, and the man headed toward the front door, lifting his hand to knock. There he stood, frozen, hand in the air. Was he waiting for something?

As if tethered to him by a thread of energy, Sofia *felt* him turn before he actually made the movement. Experiencing the moment in slow-motion, the man dropped his hand, slowly pivoted and latched onto her. Eyes clear and full of purpose narrowed, his expression grim. They spoke a thousand silent, unintelligible words in that fraction of a second. Sofia's heart slammed in her chest, and she struggled to breathe. Gathering her wits, she broke the intense eye contact, revved the car and sped down the street, away from the madness.

A few miles down the road, she pulled into an abandoned gas station, throwing the car in park. Grasping the wheel with white-knuckled hands, she rested her forehead against it as she drew heaving gasps of air into her lungs. Once she was able to regain her wits, Sofia acknowledged the truth: Heden was in the human world and he was onto her. She didn't know how much he knew, but it was evident he'd discovered her surveillance program.

She recognized the immortal world's gifted hacker from her reconnaissance. It had taken her weeks to develop a program that would go unnoticed unless he had reason to look for it. The Vampyre was extremely intelligent and close to his family. It was only a matter of time before the Secret Society was discovered.

Terror invaded her pores as she imagined relaying the news to Bakari. They were supposed to attack in a week, and he would be furious. Deciding she needed to assess how much Heden knew so she could formulate a solid plan, she headed to her hotel, dread pulsing through her shaking body.

Chapter 7

"Heden!" Arderin squealed, yanking open the door and clutching him in a smothering embrace. Drawing back, she palmed his cheeks.

"How are you here? Why are you here? Oh my god, is something wrong? Darkrip, come here! Heden's here!"

"I can see that, darling," Darkrip said, expression droll as he appeared behind her. "Perhaps he could tell us the purpose of his visit if you gave him some space."

Scowling at her husband, she grabbed Heden's wrist, tugging him into the house and closing the door. "Don't mind my extremely *rude* bonded," Arderin said, shooting a glare at Darkrip. "He's still adjusting to life outside the Deamon caves. Perhaps one day, he'll learn some manners."

"God forbid." Darkrip lifted a sardonic brow. "Hey, Heden," he said, extending his hand. "Good to see you. Why in the hell are you here?"

Heden shook his hand and heard a tiny gasp below. Looking down, he saw Calinda staring up at them.

"Daddy, you said a bad word," she whispered.

Darkrip shot Heden a grimace. "Fifty cents in the swear jar. I think the damn thing's worth about a million dollars at this point."

Arderin bent to pick up her daughter and balanced her on her hip, next to her several-months-pregnant belly. "Daddy is very sorry that he said *two* bad words, aren't you, Daddy?"

"Yes," Darkrip said, looking anything but. "I'll put an extra dollar in the swear jar today."

Callie looked at Heden, the girl's wide blue-green eyes almost melting his heart. "Can I tell you a secret, Uncle Heden?" she asked.

"Sure thing, chicken wing," he said, extending his arms to take her from Arderin. Holding her close, he rotated so his back was to her parents, seemingly giving them privacy. "Whisper it in my ear so they don't hear."

Cupping his ear with her small hand, she spoke into the shell. "I don't mind if he curses because Mommy says I get to keep all the money when I get older. As much as Daddy swears, I'll be rich!"

Heden laughed, resting his forehead against hers so he could gaze into her eyes. "You're brilliant, baby toad. Don't let anyone tell you otherwise, okay?"

"Okay," she said, nodding as she beamed.

"Oh, god, that stupid nickname," Arderin groaned. "Can you be more annoying?"

"What?" Heden said, facing her and trying his best to look innocent. "You're *little toad*, so she's *baby toad*. It only makes sense, sis."

"I hate that nickname," Arderin said, reaching for Callie's hand after she squirmed out of Heden's arms back to solid ground. "Let me get her ready for school, and then we'll talk, okay? In the meantime, go ahead and update Darkrip on why you're here. Be back in a few. C'mon, baby."

They trailed up the stairs, his sister and her mini-me, as Heden marveled at their likeness.

"I know," Darkrip said, shaking his head. "There are two of them now. It's exhausting."

Chuckling, Heden patted him on the shoulder. "You signed up for this, buddy. I told you she was difficult."

They strolled into the living room, Heden sitting on the couch while Darkrip eased into the leather reclining chair beside him. "Difficult and amazing and perfect," Darkrip sighed, relaxing into the seat. "She owns my soul." Smiling, as deeply as one like Darkrip allowed himself to, he studied Heden. "So, as much as I love the surprise, I'm guessing you're not here for shits and giggles."

"Unfortunately not," Heden said, rubbing his hands over the tops of his thighs. "First things first, you're being surveilled. Actually, we all are."

Darkrip's shoulders tensed, and he leaned forward, resting his elbows on his knees. "For how long? By whom?"

Heden held up a hand. "Let me start at the beginning. There's a lot." After expelling a breath through rounded cheeks, Heden updated his brother-in-law.

"Damn," Darkrip said, sitting back as the information washed over him. "We all thought we'd seen the last of our enemies when my father was defeated."

"Yes. It's frustrating and concerning. We have no idea who's surveilling us. However, I did recently gain a new lead."

"When?"

"About five minutes ago, outside your house. A dark-haired woman was staking you guys. Six-JRN-three-seven-two."

"What?" Darkrip asked, confused.

"The license plate of her car, which I assume is rented. I'll trace it and figure out who she is." Pulling out his phone, Heden jotted down the number in the notes section.

"You remember stuff like that automatically?" Darkrip asked, impressed.

Heden shrugged. "I've never claimed to be the smartest immortal, it's just a fact." Grinning, he acknowledged his teasing.

"He's always had a photographic memory," Arderin chimed in, floating down the stairs and into the room. "Which does *not* mean he's smarter than any of us. He just has the brain of an elephant. And about as much hot air as one." Scrunching her features at Heden, she sat beside him on the couch.

"Remind me why I love you again?" he asked, rubbing his beard.

"Because I beat you up when you were five, and you've been terrified of me ever since."

"True story," Heden murmured as Callie dashed toward them.

"I'm ready, Daddy! Can I wear my new coat today?"

Standing, Darkrip sighed and ran his hand over her raven-black curls. "It's eighty degrees outside, but you've broken me, so wear what you want."

"Stop it," Arderin scolded, lifting from the couch to swat his arm. Squatting down, she kissed Callie on the nose. "Have a good day at school, baby. We'll have fish sticks tonight, okay?"

"Yay!" Callie exclaimed, jumping up and down as if she'd won unlimited amounts of candy. "Bye, Mommy."

"Heden will update you while I drive her to school. Be back soon, princess." After squeezing Arderin's hand, Darkrip and Callie headed out the back, and the car engine sounded in the driveway.

"So, it's bad," Arderin said, sitting beside Heden.

"It's not good, sis," he said, placing his arm over her shoulder and drawing her close. "But I'll be damned if anyone hurts our family. We'll figure this out, no matter what."

"At least the timing is good," she said, snuggling into his side. "I'm working nights the rest of the week. Don't have to go in until eight o'clock tonight. It will give us time to have dinner, and you can read to Callie before she goes to sleep."

"Sounds perfect. I missed you."

"Missed you too," she said, burrowing into his broad chest.

Reveling in the joy of having her near, Heden told her everything while they waited for Darkrip to return.

Chapter 8

The next morning, Sofia sat in the coffee shop, earbuds blaring under the cloth of her sweatshirt's hood. Her fingers moved feverishly over the keyboard as she worked to restore the spyware she'd placed on the servers at the immortal compounds.

Cursing, she scowled at the error message that popped up. Although she'd completely reprogrammed the software, she hadn't been able to reinstall it. Heden was a competent hacker, and now that he was onto her, she had a feeling she was screwed. She'd always thought herself more proficient than him but also had the element of surprise. Now that he'd discovered her, he would go full force to protect his family. The Vampyre siblings were close and would sacrifice anything to safeguard each other.

Squinting at the screen, she began rewriting a section of code to see if it would allow her to infiltrate the immortals' computers through a different channel. Suddenly, a text box appeared on the laptop, the curser blinking.

Sitting up in her chair, Sofia popped the buds from her ears as the curser fully grabbed her attention. Then, three ominous words appeared: **I see you**.

Sofia's heart leapt into her throat, blood pulsing through her shocked body. Glancing around, she didn't see Heden anywhere in the café. It was pretty hard to miss a six-foot, six-inch man, so she surmised he was surveying her remotely. Understanding she was made, she began to type.

You've stumbled upon something you can't possibly understand. I suggest you leave me alone.

The curser blinked as Heden responded.

I know you're human, what you look like, and that you're spying on us. There is no way in hell you're going to hurt my family. Got it?

Air exited Sofia's nostrils as she exhaled. Sadly, the plan was already in motion. His family was already dead.

Antagonizing me is a wasted effort. I'm sorry. Things have been put into place that cannot be undone. Don't contact me again.

With shaking hands, Sofia closed her laptop. After gathering her things, she threw her empty cup in the trash, pulled her hoodie securely over her black curls and exited the shop.

Several footsteps later, she felt his presence. Even though her head was down and her sneakered soles set a steady pace, there was the unmistakable and unshakable intuition that someone was following her. Steeling herself, she clenched her jaw and pivoted.

Heden stood on the sidewalk, tall and broad under the blue sky. Cars whizzed past as their gazes held. Thick, firm lips sat in a straight line, surrounded by his beard. An austere nose led to full, dark eyebrows that bracketed ice-blue eyes. Murder swam in the clear orbs, causing Sofia to wonder if she'd ever seen anyone so angry. If so, she couldn't recall. No one had ever looked at her with such rage.

"Hello, Sofia Morelli." His deep baritone washed over her, sending chill bumps across her arms and causing the hairs on the back of her neck to straighten. "I think it's time we had a little chat."

Sofia swallowed, comprehending that she could never outrun this hulking Vampyre. He was at least a foot taller, and muscles seemed to bulge from his arms under the sleeves of his black t-shirt. Faded jeans encased the tree trunks that comprised his legs. The public setting alongside the road probably ensured her safety more than running from him anyway. Immortals were consumed with not being discovered by humans, so she doubted he'd hurt her in full view of others. Clutching the strap of her laptop bag, she faced him with every ounce of courage she could muster.

"Hello, Heden."

Those piercing eyes narrowed as he glowered down at her. "Why are you spying on the immortals? Why would one human go to all this trouble?"

Sofia blinked as she contemplated her answer. "You must know I'm not working alone."

His irises darted between hers, studying her. "Who hired you?"

She scoffed. "Oh, I'm not getting paid. In currency, at least. My restitution will come when the mission is complete."

Confusion lined his expression. "Are you seeking information on immortals? Perhaps from discovering Arderin and Darkrip aren't human? If you want data, I could supply it to you. It's natural for a human who discovers the immortal world to be curious."

She smiled although it held no amusement. "If only that were the case. Things are too far along. I'm sorry." Shaking her head, she turned and began walking again.

"Wait," he said, grabbing her bag and spinning her around. "Let me negotiate with you. Perhaps I can offer you something more valuable than whatever the person who hired you is offering."

Tears welled in Sofia's eyes as she stared up at him. The image of Francesco's smiling face filtered through her mind, sending a crack down her heart. "There is only one thing I want. One thing I've ever wanted. And I will have it, no matter the cost. The man I'm aligned with is the only one who can help me achieve it." A tear broke free, skating down her cheek, and she angrily swiped it away. "Goodbye."

"Sofia," he said, grabbing her upper arm before she could turn away.

Glaring at him, she shook him off. "Don't touch me!"

His hand fell to his side as a pleading expression lined his face. "Who hurt you, Sofia? Was it someone in my family? If so, I understand why you'd want to harm us. But please, at least give me the opportunity to make it right."

"There's no way to make it right," she said, wiping away another tear. "He's dead and never coming back! Gone, as if he never existed. Every person she loves will pay. I'm impressed you tracked me down, but your efforts are wasted. If you so much as follow me one more step, I'll send the video of your sister traveling through the ether to everyone in her residency program. Forget being a doctor—they'll think she's nuts and lock her up for decades. I could make your life a living hell and have videos ready to send to the authorities the second something happens to me. So, I'll say this one more time." Closing the distance between them, she said through gritted teeth, "Leave. Me. Alone."

Sparing him one last cursory glance, she turned on her heel and stalked away, hoping she appeared confident. But inside, she was a quivering mess.

∞

Heden watched the little human walk away as comprehension washed over him. Someone in his family had hurt her terribly. The waif of a woman had looked upon him with such pain in her translucent green-blue eyes. Never had he seen such anguish. Whoever she was trying to avenge had been someone extremely important to her.

Reaching to his back pocket, he pulled out his phone and entered the passcode. Clicking the app with the pad of his thumb, it opened onto a map. A blinking dot traveled down the street away from him, toward downtown L.A.

When Heden grabbed Sofia's bag, he'd surreptitiously planted a bug on it. The inconspicuous device would allow him to track her to whatever point she was using as home base. Once there, he would confront her.

In the meantime, he'd spend some time working on the patch he'd developed that would ensure their devices could communicate through the ether. Heden was on the right track, but it still wasn't working effectively. Now that he was beginning to fit the puzzle pieces of this bizarre mystery together, he wanted to be able to reach his family on the other side.

He sat in the coffee shop where Sofia had spent the morning. The charming café had fast Wi-Fi and strong coffee. Heden toyed for several hours but still couldn't come up with a working patch or the correct code to send messages to the immortal realm. Frustrated, he consulted his phone to see where Sofia was.

She was only a few blocks away, stationary near a hotel that was listed on the map. This must be where she was staying. After packing up his things, Heden slung his bag over his shoulder and headed to find her.

When he approached the hotel, the blinking dot appeared to be coming from the alleyway between the hotel and the strip mall next door. Moving slowly and discreetly, he slid up to the stone wall that comprised the back of the hotel. Shifting his head, he peeked around the corner.

Sofia was there, head tilted back, speaking to a man. One who was very tall and extremely broad-shouldered, with straight black hair the exact color and texture of Latimus's. His massive form was an almost exact replica of his brothers'...and his own. Feeling his eyes grow wide, Heden's brain struggled to make sense of the impossible: this man was a Vampyre.

Moreover, this man was a direct relative. The similarity of his appearance couldn't be explained any other way.

"What the hell?" he whispered.

Sofia's arms waved in the air as she spoke. The gestures were impatient and frustrated. The tone of her voice got louder with each sentence, and Heden struggled to hear their hushed words.

"No, Sofia," the man said. "We can't push off the attack. It's now or never. They might already know we're coming."

"Which is why I need more time. Give me one month. I swear, I'll hack back in again and figure out a way to get them all together so we can combine our efforts."

"I don't want them together!" he yelled, causing her to flinch. "I told you, they're strongest when they're united. We must kill them in small groups."

"Heden is on alert. There's no way I can kill Darkrip and his family now."

Rage marred the man's features. "I knew it would come to this. You're unable to kill them. Damn it, Sofia! He's an abomination, don't you see? So are his spawns. As long as Crimeous's blood flourishes, the immortals will never rise to true prominence. To their true potential!"

"I don't care about that," she snapped. "You know my reasons. And he wouldn't want me to murder them. I know that now."

"Traitor!" he screamed, grasping her around the neck with his large hand. "I'll fucking strangle you for crossing me!"

Sofia gasped, clutching at his hand and scraping it with her nails, attempting to pull it away.

It was all Heden needed to jump into action. Springing from his spot behind the wall, he jetted toward them. "Hey! Let her go!"

The man growled, his face snapping toward Heden. Replicas of his own eyes stared back at him, ice-blue and swarming with anger.

"No," the man said, the muscles of his forearm tightening as he choked Sofia. Heden reached behind and pulled a gun from his bag. Lifting it, he aimed it at the man who looked so much like Latimus. The situation was surreal.

"I won't ask again," Heden said, barrel pointed between the Vampyre's eyes where he stood two feet away. "I know this won't kill you, but it will hurt pretty fucking bad, dude. Let the human go."

He snarled, tossing Sofia aside. She crumpled to the ground, hands surrounding her throat as she gasped for air.

The Vampyre's shoulders straightened, and he turned to face Heden. "You've made a grave mistake here, *brother*. You cannot stop me!" Lifting his arms, he closed his eyes, palms facing the sky. "I will have my day. I am the one true ruler of Etherya's Earth. The one true heir. Enjoy your last days before I assume my throne."

He began to chant, the utterances a jumble of a language Heden had never heard. Clouds rushed in, darkening the sky above, as the Vampyre uttered the low-toned words. Lightening streaked overhead, booming as it illuminated the black clouds.

And then, the hulking man vanished.

Heden lowered the gun, unable to believe his eyes. The only beings he knew capable of dematerialization were Darkrip and Evie. Blood pulsed through his frame as he ran to Sofia, crouching down beside her. Deep red marks lined the pale skin of her throat, spurring a knee-jerk protective streak inside his gut. Unsure what to do with the unwanted feeling, he pushed it away to focus on the woman.

"Just breathe," he said, attempting to soothe Sofia. Those translucent eyes latched onto his as she panted, both hands resting above her collarbone.

"He shouldn't be able to dematerialize," she said, her voice hoarse. "I don't know how..." The words broke off as she began to cough. Heden rubbed her upper back, patting it gently until the coughing fit ceased.

Placing his fingers underneath her chin, he tilted her head so he could look into her soul. "Little human," he said, unconsciously running the pad of his thumb over her jawline, "what the hell have you gotten us into?"

Chapter 9

Heden helped Sofia to her feet, lifting her as if she were a feather. The woman was small, the top of her head barely cresting his collarbone. She eyed him warily, the scant freckles across her pert nose scrunching as her eyelids narrowed.

"Are you going to kill me?" she asked softly.

Heden realized he was still holding the gun in his left hand. "No," he said, engaging the trigger lock and stuffing the gun in the side pocket of his bag. "But I would like to go somewhere private, where we can talk."

She slid her teeth over her full bottom lip, gliding it back and forth as she gnawed. While she debated, Heden studied her. Never had he seen irises so clear. They swirled with shades of green and blue, magnificent as the jewels that sparkled on the fancy chandeliers at Astaria. Almond-shaped eyes under black-winged eyebrows led to a button nose and full lips. Springy dark hair sat atop her shoulders. His fist clenched involuntarily as he imagined grasping the strands in his hand. Would they be soft or coarse? Strange, but he felt compelled to discover the answer.

"I can't help you now," she said, dragging him from his musings. "Bakari will surely kill me for defecting. I thought I could do it, but I can't. I can't kill a pregnant woman."

"My sister," he said solemnly.

"Yes," she whispered.

"Who is Bakari?"

Her throat bobbed behind the smooth skin of her neck as she hesitated. "You already know."

"He called me brother and is a dead ringer for Latimus. How in the hell do I have a sibling I never knew about?"

Sofia sighed, rubbing a hand across her face. "I can't help you. I have to go into hiding. Otherwise, I'll be dead before morning. He's very powerful. More so now he's learned to transport."

Heden's eyes darted between hers. "I don't know you, Sofia, but I just saved your life. Not to be a dick, but you kinda owe me one here."

"I can't," she whispered, shaking her head.

"Um, yeah, you can," he said, picking up her bag, which had fallen off her shoulder during the tense exchange with Bakari. "I'll bet you have a room hooked up with all the fancy spyware you coded to hack into our servers. Nice job, by the way. I'll need you to show me everything. Come on." Extending the bag, he motioned for her to take it.

Sofia expelled a breath, grabbing the pack and swinging it over her shoulder. "I told you, it's too late—"

"I'll be the judge of that. Let's go. You can't fight me off, and you've lost your ally. It's time to help me, little human."

Rolling her eyes, she pivoted and began walking to the front of the hotel.

Heden's lips curved as he followed her, shoulders set and head held high. *Lots of thorns on this rose*, he thought as her hair bounced over her backpack. How many did a man have to navigate through to get to the petals? He wasn't sure, but it seemed like an interesting challenge.

They entered the lobby and elevator, Sofia pushing the button labeled "three." It whooshed to the floor, and she exited, turning left and holding the plastic card to the second door. Once inside, she threw her bag on one of the double beds.

"*Don't* touch anything," she said, holding up a finger in warning. "I need to use the bathroom, and then I'll decide what, if anything, I'm going to tell you. Give me a minute." Shooting him a glare, she entered the bathroom, clicking the lock behind her.

Heden didn't waste a moment, springing into action. Pulling the laptop from her bag, he set it on the desk and booted it up. When prompted for the password, he pulled his phone from his bag along with the USB cord. Opening the password hacking app, he plugged his phone into the computer, uncovering her credentials in three seconds flat. Once inside, he began clicking through the files.

There were so many, each labeled with names of his family and extended family. Accessing the folder named "Heden," he double-clicked the document titled "Notes." There, laid out before him, was a detailed account of the last year of his life. The spots he frequented, when he picked up his nieces and nephews from school, the women he'd dated. The Withers girls appeared on the list, reminding him of the monotony of his life. Wash, rinse, repeat.

The feeling his old existence had ended crashed over him. Enemies were detailing his every action and those of the people he loved. Peace was a beautiful illusion that was now shattered. How many unidentified foes were aligned with Bakari?

Heden clicked on another folder labeled "SS." Opening the first file, he read the name "Diabolos." It sounded familiar, as if he'd heard it somewhere before, but he couldn't place it. Was this person an immortal? If so, was he a Slayer, Vampyre or Deamon?

"Hey!" Sofia yelled, rushing over and closing the laptop. "I told you not to touch anything!"

Heden struggled to tamp down warring emotions: anger at being surveilled, and the deep, protective swell he felt toward this imp of a human. It was imperative he befriend her. She had valuable intelligence he was desperate to possess. The good news? He could be *very* charming when he needed to be, especially with women.

Pasting on what he knew to be a devastatingly handsome grin, he reached for her arm. "Sorry, I was just curious."

"Look," she said, shrugging him away, "I've monitored you for years. I get that you think you're god's gift to women. I couldn't give a damn about being seduced or getting laid or whatever you think you can accomplish with that shit-eating smile. Save it for someone else." Huffing, she began gathering her equipment to stuff inside her bag.

"Wait," he said, encircling her wrist.

"Touch me again, and I'll murder you."

Heden released her arm, unable to tamp down his smile. "You're feisty. I'm guessing by your last name, you're Italian. I've always heard Italians have a temper."

"You bet your ass we do. We definitely don't like having our computers hacked under our noses."

"Says the woman who put spyware on all my servers. Hypocritical, much?" he asked, arching an eyebrow.

"You immortals think you're so much better than us. If I hear one more person call me a stupid human, I'm going to freaking scream. I put the program on your servers because I knew I was a better hacker than you and you'd never find a trail. You'd only find it if you searched the task manager. And I was right." She crossed her arms over her chest, daring him to argue.

"Fine," he said, showing his palms. "You over-hacked me. Well done. What was it for? How did you meet Bakari, and why does he want to murder everyone on the damn planet?"

"I don't find I'm really in the helping mood right now. Sorry. Thank you for saving my life, but I have to get the hell out of here." She stuffed the laptop in her bag and began grabbing the few items in the drawers under the television, placing them in the suitcase resting on the luggage rack against the far wall.

Heden observed her furious movements, reminded of the profound pain he'd witnessed in her stunning eyes when he'd confronted her earlier that morning. She stalked into the bathroom, scooped up her toiletries and dumped them in the suitcase. When she closed it and started zipping it, he placed his hand over hers.

"I'm sorry," he said, making sure his touch was gentle. "Someone must've hurt you badly to motivate you to align with the creature I saw outside."

She stood frozen, breath slightly labored, as he held her hand.

"Whoever it was, I'm sorry. If you talk to me, I'll do my best to rectify it."

"You can't," she said, shaking her head, still staring at the felt suitcase. "It won't ever be right, and I'll never forgive myself. I should've been there with him. He was old, and I left him all alone. Now, he's gone."

"Who's gone, Sofia?" he asked, wanting to comfort her but sensing she needed space. Anguish vibrated from her body, surrounding Heden in the cloud of its pallor. It was heavy and dark, and he hurt for her.

She shook her head, a tear glistening on her cheek.

Emotion slammed his solar plexus. Unable to stop himself, he slid his palm across the back of her neck. "Who, Sofia?"

Suddenly, a rush of air washed over them, breaking the serenity of the moment. They both rotated toward the disturbance, but Heden's gaze was inexorably locked on Sofia's face. Her eyes widened, awash with fear and rage, and she whispered one shocked word: "No!"

Sofia stood, stunned, as the woman she hated with all her heart materialized into the room. Fear closed her throat, and anger welled in her chest.

"No!" she screamed again, shaking her head.

"Francesco," Evie said, standing tall and still, her tone remorseful.

"Evie?" Heden asked. "What the hell—?"

"Her grandfather Francesco," Evie repeated, gaze never leaving Sofia's. "That's who she lost."

"How do you know this?" Heden asked, his voice sounding a thousand miles away to Sofia's ringing ears.

"Because I killed him," Evie said softly.

The confession broke Sofia, who'd waited so long to hear the words. A cry burst from her throat, and she said through clenched teeth, "Say it again, you horrible bitch."

"I killed him," Evie said, clear and morose. "It's the first time I've ever regretted killing someone, Sofia. Especially a man. I did it in anger but also in compassion. It's the only way I've been able to accept it. I'll never forgive myself, but at least I can accept I alleviated some of his suffering."

"What the hell are you talking about?" Sofia vibrated with indignation as she felt Heden struggle to make sense of their cryptic conversation beside her.

"He was sick, Sofia," she said, moving forward a few inches.

"No! Don't fucking move! I know about the cancer. I could've saved him!"

Evie held up her hands, conceding to Sofia's wish and remaining still. "There was nothing you could've done, Sofia. A creature such as I can see these things. I saved him months of tubes and hospitals, poking and prodding. Your grandfather was a proud man. Do you think he would've really wanted that?"

Sofia struggled to process her enemy's words, hating that she was robbed of the chance to help Francesco. "I could've tried to help—"

"No, Sofia. It was over for him. He lived a wonderful life. He rests with Maria in the Passage now—I can feel it with every bone in my body. Knowing he's happy helps me when I'm overcome with regret."

"How *dare* you say you regret anything! You murdered him!"

"I know he was all you had," she said. Sofia wanted to retch from the genuineness in her olive-green eyes. It couldn't be real. She was a monster. "I'm sorry I took him from you before you could say goodbye. It was very unfair, and I don't blame you for hating me. It's unforgivable."

Sofia inched toward the bed, consumed with the knowledge her gun rested inside her bag. She'd bought it for the sole purpose of killing the woman who now stood before her. Could she extricate it and shoot the Slayer-Deamon before she realized her intent?

"I know the gun is in your bag, Sofia," Evie said, her voice calm and undaunted. "You don't need to reach for it." Holding out her hand, palm up, she closed her eyes. Within seconds, a handgun appeared.

"Here," Evie said, slowly approaching Sofia, gun outstretched. "Take it. Shoot me, if you must. I denied you a goodbye, but I won't deny you your revenge. It's no less than I deserve." Ever so slowly, Evie grasped Sofia's forearm, placing the gun in her hand. "If you want to shoot me, I won't fight you."

As if in a dream, Sofia watched this person she'd spent countless hours tracking gingerly back away. Once a few feet were between them, she stopped. Resolve emanated from her unmoving body.

Hands trembling, Sofia grasped the butt of the gun with both hands. Lifting it slowly, she aimed between the red-haired bitch's arresting green eyes.

"Don't do this, Sofia," Heden's deep voice said beside her. "Evie has changed. She saved so many people in our world. She made a choice to be a better person. You have that same choice. Don't become what you profess to hate."

"I've waited so long to have you right here," Sofia said, wetness clouding her eyes as she held the gun, arms shaking and heavy. "So many years."

"I know," Evie said, her tone so sad it resonated in Sofia's deadened soul. "It's okay. Shoot me."

Breath shuddered through her quaking lungs as Sofia envisioned pulling the trigger. She wanted to so badly, but her fingers were frozen. Closing her eyes, she summoned the image of her beloved grandfather. His face beamed back, so full of love and hope; so proud of the woman she'd become.

Who would she be once she shot Evie? Would her heart finally be as black as the murderer who stood silent before her? Would her soul wither to be as dark as Bakari's, mired in violence and death?

Sofia.

The word whispered through her consciousness, Francesco's smiling face still in her mind's eye. It was said in his voice, as if from heaven.

Opening her eyes, Sofia admitted the truth. She would never be able to kill Evie. She would never be able to murder anyone. The capability just wasn't there. Feeling the failure consume her, she breathed a sob and collapsed backward, her knees giving out under her.

"Hey," Heden's firm voice said as he caught her, his broad arms sliding under her arms. "It's okay. I've got you."

Unable to control her sobs, she slid down his body, onto the floor, and buried her head in her knees, clutching her thighs to her chest. Wracked with pain, Sofia acknowledged she would never avenge her grandfather.

A steady hand stroked her hair as if from far away while she cried bucket upon bucket of tears into her dark-washed jeans. Eventually, the emotion evolved into numbness, causing the tears to abate. Sucking in deep breaths of air, she grasped her legs in a death grip, wanting to disappear though a hole in the floor.

"Shhhh..." someone soothed above her, and she realized it was Heden, comforting her as he caressed her hair. It was so long since she'd been touched by another, and it should've felt foreign since he was a stranger, but it felt...good. Right. Normal.

Thinking herself insane, she lifted her head. Focusing on Evie, she blinked her eyes to clear away the remaining moisture.

"Thank you for not shooting me," she said, her lips quirking into a sardonic smile. "I very much didn't want to bleed out today. Especially since my husband has finally knocked me up."

Out of the corner of her eye, Sofia observed Heden's wide grin as he still crouched beside her. "Yeah?" he asked, joy radiating from his large body.

"Yeah," she said with a nod. "I was going to tell you the other day, when you were ogling the kids on the playground, but decided to wait. I'm a mess. Ken's over the moon. I can't wait to see how I fuck this up. Just freaking great."

Lowering to the floor, she crossed her legs, now eye-level with Sofia. "I loved your grandfather, Sofia. I know that undoubtedly means nothing to you, but he was very special to me. This probably sounds insane but killing him was something I desperately needed to do in order to become the person I am today. I think he always knew he would help me realize my true potential. It doesn't make it right, but it's the only explanation I can give you. I will do my best to help you process your grief and ensure his soul rests in peace. What can I do to rectify this?"

"I don't want your help!" Sofia screamed, still hating this woman whom she didn't have the fortitude to destroy. "I want you to leave me the hell alone!"

"That's fair," Evie said, tilting her head in acknowledgment. "I'm pretty much the evil bitch you've always thought I would be, although my husband has tempered me slightly."

Anchoring on her arms, Evie stood, placing her hands in the pockets of her brown slacks. "When you're ready to cash in on the debt I owe you, both for killing Francesco and for not shooting me today, let me know. In the meantime, you're pretty much screwed. I came through the ether shortly after Heden. Somehow, I knew my past actions had a hand in whatever the hell was happening. I researched Bakari while Heden tracked you down. Because I'm able to transport, I discovered things about him from different pockets of the world. He's dangerous, Sofia, and now that you've crossed him, he'll be out for blood. You'd be smart to align with Heden and help his family, so they protect you in return. Otherwise, it will be your murder we're dealing with next."

With those ominous words, Evie shrugged. "I'm not trying to be dramatic but, *damn*, that was a great parting line." Red lips twitched in a smile. "See you guys later. I'll update the others on what I've learned until you can uncover the rest. Take care of her, Heden."

Air swirled around the room, and in a flash, she was gone.

Exhausted, Sofia tilted her head back to look at Heden. The Vampyre stared down at her, his palm still resting on her hair above her shoulder.

"So," he said, smiling. "You're into revenge. Cool, but heavy. Have you ever thought about knitting? Or tennis? Or maybe karaoke? There's got to be a better hobby that won't get you killed."

The gravity of the moment was so tense, so profound, that Sofia lost it. There, crouched on the floor, she broke into a fit of uncontrolled laughter.

Chapter 10

Sofia struggled to swipe the tears of mirth as her body convulsed with laughter. As the gasping abated, she shook her head at Heden.

"You like to joke," she observed.

"When the time's right," he said, flashing his teeth. His fangs sat slightly pointed above his full lower lip, and her stomach lurched into a somersault. Had he ever bitten anyone with them? Would it hurt?

"And in my opinion, the time is always right for a bit of humor." Lifting to his feet, he extended his hand. "Come on, little human. We've got a lot to discuss."

Staring up at him, she realized she trusted him. There was an air of calm sureness and relaxed openness that radiated from his hulking body. The feeling was so foreign to her, she hesitated.

"I'm not going to hurt you," he said, the words a soft rush against her suddenly heated skin. "Although I'm not thrilled you've put my family in danger, I need you. Come on." He motioned his hand, urging her to take it.

Placing her smaller hand in his, Sofia felt off-balance as he pulled her up. Planting her feet on the ground so she didn't sway, she grappled with what to say. Fortunately, her stomach growled, saving her from forming the words in her mouth that was suddenly dry as sandpaper.

"How long has it been since you ate?" he asked, concern in his deep baritone.

"I...I'm not sure," she said, running her fingers through the curls at her crown. "I was too busy trying to hack into the immortal servers this morning to grab anything at the coffee shop."

"Right. Well, your stomach's obviously not with the program. Let's get you some food while we chat."

Sofia blinked up at him. "It's fine. I need to figure out—"

"Nope," he interrupted. "I've learned from my sister and Miranda that nothing good comes from a hangry woman."

"Hangry?"

"Hungry and angry. That word's everywhere. Have you been living under a rock?"

Sofia shrugged. "There's not much time to keep up on pop culture when you're hunting your dead grandfather's immortal murderer."

"Eh, that's an okay excuse, I guess." He grinned, contorting his face into something so handsome. How many women had he given that smile to? Countless, if Sofia's research held true. She'd do well to remember he had incentive to charm her. The information she possessed was extremely valuable.

"Pack up your stuff, since your location's been made, and we'll head to my sister's house."

"They're not safe now shit's hit the fan. I don't know if that's a good idea."

"It's safer we're there so I can warn Darkrip. He's powerful and can better protect us there than anywhere."

Sofia hesitated, turning her head to glance at her suitcase.

"I've got it," Heden said, plodding over and zipping it before placing it on the floor and extending the handle. "Grab your laptop and bag, and let's go."

Realizing it was futile to argue, Sofia sighed, packed up the rest of her things and slung her bag over her shoulder. "I need to return the rental car. The less traceable I am, the better. I used a false name to rent it, but you found me, which means someone else can too."

"How long until Bakari attacks us?" he asked.

"Our plan was to attack in a few days," Sofia said, swallowing thickly.

"Then we need to get our crap together. Let's go."

He exited the room, Sofia reluctantly following, and they took care of checking out of the hotel and returning her rental car. After that, they hailed a cab to Darkrip and Arderin's suburban home.

Darkrip pulled open the wooden front door, a scowl on his face. He studied Sofia under the cover of the awning. "This one's got some really fucked-up images in her head," he muttered to Heden.

"I know," Heden said, placing his arm around Sofia's shoulders. The protective gesture made something swell in her chest. "But she's seen the errors of her ways. Right, Sof?"

Sof. It was the nickname her grandfather gave her. She'd always felt so loved when he held her and spoke the word. She wanted to tell Heden to fuck off, because no one called her that but Francesco, but she couldn't seem to form any words past the lump in her throat. Capitulating, she nodded.

"Who's the old man?" Darkrip asked. "The one plastered all over your memories?"

"My grandfather," Sofia said, her voice barely a whisper. "Your sister killed him."

Darkrip sucked in a deep breath. "We're going to need coffee. And whiskey. Come on." Stepping back, he gestured them both in.

Once the door was closed and locked, he herded them to the kitchen. Sofia thought it so surreal to sit at the table where she'd watched them yesterday, still planning to kill them. She realized now, she would've never been able to go through with it.

"First things first," Heden said, setting her suitcase in the corner before lowering beside her at the cedar table. "Darkrip's going to wrangle up some food for you since you look like you haven't eaten in days. And then you're going to tell me everything, so I can head to the realm and update Sathan."

"I didn't realize I was expected to play servant," Darkrip grumbled, opening the refrigerator to scan the contents.

"Don't worry about him," Heden said, giving her a conspiratorial wink. "He's grumpy but he totally digs this Mr. Mom stuff."

"I'm imagining disintegrating you into dust with a thought," Darkrip replied as he threw some ingredients into a pan and turned on the burner.

Sofia watched their interplay, understanding they were close. How did someone as evil as Darkrip learn to accept and love others without reservation?

"It wasn't easy," the Slayer-Deamon said, his back to her as he stirred the food atop the stove. "I'm not predisposed to feel emotion. But I've chosen to live by my Slayer side, mostly because my wife possesses my soul. It's extremely difficult but worth it. I have my daughter to think about."

"Do you always read others' thoughts?" Sofia asked. "It's pretty annoying."

"He'll stop if you ask him to," Arderin said, breezing into the room in a robe, toweling her long, wet hair. "But that depends. Are you the person who's been watching my family?"

Sofia felt a jolt of guilt, although she hadn't truly done anything to harm them. Yet.

"Yes," she said, thrusting her chin up. "You all have a sense of superiority that's ridiculous considering your past transgressions. Your husband and his sister have murdered countless people, and from what I understand, the Vampyres raided and stole the Slayers' blood for a thousand years in your world."

"The human has a bit of a chip on her shoulder," Heden chimed in when Arderin's eyes narrowed. "Sofia, meet Arderin, my pregnant sister you were planning to murder. Oh, wait...who's ridiculous now?" His eyes wandered to the ceiling as he rubbed his beard.

"Well, I'm here, and those plans are toast now, so I think the tally's still: human, not a murderer; and immortals, pretty fucking terrible."

"Here," Darkrip said, slamming the plate onto the placemat in front of her. "Chicken stir-fry. I'm pretty sure I didn't poison it. Eat up."

Sofia grasped the fork from his outstretched hand, deciding death by poisoned chicken might not be so bad. These people were pissed, and she didn't much like them either.

As she ate, she detailed her activities from the past few years. Darkrip and Arderin were shocked to learn she'd discovered them during their travels to Houston. Sofia brought them up to speed, recounting how she met Bakari and the other members of the Secret Society. She informed them of the immortals who'd been brought back to life by Crimeous's cloned blood, and the multiple-pronged attack that was scheduled only days away.

"Do you think they'll still try to carry out that plan?" Arderin asked, reaching over with her fork and scooping some food from Darkrip's plate into her mouth.

"She likes food even though she's a Vampyre," Darkrip said, answering the question floating in Sofia's mind. "Correction: She likes *my* food. I can't get a damn plate down before she's stolen it all."

"Thank you, husband," Arderin garbled, mouth full of food. She placed a loving kiss on his cheek as he glowered. "Your son likes it too. I need energy before I head to the hospital tonight." She rubbed her distended abdomen. "You were saying, Sofia?"

"I don't know," Sofia said, slowly shaking her head. "Bakari is determined to kill you all, and the plan was pretty flawless. But now that he's realized I can't complete my part, I don't know what he'll do."

"How did he learn to dematerialize?" Darkrip asked. "Did he inject my father's cloned blood?"

"From my understanding, it doesn't work that way," Sofia said. "It can bring an immortal back but it doesn't transfer the Dark Lord's powers."

"Then, how?" Heden asked. "Because the son of a bitch disappeared into thin air."

Sofia inhaled a breath. "He's been studying a woman who lives in New Orleans. She's...not of this world, but not of yours either. An anomaly I haven't spent enough time researching to figure out. She possesses the knowledge of the ancient Native American shamans and understands the complexities of dark magic, the occult and voodoo. I can only guess she concocted a spell or potion that allows him to transport."

Arderin sat back in her chair. "This is all so surreal. How can we have a brother we knew nothing about?" she asked Heden.

"I don't know," Heden said, lacing his fingers behind his head as he leaned back in his chair. Sofia noticed his biceps, straining and burly outside the tight sleeves of his shirt. "There's a five-year gap between you and Latimus. I just always figured Mom and Dad took a break from knocking boots, but it looks like they had another kid. Why wouldn't the archivists record it? Since it was before the Awakening, it should've been recorded by the Slayer soothsayers and the Vampyre archivists."

"Forget the archivists. Why in the hell didn't Mom and Dad tell us? Or at least tell Sathan and Latimus? It's bizarre."

Heden expelled a heavy breath. "The Awakening happened a few years later. Maybe they were waiting to tell us all when we were older and never got the chance. I just don't know, sis. It's mind boggling."

"He bears a mark," Sofia said, looking back and forth between them as they sat on each side of her. "I heard him discussing it with some of the others. Something about a prophecy and how the one who bore the mark would be evil. I think the soothsayers and archivists decided he was better off dead and decided not to record it. Unfortunately, someone found him and raised him in the human world. He's amassed wealth and status here that you wouldn't believe. He also likes to drink human blood. Bakari believes the legend of Count Dracula is based on him. He likens himself to a god and wants nothing more than to rule your realm."

"Wow," Heden said, unlacing his fingers and running a hand through his thick hair. "Sounds like our brother's an arrogant douche."

Sofia huffed a laugh. "Honestly, he is. His arrogance is one of the things I can't stand about him."

"Why did you align with him?" Arderin asked.

Exhaling a deep breath, Sofia rested her back on the chair and twisted her fingers together as she spoke. "My grandfather's murder was very difficult for me. He was the only family I had left. When I discovered someone had killed him, I became obsessed with avenging him to ensure his soul rests in peace. I'm Catholic and believe his soul can't live eternally in Heaven without retribution."

"And what does your god think about murdering innocent people to accomplish that goal?" Darkrip asked as he sat across from her.

Sofia shot him a sardonic glare. "Obviously, that was the part I was having problems with. I just couldn't bring myself to do it. All this time wasted, and I've failed miserably." Mortified she was getting emotional, she struggled to tamp down the moisture in her eyes.

"I get it," Heden said, reaching over to cover her clenched hands with his broad one.

Through her blurred gaze, Sofia witnessed the glance that passed between Arderin and Darkrip. They were as stunned by Heden's compassion toward her as she was.

"We believe in the Passage in our world, similar to your Heaven. One must have a proper send-off to the Passage to reunite with their family there. The sentiments are not so different."

"Yes, but Heaven is real."

"So is the Passage. In my mind, at least," Heden said softly. "I was only a baby when my parents were killed, so I don't remember them. I believe that one day, I'll meet them again in the Passage."

"But you're immortal and self-healing. The chances of death are slim to none for you," Sofia said.

"Not true," he said, squeezing her hand before he sat back, resting his palms flat on the table. "Many Vampyres have perished over the last ten centuries. We all have our time, immortal or not. When mine comes, I'll accept it."

"But for now, we'd like to stay alive if at all possible," Darkrip said, his expression derisive. "Heden, we need to get this information to the others as quickly as possible. As much as I like having you here, we need to get you back to the immortal world."

"Agreed. And I'm taking Sofia with me."

"Whoa," Arderin said, her dark eyebrows forming a V between her eyes. "No way. Etherya will crap herself if you take a human through the ether."

"We have to protect her, Arderin," Heden said. "Bakari and the others will be furious she defected."

"No fucking way!" his sister shouted. "Darkrip can transport her somewhere she can hide. I'm not pissing off the goddess. It's not happening—"

"I appreciate the two of you discussing me as if I'm invisible," Sofia said, jerking to her feet as her chair scraped the floor. "But I've taken care of myself my entire life and I certainly don't need help from a bunch of entitled creatures who aren't even human. Thanks, but I'm out." She stalked to the suitcase in the corner, pulled up the handle, stacked her bag on top and began wheeling it out of the kitchen toward the front door.

"Hey!" Heden said, grabbing her arm and bringing her to a halt in the hallway. "Sorry, but you're not going anywhere, Sofia."

She pivoted, yanking her arm out of his grasp. "I've told you what you want to know. Good luck saving your family. You don't need to keep me safe, and I'm done with this." Rotating, she resumed walking.

"Wait," he called. The plea in his tone caused her to pause. "I need your help enhancing our communication equipment. I haven't figured out how to transmit through the ether. How did you do it?"

Sofia scoffed, staring at the floor. "Years of coding. You'll figure it out eventually."

Her shoulders stiffened from his nearness as the heat from his large frame enveloped her backside. Ever so slowly, he slid his palms over the soft skin where her neck sloped.

"Please," he whispered, breath burning the shell of her ear. "If you help me, I'll repay you. Whatever you ask for. If I can make it happen, I will."

"I already told you," she said, turning to stare into his sky-blue eyes. One of his hands remained on the juncture of her neck and shoulder, the skin tingling underneath. "I've lost the one thing I want, and he's never coming back."

"You don't have any other family?" he asked softly.

Sofia wanted to drown in the sympathy that lined his handsome face. "No," she said, sadness flooding her as it always did when she took time to dwell on her solitary and isolated existence. "I really want to have kids one day, but I'm thirty-eight going on menopause, so my chances are about as good as winning the lottery while getting struck by lightning."

Broad lips curved into a smile. "You made a joke. Good one."

She rolled her eyes. "Yeah. I'm hilarious."

His eyes darted between hers as the silence stretched. "Don't go into hiding," he finally said. "Let me protect you. In exchange, you'll show me how to communicate through the ether. You helped get us into this mess, but you're stuck in it now too. Let's work together, Sof. Please."

"My grandfather called me Sof," she said, her voice thick and gravelly. "I liked it."

The pad of his thumb ran over her neck, back and forth, as the corner of his smile deepened. "Yeah? I like it too. But I won't call you that if it's too painful. I just think it's cute. Not as formal as Sofia."

She was sure he could feel her pulse thrumming under his thumb. "I'm not interested in being seduced. I'm not one of your stupid Vampyre women. It won't work on me."

"Thank god," he said, displaying a mock expression of relief. "Because you're hideous."

She couldn't control the laughter that sprung from her throat. "It wouldn't be right to let a stranger call me by the same nickname as the person who knew me best."

"Then I'll just have to get to know you."

"I'm also not interested in making friends."

"Great. I have enough of those. How about super-hackers on a mission?" Stepping back, he lowered his hand, extending it for her to shake.

"The last time I made a deal like that, it led me here."

"Then let's make sure this one's better. I promise not to force you to murder anyone. Deal?"

In spite of herself, she breathed a laugh. "Fine," she said, shaking his hand. "Let's see if I can stay alive long enough to teach you how to code. You're a pretty terrible hacker." Grasping his hand, she shook.

"I'll need a lot of instruction. We might end up becoming friends anyway."

"Lord, I hope not." Smiling into his gorgeous eyes, Sofia had the nagging feeling this wager was lined with conditions and complexities she couldn't begin to understand. It should have terrified her. Instead, against all odds, her heart felt free for the first time since her grandfather's death.

Chapter 11

Bakari drove the rental car down the dirt road that led to the wooden cottage. Long strands of willows stretched from the trees above, several of them brushing the top of the vehicle. Tupelo gum trees grew out of the murky water on either side of the road, their bases broad and ridged. They'd germinated decades ago, seeing much from their quiet, stable stumps.

Stopping a few feet from the red bicycle chained to the post by the front porch stairs, Bakari observed the shack. The wood had faded long ago, but it carried the charm of a home where life thrived. Smoke emanated from the chimney, forming a snake-like swirl that dissipated through the trees above to the blue sky.

Ascending the stairs, which were sturdier than they appeared, he waited. The door creaked open, and a woman emerged, her long yellow skirt flowing as she leaned her hip on the doorframe.

"Hello, Bakari," she said, stirring the contents of the small bowl she held in her hand. Whatever was inside smelled dank, as if she'd crushed up some acrid spices or perhaps a few wayward crawdads.

"Hello, Tatiana," he said, staring into her amber eyes, offset by thick, waist-length dark brown curls. Her umber-brown skin seemed to glow under the midday sun. He'd never seen her wear a stitch of makeup, nor did she need to. She was a stunning woman who betrayed an air of superiority and confidence that surpassed his own. Whereas many accused him of being arrogant and entitled, she would never be described with such words. Her power was intrinsic...understood...cultivated, so it wasn't a threat or a curse. It just *existed*.

"I need more of the potion," he said, not bothering with niceties so he could get straight to the point and push away the imbalance she made him feel. She was the only creature on the entire planet that had ever unnerved him. Intuition informed him this meant she was dangerous, but so far, she'd been an ally of sorts. Sometimes, he felt she was just toying with him, using him as a plaything to assuage the boredom of her mundane life. But she was a powerful ally, and with Sofia's defection, he needed her now more than ever.

An onyx eyebrow arched as she lazily stirred, her arm moving in an almost hypnotizing motion. "I felt the imbalance. You were able to dematerialize. I'm happy to see the concoction worked. I've been developing that one for some time."

Bakari nodded. "I ingested the potion and chanted the spell you taught me. I transported several miles. I would like to be able to travel further distances."

Dark pupils bore into him under her questioning stare. "You'd be wise to use ancient magic sparingly. The gods do not take well to those who do not respect their eminence."

"I have no wish to anger your gods. I believe they support my cause."

The stirring halted as she contemplated him through narrowed eyes. "The gods have a respect for the world of immortal creatures beyond the ether. Be wary you don't dredge up their protective nature. You have a great battle before you."

Bakari's own eyes tapered, becoming frustrated at her lecture. "I only wish to restore Etherya's realm to true prominence. To ensure the species remain separate and free of Crimeous's blood."

"Etherya herself once loved the creature Crimeous—"

"Enough," he interrupted, frustrated at how she always spoke in riddles and platitudes. "What will it cost me to get more of the potion? I'd like to purchase enough to last me several years. I can pay you whatever price you name."

Throaty laughter surrounded him as she scoffed. "Money has no value for me. You should know this by now."

Bakari felt his jaw clench. "Then, what? There must be something you want. Something you consider valuable."

Tatiana inhaled a full breath, her nostrils flaring as she pondered. Finally, she said, "I would like a lock of hair from a child of Crimeous. Anyone who shares his blood will suffice. It will be a potent addition to some of my more sinister spells."

Bakari quickly catalogued her request. Darkrip and Evie would be difficult to extricate such a sample from. "I will get one from Calinda," he said, referring to Darkrip and Arderin's daughter.

"That will be sufficient," she said with a nod. "Once I have it, I will repay you with enough of the concoction to last several decades."

Bakari wondered what dark spells she would use the tresses for.

"I have my own reasons," she said, somehow reading the question in his expression. "You don't see broadly enough to understand them. Your mind's eye is narrowed with hate and revenge."

"Says the woman who spends all day wielding black magic in a secluded cabin," he muttered.

The corner of her lip curved. "Go. Gather what I request. I will be here when you're ready to move forward." Stepping back, she sent him one last subtle and derisive nod before closing the door.

Sighing, Bakari headed to the car, annoyed he had to return to L.A. But first, he needed to contact the other members of the society. Angered that Tatiana wouldn't just supply him with the substance he needed to transport, he debated turning back and murdering her. Since that wouldn't help his cause, he drove to the airport, determined to stay focused on the end game.

Moira turned the key in the lock on the front door of the gallery. Pulling the handle, she ensured it was secure. When the door didn't budge, she stuffed her keys in her purse and began walking home. The points of her heels made a clinking sound as she strolled upon the smooth sidewalk.

The night was clear under the full moon, allowing her to see her surroundings quite clearly. Passing the alleyway to her right, the blond hairs on her arms stiffened. Drawing her sweater tighter across her shoulders, she glanced toward the dark passageway.

A man stood back against the wall, shrouded in a dark coat and hat. For some reason, Moira froze, entranced. He lifted a cheroot to his lips, the tip glowing bright as he inhaled. The scent wafted toward Moira, and she gasped. It was the same brand of cigarettes her ex-husband always smoked. She would know the aroma anywhere, as it used to surround her battered body when he would light one after beating her.

Reminding herself Diabolos was long-dead, Moira tried to calm her pounding heart. The man's build was shadowed but reminded her so much of the man who'd caused her such intense pain.

The shrill chirp of the phone from her purse snapped her out of the nightmarish memories. Lifting the device, she held it to her ear. "Hello?"

"Moira," her current husband's voice called, "are you okay? You sound strange."

"I'm fine," she said, running her hand through her golden tresses. "Just thought I saw someone I knew."

"Are you on your way home?" Aron asked. "I'm leaving the castle now. I can meet up with you."

"I'm almost home. I can wait for you, if you like."

"No," he said, his tone warm. "Go on home so you can rest. You've been on your feet all day. I'll be there in about twenty minutes."

"Okay," she said, eyes narrowed as she watched the shadowed man throw his cheroot to the ground and stomp on it with his foot. Before sauntering away, she could've sworn he gave a slight tip of his hat. Was the action meant for her?

"Moira?" Aron called at her silence.

"Um, yeah, sounds good," she said, shaking her head to rid it of the madness. "See you at home."

"We're baby-making tonight, right?" he asked. Moira could almost see his smile through the phone.

"Oh, yeah," she said, feeling her own lips curve. "All night long, buster. Get ready."

Her regal aristocrat uttered a soft growl, causing her to chuckle. "I'm ready. See you soon, love."

Ending the call, she resumed her stroll, unnerved by how much the man in the alleyway reminded her of Diabolos. Unable to shake the morbid feeling, she kept her phone in her hand the entire way, finger near the call button, just in case.

Chapter 12

Heden decided to wait to return to the immortal world so he could spend some time with Callie before she went to bed. After Darkrip picked her up from school, they ate dinner together before Arderin went in for her shift that evening. Although Heden offered for Sofia to eat dinner with them, she declined, choosing to work on her laptop in the living room. Now she'd agreed to help the royal immortals, she wanted to disable the Secret Society's devices so they couldn't communicate through the ether.

After dinner was finished, Arderin pulled Heden outside, her grip firm on his wrist.

"Are you going to beat me up again?" he asked, letting her drag him into the back yard. "Because I'm pretty sure I can take you now that I'm fully grown."

His sister's features contorted with fury. "You're making a mistake, Heden. You can't take a human into the immortal world. What the hell are you thinking? She was planning to murder us about eight hours ago," she said, exasperated.

"Look," he said, holding his palms up, "I'm not happy about this situation either, but I can read people, sis. She's not a monster. She's a woman with a broken heart and an inflamed sense of revenge. Evie killed her grandfather, and we need to remember that."

"How do we know this isn't part of their plan? To have you witness Bakari attack her and gain your sympathy?"

Heden gave her a perplexed look. "Have you been watching human soap operas again?"

"For the love of the goddess," Arderin groaned, wrenching her hands at her sides. "This is not a fucking joke, Heden. Our family is under attack by a brother we knew nothing about and a bunch of other enemies, half of them brought back from the dead with Crimeous's blood."

"I know, Arderin," he said, placing his palms over her upper arms. "I get the gravity of the situation. We're going to fight it. Calm down. Your tantrum isn't good for the baby."

"Tantrum, my ass," she muttered, scowling as he rubbed her arms. Heden's heart splintered in tiny pieces when her bottom lip began to quiver. "I just love you," she said, shaking her head. "I love our family. I thought this was over when we killed Crimeous."

"Shhh…" Heden said, drawing her into an embrace. "It's okay, little toad. We're going to figure this out." He smoothed his hand over her dark curls.

"I don't trust her."

"I don't trust her either. But we need her, sis. She knows everything about our enemies. We have to work with her. She's also figured out how to communicate through the ether, and I want that technology implemented on all our devices." Pulling back, he lifted her chin with his fingers. "I mean, how awesome would it be to get to video chat with this handsome mug every day?" With his index finger, he pointed at his face.

She exhaled a laugh, shaking her head. "Sounds terrible."

"Blasphemy!" he teased.

Her ice-blue irises roamed between his. "You're compassionate toward her."

"Yes," he said, nodding. "I've rarely seen pain in someone's eyes as deep as hers. And yet she didn't have the heart to carry out the plan. She's all alone, and we need to help her."

"Why are you so good?" Arderin asked, cupping his cheeks.

"Being the youngest is hard," he said, answering honestly. "You all have found mates and built amazing lives for yourselves. I've always felt a bit overshadowed by how awesome the three of you are. I understand loneliness. Sofia is encompassed by it, and that makes me sympathetic toward her."

Love filled his sister's expression, spurring a warm burst of emotion in his chest. "Oh, Heden, I didn't realize you felt that way. You know I'm always here for you."

"I know," he said, affection for her swishing through his large frame. "You guys are my family, and I love you so much. It's just…I don't know," he said, releasing her and kicking the ground with the toe of his sneaker. "Sathan was always so protective of you, and you and Latimus have such a close bond. I just always felt like the fat kid left behind by the bus, running to catch up while my pants fell down around my ankles."

Arderin burst out laughing, causing Heden to giggle along with her. "It's a funny image, but now, I think I'm finally realizing why you developed the wicked sense of humor. It's a defense mechanism."

"Maybe," he said, shrugging. "It was a way to worm myself into conversation and get some attention. I mean, the three of you are pretty intense. It's hard out here for a pimp."

"Okay, Snoop," she snickered, rubbing the remaining wetness from her earlier tears off her cheek. "I get it. I'm sorry if I ever left you behind. I never meant to. I love you, Heden."

"I love you too," he said, smiling. "We're in uncharted waters here. I'm taking Sofia with me to help us. I'm determined to protect our family."

Her stunning eyes narrowed. "This had better not be about banging her. She's pretty cute for a human."

"Banging?" he asked, holding his hand to his chest in mock mortification. "I'm a virgin, dear sister. Didn't you know?"

"You're full of crap is what you are," she said, laughing as she regarded him. "Don't murk the waters, bro. We've got a lot on our plate here."

"I won't. Humans. Ew. Don't worry."

"Famous last words," she muttered. Huffing in a deep breath, she relented. "Fine. Take her to the realm. Figure out how to beat those bastards and how to contact us through the ether. I'm counting on you."

"Will do. I'd like to read to Callie before I go."

Arderin beamed at him, her white fangs glowing. "She'd love that."

After they headed inside, Arderin bathed Callie, stuffing her into pajamas with little giraffes on them that made her look insanely adorable. When Arderin left for the hospital, Heden read to Callie under the pink canopy of her small bed. Eventually, her eyelids began to droop, and he closed the book, placing a sweet peck on her forehead.

"Don't forget to give the picture to Jack," she said sleepily, looking so innocent as she gazed up at him.

"I won't," Heden said, sliding his fingers over her slick curls. Callie had drawn her favorite cousin a picture of them together, playing by the riverbank at Astaria.

"Mommy says Jack is super sweet to deliver us Slayer blood every month. Every time he visits, he tells me I'm special."

"You are special, baby toad," Heden said, already mourning that he had to leave her.

"Love you, Uncle Heden."

"Love you too." Placing a kiss on her forehead, he stood.

Once downstairs, he gave Darkrip a firm handshake. Gathering his things in his bag, he ensured Sofia had everything she needed in the pack slung across her back. They descended the wooden stairs to the back yard, and Heden held his palm to the air. Generating the ether, he guided Sofia in front of his large body. Pushing her toward the substance, they both trekked to the immortal world.

Sofia waded through the ether, the thick substance threatening to choke her. Exiting the other side, she held her hand up to the blinding rays of the sun. As she gulped air into her starving lungs, Heden appeared beside her.

"It's still daytime here," she said, coughing as she struggled to breathe.

"Yep," Heden said, his breath also labored. Searching his bag, he located a cell phone. Booting it up, he consulted the screen. "About two o'clock in the afternoon. Traveling between realms creates some serious jet lag."

"I still haven't figured it out," Sofia said, swinging the pack from her shoulders and finding the water bottle inside. Unscrewing the top, she took a large swig. "When Bakari taught me how to travel through the ether, he didn't really explain the physics to me. He just showed me how to go back and forth. Sometimes, I came through at night. Others, during the day. How do you all know how to navigate it?"

"Honestly, it's still tough for me too. I had never been to the human world until my sister moved there. Kenden taught me how to generate the ether, but I'm still not a pro. Basically, you imagine where you want to emerge on the other side. The visualization creates a portal that takes you there, but the specific timing can be off. I imagined us returning to daylight, hence it's mid-afternoon. The potency of the mind is a powerful thing."

Sofia nodded. "I studied ancient religions in college. There are so many accounts of people being able to create things with just a thought. I think humans have only scraped the surface of our capabilities."

"Let's hope so. You guys are heathens."

Chuckling at her scowl, Heden pulled up his contacts and dialed Sathan.

"Hey," his brother said, "are you back?"

"Yes," Heden said. "Any chance you can send a four-wheeler to get us?"

"Us?"

"I brought Sofia back to help us. I'm sure Evie's updated everyone on the situation. The human has defected from our enemies and is now aligned with us."

Silence stretched through the phone.

"It's done, Sathan. Can you please send your favorite brother a ride?"

"I'm at Uteria," he said, his voice gruff. "Ken is here and will be there shortly in a four-wheeler. Are you sure we can trust the human?"

"No," Heden said, "but we need her. Tell Ken thanks. I'll ping him my location."

Lowering the phone, Sofia watched him send Kenden the pin.

"Well, little human, we have about twenty minutes before Kenden gets here. In the meantime, let's get to know each other better." He sat in the plushy grass, crossing his legs and leaning back on his outstretched arms. "Sofia Morelli, before you decided to murder my family, what the heck did you do with your life?"

Sofia couldn't stop the laugh from escaping. "I told you, I'm not here to make friends. I'll help you so we can stop Bakari, but then I'm heading back to New York."

"Tell me about New York," he said, undeterred.

Sighing, she figured it wouldn't hurt to chat with him about the city she loved. It was a neutral subject. She sat down, extolling the many virtues of the Big Apple until an engine roared on the horizon. As the four-wheeler approached, they gathered their bags, slinging them over their shoulders.

Kenden arrived, his chestnut hair tussled from the wind. Sofia recognized the handsome Slayer commander from her surveillance.

"Hey, Heden," he said, shaking the Vampyre's hand. "Glad you made it home safely." When he turned to her, Sofia noticed a deep swell of empathy in his deep brown eyes. "And you must be Sofia," he said, extending his hand. "It's really nice to meet you."

She swallowed, overcome by his kindness. He emanated a calm energy filled with caring and concern. "You must be the Slayer who married the red-haired bitch."

Kenden gave her a sad smile and shook her hand. "I understand you're not a big fan of my wife." Releasing her hand, his pupils roved over her face. "I met your grandfather Francesco in Italy several years ago. He was a kind and jovial man. I'm honored to have met him, and sadly, my actions spurred the events that led to his death. I'm so sorry, Sofia."

Tears burned her eyes as she struggled with emotion.

"I wish I had known Evie then," Kenden continued. "She wasn't ready to become the person she is today. I won't make excuses for her actions, and if you want to hate us both, I certainly don't blame you."

"I think I'll always hate her," Sofia said, shrugging. "But I've realized now that I'm just not capable of the things she is...or was in the past." She noticed Kenden open his mouth to argue. "Regardless, her actions led us down the path we're all on today. I've decided to help you all to prevent needless deaths, especially of immortal children. I hope I've made the right choice."

"It's a very brave choice," Kenden said, his tone reverent. "One that few would make. It shows your character, Sofia. Francesco would be proud."

Sofia blinked away the tears that culminated from the sentiment. "I hope so," she whispered.

"Come on, Sof," Heden said, placing a strong hand on her back. "Let's get you to Astaria. We need to set up in the tech room and have a video conference with everyone. Then, you can teach me all your super-spidey hacking skills."

"Miranda's called a council meeting for tomorrow, at ten a.m. at Astaria," Kenden said as they walked toward the vehicle. "She wants Sofia to attend. It's imperative we formulate a strategy to fight our new enemies. In the meantime, Latimus and I have assigned bodyguards to the children and people we deem as targets."

Heden nodded and gestured for her to climb in the four-wheeler. She strapped herself in the front seat, Heden doing the same in the back. Kenden drove them to the train at Uteria, and they rode the high-speed rail to Astaria. Once there, Heden led her to a room in the basement.

"This is Latimus's old room," he said, gesturing to the empty set of drawers along the wall and the entrance to the private bathroom. A king-size bed sat against the far wall. "The sheets are fresh, and you should have everything you need. My room is right next door," he said, pointing with his thumb. "Why don't you take a few minutes and then meet me in the tech room? It's three doors down on the left."

"Okay," Sofia said, wondering how she'd ended up here. A guest at the Vampyre compound, ready to align with those she'd recently been plotting to exterminate. If she'd had anyone remotely close to tell this story to, they'd be marveled by the excitement. Since she had no friends, she'd have to just revel in it herself. Man, her life was a real-life fairy tale. Or nightmare, if she was honest.

"Sofia?" Heden asked, yanking her from her musings.

"I'm good," she said, throwing her bag on the bed. "Let me brush my teeth and wash my face, and I'll be there. Thanks."

He closed the door behind him, and Sofia entered the bathroom. There, under the bright bulbs, she stared into her blue-green eyes.

"Good grief, Sofia," she muttered to herself. "What the hell are you doing? Your life is a mess."

Sadly, the bare walls of the staid bathroom had no answer for her.

Chapter 13

Sofia sat beside Heden in the tech room as he held a video conference with his family. He introduced her to everyone, and she awkwardly waved, wondering if she should say something. Hi, I *really enjoyed plotting to murder all of you with your long-lost brother?* Deciding that probably wouldn't go over well, she kept her mouth shut.

They ended the call with Miranda confirming the morning's council meeting. In the meantime, Heden would work with Sofia to configure devices that would communicate through the ether so Darkrip and Arderin could be contacted at all times.

Silence blanketed the room as she sat beside Heden's large frame. Struggling to fill the quiet, her eyes darted over the equipment.

"This is impressive," she said, jerking her head toward the plethora of screens and gadgets.

"Thanks," he said, his lips barely quirking into a grin. "Let's get to work. I'd like to start with the code you used. I've tinkered with some things, but they never work." Double-clicking to bring up a text box, he began typing, his thick fingers moving over the keyboard.

Sofia observed the jumble of letters, immediately identifying several mistakes.

"No," she said, encircling his wide wrist with her fingers. "You're already screwing it up. Here." Shooing his arms away, she placed the pads of her fingers on the keys. Eyes narrowed in concentration, she opened a new text box and began clicking the keys.

The letters flowed easily, and Sofia felt comfortable for the first time since entering the immortal realm. This was her territory, her comfort zone. In front of a screen, creating something from scratch. Usually, she was alone, but she didn't find Heden's presence stifling. Being that she didn't really relish the company of others, especially when coding, she figured she'd dissect that later.

Heden watched her with laser focus, his intensity spurring her to prove her proficiency. She wasn't an expert at many things, but, *damn*, she was a freaking great hacker.

"You're using C++ code," he murmured, chin in his hand, eyes glued to the screen.

"Yes. Video game developers use this in my world to develop code so gamers can play together live." Sofia glanced over, noticing how long his black eyelashes were as he blinked at the screen.

"I didn't even think of that," he said, frustration lining his face. "I was using Xcode."

"That's a good start," she said, nodding as her fingers continued tracking. "But it has lots of limitations. You can develop apps and possibly an application that can communicate across the ether, but it's Apple dependent. I use Objective-C. It works across multiple platforms, and Android devices are much more common in Europe and Africa."

"I'm not great at Objective-C. We don't use it a lot here, but I can get better. Honestly, I'm the only one in our world who's learned to code, to my knowledge. Our realm isn't as advanced or modern as the human world, and we prefer to maintain our sedentary lifestyle."

"That reminds me of my grandfather's home," Sofia said, smiling. "It sat atop a hill on the Italian countryside and was surrounded by tons of farmland and grape vines. He taught me how to make wine from the grapes that grew there. Even though I was too young to drink it, he let me anyway." Lost in the memory, she didn't realize her hands had stopped typing.

"So, you like wine," he said, eyebrow arching. "Putting that on the list." He tapped his temple with his finger.

"What list?" she asked, confused.

"The list of items I'm keeping in my head that will help me befriend you." White fangs glowed as he grinned.

Sofia's heart slammed in her chest as she wondered if a man had ever smiled at her so genuinely in such close proximity. "Why are you so nice to me?" she asked, slowly shaking her head. "I've put you and your family in immense danger. You should hate me."

"It takes a lot for me to hate someone, Sof. Someone in my family hurt you. I'd say that makes us even."

"I don't want to be even. I just want my grandfather back."

"I know," he said, his tone solemn as he absently tucked a black curl behind her ear.

Sofia stiffened. The act was foreign, and she wasn't used to being touched.

"Sorry," he said, shoulders straightening as he pulled back. "I'm a toucher. Drives Latimus crazy, especially when I pull him into a bear hug." Holding his hands high, palms out, his expression was contrite. "It's been a long day, and I'm beat. What do you say we pick this up early tomorrow morning, after we both get some sleep?"

"Okay," Sofia said, not understanding how her voice had turned to gravel.

"I'm going to begin perfecting my Objective-C skills as soon as I wake up. If you're not up by eight a.m., I'll knock on your door. Our housekeeper Glarys is an expert at cooking food. I've never had a taste for it, but she'll make you whatever you like. Darkrip used to rave about her food when he lived at Astaria. When you wake up in the morning, just head upstairs, and you'll find the kitchen down the hallway to the left. Make yourself at home."

"Thank you," she said, humbled by his hospitality.

"Sure," he said, standing and stretching his arms over his head.

Sofia thought his biceps might actually pop the sleeves of his shirt open. They were massive.

"C'mon," he said, extending his hand to her.

She let him pull her up and then quickly broke contact with his warm hand. They shuffled to their rooms, and he stopped in her doorway.

"Goodnight," she said, head tilted back as she stared up at him.

"Goodnight," he said. Giving her a nod, he headed toward his room.

Sofia closed the door and pulled the faded t-shirt and boxer shorts from the bag on her bed. Giving in to exhaustion, she cuddled under the covers and fell to sleep.

Early the next morning, Sofia ambled up the stairs and found the kitchen. A woman with a head of curly white hair was humming as she scrambled eggs atop a stove. Sensing her presence, the woman tilted her head and smiled.

"You must be Sofia," she said, her tone warm.

Sofia nodded. "I assume you're Glarys."

"One and the same," she said, switching off the stove before pivoting to scoop the eggs onto a plate. "Sit down there at the island and let me pour you some juice. Or do you prefer coffee?"

"Coffee, please," Sofia mumbled, sliding onto the stool. The food smelled delicious, and she lifted a perfectly cooked piece of bacon to her lips. "Thank you."

"You're welcome." Glarys poured her a steaming-hot mug and set it in front of her. "I hear you're helping Heden develop technology to communicate through the ether. It will be wonderful to connect with Arderin and sweet Callie in the human world, and it's truly appreciated."

Sofia munched the crisp bacon. "Yeah, well, I don't have the best track record with immortals. Maybe this will be the beginning of a better path."

"Nothing I haven't seen before," Glarys said, waving a dismissive hand. "You should've been here when Darkrip appeared and got Arderin pregnant. Don't worry, we're used to reformed bad guys around here. I like your chances."

"We'll see," she mumbled, lifting a forkful of steaming eggs. Once finished with breakfast, she trekked downstairs to find Heden sitting in front of the screens in the tech room. His fingers flew over the keyboard, and as she approached, she noticed how broad his hands were. They could likely cup her most intimate place fully as he stared into her with those piercing eyes. Shivering, she pushed the image away. Unwanted desire had no place in the shit show she'd created.

"Hey," she said softly, not wanting to startle him.

"Hey," he said, eyes glued to the screen. "Have a seat." He gestured with his head to the chair beside him.

Sliding in, Sofia assessed his work. Realization swept over her as she comprehended he'd already written code that would allow cell phones to communicate through the ether.

"Holy shit," she said, eyes wide. "It took me years to figure out that code."

His fingers tapped with finality as he finished, hitting the Enter key with a blatant tap of his index finger. Facing her, he laced his hands behind his head, his thick lips curved into a grin. "Once you told me about C++ and Objective C, I couldn't get it out of my head. I barely slept and came in here to figure it out."

"Damn," she breathed, relaxing back in her chair. "I convinced myself I was a better hacker than you."

"Well, you figured it out first, so let's call it even." Ice-blue eyes sparkled as he regarded her. "Now that it's solved, I've got to program some phones and get them through the ether to Arderin and Darkrip. I want Jack to bring them when he delivers the Slayer blood today. Want to help me? If we work together, I think we can get it done before the meeting."

"Sure," she said, shrugging. "Since I'm here, might as well make myself useful."

They spent the next hour at the large conference table, plugging the code into various cell phones for each member of the royal family. As they toiled, they got to know each other, recounting past stories and favorite things.

"Wait," he said, eyebrow arched as his fingers stilled over the keypad of one of the phones. "You like the Jonas Brothers? Aren't you, like, way too old for that?"

Sofia rolled her eyes. "They were popular when I was younger and they've had a resurgence, okay? And who are you calling old anyway? Aren't you about a thousand or something?"

He chuckled. "Yeah, something like that. I was born right before the Awakening."

Sofia recalled what she knew of the calamitous night Slayer King Valktor killed Heden's parents, King Markdor and Queen Calla. "You never got to know your parents," she said softly.

"Nope," he said, shaking his head. "Neither I nor Arderin remember them. It's a bummer, for sure. I want so badly to meet them in the Passage one day. I hope they'll be proud of me. I've tried to do my best to live up to the reverence our people have for them."

Sofia swallowed, slow and thick. "I lost my parents when I was ten years old. It was devastating. My grandfather Francesco raised me after they died, and he was the only family I had left."

Heden lowered the phone to the table and reached across, sliding his palm over her wrist. Squeezing, his gaze bore into her. "I understand how that feels. I love my siblings so much, but they're...a *lot*. I've felt alone so many times over the centuries."

Her eyebrows drew together. "From my surveillance, you and your family seem really close."

"Don't get me wrong, we definitely are. But now they have families of their own, it just feels a little...different or something," he said, shrugging. "But I love my nieces and nephews so much. I try to spend as much time with them as I can while not imposing on their family unit or whatever. I don't know if that makes sense. It's just a different vibe now they've all settled down."

She felt her lips curve. "It makes sense. And you've certainly developed a rapport with the ladies to take up any spare time you would've spent with your siblings, no?"

Chuckling, he tightened his grip around her wrist once more before removing it. Sofia missed the feel of his warm skin immediately, sending pangs of warning through her belly.

"I might have figured out a way to charm a lady or two, but that's easy. Creating something meaningful isn't so seamless."

A black eyebrow arched. "Not even with one of your many suitors?"

His gaze roved over her as he contemplated. "Sex is one thing, but connection is another. And so is love. You must've been in love before."

"Nope," she said, shaking her head as she pretended to plug symbols into the phone. Maintaining his gaze was too uncomfortable. "I've always been a bit awkward and unconcerned with girly things like makeup and fashion. And I'm probably a contender for the 'Frizz of the Year' award," she said, pointing at her black, spiraled hair. "There have been a few men I've dated, but the sex wasn't really mind-blowing for me."

Mired in the silence, she lifted her head to find him thoughtfully staring at her. "What?" she asked, a bit exasperated.

"I just...I can't imagine how someone as fiery as you could have bad sex. Doesn't seem possible."

She shrugged. "Doesn't matter anyway. I haven't been with anyone in a long time. Revenge was much higher on my list than dating."

"Hmm..." he murmured. "Well, hopefully, we can free you up to find a nice human to settle down with once we defeat Bakari and his henchmen."

"Yeah, we need to get on that. I'm worried he's already forming a new plan now he's in possession of Tatiana's magic."

Nodding, Heden resumed tinkering with the cell. "Let's finish here and give these to Jack, and then we'll figure it out with the council."

Once finished, they gathered the menagerie of devices and headed to the foyer, where a tall, auburn-haired Vampyre was waiting. Lanky and lean, Sofia knew immediately it was Jack, Latimus and Lila's adopted seventeen-year-old son. He hadn't yet fully grown into his body but when he did, he would most likely be massive, as most Vampyres were.

"Hey, Uncle Heden," he said. "Did you figure it out?"

"Sure did, kid." Heden handed him a plastic bag. "Two phones ready to communicate through the ether. Thanks for getting them to Arderin and Darkrip."

"Sure thing," Jack said, his gaze trailing to Sofia. "Thanks for helping. I've never met a human before, except Nolan. It's really cool."

"Thanks," Sofia said, feeling a kinship with the kind teenager. "I've only met a few Vamps, but you seem nice."

Jack breathed a laugh. "I try. I've got the four-wheeler all loaded up. I'm heading to the ether now. Dad assigned a guard to accompany me, although I told him I didn't need one." He proudly puffed his chest. "I'm already outperforming soldiers in the part-time battalion who have been there years longer than me. Once I graduate, I'm going to join the army full-time. Can't wait."

"You're already an awesome soldier, kid, but better safe than sorry," Heden said, patting him on the shoulder. "Thanks for taking care of the delivery. I didn't even think to take the blood when I went a few days ago. I was rushing to get to Arderin and figure out what was happening."

"It's fine," Jack said, shrugging. "Plus, I get to see Callie. She's the cutest damn thing."

"Oh, wait," Heden said, reaching into his pocket. "Almost forgot to give this to you." He handed Jack the folded drawing. "She made me promise."

Smiling, Jack straightened the paper, expression filled with reverence as he gazed at it. "She's going to be as talented as Mom one day soon. These drawings get better and better."

"Lila's our world's da Vinci, for sure. I'd love it if Callie has her talent. I can't draw a straight line."

"But at least you're good at tech," Jack said, lifting the bag. "I'll make sure these get there safely. Want to hang and play Fortnite when I get back?"

"Only if you want to lose," Heden said, arching a brow.

"Psst," Jack said, waving his hand with the drawing in it. "I'll decimate you, old man. You've got it coming."

"Can't wait." Heden drew him into an embrace. "Be safe," he murmured in his nephew's ear.

"Will do." Drawing back, he saluted Sofia. "Nice to meet you, Sofia. Hope I get to hang with you too. You seem chill. Bye." Pivoting, he exited through the large front door, closing it firmly behind him.

Staring up at Heden, Sofia suddenly felt uncomfortable. She'd successfully helped him program the phones, which now lessened his need to align with her. Spearing her teeth into her bottom lip, she wondered what happened next.

"So…I think I should sit down and make a list of everyone who's on Bakari's team. I don't want to forget any details, and I'm sure the meeting will be uncomfortable. I can't imagine the council will be thrilled to hear how I plotted their eventual demise."

Heden grinned and extended his hand to her. "I'll protect you, little human." Shaking his hand, he urged her to take it. "Come on. I've got a notebook in the tech room with your name on it."

Against her better judgement, she slid her hand into his, heart pounding at the way it fit so perfectly. He tugged her toward the stairs, and she followed, clutching onto him although she already knew the way.

Chapter 14

Heden sat in the conference room at Astaria, observing Sofia as she stood at the head of the table meticulously describing each person on Bakari's team and their motivations. Every few seconds, his gaze would wander to the rest of the council members, searching their reactions and body language. Latimus was tense, his face marred with his ever-present scowl as Sofia recited the intel, but that was normal for his stoic brother. Lila sat beside him, her expression much more open and receptive.

Aron sat beside Moira, whom Miranda had asked to attend due to the fact her once-deceased husband, Diabolos, was a member of the Secret Society. Aron absently rubbed her stiff shoulders as she listened to Sofia's calm voice, her features slightly laced with fear.

After speaking for thirty minutes, Sofia gently laid the notebook on the table. Reaching for the plastic cup of water, she lifted it to her lips, her hand slightly shaking.

Empathy swelled in Heden's chest as he watched her. She was literally a world away from her own, endeavoring to help them even though many in the room were shooting her looks filled with anger and mistrust. Yes, she was partly responsible for their predicament, but she wasn't the leader and had only joined Bakari's cause due to her extreme grief following Evie's actions. No one was innocent here. They all had blood on their hands, and Heden felt the need to protect the human and remind everyone of that important fact.

"Thank you, Sofia," Heden said, straightening in his chair. Addressing the council from his seat, he intentionally made eye contact with each one as he spoke. "I want to remind everyone that Sofia is here of her own free will. She could've chosen to stay in the human world and left us to fight for ourselves without her intel. She also helped me write the code that allows the new phones I gave each of you to communicate through the ether," he said, gesturing his head toward the device resting on the table in front of Ken, who sat to his left. "She is our ally, and I expect her to be treated that way."

"And I killed her grandfather," Evie said, eyebrow arched. "She had every reason to join Bakari when he approached her. I can read the thoughts swirling in this room, and your distrust of her is misplaced. If there's anyone you should be angry at, it's me."

Miranda stood at the opposite end of the table from Sofia. "I suggest we let any residual anger go now. We've got bigger problems to tackle and must be united. If anyone has a problem with that, let's discuss it now."

Miranda's gaze traveled back and forth between Sathan and Latimus, both of whom sat with lips drawn into thin lines and muscled arms crossed over their chests. "I'm speaking to you two, in case you didn't get the memo."

Sathan's gaze traveled to Sofia's. "Can we trust you, Sofia Morelli?" he asked in his deep baritone.

Sofia sighed, sliding into the leather chair behind her. Resting her hands atop the table, she clasped them, her fingers fidgeting. "I realized recently that I just don't possess the will to end another being's life. Even if those beings are quite dismissive of humans and have committed some pretty terrible deeds." Eyes narrowed, she shot Evie a glare. "You all seem to have a distaste toward humans that baffles me, especially since we're certainly the most evolved species on the planet."

Latimus mumbled something under his breath, and Heden glowered at him, causing his brother's scowl to deepen.

"In the end, I'm pretty sure I'm insignificant to you, especially now that I've given you all my intelligence and you have nothing left to gain from me. So, I guess the question really is, can I trust *you*?"

Sathan inhaled a breath and straightened in his chair. "We appreciate your help, Sofia. I'm willing to move forward and cement an alliance with you. It would be unwise to turn away someone with your programming skills. As our plan to protect our families and subjects progresses, we might need your assistance after all."

"I second that motion," Miranda said.

"All in favor?"

A resounding "aye" reverberated through the room, with everyone in agreement—even Latimus, who seemed to have the most reservations. Miranda nodded and sat, training her gaze on Kenden.

"Ken, please update us on the heightened security measures you and Latimus have put in place."

"We've identified the threats based on Sofia's intel, which she supplied to me and Latimus last night," Kenden said, his tone firm and assured. "It seems Vadik and Melania are focused on attacking at Valeria, Diabolos at

Uteria, Ananda at Astaria, and Bakari at Takelia. It's possible those plans have changed with Sofia's defection, but we've increased the number of soldiers at each compound and all are on high alert. Bodyguards have been assigned to the children of everyone in this room, and Larkin will be personally guarding Aron and Moira."

Moira clenched her hands atop the table as she spoke. "I saw a man the other evening who reminded me so much of Diabolos. I was so sure it was my mind playing tricks on me. I can't believe he's alive."

"He's not going to touch one hair on your head, Moira," Miranda said. "Take it from me. Larkin is a fantastic soldier, and I have utmost faith in his abilities to protect you and Aron."

"Thanks, Miranda," Larkin said, covering Moira's hands with his own as he sat beside her. "I've got you guys. I'll be moving into the downstairs bedroom as soon as we adjourn and won't leave your side until that bastard is dead for the second time."

Moira thanked the kind soldier, and the meeting changed direction so they could strategize and move forward. After a thorough discussion, it was decided Darkrip was capable of protecting Arderin and Callie in the human world, especially now their phones could communicate through the ether. Latimus and Kenden would work with their soldiers to beef up security first, then track down the enemies and systematically disable them until they were captured or killed.

"What should we do about Melania?" Miranda asked. "Being that she's the wife of Valeria's governor?"

"Sofia has assured us Camron has no idea his wife is involved. At this point, I think it's better to surveil her and see if we can gather some intel. She's not a trained soldier like some of the others and could end up leading us to Bakari."

"Okay, Ken, I'm on board with that. Hopefully she'll slip up and inadvertently give us a clue."

"We're forgetting one key player here," Sofia said once the plan to stop their enemies was set. "Tatiana Rousseau, who lives on the outskirts of New Orleans. She's been supplying Bakari with the dark magic that allows him to transport, but I don't think she's aligned with him in the cause."

"What leads you to believe that?" Miranda asked.

Sofia's eyes narrowed as she contemplated. "I spent some time surveilling her movements around her Louisiana home, gathering intel for Bakari. She doesn't really seem interested in forming an alliance with anyone, human or immortal. I get the feeling she's..."—she waved her hand, searching for words—"interested but detached, if that makes any sense. It would be helpful if we could discern her motivations and see if she's open to helping our cause instead of Bakari. She doesn't use electronic devices, so I can't hack her that way, but I could create some sort of surveillance system I could implant in and around her cabin. I'd obviously need help and would need to be inconspicuous."

"I can help you," Heden found himself saying before he realized the words had left his mouth. "We can create a surveillance program together, and I can protect you in the human world while we work."

Sofia's blue-green gaze studied him. "I've protected myself well enough on my own, thank you very much, but I could use your technical skills. It will cut the development time in half."

Heden nodded, feeling his lips curve at her dismissal of his protection offer. "Okay, let's do that. We can secure an Airbnb in the human world near Tatiana's home and work from there. As long as the Wi-Fi is strong, we'll be good to go."

"You'll need to carry some weapons through the ether, Heden," Lila's sweet voice chimed in. "I don't want anything to happen to you in the human world."

"Will do, buttercup," he said, giving her a wink. "Sofia and I will each carry a gun, and I'll strap an SSW to my belt as well. I'm not as well-trained as Latimus but I trust I can protect us there."

Lila nodded, concern lacing her gorgeous features.

"Okay, we all have our assignments," Miranda said as she rose, spine straight with resolve. "Ken and Latimus are running point, but we must all stay in constant communication. In the meantime, I'm going to go check on Tordor at school. The guards assigned to him are awesome, but I just need to hug my little man."

"I'll go with you," Sathan said, gripping her hand.

She smiled, squeezing as she stared down at him with love.

"I'm going to do the same with Adelyn and Symon," Lila said to Latimus, referencing their two youngest children.

"Okay, honey," Latimus said, brushing her pink lips with his. "I'll be home when it gets dark. Love you."

"One more thing," Evie said, standing and placing her hands in her back jeans pockets, her expression wary. "I was going to wait to tell you all but I'm currently ten weeks pregnant. It's important you all understand another child with my father's blood exists."

"Oh my god, Evie!" Miranda chimed, rushing around the table to give her a hug. "That's amazing! I'm so excited for you."

Evie pulled back and arched a brow. "That makes one of us. I hope the little bugger isn't as evil as my father. We'll see."

"Hey," Kenden said, pulling her to his side. "This baby is going to be filled with the blood of Valktor, Rina and my parents, who were wonderful people. Callie is such a sweet little girl, and I know our child will have the same qualities, sweetheart."

"I had to marry an optimist," Evie muttered under her breath.

"I think it's fantastic," Lila said, breezing toward Evie and enveloping her in a strong hug. "I'm here if you need anything, Evie."

"Thanks, guys," Evie said, wiping her palms on her jeans once she was free of Lila's embrace. "I'm going to do my best here. Thank the goddess I have Ken."

Her husband placed a kiss atop her crimson hair, and several others approached to congratulate Evie. Heden trailed to Sofia's side as she stood at the far end of the table, her expression impassive.

"Hey," he said, cupping her shoulder. "Thank you for helping us. I'm excited to create something with you in the human world. I've never collaborated with a programmer as competent as you."

She nodded, her gaze trailing to Evie. "Isn't anyone worried the child will be evil?" she asked softly.

"We all have our paths to chart, Sof. I believe in free will and choice. Hopefully, if Evie and Ken nurture the baby correctly, it will grow to be good and just. Callie is an amazing child, and I've never seen one speck of Crimeous's darkness in her."

"I guess," she said, kicking the carpet with the toe of her sneaker. "Only time will tell."

"Thank goodness we have a lot of time."

"Speak for yourself," she muttered. "I feel it slipping by so quickly, more and more as I age."

"Then let's not waste it," Heden said, squeezing her shoulder before releasing her. "Let's head to the tech room and find a place near Tatiana's where we can work."

Nodding, the human followed him from the conference room.

∞

Once he and Sofia were prepared for their journey into the human world, Heden went in search of his siblings. They'd agreed to meet that afternoon to discuss the almost unbelievable fact they had a brother they knew nothing about. Entering the conference room at Astaria, Heden smiled at Sathan.

"You need me to set up the video conference with Arderin?" he asked, sitting to Sathan's right while Latimus flanked him on the left of the large table.

"No," Sathan said, his face a mask of concentration as he fiddled with the laptop. "I think I've got it." Maneuvering the mouse, he smiled when Arderin's face appeared.

"Hey, guys," she said, waving. "This is so freaking cool. I'm so glad we can communicate through the ether now."

"It's all due to Sofia," Heden said. "She's a really valuable asset to our team."

"I give you a day before you bang her," Arderin said, rolling her eyes.

"Can we get to the discussion at hand?" Latimus asked, annoyed. "I have shit to do and a kingdom full of people to protect, and I really don't give a crap about who Heden is seducing at the moment."

"Chill, Latimus," Heden said, resting his chin on his hand. "I already told you, I won't use my seduction skills on Lila. You're welcome, by the way."

Latimus scowled while Sathan chuckled. "Okay, kids, let's get to it. I can't believe we have a brother. One who seems intent on destroying us and our kingdom. The way I see it, we need to figure out three things: why he wants to harm us, what powers he and his team possess, and if we can turn him back to our side."

"Agreed," Latimus said. "Sofia said he has a mark on his leg he discussed with the Secret Society. Supposedly, it represents his nefarious nature. I don't recall ever reading about that in the archives."

"Me neither," Sathan said. "We poured over the archives and soothsayer scrolls extensively when we were searching for Evie. There was no mention of another Vampyre royal child."

"How could they keep it from us?" Arderin asked. "Do you two remember her being pregnant before she was pregnant with me?"

"My memories are kind of mashed together," Sathan said. "I would've been about four or five when she was pregnant with Bakari. I think because I was so young, and she got pregnant with Arderin soon after she lost Bakari, the pregnancies just morphed together in my mind."

Heden nodded. "Maybe they were waiting to tell us until we were older. Telling young kids about a dead brother isn't an easy conversation."

"I think that's the most logical explanation," Sathan said. "Sadly, they didn't get to see us grow much older."

Silence pervaded the room as they contemplated. Finally, Heden said, "Well, Sofia and I will do our best to surveil Tatiana and figure out what powers she's bestowed upon Bakari. In the meantime, Sathan, I think you and Miranda should search the soothsayer manuals and Vampyre archives and see if there's any mention of Bakari."

"And Kenden and I will work on revamping the army. It's going to be a huge project. I was so sure we'd entered an era of peace. Now that we have kids and families, the stakes are even higher," Latimus said, running a hand over his face.

"We have to hold out hope we can eventually turn him," Arderin said. "After all, he's our brother. Blood means something to us, and perhaps one day, we'll be able to show him how important family is to us."

"Sofia said he's a purist," Heden said. "That he believes in true bloodlines and separation of the species. He absolutely hates the direction we've taken the immortal world, combining the species again and bearing hybrids."

"Where do those beliefs come from?" Latimus asked.

"I don't know," Heden said, shaking his head. "He's been in the human world for a thousand years. There are so many things he's been exposed to. It will be difficult to figure it out, but as we study him more, hopefully, we'll make some headway."

"I hope so," Sathan said, patting Heden on the back. "The first step is your journey with Sofia to perform reconnaissance on Tatiana. I wish you safe travels, brother."

"Thanks, Sathan," Heden said, determined to help his people.

"I love you guys," Arderin said, blowing them a kiss. "Stay safe."

Resolved to protect their realm, the royal siblings got to work.

Chapter 15

Bakari observed Callie as she played with the other children on the playground beside her school. She was a natural leader, directing her fellow classmates in a game of dodgeball before heading to the swings. Every student was given two minutes on the swing, monitored by Callie, before another could take their place. They followed her direction seamlessly, planting seeds in Bakari's mind as he watched the interplay. Once she was fully grown—if she stayed alive that long—her ability to guide and command others would be a huge asset. Filing that away, he waited.

The teacher announced recess was over, and Callie scowled, crossing her arms over her chest and asking for more time. Darkrip appeared, causing Bakari to sink further behind the tree. Now that Sofia had defected, Darkrip would be on high alert and was most likely volunteering at the school in order to protect Callie.

Fury for the stupid human filled Bakari's gut, and he cursed himself for ever approaching Sofia. He'd been able to sense her hate and thought it would make her a powerful ally in his quest to murder the immortal royals and set things right. Plus, he'd needed her hacking skills. It was a grave mistake and quite costly. Determined not to make another one, he watched the kids trail back inside the school.

Once the last bell rang and Darkrip loaded Callie into their SUV and drove away, Bakari approached the swing. There, tangled in the metal rings that hung from the base, were three dark, curly hairs. Absconding them, he placed them in his pocket. He would ensure they made it safely to Tatiana, so she would supply him with enough potion that he could transport as he wished in the land of humans and immortals.

Then, he would focus on killing his family.

Smiling at the thought, he ambled toward his rental car to begin the journey to LAX, confident it would be one of the last times he had to travel by such primitive methods.

※

Jack was helping Arderin load the canisters of Slayer blood into the refrigerator when he heard excited footsteps pound up the wooden stairs of the back porch. The door slammed open, and Callie ran inside.

"Jack!" she called, giggling as he lifted her into his arms and swung her around.

"Hey, munchkin," he said, rubbing his nose against hers. "I missed you."

"Who's that?" she asked, eyeing the man who stood in the corner of the room.

"That's Bryan. He came along with me to make sure I'm safe. Did you have fun at school today?"

Nodding, she grasped his cheeks in her small hands. "I missed you so much. Did you bring me a present?"

"Hmm..." he said, squinting at the ceiling. "I think you're too old for presents."

"No way!" she said, shaking her head. "You can always get presents, even if you're a big girl. Mommy tells me that every time she makes Daddy buy her stuff."

"It's not *that* often," Arderin said, flicking her hair over her shoulder. "I mean, I have to keep up with these L.A. humans to blend in, and they have nice purses. What can I say?"

"Yes, I think I've bought each one featured on *Real Housewives*," Darkrip said, stalking over and placing his arm around Arderin's waist. "You're expensive, princess," he said, nipping at her lips.

"Don't make me bite you back, husband," she murmured.

Callie scrunched her nose. "They kiss all the time. It's so gross."

"They love each other. My mom and dad do the same thing, but I've gotten used to it, kid," Jack said. Although he was adopted by Lila and Latimus, several years ago, he'd begun calling them "Mom" and "Dad" as opposed to their formal names. He couldn't remember how it happened exactly, but it had naturally progressed. Jack could still remember his biological parents, both of whom passed years ago, and he felt extremely lucky to have been blessed with two sets of amazing parents.

"I love you," Callie said, placing a wet kiss on his lips.

"I love you too, munchkin," he said, smiling. Jack loved his family with his entire heart, but he had a connection with Callie that was unbreakable. It had always been there, since the moment he first laid eyes on her as a baby, and it coursed through him, so strong and true. "Uncle Heden gave me your drawing. It's really good. Thank you."

"You're welcome," she said, the tips of her incisors not quite as pointed as his since she was only half-Vampyre. "It was for your birthday last week. Now that you're seventeen, Mommy says you might break Aunt Lila's heart and live on your own."

"I don't have any plans to leave yet. Where else can I find the bangin' mac and cheese she makes?"

Her eyes roved over his face. "I got a new book. I can read most of the words. Can I read it to you before you go?"

"Heck yeah," he said, setting her on the floor. "In the living room?"

She nodded, black curls bouncing as she pulled him into the dim room. After turning on the lamp, Callie grabbed the book and settled into Jack's side. He held her as she read, so proud of how smart she was to already be reading so proficiently at six years old, although some of the words were stilted at points.

Eventually, Arderin headed to the hospital, and Callie's stomach growled. Jack left Callie to her dinner, promising to bring her a present next time he visited. With Bryan by his side, they reentered the immortal world, and Jack headed home to convince Lila to whip up some of the mac and cheese he was now craving.

Chapter 16

Heden strapped his bag over his shoulder and jumped out of the four-wheeler. Extending his hand, he helped Sofia hop down and walked to the edge of Etherya's Earth, where the wall of ether stood between them and the human world.

"Be careful," Latimus said. "And keep an eye on this one."

"I understand you don't like me," Sofia said, scowling. Heden admired her strength. Latimus towered over her, but she faced him like a champ. "I don't really give a crap. I'm not here to make friends."

"I don't really understand why you're here," Latimus said, crossing his arms over his chest. "You've got nothing to gain by helping us."

"I want to set things right," Sofia said, chin thrust high. "I don't want any harm to come to your pregnant sister or your children. Once I accomplish my goal, I promise, you'll never see me again. I've already spent too much time with arrogant immortals."

Latimus's lips drew into a thin line. "Damn it," he muttered.

"What?" Sofia asked, perplexed.

"I like your spunk, okay? It's annoying. I told myself I wasn't going to let you off the hook for putting my entire family in danger."

"She has a way of growing on you, bro," Heden said, patting Sofia on the back. She promptly swatted his hand away, causing him to chuckle. Man, he loved her fiery spirit. It was extremely attractive.

"Don't fuck this up, Heden," Latimus said. "We're counting on you."

"Love you too, bro. I know that's what you meant to say." With a wink, he turned to Sofia. "Ready?"

She nodded and walked toward the ether. Inhaling a deep breath, she began to wade through.

Heden took a step forward but was halted by his brother's firm grip on his arm.

"I've already lived through Sathan not being able to keep his dick in his pants. It almost ended in disaster. I see the way you look at the human. Be careful, Heden."

"Man, you are some kind of Debbie Downer, Latimus." Heden carefully extracted his brother's hand from his arm. "I'll kindly remind you that Sathan's intense need to be with Miranda is what eventually reunited our kingdoms. And I'm pretty sure I'm an adult and can do whatever the hell I want with my life."

Latimus's nostrils flared. "I just don't want your dick to get you into trouble."

Heden chuckled and rolled his eyes. "You're dramatic in your old age, bro. Go home to Lila and get laid. I'll be fine."

"Hey," Latimus called when Heden was almost to the ether, causing him to turn. "Call me if you need me. I mean it."

"Awww..." Heden said, lifting his hand to rub his heart. "I just got all warm and fuzzy inside. Thanks, Latimus. Now, tell me how much you love me and that I'm your favorite brother."

Latimus glowered. "Everything's a joke to you. I should've known." Pivoting, he stalked to the four-wheeler. Once he was behind the wheel, he lifted his hand in a wave, the gesture poignant.

Heden smiled, knowing that was his stoic brother's way of wishing him well. Straightening his spine, he entered the ether and waded through.

Sofia stood on the other side, pilfering through the bag she'd carried through. Pulling out a phone, she illuminated it under the rapidly darkening sky. "Should we call an Uber to the Airbnb?"

"Sure," he said, giving her a nod. Sofia had secured an Airbnb reservation in the human world for a small two-bedroom cottage a few miles from where Tatiana lived. It was on the outskirts of a rural bayou town and it would offer them the inconspicuous location they needed.

Her phone pinged as it confirmed the rideshare, and two minutes later, a woman in a black Camry pulled up. She chatted companionably with them on the ride, her Southern accent deep. Once they were at the house, Sofia punched the code into the keypad, and they entered.

After taking a small tour, Sofia took the room with the double bed, and he took the king since it would accommodate his larger frame. He quickly showered in the private bathroom and headed to the kitchen. The Slayer blood he'd deposited in the fridge would last weeks in the human world. Hopefully, it wouldn't take that long to study Tatiana and determine if they could recruit her to support their cause. They'd secured the rental home for a few days and would evaluate extending once they deciphered how difficult the surveillance would be.

Sofia padded out of her room, feet bare below smooth legs and thighs barely covered by cute, thin shorts. She wore a tank top that hugged her small frame, and Heden noticed her nipples were pebbled underneath the ribbed fabric. A black bra strap peeked out from underneath one of the tank's straps but the garment didn't offer much coverage. Blood coursed through his body as she approached, heading straight to the organ behind his fly.

"Hope you don't mind that I'm in my scrubs," she said, combing her fingers through her wet curls. "I work better if I'm comfortable."

Heden swallowed, feeling his throat bob. "Fine with me. I'm usually a jeans and t-shirt kind of guy."

"Whatever works," she said, shrugging. Reaching into the fridge, she pulled out one of the beers and popped it open. "What? The owner said we could have whatever the last guests left behind. Why waste perfectly good beer?"

His lips curved. "Excellent point. I'll take one too."

She grabbed one and extended it to him, and once he'd opened it, they clinked the bottles. "To a successful mission."

"Let's get to it then," she said, sipping the beer.

They set up her laptop on the desk in the main room, Sofia facing it as Heden pulled up a chair to sit behind her. She began typing, fingers moving furiously as she connected to the Wi-Fi. Once complete, she opened the internet browser.

"First things first, we need to download a secure VPN. I suggest Surfshark. I've used them extensively, and our work will be untraceable."

"I think NordVPN is better," Heden said, eyebrows drawing together. "I use that in the immortal world, and they have military grade encryption."

"That's just a marketing ploy," Sofia said, waving her hand. "All the major VPNs have top-notch encryption."

"Yes, but Nord has an anonymous payment structure."

"I can maneuver our Surfshark account to be anonymous, and it has much faster speeds than Nord."

Heden smiled at her, his gaze roving over her face. It shone with just the barest hint of freckles under the bulb of the overhead light, causing him to wonder if they got darker when she was out in the sun. Did they blend in with her smooth olive skin?

"Earth to Heden," she chimed.

He took a swig of his beer, slow and lazy, loving how the frustration on her face only increased. For some reason, stirring her ire was insanely enjoyable.

"Sofie?" he asked, arching an eyebrow.

"Yes?"

"Are you going to argue with me over every single thing we try to complete on this laptop? Because it's extremely cute, but I don't think we're going to get a lot accomplished."

Her features drew together. "I have no desire to be cute or anything remotely close. I just think you're wrong about the VPN."

"Fine. We'll use Surfshark, but just know, I'm only capitulating in this first battle. You won't win so easily next time."

"Whatever," she muttered, turning to face the laptop. She loaded the VPN and proceeded to set up an anonymous account as promised.

Watching her maneuver the various programs and text prompts with her agile fingers caused pangs of arousal to curl in his stomach. Heden had mostly spent time doing one thing with women: getting his groove on. Although that was extremely pleasurable, he never really took the time to get to know them on an intellectual level. It was most likely a defense mechanism, since he'd convinced himself he preferred to remain unattached, but it also led to him not forming the connection he'd begun to recently contemplate.

As he'd slowly opened himself to considering something more, this waif of a human had appeared in his path. Smart, adorable and feisty as hell, it was almost as if she was sent by divine intervention, if one believed in that sort of thing. Although he didn't yet know her well, Heden could see himself spending time with her, writing code and playing the video games she'd told him she loved when they'd chatted in the grass upon entering the immortal world.

Not only would she understand his need to decipher things and create new technology, she would be an asset in that undertaking. Heden wasn't too proud to admit she was a better programmer than he was. It was extremely sexy, and he found himself imagining what it would be like to whisper in her ear as he held her trembling body to his and asked her to code something just for him. Man, the image was so hot to a tech dork like him.

"What do you think?" she asked, looking at him over her shoulder.

"Sorry, what?" he asked, overcome by the smell of her damp hair.

"I think we should use the mini wireless cameras for inside the cabin, and the waterproof Nannday wireless cameras for outside. Thoughts?"

"Sounds good," he said, reminding himself to stay on task.

They proceeded to have several more discussions around the various technology to employ in surveilling Tatiana, and Heden reveled in each one. Sofia was extremely fun to argue with, although it was good-natured, and he sometimes would draw out the debate just to see her cheeks redden. Would her entire body flush like that as they made love?

Reminding himself he should probably keep it in his pants, they eventually finished the prep work. Tomorrow, they would head to the electronics store in the small town square and purchase the equipment they needed. Then, they would figure out how to install it in Tatiana's home—not easy, since Sofia had already observed she rarely ventured out.

Once they were both in their own beds, Heden turned out the light and stared at the darkened ceiling. He imagined having Sofia's body against his side, cuddling into him as her skin cooled. Smiling softly, he realized he wanted to seduce her. Latimus and Arderin's warnings be damned. Heden had never denied himself the opportunity to make love to a woman, and he wouldn't lie to himself about his desire for the human.

It was there, a latent pulsing through his entire body, and he meant to navigate around every thorn to get to her soft petals. Content in his resolution, he willed himself to sleep, wondering if he would dream of her in the balmy Louisiana night.

Chapter 17

Bakari sat at the makeshift table in the dirty cave, surrounded by the members of the Secret Society. As he brought them up to speed on Sofia's defection, he scanned their faces, judging their reactions. Ananda and Vadik were stoic, which was to be expected since both were usually emotionless. Diabolos' angular features were filled with rage, while Melania appeared terrified.

"It's unacceptable that you didn't tell us of her defection until now, Bakari," Diabolos said. "I had a perfect opportunity to kill my bitch wife a few days ago but didn't want to give up the element of surprise. Now, it's lost to us. What a waste."

"Sofia disabled the devices from communicating through the ether as soon as she defected, and I had other tasks to complete in the human world," Bakari replied, feeling his nostrils flare. "I delivered strands of Calinda's hair to Tatiana, and she supplied me with these." Pulling several vials from his bag, he sat straighter in his chair. "They will allow us to transport as Darkrip and Evie do. It's an invaluable asset. I will leave each of you with one container. You must place it on your tongue at least sixty seconds before you want to transport. Once you ingest it, the capability will last for several hours. There is a chant that will activate the serum, which I'll teach you before we leave today. Understood?"

The team nodded, and Bakari slipped the vials across the table, one to each of them.

"I have no idea what to do," Melania said, worry lining her pretty but cold features. "I saw Lila yesterday, and she said nothing to me, which means they're waiting for me to slip up. I can't let Camron discover my alliance with you. I think I have to defect as well."

Bakari sighed and ran his hand over his slick hair. "If you must, I won't object. I learned a lesson from Sofia. No one should be in this society unless they are one hundred percent on board with murdering the royal family and their offspring. There is no place for wavering."

Melania's eyes narrowed. "I want Lila, her vile bonded mate and her children exterminated from the planet, but I won't chance being caught. I'm sorry," she said, eying the other members. Standing, she placed the vial on the table. "I wish you all luck and will revel in the death of our enemies, but I must defect." With a nod of her head, she departed the cave.

"Anyone else?" Bakari asked once she was gone. "It's better if you leave now than wait until we've devised a new plan."

"I'm still committed," Vadik said. "I will avenge Crimeous until my dying breath."

"I'm not going anywhere," Diabolos said.

"Me neither," Ananda chimed.

"Good," Bakari said, standing and lifting the new tablet he'd secured so Sofia couldn't track his previous one. "I've formulated a new attack strategy. Now we've lost the element of surprise, we must change our tactics. I have secured samples of some deadly chemical toxins from the human world. They will poison any Slayer upon ingestion. Since they're rare, the immortal physicians will have trouble identifying them, which means they'll struggle to find a cure for anyone who consumes them.

"I'm giving you samples to have on hand in case you find yourself in the position to poison any of our targets. I don't foresee that happening, since Kenden and Latimus have increased security immensely around their families and across the realm, but it could happen. I have an appointment with a chemist next week to purchase a stockpile of chemicals so we can plan a full-scale attack." He slid a black baseball-sized pouch to each of the associates.

"Are you planning to attack the subjects of the kingdom now as well?" Ananda asked.

"That wasn't the plan initially, but I believe it will be required in order to exterminate the royals. If their efforts are divided across the realm, it will make it easier to find an opportunity to attack the family members. Chaos creates instability. The sovereigns will be so focused on protecting their people, it will create an opening for us."

"I thought you wanted to rule Etherya's realm for yourself. Will there be any subjects left to rule if you poison them all?" Ananda asked, eyebrow arched.

"Vampyres' self-healing bodies will not be harmed by the chemicals. I just need to make sure I leave enough Slayers alive to supply us with blood. I will build a better kingdom with the subjects that are left after the attack. The species will remain separate and pure, as the goddess intended."

"And what about the Deamon prison?" Vadik asked. "I still think our best option is to jailbreak the prisoners there and have them fight with us. They still worship Crimeous and will align with me as their commander."

"The security system is extensive there, thanks to Heden's programming and the well-trained troops. It's better if we poison the subjects first to create some diversions and hope they pull soldiers from the prison."

Vadik considered. "Being able to transport gives me the ability to get inside."

"Yes, but if you are caught, we'll have lost our most skilled combat warrior. I would rather wait until their resources have been stretched."

"I see the logic in that. I will wait, but I'm ready to move forward. I fear we've already squandered our best opportunities."

"Me too," Diabolos mumbled. "We're down to four members, and our chances of success diminish each day."

"This will not be a fast coup," Bakari said. "It is imperative we think each detail through. I know you all are anxious to prevail. I am as well. But it took centuries for the kingdom to devolve to this point. It will not be fixed in days or even weeks. I ask for your patience so we may form an infallible plan. It is better to toil a few weeks in caution than fail."

"I agree," Vadik said. "I don't want to come this far only to crumble at the end."

"All right," Diabolos said. "I will be patient, but you must stay in contact with us, Bakari. I want regular updates."

"Our new devices can't communicate through the ether but they also can't be tracked by Sofia. I will make sure to travel to the realm and update you as often as I can."

"I am determined to succeed," Ananda said, "and I will keep watch on my niece's children and look forward to your brief once you secure the chemicals from the scientist."

"Thank you," Bakari said, rising. "If there are no more questions, we can adjourn."

After the members all nodded with resolve, Bakari dismissed them, more determined than ever to prevail.

Chapter 18

The next day, Sofia and Heden traveled by rideshare to the electronics store, purchasing several wireless cameras and other various electronics they needed for their surveillance. Once they had everything, they instructed the driver to drop them off half a mile from Tatiana's property. After traversing the forest, they came upon the clearing where her house resided. Hiding behind a large willow tree, they observed the cottage.

A winding trail of smoke curled from the chimney even though it must've been eighty degrees outside. Heden thought it smelled quite rotten and wondered if the mysterious woman was cooking something nefarious in a cauldron in the fireplace. From what Sofia had told him, Tatiana liked to concoct different brews for her spells and chants.

"Should we go closer?" Sofia whispered, palm flat on the brown bark of the tree.

"Let's give it another few minutes," he murmured. "Maybe she'll give us an opening."

Sure enough, only a few moments later, the front door creaked open and a woman appeared. She had long, curly brown hair and smooth russet skin under a flowing blue dress. Flat sandals adorned her feet, and she trailed to an open-top Jeep in the driveway. Sitting behind the wheel, she started the car, revved the engine and pulled onto the gravel road.

Wanting to shield them, Heden gently pushed Sofia further behind the tree, crouching into her as the car drove off in the distance.

"Now's our chance," Sofia said, squirming against him in an effort to dislodge from his protective stance. Wriggling, she turned to face him, sending daggers of arousal through his veins. "Let's hang the inside cameras first."

Heden stared at her upturned face, unable to move as her small breasts jutted against his chest. His fingers tensed slightly on the rough bark of the tree as they bracketed her head. Frozen, his gaze roved over her pert nose, delectable freckles, and limitless eyes.

"Hey," she said, placing her palms against his pecs and pushing. Her features drew together when he didn't even budge. "She could come back any minute. Let's go!"

Desire coursed through him as he inched forward, aligning their bodies until he could feel her rampant heartbeat against his own. Unable to stop himself, he slid his hands behind her neck, placed his thumbs against her jaw and tilted her face to his.

"What the hell are you doing?" she rasped, lips shining from where her wet tongue darted to lather them.

Short breaths escaped his lungs. "I want to kiss you, Sofie."

"Now?" she almost squeaked. "We might only have minutes to infiltrate Tatiana's house, and you want to kiss me now?"

Exhaling a laugh, he nodded. "Now. I'll make it quick, I promise." He waggled his eyebrows.

Curious blue-green eyes darted between his.

He gently nudged her nose with his. "Please, Sof." Ever so gently, he ran his lips over hers. "By the goddess, your lips are so soft."

"Heden—"

Opening his mouth, he closed over hers, inhaling his own name from her lips.

A high-pitched mewl escaped her throat, causing his body to tighten further as he maneuvered his lips over hers. Needing to taste, he slipped his tongue inside her warm mouth, feeling her body tremble as he plundered the wet depths. She tasted like rose and honey, rolled into a flavor so sweet he craved more. Cupping her neck with his broad hand, he slid the other across her collarbone, over the side of her breast and around her trim waist before gliding it over her jean-clad ass. Undulating his hips into hers, he clenched the ripe globe, groaning into her mouth.

Her fingernails speared his chest through his black t-shirt, the pleasure-pain driving him wild. In retaliation for the sexy gesture, he softly sucked her bottom lip through his teeth, alternately flicking it with his tongue. Her eyes blasted open, staring into his as she panted beneath him. Gaze locked with hers, he swiped his tongue over her lips and rested his forehead on hers.

"Damn, Sof," he mumbled against her lips. "You taste like heaven."

Her eyes were so deep, Heden was sure he could see her soul. With two words, she ripped him open. *"Don't stop."*

Growling with lust, his free hand fell to her rear. Clutching her ass with his palms, he lifted her as if she were a feather, loving how her legs instinctively wrapped around his waist. Seating his pulsing length into her core, he devoured her mouth.

His spunky human gave as good as she got, thrusting her fingers in his thick hair as she jabbed her tongue inside his mouth. Lifting to meet it, his tongue warred with hers...licking...sucking...sliding over each other until Heden thought he might die if he didn't bury himself inside her. Groaning in frustration, he broke the kiss and buried his face in her neck.

Her body trembled as she spoke in his ear. "Heden?"

"I'm sorry," he said, squeezing her with his burly arms. "It's just so much. Your taste and your smell. I have to stop."

Heden felt the doubt course through her gorgeous body. Lifting his head, he locked his gaze with hers. "Not because I want to stop, Sofie," he said, shaking his head. "Because if I don't stop now, I might not be able to. I want you very badly, little human."

Her tiny nostrils flared. "You do?"

The corners of his lips curved. "I do. But we have a job to do, and I'd rather get that out of the way so I can focus on you."

His ego swelled at her expression of extreme disappointment. She nodded.

Lowering her, he set her on her feet and straightened, running a hand over her ponytail. "I think I messed it up," he said.

Lifting her hands, she maneuvered the band and reformed a perfect ponytail in five seconds flat. "All good. Let's go."

With a tilt of his head, they began walking toward the cabin. Heden noticed how tightly she clutched the bag in her hand, her knuckles almost white. She seemed frazzled by their kiss, and he recalled their conversation in the tech room where she told him she didn't date often. Pursuing a pretty woman was second nature to Heden, but he reminded himself that not everyone was as comfortable with casual flings. Wanting to put her at ease, he slid his hand over the juncture of her neck and shoulder.

"Don't tense up, Sofie. It was just a kiss. I promise, I won't ravage you unless you beg me."

"Beg you, my ass," she muttered, swiping his hand away. Approaching the front door, she pulled some small tools and crouched, eyes narrowed as she began to pick the lock. "In your dreams, Vampyre."

Heden grinned, watching her deft fingers, loving how she'd slipped back into their jibing banter. It was comfortable for her and would put them back on even ground. The last thing he wanted was for her to shut down around him.

A click sounded, and she stood, triumphant. "Let's go," she said, pushing the door open and waving him inside. "Remember the plan?"

Heden nodded. Striding to Tatiana's bedroom, he secured the small camera to an inconspicuous location on her dresser, facing the bed. It would be impossible to notice it unless one knew to look for it. Heading back to the main room, he saw Sofia fastening the camera below the mantel above the fireplace.

"Done," she said, swinging her pack over her shoulders. "And I hung the one under the counter too. It has a clear view of the fireplace. Let's hang the outside cameras quickly."

They closed the door behind them, careful to reset the lock, and each trailed to a tree on opposite sides of the home. Once the cameras were secure, Sofia lifted the monitor from her bag. Observing the screen, she double-checked everything.

"Two outside cameras, one bedroom, and two main room. All are submitting signals. Let's go."

They trekked back through the woods, navigating the dense brush and overgrown bushes until they came to a gravel road almost a mile away from Tatiana's cottage. Sofia called the rideshare and showed him the screen. "Five minutes."

The car pulled up, and they hopped in back. Heden could sense her excitement at the seamlessness of the mission. For his part, he wasn't so convinced.

Upon walking into their rented house, Sofia threw her bag on the counter, triumphant.

"We did it! I'll run the feed to my laptop so we can watch from there."

Heden studied her. "Don't you think it was just a tad too easy? I'm wondering if she knows we're here."

Sofia inhaled a deep breath, pondering. "You could be right. She's wily and observant. What would she gain by letting us place the cameras?"

"Perhaps she wants to assess our capabilities. See what she's dealing with."

Sofia bit her lip, chewing thoughtfully. "Or maybe she wants the cameras in place so we only see what she wants to show us. It would be a way to manipulate our surveillance of her."

"True," Heden said, striding over to the laptop on the desk in the large room. "Let's bring up the feed."

Sofia trailed over and configured the laptop to show them the different angles. Locked on the feed from the fireplace image, their shoulders stiffened as the front door opened and Tatiana walked into the dim living room. Slow and meticulous, she searched the room, gaze traveling as she surveyed. Walking toward the mantel, she stopped in front, facing the camera.

Amber eyes glistened from the glow of the fire as Tatiana stared through the laptop monitor. Full red lips turned into a smile. Tipping her head, she nodded, acknowledging their surveillance.

"Shit," Sofia breathed. "She's onto us."

"Yes," Heden murmured as Tatiana trailed away, seeming to disregard the cameras as she began unloading the grocery bag on the counter. "But she didn't tamper with the camera or remove it. It's almost as if she wants us to watch her."

"Why?"

"I have no idea, but let's not squander it. I say we take turns. One hour each. Sound good?"

"Sure," Sofia said, glancing at her watch. "It's almost two o'clock. I'll take the two to three shift, and we can alternate from there."

Heden couldn't stop his grin, realizing she was now fully focused on their mission and avoiding acknowledging their earlier liplock. "Did you want to discuss the fact we were sucking face earlier? Because I don't think I'd mind revisiting that."

"I'm good," she said, her expression resolved. "I'm here for one purpose and would like to focus on that."

He studied her, deciding not to push it...for now. "Okay, Sof. You can take the first shift." Unable to help himself, he reached for the dark curl that had escaped her ponytail. It was soft under his fingers, and he reveled in her tiny shiver. "Come get me when you're ready to switch." Already missing the feel of her silky hair between his fingers, he gave her a nod before heading to his room.

Firm in their plan, they began to study the woman who, for unknown reasons, wanted to be observed.

Ananda studied Lila as she picked up her two youngest children from school. Located a few blocks from Lynia's main square, the property was heavily protected by swarms of soldiers, undoubtedly placed there by the brute Latimus.

Ananda hated the Vampyre commander, not only because his bastard brother King Sathan had banished her from the royal compound of Astaria centuries ago, but because the man was a heathen. Shivering at the thought of his filthy, blood-soaked hands touching one inch of her niece's skin, Ananda scowled.

Lila was supposed to become queen. Ananda's aristocratic sister, Gwen, had ensured the betrothal when Lila and Sathan were babies. When Gwen and Theinos passed, Ananda proclaimed herself Lila's advisor, intent on molding her into the perfect aristocratic wife and queen. Despite her best efforts, Sathan had treated Lila like garbage and cast her aside when he fell for the Slayer whore Miranda.

When Bakari had resuscitated Ananda, she'd been distraught to learn the warmonger Latimus had bonded with her niece. Disparaging all of

Ananda's training, Lila seemed to love the barbarian back even though it went against every natural order in the immortal world. Betrothals were sacred and traditions were revered, and Ananda would be damned if she stood by and let the immortal royals destroy centuries of evolution.

Bakari shared her beliefs: a sense Etherya created the species to be separate, and traditions should be upheld. Pledging her loyalty to him was effortless, and she felt he would set things right. Ananda would do everything in her power to help him.

Lila held her two-year-old adopted Vampyre son, Symon, giving him a kiss as she swung him through the air. Then, she lifted Adelyn, the little girl who shared Lila's violet-colored eyes even though she was a Slayer and Lila was a Vampyre. Ananda felt the bile bubble in her throat. How could her niece love a Slayer child as her own? It was an abomination, born of a disreputable Slayer mother who discarded the child without a thought. Ananda was determined to save these people from themselves. The level of desecration of their sacred customs was maddening.

From across the field, Ananda observed Lila grab the backpack that held the Slayer blood and food the children had carried to school. It had been tough with all the soldiers milling around, but Ananda had been able to sneak in and sprinkle the poison flecks Bakari had given her over the food that remained in the lunchbox. If ingested, it would kill Adelyn almost immediately since she didn't possess self-healing abilities.

Ananda hoped it would send a message to her niece and the rest of the royals, for she was tired of waiting to kill the ones who had so little disregard for the rules of Etherya's realm. The Secret Society had plotted extensively and had begun to fracture. The time to attack was upon them. Clutching her hands, Ananda sent a prayer to Etherya, hoping they would succeed in their quest.

∞

Darkness fell upon the small cottage, causing Sofia to straighten on her bed as she looked out the window. Upon defecting from Bakari's team, she'd disabled their communication devices, rendering them unable to transmit through the ether. Now, she was working to trace their devices and track them through the GPS settings. Unfortunately, she'd been unable to locate them and realized Bakari must've supplied them with new contrivances. That would make her task more difficult, but she was determined to find a way to surveil the Secret Society.

Rotating her neck, she squeezed the tension away from her shoulders. Feeling her stomach growl, she shut down her laptop and padded to the kitchen. Scowling at the meager contents of the fridge, she closed the door and reached for her phone.

"I need to order food," she said, approaching Heden as he sat at the desk watching the laptop screen. "Any update on Tatiana?"

He shook his head, and Sofia noticed the broad muscles of his back flex under his black t-shirt. Good lord, he was massive. Earlier, when he'd given her that earth-shattering kiss, Sofia had felt his body vibrate against hers, full of lust and desire. Not even understanding how someone as viscerally sexy as Heden could want her, she studied him.

Sofia had always considered herself awkward and a bit standoffish. She rarely put herself in situations where men hit on her, and if they did, her first instinct was to rebuff their advances. At first, it stemmed from her lack of understanding of intimacy. The idea of sex was complex to her, and she had a hard time imagining opening herself up to anyone. The few men she'd been with had often commented that she needed to relax. Frowning, Sofia wondered how in the hell you were supposed to relax when a man was spreading your legs open and doing all sorts of intimate things to your innermost place. How did you trust someone when you were that raw? For someone who'd lost her parents so young and only had her grandfather as a confidant, it was a foreign concept.

Discovering Evie and blazing a path of revenge had given Sofia a new excuse. After all, there wasn't really time to date when you were pursuing your grandfather's immortal murderer. It had blanketed her in purpose, and she'd convinced herself she didn't need sex, intimacy or love. Although she definitely wanted children, she was lucky to live in modern times and considered artificial insemination by an anonymous donor an acceptable option.

Heden mumbled an answer to her question, hand over his chin as his gaze stayed fixed to the screen, although the words didn't register to Sofia. Instead, she moved closer, as if pulled by an invisible tether, suddenly aching to touch the pale skin of his neck above those magnificent muscles.

How would it feel to have him loom over her, his hulking body tense and ready to claim her? Would it hurt? After all, he was colossal compared to her. Flashes of other lovers ran through her mind as she recalled the sometimes clumsy experiences. Men telling her to calm down and lamenting how hard they had to work to bring her to orgasm. Most times, they were unsuccessful, and she chalked it up to her just not being great at sex. The thought of disappointing Heden, whom she knew to be a prolific lover from her surveillance, made her inwardly cringe.

"Sofie?" he called, head turning as he stared up at her. "Did you hear me?"

She stared into his ice-blue irises, losing herself to their depths. When she'd first focused on them, on the bustling L.A. sidewalk, she'd felt her heart leap into her throat. He was one of the most handsome men she'd ever seen. When he'd kissed her earlier, her entire body had gone up in flames, and she'd been terribly disappointed when he'd ended the embrace. Perhaps it was for the best. She would never be able to please someone as experienced as Heden.

"Yeah," she said softly, clenching her fist at her side in an effort to control her desire to reach for him. When had the arousal taken hold? From that first moment in L.A.? When he'd shown her such kindness in front of his family, even though she'd put them all in such danger? When he'd stared at her with those gorgeous eyes as she trembled in his arms, his deep baritone telling her how much he wanted her?

Damn it. Her attraction to him was something she hadn't anticipated, and it worried her. They needed to work together and would be in close proximity for the foreseeable future. Now that she'd kissed him, the craving had taken hold deep in her gut, and she was unable to squelch it. Anxiety at the loss of control swamped her, and her heart began to pound in her chest.

"Hey," he said, reaching up to gently cup her cheek. "You okay, Sof?"

"I, uh..." She struggled to breathe against his warm palm. "Yeah, I'm fine. I need to order some food."

He nodded and stood, stretching his beefy arms above his head.

Sofia swallowed thickly as she gripped the phone in her free hand. "I'm thinking Chinese since it's easy. Do you want anything?"

"Nah," he said, shaking his head. "Wish I liked food. Just Slayer blood for me."

There must've been a question in her expression because the corner of his lip curled. "Go ahead and ask me, Sofie."

"Ask you what?" she rasped, hating that she couldn't control her breath.

He stepped closer and brushed a wayward tendril at her temple behind her ear. "If I've ever drank from a human. You're dying to know."

"I am not," she said, defiant even though his words were true. "I couldn't care less. Like I said, I know how many women you seduce and understand it's just a game to you."

Hurt flashed in his eyes, and guilt squeezed her heart. "It's not a game, little human. I'm honest with every woman I pursue."

"Honest that you're only looking for one thing. I'm not interested in that."

His eyebrow arched. "Your scent would indicate otherwise."

Sofia felt her cheeks enflame with embarrassment. "That's just a chemical reaction. I know Vampyres have heightened senses for arousal. It doesn't mean anything."

His tongue darted over his full lips, causing them to glisten under the pale light of the living room fixture. The action spurred a flush of moisture between her thighs, compounded by the heat emanating from his thick body.

"Honestly," he said, stepping forward so their bodies brushed, "it means something to me, Sofia. I don't play games, so let me make this clear. I want you, and judging by how your body is reacting to me, you want me too. I think it would be easier to work together if we relieved the sexual tension, but that's up to you. I'm not in the business of forcing women into something they say they don't want. So, why don't you think about it and let me know when you've decided? Until then, I've got plenty of things to keep me busy. I'm still tweaking the coding so I can improve the comm devices so Latimus and Ken can implement them to the soldiers throughout the realm. I'll let you take the next shift while you eat."

Lowering, he spoke softly in her ear. "I've always been taught that drinking from humans is a waste of effort, but I'd make an exception for you, Sofie. I'd start here," he said, placing his finger on her pulsing vein and slowly tracing the length. "Then, I'd suck you until you screamed in my arms. All you have to do is ask." Straightening, he gave her a wink. Lowering his hand, he stalked to the refrigerator, grabbed a thermos of Slayer blood and headed toward his room, closing the door behind him.

Sofia missed his touch immediately. Expelling a breath, she lifted her phone, noting how badly her hand was shaking. Would it truly sate the sexual tension if they made love? Or would it make things worse if they had a disastrous sexual encounter? How could she continue to work with him if she disappointed him in bed?

Annoyed at the questions swirling in her mind, she ordered food from the delivery app and sat down to watch the screen. Tatiana was stirring something in the cauldron above her fireplace, the movements slow and measured. Suspending her hand above the pot, she sprinkled in what looked to be hair, although Sofia couldn't be sure. Who was it from? An animal, or perhaps an immortal being?

Picking up the pen that sat atop the notebook, Sofia noted the occurrence. She and Heden had various notes they'd taken during their surveillance so far, and tomorrow, they would compile them and look for patterns. For now, Sofia sank into the chair to watch the mysterious woman as she waited for her food, determined to push a certain attractive Vampyre from her thoughts.

Chapter 19

The next morning, Heden emerged from his bedroom ready to study the notes they'd taken on Tatiana and report back to Sathan. Thanks to Sofia's shared coding knowledge, he could now video chat through the ether, which was invaluable. Not only that, it allowed him to check in with his family as well.

Noting the time, he pulled up the video call app on the laptop and rang Arderin. She answered on the second ring, propping the phone against the wall as she dressed Callie.

"Hey, baby toad," Heden said, grinning as his sister stuffed the tyke into a shirt. "Is Mommy being rough with you?"

"Mommy is overworked and pregnant, and Daddy should be doing this crap," Arderin said. "He's downstairs with Evie and Latimus. They're meeting this morning to discuss the heightened security measures across all the worlds. With Darkrip protecting us here, and Latimus and Ken on high alert in the realm, there's a lot going on."

"Mommy's grumpy," Callie said, frowning. "She says I can't go to school without Daddy anymore. I have to say he's a vault-a-neer."

"That's *volunteer*, baby toad, and it's what you need right now. We can't have anything happen to you."

"I told Mommy I can use my powers if I need to. They're really strong now, and I can hurt any of the bad men who try to get me."

"What's the rule about using your powers, baby?" Arderin asked, a warning in her tone.

Callie sighed and rolled her eyes. "Only in the house when you or Daddy are here. But that's so *boring*. My powers are special, and I want to use them."

Arderin's face fell as she smoothed her hand over her daughter's cheek. "Please don't argue with me today, baby. I'm tired, and your brother is kicking up a storm."

Callie touched Arderin's belly with her hand and gasped. "I can feel it."

"Yep, that's our little Creigen. He's going to do whatever his big sister does. I hope she can teach him to keep a secret."

"I can," she said, crossing an X over her heart. "I promise. I'm sorry, Mommy. I know you get mad when I use my powers."

"How can I get mad at you? Can you tell Uncle Heden to have a good day?"

Callie did as she was told, waving before her gaze trailed upward. "Hi, Sofia. Are you having fun with Uncle Heden?"

Heden smiled up at Sofia, who stood silently at his back. Her face was swollen with sleep, causing her to look innocent and unguarded. His throat tightened as he imagined her waking atop his chest, smiling into him, open and bare. By the goddess, he yearned for it.

"Hi, Callie," she said, waving at the phone. "You look pretty. Are you heading to school?"

Black curls bobbled as she nodded. "Daddy comes with me every day now. He says it's annoying but necessary. I think he gets annoyed a lot."

"Ain't that the truth," Arderin muttered. "I've gotta get this show on the road. Did you need to talk to Darkrip?"

"No," Heden said. "I'll call him later, once Sofia and I have compiled the notes, but he and the others should know Tatiana's aware of our surveillance. We don't understand why she's letting us observe her, but it must have some purpose."

"Strange," Arderin said, eyebrows drawing together. "Well, Sofia did say Tatiana didn't appear to have any alliances. Perhaps she's studying you guys too. Be careful, bro."

"I will. Kisses and hugs. Tell Darkrip and Latimus I'll call them later."

Callie blew him a kiss, and the screen went dark.

Sofia appeared slightly uncomfortable as she scratched her head under her mess of tight curls. "I need to shower, and then we can sit down and go over everything."

Heden nodded. "I walked into town and got some eggs, bread, chips—that kind of stuff. Want me to fry up some eggs while you shower?"

A dark eyebrow arched. "You know how to cook eggs?"

"I watched a YouTube video while you were sleeping. Seems pretty self-explanatory."

Chuckling, she shrugged. "Okay then. Fry away. I'll be out in a few."

Heden got to work in the kitchen while the pipes of the older house creaked overhead. Needing to create space on the small island, he accidentally knocked her purse off as he cleared everything. Bending down, he began stuffing everything back in and froze when he saw her license.

Taking note of the information, he set the purse on the nearby chair and waited for her to enter.

"Perfect timing," he said, scooping the eggs onto a plate. "Salt and pepper?"

"Sure," she said, sitting on the island stool and taking the dish and shakers from him. Grabbing a container from the fridge, he sat beside her, joy coursing through him when she closed her eyes and smiled.

"These are delicious," she said, swallowing and scooping up another forkful. "Great job, Vampyre. You can officially cook eggs."

He took a swig of the Slayer blood, thrilled with her praise. "So, I figure it should take us about a few hours to go over the footage and summarize the notes. Then, I need to call everyone and update them. All in all, we'll be done by four or five. In the meantime, we'll continue to surveille Tatiana, but she goes to bed rather early. She was asleep by nine-thirty last night."

"Yep. Can't say I blame her for that. I've never been a night owl."

"You didn't party when you were younger?"

She scoffed. "Party? Um, yeah, no. I'm kind of a loner, in case you haven't noticed. I'm a huge geek who likes programming and video games. Doing that by myself is actually pretty fun."

"Maybe you just haven't met anyone who shares your interests. I like those things too, you know? Latimus could never understand why I'd hole myself up in my room to write code or play with virtual technology. You like what you like, nothing wrong with that. Still, it's nice to go out and enjoy life sometimes."

"I guess," she muttered.

"Especially on your birthday."

Her shoulders tensed. "Yep, I guess that would be a good day to go out and party."

"Great, then we'll do that tonight once Tatiana falls asleep."

"Oh, it's not my birthday."

Heden almost laughed at her lack of eye contact as she stared at the plate. "Wow, you're an awful liar. I accidentally knocked your purse over when I was cleaning the counter. Today's your thirty-ninth birthday. That's exciting, Sofie. We have to celebrate."

"I don't really celebrate my birthday, but thanks." Standing, she carried the plate over to the sink and began washing it.

"That's unacceptable, and I'm not taking 'no' for an answer, so you can give up that notion right now. I think it's time you had some fun, Sofia."

Heden could sense her frustration as she shut off the faucet and dried her hands. Leaning back against the sink, her features drew together. "First of all, we're in the middle of a shit show I had a hand in creating. Having fun is very low on my list. Secondly, I know you're not familiar with the human world, but thirty-nine isn't exactly a milestone birthday.

I'm totally fine just hanging here and completing the multitude of tasks at hand. Thanks though."

"I love that you think you have a choice here," Heden said, reveling in the way her cheeks reddened as they continued to argue. "We'll go out once Tatiana's asleep. End of story. For now, let's get started on the footage."

"You can go out and have all the fun you want," she said, nose in the air as she trailed to the desk. Sitting down, she brought up yesterday's footage so they could study it.

"Oh, I plan to," Heden said, sitting beside her. "With you by my side. Can't wait."

A muscle clenched in her jaw. "You're infuriating."

"You love it," he whispered in her ear.

Planting a palm over his face, she pushed him away. Heden nipped at it, reveling in how fun it was to tease her. Her nostrils flared, and he damn near giggled.

"You have the maturity of an infant."

"Aw, that's so sweet. Miranda says the same thing. I assure you, I'm very mature when the situation calls for it."

"Sex," Sofia muttered. "Always sex with you. Give me the damn notebook. I want to compare the notes we took."

Heden grabbed it and handed it to her, pulling it back when she reached for it. Her frustrated grunt went straight to his dick, causing it to harden beneath his jeans.

"Give it to me, you heathen." Grasping the notebook, she roughly dragged it from his hands.

"Man, you're a tiger," he said, aching to carry her to bed and seduce her hesitancy into flames of need. "It's so fucking cute, Sof."

She shot him a glare from the corner of her eye, filled with restrained laughter. Nice. His gorgeous human was warming up to him after all.

"So," she said, ignoring his comment. "I've noticed she seems to be showing us what she puts in the cauldron, but why?"

Heden tucked a wayward raven-black curl behind her ear. The action was becoming a habit he never wanted to break, for it gave him a reason to touch her. "That she does. Let's try to discern what the items are, and then we can research them and find a pattern."

Sofia pulled up the footage, and they got to work, Heden deciding he'd give her a break from his teasing before turning on his full charm later that evening. It was his little human's birthday, and he was determined she'd loosen up and enjoy it.

They toiled for hours, meticulously detailing the items Tatiana dropped into the steaming broth. Since some of the footage was grainy, considering she kept her cottage dim, they did their best to decipher the ingredients. Eventually, they came up with the following list:

- Dark, curly hairs (from Arderin or Callie perhaps?)
- Eyeballs of a small animal or rodent
- A frog's tongue
- Alligator skin
- Drops of a red unidentified substance (Sofia and Heden both feared it was Crimeous's cloned blood)
- Long leaves from the Cypress trees that lined the bayou
- Various herbs and spices that remained unknown

Once the list was compiled, they called Sathan and updated him so he was prepared for the evening's council meeting.

"Thanks, Heden," Sathan said, running his hand through his thick hair during their video chat. "This is good intel, but I don't like the unknowns. Sadie and Nolan are cataloguing the results from the apple Adelyn brought home from school with her yesterday."

"Why?" Heden asked, looking worried. "Did something happen?"

"Latimus has been sending all her uneaten food to the doctors to test, thinking our enemies might try to get to her that way. Sure enough, the apple she brought home yesterday was poisoned. Sadie and Nolan are identifying the various substances now. They could be some of the same ones Tatiana is using. Who knows? We're guessing here."

"We'll figure it out, bro," Heden said, features drawn together, "but I can't believe someone got past Latimus's guards at the school."

"A woman posing as one of the children's grandmothers seems to be the culprit. The soldier who let her in didn't deem her a threat because she appeared frail. It was most likely Ananda."

"Damn," he said, lacing his fingers behind his head. "Latimus's troops are slacking."

"We're years removed from the war. I think we've all become a bit complacent. If there's a silver lining in this situation, it's that we can identify weakness in our men and retrain them to be more effective."

"Ken and Latimus will be swamped, but it's for the best."

"Agreed. How's the human doing? She hasn't defected yet, right?"

"Still kicking, although your brother could drive a saint mad," Sofia said, batting her eyelashes.

"Honestly, I'm with you on that, Sofia. Keep him in check, okay?"

"Ten-four," she said, saluting the screen.

"I'll shoot you an update after the meeting wraps up tonight. In the meantime, how's the coding coming for the devices? I want all our soldiers equipped with the most up-to-date technology, just in case we need to quickly order a battalion to L.A. That's obviously a worst-case scenario, but I want to protect Arderin and Callie at all costs."

"Good," Heden said. "I just need to tweak a few more things and I should be able to roll it out to Ken and Latimus so they can install it on all the soldiers' devices."

Sathan nodded. "Thanks, Heden. You're actually pretty helpful when you're not focused on driving me or my wife insane."

"You're my favorite brother too, Sathan. Don't tell Latimus because I told him the same thing last week. Good luck at the meeting."

They signed off, and Heden turned to Sofia, fangs resting atop his bottom lip as it curved. "So, it looks like we're done here. There's a happy hour calling our name."

"We have to watch Tatiana," Sofia said, pointing to the laptop. "She won't go to bed for several hours."

"Not to state the obvious, but Tatiana's life is as boring as yours." Sofia glowered at him. "It's true. All that woman does is stir the pot. Literally. And not in any way remotely fun. Come on, Sof," he said, extending his hand to her. "Let's get ready. Throw on your heels and let your hair down."

"I hate heels," she said, rising from the chair. "They're extremely uncomfortable."

"Well then, throw on your sneakers, and let's go."

"I'd rather just stay and write some code to create a program that can help us catalog Tatiana's ingredients and movements. And I need to keep trying to locate Bakari."

"Nope," he said, grabbing her wrist and dragging her toward her bedroom door. "Coding will be here tomorrow. It's your birthday. Meet you back out here in ten minutes."

Sofia rolled her eyes and entered her room, locking the door behind her, showing him she had no intention of meeting him anywhere. Ten minutes later, he began pounding on her door.

She held firm.

Fifteen minutes later, he began singing "I Want It That Way" by the Backstreet Boys at the top of his lungs. Sitting on her bed, Sofia covered her ears. It was no use. Every time she thought he might stop, he began belting another tune. Sighing, she changed her clothes, questioning what the hell she was doing. After two verses of "Bohemian Rhapsody," she thought her eardrums might start bleeding.

"I can do this all night, Sofie," he called through the door. "I haven't even started on Madonna yet. Let's see, should I sing 'Like a Prayer' or 'Lucky Star'"?

Furious, she yanked open the door. "Stop. Fucking. Singing."

"Oh, sweet," he said, eyes roving over her frame. "You put on sandals. Much better than sneakers. You look hot. That shirt is silky." He slipped a finger under the thin strap of her tank top.

"It's comfortable, okay? It's hot as balls down here, and the fabric is cool."

"It's sexy," he said, waggling his eyebrows. "C'mon. Let's go. Unless you want to hear 'Toxic' by Britney. I'm awesome at that one."

Sofia groaned. "Fine. We'll go out for *one* drink." Closing the bedroom door, she grabbed her purse from the counter. "But that's it."

"Oh, yeah, totally," he said, making an X over his heart. "Promise."

"I think I saw your six-year-old niece make the same gesture today. Do you realize how ridiculous you are?"

"Who do you think taught it to her?" he asked, striding over and lacing his fingers through hers. "And I think you like that I'm completely ridiculous and make you laugh. Admit it. Just a little." He squeezed her hand.

"I hate it," she teased, scrunching her features at him.

"Not for long. Shots will make you love me. I get so much hotter after a few shots, and my sense of humor is off the charts. C'mon, Sof. Time's a wastin'."

She let him pull her through the door and onto the gravel sidewalk. Her hand swayed in his as they walked under the late afternoon sun. She should've pulled it away but found it impossible. Their palms seemed to fit together perfectly, and she begrudgingly admitted she liked the image of her smaller hand in his. It made her feel protected and...accepted somehow. Heden seemed to genuinely like being in her presence, and that melted something in her stoic heart.

Smiling, she let herself enjoy their time together as they trailed along. After all, it was temporary, and he would soon return to the immortal world and resume his life of being the realm's tech whiz and serial dater. For now, she would allow herself to be charmed by a handsome man who, despite their circumstances, was attracted to her. Sofia hadn't created any cherished memories since her grandfather died. Could she possibly create some with this affable Vampyre?

Forging ahead, she admitted there was only one way to find out. They approached a small bar that had a flashing "Beer" sign in the window. Heden held open the door and gestured to the darkened interior.

"After you, birthday girl."

Inhaling a deep breath, Sofia stepped inside.

Chapter 20

Hours later, Heden was onstage, karaoke mic in hand, belting a Garth Brooks tune at the top of his lungs. Sofia snickered from the bar as he motioned to her, begging her to join him.

"No way, buddy," she yelled, lifting the half-drunk tequila shot. "I'd need a thousand more of these to do karaoke."

"That's the love of my life, folks," he slurred into the microphone, causing Sofia to giggle. "She's the greatest human I've ever met."

"You're not so bad yourself," she called, thoroughly enjoying their exchange. The song finally ended to raucous applause from the patrons scattered throughout the bar, and Heden plodded toward her, sliding onto the bar stool.

"Two more tequila shots," he said to the bartender. "Have to get her drunk for her birthday."

"I'm good," she said, exchanging a look with the bartender. "We'll let you know if we need another."

"You still have half left. Who drinks half a shot? Come on, woman."

Sofia chugged the shot, grabbing the lime as her eyes watered. After sucking the juice, she threw it on the bar. "No more shots," she said, wiping her mouth. Heden stared at her, desire swimming in his eyes. "Don't look at me like that."

"Like what?" he asked, leaning closer. "Like I'd rather you suck me instead of the lime?"

Sofia laughed in spite of herself. It was difficult to act indifferent toward him after all the shots she'd imbibed. "Yes, exactly like that."

"But it's true," he growled, resting his forehead against hers. "You look adorable, all drunk and tipsy. Your cheeks are glowing. Let's blow this joint. I want to take you home and ravish you."

Fear flooded her as she slowly pulled away. Celebrating her birthday with Heden was one thing, but letting her guard down completely was another. She wasn't ready for that and doubted if she truly could be.

"We can go, but we're not hooking up."

His lips formed a pout. "Why do you hate me?"

She laughed, admiring his persistence. "I don't hate you. But you're really drunk, and I'm mostly drunk, and we need to sleep. I appreciate you celebrating with me, but it's time to go."

They paid the tab, Heden stuffing the bills she laid atop the bar back in her purse and insisting on paying from his stash of human currency. On the way home, they stopped to grab a slice of pizza for Sofia, and she scarfed it down as they stumbled under the full moon. Once back at the house, Heden kicked off his shoes and began undressing in the living room.

"No way," Sofia said, clutching his wrist and leading him into his bedroom. "You'll undress in your room like a civilized person and pass out on your bed, not the couch."

"I should be taking care of you," he said, sliding his hand behind her neck. "Why are you taking care of me?"

"Because you're drunker," she said, giggling. Man, he was wasted, but she was certainly tipsy.

"Help me undress," he said, lifting his arms. "I can't get it off."

"You're such a baby," she said, grasping the ends of his shirt. As soon as she pulled it off, she realized her mistake. His chest was a masterpiece, chiseled with a firm six-pack. Black, springy hairs covered his pecs and whirled around his nipples. Sofia's mouth began to water as she imagined sucking him there.

"Yesss," he hissed, reading her thoughts. "Please, Sofie. You're the perfect height to kiss me there. Please, baby. I want your mouth on me."

Emboldened by the liquor coursing through her veins, she lifted her hand and swirled her fingers through the prickly hairs. With her thumb and forefinger, she pinched the tiny nub and then flicked it with her fingernail.

"Fuck," he breathed, sliding his fingers to gently clench the hair at her nape. "Yes, Sofie. Please. I'm dying for you."

The words sent a rush of wetness to her core. Never had she heard such raw desire in a man's tone. Taking pity on him, she slowly eased toward him and rested her lips over his nipple. Extending her tongue, she licked the sensitive bud.

"Oh, god," he moaned, fist tightening in her hair, the possessive gesture causing pangs of desire to shoot low in her abdomen. Wanting to please him, she began lathering him fully, her wet tongue slathering his nipple with her saliva. His massive body shook against her, and she reveled in the knowledge she could make him shudder.

His free hand encircled her wrist, dragging it toward his fly. With deft fingers, he slid the zipper down and pulled his length through the hole in his boxer briefs. As she continued to lick his straining nipple, Sofia's eyes widened. His cock was massive, thick and throbbing, the veins pulsing under the purple head.

"Is this okay?" he whispered, bringing her hand to his shaft. "I don't want to pressure you, sweetheart."

She nodded, inching her fingers around his length, realizing she barely surrounded him fully. His girth was almost the span of her hand.

"Stroke me," he commanded, his voice gravelly.

She followed his directive while her tongue resumed its assault on his nipple. He spoke words of longing and desire, the vibration of his silky baritone at her temple causing her to body to shudder. Lifting her hand, she licked her palm, wanting to add a layer of lubrication against his sensitive skin. Encircling him again, his large frame quaked as he lifted her chin.

"Sofie," he murmured against her lips. "I'm about thirty seconds from coming in your hand. If you don't want that, let me go now."

"I want it," she whispered, stroking his bottom lip with her tongue. "I want you—"

His lips devoured the words, overtaking her mouth as he groaned against her. Broad hips jutted into her hand as she stroked him, his tongue sweeping every inch of her mouth. Never had Sofia been kissed so thoroughly—or so desperately—and it snapped something inside her soul.

Opening her eyes, she watched him through slitted lids, arousal evident in every inch of his gorgeous face.

Ending the kiss, he stared into her eyes. "Sofie," he cried softly, hand fisted in her hair.

"Heden."

Suddenly, his huge frame began to jerk, and Sofia realized he was coming. Exulted that she could bestow such pleasure, she held tight as he climaxed in her embrace. He groaned her name and buried his face in her hair, his lips resting on her neck. Slowly, his body began to relax, and she felt a small sensation on the sensitive skin of her nape.

"Are you sucking me?" she asked, her voice husky.

"Mmm hmm," he said, chuckling softly. "I'm going to pierce this vein one day, little human. Get ready. But I'll ask you first." Lifting his head, he gazed at her, his eyes glassy. "Deal?"

"Deal," she said, shivering in anticipation.

He expelled a large breath. "Wow, I made a mess. Let me run to the bathroom and I'll return the favor, okay?"

"You don't have to," she said as the anxiety about being with him slowly began to creep back in. "I'm not sure if it's a good idea we have sex, Heden. Especially since we're drunk."

"My practical human. What would I do without you?" He placed a sweet peck on the tip of her nose.

"I'm serious," she said. "Sex is a big step for me. I'm not sure it would even work between us."

"Okay, sweetheart. I don't want to make you uncomfortable. Let me clean myself up in the bathroom, and then maybe I can just hold you for a while? I don't want tonight to be over yet."

She nodded and watched him trail to the bathroom. Wanting to freshen up, she headed toward her own room, where she washed her face and brushed her teeth before changing into her shorts and t-shirt. Or should she wear something else? She took a moment to pilfer through the meager contents she'd brought with her.

After agonizing for several minutes, she decided the shorts and t-shirt were fine. Heading back to his room, she approached him where he lay on his stomach on the bed. Lifting her hands to her mouth, she stifled the laugh. Her Vampyre was naked, stretched out on the bed, fast asleep.

Leaning over, she tapped his face with her finger. He didn't budge. Chalking it up to the fact they definitely weren't meant to have sex tonight, she turned to leave. A hand snaked around her wrist, fast as lightning. In two seconds flat, she was under his naked body, attempting to catch her breath.

"I can smell you when you're near, little human," he said drowsily, nuzzling her neck as he cuddled into her body. "Just give me five minutes, and I swear, I'll rock your world."

Sofia snickered, noticing his eyes were already cemented shut. "I think you're going to be asleep in five seconds, buddy."

"Then sleep with me," he said, throwing his leg over her thighs. His arm already encircled her waist, and he nudged further into the crease of her neck. She was wrapped up in his warmth so tightly, escape was impossible.

"Relax, Sofie," he warbled against her skin. "We're just sleeping. Let me hold you."

The cadence of his breath was calming as it washed over her, warm and intimate. His expression was open, and he looked extremely young. How old would he be if he were human? Sofia guessed twenty-seven or twenty-eight, max. He must've gone through his immortal change in his late twenties. Smiling, she realized that made her the "older woman" in a way, although in reality, he was many centuries older. What would people think if they saw them together? Would they think her a cradle robber?

Biting her lip, she traced her finger over his beard. It was scratchy under his soft lips, and she gave them a caress as well. Realizing she was trapped in the most delicious way, she gave in to the exhaustion and tequila. As her Vampyre held her close, she succumbed to her dreams.

Chapter 21

Sofia awoke to the most pleasurable sensation. A soft finger was tracing her face. It flitted over her brows, down her nose and stopped at her lips. Lifting her lids, she saw Heden looming above her, head resting on his hand, elbow propped on the bed.

"Hey," she said, her voice raspy from sleep.

"Hey," he said, his baritone causing every nerve ending in her waking skin to sizzle. "You look so pretty when you wake up, Sof."

She breathed a laugh. "I have morning breath, and my eyes are crusted over. Ew."

Chuckling, he placed a soft kiss on her lips. "Don't care. You're gorgeous. I loved holding you while I slept."

"Eh," she said, shrugging against the pillow, "it was okay."

"You spout lies, woman," he said, winking. "You adored sleeping in my arms. Admit it."

Heart thrumming in her chest, she searched his gaze. "Maybe a little."

His fingers continued their mesmerizing caress over her cheek. "I really blew it last night—literally and figuratively."

Sofia snickered. "You did. Everywhere."

His deep chuckle rumbled through his chest. "I'm so sorry. I was ready to show you what an amazing lover I am and I passed the fuck out. It's appalling, and I'm pretty embarrassed. I'd like to make it up to you."

"It's fine. Being intimate with someone is hard for me. It's probably good we just slept together."

Ice-blue eyes roamed over her face. "Do you want me to make love to you? We don't have to go all the way. I can make you come."

Cold daggers of fear shot through her heart. What if he couldn't make her come? She already felt awkward knowing she'd just woken up, which meant she definitely wasn't at her best. Would she close up with him? Worried, she chewed her lip, contemplating.

"It's okay, little human," he said, his smile so endearing her heart splintered. "I won't push you. We can accomplish what we need to today and try again tonight. What do you say?"

Sofia swallowed, terrified to disappoint him. "I might not be ready tonight. Or maybe I will. I don't know. I don't want to lead you on."

"I'm not worried about that at all. You're a straight shooter, Sof. If you feel ready, that's great, and if not, I'll just make out with you. For a reaaaaaally long time."

Her laugh surrounded them. "Deal."

"Come on then," he said, giving her one last poignant kiss. "I'm going to hop in the shower. You're welcome to join me."

"Um, yeah, I think I'll take my own, but thanks."

"Your loss. But I'll make it up to you one day." After waggling his brows, he disentangled from her and stood, stretching his arms above his head. Yawning, he smiled down at her, seemingly unconcerned with his nakedness. His shaft jutted up from the dark thatch of hair between his thighs as if it was searching for her.

Sofia let her eyes wander over his body, unable not to look at his magnificence.

"Like the merchandise?" he teased.

"Yep," she said, sitting up and rolling her neck. "It's not a bad view."

"My ego needed that. Keep it coming. See you in a few." He stalked to the bathroom and shut the door behind him.

Sofia plopped back down on the bed and gave a tiny squeal. It was so unlike her to be giddy, but she'd spent an extremely intimate night with a man and actually felt happy. Reveling in the unfamiliar feeling, she thanked the heavens for her good fortune and headed to her room to shower.

Vadik observed Evie as she puked her guts up behind the newly planted oak tree on the outskirts of Takelia. She was visiting the Deamon prison with Latimus and Kenden to ensure the security was tight. It was a futile folly, and Vadik felt his lips curve in a sinister smile. Now that he had the ability to transport, his power was limitless.

He would never understand why the red-haired usurper denied her heritage. Crimeous had been his lord and king, and Vadik still worshiped him with unparalleled reverence. There had been a cold and systematic righteousness to the Dark Lord's actions. Through torture and murder,

Crimeous had instilled fear in the land and upheld a sense of structured order. Vadik thought him the most valiant leader on all of Etherya's Earth.

When Evie had killed her father with the Blade of Pestilence, Vadik had screamed words of betrayal at the daughter who'd been deemed his successor. How could she toss aside her heritage and her unimaginable powers to live a squalid life amongst the Slayers and Vampyres? It was such a massive waste of resources and abilities.

Eyes narrowed, Vadik saw Kenden approach his wife and rub her back as she vomited into the grass. Crimeous's blood was malicious and it would cause Evie extreme sickness—not just in the morning, but all day, every day until she gave birth to the spawn. *Good.* The ungrateful bitch deserved to suffer. She might disparage the opportunity she'd been given, but Vadik never would. He would take her place and restore Crimeous's name to the prominence it deserved.

Pondering Bakari, Vadik admitted their goals were not the same. Bakari was arrogant and wanted power for himself. He didn't worship Crimeous as lord. But they were both aligned in their hatred of the immortal royals and both believed in a systematic approach for life in Etherya's realm. That shared goal would cement their alliance, at least until all the royals were dead. After that, Vadik wasn't so sure, but he would deal with that once their current objectives had been achieved.

He'd learned there was a value to living in the moment. He'd already waited years to take his revenge and understood it might take several more decades to fully achieve his purpose. That suited him just fine. There was a beauty in patience, as there was in so many things others deemed unnecessary.

Suddenly, Evie lifted her head, and Vadik froze. The bitch's green eyes locked onto him, and he stood his ground, refusing to sink further behind the tree. A voice wafted through his head: *You'll never succeed, Vadik. I'll always be one step ahead.*

Throwing back his head, he laughed, dark and sinister, denying her words. Lifting his hands in the air, he began chanting the phrases Bakari taught him from the human woman who wasn't so human after all. Black clouds whirled overhead, and he felt his body disintegrate into nothing.

Opening his eyes, he looked down on the burning lava of the Purges of Methesda. Staring into the glowing embers, he spoke to his king. "I promise, my lord Crimeous, I will avenge you until my last breath. Your eminence will reign once more!" Tilting his face to the sky, he prayed to Crimeous, hoping he would hear as he suffered in the Land of Lost Souls.

Chapter 22

Heden and Sofia trailed through the woods as they discussed next steps regarding Tatiana. The day was gorgeous, and Heden had suggested they take a hike to soak up the rays. Every time they reached a stump or dead log, Heden would reach over and offer to help her navigate over or around it. Sofia was an avid traveler and hiker and didn't really need his assistance, but she figured it wouldn't hurt to accept chivalry from her handsome companion. Plus, it added to his burgeoning ego, which should've been off-putting, but instead, Sofia found it rather endearing. His persistent efforts to seduce her were secretly thrilling, although she kept that info close to the vest.

"You must really enjoy being in the sun after all those centuries of darkness," she said.

"You have no idea, Sof," he said, stepping over a log and turning to lift her by the waist and place her on the other side as well. Damn, the gesture was so freaking charming. "It's absolutely amazing, although it took me a while not to burn. Now, I wear sunscreen. Most Vamps do."

"I'd imagine your skin was ill-prepared for the radiation, so that makes sense. Do you enjoy watching sunsets? If so, you have to visit Italy. The sunsets on the coast at Positano are so beautiful. You'd love them."

"I've never been," he said, shaking his head. "Maybe you can take me there one day."

"I'd like that."

"So, I think we've gathered all the intel Tatiana is going to give us. She's obviously controlling what we see. It's time to approach her. Should we just visit her when she's home?"

"That seems best," Sofia said, contemplating. "I mean, honestly, if she wanted to harm us, she could've done so by now. As you saw from Bakari's transportation, she has powers I don't even claim to understand. I have no idea how she's learned to wield powers that should only exist in the immortal realm."

Before Heden could answer, a possum scuttled out of the nearby bush and ran across their path, startling them both. As his hand gripped hers, a woman appeared to walk from the bush, although the clearing had been quiet moments earlier.

Standing tall, she crossed her hands in front of her abdomen, assessing them. Sofia clutched Heden's hand, and he squeezed back, assuring his protection.

"Hello, Tatiana," he said with a tilt of his head. "We were just strategizing on the best way to approach you. Thanks for saving us the hassle."

Her dark eyebrow arched. "Anytime. I find it's easier to eliminate unnecessary actions. Although you and I have much time left on the Earth, your human here only has decades."

"So, you're an immortal?" Sofia asked.

"I'm..." She hesitated, seeming to ponder her response. "Not of either world. Not completely. I don't mean to speak in riddles, but my heritage is not what I've come to discuss with you. There will be time for that later. For now, I'd like to see if I misjudged your intelligence. After all, you two seem to possess quick intellects. Tell me what I want to know."

"You let us surveil you because you wanted us to see what you put in the cauldron."

"Yes," she said with a nod. "Go on."

"Your main concoction enables transport, but that one was easy," Heden said. "Based upon your ingredients, we also believe you've created serums that can heal and also bring a corpse back to life. We're worried about that one because it requires Crimeous's cloned blood."

"Very good," she said. "You're correct, although you've only identified three of the several potions I created while you observed me. The other brews aren't important now, since the ones you named are the only ones I gave Bakari."

"We'd like to ask for your alliance," Heden said, releasing Sofia's hands to show Tatiana his open palms. "I would be forever grateful, and the royal immortal family would repay you with anything you request. We would leave no stone unturned to secure any restitution you desire."

Tatiana smiled, the action contorting her face into one more exquisite than Sofia had ever seen. Amber eyes glowed above her full lips, and her brown skin was luminous in the rays of the sun that filtered through the trees.

"I appreciate your request, son of Markdor, but I cannot honor it at this time. It is not yet time for us to align, although that day will come soon enough. For now, I have shown you what you need to fight Bakari and the Secret Society. Take the knowledge I've imparted and discern what he wishes to use the potions for. I have faith you and the human will figure it out."

"Please," Sofia said, unashamed at the pleading tone in her voice. "I know you have no allegiance to Bakari. Is there anything we can do to secure your help?"

Tatiana slowly approached and lifted Sofia's chin with her ring-clad fingers. Several inches taller, she spoke softly down to her. "I sense your guilt, Sofia. Know that you are absolved. I've spoken to your grandfather in the great beyond. He is so very proud of you. All humans make mistakes, but it's the choices they make in their darkest moments that count. You were quite brave to defect, and that decision will be rewarded. More than you can ever know now."

Sofia's eyes burned at the mention of her beloved grandfather, and a tear trailed down her cheek. "Does he know I tried to avenge him?"

"He doesn't need vengeance, my dear. He never did. Francesco lived a long life full of love and laughter. If we could all be so lucky. His only wish now is that you find the same."

"I don't care about that," she said, swiping away the tear. "I just need him to know I'm sorry."

"Apologies have no meaning in the great beyond," she said, gently shaking her head. "He only wishes for you to be happy."

"Please tell him I love him," Sofia whispered, barely able to speak.

"He knows, Sofia. With all his soul." Lowering her hand, she turned to face Heden. "And you, son of Markdor. You will have a great choice to make as well. Sofia has done her part. I am confident you will do yours."

Heden's fangs glistened as he grinned. "Not to squelch the melodrama, lady, but you sure do talk in some serious riddles."

Throwing her head back, Tatiana broke into a jubilant laugh, her entire body quaking under her flowing green dress. "That I do, Vampyre." Stepping back, she regarded them. "I let you into my home, but that is now over. Please do not enter my property again without permission. I don't take lightly to those who do, understood?"

"Yes," they said in unison, their tones contrite.

"The cameras have already been disabled. You have everything you need. Take the knowledge you have back to the immortal world and help your family defeat the Secret Society. Sofia will question whether she should accompany you, but you need her. Don't let her waver. She is invaluable to your future, Heden."

"Yes, ma'am, Ms. Tatiana," he said.

"I like that. 'Ms. Tatiana.' I believe I shall request to be called that more often. Best wishes, my new friends. May your goddess Etherya and your Catholic god work together to ensure your success. For now, goodbye, until we meet again."

Lifting her palms to the sky, Tatiana tilted her face and closed her eyes, chanting words indecipherable to Sofia but similar to those Bakari had chanted in the alley in L.A. Wind swirled as the clouds above darkened, and she vanished into thin air, leaving only a swirl of dead leaves behind.

"Wow," Sofia said, expelling a breath. "That was heavy." Heden stared at her, his gaze reverent. "What?"

"You're just really beautiful when you cry," he said, inching closer and cupping her jaw. Slowly, he wiped the wetness away. "I'm so damn sorry about your grandfather, Sofie. I wish I could bring him back for you."

She sighed, basking in the warmth of his caress. "Her words gave me comfort, and I hope they're true. Perhaps he really is content up there and wants me to move on and focus on my own happiness. I wonder what she meant by 'the great beyond.' I'm guessing it's Heaven."

"It's the Passage. Only barbaric humans believe in Heaven."

Sofia breathed a laugh and made the sign of the cross over her chest. "I'm pretty sure you just damned yourself to Hell."

"No way. In our lore, there's the Land of Lost Souls and the Passage, similar to your Hell and Heaven. Hell doesn't exist, so I can't end up there."

"Well, Heaven definitely exists," she said, loving their banter. "There's nowhere else my grandfather could possibly be."

"Only the Passage exists, little human. Everybody knows that."

"Well, I guess there's only one way to find out. We're both going to have to die."

"If it means winning an argument with you, I'm down," he teased.

Sofia's features scrunched as she stared up at him. "Do I really argue with you that much?"

"About every damn thing, Sof. It's fucking adorable. I get so hard when you insist you're right."

Sofia's eyes widened, and her gaze traveled to his fly.

"Yep, right now. Want to bang on the old log? I'll take the bottom so you don't scrape your delectable skin."

She pulled away and swatted his chest. "I'm not *banging* you on a dirty log in a forest. Good grief, you're annoying."

"I'll show you annoying, woman," he said, bending down to pick her up. Sofia yelped as he threw her over his shoulder and began walking back toward the house.

"Put me down," she squealed, lightly pounding his back with her fists.

Heden smacked her jean-clad ass with his broad palm, causing her to squirm atop his shoulder. His hand smoothed away the sting, and then he nipped the juicy globe. Sofia gushed so thoroughly in her panties she thought they might melt away.

"Holy shit," he murmured, inhaling as he walked. "I smell your arousal, honey. It smells so damn good."

"I'm not aroused at all," she lied, wriggling against him in the hopes he would do it again.

"Don't lie to me, Sof," he said, placing another playful slap on her ass. As he took measured steps, he soothed his palm over the sensitive cheek. God, she loved it. Relaxing into him, she realized how safe she felt in his arms.

"I'm going to carry you like this all the way home," he said, placing a kiss on her butt. "You feel so good against me."

Although hanging over his shoulder was quite uncomfortable, it did give her a great view of his magnificent backside. Sliding her palms over his ass, she squeezed, loving the feel of the tight muscles beneath as he walked.

"You squeeze mine, and I'll squeeze yours back," he growled, clutching her ass cheek in his hand.

"Is that supposed to deter me?" she asked, laughing.

They proceeded to honor that arrangement the entire way home, Sofia's delight echoing through the forest lined with withered trees and curious critters who came out of hiding to see what all the fuss was about.

Once home, they logged onto the laptop to verify the feed had been cut. Sure enough, every camera angle was black and inactive. Sofia removed the program from the hard drive, thankful they had already saved the segments of video showing Tatiana adding the various ingredients to the cauldron.

After video chatting with his family and updating them on the meeting with Tatiana, Heden discussed next steps with Sathan as Sofia sat beside him.

"Great job, bro," Sathan said.

Heden appeared pleased by the praise, and Sofia realized Sathan was the only father figure he'd ever known. Although they were brothers, she could tell he looked up to the king and found it sweet that he basked in the acclaim.

"At this point, it's probably best for you to head back to Astaria. You can focus on updating the military devices to communicate through the ether and also work with Sadie and Nolan to identify the toxins we found in Adelyn's lunchbox. The chemicals are new to our realm, and we want to identify them so we can have a cure ready if someone accidentally ingests them."

"I could write a program that could help the docs catalog and analyze the results faster. Those two love to write things on paper. It's outdated as hell."

"Agreed," Sofia chimed in.

"You're welcome to accompany Heden, Sofia," Sathan said. "We could use another programmer with your skills. I don't want to detract from your life in the human world, but if you're willing to help us for a few weeks or months, I won't turn it down."

Sofia chewed her lip, contemplating. Was there anything tethering her to the human world? Not really. For years, there had been no purpose to her life except exacting revenge for Francesco. Sadly, no one would miss her if she left.

But there were other things to consider now that she was free of her quest for vengeance. She wanted to bear a child of her own and was pushing forty. There was only so much time left for her to conceive. Each moment she spent in the immortal world was one that lessened her chances of being a mother. After being alone for so long, she was ready to love and nurture a baby.

Glancing at Heden, she noticed his imploring smile. "Come on, Sof," he said, nudging her shoulder with his. "Come back with me for a few weeks at least. I'm not ready to let you go yet."

Sathan cleared his throat, acknowledging he understood their relationship was no longer purely platonic. "Why don't you two discuss tonight? You have the house for one more night, right?"

"Yep," Heden said. "Let me work on our girl here. I'll do my very best to charm her into coming home with me."

"I bet you will," Sathan muttered, although it was good-natured. "Sounds good. Text me before you come back through the ether. Sofia, I hope you choose to come to the realm. We're thankful to have you on our team."

"Thank you, Sathan," she said, swallowing over the lump that formed in her throat. She was honored to be accepted by the people she'd wronged not so long ago.

Heden clicked off the chat and turned to her, fingers laced behind his head. "So, little human, we have all night. What do you want to do?" He waggled his eyebrows.

"Well, I'm not just going to jump into bed with you. Good lord. Is it really that easy for you with women?"

He shrugged. "Most of the time, yeah. I like that you're difficult though. It keeps me on my toes."

"Difficult, my ass," she said, standing and placing her hands on her hips. "I'm one hundred percent sure *you* are the difficult one in this relationship, but I won't argue with you."

"That's a first," he said, standing and running his hand through his thick hair. "So, what should we do with our last night in Louisiana?"

"Well, I'm starving and could definitely eat. This might sound lame, but I saw on Yelp there's a bar in town that has a bunch of arcade games and yummy appetizers. Is that super dorky?"

"Fuck yes, and I love it," he said, inching closer. Cupping her jaw, he tilted her face. "Please tell me they have Ms. Pac-Man."

"And Galaga and Space Invaders..." she said in a sultry tone.

"Keep going..." He inched closer to her face.

"And Centipede and Street Fighter II..."

"Damn it, woman, I'm going to come in my pants. Tell me one more. It's all I can take."

Sofia licked her lips, the movement slow and deliberate. "They have..."—she lifted to her toes and whispered—"Mortal Kombat."

He captured her lips, his tongue consuming her as he groaned.

Sofia threaded her arms around his neck, thrusting her body into his. Their tongues warred with each other as small moans of desire escaped their throats. Clenching his hair with her fingers, she tugged and felt his resulting shudder.

"I've never heard anything as sexy as you spouting vintage arcade games to me," he whispered against her lips. "Fuck, Sofie, you're incredible."

She chuckled and shook her head. "I'm a huge geek."

"You're my geek, woman. Get used to it." He playfully slapped her butt. "Come on, let's get you fed so I can ravish you."

She nodded and gave him one last kiss. "Let's do it."

Armed with their wallets and Sofia's empty stomach, they headed out into the temperate evening for what Heden insisted on calling their "dork date." To her, that sounded just about perfect.

Chapter 23

Sofia proceeded to have the absolute, hands-down, best date of her life with Heden at the arcade bar. The games were plentiful, and the food was fantastic. After several hours of competition, they were tied at five wins per person on the various consoles. Now, they were playing a hot and heavy two-player game of Ms. Pac-Man for winner-takes-all bragging rights.

Heden's thick fingers deftly maneuvered the tiny joystick, causing Sofia to wonder how in the hell he could be so agile with hands so large.

"My hands are magic, Sof," he said, eyes never leaving the console. "Don't doubt me. You'll see soon enough."

"In your dreams," she said, rolling her eyes.

"It's my only dream," he said, glancing up to wink at her. He finished two more levels before being eaten by the yellow ghost and dying a quick but painless death.

Sofia took the seat and proceeded to handily defeat the next four levels, only losing her last life once she'd squarely beaten Heden.

"Damn, you're good," he said, shaking his head as she rose. "I admit defeat. You own my body for the next twenty-four hours. I'm your humble servant."

Sofia threw back her head and laughed. "I'm pretty sure that's *your* prize, not mine."

"Fuck yes," he said, pecking her on the lips. Threading his fingers through hers, he led her out of the bar and down the darkened sidewalk.

"This will probably sound strange, but you're the first person I've felt this free with since my grandfather." Slightly embarrassed by the admission, she awaited his response.

"That means so much, Sof," he said, squeezing her hand. "I feel the same. It's been hard for me since everyone and their damn mother started falling in love and having babies."

"How so?" she asked, glancing up at him.

"I've always been close with my siblings but still...*apart* from them in a way. Sathan always had his duties, Latimus had his army, and Arderin was always buried in a book studying medicine or driving Sathan crazy." He grinned. "That was always *really* fun to watch, by the way."

Sofia chuckled, and he continued. "We were tethered together because it was just the four of us, even if I was the most aloof. As they all bonded and had kids, the separateness I'd felt expanded even more. It's hard to explain because I still love them all so much, but I've just been kind of drifting, I guess. Then, one day, the craziest thing happened."

"You met the most gifted hacker you'd ever seen?" she teased, beaming up at him.

His features contorted playfully. "Do you even know how to turn on a laptop? I can show you. You're a pretty crappy programmer."

"Says the man who didn't even know C++ code," she mumbled.

"Anyway," he said, winking, "I met this really awful hacker, but she was so damn cute, and I felt this instant connection with her even though she was trying to murder my family. It's the love story every young man dreams about."

Sofia rolled her eyes at his teasing. "Even though you're making fun of me, I get it. I think you and I both see the world the same way. Like, we don't quite fit into a lot of the situations we're presented with, so we forge ahead and create ways to exist in our reality even if it isn't comfortable. Outwardly, we function really well, but we don't really feel connected to a lot of people."

Their hands swung as they clung to each other, digesting her words. "That's exactly how I feel, Sof. Damn. You get it."

"I get it," she said, squeezing his fingers. "It's nice to find someone else who does."

Blue eyes glimmered with reverence and emotion as he gazed down at her. They continued to trail along, talking about everything and nothing, and Sofia realized how much she would miss him when they did ultimately part. In such a short time, she'd become so comfortable with him. It was poignant, and she was extremely thankful he'd seen the goodness and pain warring within her, almost before she recognized it herself.

Their words tapered off as they trailed inside, each exhibiting a reverent shyness that was atypical of their personalities. A lamp shone atop the bedside table from Heden's open bedroom door, the lone light that permeated the otherwise dim house.

Heden slowly approached her. "Sofie," he whispered, palming her cheeks with his strong hands, "I want you so much."

She stared into his gorgeous clear irises, anxiety slamming inside her pounding heart. "Okay," she said, nodding hesitantly. "But I've never really been great at this, so go easy on me."

"Impossible," he breathed, lowering his lips to hers.

Enveloped by his strength and his musky scent, she clutched him closer, whimpering as his tongue invaded her mouth. It slid over hers, claiming it, warring with it, until she was breathless.

Gently breaking the kiss, his gaze, blazing with desire, bore into her. "You're absolutely perfect. I can't think of one thing you could do to my body that I wouldn't enjoy. I mean, you're not the greatest coder I've ever seen, but other than that—"

"Stop teasing me," she said, swatting his pecs as he grinned. "I'm so nervous."

"Don't be," he said, dropping his hand to clutch her wrist. Pulling it to his chest, he placed her palm over his pounding heart. "It always beats like this when I'm around you. I don't think I've ever wanted anyone more."

"That's a good line."

He lifted her hand from his chest to nip her palm. "I mean it, Sof. There are no lines with you. Just you and me and my insatiable desire for you. You ready?"

"I'm ready." She threaded her arms around his neck. "But I am a bit intimidated. You're freaking huge. What if it doesn't fit?"

His warm chuckle surrounded her, causing embarrassment to warm her cheeks.

"Stop laughing! It's a valid concern, especially with someone as massive as you."

"Oh, I'll fit, honey. I'm going to have you flowing for me before I even consider fucking you. When you're ready, we'll know."

"Should we use a condom?"

"It's impossible for humans and Vampyres to spread disease or impregnate one another, but I'll wear one if you want. I want you to feel safe with me, Sof."

The tender words almost shattered her heart. "I feel so safe with you. It's…liberating. And it's not every day you can have sex with no consequences, so…let's bareback the shit out of each other."

"Dude," he said, shaking his head. "That's the hottest sentence anyone's ever spoken to me."

"And yet being called 'dude' is incredibly disconcerting."

He breathed a laugh. "Let me make it up to you, dude. I swear, I'm good for it."

Sofia couldn't stop her laughter. "You're incorrigible." Emotion swirled through her, igniting a maelstrom of feeling as he lifted her. Instinctively, she wrapped her legs around his waist, crossing her ankles behind his back.

His mouth pillaged hers as he stumbled through the bedroom door, stopping beside his bed. Anchored by her legs, she drew back, yanking at his t-shirt and pulling it off his shoulders. In between kisses, he freed her of her shirt, and she pressed her torso to him, craving contact.

Heden's lips blazed a wet trail across the curve of her jaw and then down the sensitive skin of her neck, coming to rest at the juncture of her shoulder. Groaning, he sucked her there, and Sofia knew he was imagining drinking from her. The thought sent a rush of lust through her shaking body, and she gasped.

"You okay?" he asked, lifting his head to gaze into her eyes.

She nodded, desire causing her skin to flush.

"You want me to pierce you with my fangs right there on your pretty neck, don't you, honey?"

"Yes," she whispered.

"I will, but first, I need to make up for last night. Man, you must think I'm so lame. At this point, I'm lower on the sexiness scale than Screech from *Saved by the Bell*."

Sofia threw her head back, overcome with laughter. "How in the hell do you know about that show?"

"Come on, woman," he said, nipping her lips. "It's a classic. I pride myself on staying up-to-date on human pop culture."

She traced her fingers over his cheek, stopping at the soft hairs of his beard. "I have a feeling I'm going to be torn between laughing and climaxing over the next few hours. Of course you wouldn't be serious during sex. It would ruin your comedic reputation."

"Sofie, if you think I'm not serious about you, you haven't been paying attention."

The words threatened to rip her heart from her chest, and she told herself to calm down. If she wasn't careful, she'd end up falling for him. This man who wasn't a man, and someone she had no future with. Determined to stay in the moment, she focused on his handsome features.

"Let me set you down for a sec," he said. After she uncrossed her legs, he slid her down his body until her feet hit the floor.

Feeling wobbly, she gripped his biceps.

"Hold on to my shoulders," he said, slowly kneeling before her. When she complied, he removed her sneakers and socks, taking his time as he slowly divested her of the garments. Reaching for the button of her jeans, he grinned up at her, holding her gaze as he unclasped the button.

"Your bra is pretty," he said, his voice husky as his irises roved over the small mounds of her breasts covered in black lace. She didn't have many appealing undergarments, considering them impractical, but this bra was her favorite. She'd worn it tonight hoping he might see it and glowed at his compliment.

He slid the zipper of her jeans down, and she threaded her fingers though his thick, wavy hair. He growled, closing his eyes as she squeezed. "That feels so good," he said, lifting his lids to drill into her. "When I'm inside you, I want you to clutch my hair and anchor yourself that way. I love having my hair pulled and my scalp scratched."

"Okay," she said, digging the tips of her nails into his scalp and dragging them across.

"Fuck," he breathed, closing his eyes again. "Not right now, honey, or I'm going to blow my load in my pants. Later though. Don't forget."

"I won't." He commenced ridding her of her jeans, dragging them off each leg and tossing them to the floor. She was left standing before him in only her bra and red cotton underwear. His gaze darted over her hips and the intersection between her thighs as he grasped her hips. Pulling her toward him, he buried his nose in the cloth-covered juncture and inhaled deeply.

"Heden."

"Shhh..." he said, nuzzling her with his nose. "You smell so good. Let me have this much of you. For just a minute...or maybe forever..."

There she stood, grasping his hair, his face buried in her most private place, more open to him than anyone she'd ever known. The moment felt special...reverent in some way...and she felt the sting of tears. Through the moisture, she smiled at the strong man who bowed before her.

After a small eternity, Heden lifted his head and ran his hand over her mound. As her flushed body trembled, he hooked his fingers over the top of her panties and slid them down, tossing them near her jeans. Standing, he gripped her hand and led her to the bed. Sitting on the side, he drew her in between his open legs.

"You still have your pants on," she said, feeling her lips curve into a slight frown.

"I want to take my time with you," he said, grasping her other hand and pulling her down to him. "Kiss me, Sofie."

She followed his command, opening her mouth over his and slipping her tongue inside. As he moaned, she straddled his thick thighs, sitting atop his jean-covered erection.

His hands caressed her back, flirting with the tips of her curly hair, as his tongue warred with hers. When he slid his hand down over her hip and thigh and rested his fingers atop the triangle of black hair covering her deepest place, she gave a high-pitched mewl.

His chuckle both aroused and frustrated her. Self-doubt rushed in, and she reminded herself to remain calm and open.

"I like to laugh during sex, Sofie," he said, gently fingering her soft curls down below. "It's something that's supposed to be *fun*. I'm never laughing at you, so don't tense up. If you relax enough, you might just laugh along with me."

"I've never really had fun while having sex."

"You poor, sheltered human. I can't wait to change that narrative. You're going to have so much fun with me, I'll ruin you for anyone else. Ready?"

Sofia stared at him, worried he was right. "Ready," she whispered.

Nuzzling the tip of her nose with his, he lowered his finger to her opening, circling it, testing.

"Fuck. You're so slick, baby. Feel that?" He rimmed the swollen lips of her core, causing her to purr, and slipped a thick finger inside. Instinctively, her body clenched him, his teeth gritting as he breathed against her lips. "God, Sofie, you're so tight."

"It's been a long time," she said, trying to remember the last time she'd had sex. Many years ago, for sure.

"I'm not sure I'll survive fucking you," he said, stealing a kiss from her lips as he pumped his finger in and out of her tight, wet channel. "But I don't think I'll give a damn. What a way to go."

Sofia giggled, taken with the intimacy of the moment and his gentle teasing.

"She's laughing," he said, mock surprise in his tone. "Look who's loosening up."

"In more ways than one," she said, snickering at the double entendre.

"Oh, man. Don't make me give you a 'that's what she said,'" he said, shaking his forehead against hers. "Once you get me started, I'll go on forever."

"That's what she said," Sofie chortled.

Heden laughed, overtaking her lips with his and consuming them in a heated kiss. "Don't steal my material," he murmured against her lips. "That will get you punished."

"Oh, yeah?" she taunted. "How?"

He inserted another finger, stretching her swollen folds. Sofia exhaled a groan, her head lolling back as she struggled to breathe. It was so intimate, so freeing, to straddle him while he explored her innermost spot. Gathering some of her silky moisture, he spread it to her clit, causing the skin there to become slippery. Reintroducing his thick fingers to her channel, he rubbed the heel of his hand against her sensitive nub. Sofia rocked against him, the back and forth motions of his fingers and hand causing bursts of pleasure to shoot through her body. They spiked from her core, connecting with every nerve ending in her straining frame, lifting her from her body to a place where only pleasure existed.

Grasping his shoulder with a vicelike grip, she reached behind, attempting to unhook her bra. Frustrated, she grappled with the hook until Heden lifted his free hand, snapping the garment open in seconds.

Sofia stilled, panting as she eyed him warily. "Should I be jealous that you know how to do that so well?"

"Yes," he teased, scrunching his features at her as he nipped her lips and tore the bra from her body. "I'm the greatest lover the immortal world has ever seen. In fact, I have several ladies you can ask for references—"

"Shut up," she said, swallowing his words as she kissed him.

"Mmmm..." he said, lifting his hand to her breast and cupping the small swell. "I like this dominant side of you. We need to get a whip for next time. I'll go first."

"You wish—" She broke off, gasping as he pinched her nipple.

His fingers resumed their pace below, the heel of his hand grinding against her. Heden's gaze lowered to her nipple, now firmly pressed between his fingers. "Look at that sweet little nipple," he growled, tugging on it as she moaned. "You like that."

"Yes," she whimpered, her head falling back as she arched toward him.

"Poor baby," he murmured, releasing her breast and gliding his hand up to fist her hair. Tugging her head back further, he grazed his lips across her collarbone, moving closer to the tip of her straining nipple. "You're so wound up. Let me help you."

Extending his tongue, he licked around the nub, leaving a wet trail that encircled her breast. Lifting her head, she cemented her eyes to his, pleading. As her hips gyrated over his hand pistoning into her deepest place, his gorgeous gaze held hers. Extending his tongue, he touched the tip to her nipple.

Sofia bucked, feeling the orgasm build, reaching ever higher toward the moment she would explode all over him in a fit of spent desire. Never had she seen anything as sexy as Heden flicking her nipple with his tongue as he stared up at her, silently begging her to come.

Out of nowhere, a slight fear began to choke her. She was mad for this man who was so intent on giving her pleasure. What if she became addicted to his touch? His friendship? His...*love*? Happy-ever-after with a Vampyre was impossible—Sofia knew this in her practical heart. What the hell was she doing, opening herself so thoroughly to someone she had no future with?

"Don't leave me, honey," he murmured against her breast. "Come back to me."

"What are we doing, Heden?" she cried, desire warring with the terror inside.

"Hey," he said, gaze locking with hers. "Don't bring that stuff in here. It's just you and me right now. Nothing else. Stay with me, baby." His fingers continued the madness below, threatening to shatter her.

Moving his lips to her ear, he spoke reverently in his low-toned voice, the deep timbre soothing. "You're mine, Sofie," he declared, clutching her to him as he loved her. "*Mine*. I've been searching for you for so long, I didn't even know it."

Lifting his head, he locked onto her eyes. "Now, I want you to take my fingers and move that sweet little clit against my hand."

Sofia whimpered as her hips gyrated.

"You're beautiful and perfect, and I want you to come for me."

Following his directive, she lowered her lids and called his name.

"I'm right here, baby. I'm so fucking turned on for you. I can't wait to claim you and make you mine." Grasping her hair, he drew her head back, lowering his head to her nipple. "Let *go*, Sofia." Closing his teeth around her nipple, he gently bit the delicate nub.

It was the jolt she needed, sending Sofia headfirst into a massive orgasm. Grasping Heden's firm shoulders, she lost control of her muscles, unable to restrain the violent spasms. Crying out, she clenched her eyes shut as prickles of pleasure and fire shot to every pore of her burning skin. Somewhere in her dazed mind, she remembered she was supposed to be scared of her feelings toward him, but she didn't have the ability to hold onto the fear. It flew away into the night, dispelled toward the stars and moon along with any lingering reservations about the intense intimacy. Her magnificent Vampyre had dissipated them all. Inhaling huge gulps of air, she buried her face in his neck and drew him close with her quivering arms.

He held her, quiet and serene, which was quite a feat for her talkative immortal.

Squeezing him, she laughed into his pecs and gave them a sloppy kiss. "Somebody's quiet," she mumbled into his slick skin. It warmed her to know he'd gotten sweaty and sticky just from making her come. The thought of him oozing sweat as he loomed over her, his thick cock inside her, sent a fresh round of shudders through her spent body.

When he didn't answer, she lifted her head and cupped his jaw. "Heden?"

Removing his fingers from her, he lifted them, palming her cheek. There was something so sexy about feeling her own wetness against her flushed skin. But even better was the way the handsome man stared at her. Sofia had never seen such pleasure swimming in another's eyes.

"You're happy," she said, rubbing his beard.

"So happy," he said, his expression one of wonder and affection. But there was something else too. Something she struggled to read.

"What's wrong?"

"I was worried there for a second," he said, running the pad of his thumb over her lower lip. "That you weren't going to trust me and let go."

"There are a lot of unsaid things between us, Heden, that's all. It shook me for a minute."

"I know," he said, his other hand stroking her back. "I wish we had more time. I want years with you, Sofie. Centuries. However long it takes until you get tired of me and tell me to go to hell. Which I don't believe in," he said, lifting a finger.

She laughed, her heart jolting at his touching words. "I don't have centuries. I wish I did. Time's a bitch."

"It sure is, little human." He stood, holding her in his arms as he turned down the bed. Placing her gently beneath the covers, he slipped off the rest of his clothes, gazing at her the entire time. Lowering beside her, he pulled her against him.

Sofia rubbed the scratchy hairs on his chest, needing to at least acknowledge the unknowns. "I'm afraid to come back with you to Astaria. I experience some pretty intense feelings around you."

"Same," he said, running his hand over her back. Her gaze rested on her fingers plucking at his chest hairs as he stared at the ceiling. "I feel so connected to you, Sofie. I know it's only been a short while, but there's just something about you."

Ever so slowly, she slid the silken skin of her leg over his thighs and glided to sprawl atop his massive chest. "There's something about you too. When you're not making fun of me."

He grinned, running his fingers through her hair. "Me? Never."

Sofia slithered up his body, aligning her lips with his. "Make love to me," she whispered.

Breathing her name, his palms ran down her back, stopping to clutch the globes of her ass in his hands. Maneuvering her over his frame, he aligned the tip of his cock with her wet opening.

"God, Sofie," he said against her mouth. "You're still so wet."

Anchoring on his pecs, she straddled him, attempting to push herself onto his cock. Feeling the thick head inch inside her sent shards of arousal though her still-flushed body. She worked her hips, becoming frustrated that he seemed to be holding back.

"You can push harder."

"I don't want to hurt you. And I'm not sure if this way is best for our first time."

"Want me to flip over?"

"Hold on." Grasping her in his arms, he flipped them, rolling atop her and stroking her hair as it fanned on the pillow. "I wasn't worried before, but I'm a bit worried now. You're really tight, honey."

"So stretch me open," she said, biting her lip.

His fingers found her opening and gathered her silken moisture. Lifting to her clit, he began to stimulate it. Sofia's hips gyrated against his ministrations, the pressure so intense as he circled her swollen nub. Gliding to her opening, he jutted two fingers inside. Sofia told herself to relax, wanting so badly to please him.

"You're fine, honey," he said, moving his fingers inside her deepest place. "The more you tell yourself to open up, the harder it will probably be."

"How do I turn my brain off?" she asked, only half-joking.

"Think about other fun stuff. What's your favorite color?'

"Blue," she moaned, hips undulating against his hand.

"Dogs or cats?"

"Dogs."

"Beach or mountains?" He inserted a third finger, the stretching sensation pleasurable and uncomfortable all at once.

"I, uh..." She mewled softly. "Beach. Positano or Greece."

"Good answer." Removing his fingers, he aligned the head of his shaft with her opening. His finger resumed circling her clit as he loomed over her. "Favorite Vampyre?"

"You," she cried, arms encircling his neck. "Oh, god, Heden. Please."

He began pushing inside, tiny juts that filled her so completely she thought she might burst.

"You with me, Sof?" he asked, eyes boring into her.

"Yes," she said, gliding her hands to his head. Remembering his earlier directive, she grabbed the thick strands.

"Yeah, baby," he said, increasing the pace of his thrusts. "Tug my hair hard. I love it. You won't hurt me."

Needing to please him, she clenched tight, alternating between pulling the strands and scratching his scalp with her nails. With every motion, he groaned and pumped further inside her. Opening herself up to him, she spread her legs as wide as they would go, showing him with her body how much she trusted him.

"I need to fuck you harder," he growled, fangs bared as he stared down at her. "If I hurt you, tell me right away, okay?"

She nodded, her hair swishing over the pillow.

Anchoring on his palm, he began thrusting into her, still rubbing her clit with his other hand. Sofia could feel the head of his shaft pounding her core, and she wanted to weep with joy. Seeing him so lost to desire filled every chasm of doubt she'd ever had.

"Sofie..." Beads of sweat lined his forehead as he moved above her, the sight visceral and raw. They began to drip over her skin, and she loved that he was as consumed by the experience as she was.

"Nothing has ever felt this good," he groaned, hammering her with his pulsing cock. "Do you know how good you feel, baby?"

Her engorged clit tingled under his fingers. "I'm going to come again," she wailed.

"Yes, honey. Come all over my cock. Damn it...I'm going to lose it."

Her body snapped, and she succumbed to the pleasure, closing her eyes as he hammered into her, screaming her name. The walls of her core convulsed around his silken length until she felt him start to shudder. Stuffed to the brim with his magnificent cock, she felt it begin to pulse and then jet his release into her deepest place. Spearing his scalp with her fingernails, his colossal frame jerked above her several times until he collapsed in a heap over her trembling body. Laughs of pure joy escaped her throat, and she clutched him tight, needing to hold every fragment of his skin to hers.

He groaned into the soft curve of her neck, subsequent quakes wracking his frame. "Good lord, Sof. You fucking strangled my cock to death."

Unable to control her sultry chuckle, she ran her nails over his scalp, reveling in his resulting shiver. "You asked for it, buddy."

"Hell yes, I did. Man, your pussy is amazing. Like, it deserves an award. An Oscar or an Emmy or something."

"You're such a tool," she teased. "And I'm glad it felt good."

Grunting, he lifted his head, resting it on his hand as he undulated his hips against hers. "It felt fucking amazing. I'm staying here forever. My cock has found its permanent home."

She giggled, jutting right back into him. "As fun as that sounds, I'll eventually have to get up to pee."

"Never," he said, smacking a wet kiss on her lips. "Sorry, but you're never allowed to move again."

"We'll see, Vampyre."

They lay there, sated and lazy, staring into each other as their bodies cooled. Sofia trailed her fingers over his back as he slowly combed his fingers though her hair on the pillow.

"You look so gorgeous right now," he whispered after a while.

"So do you."

Tracing his thumb over her lip, his expression grew serious. Sofia knew he was thinking of the future and the inevitable end of their relationship somewhere down the line. "Please come back to Astaria with me. Give me two months. After that, we'll sit down and reevaluate."

"Heden," she said softly, shaking her head atop the pillow.

"Please, Sof. I can't let you go yet. I mean, I physically can't. I'm still inside you."

The chuckle rumbled in her chest. "It's a big risk for me. I want to have kids, Heden, and I'm running out of time for that. Every day I spend there with you is a day in a future that isn't mine."

Sighing, he cupped her jaw. "I don't want to take anything away from you, but two months is nothing."

"Not to you—"

"I'm not trying to diminish your dreams, Sof. I just want so badly for you to make mine come true a little while longer."

"Damn," she said, trailing her fingers through his hair. "That was a good one."

"Yeah?" He squinted at the ceiling. "I was thinking maybe it was too heavy. Have to make sure the levity is just right."

"Your comedic timing is intact," she said, giving him an affable eye roll. Contemplating, her gaze roved over his attractive features. "Okay," she finally said. "Two months. And then we'll reevaluate."

"Yippee!" he said, sliding his arms around her and squeezing tightly. "I'm going to make you so happy, honey. I swear, these are going to be the best two months of your life."

Sofia hugged him back, knowing he spoke the truth while acknowledging how much harder that would make her eventual departure. Pledging to enjoy the moment, she lifted her lips to his and allowed him to kiss her fears away for now, knowing they would return in the not-so-distant future...

Chapter 24

After the sun rose, they packed up their bags and tidied up the house, ready to depart to Astaria. Once finished, Heden closed the door behind him with a firm thud.

"Ready?" he asked, extending his hand to Sofia.

Nodding, she placed her hand in his.

He led her to the soft grass beside the house and held his palm in the air, generating the ether. Placing a protective hand on her back, he urged her to walk through first.

They emerged on the other side, the sun blazing above. Kenden was waiting by a four-wheeler and lifted an arm in a wave. Hopping into the vehicle, he caught them up on Vadik's appearance at the Deamon prison and his subsequent vanishing act.

"I didn't sense any malice in Tatiana's demeanor when we met her," Heden said. "I can't understand why she supplied the potions to Bakari and, by proxy, his allies."

"I don't think she sees it as helping them," Sofia said. "There's an underlying control in playing nice with both sides. After all, she also gave us intel. Perhaps she's letting things play out and doing what she feels is right in her gut."

"Maybe," Heden said, "but I don't like it. Vadik's interest in the Deamon prison is worrisome. If he figures out a way to spring the prisoners there, we'll be thrust right back into war. There are almost a thousand Deamons housed there."

"Latimus and I are all over it," Kenden said. "The troop count there has been increased tenfold, and the security system you implemented when it was built is fantastic. In the meantime, Sadie and Nolan definitely need some sort of program to analyze and catalog the various chemicals we've been finding faster. Moira and Aron found traces in the tomatoes in their garden as well. I want cures developed as soon as possible. We don't know how many toxins they have stockpiled, and if they somehow begin poisoning subjects, we want to be prepared."

"Done. Sofia's pledged to help us for two months. The little human is going to save us all." He squeezed her shoulder as she sat in the front seat.

"Not sure about that, but I'm happy to help," Sofia said, sliding her hand over his and squeezing.

Heden noticed Kenden smile at the reverent gesture.

"Have they found any chemicals at Astaria?"

"No," Kenden said. "Etherya's protective wall around Astaria prevented Crimeous from transporting there. As far as we can tell, the same holds true for the transportation serum. It can traverse them anywhere in the kingdom except Astaria."

"Good. That means I don't need to have a guard with me every time I want to steal kisses from Sofia by the river. I'm not down with the cockblock."

Kenden arched a brow. "Stealing kisses, huh?"

"Yep, we're totally banging," Heden said. "Don't tell Latimus. He's a stick in the mud."

Sofia pivoted and shot him a glare. "Did you think of maybe asking me before you told Kenden we're together? Sheesh."

"Come on, Sof," he said, tugging her ponytail and laughing when she batted his hand away. "Ken already knows I'm a stud. It would make sense you couldn't keep your hands off me."

"Well, I'm happy for you guys," Kenden said, white teeth flashing as he beamed. "I want you to find happiness, Sofia. I feel terrible at the pain you've experienced over the past few years, and Heden's pretty awesome."

"Thanks," she grumbled, arms crossed over her chest.

Once they made it to Astaria, Kenden jumped out and proceeded to the barracks. Sofia slung her pack over her shoulders and began stomping toward the castle. Judging by the set of her shoulders and overall energy output, she was *pissed*.

"Sofie," Heden said, grabbing her wrist once they'd entered the house through the back door.

Turning, she shook off his arm. "Don't look at me all cute and innocent!" She stomped her foot on the ground. "You had no right to tell Kenden we're together."

His brow furrowed. "I didn't think you'd care. Are you embarrassed to be with me?"

She expelled a breath and lifted her fingers to her forehead, rubbing harshly. "Of course not. But I don't want your family to think I just came here for some extended booty call or something. I came to help because I still feel bad I had a hand in creating this mess."

"I know," he said, inching closer and sliding a hesitant hand over the skin above her shoulder. "But I thought you also came to hang with me, maybe just a little bit. I'm so honored you're here and that you're with me. I want to tell everyone."

"You want to tell everyone you're with a human? Won't they think you're slumming or something?"

His lips curved. "Not with you. You're one of the good ones." Drawing her close, he cupped her cheek. "I'm sorry. I didn't mean to tell people if you weren't ready. But we're going to be working together a lot, and it's pretty obvious you're crazy about me."

She rolled her eyes. "You're infuriating."

"Tell me you're insane for me," he murmured, lowering his face to hers.

"No."

Brushing his lips over hers, he grinned at her resulting tremble. "I'm so crazy for you, Sof. I don't want to hide it. I should've asked you first, and I'm really sorry I didn't. I want to tell my family about us. Is that okay with you?"

Translucent blue-green eyes darted between his. "I'm just worried it will set them up to believe I might stay here for the long-term. I can't, Heden. We both know that."

"All they'll think is that I'm happy. I don't think I've ever dated anyone for two months. They'll most likely think it's a miracle."

A laugh escaped her throat. "Is that supposed to make me feel special or something?"

"You are special," he said, giving her a sweet kiss. "Please don't be mad at me, honey."

Sighing, she glared at him. "Fine. You can tell everyone, and I'm not mad. But don't expect my time here to be an all-out sexcapade. I have a job to do, and I plan on accomplishing my tasks before I leave."

"Ohhh, a sexcapade. I love that word. Let's do that instead," he teased.

"No way, buddy." She grabbed the straps of her pack. "Should I stay in Latimus's room again?"

"You can, but I'd really like you to stay with me, Sof." He grasped her hand. "I'll leave it up to you, but I can be pretty persuasive." He waggled his eyebrows.

She bit her lip. "What if you get tired of me?"

"No fucking way. Come on. Let's unpack and make a plan."

"I'm pretty much used to living alone," she said, trailing behind him as they walked through the foyer and down the carpeted stairs. "I might be really difficult."

Approaching the door to his room, he turned and gave her a brilliant smile. "Little human, I'd expect nothing less from you." Giving her a wink, he watched her walk into Latimus's room before he entered his own. He gave her twenty-four hours before she gave up and just moved everything into his room. After all, they only had so much time, and he was determined to make the most of it.

Heden gave Sofia a proper tour of the castle, which was enormous, telling her to make herself at home. When they passed through the kitchen, Glarys looked up from the pot she was stirring atop the stove and gave Sofia a huge smile.

"Back for more, Ms. Sofia?" she asked, blue eyes twinkling under her short cap of white hair.

"Yep," Sofia said, biting her lip. "But I don't want to put you out. Honestly, I'd love to help you. My grandfather made a mean sauce, and I could whip it up anytime."

"Well, that's a lovely offer, dear. Jack and Lila love pasta. I'll have you make it next time we have a family dinner."

"Sure thing. Thanks for your hospitality, Glarys."

"I trust Heden is taking good care of you?" Glarys asked, hand propped on her hip.

"Oh, I'm taking very good care of her," he said, striding over to plant a smacking kiss on Glarys's forehead. "She's the second hottest babe in this joint after you, Glarys. I've got to treat her right."

The housekeeper's face turned an endearing shade of red. "You boys are all such flirts. Go on and let me work. I don't have time for your teasing."

"Oh, I'm not teasing. One day, you'll run away with me." Looking at Sofia, he lifted his hand to his mouth as if to hide his words from Glarys and whispered loudly, "She's mad for me."

"Get out of here, boy," Glarys said, swatting him with her dish towel. "Nolan and Sadie are in the infirmary waiting for you. Take this banana to Nolan, please. He only ate half his sandwich at lunch."

"Yes, ma'am," Heden said, taking the fruit. "You're too good to us."

"Oh, I know. Now, let me get back to work."

Heden led Sofia through a hallway and down a dim stone stairway. Once it bottomed out, she noticed cells on each side, lined with metal bars.

"It was our dungeon during the War of the Species," Heden said, trailing beside her. "Those were dark times. I'm so glad they're over."

"Hopefully, we can save your people from another round of darkness," Sofia said.

"By the goddess, I hope so."

They walked through a door that led to an infirmary, fluorescent lights shining above three stretchers and a back wall lined with drawers and cabinets. Two people stood at the counter, one furiously scribbling notes as the other gazed into a microscope.

"These are our realm's esteemed physicians. Sofia, meet Nolan and Sadie."

"Hello, Sofia," Nolan said, turning from the microscope and extending his hand. "It's so nice to meet you."

"Hi," she said, shaking his hand and then Sadie's, which she realized was missing the two smallest fingers.

"I was burned a long time ago, and they're gone forever," Sadie said, referencing her fingers. "Hope it doesn't freak you out."

"Not at all," Sofia said, "although you seem to have healed nicely. You aren't scarred around your hand."

Sadie grinned and glanced at Nolan. "That's because my amazing husband here, along with Arderin, created a serum that healed my skin. It's why Arderin came to Houston when you discovered her and Darkrip all those years ago."

"Life really is a series of strange coincidences, isn't it?" Nolan asked.

"It is," Sofia said. "Well, the serum seems to have worked. And Heden tells me you just had your first child. That's fantastic. Congratulations."

"Oh, can I show you some pictures?" Sadie asked, pulling her phone from the pocket of her white lab coat. "Yes, I'm one of those mothers. Daphne is with her nanny at Uteria today, and I miss her so much even though we'll head home and see her in a few hours. Want to see?"

Sofia nodded, stepping forward to look at the doting mother's pictures. The baby was adorable, with a swath of brown hair and large hazel eyes. "Wow, she's beautiful."

"I know," Sadie said, clutching the phone to her breast. "She's the love of my life—along with my husband, of course."

"Thank you for remembering me, darling," Nolan said, kissing her sweetly.

Sofia studied them, questions swirling in her mind.

"Sadie used a sperm donor," Nolan said, smiling. "Sadly, I can't give her children since I'm human, but we found an anonymous donor at Uteria who had an amazing profile."

"There's nothing sad about it," Sadie said, squeezing his hand. "Nolan is an incredible father, and Daphne loves him with all her heart."

"I'd love to hear about the process you went through to conceive sometime," Sofia said. "I've considered artificial insemination as an option in the future."

Sadie smiled. "We'll make a plan to hang one evening while you're here, and I'll answer any questions you have. Heden informed us you're staying for two months."

"Yep," Heden said, sliding his palm over Sofia's shoulder. "And we're going to create some software to get you two dinosaurs off paper and into the modern world. It's about time I created an EMR system for you anyway, so we'll create that along with a program to help you analyze the chemical test results."

"On that note," Nolan said, gesturing to the microscope, "we were just studying samples from the poisons found in Adelyn's lunchbox and Aron's garden. The chemicals are all combinations of extremely rare synthetic and naturally occurring toxins in the human world. Whoever put them together for Bakari is an expert chemist, and the multitude of combinations is staggering. Sadie and I can create several different antidotes but we need to catalog the probability of which chemicals will be used most. Does that make sense?"

"Yes," Sofia said, wheels already turning in her mind. "I can create a program where we log the quantities of each chemical and write an algorithm that determines which ones have the highest potency and ability to form stable bonds with the others. It should only take me a day or two at most."

"She's a pretty terrible programmer," Heden teased, shrugging affably, "so I'll help her, of course."

Sofia shot him a glare. "I run circles around him, and he's insanely jealous."

"Well, I'm sure you're better than I am at anything remotely involving computers, so I defer to you both," Nolan said.

"Let me look over your results so far and take some notes, so I can make sure I write the software to the specifications we need." Approaching the counter, Sofia pointed at the white papers lined with scribbled notes. "Can I have a look?"

Sadie nodded, and Sofia took multiple screenshots with her phone. After discussing specifics with the physicians for several minutes, she turned to Heden. "Can we head to the tech room? I want to start this while it's fresh in my mind."

He smiled and nodded. "Let's get crackin'."

Chapter 25

Several hours later, Heden sat beside Sofia as her fingers sped over the keyboard. They were both plugged into the same hard drive and adding to the code along the way.

"No," she said, squinting at the large screen hanging above them on the wall. "I don't like that. Let's do this instead." She erased the last lines of code Heden had written and replaced it with cleaner symbols to create a more seamless pathway.

"Damn, that's good. It will allow the docs to click through the various screens of the software without having to save along the way."

"Yes," she said, eyes glued to the monitor. "Although it seems small, automatic saves will create more efficiency as they catalog information."

Heden studied her, incredibly turned-on by her intellect. He'd rarely met someone whose mind fired as quickly as his, although his siblings were all quite intelligent in their own ways, especially Arderin. Desire pulsed in his veins as he watched Sofia code, blood surging to his shaft.

"How much longer do you think it will take before we have a working software program we can test?" he asked, his voice gravelly from the thrumming arousal.

She pursed her lips. "Two hours, tops. I'm killing it over here. You're slacking though." Gazing at him, she gave him a brilliant smile.

By the goddess, she was gorgeous. Heden had been lucky to be with many beautiful women over the centuries, but surface beauty only went so far. Not only was Sofia insanely stunning with her blue-green eyes, button nose and beaming smile, her astuteness was so damn sexy. Deciding he was going to seduce her right in front of the computers as soon as they had a functional prototype, he got to work.

"I'm on it," he said, focusing on the screen.

For the next two hours, they toiled, Heden's concentration so intense he coded like a damn genius.

"Crap, that's awesome," she said as they were finishing up. "You wrote that last section in record time. What's gotten into you?"

Finishing up the last line of code, Heden exported the program to the desktop and brought it up onscreen. "Done. Let's let it sit for a few minutes while we take a break."

"Okay," she said, shrugging. "Want to head outside and take a walk? We should probably get some fresh air."

"In a minute," he murmured, so aroused from watching her program for the past several hours he thought he might lose it in his pants. Standing, he padded over and closed the door, turning the lock before pivoting to face her.

"Or you could lock us in the tech room?" she teased, eyebrows arched.

"I've never seen this room as sexy, but now that I've seen you code here, all I can think about is seducing you in front of the computers."

Her throat bobbed as she swallowed. "Don't we need to get the program to the doctors for testing?"

"What I'm imagining won't take too long." Grinning, he placed his hands on his hips. "Do you want me, Sof? Because I'm burning for you right now."

White teeth toyed with her lip. "Yes," she whispered.

Focused on her, he bunched the bottom of his t-shirt in his hands and pulled it over his head, tossing it to the floor. Her eyes grew wide as he began to unbuckle his belt.

"Are you going to strip in front of me?" Her nervous snicker sent shivers along his spine.

His hands froze. "If that's what you want." He arched his brow, awaiting her reaction.

"It's definitely what I want," she said, her voice raspy.

After unfastening his pants and shucking them off along with the rest of his clothes, he sauntered toward her. Extending his hand, he said, "Stand up, little human."

She tentatively slipped her hand into his and stood, her upturned face flushing red.

"Lift your arms," he commanded softly.

Her tongue darted out to bathe her lips, and his knees almost buckled. "Sofia. Lift your arms."

She complied, lifting them in the air, and Heden pulled the shirt from her body. Reaching behind, he unclasped her bra and tossed it to the ground.

"Now I know why you were coding like a bat out of hell," she said, sliding her palms over his pecs. "You had a reward in mind at the end."

"Fuck yes," he breathed, reaching to unbutton her jeans. Sliding the zipper down, he urged her to remove her sandals and quickly discarded her clothing. "I want you to write some code just for me."

"While I'm naked?"

"Holy shit. Yes, Sofia, while you're naked. Come here."

Sitting in the black office chair, he tugged her to sit on his lap so she faced the multitude of screens lining the desk and wall. The smooth skin of her back was warm against his chest, and she wriggled her ass over his straining cock.

Heden hissed, positioning her so she could sit still while she typed. Dragging the keyboard toward them, he spoke low into the shell of her ear, "Write something for me while I touch you."

She exhaled a ragged breath and placed her hands over the keyboard. Bringing up the text prompt window, she began to type.

"Mmmm..." he said, nuzzling her nape while his palm roved over her quivering abdomen. "You're using Java. Hot, but super easy."

She breathed a laugh. "I can't write complex code while you're doing that to my neck."

"This?" He lightly scraped his fangs over her pulsing vein. "I haven't drunk from you yet. Are you ready for that, honey?'

"Yes," she moaned, squirming against him.

Her fingers blazed over the keyboard, writing some generic code as he grew even harder beneath her. "Do you know how sexy you are when you're coding? It's so fucking hot, Sof."

"I've always seen it as pretty boring," she mumbled, head falling back on his shoulder to allow him better access.

"No way." His fingers trailed down her stomach to the springy patch of hair that covered her core. Searching, he found her folds, swollen and thick, and almost wept with joy. His tongue began sweeping over her neck, dousing the sensitive skin with his saliva so he wouldn't hurt her when he impaled her.

"Will it sting?" she asked, lids heavy as her hips undulated over his fingers.

"No, baby," he murmured. "My saliva will shield you from the pain. You ready?"

She purred in assent, her lithe body flushed and aroused. Sliding his finger to her clit, wet with her moisture, he began circling the enflamed nub as he aligned his fangs over her vein. Heart pounding in his chest, he sank his teeth into her tender nape.

Sofia cried his name, body arching as he growled against her. Blood flooded his mouth, thick and spicy, and he closed his eyes, overcome with pleasure. His sexy human writhed against him as he drank her essence, his need for her so intense he wondered if he would ever escape it. Although he couldn't read her thoughts from direct drinking as he could a

Slayer's, her energy surrounded him, pure and clear. Heden felt her spirit, fiery and vibrant, and became drunk on the woman who'd consumed him.

Needing to connect with her in every possible way, he slid her over his thighs, aligning his shaft with her drenched opening. Holding her steady, he pushed into her from behind, sanity fleeing as the tight walls of her pussy squeezed him.

"Oh, god," she wailed, reaching behind to clutch his lower back as she searched for an anchor. "Yes, fuck me this way."

Listening to his woman, his hips jutted into her, spearing his shaft into her core, increasing the pace until he was drowning in ecstasy. Full with her lifeforce, he broke the connection with her neck and searched for her lips, moaning when she cemented them to his.

His tongue invaded her mouth, pumping in tandem with his cock as he hammered into her. Wanting to give her the immeasurable pleasure she was bestowing upon him, his fingers found her clit and flicked it mercilessly.

"Come all over me, baby," he growled against her mouth. "Fuck, this is so hot."

"You're so deep inside me...oh, *fuck*...I'm coming..."

Her body bowed, mouth open in a silent wail as she began to shudder atop his massive frame. Feeling her walls spasm around his shaft was mind-blowing, and he pumped into her, drawing out the pleasure until he was sure his balls would explode. Gritting his teeth, he buried his face in her neck and let go, releasing into her wet depths as she shattered against him.

They cried each other's names, quaking and raw, connected in the most primal way.

Heden slid his arms around her waist, drawing her close, craving every inch of her skin. Heaving large breaths into his lungs, he spurted the last drops of his release, unable to comprehend the intense pleasure. Making love to Sofia was his every dream come true. Passionate, intelligent, sexy...she was *everything*, and he was quickly becoming possessed by this waif of a human.

Wanting to heal her bite marks, he began licking the tiny wounds, reveling in her shiver as she sank further into him. The gesture shifted something in his heart, revealing a possessive streak he'd never felt before. By the goddess, he wanted to hold this woman forever and never let her go.

"You okay, honey?" he asked, making sure the wounds closed.

"So okay," she said, eyes closed as she smiled, head thrown back on his shoulder. "I'm never moving again. You were onto something with that. I just want you inside me forever."

The words sent a jolt of insane joy through his body. "Same," he murmured against her skin.

Sadly, reality crept in, and Heden's release began to seep down their thighs. Sighing, he placed a kiss on her temple and gently urged her to stand. Rising on wobbly feet, he strode to the table in the center of the room and grabbed the tissues. Trailing back to her, he crouched down and began wiping the evidence of their loving from her thighs.

She sifted her fingers through his hair, sending spikes of pleasure through his sated body, and he grinned up at her, humbled by the emotion swimming in her gorgeous eyes. For someone used to casual flings, he didn't normally experience deep connection with his lovers. But there was nothing casual about Sofia, and he understood she didn't often open herself to men. He was incredibly humbled by her trust and vowed to be worthy of it.

And, if he was honest, he was feeling some pretty intense affection toward her too. Casual was second nature to him, but it was impossible to feel that way toward Sofia. Although it had only been a short while, they were a match in so many ways. Perhaps that was why he felt so close to her even though it didn't make a ton of logical sense. Logic was rarely effective in matters of the heart, and Sofia had bewitched him with her adorable, stubborn personality and voracious intellect.

Tossing the tissues in the wastebasket, Heden stood and grabbed a few more to clean himself. Once finished, he pulled her close and rested his forehead against hers. "Want to take a shower with me before we show the program to the docs?"

Biting her lip, she nodded. "That sounds...functional. I'm in."

"Functional?" he scoffed. "I'll show you functional, woman." Bending his knees, he slipped his hands under her bottom and lifted her, loving how her legs encircled his waist almost by instinct. Placing a peck on her lips, he said, "This is going to be the best shower of your life."

Her dark brow arched. "Well, don't keep me waiting."

Heeding her words, he carried his naked human to his large bathroom, confident in his abilities to prove his statement true.

Once dressed, they summoned Nolan and Sadie to the tech room to show them the program. After a brief tutorial, Sofia and Heden promised to help the physicians use the software over the coming weeks. The docs were extremely thankful, and Sadie gave them both a smothering hug before she and Nolan boarded the train home to Uteria.

Night settled in, and Sofia raided the kitchen, devouring the leftovers Glarys had stocked in the fridge. Heden sat with her, drinking Slayer blood as they recounted stories from their pasts. Afterward, Heden led her downstairs to his room, remarking that he wanted her to move her stuff in so she would have everything on hand. After a few minutes of protest, his little human conceded and stuffed her scant belongings in his vacant drawers.

They brushed their teeth side by side, Heden sensing her nervousness as she scraped the bristles over her teeth.

"What's wrong, Sof?" he asked, spitting in the sink. "Don't close up on me now. I just got you here."

She eyed him in the reflection. "It's just moving kind of fast, don't you think? Are we going to crash and burn?"

Finished with his dental ritual, he slid behind her and cupped her shoulders while she finished flossing. "Do you overthink everything, little human?"

She shrugged and leaned down to rinse. "Pretty much. Do you ever weigh the consequences of anything?"

Chuckling, he led her to bed, urging her out of her clothes so she could wrap her naked body around him. Clicking off the lamp, he held her close, loving how she snuggled into him. "I'll let you worry about everything for both of us. I'm a fan of doing what feels right in the moment. After all, you only get one shot at life. Might as well take full advantage."

"That's especially true for a human," she mumbled against his chest.

"Then that's all the more reason for you to relax and enjoy the moment, Sof. The way I look at it, I thoroughly enjoy spending time with you, and since our time is temporary, I want to do it as much as possible. Who cares about anything else?"

"I enjoy spending time with you too," she said, yawning. "You make me laugh. I didn't realize how much I needed that."

"I want to make you happy, sweetheart," he said, running his lips over her springy hair. "For whatever time we have. Don't analyze it to death, okay?"

"Okay," she murmured. "Do you want to have sex? I'm beat."

He breathed a laugh. "I'm not really into banging half-conscious chicks, but thanks. You're almost passed out. I'm fine just holding you, honey."

And he was. Heden, who enjoyed a good cuddle but made sure to extricate himself from romantic situations that were in any way profound, had essentially begged the human to move into his room. That in itself was a major departure from his normal behavior. Contemplating, he wondered why it didn't scare the shit out of him. After all, he'd always been so confident he didn't want a commitment and didn't do "serious."

But his thoughts on the matter had changed somewhat recently, and he'd slowly opened up to the possibility of more. Letting his thoughts wander, he imagined creating all the things he'd deemed too traditional with Sofia. A home of their own. Marriage. Children. Strangely, the idea of building those things with her didn't elicit any doubt or hesitation in his heart. Although they could never have those things together, he did find it encouraging that he was evolving. He'd have to make sure to tell Miranda so she'd stop making fun of him for being a serial dater. Maybe, after a thousand years, he was maturing after all.

"What are you laughing at?" Sofia whispered, her voice heavy with sleep.

"I think I'm excited at the possibility of adulting. Miranda's going to be thrilled."

She chuckled. "Welcome to the world of responsibility and accountability. Nice of you to stop by."

"If you live here, I'm never moving." He kissed her temple.

Marveling at his acceptance of something more, the wheels churned in his brain as his woman fell asleep in his arms.

Chapter 26

The newly cemented couple fell into a pattern, working together to program software that would improve the kingdom. Sofia absolutely adored Sadie and Nolan and enjoyed helping them with the new technology. Heden focused on improving the military communication devices, and after a week, he was ready to install the updated patches that would allow them to communicate through the ether.

Sofia also worked with Heden to create an electronic medical records system for Nolan and Sadie, so they could migrate away from paper charts. The EMRs were an extensive project, but with their combined skills, they plowed through it at a breakneck pace.

Three weeks into Sofia's stay at Astaria, her phone buzzed as she sat in the tech room writing code. Heden was at Takelia, doing a routine security system check at the Deamon prison with Kenden, and Sofia squinted at the unfamiliar number.

"Hey there," an upbeat voice chimed. "Not sure if Heden programmed my number, but it's Miranda. What are you doing right now?"

"I, um…" Sofia rubbed her neck, wondering what the Slayer queen needed. "I'm just working on the EMRs. Are you looking for Heden? He's at Takelia."

"Oh, I know, and he'll be occupied for several more hours. We're kidnapping you, Sofia. It's time we get to know the woman who's stolen our resident bachelor's heart."

"Kidnapping me?"

The door to the tech room swung open, and Sadie and Arderin burst in. "Yep. Arderin brought Callie for a checkup with Sadie, and she's here for the night. The kids are with the nannies, and we need a mom's night out. Also, we just want to grill you. Arderin and Sadie will walk you to the bar—it's not far from the castle. See you there soon."

The phone clicked, and Sofia stared at the two women who had huge smiles plastered over their faces. "Come on, Sofia," Arderin said. "We didn't get off on the right foot, but you've somehow smitten my immature-as-hell brother, and I'd like to set things right. Let's go."

Sofia sat back in her chair, wary. She wasn't really a spontaneous person and had absolutely nothing in common with these immortals. Her purpose in their world was clear, and she didn't want anything to detract from it. "I have a lot of work to do on the EMRs..." she said, hating how lame the excuse sounded.

"Nope," Arderin said, marching over and grabbing her wrist. "I'm pretty sure I can pick you up and carry you over my shoulder, although I'd rather not have to do that since I'm about a million months pregnant. It would be great if you just concede and accompany us willingly." She tugged Sofia's wrist.

"Please, Sofia," Sadie said in her sweet voice. "I can answer all your questions about my pregnancy, and we can have a few drinks. What you've created for us so far is amazing, and I think you deserve a few hours of fun."

Sofia's gaze trailed between them. "Will Evie be there?"

"Yes," Arderin said, giving her a compassionate smile. "You don't have to hang with her if it's too uncomfortable. She really wants to make things right, but I understand if you're not ready."

"I might never be ready," Sofia mumbled.

"And that's okay. But I will remind you that you staked out my house, contemplating my eventual murder, and I've completely let it go." Looking to the ceiling and pursing her lips, Arderin said, "Damn, I'm so evolved. It's pretty fucking awesome."

Sadie laughed and trailed over to Sofia. "Come on," she said, extending her stubbed hand.

Inhaling a breath, Sofia encircled the kind woman's hand, hoping she wasn't setting them all up for disaster. There were some pretty complex dynamics in their group, and a fallout wouldn't be pretty.

"Wow, Heden was right. You're a worrier. That's probably good because he hasn't worried about one damn thing in his life. Let's go, ladies. I hear a virgin daiquiri calling my name." Flipping her long hair over her shoulder, Arderin trailed from the room.

"This is probably a terrible idea," Sofia said.

Sadie shrugged. "Then let's get it over with."

Sighing, Sofia followed the immortals to the bar.

Three hours later, Sofia was pleasantly surprised at how much she was enjoying herself. They sat at a high-top table munching appetizers as the server supplied them with endless rounds of beer, wine and virgin drinks for Arderin, Evie and Moira, who'd informed them earlier she was pregnant, followed by a round of raucous cheers. Sofia figured the restaurant wanted to take exceptional care of the queen and her family, so the doting service made sense.

Flanked by Sadie and Lila, Sofia enjoyed getting to know them as they told stories of how they each fell in love with their husbands. Miranda and Arderin sat across from her, Moira and Evie at opposite ends of the long wooden slab. So far, Evie had been pleasant and unassuming, and Sofia wasn't as uncomfortable around her as she'd anticipated. Perhaps it was due to the red wine, which Miranda kept surreptitiously pouring into her glass each time it was low.

"Are you trying to get me drunk, Miranda?" Sofia asked, hiccupping.

Laughing, Miranda nodded. "Oh, hell yes. We want you to spill the beans, Sofia. How in the hell did you get Heden to commit to spending two months with you? I'm used to him running away from most women after two hours."

"I don't know," she said, shrugging. "I told him I wasn't interested and to leave me the hell alone, but I think he just saw it as a challenge or something."

"Brilliant," Miranda said, lifting her glass in the air. "I get so excited when our men are thrown off-balance. Great job, human. Cheers!" They clinked their glasses, sharing smiles as they sipped.

"I mean, it won't last forever. I eventually have to go back to the human world, and I also want to have kids. I'm not getting any younger. But for now, I'm really happy. He says I worry too much and need to live in the moment, so that's what I'm focused on doing."

"Good for you," Arderin said. "And you never know how things will work out. Every one of us was sure we'd never find a mate, and we're all stuck with one for better or worse at this point."

Evie rolled her eyes. "True story."

"Come on, sis," Miranda said. "You love Ken so much. You're not fooling anyone."

"I have to maintain my nefarious reputation, Miranda. Chill." Munching a fry, she winked at her half-sister.

"Have you considered artificial insemination with Heden?" Sadie asked. "It was a perfect option for me and Nolan."

"Yes, but Nolan is immortal, and I'm not. I wouldn't want to sign Heden up for having kids with me and watching all of us eventually grow old and die while he lives on. That's way too heavy to contemplate. And our relationship is still so new anyway. I'm sure he'll get tired of me eventually. We'll both move on, and I'll live out my days in the human world."

"Well, I know my brother, and he's never conveyed interest for a female on a level remotely close to what he expresses for you. Watch out, human. I'm not sure he's going to let you go so easily." Arderin reached over and grabbed a fry from Evie's plate, grinning at her sister-in-law's scowl.

"So, let's get to the topic we all really want to discuss," Miranda said, placing her palms on the table. "How's the sex? Is it incredible?"

Arderin plugged her fingers into her ears. "Gross," she said, eyes squeezed shut.

"It's so damn good," Sofia said, sighing like the lovesick sap she'd convinced herself she'd never become. "It's always been hard for me to open up with men, but I'm so comfortable with him. It's strange and awesome, all at the same time."

"Damn straight," Miranda said. "Our boy's doing you right. Well done, Heden."

They shared a companionable laugh and settled into conversation, Sofia reminding herself to take it easy on the wine. Finally, after several hours, Darkrip materialized at Arderin's side.

"Not to be a downer, ladies, but my wife made me promise I'd show up here if she wasn't home by eleven. You ready, princess?"

"Yes," Arderin said, her lips forming a pout. "Although, I was having so much fun. We have to do this again, ladies."

"Absolutely," Miranda said, gesturing to the server for the bill. "Sofia, I think I speak for the group when I say you're really cool, and we're in awe you accomplished what so many others couldn't. You've turned Heden into an adult. We all owe you a debt of gratitude."

Drunk from the multiple glasses of cabernet, Sofia giggled. "Thanks, guys. I really like you too. Thanks so much for dragging me out tonight. I think I really needed it."

"Anytime."

They all hugged goodbye, and Arderin disappeared with Darkrip. Evie offered to transport everyone else home and whisked them away one by one before reappearing again. Finally, Sofia was left alone in the empty bar with the woman who'd murdered her grandfather.

"I can walk to the castle," Sofia said, kicking the wooden floor with her sandaled toe. "It's not that far, and we walked here."

Evie's green eyes traveled over her face. "Can we sit for a second?"

"Sure." Sofia slid onto the stool as Evie did the same.

Evie spoke, her tone contrite and thoughtful. "I was trying to think of something I could give you, since I took so much from you."

Sofia squirmed, feeling uncomfortable. "Evie—"

"Wait," she said, holding up a hand. "I know this is awkward, but I'd like to finish if you'll hear me out."

"Okay."

Her gaze fell to her lap. "I can't change the past. I'm pretty damn powerful, but even the daughter of the evil Deamon king has her limits." Lips forming a repentant smile, she shrugged. "But I did spend some wonderful years with Francesco when he was young, and I have so many stories from our time together. I'd like to share them with you, to help you remember him and maybe get to know a side of him you never experienced. If and when you're ready. I know you might never be, but I wanted to at least offer."

Sofia studied this woman whose past was comprised of such terrible deeds but who also seemed to have genuinely turned over a new leaf.

"I know," Evie said, rolling her eyes. "It's almost too good to be true. Sometimes, I wake up in a cold sweat and think I'm right back in the Deamon caves and that bastard is torturing me and my mother. Other times, I get lost in nightmares where I'm murdering someone who hurt me, usually a man, and I'm reveling in the pleasure. It's hard to comprehend that I've changed—certainly for you, but even more for me. Ken is my rock, and I couldn't do it without his love. It...*shifted* something in me. I know that sounds corny, but it's the only explanation I have, so I'm going with it."

"How long did Crimeous torture you?" Sofia asked softly.

Evie's gaze was clear and strong. "Several centuries, until I realized I needed to seize control and power for myself. I did it through the only methods I understood. It took a hundred lifetimes for me to learn another way. Francesco saw a glimmer of goodness in me, and it broke me until I snapped. My final action toward him was reprehensible and uncharacteristic of the time we shared together, but it also was the catalyst that set me down this new path. That probably sounds ridiculous to you, but it's true."

"He used to talk about you all the time," Sofia said, the sting of emotion causing a rasp in her voice.

"Yeah? That's nice to hear. I cared about him very much. So much that when he pushed me to be better, I wanted so badly to listen, but I wasn't ready, and he paid dearly for that."

"How bad was his cancer? I wish I could've helped him."

"I know," Evie said, nodding as compassion washed over her stunning features. "He was riddled with the disease in several of his major organs. I knew that if you found out, you'd traipse him all over the world to find a cure. I honestly wasn't sure he'd want that, so I convinced myself there was a humaneness in my actions."

"You knew about me?"

"Of course. I kept up with Francesco over the years and would observe you two together. Your love for him is so pure. It's really beautiful, Sofia. He's the only person you've ever loved in your entire life besides your parents. Maybe you're on your way with Heden. It would be great for you to experience that. Take it from me, love is pretty damn powerful."

Sofia's fingers fidgeted atop her thighs. "We don't have a future, so I hope I don't fall in love with him. I'm not really in the market for a broken heart."

"Unfortunately, broken hearts usually find someone when they least expect it. Regardless, it's nice to see you happy. I'm so sorry I caused you so much pain. My offer stands, and you can redeem it anytime you're ready. Just let me know."

"Okay," Sofia said, standing and stifling a yawn. "Thank you, Evie."

"Let me transport you. You're buzzed, and it's dark as hell outside. Heden would kill me if I let you walk home alone."

"All right."

Evie instructed her to slide her arms around her neck, and in a moment, they were outside Heden's closed bedroom door. "Give him hell, Sofia. Goodnight." Closing her eyes, she vanished.

Heden swung open the door, fangs glistening in the nearby lamplight as he smiled. "Did you have fun, honey?"

Biting her lip, Sofia nodded. "I actually did. Everyone is so cool. How did the prison security systems check out?"

Encircling her wrist, he drew her into the room and closed the door behind them. "Do you think for one moment that I'm going to talk about prison security systems with you when you've just appeared at my door tipsy and adorable as hell?"

Chuckling, she glided her palms up his chest and linked her hands behind his neck. "Did you want to discuss something else?"

Growling, he lifted her and devoured her mouth. Carrying her to the bed, he sprawled them over the green comforter. Smiling down at her, he waggled his eyebrows.

"What I have in mind doesn't require talking."

Overcome with emotion and desire for her handsome Vampyre, she let him show her that his mouth was quite useful, and it was indeed occupied with many other activities besides talking for the next several hours.

Bakari entered the lobby of the office building and showed his credentials to the night guard. Verifying his false name on the visitor list, the guard gave him a pass and instructed him to head to the back warehouse. Black shoes clicked on the cold floor as he walked under the fluorescent lights. Arriving at a metal door, he rang the bell.

Several moments later, a man in a white lab coat pulled the door open. "Hello, Bakari. Right on time as usual."

"Hello, Dr. Tyson."

Waving him through the door, he asked, "The guard didn't give you any trouble?"

"No," Bakari said, following him into the warehouse. "I was on the list as you instructed. My car is parked at the loading dock."

"Perfect. The last two canisters are ready for transport. This batch is particularly potent. It's an extremely rare combination. Finding an antidote would require extensive cataloguing by a very advanced software program."

"Two of my enemies are expert hackers, but hopefully, the different combinations will overwhelm any analytic software they create. I appreciate your attention to detail."

"You have my payment?"

"Yes." Reaching in his pocket, Bakari pulled out the vial of Crimeous's cloned blood.

"Excellent," Dr. Tyson said, holding it up to inspect it against the stark ceiling light. "There are so many formulas I can create with this."

"Should I even ask what you have in mind?"

"That wasn't our deal, Bakari, and besides, you'll know soon enough. After all, you weren't the only immortal raised in the human world." Dr. Tyson's incisors glistened behind his slightly sinister smile, relaying the Vampyre portion of his heritage.

"I'll leave you to it then. I wish you the best, Quaygon."

"Dr. Tyson is fine," he murmured. "Can't have anyone overhearing my immortal name."

"Thank you, Dr. Tyson."

They shook hands, the chemist instructing several of the warehouse employees to help Bakari load his car.

Once the containers were loaded, Bakari left the St. Louis warehouse, wondering when he would see Dr. Tyson again. Bakari would most likely need his help to assume his rightful place as sovereign over Etherya's realm. For now, he was content to let Dr. Tyson stew in the human world, which was insignificant—but if he chose to enter the immortal world without Bakari's permission, there would be consequences.

Quaygon, son of Letheria, was a hybrid and therefore an abomination. If he knew what was good for him, he'd live out the rest of his days with the heathen humans. Otherwise, he was doomed.

Chapter 27

Latimus and Kenden worked around the clock to secure the realm while Heden and Sofia completed their tasks. The royal family worried the Secret Society would launch a surprise attack, most likely by poisoning or attempting to spring the prisoners from the Deamon prison at Takelia, but so far, things had been relatively quiet. Besides the chemicals found in Adelyn's lunchboxes and Aron's garden, nothing else had been uncovered.

A week after her ladies' night out, Sofia was in Heden's bathroom securing her hair into a bun when she heard him enter the bedroom. Giving her reflection one last check, she headed to greet him.

"Hey, sweetheart," he said, bending down and giving her a gentle kiss. "You ready for dinner?"

"Yep," she said, excited for the meal she'd prepared. She'd come downstairs half an hour earlier, while the sauce simmered, to quickly shower and tame her hair. "I hope everyone likes Grandfather's sauce."

"They're going to love it," he said, gliding his hand over her shoulder. "You look pretty."

"Thank you," she said softly, humbled he was attracted to her even though she wasn't one of those women who gobbed makeup all over their face. Heden seemed to genuinely think she was beautiful, and it softened something inside her austere heart. "You know, if we were a couple in the human world, people would think I was your sugar mama."

"How so?"

"Because I'm years older than you—in appearance anyway. How old were you when you went through your change?"

"Twenty-eight," he said, grinning. "Yeah, I was going to buy you some Depends pretty soon. You're ancient."

She whacked his chest. "Don't give me a complex. I'm already worried you're going to wake up one day and think I look like Betty White."

"Dude, Betty is hot. All the Golden Girls are. Blanche? Man, I'd be all over that in a second."

Sofia snickered. "I bet you would. She was pretty feisty."

Inching closer, he gently traced the skin of her face. "I think you're gorgeous, Sof. I look at these tiny lines," he said, rubbing the tender skin at the edge of her eye, "and I know they were formed by each laugh you had in your past. I hope I contributed at least partly to forming them. It's a small mark to remind you of our time together."

"Wow," she said, basking in his praise. "I've never heard wrinkles described so eloquently."

Fangs flashed as he grinned. "I adore every part of you, even the wrinkles, although you can barely see them. I get a close-up view because I get to kiss you every day."

Heart pounding from his words, she stepped toward him and placed her palms on his pecs. "Every day for another month. I can't believe I've already been here four weeks."

A slight sadness pervaded his expression. "Me neither. It feels like longer."

"Does that mean you're ready to get rid of me?"

"That's something I can't even joke about, Sof. Not even if I wanted to. I'm not ready to think about you leaving me."

It was a discussion they needed to have, but they had a few weeks to let it simmer. Thankful for the reprieve, she slid her arms around his neck. "But I'm here now."

"Thank the goddess." Leaning down, he enveloped her in a smothering kiss. Afterward, he stared deeply into her eyes...into her soul. "Let's get this dinner over with so I can seduce you. I'm determined to make you addicted to my body so you can't ever leave."

"Does it work that way?" she teased, squinting at the ceiling.

"I sure fucking hope so. Come on." Sliding his palm over hers, he led her up the stairs and to the kitchen.

Sofia worked with Glarys to prepare the noodles and garlic bread while the sauce simmered. Tasting it, Sofia closed her eyes in ecstasy. It was perfect.

She and Glarys carried everything into the large dining room. The family was settling around the table: Latimus, Lila and their three children; Miranda, Sathan and Tordor; Evie and Kenden. Once everyone was seated, Sathan said a prayer to Etherya, asking her to watch over Arderin, Darkrip and Callie in the human world. Acknowledging Sofia, he also mentioned her Catholic god in his prayer, the inclusion of her beliefs making her feel so accepted.

Everyone dug in—even Heden, who announced he was going to try the sauce even though he wasn't a fan of human food. Sofia watched him out of the corner of her eye, wanting so badly for him to enjoy it.

"This is amazing, Sofia," Jack said. "Holy crap. I might eat the whole pot."

"Thank you, Jack," she said, feeling her cheeks warm. "I'm glad you like it."

"It's really good, honey," Heden said, squeezing her hand after he swallowed his first bite. "Thick and flavorful. I'm impressed. You might make me a food lover after all."

Thrilled he liked it along with everyone else, the dinner went on with lots of laughter and wine. Once Glarys served dessert and the kids left the table to play in the sitting room, the mood grew a bit more solemn.

"How were the rounds today, guys?" Miranda asked Kenden and Latimus. "Anything we should be concerned about?"

"It's strange," Kenden said, shaking his head as he toyed with his coffee mug. "There are four people plotting to attack us, but they haven't yet. Of course, the Secret Society knows we've beefed up security, but they also have extraordinary powers. I'm wondering why they're waiting."

"Do you think we should consider bringing Melania in for questioning?" Miranda asked.

"Lila has a soft spot for Camron and doesn't want to call attention to Melania's previous dealings unless completely necessary," Latimus said, squeezing Lila's shoulder.

"I know you all probably think it's weak," Lila said, compassion in her stunning features, "but it will break Camron's heart if he discovers her treachery. As we've discussed, it seems she's defected from the Secret Society. Her whereabouts over the past few weeks has been transparent and conspicuous. It's as if she's sending us a message she's no longer plotting against us. I don't want to out her if that's the case."

"Isn't Camron the one who treated you like shit after my father maimed you?" Evie asked.

"Yes, but we made amends, and I don't want to hold a grudge. He's one of my oldest friends, and I'd like to shield him from any pain if I can. Of course, if you think you need to question her, I trust you." She smiled at Latimus. "But I can't imagine she possesses any more knowledge than we already have."

Evie arched a brow. "One day, I need you teach me how to be a saint, Lila. Good lord. It's vomit-inducing."

Lila bit her lip, her fangs squishing the soft flesh. "Thank you?" she said, her tone teasing and hesitant.

"Okay, stop torturing Lila," Miranda said. "Moving on from Melania, where are we with the four remaining members of the society?"

"They're impossible to trace since they have the ability to dematerialize," Kenden said. "The best we can do now is to monitor every inch of the kingdom and ensure the troops are alert. I wish I had a better plan, Miranda. It's hard to fight an enemy who's waiting in the wings to attack. Latimus and I would love to take the offensive, but it's been impossible to capture any of the society members so far."

"You both are doing a great job," Sathan said. "The enhanced security at the compounds, the kids' schools and the Deamon prison is phenomenal. So far, we've thwarted any catastrophes. We'll continue to do our best and stay alert."

"Sadie and Nolan have created several antidotes from the data they've analyzed through our program," Sofia chimed in. "If there is a chemical attack, I'm confident we've identified the chemical combinations they're most likely to use."

"Good," Sathan said. "You two created that program in record time. How are the EMRs coming?"

"That's a much more extensive project," Heden said. "We anticipate being done with it in about three weeks, give or take."

"Perfect timing. I know you're with us for another month, Sofia. We appreciate you helping Heden bring our realm into the twenty-first century."

"And thanks for the amazing pasta," Miranda said, lifting her glass. "I'm going to have seconds, so don't you all even think of making fun of me."

They toasted Sofia as Heden gave her a wet smack on the cheek.

"Thank you all for having me at your family dinner. I still feel terrible I aligned with Bakari in the beginning. It means a lot that you can forgive me."

"You've more than made up for your past transgressions, Sofia," Sathan said, "and we really like who Heden is around you. Hopefully, you'll come visit us after your two months are up. We need you to keep him in check."

"They love me," Heden said, rolling his eyes. "Don't listen to a word my idiot brother says."

They settled into their post-meal food comas, the night eventually winding down as everyone started to head home. Sofia helped Glarys clean the kitchen before Heden led her downstairs. They played video games for a while in the tech room, Sofia loving every minute of their competitive jibing, until they could no longer stifle their yawns. Once they were in bed, she slid over him in the darkness.

"Push into me," she whispered, straddling him as she sprawled atop his body.

Grasping her hips, he inched his shaft into her wet sheath. Anchored on her outstretched arms, she stared into his eyes, so clear even though the room was dark.

"How am I going to let you go?" he whispered, breath heavy as he undulated into her.

"Don't," she said, lowering her lips to his. "Let's pretend a few weeks longer."

"That's the problem, sweetheart," he murmured against her lips. "I'm not pretending."

Sentiment swelled in her chest. "Neither am I."

His broad hand fisted in her hair, cementing her lips to his. Their tongues collided, wet and silky, as they loved each other. As she moved atop his trembling body, she rubbed her sensitive nub against the base of his shaft, bursts of pleasure igniting throughout her body as he filled her. Succumbing to desire and emotion, she exploded, writhing over his large frame as he cried her name.

After they were spent, she lay against his cooling skin, tears prickling her eyes. Thankful for the shadow of night, she willed them away, not wanting him to see. Crying had no place in their predicament and would only make their separation harder. Twirling the coarse hairs of his chest under her fingers, she memorized the texture...counted the cadence of his breaths...inhaled the musky scent of his skin...

Once she was alone in the human world and decades without him stretched before her, she would recall these memories and hope they brought her peace.

Chapter 28

Sofia was in the tech room two weeks later, programming one of the modules on the EMR, when Latimus stormed in.

"I can't believe I'm going to say this but I need your help, human."

Sofia turned in her chair, wondering how in the world she could help the colossal soldier. "Sure. What's up?"

"One of our soldiers' weapons discharged when he was putting it back in the barracks, and it tripped the security system. Heden won't be home from Uteria for another hour, and I can't turn the damn alarm off."

"Yikes," she said, rising. "I'm not familiar with the system but should probably be able to figure it out. Lead the way."

She followed Latimus up the stairs, through the foyer and down a long hallway before he turned a sharp left instead of heading to the barracks.

"Isn't it through there?"

"This way," he commanded with his deep baritone.

Pushing open two wooden doors, Sofia followed him into a large, dark room.

Suddenly, the lights illuminated, and several people yelled, "Surprise!"

Sofia froze, not understanding what the hell was going on. Eyes searching the room, she located Heden standing on a platform in the corner that looked to be a DJ booth. He gave her a wave and a goofy grin.

"Am I being punked?" Sofia asked.

"Welcome to your belated birthday party, Sofia," Miranda said, walking toward her. "We love to throw a party around here, and things have been really tense, so when Heden told us your birthday was a few weeks ago, we thought we'd throw you a bash."

Stunned, Sofia looked at the faces of the royal family as they smiled back. Guilt flooded her that people she'd put in so much danger would go out of their way to celebrate her. "Wow. This is really nice, guys, but I don't need a party. I told Heden I don't really celebrate my birthday."

"Which is all the more reason why you should," Lila said, walking over and drawing her into a warm embrace. Whispering in her ear, she said, "I know you've been alone for your past several birthdays since your grandfather passed. Let us celebrate you."

Sentiment flooded her. "You all do understand I'm ancient for a human, right?" She smiled up a Lila and looked around the room for confirmation.

"Your whole life is ahead of you, Sof," Heden said from the DJ booth, his voice amplified by the microphone attached to the headphones he wore over one ear. "Plus, you get to hear my awesome DJ skills. I'll play the Jonas Brothers if you're lucky. Let's get this party started, people!" Spinning the record with his thick arm, music began to blare from the speakers, and the lights in the room dimmed.

"He's the self-proclaimed best DJ in the immortal world," Miranda said over the music, affectionately rolling her eyes. "Most of the time, we can't get him to stop once he gets going. He won't admit this to you, but he's so freaking excited to show you his 'skills.'" She made quotation marks with her fingers. "It's the same excitement I see in Tordor's eyes when he plays me a new song on the piano. He wants to impress you, Sofia. It's so cute."

Sofia bit her lip. "It is pretty cute."

"Come on," Lila said, drawing her onto the dance floor. "Adelyn loves this song."

Letting her hesitation go, Sofia relaxed and began dancing with Lila, Adelyn, Miranda and Tordor. She thought the children so cute as they jumped and moved to the music. Glancing at the wall, she noticed Latimus standing, arms crossed as he chatted with Sathan.

"Your husbands don't dance?"

"Sathan will dance slow ones with me. He's actually a great dancer. But Latimus is an old fuddy-duddy."

"I can usually coax him onto the dance floor if I promise him favors in return," Lila said. "You know, like giving the kids a bath when it's supposed to be his night. Things like that."

"Bullshit, Lila," Miranda said, laughing. "We know *exactly* what kind of favors you offer him. She's too proper to say it out loud."

Even under the strobe lights, Sofia noticed her blush. "A lady never tells."

Thoroughly enjoying the exchange, Sofia glanced toward the DJ booth. Heden was in his element, bumping along to the beat as he held one earphone to his ear. Gaze lifting to hers, he winked, causing her knees to quake. Holy hell. He was so fucking gorgeous. Sometimes, it baffled her that he even spoke to her, much less wanted her.

"Uh-oh," Miranda said. "Sofia's drooling. Heden's going to be thrilled."

"Sorry, but he's hot," Sofia said, shrugging as she danced. "The hottest guy I've ever been with."

"Keep it in your pants, Morelli," Miranda teased. "There are children around."

They danced for an hour, taking breaks in between to grab drinks and attempt to pull the reluctant dancers onto the floor. After some serious pleading, Miranda was able to get Heden to turn up the lights and step away from the DJ booth so they could sing Sofia "Happy Birthday" and eat the cake.

Sitting at the long folding table on the side of the room, Sofia ingested the most amazing cake of her life, courtesy of Glarys. She'd finished her work in the kitchen and was now seated with them at the table, the close-knit family lost in conversation, teasing and good cheer.

"Evie wanted to come but she wasn't feeling so hot," Miranda said, sitting to her left. "She said you guys had a nice talk though."

Sofia nodded, swallowing the last bite of the scrumptious cake. "I hated her for so long and might never be able to forgive her, but the hate has dissipated into a dull ache. I don't want to despise her. My religion teaches forgiveness and atonement. But it's so hard because she took someone away from me whom I loved very much."

"I know," Miranda said, squeezing her hand. "It's such a fucked-up situation. Welcome to our family, Sofia. When I first met Evie, she instigated some things that caused me to lose my first child when I was several weeks pregnant."

"Oh, Miranda," Sofia said, feeling her heart splinter in her chest. "I'm so sorry."

"Me too. It was devastating. But I agree with forgiveness and atonement too. I can't even imagine the level of torture Evie experienced in her early life. I truly believe, if she'd learned another way, her Slayer side would've shown through. Sadly, it took her a really long time to figure it out."

"I'm trying, Miranda. I really am. I don't have time to live with hate in my heart. I want to have my own child—or children, if I'm lucky—and there's no place for lingering animosity in the next chapter of my life."

"Have you and Heden spoken about what will happen when your two months is over?"

Sofia sighed, surreptitiously glancing at Heden where he sat a few seats away, chatting with Lila. "I have to make a clean break after we part. I've thought about it a lot. Maintaining a connection with him will be too hard and will make me want things I can't have. It will prevent us both from moving on and having a full life."

"Is he on board with that?"

Sofia chewed her bottom lip. "I know he's into casual, so I honestly have no idea how he sees this thing with me. He'll probably be ready for some space once I head back home."

"I'm not so sure," Miranda murmured. "I think he's pretty crazy about you, Sofia."

"It hasn't been that long. He has centuries to find someone else."

"An eternity does him no good if he's already found his soulmate."

Sofia wrinkled her nose. "You believe in that stuff?"

Miranda arched a brow. "I didn't until I met Sathan. I think I fell in love with him when he knocked me unconscious with the butt of his knife."

"Sounds romantic," Sofia said, snickering.

"Right? So fucking weird, but there you have it. My feelings for him were pretty much there from the beginning. I think when you know, you just know. I'm not really sure length of time matters when there's a powerful connection."

Sofia pondered her words, wondering how Heden saw their relationship deep down. From her perspective, there was no doubt: it was the most intense of her life. Sure, she'd dated a few men for a year or two, but that was before she began her quest for vengeance, and she hadn't felt one tenth the desire she felt for Heden. But more than the sexual connection, which was incredible, she enjoyed their banter and similar interests.

His intelligence didn't hurt either. Although she teased him about being a terrible hacker, he was magnificent with everything tech. An impressive feat since he lived in a world where computers were still anomalies. The fact he'd taught himself to be so proficient and that he used those skills to protect his people was exceedingly admirable.

There was something else that tethered them together too. A shared understanding of what it felt like to be alone even when surrounded by others. Heden's stories of how he sometimes felt like an outsider even though he and his siblings loved each other deeply resonated with Sofia. They'd both learned to function as independent, sometimes isolated beings in a world where others didn't quite understand them.

Heden would occasionally tell her of his frustration at being misunderstood by his family. Although his demeanor was jovial, he took the safety and security of the realm seriously and strove to support his family. His siblings, who were all more serious and stoic, didn't understand he'd developed his own way to cope with the world; his own path to functioning the best way he knew how. Sofia had expended the same effort, attempting to live in a world where she just didn't *fit* sometimes. In a way, they both coped with their aloofness and disconnectedness similarly, and she felt that led to a deep, unspoken understanding between them.

He must've noticed her watching him because his gaze drifted to hers, and he gave her a toe-curling grin. Narrowing his eyes, he mouthed, "I want you," and she shuddered. Would she ever feel arousal this consuming for another man? It was unlikely. Their chemistry was undeniable.

The party wound down, Lila and Latimus gathering the children to head home while everyone dispersed. Once they were alone, Heden tugged her toward the empty dance floor.

"Stay here," he said, rushing to the DJ booth and dimming the lights. He pushed some buttons on the console and stalked back over to her. Pulling her into his arms, she laughed when she heard the song.

"'When You Look Me in the Eyes,'" she said, unable to contain her smile. "It's one of my favorite Jo Bros songs."

"I'm not a huge fan, but it's pretty catchy." Sliding his arms around her waist, he held her until there was no space between them. Encircling his neck, she laid her head on his chest. They swayed, his firm heartbeat under her ear, and Sofia began to feel the slide. Into heaven. Into happiness. Into love.

Regardless of whether it made sense or not, she was falling in love with this Vampyre she had no future with. The result of the deep emotion would leave her brokenhearted and shattered, but in this moment, aligned with his strong body, she just couldn't bring herself to give a damn. There would be time for heartache and tears later. For now, she just wanted to enjoy the overwhelming feeling.

When the song ended, Heden turned off the equipment, and they headed downstairs. Beside his bed, he kissed her, slowly removing their clothes until their burning skin was exposed. Lying on his back, he dragged her over his body so she straddled his broad shoulders, facing the foot of the bed. Drawing her core to his lips, he began making love to her with his tongue.

Sofia purred, stretching out over his frame, sliding down to grasp his shaft. Drunk from the sensation of his ardent tongue upon her sensitive folds, she took him in her mouth, hoping to give him even half the intense pleasure he was bestowing upon her.

"Yeah, honey," he moaned, flicking her engorged clit with his tongue. "That feels amazing."

Sucking his thick shaft, her hand worked in tandem on the base as her lips milked him. Reveling in his tremors beneath her, she opened her legs wider, spreading herself so he could spear her with his tongue.

Their groans became frantic, and Sofia cupped the sack below his cock, his hips undulating in response. "I'm so close, honey. Pull away if you don't want me to come in your mouth."

Not on your fucking life, she thought, increasing the pace of her hand as she hollowed out her cheeks, creating suction.

He growled her name and placed his fingers on her clit, rubbing furiously as he licked her sweet juices.

The orgasm blinded her, causing her to splinter atop his body as he buried his face in her core. Moments later, he exploded in her mouth, his release pulsing against the back of her throat as her lips drained it from his straining shaft. Swallowing, she collapsed over his body, cheek resting on his thigh as she struggled to breathe normally.

"Good grief, Sofia," he murmured into her slick folds, causing her body to quake. "That was insane. I could drink every drop of you."

"Mmmm..." she purred against his skin. "So good."

Chuckling, he softly caressed her bottom as they floated back to Earth. Content to lay there forever, Sofia uttered a frustrated grunt when he shifted and contorted her body in his arms.

"I need to brush my teeth," she mumbled against his chest, wriggling into him.

"In the morning," he murmured, hand trailing over her back. "Can't move."

"You're my favorite body pillow," she said, unable to keep her eyes open.

"You're my favorite everything, Sof."

Sofia clutched onto the poignant words as sleep hauled her to the other side of consciousness.

Chapter 29

With one week left in the immortal world, Sofia felt the looming departure settle in her bones as she tried to stay upbeat. After all, there would be so many years to mourn the loss of her Vampyre lover, and she wanted to enjoy the time they had left together.

Heden had texted her earlier, the missive causing her to snicker as his texts usually did.

Heden: Surprise date tonight. Will pick you up at six p.m. outside Chez Heden (aka, my room, duh!). Wear comfy shoes, not because we're going to bang (I mean, obviously we'll do that later) but because we're going to walk a bit. And maybe wear a dress if you brought one. Will make said banging easier later. Mwah.

Biting her lip to contain her smile, she texted him back that she would be ready.

She'd brought exactly one dress, dark blue and flowing above her knees. It was comfortable and paired perfectly with her sandals, which were extremely comfortable. She even applied some makeup from the one scant palette she'd brought. Eye shadow and mascara, but it was something. This would most likely be their last private date, as they would spend Sofia's last week in the realm teaching Nolan and Sadie how to use the EMRs—an extensive task since neither was very tech-savvy.

A knock sounded on the door, and Heden walked in, his eyes lighting up when he saw her.

"Hey," she said, sliding her earring through the tiny hole in her ear. "You look nice." He was wearing a collared button-down shirt instead of his normal t-shirt, along with jeans, a black belt and loafers.

"Yeah, I took it up a notch when I woke up early this morning and got ready before heading to Takelia. How did the programming go today?"

"Amazing. I tested everything, and the EMRs are ready. We'll roll it out to Sadie and Nolan next week."

"Can't wait," he said, encircling her wrist and tugging her close. "Did you put on makeup?'

"Yeah," she said, suddenly feeling like an idiot. "Does it look bad?"

The corner of his lip turned up as he slowly shook his head. "It looks awesome. Sometimes, I look at you, Sof..." The words trailed off as he brushed a tendril of hair behind her ear. "You're just so pretty. I'm really honored to be with you."

Tears stung her eyes as a flush of desire flooded her core. "Thank you," she whispered, swallowing thickly. She would've liked to say more, but her throat was suddenly choked with emotion.

"Ready to go?"

Smiling, she nodded. "Where are you taking me?"

He arched a brow. "What part of 'surprise' didn't you understand when I texted you earlier? Come on, woman. Let's go."

Sliding her palm over his, she squeezed for dear life as he led her from the room.

∞

Sofia's hair whipped in the wind as Heden drove them from Astaria, across the open fields for several miles until they entered a clearing. Pulling up to a sprawling home with a red-tiled roof, he helped her from the four-wheeler, and they approached the front door.

"Hello, Prince Heden," a man said, opening the door. He had white hair and sparkling light green eyes. "You are right on time."

"What's up, Genarro?" Heden asked, shaking his hand. "And seriously, chill with the 'Prince' stuff. I think you're the only one in the kingdom who calls me that."

"I have reverence for your family," Genarro said, bowing gracefully. "I would never disparage your title."

"If it impresses the lady, I'm fine with it." Glancing down at Sofia, he muttered, "Are you impressed?"

She giggled. "Sure. I'm always impressed with *Prince Heden*."

"Oh, brother," he said, rolling his eyes. "Something else she can tease me about. Great." Grinning, he asked, "Is everything ready, Genarro?"

"Yes, your highness. This way."

Genarro led them through the house until they came to a sprawling back patio. Gasping, Sofia walked toward the balcony's edge, eyes wide as she gazed over the sloping hills. "It's a vineyard," she whispered.

"I thought it might be similar to the one your grandfather owned."

Sofia inhaled the vibrant air, overcome with the songs of the birds and aromas of something so familiar to home. "It's magnificent." Staring up at him, she basked in his thoughtfulness. "Thank you."

"Come on," he said, extending his hand. "Let's explore."

They strode down the stone stairs from the balcony, Sofia's sandals landing on the soft ground. Navigating the vines at a slow, reverent pace, she explained to him the inner workings of being a vintner, which she'd learned from Francesco all those years ago. She'd spent so much time with him between the vines, learning and laughing, and the memories flooded her as they strolled. Plucking one of the grapes from the stem, she placed it on her tongue, flavor saturating her taste buds as she chewed.

"Let me taste," Heden said, waggling his eyebrows as he touched his lips to hers. Swirling his tongue in her mouth, he groaned, her knees buckling at the primal sound. "Mmmm... Tastes so good."

Sofia beamed, swallowing the tart fruit. "I think you ate more of me than the grape."

"Now you're catching on," he said, winking.

Hand in his, they trailed to the end of the vines, and Sofia noticed the table set for two under the setting sun.

"Wow," she said, almost in awe of the romantic setting. "You really went all-out."

Turning to face her, he cupped her cheek. "You're leaving me in a week, unless you want to stay longer..." The words trailed off, and Sofia remained silent, heart pounding in her chest, not wanting to sully the beautiful moment with hard discussions and melancholy realities. "Well, anyway," he continued, shrugging, "I figured you deserved a romantic dinner. You haven't strangled me yet, so I figured you kind of liked me."

"You're okay."

Fangs glistened as he flashed her a gorgeous smile. Pulling out a chair, he gestured for her to sit and then took his place across from her.

A brown-haired woman appeared, bottle in hand. "Would you like to taste, Ms. Sofia?"

"This is Genarro's daughter. She married a Slayer a few years ago and loves to cook for him. Tonight, I've hired her to cook for us." Lifting his gaze, he said, "Luciana, your husband tells me you're a natural chef. Pretty impressive for a Vampyre."

"I love it," she said, lowering the wine to Sofia's glass, a question in her expression. Sofia nodded, and Luciana poured her a taste.

Swirling the red liquid, Sofia took a sip, eyes closing in ecstasy. "It's fantastic. A blend of...let me see..." Taking another sip, Sofia said, "Cabernet Franc, Merlot and Montepulciano?"

"Yes," Luciana said, eyebrows lifting in wonder. "That's impressive."

"I love wine," Sofia said. "It's excellent. I'll take a glass, thank you."

Luciana poured them both a glass and scuttled away, telling them she'd return with a salad and the main course after sunset.

Reaching over, Heden offered his hand, and Sofia slipped hers into his warm grasp, contentment filling her every pore.

"Are you happy?" he asked, his thumb moving back and forth across the smooth skin of her hand, the caress mesmerizing.

"So happy," she said, voice gravelly from emotion. "This brings back so many memories of Grandfather. Thank you, Heden. It's so incredibly thoughtful."

"Tell me about him. I'd love to hear your stories."

So, she did. Under the setting sun, she told him how Francesco had held her when her parents died, promising to love her with all his heart and raise her as his own. He'd taught her to dance and how to cultivate wine and had let her cry upon his shoulder when the first boy she'd ever kissed told her she was ugly when they ended their brief teenage relationship.

"Was he blind?" Heden asked.

Sofia breathed a laugh. "No, he was just awkward, and so was I. Young love is messy. I look back on those years and think of all the life I've lived in between. I'm at least a third of the way through, if you look at it mathematically. So strange it will all be over one day. My father's grandfather lived to be one hundred and ten, so at least I've got some good genes."

"I bet you'd be even hotter than Blanche at one hundred and ten," he said, sentiment glowing in his eyes, reverent and sad. "I'd love to see it, Sof. We could have a huge party for you."

Her eyes darted between his, communicating with her gaze what she wouldn't with her words. There would be no more shared birthday celebrations once she returned home. There couldn't be.

Thankfully, Luciana appeared, salads in hand, and they commenced eating, the conversating traveling to safer subjects.

"Do you like the salad?" Sofia asked, ingesting another forkful.

He nodded. "I've come to appreciate eating since it's one of the things I get to do with you. Food is pretty good. You humans and the Slayers might be onto something."

They ate under the newly risen moon, Heden recounting his own stories of growing up after the Awakening. He spoke of his bond with his siblings and Lila, love evident in his tone but also a latent twinge of loneliness.

"It must've been difficult being the youngest," she said sympathetically.

"Yeah," he said, sipping his wine. "It's so hard to explain because I love my family so much. I'd die to save any of them from pain or danger. But they're all really intense. I've always been pretty chill, and I think it's hard for them to understand me sometimes, and vice versa."

"I get it," she said, finishing the last of the amazing gnocchi Luciana had prepared. "Sometimes, I have trouble making connections with people since I'm an only child. I learned how to function on my own and actually think that's pretty awesome. Humans always want to paint some sad story about women living alone, especially at my age, but I actually kind of dig it. I get to do what the hell I want, when I want, and I don't have to confer with anyone else. It kind of rocks."

Heden chuckled. "You are pretty independent, although we've managed to get along pretty well."

"We have. I think we're pretty compatible."

"It's probably just the bangin' sex."

Sofia snickered. "The bangin' banging."

Throwing back his head, Heden laughed, looking so handsome in the moonlight. "Yep, the bangin' banging. Speaking of, your dress is pretty. Once we have dessert, I want to worm my way under it."

"Well, folks, he's not a subtle man," she murmured into her glass.

"No one would ever accuse me of being subtle," he said, arching a brow.

Dessert arrived, and they devoured the tiramisu, Sofia commenting it was some of the best she'd ever had. Finished with the meal, they slowly traversed the rolling hills, Heden tugging her toward the thick trees that lined the vineyard.

Gliding her toward one of the trees, he gently pushed her back into the bark. Lowering his lips to hers, he kissed her softly, sweetly, until their desire began to smolder. Sofia reached for his belt, unclasping it and sliding the zipper down, urging his clothes from his hips. His hands trailed down her sides, bunching the fabric of her dress, baring her to him.

When he lifted her with his strong arms, she encircled his waist with her legs, panting with longing as she looked into his ice-blue eyes. Pushing the slip of fabric that covered her mound aside, he aligned the head of his cock with her dripping opening.

"Sofia," he whispered, staring into her soul. "You're mine."

She nodded, clenching her hands behind his neck. "Always."

Cementing his lips to hers, he thrust into her, the movement filled with an urgency that conveyed their impending separation. Groaning in ecstasy, she threw her head back against the tree, his hips pumping into hers as he murmured words of love against her neck. As his thick shaft slid along the engorged folds of her core, he licked her nape, preparing it for his invasion. Pointed fangs dragged across her pulsing vein, and he impaled her, hand clenching in her hair as he fucked her, deep and thorough.

Sofia felt every inch of him inside her, his cock and his fangs spearing her as he clutched her close. The moment was so intimate, she felt raw...wrung out...so open she barely retained her grasp on reality. But her beautiful Vampyre supported her, held her when she might've floated away, loved her as she fell apart in his arms. Never had she felt so safe.

I love you.

The words flitted through her frazzled brain, true on the most visceral level. She wouldn't speak them aloud—that wouldn't be fair to either of them—but she would clutch them as tightly as she held her lover's shoulders, knowing with all her heart they were true.

The base of Heden's shaft stroked her swollen clit as he hammered her, the action so pleasurable her eyes rolled back under closed lids as she moaned his name.

"Don't forget this, baby," he said, unlatching from her neck and bringing his lips to the shell of her ear. "I need you to remember how good we are together."

"I won't," she cried, fingers fisting in his thick hair. "Oh, god, it's heaven."

"Come all over me, baby," he commanded. "Fuck, you're so tight. It feels so good, Sofie."

Stars exploded behind her eyes as she began to come, mouth open in a silent wail as he pounded her. Her walls convulsed around him as he jutted into her, drawing out his pleasure as she came. Burying his face in her neck, he began to spurt into her core, seeds of his release pulsing inside her as he claimed her for one of the last times.

Overcome with sadness, her arms clasped him so tightly the muscles spasmed. There, against the rugged tree trunk, they held each other as they struggled to reclaim their breath.

Eventually, he slipped from her warmth, drawing a handkerchief from his pocket to wipe away his release.

"Since when do you carry a handkerchief?" she asked, one eyebrow arched as he slyly grinned.

"Since I decided I was going to fuck you against a tree in a vineyard a few days ago."

"Hmm." Her features maneuvered into a mask of mock consideration. "Good lookin' out."

Their sated laughter permeated the sloping valley as they cleaned up and headed back through the vines, slow and unhurried. Heden eventually drove them home, looking adorable as hell when he asked her if she'd had a good time once they reached Astaria.

"I had an amazing time. Thank you, Heden."

"You're welcome, honey. I like making you smile."

It just so happened he was in luck, because Sofia rewarded him with what was possibly the most brilliant smile of her life before he led her inside the castle.

Chapter 30

Heden and Sofia spent the next week training Nolan and Sadie. Since neither was proficient at technology, the training required immense patience and lots of demonstration. Thankfully, the physicians eventually felt comfortable enough to implement the program, and their era of using paper charts came to an end.

Proud of the "Dinosaur Doctors," as he lovingly called them, Heden suggested they go out to celebrate, and they ended up at the bustling pub in Uteria's main square. As they chatted over beers and wings, Sadie asked Sofia when she would head back to the human world.

"I...well, probably in a few days," Sofia said, eyeing Heden as he sat silently beside her. "The EMRs were my last project. Between that, the chemical analyzation program and the updated military comm devices, Heden and I accomplished a lot. I guess it's time I get back to my own life though."

"I'm really sad to see you go," Sadie said, reaching over to grasp her hand. "Promise you'll contact me if you need anything, especially if you decide to go forward with insemination. I'd love to be a resource for you."

"I will." Sofia squeezed her hand, so thankful for such genuine friendship over their short acquaintance. "I'm going to miss you guys so much."

"Sofia has promised to show me the sunset in Positano," Heden said, sliding his arm over her shoulders. "She's got another thing coming if she thinks I'm letting her off the hook with that one." Grinning, he winked at her.

Sofia smiled back, although the action was forced. Of course he would remember the conversation they'd had in the forest all those weeks ago, before their discussion with Tatiana. She had indeed promised to show him the blazing sunset she adored but realized now, she could never keep that promise. Their relationship had evolved so rapidly yet so organically, she feared she'd already lost herself.

The past weeks had been filled with deep reflection. Sofia understood the possibility of finding a partner as remotely compatible as Heden was unlikely. They were almost too perfect for each other, and that terrified Sofia because it made her want to give up every single dream she'd ever had and beg him to let her stay.

But to what end? Yes, she could stay in the immortal realm and have a few good decades with him before she truly began to age, but what about when she turned sixty? Seventy? Eighty? He would still be locked in his immortality, young and vibrant, while her body began to fail. He would feel obligated to care for her, perhaps through illness or dementia, and then he would watch her body grow frail until she eventually passed.

And what of their children? Heden had floated a few comments over the past few weeks, commending Sadie and Nolan's choice to have children through artificial insemination. Sofia understood he was testing the waters, judging her reaction to see if she was open to discussing the possibility. So far, she'd shied away. In her dreams, she was able to bear his child, a boy or girl with ice-blue eyes and thick hair, with his jovial disposition and accepting nature. But her dreams were impossible, and her only option was to have a human child. One that would also grow old and wither before his eyes, dying decades after she did, leaving him alone in grief or pain.

Sofia cared about Heden too much to let him make those choices. So, she would make the hard decisions for them both. He was the optimist between them, the one who pushed her to see possibilities when a solution seemed bleak. Understanding this, she knew he would fight her on the decision. Her strong and compassionate Vampyre would most likely ask her for more time, wanting to nurture their connection. The sentiment was moving, but Sofia was a realist. She comprehended that as she aged, their happiness would wane. Unwilling to set them both up for heartache, she stood firm in her resolve to go home in a few days, and with great difficulty and remorse, she would ask him for a permanent end to their relationship.

It would be too hard to see each other over the years. Too many memories tied up in what they could never have and the differences that would always keep them separate. Although Sofia longed to show him the sunset from the cliffs of the Amalfi Coast, she would bury that dream deep inside. Maintaining any sort of contact with him after they parted wouldn't be fair to either of them.

"Dang, Sof," Heden said, yanking her from her musings. "You got all serious there. You okay?"

"Yeah," she said, waving her hand. "Sorry. Let's chug these beers. I want to meet Daphne before we head home."

Emitting a positivity she certainly didn't feel, she focused on enjoying the time she had left with the wonderful people she'd come to love in the immortal world.

Heden observed Sofia as she cooed to Daphne, joy evident on his little human's face. He'd driven them to Sadie and Nolan's home at Uteria, which they'd purchased from Kenden when he moved to Takelia, and his woman had gravitated toward the baby immediately.

As he watched, she rubbed her nose against the little girl's, her gaze reverent. It was a poignant moment showcasing Sofia's intense desire to become a mother herself. Heden had dropped hints over the past few weeks that he was open to discussing different possibilities of how they could have children together, but so far, she hadn't taken the bait. He understood why. That discussion led down a rabbit hole neither of them were ready to traverse. But their two-month window was rapidly closing, and they would have to tackle the issues eventually. Realizing he didn't want to draw it out any longer, Heden decided he'd bring it up tonight and wouldn't let Sofia dodge the conversation any longer. It was time to discuss their future—or lack thereof—and make some hard decisions.

They said goodnight to the new parents, Sofia reluctant to release Daphne until the last moments, and hopped into the four-wheeler to head to Astaria. Under the full moon, silence stretched between them, both of them quietly acknowledging the impending discussion. Once back at Astaria, Heden led her to the soft grass that lined the meadow beside the castle. Smiling down at her, he tucked a wayward strand of her springy hair behind her ear.

"You looked pretty damn awesome with that baby in your arms tonight, Sof," he said, hoping to keep the tone light.

"Yeah? She's so freaking cute. I didn't want to let her go."

His gaze roved over her face. "I'm not sure I'm ready for kids yet, but I'm willing to discuss it with you. I think it's time we did."

Inhaling deeply, she nodded. "We're at different places in our lives, Heden. You have so much time. It's unbelievable. I wish with all my heart I had more. But I don't, and unfortunately, I can't change that. I'm ready for the next chapter of my life. I'm ready to be a mother."

A cold wave of anxiety coursed through him. Although he'd toyed with the idea of having kids with Sofia through insemination, the idea still seemed so faraway. For someone who'd been a proclaimed bachelor for centuries, the stark change was daunting.

"I know," she said, shrugging under the moonlight. "It's scary. I don't expect you to be ready for such a drastic change. I'm pretty sure you entered into this thing with me intending for it to be casual. That's your M.O., and I always understood that."

"It was, for so long," he said, realizing he'd changed so much since meeting her. "But I don't think it was ever really casual with you, even if I convinced myself in the beginning. It certainly isn't casual now."

Her lips formed a sad smile. "Well, I'll wear that on my sleeve. I tamed the immortal world's resident bachelor."

Heden chuckled. "You've done that and so much more. Is there any way we can at least try to make this work? I'm willing to put in the effort if you are."

"It's not about effort," she said, shaking her head. "I wish it was that easy. But there are fundamental differences between us we can't change. I'll always be human, and you'll always be immortal. I won't sign you up for a temporary lifetime of unknowns and heartache. I care about you too much, Heden."

His heart slammed in his chest. "I care about you too. So much, Sofie."

"I know," she whispered, placing a palm over his chest. "Please, don't make this harder than it already is. I want to remember our time together fondly."

"I'll still come visit you in the human world."

"No," she said, eyebrows drawing together. "That's impossible, Heden."

"What are you talking about?" he asked, confusion and fear twining together in his gut. "Of course I'll come and see you. You still have to show me the sunset at Positano."

Her chin warbled as those magnificent eyes flooded with tears, glistening as she struggled to speak. "We can't. I know it seems harmless now, but it will end up causing us so much pain if we clutch onto something that isn't real."

"Something that isn't real?" he asked, her words causing a sharp pang in his solar plexus. "Are you fucking serious? How can you say that?"

"Don't curse at me," she said, lowering her hand and glaring up at him. "We both knew what would happen here, Heden. I won't let you disparage me for making hard choices we both know deep down are right."

"So, what? You're just going to leave and never see me, never talk to me again? How can you walk away so easily?"

"This isn't easy for me!" she cried, arms slicing through the air as she stared at him in disbelief. "Don't you think I want to stay? I've almost caved a hundred times and asked you if I could stay longer."

"Yes," he said, reaching for her hand. "You can stay as long as you want. Months. Years. Decades. Please, Sof, don't give up on us. We need more time. Can't you see that?"

"I don't have time," she said, swiping away an errant tear. "It's so damn frustrating you can't understand that. I keep telling myself it's impossible for an immortal to comprehend things like aging and death, but it's maddening you refuse to see it."

"Oh, I refuse to see it? I understand death and loss more than you'll ever know. My parents were taken from me before I ever got to know them. I grew up searching for bonds I never truly understood. Alone. Aloof. Disconnected from everyone, even my family, in so many ways. I love them so much, but they all had a purpose, while I floundered, struggling to find my place. It's pretty much how I've functioned my entire life. You're the only person outside my family I've even considered opening my heart to, and you toss it away like it's nothing."

"Well, I'm sorry the first person you decided to be an adult with came with her own set of fucked-up issues. That's life, Heden. It's really intense and hurts a hell of a lot. Sorry I couldn't be some immortal princess who could wait forever for you to decide when you're ready to have a family. I'll never be that person. I hope you find her one day. For now, it's better if we end this on the best note possible."

"I didn't even contemplate I'd never see you again after you left Astaria," he said, overwhelmed at the thought of losing her. "I always entered into this with the hope we'd at least be friends."

"For how long? Until one of us marries? Until I have a child and focus on raising her? We're worlds apart, Heden. It will never work. We have to let each other go."

"How?" he asked, stepping forward and cupping her face. "How can I let you go? I won't do it, Sof."

"I'm so sorry," she whispered, nostrils flaring as her eyes shimmered. "I wish it didn't have to be this way. It has to end."

"Sofie," he whispered, lowering his lips to hers. "I can't."

"Please don't hate me. This is already so hard for both of us." Lifting to her toes, she spoke against his lips. "Make love to me. Once more, so we can remember. *Please*, Heden."

Feeling the sting of tears behind his own lids, he captured her lips in a passionate kiss as he swept her into his arms. Carrying her through the darkened castle, he entered the room where they'd spent so many weeks laughing and loving. Frantically, they tore at each other's clothes, aching to connect in the most primal way. Spreading her legs, he slipped inside her, needing to show her how much he cared for her...how much he...*loved* her.

Threading his fingers through her hair as it fanned across the pillow, he stared into her soul as he undulated his quivering body into hers. She gazed back, regret and sadness lurking in the depths of her luminous eyes.

"Sofie," he whispered, emotion threatening to choke him.

"Don't say it," she said, covering his lips with her fingers as she shook her head upon the pillow. "Please. You'll break my heart."

But instead, his own shattered deep in his chest as she rejected the words he'd never even thought to say to another. Overcome with pain and sadness, he loved her with every movement of his hips, every kiss upon her silken skin, every moan that escaped his lips as her velvet walls squeezed him tight.

And when he could take no more, he emptied everything into her. His pain and heartache and longing that they could change their impossible circumstances. Afterward, as he stroked her cooling skin, he felt the drop of a single tear upon his chest. Cursing every god who'd created them to be so different, he stewed in the unfairness of life in general.

In the morning, he woke, reaching for her and finding the bed empty. Searching the room, he noticed her stuffing the last of her things into her pack.

With a gentle smile, she sat on the bed. "We've finished all our programming tasks, so there's really no reason for me to stay," she said, smoothing a hand over his cheek. "I'm going to head through the ether. Please tell everyone I said goodbye. It was so amazing getting to know your family. I wanted so badly to tell them myself, but I realize now, it's time to go. Drawing this out any longer will just lead to more heartache. I don't want that for us, Heden."

Heden swallowed thickly. "This can't be goodbye, Sof. You're shredding my heart over here. Please stay a little longer. Give me another week at least. Then you can give everyone a proper goodbye."

She pursed her lips and gazed toward the ceiling, chin trembling as she fought off tears. "I can't. I want to so badly, but I can't. Every day I stay, my feelings for you grow exponentially." Locking her gaze with his, she rubbed her thumb over his lips. "Thank you for seeing the best in me. I'm so thankful for you. Be happy, Heden. Please. I can't do this if I know you won't be happy."

"How can I be happy without you?" he whispered, clutching her wrist.

"You'll find a way, little immortal," she said, smiling through her tears as she replicated the affectionate nickname. "I know you will. Goodbye." Leaning down, she gave him a reverent kiss as he caressed her hair for the last time.

And then, she was gone, sure as the wind that whipped through the leaves of the old oak trees on the edge of Astaria.

Cupping his face in his hands, Heden began the long, arduous task of letting her go.

Chapter 31

Heden arose that morning, numb and listless, wondering how he would carry on without her. After barely a few months, Sofia had bewitched him so thoroughly he thought his heart might never recover. He threw himself into helping Sathan, Kenden and Latimus, spending much of his time testing the security systems on the train, at the prison and on their servers. The tasks were mundane but time-consuming and kept him from thinking about Sofia every second of the day.

But at night, when he crawled into the bed he now thought of as theirs, he yearned for the softness of her body against his. For the way she would nuzzle into his side and throw her silken leg over his thighs.

Sometimes, as he sat in the tech room, he would reverently gaze at the chair where she'd sat for so many hours, programming beside him as they worked to improve and protect the kingdom. She'd had nothing to gain besides helping them, and he remembered this whenever the anger surfaced.

With snake-like precision, it would seethe into his veins, making him queasy as he inwardly railed at her for leaving. For not even attempting to give them a chance. But after a while, the bouts of anger would always dissipate, and he would see their situation from her point of view. If the tables were turned, he would never want her to watch him grow old as she stayed locked in immortal youth. He could imagine her gazing at him with pity as his body became withered and brittle before he eventually passed on. It was a terrible sentence to impose on anyone.

He would often wonder if she'd decided to move forward with a donor, wishing with all his heart he could give her children. The idea had seemed so daunting when they'd spoken under the moonlight, but now, as he lived in the agony of her absence, he would give anything to have a child with her.

As the weeks dragged on, he thought the pain might lessen, but strangely, it continued to grow—into something pulsing and latent and ever-present, deep inside his heart. Recalling the words he'd almost uttered to Sofia the last time they made love, Heden accepted that he'd fallen in love with a woman for the first time in his long, connection-free life. How fitting it had been with her, a woman so much like him in so many ways but so fundamentally different in others. At times, the irony would overwhelm him, and he would recall the memories they'd created during their short but passionate affair. They helped him navigate the pain, and he was truly thankful for them.

Sometimes, he would walk to the spot where they'd had their last impassioned argument, on the soft grass under the stars, and gaze up at the moon, wondering if she was doing the same in her world. Did she miss him? Did she think of him even half as much as he obsessively thought of her?

One night, several weeks after her departure, Heden stood in that very spot under the moonlight. Breathing a laugh, he rubbed his hand over his heart as he remembered how furious she'd been when he was belting pop songs outside her door in Louisiana. It was nights like this, when he felt so lonely without her, he would steep himself in the memories of her fiery spirit.

And it was there, as he lowered to sit upon the grassy knoll, he realized something very important: He had to find a way to be with Sofia.

The realization was intense because it entailed a plethora of unknowns and even more terrifying realities. The loss of his bachelorhood. Building a life with someone. Shifting focus from himself to a unit they would form together.

The possibility was daunting and yet it felt...right. Natural. True.

Heden understood Sofia's concerns about their seemingly insurmountable obstacles and differences and knew he had to figure out a way to overcome them. It would be difficult, but for the goddess's sake, he was an extremely intelligent person. With his intellect and skills, there had to be a way for him and Sofia to build a life together, where they could have biological children and an immortal future. The possibility had to exist if he just tried hard enough, didn't it? Wracking his brain, different possibilities began to churn in his mind.

Lost in thought, he didn't hear his brother behind him until he squeezed his shoulder.

"Hey, Sathan," he said, turning. "Is everything okay?"

"There's an outbreak at Uteria. Fifteen Slayers sick and vomiting. It's possible the attack has begun."

Standing, he cupped his brother's arm. "What do you need from me?"

"We're heading there in a four-wheeler in fifteen minutes. I'd like you to come if possible. We need all hands on deck."

"Okay," Heden said. "I'll be ready."

Sathan studied him with his dark eyes. "Are you okay, Heden?"

Sighing, he rubbed his neck. "Not really, but I want to help. I've got a lot of shit to figure out, Sathan."

"I'm so sorry, brother," he said, concern lining his angular features. "She was special. I wish things had been different for you both."

"Me too."

Silence ticked between them. "Did you fall in love with her?"

Heden's lips curved. "Yep. I sure did."

"Damn. That's rough, bro. Is there anything I can do?"

"Let me help you at Uteria," Heden said, patting him on the back as they began to trek toward the castle. "We can't let those bastards hurt our people."

They strolled in silence until they were at the barracks. Before Heden could head inside to prepare, Sathan clutched his forearm. "Heden?"

"Yeah?"

"I'm really proud of you. You've turned into such an amazing man. I'm honored to be your brother."

Heden felt his nostrils flare, and pride swelled in his chest from the heartfelt words. His oldest brother was a father figure to him in so many ways, and the assurance gave him strength. "Thank you, Sathan. That means a lot."

His brother gave a nod. "Go on. We're rolling out in ten."

Heeding his directive, Heden headed inside to prepare to help his people.

The sickness spread across the kingdom, vicious and vile, leaving destruction in its wake. Armed with the antidotes they created, Nolan and Sadie did their best to test the patients for the exact combinations in their blood and supply the appropriate cures. Their success rate was eighty-five percent in the first week, thanks mostly to the software Sofia and Heden had created that allowed them to work so quickly. The other fifteen percent were Slayers with compromised immune systems who would've most likely succumbed to other viruses or flus if exposed.

Vampyres' self-healing bodies were immune to the toxins, allowing an influx of soldiers to sign up for the army. Years removed from war, many of the troops had been transitioned to law enforcement positions and would need to be retrained. Although the chemical warfare required a different type of soldier, Sathan and Miranda felt it was only a matter of time before Bakari and Vadik decided to employ some type of ground offensive. Preparation was essential.

Along with helping Sathan and Miranda try to curb the pandemic, Heden threw himself into researching everything he could about immortality, Etherya's history of granting requests to immortals and even old wives' tales that circulated throughout the kingdom. He spent countless hours examining the archives at Astaria, Valeria and Uteria, meticulously searching for evidence Etherya had granted immortality to anyone other than Nolan. There were no other instances in the age-old scrolls and manuals, but Heden remained determined. If there was a way to solve their conundrum, he would find it.

Two weeks into the pandemic, Heden was at the Deamon prison at Takelia, implementing some enhanced security measures on the server. Evie had come up with the idea of implementing call buttons throughout the prison, connected to a pager she wore at all times. Heden, Kenden and Latimus thought it brilliant since, upon being paged, she could transport inside and essentially freeze the inmates in place. Although the Secret Society had the power of dematerialization, Evie had the ability to control people's movements with a thought.

Finishing up, Heden completed his last item on the checklist, confirming each call button was wired properly. Pleased everything was online, he began walking from the room that housed the main servers.

Out of nowhere, a man appeared in his path, blocking the doorway, holding an eight-shooter aimed at Heden's chest.

"You must be Vadik," Heden said, lifting his hands, palms facing forward as he attempted to stay calm. "Man, you Deamons are all really fucking pasty. Crimeous could've at least given you some self-tanner, being that you lived in the caves for all those centuries—"

"Shut up!" Vadik spat. "Disable the security system now, or I'll lodge eight pellets in each chamber of your heart so fast you'll be dead in seconds."

"Uh, yeah, not gonna do that," Heden said, his jibing tone unrepresentative of the fear coursing through his veins. With his mind, he called to Evie, having no idea if she'd hear him since she was at the governor's mansion—but it was worth a shot. Then, he sent a quick prayer to Etherya, asking for protection, and reached for his phone in his back pocket.

Vadik cocked the eight-shooter, causing Heden to freeze again. Shit. The guy looked like he meant business.

"There are two guards in the hallway—"

"They're dead," Vadik interrupted. "That's what happens when you're ill-prepared to fight an enemy who can materialize out of thin air. No one will hear you if you scream. Disarm the security system."

"Look, dude, I'm not going to disable the system. You can try yourself, but it's encrypted in about a thousand ways I'm pretty sure you'll never understand. What's your objective here?"

"To distract you so I could gain the upper hand, of course," a deep voice said behind him.

Pivoting, Heden looked into his brother's eyes as he sneered back. His face was a mask of hatred and arrogance, cold and unyielding. Steeling himself, he said, "I don't understand, Bakari. Why do you hate us so much? I wasn't even born when you were abandoned in the human world. I'm sorry it happened, brother, but it doesn't have to be this way. We can start over."

"Start over?" Bakari scoffed. "This world has devolved into chaos, filled with hybrids and weaklings. It's appalling. None of you can be saved. I must exterminate you and start anew." Lifting an eight-shooter, he aimed it at Heden's heart. "Look at you, in love with a human, for the goddess's sake. You're an *abomination*."

"I'm not going to help you, Bakari," Heden said, refusing to rise to the bait. "So, you can shoot me or you can leave, but it's not fucking happening."

"There is another who could disarm the system," Bakari said, arching a brow. "If you force me to bring her here, I will."

Heden shook his head. "You'll never find Sofia. We spoke about her post-immortal world plans extensively. She always planned to go off the grid once she went home. I'm confident you have no idea where she is."

"Is that so?" Bakari asked, his tone chilling. "Diabolos, bring in the human."

Heden whirled, his heart leaping in his throat at the thought of them holding Sofia hostage. A Slayer entered the room, a squirming woman in his arms, head covered by a brown cloth. Jumping into action, Heden lurched for the newly minted call button against the wall. Depressing it, he rushed toward the Slayer, intent on rescuing Sofia, but a million shards of pain exploded in his chest, and he gasped for air.

Sofia's beautiful face flashed through his pain-riddled mind, the last thing he saw before everything turned to darkness...

Ananda pulled the cover from her head, her lips forming a cruel smile as she watched Heden bleed out on the floor. "He bought it. He thought I was Sofia."

"Yes," Bakari said, pleased his plan had worked. "He has no idea we haven't been able to find any traces of her in the human world. We must hurry. If the four of us work together, we can each transport twenty-five Deamons per minute to the cave."

They closed their eyes and began to chant, dematerializing from the main security room to the cell block that held the prisoners. Vadik and

Bakari systematically shot each Vampyre guard with their eight-shooters until all nine were dead. Then, they began extracting the prisoners.

In a relentless cycle, they chanted the spell, transported a prisoner to the designated cave near the Purges of Methesda and returned to grab another. Two full minutes passed before Evie materialized into the cell block, Latimus and Ken running in behind her, soldiers flanking them.

Evie stared at them, palm held high, frustration lining her expression.

"Tatiana gave me a potion that prevents your freezing spells, Evie. Your powers are useless here." Yelling toward Ananda and Diabolos, Bakari said, "Keep transporting the prisoners. Vadik and I will fight them off."

"You can fucking try!" Latimus snarled, running toward Bakari, an SSW in his hand.

Bakari lifted the eight-shooter, and Latimus knocked it to the ground as if it were a feather. Reaching for his SSW, Bakari extended the glowing blade. "Okay, brother. Let's see how strong you really are."

They began to spar, blade crushing against blade, as Kenden and Evie rushed Vadik, weapons drawn. The immortal troops backed them, battling the wayward Deamon prisoners who were fighting with their bare hands. Now free of their cells, they fought for their lives.

The skirmish escalated as Ananda and Diabolos appeared and vanished in the background, transporting an inmate each time they disappeared.

"We have to stop them from freeing the prisoners!" Kenden yelled above the scuffle.

Pushing against Bakari's wide body, Latimus plunged his shoulder into his brother's chest, causing him to gasp and fall back. Seizing the opportunity, Latimus sprinted toward Diabolos, who was clutching a Deamon in his arms, about to dematerialize. Lifting his Glock, he shot the Slayer between the eyes.

Diabolos wheezed, eyes growing wide, before falling to the ground in a heap.

"Should I use the healing serum?" Ananda asked Bakari.

"No," Bakari said, recovering. "We don't have time. Grab one more prisoner and retreat!"

Evie approached, encircling Bakari's neck with her hand. "You son of a bitch," she said, squeezing. "It wasn't enough for you to have unlimited riches in the human world? Why are you intent on attacking us?"

Bakari grabbed her back, squeezing her throat as they stared each other down, both gasping for air. "I am the true sovereign, Evie," he said through clenched teeth. "We'll never waiver in our efforts to exterminate you. You've all become complacent, and it gives us ample opportunity to strike. You know this to be true. Until we meet again, good luck with your nightmares. I know they haunt you, and that brings me great joy." Closing his eyes and beginning the chant, he vanished into thin air.

Lifting his lids, Bakrai observed the musty cave. Ananda and Vadik appeared, a Deamon in each of their grasps. Taking a mental headcount, he tallied their efforts.

"We extricated almost two hundred," Bakari said, mulling as he struggled to catch his breath. "It's a good start."

Vadik nodded. "We'll begin to clone more soldiers using Crimeous's blood. I'm confident we can figure out the process, especially with Dr. Tyson's help."

"Yes," Dr. Tyson said, stepping from the shadows. "I don't really like the immortal world, but I'm interested in the science. I will help you in exchange for the terms we discussed. I look forward to partnering with you all."

"Should we at least try to extricate Diabolos' body and bring him back to life?" Ananda asked.

"No," Bakari said. "It's too dangerous. May his soul find peace in the Passage."

"I doubt he'll end up there," Ananda muttered.

"Shall we begin the next phase?" Vadik asked.

"Yes," Bakari said. "We will blaze this next chapter with thought and care. We must plan small attacks to divide them, and large ones when we are sure we cannot fail."

"Then we'd best get to work," Dr. Tyson said. "Vadik, please show me where you've stored the equipment you stole from the human world."

Vadik led the hybrid immortal down the long chamber as Ananda eyed Bakari. "Your disdain for the hybrid is palpable."

"He is necessary for now. Once he's served his purpose, he can return to the human world or die."

"We're all expendable to you, aren't we, Bakari?"

"Yes," he said, unwilling to waste the effort to lie. "But you've always known this."

"I have," she said, one eyebrow arching. "I find it rather...entrancing, in a way. At least we have no illusions about who you are. Excuse me, but I feel I need to rest for a few moments. That was a lot of action for my old, withered heart." Shuffling away, she ambled toward one of the chambers of the cave.

Lifting his arms, he addressed the Deamons. "Children of Crimeous, I am your leader now. In exchange for your freedom, we will begin a new war. One we will not lose. I, Bakari, son of Markdor, ask for your allegiance!"

The former prisoners cheered in assent, the sound invading every cell in Bakari's body, causing him to feel like the king he would one day be. Reveling in the glory, he silently thanked Etherya for today's victory.

Evie transported to Heden's side immediately after the battle, leaving Kenden and Latimus to deal with the released inmates. Crouching down beside him in the security room, she felt his pulse. Nothing. Flipping him over, she noted the extensive damage. Eight small wounds fractured the skin above the eight chambers of his heart, bleeding and open. Pulling her shirt over her head, she covered the wounds, hoping to stop the gushing, and placed her hands over his chest. With precise movements, she began performing CPR.

"It won't work," a voice said beside her. "There's too much damage."

Evie looked up at the stunning woman. "I'm open to suggestions, Tatiana."

Bending her knees, Tatiana placed her hand above Heden's chest, palm open. Closing her eyes, she inhaled a deep breath. Slowly circling her hand over his body, she assessed.

"The bullets were infused with a poison Crimeous used to employ for his weapons. It won't allow his body to self-heal. Several of the bullets missed a direct heart chamber, but without combatting the poison, he's doomed."

"Do you have a potion?" Evie asked.

Tatiana pulled a vial from the pocket of her flowing dress. "It isn't specific to this poison, so I don't know if it will work, but I think we must try."

"Do it," Evie said.

Tatiana sprinkled drops over Heden's face and chest. "Transport him to the infirmary at Uteria. It is the most advanced. If he doesn't regain consciousness in a few days, you must employ other methods."

"Such as?"

"He loves the human, perhaps more than he realizes. You know that has the power to heal. Good luck, daughter of Rina. You must transport him now."

"Why are you helping us, and why in the hell are you helping Bakari? It seems like a waste of effort to help both sides."

Tatiana's eyebrows lifted. "So you will owe me. I always need favors from one as powerful as you, and it is imperative I have things of value to offer Bakari. You will understand one day. Now, go."

Gathering Heden in her arms, Evie whisked him to Uteria.

Chapter 32

Sofia stood on the balcony of her rented home overlooking the magnificence of the Tyrrhenian Sea. It had been an act of wistful spontaneity to move into a home that overlooked the sunset she'd wanted so badly to show Heden. It was quite uncharacteristic of Sofia's stoic demeanor, but she'd changed so much in the past few months, she barely recognized herself. Perhaps she wasn't so stoic after all.

Lost in nostalgic memories of her romantic, sometimes infuriating, always amusing Vampyre, she counted the days since she left him. Eighty-seven days, four hours and thirty-three minutes. Check that. Lifting her wrist, she noted the time. *Thirty-four minutes.* Sighing, she watched the waves crash upon the shore, contemplating if there would ever come a time when she didn't feel so empty.

When she'd first returned home, she'd sold her flats in New York and Florence along with most of her possessions. Wanting to start fresh, she'd moved to Positano, hoping the lovely seaside town would refresh her spirit. Needing to stay inconspicuous, on the off chance Bakari came for revenge, she searched available rentals. Since she spoke fluent Italian, she'd charmed the owner of the small home she now occupied, agreeing to pay him a year up front if he took cash. The man smiled with glee and gladly took her euros. Afterward, she was set; ready to resume her life and have children.

She met with a gynecologist in town who recommended some highly regarded sperm banks in Naples. Instructing Sofia she could browse through anonymous profiles online, she set about looking for a donor. Many of the profiles were outstanding: men with doctorates and PhDs, semi-professional athletes, CEOs of large corporations. But none of them had what she truly wanted: sky-blue eyes with a killer sense of humor and a brilliant intellect. Sadly, none of them were Heden.

Of course, she could never have Heden's child, but that didn't stop her from wishing. For things she couldn't have and dreams that would never come true. After almost three months of filtering through profiles, Sofia decided to put looking for a donor on hold. The gynecologist had given her a thorough exam, and her egg count was excellent for a thirty-nine-year-old. The kind physician thought her prognosis favorable to get pregnant into her forties, although she did offer to help Sofia with fertility treatments if needed. It was all so daunting to someone whose heart was a shattered, broken mess, and she realized she needed to take some time to mourn the loss of the love of her life.

How had it happened? Sofia had no idea. Not so long ago, Heden had been the hacker she was determined to beat, an enemy she wanted to destroy. Now, almost half a year later, he was the person who consumed her every thought. Gaze drifting to the moon, which sat low on the horizon as the sun set miles away, she wondered if he ever did the same. Did he look at the celestial satellite and think of her, hoping she was gazing back?

Sofia wasn't sure, but she hoped he missed her terribly. It was what he got for being so damn charming and making her fall madly in love with him. Jerk. Breathing a laugh, she realized he would think her inner rantings hilarious. He'd peck her on the cheek and tell her how cute she was when she was mad at him. Oh, how she'd give anything to be mad at him one more time, so they could make up and whisper words of forgiveness as they loved each other.

A rustling sounded to her left, and she gasped. Evie appeared from nothingness, a determined look on her face.

"Evie?"

"I'm sorry if I startled you," she said, holding up a hand. "But it's been a week, and Heden hasn't regained consciousness. I've been searching for you for three days. Nice job, by the way. I'm impressed at your ability to disappear off the face of the damn planet."

Sofia's heart leapt into her throat. "Heden's unconscious?"

Evie nodded, lips drawn into a firm line. "The Secret Society attacked the prison while he was updating the security systems. They killed the two guards outside and shot him with an eight-shooter. The bullets were also poisoned. He's on life support."

Sofia covered her mouth with both hands, heaving in breaths. "Oh, my god. I have to go to him."

"Yes," she said, nodding. "That's why I'm here. We hope having you near might help him wake up. Grab whatever you need, and I'll transport you."

Flinging open the sliding glass door, Sofia stuffed items in a bag, barely even registering what she was packing. Overcome with fear that he would die, she slung the bag over her shoulder. "Let's go."

Threading her arms around Evie's neck, they dematerialized to Uteria.

Heden swam in the murky waters, the liquid dark and stifling. Sofia was yelling at him, and he wondered what he'd done to piss her off. Was she still mad he was singing outside her door? Wait...that wasn't it. Maybe she was upset about him telling Kenden they were together. Wading through the water, he remembered her forgiving him for that rather quickly. What in the heck had he done? He wanted so badly to figure it out, but his brain was incredibly fuzzy, and he was having a hard time stringing thoughts together.

"I mean it, Heden," her voice called, filled with passion and...fear? "You'd better wake the hell up. There's no way I broke my heart into a million pieces so you could die first. Wake the fuck up! Now!"

Heden wanted to laugh at how bossy she was. He was extremely comfortable, thank you very much, and didn't quite feel like leaving the water yet. No, it was inviting and warm, and he felt himself slipping further into the shadowy depths...

An eternity later, her voice returned, stubborn and commanding as ever. "If you don't come back to me, I'll never see you again. Never get to hold you. Please, Heden. Come back to me. I'll stay here forever. I don't care anymore. Just, please, don't die."

The words registered in the far reaches of his mind, and he ached to hold her. He hated when his Sofie cried, although she was beautiful when tears streamed down the smooth skin of her cheeks. Wanting to comfort her, he tried to reach for her, but his arms wouldn't move.

"Sofie?" he called, drowning in confusion as to why his body wasn't functioning. "Where are you, honey?"

Sobs surrounded him, and he fought against the invisible confines, clenching his teeth as he thrashed to escape. It was no use. His muscles felt like liquid and air, heavy and light, all at the same time. Frustrated at his inability to reach her so he could hold her and kiss away her tears, he succumbed to the darkness once more.

Sofia sat beside Heden's bed, clutching his hand as she prayed. Eyes raw from crying, there were no tears left to shed. After three days, his prognosis was the same: he couldn't survive without life support.

Eyeing the tube that fed into his lungs, she watched the machine pump air. Once. Twice. Again. Over and over. The monotony was grating to her nerves, and she gritted her molars together in frustration.

"Any change?" Nolan asked, approaching her and sliding a supportive hand over her shoulder.

She shook her head. "I don't understand. He was supposed to live forever. If I had known…" Emotion clogged her throat as she struggled to speak. "I never should've left."

"There's nothing you could've done, Sofia," he said, compassion lacing his British accent. "Sometimes, these things just happen."

"I wish there was something I could do."

"Me too. In the meantime, Glarys sent lasagna over. I've been instructed we're both meant to eat it for lunch, or she'll come looking for us."

Sofia's lips formed their first tentative smile in days. "Did she send along fresh grated parmesan to put on top?"

"She wouldn't be Glarys if she didn't. Let's go to the break room and eat. I think you need a few minutes away from this stuffy room."

Nodding, she grasped the hand of the only other human in the realm. Together, they warmed up the dish the kind mother figure had prepared.

※

Heden hiked in the woods, tickled by how much fun he was having with Sofia. Who knew a human could be so damn adorable and engaging? Turning to pick her up and lift her over the log, his eyebrows drew together. Where was she? She was behind him a moment ago.

"She's not here, my friend," a female voice called to his right.

Pivoting, he smiled at Tatiana. "Hey, super confusing riddle lady. How's it going?"

She gave a good-natured shrug. "Fine for me, but you've seen better days."

Glancing around, he searched the forest. "Is that why Sofia disappeared? I swear, she was right beside me."

"You're lost in the memory of the hike you took before you met me in the woods," Tatiana said. "It's a pleasant memory for you, and you find it safe. But it's time for you to return home, son of Markdor. Your time in Etherya's realm isn't yet over."

The words were perplexing. "Am I in the Passage?"

She shook her head. "You're in the in-between. It's a paradoxical place, tough to understand even for one as bright as you. You seem to be stuck here, and I think you know the reason why."

Heden's eyebrows drew together. "I can't imagine why I'd want to be stuck here. I'd much rather be at home with my family. And with Sofia."

"Ah, but you have no home with Sofia. It is an unfortunate but unwavering truth. This causes you much pain and hiding here is as good a place as any."

Resting his hands on his hips, he plopped his foot on a nearby log, contemplating. "Are you saying I'm stuck here because I don't want to go home and accept reality?"

Tatiana's head tilted to the side. "Perhaps. What do you think?"

Heden inhaled the fragrant air, mulling her words. It was true that here, in this place, the agony of Sofia's absence didn't hurt so much. He didn't have to suffer with the knowledge they were forced to live separate lives due to factors beyond their control. Instead, he was just...numb. It was a welcome reprieve from the pain he'd experienced over the past few months.

"I know it feels better," she said, "but that is an illusion. You are stronger than the shell of the person you are here. Running from your pain won't heal you. It will only create more for the ones you leave behind."

He toyed with his bottom lip with his fangs. "Living in that world is so damn hard. I don't understand how to live without her."

"Then don't."

He sighed. "She's adamant she doesn't want me to witness her grow old. That it's better we part."

"I think she is correct in that assertion."

"But you're telling me to go back," he said, frustration curling in his gut. "So she can just leave me again? Sounds pretty shitty to me."

Tatiana crept forward, leaves crunching under her sandaled feet. When her face was inches from his, she grinned and tapped his forehead with her finger. "For someone so smart, you are blind to so much. Go home, Heden. You have lived your life without purpose for so long. Although you do much to help your people, you shy away from hard choices. This has to change for you to realize your full potential."

Heden chuckled. "Are you telling me I need to 'adult'? Because I'm pretty terrible at it."

Throwing back her head, she gave one of the deep throated laughs he was beginning to expect from her. "Yes," she said, amber eyes glowing. "You need to 'adult.' It baffles me how each new generation of humans denigrates their languages. Wait until you see the millennials' children's children. You will think them insane."

"You can see the future?" he asked, awed by the prospect. Not even Evie was that powerful.

"I function differently in the world than most creatures. Time is not a constant for me. You will discover soon enough. For now, go home. Each moment you stay here increases your family's suffering along with Sofia's."

"I don't want that," he said, kicking the leaves at his feet with his sneaker. "How do I go back?"

"Can't you hear?" Tatiana asked, pointing to the sky. "She's calling you. All you have to do is answer."

Sofia's voice filtered through the clouds, soft but vibrant. "*Heden. Please come back to me.*"

Closing his eyes, he concentrated, focusing on her words in the dark void.

"Good," Tatiana said, sounding a million miles away. "Tell Miranda to pull the loose brick along the soothsayer chamber far wall."

"What?" Heden asked, lost in another one of her riddles. He fought to open his eyes, but they were cemented closed. Directing all his energy to Sofia's muffled voice, he swam toward it through the obscure dimness. Feeling as if he might suffocate, he struggled to reach her.

Sofia felt something brush against her cheek and batted it away. When the nagging jolt persisted, she rose from her slumber to tell whoever it was to cut it out. Rapidly blinking her eyes, she immediately understood she'd fallen asleep beside Heden, face planted on the hospital stretcher. After imploring him for several hours to wake up, she'd laid her cheek against the soft sheet beside his abdomen to rest for only a minute...

His fingers twitched, and she gasped, shooting from the chair. Eyes still closed, he lifted lethargic arms to the tubes at his throat, trying to pull them free.

"Nolan!" she screamed.

Both physicians rushed in, Sadie immediately reaching for the tubes while Heden gulped for air and Nolan held down his flailing arms. Terrified, Sofia waited.

Sadie removed the hoses and gently slapped her fingers on Heden's face. "Heden! Heden!" she called. "It's okay. I need you to breathe on your own. You can do it."

Her massive Vampyre sucked in a huge breath, eyes flying open as he searched the room.

"Oh, my god," Sofia cried, rushing to stand beside Sadie. "You're awake. You came back to me." Making the sign of the cross, she looked to the sky. "Thank you."

"She's a heathen," he almost whispered, his voice raspy from the tube. "Thinks heaven is real."

Sadie laughed. "Does she now?"

Sofia sat on the bed and leaned over him, throwing her arms around him as she placed ardent kisses over his face. "How can you already be making fun of me? Oh, Heden, I was so worried for you."

"I'm here, Sof," he murmured, running his hand over her hair. "I missed you so much."

"I'm never leaving again. Screw the consequences. I can't do this without you."

"Sofia," he said softly, caressing her face with his fingers. "I think you look more and more like Blanche every day. It's so hot."

Head falling forward, she laughed upon his chest, overcome with joy that he'd returned to her. Holding him tight, she resigned herself to their future—whatever it may hold. The alternative was now unthinkable.

∞

Two days later, Heden sat in Sadie's office holding Sofia's hand as the physician discussed his prognosis.

"The poison from the bullets somehow wormed into the vessels around your heart, Heden. It's created a strange phenomenon where your arteries carry the poison away but the veins transport it right back. After consulting with Nolan, we think you're going to have to do some old-school rehabilitation."

"What does that entail?" Heden asked.

"Five hours each day on the treadmill, spread out intermittently. This will cause your heartbeat to accelerate, and the arteries will be able to flush the poison from the area around your heart to your kidneys and liver so they can filter it from your body. If you follow the regimen for three months, we think your body will be completely decontaminated and back to normal."

"Okay," he said, feeling weak as he ran his thumb over Sofia's soft skin. "I'll do whatever I have to do to recover."

"Can I help him?" Sofia asked.

"That's up to Heden. I'm sure he'd love moral support, but that's for you two to decide."

Sofia nodded and helped him stand. Since his heart wasn't functioning at full capacity, the most mundane task drained his recovering body. "Lean on me," she said, lifting his arm and placing it across her shoulders. They shuffled back to the infirmary bed, which Heden was thankful he would be discharged from tomorrow.

Lowering onto the bed, he struggled to catch his breath as he caressed Sofia's face. "You're the sexiest nurse I've ever had."

She grinned. "Damn straight. I'm going to help you kick your recovery's ass. I almost lost you, and I want that poison out of your body as soon as possible."

Heden studied her, his irises roving over her face. "Does that mean you're staying?"

"Yes." Her tone was unwavering. "I'm here and I'm not going anywhere. We'll get you better and then we'll forge ahead with what we've got. I thought about it a lot while I prayed over the past few days, and honestly, we have a lot of challenges others will never face, but almost losing you changed everything. I have no ties in the human world, and I can have a human child just as easily here as I can there. We can figure out how to make this work."

While his heart swelled from her desire to stay with him, something felt...*off*. She'd been so sure of her decision to leave before his injury, and he didn't want that to be the only reason she decided to stay.

Licking his lips, he said, "Are you sure, Sof? There are still so many obstacles for us."

His little human palmed his cheeks and began to piece together his shattered heart. "I love you," she whispered, eyes clear and brimming with emotion. "I don't give a damn about the obstacles right now. This is all that matters." Lowering her hand, she covered his heart.

"Sofia," he breathed, drawing her close so he could thread his fingers through her hair. "I love you so much. I wanted to tell you before you left."

"I know," she said, her smile so bright. "You don't have to say the words for them to be true, Heden. I feel it. It's so amazing."

Brushing her lips with his, he gazed into her blue-green eyes. "Is love going to be enough?"

"Yes," she said, capturing his lips with hers. "It has to be."

There, in the staid, sterile room, he kissed her, overjoyed at being in her arms once more. But a nagging fear lingered in the far reaches of his mind: they hadn't yet overcome the tremendous issues that led to their separation. Pushing it away, he clutched onto the moment, thrilled his beloved human had returned.

Chapter 33

Sofia threw herself into Heden's recovery, ensuring he stayed on schedule with his workout sessions so the ominous toxins would exit his body. He was a fun patient, albeit rather annoying, as he would attempt to pull her onto the treadmill, stating he'd rather exercise with her—naked. She loved his jibing but also urged him to take his rehabilitation seriously. Almost losing him had shaken her to her core, and his complete recovery was her ultimate goal.

They fell back into their seamless pattern, settling into the life they were only supposed to share for two months. Although Sofia was infinitely happier with Heden, concerns lingered in the back of her mind. She'd committed to stay with him for the long haul, and that was easy, for she now accepted she loved him, body and soul. But that promise also led to a multitude of unknowns.

Since having biological children together was impossible, they decided once Heden was healthy, they would search for a human donor. She'd always been fine with artificial insemination when she was single, but for some reason, it didn't sit well with her now they'd cemented their relationship. Sighing as she sat in the green grass under the moonlight one evening, she acknowledged the truth: she wanted Heden's babies. With sky-blue eyes and thick, black hair, they would be beautiful. In her dreams, they inherited his buoyant personality and her practical common sense. She could almost see their faces when she closed her eyes and concentrated.

They'd discussed adopting immortal children, but Sofia had always longed for biological children. Ones that would have Francesco's features and sparkling eyes. Heden understood that desire, and they decided having human children was their best alternative. She knew Heden would love them with all his heart for the finite lives they would live. He would raise them with her and be there for them when she passed on, until they eventually left the Earth as well. Would their children ever fall in love? How would that be possible if they lived in the immortal world?

There were other challenges too. Bakari's presence in the immortal world was a chilling perplexity, and he was a menacing nemesis who loomed in the backs of all their minds. Their mortal children would be vulnerable, and she and Heden discussed various methods to keep them safe. With their skills, Sofia knew they could create several kick-ass security systems that would protect their family and others in the realm, but the Secret Society still posed a serious threat.

Blowing a breath through her puffed cheeks, she pushed away the unknowns. They were just too overwhelming. Once Heden was healthy, they would sit down and discuss all the complexities and heartache that came with their future predicament. For now, it was best to soldier on and focus on his rehabilitation.

"Hey, sweetheart," Heden said, approaching from behind and sitting next to her. "You look like you're pondering the mysteries of the universe. Did you figure them out?"

"Nope," she said, pasting on a smile, determined to stay the course. "I just really like it out here. There's something peaceful about this spot."

"I came here so many times when you were gone," he said, taking her hand and lacing their fingers. "I'd look at the moon and wonder if you were doing the same and possibly thinking of me."

Swallowing thickly, she remembered her desolate loneliness without him. No obstacles were insurmountable enough to cause her to want to feel that despondent again...were they? "I did the same," she whispered, clenching her fingers over his. "Living without you was awful."

"Yeah," he said, tucking a strand of hair behind her ear. "It pretty much sucked."

Reminding herself to be thankful for what she had, and that Heden had survived his attack, she rested her head on his shoulder. Together, they would discern how to navigate their complicated future, for their connection was too pure and their love was too magnificent to squander.

※

Heden strode atop the treadmill, his body growing stronger each day. Sofia had been home for weeks, helping his heart heal infinitely more than any exercise could. Each day, he would send a prayer of thanks to Etherya for bringing his love back to his life.

But Heden read people well, and he understood Sofia still had reservations. Hell, he had them too. They had discussed various possibilities for their future: living in the immortal realm versus the human world, having human children, how they would raise human kids in a world tailored to Slayers and Vampyres. There were just so many challenges they would have to navigate. But Heden loved his little human and knew he would be miserable without her by his side for as long as they had. Unable to set her free, he let her resume their life, telling himself it was the only option.

One day after his rehab session, he sought out Nolan. Sitting in the infirmary, they chatted about the choice Etherya had given him when she granted his immortality.

"She seemed quite thankful I trudged through the ether in an attempt to save Sathan," Nolan said. "She warned it took great effort for her to offer me immortality, but she seemed...curious. Afterward, she informed me I am the only creature in her expansive lifetime she's ever manipulated mortality for. I got the sense she was...*intrigued* in some way and wanted to observe the results of such a massive transformation."

Heden nodded, contemplating. "I want so badly to ask her to do the same for Sofia. Since you have firsthand experience with the goddess and the enormity of her decision to grant immortality, what do you think my chances are?"

Nolan inhaled a deep breath as he pondered. "Etherya warned me something so expansive requires great effort and sacrifice. Remember, she offered me two choices: immortality, or death. It wasn't a 'wine and roses' scenario," Nolan said, making quotation marks with his fingers. "Lost to terror, I chose immortality and regretted that decision for almost three hundred years. A condition of her offer was that I could never enter the human world again. Once I realized I would never see my family again, I became despondent and extremely unhappy. Thank goodness Sadie came along, or I fear my future would've been almost unlivable."

"I'm so glad you found her, man," Heden said, patting his shoulder. "You two are so damn cute together."

Nolan beamed. "I love her so much. Sometimes, I'm still baffled I have a family. It's more than I ever hoped for during those long, lonely centuries."

Looking to the ceiling, Heden rubbed his beard. "I wonder what sacrifices she would require of us if we requested she turn Sofia immortal."

"I don't know," Nolan said, "but I hesitate to offer you hope, Heden. As I said, I'm the only being she's ever manipulated mortality for. When my transformation was complete, she was ravaged and spent. She fell to the ground and wept, and the sky opened up to a magnificent storm filled with black clouds and torrential rain. I was petrified, but Sathan led me to Astaria and took me in, thank goodness. It was all quite extraordinary. I'm not sure she was supposed to change me, if that makes sense. It seemed the forces of nature were quite angry at her choice to turn me."

Heden nodded, hands on his hips as he stared dejectedly at the floor. "It sounds daunting, but I have to try."

"Well, there's no worthier cause than love, my friend," Nolan said, cupping his shoulder. "I wish you the best of luck."

That evening, Heden approached Sathan as he sat in his office. Lowering into one of the broad-backed leather chairs facing his desk, Heden implored him to speak to Etherya on his behalf.

"I know she used to converse with you by the river," Heden said. "You're the only immortal she's ever appeared to on a regular basis. I've never seen her in the flesh and have sent her a thousand pleas over the last few weeks, to no avail. I think she's ignoring me," he said, scowling.

"The goddess is fickle, brother," Sathan said, leaning back in his chair. "She hasn't appeared to me for years now. She prefers to observe from afar and stay out of our affairs. Several times over the centuries, she told me the Universe becomes displeased when she interferes in our free will. Each time she does it, she suffers. Now that Crimeous is gone, I think she's content to watch over us and let us be."

"Well, that pretty much sucks since I've fallen in love with a mortal. Damn it, Sathan. I wish I could change our predicament."

"I thought you and Sofia had decided to build a life here."

"We have, but it's not ideal. I'm so bummed I can't give her biological children, and raising mortal children here is going to present a ton of problems. I just..." He rubbed his forehead, frustrated. "It just fucking sucks."

"I will try to summon the goddess," Sathan said. "Let me see if I can attempt to sway her."

"Thanks, bro," Heden said, feeling a tiny swell of hope in his heart. "I'll continue to do the same, although I think she'll appear to you before me. Let me know."

The weeks wore on as Heden completed his physical therapy. Each night, as Sofia snuggled into his side, he reminded himself he was extremely fortunate to have found a woman who was so damn amazing. His little human was a coding whiz, a video game lover, funny as hell and absolutely gorgeous. Even with their obstacles, finding her had been exceedingly fortuitous. Vowing to focus on the strengths of their magnificent connection, he reveled in her smell and the softness of her smooth skin.

Until the day his brother approached him as he was climbing down from the treadmill. Wiping his brow with his towel, his eyebrows drew together at Sathan's downcast expression.

"What's wrong, Sathan?"

His brother slid his broad hand over his shoulder. "I'm sorry, brother. Etherya finally appeared to me. She was quite angry I summoned her and told me she's also heard your prayers. They won't do any good, Heden. She's immovable on offering Sofia immortality. She warned me not to ask her again, or there would be consequences. I'm so damn sorry."

A long breath left Heden's body as he collapsed on the workout bench, running his hand through his hair. The news was deflating and heavy.

After Sathan consoled him, Heden headed to shower, contemplating his next move. Perhaps there were other creatures with Etherya's powers on the Earth, possibly living in the human world. It wasn't likely, but Bakari, Evie and Tatiana had all resided there, so it wasn't impossible. Could there be some other being or force who could grant his request? Unwilling to be deterred, he toweled himself dry and plodded to the kitchen to find his love.

She was cooking chicken marsala in a large pan and smiled at him as he entered the expansive kitchen. The jolt in his solar plexus was palpable. Sofia's broad grin was the most beautiful thing he'd ever seen. Vowing to be worthy of the innumerable sacrifices she was making to live with him in the immortal realm—until he could hopefully figure out a better solution—he lifted her in his arms and twirled her in time with her melodious laughter.

Chapter 34

Bakari sat in the darkened cave flipping through the withered book. The spine had long ago begun to fray, and he was careful with the pages lest he damage them. The journal archived his history in a way, and for someone who had no ties—who had no family—it gave him purpose on a planet he wasn't meant to inhabit for more than a few hours.

The first pages had been written by Zala, centuries ago, when she'd exhumed his small body and resuscitated him. The ancient witch had been quite powerful and had raised him to comprehend they both were different...separate...alone. Later, she taught him separateness led to fear, and if fear was exploited properly, it was a powerful motivator. In those early decades of his life, Bakari understood he could wield much power and cause much pain by manipulating people's anxieties and phobias.

Tracing the faded parchment, Bakari read the words Zala had scrawled, detailing the extensive spells she'd cast upon him when he was just a babe. When he'd first read them at the tender age of ten, he was overcome with curiosity.

"What spells did you cast on me, Zala?"

"Ones that made you able to survive on the blood of creatures like me instead of the others."

"What others?"

"They don't deserve you, my boy," she'd said, caressing his cheek. "It's no matter now. You're here, and you shall never know of them. Not so long as I exist."

Thus had ended the cryptic conversation, which, strangely, he still recalled to this day. Zala had also trained him to eat food, so his thirst for blood became an anomaly that added to his separateness along with his severely pointed incisors, which were quite different from the scant others he came into contact with during his formative years.

Once Zala passed on, Bakari entered many new phases of life. In some, he was kind. In others, he was murderous. He loved many beautiful women, amassed great wealth, which he squandered and regained, and had a thirst for blood, both for nourishment and for taste.

He could never discern why he craved drinking from people's veins, for humans had long ago lost their thirst for cannibalism. But he ached for it all the same and would sate his thirst by draining others and disposing of them like the meals they were. Only when he met Xen did he truly begin to understand.

Xen practiced medicine in a small rural town outside of Yangzhou, China in the 1600s. Bakari had long ago accepted he would never age, nor grow ill, and he dedicated this portion of his endless life to researching Eastern medicine in the hopes of finding the reasons why. He thought perhaps the doctrine would hold some clues as to why he wasn't quite...human.

When he walked into the medicine woman's tent, Xen stood beside the crackling fire and gasped. Pointing at him, she exclaimed, "Xīxuèguǐ! Jiangshi!" He would later learn they both translated to "bloodsucker" and "vampire." Desperate for information, Bakari befriended the woman, hoping she could explain his strange heritage.

He was charming when he expended the effort and soon seduced Xen under his spell. Deep in love, she gladly imparted her knowledge to him as he held her each night, softly stroking her skin. She informed him of the ether and the immortal world beyond and the stories it held. When pressed on how she'd come to possess this knowledge, she explained it had been passed down her family line through generations by song and folklore. She didn't know which one of her grandfathers' grandfather originated the tales but knew they'd generated many centuries ago. Bakari realized yet another dead end in his life, as he would never know how Xen's ancestors discovered the immortal world so very long ago.

Once his time with Xen was over, Bakari relocated to the Transylvanian region of Romania. There, he made use of the vast libraries built during the European Renaissance and tirelessly researched any mentions of the immortal world. The progress was slow, leading him down a spiral of frustration and anger, and he killed and drained many during this time of his life. It was here the legend of Count Dracula was born, most likely from his murderous actions.

Eventually, through painstaking efforts, Bakari found others like him. Others who were from the world humans couldn't even fathom. Some of them shared their knowledge, and Bakari realized his true heritage as the child of the revered Vampyre royals. Once he learned to generate the ether, he stepped through to observe the realm that had cast him out so long ago. To his dismay, they were embroiled in a bloody war he wanted no part of, for he'd seen enough human war to last a hundred lifetimes. Deciding he'd return once the species eradicated each other, he returned to his comfortable life in the human world.

But over time, vile seeds planted over his entire life began to grow and curl in his mind. He was akin to a god in the human world, massively wealthy as all human gods were, and he felt he deserved the same in the realm of his birth. After all, he was the son of Markdor and Calla. How dare the immortals not even acknowledge his presence upon the Earth? How dare they not respect him as the humans did?

As his rage grew, so did his quest for vengeance. Convinced the immortals were weak creatures who needed to be curbed by an intelligent and omnipotent leader, he decided he would let Crimeous defeat them and then murder the Deamon king himself, understanding he burned in the sunlight. Frustrated his siblings, who were king and commander of the Vampyre army, hadn't discerned that yet, he convinced himself they were too stupid to rule the realm. They must be exterminated so he, the true sovereign, with his centuries of acquired knowledge and intellect, could reign.

Of course, his plan failed, as his siblings actually defeated Crimeous with the help of his powerful spawns. Bakari hated Evie with a passion he couldn't explain, and he'd been convinced she would fail. But no, she had prevailed along with the others, and they had proceeded to denigrate the kingdom into one of hybrid spawns and a false utopia. It went against everything Bakari had been taught. Everything he believed deep in his soul.

Zala had ingrained in his young mind all those centuries ago that there was a pureness to remaining separate. A natural order that must be maintained. When Bakari learned of Etherya, he understood she created the species that way. After all, if there was no value in separateness, his entire life was a lie. It was his difference that made him special. There was a systematic order that made the planet churn. Without those mechanisms in place, the world would devolve into chaos, and his presence upon it would mean nothing.

Dedicating his life to Etherya and what he believed was her true vision, he determined only he could save her realm. He must exterminate the immortal royals and their vapid spawns before they denigrated all that was right and holy. His mind was crazed with the potential successes he would attain. He would now be preeminent in two worlds, unstoppable in his quest to make things function on a higher level than others could ever begin to see.

And then, he would look out upon his planet and bask in his moment of exaltation. The moment where he was no longer separate but the one they all aspired to be. By the goddess, it would be *glorious*.

There would be many steps along the way. Bakari was slowly realizing Callie might be more integral to his scheme than he'd originally anticipated. It was no matter. He could convince her to fight with him—of that, he was sure. Crimeous's blood and dark tendencies ran through her quite vehemently, even if Darkrip and Arderin chose not to see it. Once she aligned with him and they succeeded, he would murder her, of course, but it would be nice to exploit her potency while he could.

Pondering the possibilities, he closed the withered archive and sat back in his chair. Lifting the goblet, he drank the human blood Zala had ensured he would thrive on for his long life. Stewing in the vast possibilities of victory, he resumed plotting his next moves.

Chapter 35

Heden and Lila sat on the park bench as Sofia rolled in the grass with Symon and Adelyn. His woman's laugh was infectious as she lifted Symon in the air, holding him high as he giggled with mirth.

"She's so wonderful with children," Lila said, fangs slightly squishing her lower lip as she smiled.

"She's fucking amazing. She's going to be an incredible mother."

Lila chewed her lip, her eyebrows drawing together as she stared ahead. "So, you are going to choose a human donor?"

"It's the best choice we have," he said, arm stretched over the bench as it surrounded her shoulders. "Now that I'm completely recovered, we're ready to move forward."

Lila nodded, her expression thoughtful.

"Okay, buttercup, what's the deal? I thought you of all people would be on board with making a family from non-traditional methods."

"It's not that," she said, her words thoughtful. "It's just…"

"Go on."

Lifting her stunning lavender eyes to his, he felt them bore into his soul. "She's stuck in a world that isn't hers, Heden. A world where she's going to eventually age, and her body will break down. You'll still be healthy and vibrant as she deteriorates, and then you'll have to do it all over again with your human children. I know it doesn't seem so bad now, but what about the future? I fear you're not allowing yourself to see how difficult this is going to be. For both of you."

The images flashed in Heden's mind. Of Sofia becoming ill and him having to nurse her, possibly for decades, before she perished. Of their human children growing up in an immortal world, so different from everyone else, continuing to age as their friends lived in immortality.

Then, having to care for them before they died. It was extremely overwhelming.

"We've discussed so many possibilities for our future. I offered to live in the human world with her, but she doesn't have any family there, and all of you are here. Plus, we'd have to move every few years or live in hiding, so people wouldn't wonder why I never age. Eventually, I'd have to start telling people she's my mother, or my grandmother, whenever we move to a new place. Kinda creepy. Here, everyone knows our situation."

"But can she really be happy with that, Heden? Deep inside? She already told you the first time she left what her true wishes were. She only pushed them aside because you almost died. Do you really think they've changed?"

Heden studied Sofia as she played a game of tag with the kids next to the swings. "Probably not. But what the hell are we supposed to do, Lila? We love each other."

She scrunched her nose and gave him a contrite arch of her blond eyebrow. "Can I say something kind of harsh?"

"Yikes," he said, grimacing. "I don't think I'm going to like this."

Laughing, she shook her head. "You might not."

"Okay, lay it on me."

Inhaling deeply, she said, "I think if you truly love her, you have to let her go. There's a selfishness in molding your love to this future you've decided to make. I understand the need to be with someone desperately, believe me, but sometimes, you just have to have the fortitude to walk away when you know in your gut it isn't right. I had the strength to walk away from Latimus, and our relationship became something so much better in return. When you act in fear, you limit your possibilities."

Sighing, Heden squeezed her shoulder. "So, you're telling me I'm a selfish prick? Low blow, buttercup."

"Oh, Heden, you know I love you," she said, her tone so genuine.

"Chill, Lila, I'm joking." Pulling her into his side, he placed an affectionate kiss on her hair. "I know you'll always secretly love me more than Latimus."

Chuckling, she smiled. "Be glad he's not here to hear you say that. He might murder you."

Heden chomped his gum as he grinned. "I can take him."

Lila snickered. "Okay," she said, rolling her eyes.

They sat in silence, letting her words sink in. "Honestly, Lila, you're right. About everything. Living here and raising mortal children while I live on is going to be really tough. I just don't see another scenario."

"Have you asked her what she wants?" Lila's irises searched his. "Deep down in the far reaches of her heart? I think you should."

He rubbed the back of his neck, pondering. "I think I'm afraid to ask her," he murmured.

"All the more reason you should."

"Damn, Lila, why are you so smart? It's exceedingly unfair considering how gorgeous you are. Most people barely get one or the other."

"You're the smartest person I know, Heden," she said, resting her head on his shoulder, "and that's why I know you understand this scenario won't make either of you happy. If you choose to go forward, I'll support you, of course, but I think it's a mistake. I'm so sorry to say it. I truly am."

"Thanks, buttercup," he said, resting his cheek on her head.

Lost in silence, they observed their loved ones play as the gravity of future choices loomed in the air.

That night, as Sofia was prepping for bed, Heden gently cupped her shoulders. "Can we talk for a minute?"

"Whoa," she said, eyeing him in the reflection. "You're never this serious. Did someone die?"

"I just want to chat, Sof. Come on." Grabbing her hand, he led her to the tech room.

"In here?" she asked.

"Yeah," he said, sitting on the edge of the large table in the middle of the room. Drawing her between his legs, he ran his finger over her collarbone. "If we talk near a bed, we'll probably just end up boning before we finish two sentences."

Her eyebrow arched. "In case you've forgotten, we've done quite a bit of boning in this room as well."

Chuckling, he squeezed her wrists. "That we have. So, now that I'm back to one hundred percent, we need to talk about the future. I know we've discussed different options these last few months, but I think it's time to nail down exactly what we want."

Wary eyes darted over his face as her expression grew more somber. "Okay. You start."

He took a moment to consider his words. "When you left all those months ago, it was because you felt it best we part forever rather than leading lives that would ultimately cause us both to suffer. I'm wondering why you changed your mind."

Blowing air through her extended bottom lip, it fluttered the hair above her brow. Extricating from his touch, she stepped back, easing to perch on the edge of the computer desk. Crossing her arms over her chest, she said, "Because you were hurt and almost died. That put a lot of things into perspective for me."

Heden also crossed his arms, tapping his foot as he studied her. "There's a difference between changing perspectives and changing your mind, Sof. I'm wondering if you still feel the same about our situation but you're pushing it aside because of what happened."

White teeth gnawed her lip. "I almost lost you. It made me realize I had to spend whatever time I had left with you, no matter what the cost."

"And what would be the cost?"

Annoyance pervaded her features. "Why are you interrogating me?"

"Because we never truly discussed this, and I think that was a huge oversight for both of us. We just headed straight back into the life we were only supposed to have for two months."

"So, are you saying you want it to end? Wow, I didn't see that coming."

"Of course I don't want it to end. I want it to stay just like this forever."

Realization entered her eyes. "But it won't be like this forever," she said softly.

He shook his head. "We've probably got three, maybe four more decades before things begin to drastically change. I need to know if you're okay with that."

She lifted her hands in a shrug. "What do you want me to say?"

"I want you to be honest."

Her gaze fell to the floor, and Heden could see the wheels churning in her mind.

After a fitful bout of silence, he said, "The thing is, I don't think you really changed your mind, Sof. I think you just compromised your beliefs because you love me."

"I do love you," she said, those stunning eyes blazing with emotion. "That requires sacrifice. I have no problem with that."

Standing, he strode toward her and cupped her face. "But I have a problem with it, little human. I would be some piece of shit if I let you choose a life with me when you truly didn't feel it was the right path. And honestly, as much as I hate to say it, I'm not sure it's the right path either."

"I don't know what to think." Her frustration was palpable. "I don't want to live a life without you, but I also don't want to saddle you with my death and our children's deaths. The thought tears me apart. It's maddening."

"So, you haven't really changed your mind."

A single tear slid down her cheek, and he wiped it away as she whispered the words that sealed their fate. "I haven't really changed my mind."

Inhaling deeply, he caressed her face, committing it to memory so it would live there for centuries to come. "I have to let you go, Sofia," he said, placing his forehead against hers. "I didn't get it before, but I do now. Maybe it's because I almost died. Just thinking how much you suffered for three days while you watched over me and begged me not to leave you...I can't imagine how painful that was."

"It almost broke me," she said, shaking her head. "It was awful."

"And you want to save me from the same pain. From suffering while I watch you slip away, knowing I can never save you."

"Bingo," she said, shoulders lifting. "I don't want you to have to watch me die. To watch our children die. To raise children in a world where they can never find love. What if our mortal children fall in love with an immortal? We've relegated them to the same predicament we're in now, but I might not be around to help you navigate it with them. There are so many disasters I want to shield us both from, Heden." She cupped his jaw, tender and reverent. "I love you so much, I'd live without you to prevent that heartache for you. For *us*."

Heden finally understood. After all his consternation and anger and pain from her leaving all those months ago, he finally comprehended she had done it for love. It was such a magnificent gift, and he was humbled she had the foresight to see what he couldn't.

"You're so amazing, Sof. I wish I could change things for us."

"I know. It fucking sucks."

Placing a sweet kiss on her lips, he pondered their next move. As the idea formed, he knew in his heart it was right. "I have a proposal."

"I think we just decided I have to say no to any proposal."

Heden chuckled. "Were you this funny when we met? I don't remember you being this funny."

"You rubbed off on me. It's a nice side effect of dating a self-proclaimed comedian."

Smiling, he ran his thumb over her lips. "Let's spend a week at your home in Positano. You promised me a sunset, and I'm not letting you renege. We'll spend seven more sunsets together, and then we'll say goodbye properly. Something worthy we can hold onto once you're old and I'm still incredibly handsome."

Tears streamed down her face as she warbled a laugh. "That sounds perfect."

"Okay, little human. We'll make the rounds this week so you can hug everyone here one last time, and then we'll head to Italy. I'm excited to see your home."

"Italy was always home for me until I met you. Now, I want to live here, even if I'm not physically with you." She tapped his chest over his slowly breaking heart. "If you'll have me."

"You'll always live here, Sof," he said, covering her hand as her palm rested over his heart. "I love you with all my soul."

"I love you too." Standing on her toes, she kissed him.

Heden drew her close, burying his face in her neck so she didn't see his own tears swimming in his eyes.

Chapter 36

The week in Italy was the absolute best of Sofia's life. After saying some heartfelt goodbyes to the people she'd come to love in the immortal world, Heden accompanied her through the ether to Positano. He'd been awed by the quaint seaside town, bustling yet charming with its cliffside buildings and gorgeous scenery.

They set off to enjoy all Sofia's favorite things: Italian wine, delicious pasta, walks across the pebbly beaches. The balcony of her secluded rental home sat high on the cliffs in a perfect location to watch the sunset each evening. The first night, they held each other on the balcony, Sofia gazing at Heden while he gaped, open-mouthed at the glory of the setting sun.

"You were right, Sof," he said, his eyes slightly glassy. "It's so damn gorgeous. I'll never see a sunset again without picturing this one with you. Thank you."

Locked in a gentle embrace, they stood, heads resting against each other, silent and content above the ocean.

Sofia introduced him to some of the local merchants. One of them, who passersby seemed to lovingly address as "Uncle Tony," helped Sofia identify which of the gigantic lemons would make the best lemonade. Once they trekked home, Heden drank her homemade concoction, surprised by how much he enjoyed it.

"I think I'm officially a food and drink lover," he said, toasting Sofia with the glass. "It's fantastic, honey."

Their days were filled with laughter and teasing, their nights with poignant passion. Each evening, after they made love, they would get lost in deep conversation, agreeing it wouldn't hurt to dream just a little bit longer.

"I like Bianca or Isabella," she said late one night as her body cooled upon the bed, fresh from their heated lovemaking session.

Tracing his finger over her cheek as his head rested on his palm, he squinted. "Bianca is good. I don't think I'm a fan of Isabella. What about Marcus for a boy? I've always liked that name for some reason."

"We'd name a boy Francesco," she said, her gaze questioning. "Wouldn't we?"

He feigned contemplation, squeezing one eye shut. "I think we should just go with Screech. We can carry on my family tradition of prematurely blowing my load."

Sofia burst into laughter, overcome by his teasing. "Please, tell me you're kidding."

"I'm kidding," he said, kissing her softly on the lips. "I would be honored to have a boy named Francesco with you, honey."

Sofia swallowed, lost in the sentiment in his eyes. Her nostrils flared as the tears began to well.

"Don't cry, sweetheart," he said, his face a mask of pain. "You promised if we discussed this stuff, you wouldn't get sad. Maybe we should stop."

"I'm okay," she said, shaking her head on the pillow. "I just wish so badly it was true."

"Everything about our love is true, Sof. Please don't forget that. I need you to hold onto it."

"I will," she whispered, drawing his lips to hers. "Love me again before we fall asleep."

Lost in the promises of a tomorrow that would never come, they loved each other until exhaustion overtook their ravaged bodies.

Finally, the last night arrived. Sofia awoke solemn and cranky, but her jovial Vampyre would have none of it. Urging her to don her bathing suit, they walked to the ocean and swam in the warm summer water. Somehow, Heden managed to loosen her bikini top and threatened to feed it to the fish. Sofia pleaded for it back, mortified, until he assured her no one was around to give a damn.

A slight fear shot down her spine at the notion Bakari could be lurking in the distance, waiting for the opportunity to attack them while they were unaware. But Heden convinced her they were safe, enveloping her in his strong embrace, reminding her how protected she felt in his arms. Observing the private pebbled beach that bordered the stairs leading up the hill to her home, she accepted their solace and relaxed. He somehow lost his shorts a few moments later—which Sofia was pretty damn convinced was intentional—and their squeals of laughter echoed off the cliffs as they skinny-dipped.

As the sun began to inch toward the horizon, Sofia emerged from her shower, throwing on a light yellow dress to combat the summer stickiness. Joining Heden on the balcony, she maneuvered in front of him to watch the sunset.

His front bracketed her back as his arms encircled her waist. Silent and thoughtful, they watched the ocean consume the glowing orb. Warm breaths caressed her neck as he inhaled behind her, calm and sure. As the ember-red half-circle eased into the void, he rested his lips against the shell of her ear.

"I love you."

Tears streamed down her face, free and unabetted, as she clutched onto the words. The coarse hairs of his beard caressed her neck as he nuzzled the delicate skin of her nape. "By the goddess, Sof, it's more than I ever hoped for. These feelings I have for you, they're so encompassing. You make me so happy. I'll never be sorry."

Her body shook in his arms, words impossible due to her sobbing. Sinking into him, she drew upon his strength, thankful he was there to support her inconsolable tears.

"It's okay, little human," he murmured, hands gently gathering her dress and lifting it. Sounds of clothes rustling registered in her ears, and she felt him searching, finding her wetness. He slipped inside her, joining them as the rays of the dying sunset illuminated their skin. Turning her head, she searched for his lips, kissing him with all her ardor as he pumped into her most intimate place.

"Look at me, Sofia," he said against her lips.

Opening her wet eyes, she stared into his soul.

"Please don't be sad," he said, undulating against her quivering body. "There's so much time for that later. Please, just focus on loving me."

"I love you so much," she cried, gliding her hands to fist in his hair. "I'm so sorry."

"No, baby," he said, his breathing harsh and labored. "No apologies. You're perfect." His fingers found the place between their bodies that drove her wild and brought her to the edge of sanity.

"My beautiful Sofia," he whispered.

"Heden," she cried.

Together, they shattered, their bodies depleting against one another as they both rejoiced and mourned their love. Trembling, they held each other, murmuring words that had no meaning except in the far reaches of their hearts. Heden surrounded her with his arms, carrying her to bed and pulling her into his cooling frame.

The bedroom curtain whipped, lazy and sluggish, from the nighttime breeze as she spread herself over every inch of his body. Slumber engulfed her for a while until he roused beneath her. Unable to move, lethargic with sorrow, she watched him dress. Once his things were gathered, he sat upon the bed.

His thumb traced over her cheek as they memorized each other one more time. Silently, he nodded, acknowledging her pain. She nodded back and reached up to catch the lone tear that trailed down his cheek. Smoothing the wetness over his skin, she smiled as much as her trembling lips would allow. He grinned back, reverent and sad.

Lowering, he kissed her, sweet and soft.

Sofia's heart leapt when he stood, most likely attempting to follow the man who'd stolen it.

From the doorway, he gazed at her for an eternity that only lasted a moment.

And then, he pivoted and returned to the immortality that made their love impossible.

Burying her face in the pillow, Sofia cried the tears she'd promised him wouldn't fall when he left her to resume his infinite future without her.

Chapter 37

Miranda grunted as she pulled at the brick that slightly jutted out from the wall. Frustrated it wouldn't budge, she flattened her foot along the wall as leverage and tugged again. Nothing. Annoyed at the stubborn rock, she collapsed on the floor in a huff, contemplating what tools she could use to move the damn thing.

"You still trying to find the loose brick?" Kenden asked, striding into the soothsayer chamber.

"Yeah," she said, angrily rubbing her forehead. "Every time I think I find one that sticks out, I look at it five minutes later and it seems even with the others. My eyes are going to cross soon."

"Hmm..." Kenden said, approaching her and extending his hand. He pulled her up and rubbed his chin as he contemplated the wall. "What exactly did Tatiana say to Heden again?"

"From what he remembers, she said, 'Pull the loose brick along the soothsayer chamber far wall.' This seems to be the far wall," Miranda said, gesturing to the open doorway across the room. "Do you see a stone that sticks out?"

"No," Kenden murmured, eyes narrowed. "They all seem pretty uniform. This chamber hasn't been used in centuries. It's possible any loose brick cemented to the ones around it over time."

"Maybe," Miranda said. "From what we know of Tatiana, she knows some pretty weird and important stuff. I'd really like to chase this rabbit hole and figure it out."

Kenden smiled. "Then I have no doubt you'll find it, Randi. When you're determined, nothing will get in your way."

Miranda nodded, running her hand along the cold wall. After a moment, Kenden said, "We could always check the abandoned soothsayer chamber at Restia. Tatiana didn't specify which compound, did she?"

"No, but that chamber was much smaller and only held copies of the most significant main scrolls in case something happened to this chamber. This is where the goods were kept."

"I vaguely remember the head soothsayer at Restia. He was young and quite zealous about his role in preserving our history. Sadly, he passed in the Awakening, but I remember his fervor for maintaining the soothsayer chamber there." Shrugging, he said, "I mean, it's worth a shot."

Miranda pursed her lips. "Okay. Want to come with me?"

"Sure. I'm up for an adventure. I'll drive us in a four-wheeler."

They set out through the open fields, catching up on their families and the state of the kingdom. Kenden and Latimus had been exhaustively rebuilding the army, and Evie and Larkin had been leading missions to far reaches of the realm in search of caves or natural structures where Bakari and his team of escaped prisoners and associates were hiding. So far, they'd found nothing. Perhaps the Secret Society had created a cloaking spell to hide their location from the naked eye. Perhaps they were in an uncharted part of the kingdom near the Purges of Methesda. Regardless, the immortal world was now on alert and involved in a conflict with unpredictable foes. Miranda was determined to keep her people safe and unharmed.

"Sadie informed me there haven't been any new cases of chemical poisoning in three weeks," Miranda said. "What do you think Bakari is waiting for?"

"I can't say for certain, but he's now got a battalion of soldiers as well as chemical weapons and magical powers. If it were me, I'd study the enemy and remain patient until I figured out the most effective ways to attack. He's most likely building his army, perhaps even cloning more."

"We have to find him, Ken. We can't let that happen."

"I know," Kenden said, squeezing her hand atop the leather seat. "Latimus and I will be done with the current round of training next week, and we're going to join the search. Jack is going to lead the next training round, and I'm confident he'll do a great job. Darkrip has offered to help, but he's stretched thin now Creigen's here. Evie has been relentless in tracking the unmapped land at the outer stretches of the kingdom, although I'm worried she's putting herself in danger."

"Evie's the toughest amongst us all," Miranda said, wanting to assure him. "She'll be fine."

"I hope so."

"You're going to be a father," she said, thrilled for her cousin. "I'm so happy for you, Ken."

His lips curved as he gave her a loving grin. "Remember when it was just you and me all those years ago? Things have changed so much."

"But you're still my ride or die, Ken."

"You're still mine too, even if you continue to listen to that human heavy metal garbage."

"Shut up," she said, swatting his arm. "You *will* come to appreciate Metallica one day. When that day comes, I'm going to do a freaking dance of joy. Just you wait."

Kenden pulled up to a sloping green-thatched hill housing a wooden door. Hopping from the vehicle, Miranda pulled the key she kept in her safe at Uteria, inserted it and turned the lock. The door clicked open, and Kenden illuminated his flashlight so they could step inside.

"Yuck," Miranda said, fanning her hand in front of her face. "It's so musty in here."

"I don't think anyone's been in here for centuries," Kenden said, slowly illuminating the chamber with the flashlight. Scrolls aligned the dusty tables and shelves that permeated the room. Clicking her phone, Miranda turned on the flashlight app.

"Wow," she said, fingers trailing over the felt that housed some of the scrolls on the center table. "These are ancient." Setting her phone down, she began to extricate some of the parchments from the felt bags.

They poured over them for half an hour, reading about the history of Etherya's Earth and the goddess's two beloved species. After categorizing them more efficiently in the chamber, Miranda began examining the far wall.

"I don't see any loose stones," she said, running her palm over the smooth surface.

"Me neither," Kenden said, crouching to examine the lower part of the structure.

Suddenly, Miranda gasped. "This one's loose!"

Kenden stood, grabbing the brick and helping her jerk it back and forth. Suddenly, it popped free and dropped to the ground. Eyes wide, Miranda grabbed Kenden's flashlight and shone it through the small hole.

"Holy shit," she breathed, maneuvering the flashlight. "There's a whole room filled with more scrolls."

Kenden's eyebrows narrowed. "There was only supposed to be one soothsayer chamber room at each compound."

"Well, someone built another one, and it looks like they went out of their way to keep it secret. I'll bet there's a hidden one at Uteria too."

"Damn," Kenden said, grasping onto one of the bricks by the hole. "Let's see if we can make a big enough opening to crawl through."

After grabbing some tools from the four-wheeler, they began to demolish the wall. Finally, they created an opening large enough to squeeze through.

Miranda began opening the parchments, careful not to damage them. Her heart began to pound as she realized their significance. "They all have 'Hidden Prophecy' in their titles. Like this one," she said, showing it to him and reading aloud.

Addition to the Restian Hidden Prophecy Soothsayer Scrolls by Ethu, the Youngest Soothsayer.
Enclosed, please find the hidden prophecy of the Vampyre Prince Bakari. The Eldest Soothsayer did not sanction this scroll as he will not sanction my others. He does not concur with my choice to keep a separate secret archive, but I believe our children will need to know the history of the realm, even the history others deem too dangerous or insignificant. If the scrolls at Uteria are destroyed, my hope is that these scrolls will preserve our chronicles. If I am punished for my deeds, I will consider it a worthy retribution.
Peace be to all of Etherya's creatures."

"Well," Miranda said, arching a sardonic brow, "guess somebody tried to tell us about Bakari after all."

Kenden scanned the scrolls, awe in his features. "How many more warnings are in these hidden prophecies? My god, Miranda, we could have so many enemies we know nothing about."

Inhaling a deep breath, she nodded. "Let's get to cataloguing them. The more we know, the better."

They collected the scrolls with care, wanting to preserve the withered parchments so they could analyze them at Uteria. When they'd almost finished gathering them, she lifted a scroll that had a strange symbol on it.

"Have you ever seen this mark?" she asked.

"No. It doesn't look like any of Etherya's creatures' written languages."

"I want to open it."

Kenden nodded. "Gently."

With careful movements, she broke the wax seal and unrolled the paper. Reading aloud, her tone became more concerned as she advanced.

Addition to the Restian Hidden Prophecy Soothsayer Scrolls by Ethu, the Youngest Soothsayer.
Be it known that the Elves have all but perished from the land. They were not Etherya's creatures, and we did not revere them, but they were a simple people, and we wished them no harm. Our magnificent King Valktor visited their realm, hoping to abet them, but it was too late. He returned with their prophecy scrolls, which we have catalogued.
The Eldest Soothsayer deemed some of the prophecies impossible, and they were discarded, but I believe all divinations must be catalogued for historical purposes. Below, you will find the hidden Elven prophecies, listed in the order I deem most important.
Peace be to all of Etherya's creatures.

Elven Prophecy #1
A lone Elf will survive our kingdom's destruction. He will evolve into a powerful being, castigated by the goddess Etherya. Embroiled in his hate, he will spawn children upon the Earth who will cause great devastation. The firstborn spawn of his firstborn spawn will align with the marked Vampyre prince to destroy Etherya's realm as we know it, and it will exist no more..."

Swallowing thickly, Miranda gazed up at Kenden. "The firstborn spawn of Crimeous's firstborn spawn," she said softly.

"Callie," he murmured.

Miranda nodded. "We have to show this to Darkrip as soon as possible."

Kenden nodded, his expression pensive. "Come on. Let's get everything in the four-wheeler and head to Uteria. There's so much to categorize, and this might only be the beginning."

Consumed with a latent foreboding, they collected the secret prophecies, intent on identifying the new threats they most assuredly held.

Chapter 38

Heden sat at the Bourbon Street coffee shop attempting to focus on his research. Difficult, since his eyes kept darting to the door every five seconds. He hoped the handwritten note he'd left on Tatiana's door would implore her to show. Nervous, he tapped on the keypad, awaiting her arrival.

The bell above the door rang, and she breezed in, the airy skirt of her long dress flowing behind her. Her smile was kind as she approached the table. "May I?" she asked, gesturing to the vacant seat across from him.

Nodding, he rubbed his damp palms on his thighs. "I wasn't sure you'd show. I stopped by your house multiple times before I realized you weren't really living there anymore."

"I've been spending time at some other places I enjoy upon the Earth. But your note did intrigue me."

The server came over, and Tatiana ordered an herbal tea before continuing. "So, you didn't return to the immortal world after leaving Italy?"

He shook his head. "I figured it was worth a shot to see if you could use your super-potion powers to create something that could turn Sofia immortal and allow us to have biological children together." Breathing a laugh, he ran his fingers through his hair. "When I say it out loud, it sounds insane."

Tatiana slowly stirred the steaming liquid the waitress set in front of her with the tiny metal spoon that accompanied it. "You both had a magnificent goodbye. Is that not enough?"

"I said goodbye because our relationship in our current form won't make either of us happy. It took me a while to get that, but I get it now. Even with that knowledge, I'm determined to figure out another way."

Amber irises studied him as she blew steam from the tea. "And what makes you think I know of another way?"

"The conversation we had in the in-between. You seemed to indicate there was hope."

Her eyes narrowed. "Hope for happiness between a mortal and an immortal is futile."

"I know," he said, running a frustrated hand over his face. "I was hoping you have some potion or knowledge to help me figure out how to grant Sofia immortality."

Setting the cup in the saucer, she slid a hand over his wrist. "I'm so very sorry, son of Markdor. Truly, I am. Your love for her is palpable. There is only one on the planet who can grant immortality."

"Etherya," he said, clenching his jaw.

"Yes."

"I've prayed and pleaded to her so many times, but she won't appear to me. She finally appeared to Sathan and told him she won't even consider it."

"The Universe was extremely displeased with her when she granted Nolan immortality. I understand her decision."

Defeated, Heden sat back in his chair. "I've researched every human library and every archive and soothsayer manual in the immortal world. I just don't know what to do, Tatiana. How can I give up?"

Her lips compressed as she looked out the window, contemplative and pensive. Finally, she trained her gaze upon him. "Although time is your enemy, I think you must take some. Time to think. Time to truly process your emotions and the gravity of the choices you face. Only then will you find the remote possibility of a solution."

"So, you think there's hope? I'm so afraid of losing faith, Tatiana."

"There is a beauty in your love. Both of you were two solo puzzle pieces searching to be whole. You're extremely close to locking in place, but like any puzzle, if the edges are bent, the pieces remain unconnected."

"Wow," he said, rubbing his beard. "I need to write this stuff down. Your riddles are insane, lady."

Her rich laughter washed over them, and she sipped the last of her tea before standing. "Take some time, Heden. You will know how much you need. I truly wish for all your dreams to come true. Until we meet again, know that I am sending you positive vibes through the ether." Giving him a nod, she exited the shop, the bell ringing solemnly behind her.

Frustrated and sad he still had no discernable solution, Heden packed up his laptop and headed back to the immortal world.

Several weeks later...

Heden gritted his teeth, punching the hanging bag with his bare fists. Sweat dripped down his brow as he unleashed every unwanted emotion on the lifeless target. He'd been frequenting the gym at Astaria often since his return from the human world, hoping the uptick in energy would help spur his brain into solving the conundrum of building a sustainable life with Sofia.

So far, no such luck.

Latimus stalked in, his face an unreadable mask as usual. Normally, Heden would make fun of him for his perma-scowl, but he just didn't feel like jibing with him today. Or any day, really. He'd become so sullen and withdrawn since his return, he knew his family was worried. Unfortunately, he just couldn't seem to shake the funk.

"How was your visit to the Slayer military hospital?" Heden asked.

"Fine," Latimus said, although frustration emanated from his massive frame. "This new batch of chemicals has a twenty-five percent mortality rate in Slayers. Bakari's becoming more effective even with the program you and Sofia created."

"Damn," Heden said, sighing. "I can try to make some tweaks, but I'm pretty sure the software is already functioning at its highest capacity."

"I'll let you know if we need you to reconfigure anything. For now, we're on top of it." Latimus grabbed the punching bag. "Throw some stationary punches. I'll hold it steady."

Complying, Heden began a series of rapid-fire jabs, the resulting pain upon his knuckles a welcome distraction from his completely fragmented heart. After a few minutes, he began to wheeze.

"All right," Latimus said in his deep baritone. "That's enough. Take a break. Here." His brother thrust a canister at him.

"Thanks," Heden said, gulping the water as if his life depended on it. "Whew, that's good." He wiped his brow with his forearm.

Latimus crossed his arms and regarded him, foot tapping on the blue mat. "You look like shit, Heden."

A laugh escaped his throat. "Thanks, bro. You're pretty fucking hideous too."

Latimus scowled. "I mean it. You must've lost twenty pounds since you returned from the human world. You're chiseled because you spend hours in here every day, but you still look thin."

"Sadie said I might have some lingering health effects from my wound. If I keep working out, I'll be fine."

"It's not from your injury, and we both know it."

Sighing, Heden sat on the nearby workout bench. "What do you want me to say, Latimus? That I miss her? That I'm a fucking shell of a person without her? Even if it's true, I just can't figure out how to change our impossible situation."

His brother stood stoic, the mindless tapping of his foot driving Heden insane. "Dude, if you're just going to stare at me all day, I'm out."

Latimus's eyes narrowed. "I'm just remembering a conversation we had many years ago, when I was distraught after Lila's maiming. I was so sure there was no way we could be together. There were so many obstacles in our way. But you convinced me anything was possible if I wanted badly enough to make it happen."

"That was true," Heden said, shrugging. "You guys certainly had some struggles, but there was always a way forward if you fought hard enough. I'm glad you figured it out."

"I'm wondering why the same doesn't hold true for you."

"Um, because I'm immortal, and Sofia is human. A future together is impossible for us. Every scenario we imagined is ultimately filled with so much heartache and pain. Until I can find a way around that, we just can't be together, Latimus. It breaks my heart, but I won't put Sofia through that. I can't put either of us through that. It's just fucking awful."

Latimus stood firm, contemplating.

"Dude, you're annoying the hell out of me."

"If I recall," Latimus said, eyes searching the ceiling as he placed his hands on his hips, "you said something to the effect of 'If I ever meet someone for whom I feel half the emotion you and Lila feel for each other, I'll never let her go.'" Piercing him with his gaze, he asked, "I think that was it, right?"

"Yes, but our situation is different—"

"Bullshit," Latimus interrupted. "I don't think it's different at all."

Heden scoffed. "Okay, awesome. Tell me how in the hell I'm supposed to build a life with a mortal. Can't wait to hear it."

His brother shook his head, disappointment in his eyes. "You've always been afraid of committing one hundred percent, Heden. For the goddess's sake, I think you seduced over half the women in the kingdom. To what end? What was the purpose? It's time for you to truly commit to something. It's going to require sacrifice and hard choices. That's what people do when they love each other. They throw it all on the line and never accept defeat."

Heden stood, palms exposed as he slashed his hands in frustration. "I've made a thousand hard choices—"

"No, you haven't," Latimus said, stepping forward. "You're amazing at helping us with the weapons and the tech, but that's easy for you, Heden. Finding a way to be with Sofia is going to be extremely difficult. It's time you put that brain of yours to good use and figure out a way to make sacrifices to be with her."

"Sacrifices? I'd make a million sacrifices to be with her if I could."

"How? What methods have you truly employed?"

"I prayed to Etherya a thousand times, asking her to bestow immortality on Sofia. When she finally appeared to Sathan, she basically told him to tell me to fuck off. I approached Tatiana, and she just spouted her usual riddles, so that didn't help. I researched every immortal archive and human library I could. I'm not sure what else you want me to do here, bro."

"So that's it?" Latimus said, lifting his hands. "A few prayers, some rejections, some research and you're done? If someone told me I'd have to live without Lila for an eternity, I'd blaze the damn planet until I found a way to be with her."

Heden opened his mouth to speak and promptly closed it. What was he missing? Was there something else he could've tried? Tatiana had told him to take time to digest things, but he'd come up with absolute shit. Maybe there was still something he hadn't considered...

"Now you're getting it," Latimus said. "Finding a way to be with Sofia is going to be *hard*, Heden. You want to sit around and mope all day? Fine with me. But I have a feeling you'd rather discern a way to be with the love of your damn life. So, figure it out. We live in a world of magical creatures and potions that can bring people back to life, for the goddess's sake. There has to be a way you can figure out how to live with a mortal."

Heden's eyebrows drew together as he contemplated.

"You always tell me how damn brilliant you are. Use your intellect and find a solution."

"Damn it," Heden said, lowering back to the bench. Gripping the sides, he clenched his fists. "I have no idea what else I can do."

"Did you talk to Evie? She shares Etherya's blood. Maybe she can help you."

Heden nodded. "Yeah, but that was before I did the bulk of my research. I learned a lot about human rituals from lots of different cultures. There are some really fascinating stories of otherworldly things that happen over there. I wouldn't be surprised if there were more immortals who have frequented the human realm over the centuries than we even know."

Latimus's lips drew into a thin line as he contemplated. "Maybe Evie could use her powers along with some ancient human spell or something to try and bestow immortality on Sofia. I don't know, Heden, but I think you're giving up too easily."

Feeling his heartbeat accelerate as numerous possibilities began to filter through his mind, Heden stood and approached his brother. Grabbing Latimus's face, he tried to place a walloping smack on his forehead. Latimus shoved him away, causing Heden to laugh.

"Damn, Latimus, I really needed that kick in the ass," he said, smiling for the first time in the goddess knows how long. "It's nice to see your surly personality put to good use. Now, tell me I'm your favorite brother and that you love me."

"Get the hell out of here so you can figure out a way to bond with the human and leave me alone."

"Oh, I'm going to figure it out," Heden said, excitement coursing through his veins as he gathered his sweat-soaked towel and slung it around his neck. Trailing to the door, he continued. "And then I'm going to bond with Sofia, and we're going to build a huge house right next to yours and Lila's, and you'll get to see me every second of every day. You're gonna love it!"

"I'm banning you from Lynia!" Latimus called after him.

"No way, bro! You're stuck with me."

Chuckling as he trekked to his chambers, he swore his heard his brother mutter a curse before he was out of earshot.

Heden recommitted himself to the task of finding some way, any way, to create a sustainable future with Sofia. The next day, he approached Evie armed with the knowledge he'd gained from months of meticulous research. Although she was sympathetic to his cause, she was adamant no amount of effort would allow her to bestow immortality upon Sofia. Even with her potency, there was no entity besides Etherya who had the capacity to render someone immortal.

"Are you absolutely sure?" he asked as they sat in front of her mahogany desk at Takelia.

"I share Etherya's blood, and that gives me a certain...*insight* into her powers," Evie said. "You can choose to believe me or not but trust me when I say, Etherya is the only one on the planet powerful enough to manipulate mortality or immortality."

Heden sighed and ran his hand through his hair, frustrated at his inability to elucidate the situation. He had always been able to find a solution to even the most indiscernible problem, and his inability to build a sustainable future for him and Sofia was maddening.

Evie encircled his wrist, squeezing as empathy welled in her green eyes. "You're trying so hard, but sometimes, you just need to take the simplest path."

His eyes darted between hers. "I'm open to suggestions."

"I *feel* your love for her, Heden. It's amazing. I think you need to speak to Etherya directly. I think she'll be swayed by the sentiment in your heart."

"I called upon her so many times, Evie," he said, shrugging. "She wouldn't appear to me. And when she finally spoke to Sathan, she was clear it was a no-go."

Evie grinned. "My advice? Try again. And don't stop trying until she appears to you. I mean, what the hell have you got to lose? And lord knows, you've got nothing but time."

Heden bit his lip. "Are you telling me to piss off the goddess who can decimate me with a snap of her fingers?"

Her scarlet eyebrow arched. "I think that's exactly what I'm telling you. She'll either grant your request or disintegrate you on the spot for driving her insane. Either way, you'll get a dramatic conclusion."

Laughing, Heden stood and embraced her. "Okay, I'm down. But remember to hide my porn if she murders me. I'll text you a picture of my stash so you know where I keep it."

"Ohhhh," Evie said, pulling back and waggling her brows. "I'll put it to good use." Cupping his jaw, she smiled reverently. "I wish you luck, my friend. You and Sofia deserve all the happiness in the world."

Since Evie was one of the most omniscient people he knew, he chose to heed her advice and forged ahead. That evening and each night after, he trekked to the river, standing upon the spot where he knew the goddess spoke to Sathan. For hours, he would call to Etherya, begging her to appear, to no avail. Undeterred, he continued the ritual, firm in his belief if he summoned her long enough, she would surface. As Evie had pointed out, he had nothing if not time.

One night, as the gurgling river kept him company, Heden sat on the soft grass, silently praying to the goddess, begging her to materialize. So far, hours had ticked by, and his pleas had gone unanswered. Unwavering in his palpable desire to build a life with his beloved, he sat patiently, eyes closed as his fingers twined together.

Suddenly, a rustling sounded to his right, and he lurched to his feet, hoping this would be the night she finally emerged. Bright light materialized from nothingness until her image appeared, floating and airy. Long, blood-red curls flowed down her back above her white, ethereal dress.

"Hello, son of Markdor," she said, the anger in her tone sending a jolt of fear down his spine. "I have heard your pleas, and they disturb my peace immensely. I implore you to stop your prayers. They are wasted and fruitless."

"My goddess," he said, bowing on one knee. "I am honored with your presence."

"Rise and tell me why you insist on pleading for something you know I will never grant."

Standing to his full height, he contemplated his words, wanting to make sure his appeal was seamless so it enhanced her chances of changing her mind. "My goddess Etherya, you must be able to sense I love the human with my entire soul. I beg you to take pity on us and grant us the ability to have a future."

The goddess's eyes narrowed. "Sofia Morelli is destined to remain human, and this cannot be changed. I find your entreaty a nuisance."

Licking his dry lips, he forged ahead. "I understand you made the human physician Nolan immortal. Why can you not bestow the same gift on Sofia?"

The goddess's beady eyes bore into him, her figure floating above the grass. "Nolan acted honorably when he followed King Sathan through the ether in an attempt to save him. I conferred immortality on him in return for his deeds."

"Sofia has done so much to help our kingdom, Goddess," he pleaded. "To help your people and mine." He detailed all Sofia's efforts, making his case for her worthiness. Once finished, he asked, "Knowing all that, doesn't she deserve immortality?"

Etherya blinked, slow and thoughtful, the silence threating to choke him. Then, she opened her mouth and said firmly, "No."

Heden's heart lurched to his knees. "No? How can you say that, Etherya? I can't think of anyone who deserves immortality more."

"Quiet!" she said, slicing her hand through the air. "Do not anger me, son of Markdor, or I will vanish and leave you to your heartache."

"I'm sorry, Goddess," he said, bowing his head in contrition. "I just want so badly to build a life with her. She's...the love of my life."

He thought the goddess might have sighed. "The Universe was displeased when I bestowed immortality upon Nolan. It was a rash decision but one I do not regret. Unfortunately, an imbalance was created when I granted him immortality. I do not want to displease the Universe further."

Heden stayed silent, wracking his brain for stronger arguments he could make to change her mind.

"But my heart is intrigued by your persistence. You must truly love the human to beg so passionately."

"I do, Goddess. With all my heart."

Silence stretched as she studied him. "Then, perhaps you could help me."

"Help you?" he said, lifting his gaze to hers.

"Yes," she said with a nod. "Help me restore balance and relieve the Universe's displeasure."

Heden's irises darted between hers. "How?"

Lifting her chin, she said, "You could choose to become human."

Heden's eyelids fluttered in quick succession, unsure he'd heard her correctly. "Become human?"

"Yes. I would extricate your immortality and render you human. You would function as a human, requiring food and water, and would eventually die as all humans do."

A thousand emotions ran through Heden's body as he deliberated. Locking his gaze with hers, he asked, "Would I be able to have human children?"

"Yes." She tilted her head. "You would be able to impregnate human females. You would be human in every sense of the word. Your body would resume aging from the day you went through your immortal change and advance in years until its eventual end."

Running his fingers through his thick hair, Heden struggled to catch his breath. The possibility was overwhelming.

"I will give you one day to consider. It is a formidable task for me to undertake, but I will do it to rebalance the Universe and to thank you for your efforts across the kingdom. You have done much to help my people. If you wish to accept my offer, meet me here tomorrow under the waxing moon. I will not make this proffer again. Choose wisely, Heden, son of Markdor." Lifting her hands, palms facing the sky, she closed her eyes and vanished.

Heden expelled a huge breath through puffed cheeks, the gravity of the choice before him enormous. Lifting his phone from his back pocket, he called Sathan.

"What's up, Heden?"

"I need to have a video call with you, Latimus and Arderin tomorrow morning. It's important."

"Are you okay?"

"Yes. I think I'm actually more okay than I've been in a long time. Can you coordinate the call? I'll need at least an hour, and I feel like everyone will take it seriously if you schedule it."

"I'll do it as soon as I hang up. Are you sure you don't need anything? Miranda and I are at Uteria, but I can come to you."

"I'm good, bro," he said, beginning his trek back to Astaria. "Actually, I'm really fucking good. Talk to you tomorrow."

Stuffing his phone in his back pocket, Heden headed toward the darkened castle, his heart so full with possibility he damn near skipped home.

Chapter 39

Sofia sat in the coffee shop, scrolling the wheel of her wireless mouse as her chin rested on her fist, elbow propped on the table. She was spending her fortieth birthday filtering through endless sperm donor profiles. *Happy birthday to me*, she sang sarcastically in her mind.

She'd put off searching for a donor after Heden left because her heart was a heap of broken mush that would most likely never recover. But time had a way of kicking your ass, and she decided she'd resume on her fortieth birthday. So, here she was, in the Italian coffee shop with great Wi-Fi and amazing cappuccino, deciding which man's sperm she wanted shoot up her vagina. *Happy birthday, indeed.*

As she continued to absently scroll, a text window suddenly popped up on her screen. Three words appeared from the blinking curser: **I see you.**

Sofia gasped, immediately searching the coffee shop. They were the first words Heden had written when he'd hacked into her laptop in L.A.

Thick heartbeats threatened to close her throat as she placed her fingers on the keyboard. **Heden?**

The curser blinked. Once. Again. Several times, driving her insane. Struggling to breathe, she waited.

Finally, a message appeared: **40.874240, 14.656890.**

"What the hell?" she murmured, struggling to decipher the numbers. Dragging the curser, she copied the digits and pasted them in the internet search bar.

"They're coordinates," she whispered, striving to understand what was happening. Plugging them into a map application, she noted the longitude and latitude coordinates corresponded to a town called Moschiano, which was about a two-hour drive away. Contemplating, she chewed her lip. What did the mysterious coordinates represent? Had Heden sent them to her?

Pulling out her phone, she dialed his number. They'd promised each other they would never make contact even in emergencies, but she didn't give a damn. Each ring of the phone frazzled her shattered nerves until his voicemail picked up.

"Of course you let it go to voicemail. Bastard." Huffing with frustration, she pondered a moment longer and then gathered her things and headed to the rental car office a few blocks away.

Several hours later, she slowly navigated a gravel driveway that opened up to an expansive property. Acres of open land stretched in the background as she pulled up to a green-shingled house. Stepping out of the car, she closed the door and approached the archway. Opening the metal gate, she stepped through, hesitant and unsure.

"Heden?" she called, tentatively walking over the flat stone patio. "Hello? Is anyone here?"

Advancing forward, she saw the edge of the balcony and approached the flat surface of the balcony's edge. Peering over it, she broke into a huge smile.

"Hey, little human," Heden said, waving up at her from the ground below. "Took you long enough. I've been waiting forever."

"Heden!" Squealing, she vaulted down the stairs and ran to him, leaping into his arms, causing him to emit an "oomph" when he caught her. Wrapping her legs around his waist, she rained kisses all over his face, his beard tickling her lips.

"Damn, Sof, you almost knocked me over. I hope that means you're happy to see me."

"You're so thin," she said, concern smothering her as she ran her hands over his shoulders. "Are you okay? Is it something from your injury?"

He smiled, his gaze reverent as it roved over her face. "I've been pretty fucked-up and haven't really been drinking a lot of Slayer blood. It's hard to nourish yourself when you're not sure how the hell you're going to make it through another day."

"Oh, Heden," she said, his face blurring from the tears in her eyes. "I missed you so much too. Can you stay for a while? Maybe I can try to fatten you up with some pasta."

His eyebrow lifted. "That statement might prove truer than you think," he murmured.

"Huh?"

He kissed her and set her gently on her feet. Reaching behind his back, he pulled a single red rose from the back pocket of his jeans. "Happy Birthday."

"Thank you," she said, taking the flower and inhaling the fragrant scent. "I think I'm supposed to be washed up now, but I feel pretty good."

His irises raked over her. "Did you move forward with a donor?"

Sighing, she shook her head. "I only started looking again today. Told myself I'd resume on my fortieth birthday. Whether I like it or not, time's a tickin'."

Extending his hand, he urged her to take it. "Walk with me."

Sliding her palm in his, she squeezed. "Did you bring me to an abandoned winery to bang me against a tree again? I'm open, but I think this place has seen better days."

Throwing back his head, he laughed, loud and deep. The sound sent thrills of pleasure through her body. Although he'd lost weight, he still towered over her and looked delicious in his jeans and black polo shirt. "I brought you here because this place is for sale."

"Okaaaay," she said, glancing up at him as they strolled between the deadened vines. "I didn't realize Vampyres were into deserted human wineries, but I've been wrong before."

"Actually, I find I'm not really invested in Vampyre interests these days. I've become much more enthralled with human interests."

"Heden," she said, stopping short and facing him. "What in the ever-loving hell are you talking about? You're not making any sense. Why are you here?"

He licked his lips, and Sofia realized he looked incredibly nervous. When he opened his mouth to speak, she thought something was different but couldn't put her finger on it.

"I finally made a choice, Sof," he said, a reverence in his tone. "A commitment that required sacrifice and deep reflection."

"Well, I'm proud of you. What was the choice?"

He struggled to speak as he pushed a strand of hair behind her ear. Licking his lips again, she noticed his teeth. "Where are your fangs?" she asked, squinting at the strange image. His incisors didn't form the points they had in the past. "Did you…shave them down?" Looking around, she felt off-balance. "Am I stuck in one of Tatiana's weird visions or something?"

He gently grasped her upper arms, rubbing them in a soothing caress. "I didn't shave them down, Sof. They disappeared."

"Disappeared," she repeated, wondering if the bizarre conversation was ever going to make sense. "When?"

"When I accepted Etherya's offer."

Blood pulsed through every vein in her body as she whispered, "What offer?"

His chest heaved with labored breaths as he beamed down at her. "Her offer to become human."

Sofia sucked in a breath, exhaling it slowly as she stared up at him. "That's impossible."

"No, little human," he said, shaking his head, "it's extremely possible and it's already been done, so I hope you still kinda like me because reversing it actually *is* impossible."

The forgotten rose slipped from her fingers as disbelief coursed through every cell in her trembling frame. Tentatively, she laid her palms against his cheeks. As wetness pervaded her eyes, she stroked his face, searching for evidence he spoke the truth.

"You're human?"

He nodded, eyes closing as he nuzzled into her hands. "God, Sofie, I missed your touch. It's amazing to feel your soft skin again."

"How did you convince her to turn you human? What does that mean? Are you mortal now?"

Lifting his lids, he placed his hand over hers upon his cheek. "Yes, sweetheart. I'm human in every way. I'm going to start aging from twenty-eight and advance just like you."

Puffs of air jetted from her lungs as her chin trembled. "Does that mean you can give me babies?"

"As many as you want, Sof," he said, elation encompassing his every feature. "I mean, within reason. I just came around to the notion of this whole wife and kids thing, so let's not go overboard."

Giving a jubilant laugh, she gazed at him with wonder. "But what about your family? How could they agree to this?"

"I love them so much, Sof, but they have families of their own now. Something they've created that's so magnificent for each of them. I want to create that with you."

Overwhelmed by how much he'd given up so he could build something with her, the tears that had been threatening to fall slid down her cheeks. "Heden, how could you do this? It's such a huge sacrifice. You're forfeiting eternity to be with me for less than a century in the best of scenarios."

"I'm relinquishing an infinity of loneliness to spend a lifetime with you. There's no contest, honey. I'd choose that option every day and twice on Sunday."

"I can't even imagine how you made this decision," she said, caressing his face. "It's such a gift."

"You know what's awesome? I've got a lifetime to make you understand how simple it was to make this choice. Nothing has ever felt truer than deciding to spend the rest of my life with you, Sof."

"Come here," she cried, pulling him close and devouring his lips, lost in the splendor of his astonishing decision. Their tongues slid over each other, familiar and passionate, until she thought her knees might buckle. "I'm so humbled by you," she whispered, brushing his lips with hers. "I don't even know how to begin to thank you. My god, Heden. We're going to have a future together. It's amazing. I'm overwhelmed."

"I mean, we could still bang against one of the trees," he said, jerking his head toward the nearby forest. "You kinda owe me one here."

Her laughter erupted over the sloping hills as she held him close. "I'll bang you anywhere. Everywhere. If that's what I have to do to even this out, I'm in." Caressing his cheek, she said, "I love you so much."

"I love you too," he said, placing his forehead against hers. "And I can't wait to build our life together. It's going to be fucking awesome, Sof."

"Does this winery have something to do with it?"

Lifting his head, he gazed over the withered vines. "It's just a thought, but I know you love to make wine, and you're great at it. Also, you're loaded, and I have no money except Vampyre lira, which is only good in the immortal world. I thought we could maybe buy this place and spruce it up and bring it into the twenty-first century. We could create the first virtual winery, where people could see 3D renderings of each glass on an app and order various tastes or quantities. I don't know, I'm spitballing here."

"I love it," she said, wheels already churning in her mind. "And we could create a rewards system through the app where they accrue points to win trips to visit the winery. And we could develop a virtual hub where people can log on from across the world and drink wine together while connecting online."

"Like Facebook for wine."

"Exactly."

"Damn, that's a great idea. Let's look around. I want to see the whole property. The owner lives a few miles away and said we could have free rein of the place."

"Does that include the woods over there?"

"Sofia," he said, his grin so sexy she felt a rush of moisture between her thighs. "You've brought this up a few times now. If you want to ravish my body, you have to ask me nicely."

Standing on her tiptoes, she softly pecked his lips. "Heden, will you please let me ravish your body?"

Reaching down, he grabbed her hips, lifting her over his shoulder as he proceeded to march toward the forest. "Little human, I thought you'd never ask."

Her blissful giggles radiated across the gentle slopes and rows of vines as her beloved granted her request.

Epilogue

Four years later...

Heden heard the euphoric sounds of children playing as soon as he stepped onto the soft grass. Trailing through the vines, thick with ripe grapes, he broke into a huge grin as the little girl ran toward him.

"Papa!" she said, arms outstretched as love washed over his skin. Crouching down, he picked her up and balanced her on his hip, pretending to eat her ear.

"Yum! An ear all for me. It's so scrumptious."

Her high-pitched giggles expanded his heart so much he thought it might burst. "You can't eat my ear. Ew!"

"Sure can. Just you wait. Were you a good girl for Mama?"

"She was a really good girl," Sofia said, walking toward them, their son perched on her own hip. "Bianca is a big girl now, and I'm so proud of her."

"I'm big too," Francesco said, his tiny lips forming a pout.

"You're big too, Frankie," Heden said, leaning over to kiss his cheek and then Sofia's lips. "Hey, honey."

"How was the drive back from Rome?"

"Not bad. I only sped a little," he said, winking. "After two days with stuffy investors, I was ready to get home."

"I'm so excited the venture capitalists love our virtual wine club idea," she said, excitement lacing her stunning features. "I can't believe we're fully funded for launch. Great job with the meetings. Wish we could've gone with you, but it would've been too much. Someone had to take care of the wonder twins here."

"Thanks for taking one for the team. I definitely owe you unlimited babysitting breaks for a month. And maybe unlimited banging breaks too."

"What's banging?" Bianca asked.

"That's when you hit something hard, like a wall or a tree," Sofia said, shooting Heden a stern glare.

"Really hard," Heden said, waggling his brows. "And over and over—"

"Okay, Papa's really tired and needs to stop talking right now. Good thing Mama made some pasta. Who's hungry?"

The twins cheered as their parents set them on the ground and ran to the house, breaking into a sprint to see who was faster.

Closing her eyes, Sofia sighed. "I'm exhausted."

Chuckling, he pulled her into a warm embrace. "They have way too much energy, that's for damn sure." Palming her cheeks, he stared into her blue-green eyes. "I missed you, Sofie. Damn, you look so pretty right now. Even with dried food on your shirt," he finished, snickering.

Her features scrunched. "I think there's a compliment in there somewhere?"

Laughing, he consumed her lips in a passionate kiss. Resting his forehead on hers, he said, "I picked up the new virtual reality game with the awesome reviews. I thought we could play it once the kids are asleep. Naked, of course."

"Mmmm..." she said, arms squeezing around his neck. "That sounds naughty. I'm so in."

Brushing one more sweet kiss over her lips, he straightened and threaded his fingers through hers. Together, they strode to the home they'd built under the glow of the late afternoon sun.

"Miranda called today," Sofia said. "Everything's set for Tordor's birthday party at Uteria next weekend. I told her I'd help cook, but she said Glarys and Jana have it covered."

"I can't wait to see everyone. We haven't been there since Christmas."

"It's so awesome of your family to celebrate Christmas with me even if they don't believe."

"You're family now, honey. It's an important holiday for you, and it's really fun to celebrate because it brings everyone together."

"Maybe we can have everyone come here next Christmas. I'd love to decorate the house and get a tree and host."

"Let's bring it up at Tordor's party. I'm sure they'd love that. Did Miranda have any updates on Bakari when you spoke?"

Sofia shook her head. "After the last attack three months ago, he's been quiet. Latimus estimated he lost a hundred Deamon soldiers in that attack, so Miranda thinks he's cloning more. They still have no idea where he's hiding. She thinks it's in the immortal world, but he could also have a base here. It's terrifying," she said, worry crossing her features as she glanced toward their children in the distance.

"I've got you, sweetheart," he said, clenching her hand, his tone reassuring. "I have the utmost faith in Latimus and Ken. They'll be ready for the next attack. And we're armed here with weapons and the kick-ass security system we programmed. We're smarter than the Secret Society. I won't let anything happen to our family."

Their children called to them, beckoning them inside, and Sofia clutched his hand. Gazing up at him, she whispered, "Thank you. For loving me and protecting us and for our babies. I love you all so much."

Turning to face her, he tucked a black curl behind her ear. "Thanks for being a terrible hacker. Otherwise, I never would've had to correct all your work, and we never would've fallen in love."

Chuckling, she shook her head. "You're still jealous I'm better than you. When will you let it go? Just accept it, buddy."

"Give me a few decades. Maybe I'll get over it then."

"That I can do," she said, tugging him toward the house. "If we're lucky, I can give you many more decades."

"I think we're pretty damn lucky, Sof, so I like our chances."

Full lips curved into a poignant smile, she whispered, "So do I."

Rejoining their children, they headed inside to enjoy the magnificently mundane task of eating family dinner.

Acknowledgments

Thanks so much to everyone who's waited *almost* a year for this book! I felt it was important to take some time and launch a new series to keep things fresh. Although I love writing my new books, Etherya's world and the complex, funny, amazing characters who inhabit it will always be my first love because it was, well, first! Rest assured I'm not done with this world and will keep writing books for our amazing immortals (and humans!) until the stories no longer appear in my head. Can you guess which characters are next? I planted a few very vague seeds in this book, but you'll have to wait to see! I hope to publish at least one Etherya's Earth book per year (more if they flow faster) along with the new series that I'm currently writing (and some that only exist in my head right now!). Thank you all for being on this journey with me, and I'll see you in the next book.

Special thanks to Sharan D. for her unwavering support. She's always one of the first to read my books and leave a review, and I think I forgot to mention her in the acknowledgments of my last book, which was a huge oversight. You're awesome, friend. Thank you!

Thanks to Jaime who let me use her awesome line about hiding the porn. Ha! It was a perfect line for our sexy jokester, Heden, and you did him justice!

And thanks to all of you who read these books and get lost in these worlds with me. You'll never know how much it means to have you along for the ride. Until next time, stay well and don't forget to seize your dreams!

The Cryptic Prophecy

Etherya's Earth, Book 6

By

REBECCA HEFNER

This book is a work of fiction. Names, characters, places and incidents are the product of the author's imagination and are used fictitiously. Any resemblance to actual events, locales or persons, living or dead, is coincidental.

Copyright © 2021 by Rebecca Hefner. All rights reserved, including the right to reproduce, distribute or transmit in any form or by any means.

Cover Design: Author CD Gorri
Editor: Megan McKeever
Proofreader: Bryony Leah

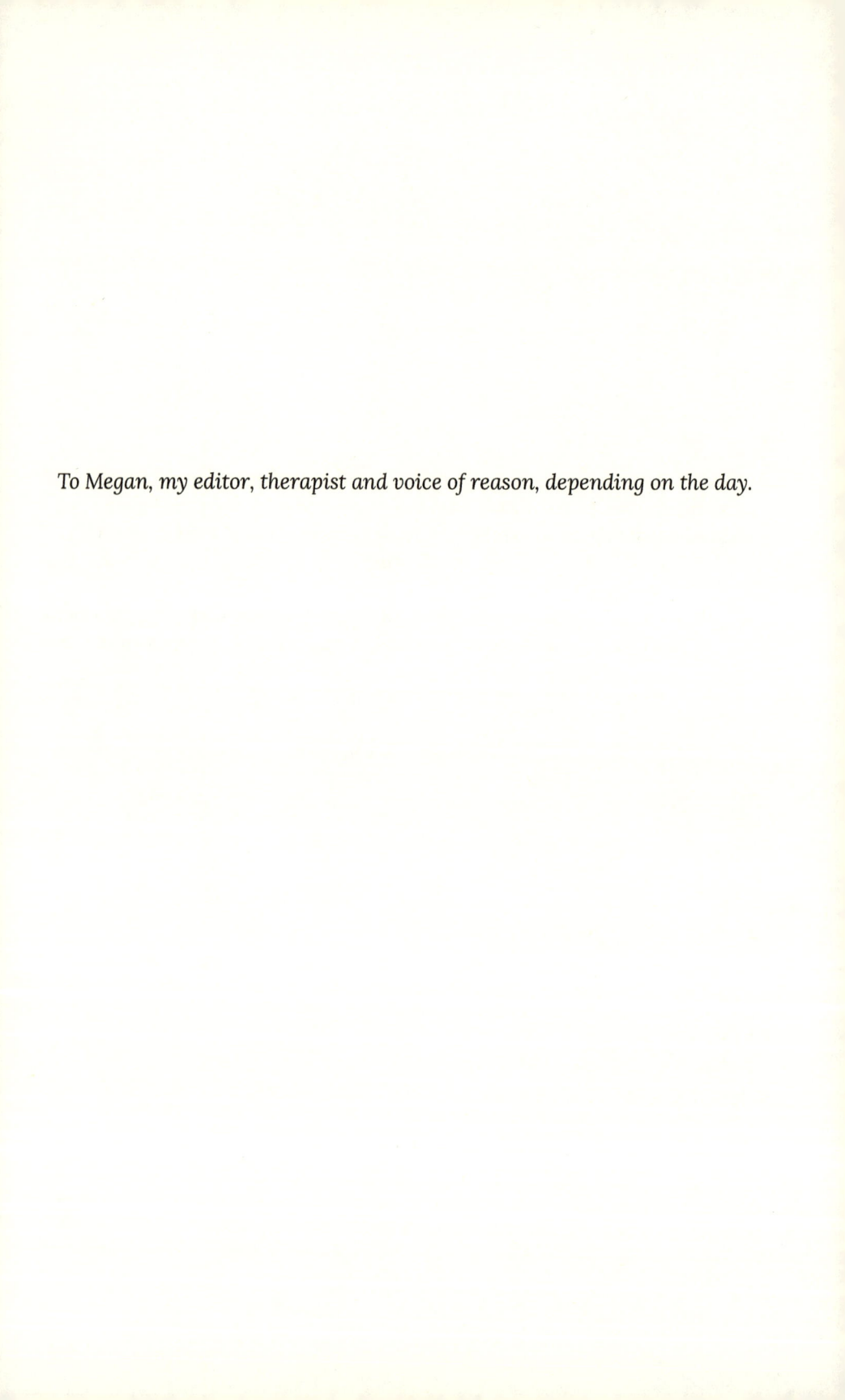

To Megan, my editor, therapist and voice of reason, depending on the day.

A Note from the Author

Hello, awesome readers of Etherya's Earth. I am so happy to begin this new phase of the series. If you're anything like me, you enjoy series where several couples fall in love and their children grow up to get their own love stories as the series progresses. The Cryptic Prophecy is the first book in the second generation of Etherya's Earth where we'll see the children of Miranda, Latimus, Darkrip and Evie fall in love, and I can't wait to bring them to you.

For now, enjoy Callie and Brecken's story as our beloved immortals chart a new path that will change their world forever. These two had some explosive chemistry, and Brecken ended up being really hot *and* romantic, which was perfect for our kind, sassy Callie. Also, Darkrip turned out to be slightly overprotective, which was so fun to write and had me snickering along the way. Happy reading, and thank you for taking the journey with me and the people who live in my head!

An excerpt from the diary of Calinda, daughter of Darkrip and Arderin

Dear Diary,

    I'm writing to you from L.A. for one of the last times ever. Today, Mommy and Daddy told me we were moving back to the immortal world so we could be close to our family. Now that Mommy is a doctor, she wants to help people in our kingdom when they're sick. I'm proud of her, but it makes me sad because I really like it here.

    Mommy says I'll make friends in no time, but I'm not so sure. In the human world, I have to hide my powers, but she says everyone will know about them in the immortal world. She and Daddy say I'm special, but I'm worried having powers will make the other kids think I'm weird.

    Tomorrow is my seventh birthday, so I'll be enrolling in second grade at Takelia when we move. Daddy has been named Ambassador by Uncle Sathan and Aunt Miranda, so he's going to help make sure the compounds keep getting along. Mommy said it was the perfect job for him before she giggled, and then Daddy gave her a weird look where his face scrunched up. They're funny when they look at each other that way, and then Daddy always whispers he'll get her back once they go to bed. I don't understand how you can do anything when you're sleeping, but whatever.

    Anyway, I'll keep you updated on how school goes. Hope it isn't awful. Wish me luck!

Love, Callie

Chapter 1

The Vampyre compound of Valeria, seventeen years after Heden married Sofia

Brecken, son of Maddox, would never forget the day his life changed forever. His boss—well, technically his boss's son, Zadicus—called him over with an absent hooking of his fingers as he stood by the window in the sitting room of his expansive mansion at Valeria.

"Come, Brecken," he said, eyes narrowing as he gazed out at the manicured lawn. "I have a question for you."

Brecken approached, only slightly gritting his teeth at the command. He wasn't a fan of Raoul's son, but he needed the income his job as bodyguard provided, so he put up with Zadicus's arrogance and dismissive attitude. Many aristocrats still treated laborers and soldiers as "beneath" them, although King Sathan and Queen Miranda discouraged it.

"Yes?" Brecken said, placing his crossed hands on the buckle of his belt as he stood in a wide-legged stance, waiting. He was a few inches taller than Zadicus, which brought him great pleasure for some reason. Perhaps it was because he knew he could kick the haughty prick's ass. Not only because of his size, but because he thought Zadicus rather soft. Of course, if ever accused of it, his ward would scoff and assert his dominance over all the other aristocrats he defeated in his weekly boxing matches.

It might be a good defense to some, but Brecken understood the matches were carefully planned in plushy-floored boxing rings with felt-covered ropes. Much different than the dirty fields where he'd scraped and clawed his way to becoming a formidable soldier. Brecken had worked hard to tone his body and his mind, and his commanding officers took notice.

When Raoul decided to hire a personal bodyguard for his son, Brecken's good friend Jack, adopted son of Latimus, suggested he apply. There had been scattered attacks from Bakari's Deamon army at Valeria and Uteria over the years, and many wealthy aristocrats felt safer having private security at their homes. They could afford it, and it created jobs, so Brecken kept his opinion on the matter to himself. It seemed a bit much since all the compounds were protected by immortal soldiers, but if a rich Vampyre or Slayer wanted a bodyguard in their personal space, who was he to argue? Although Brecken hadn't wanted to leave the army, the pay was substantially higher and allowed him to help support his mother and five sisters at Lynia. After some contemplation, he applied for the job and was hired within a week.

Several years in, he was used to his eccentric ward and could tell Zadicus disliked having a watchdog as much as Brecken disliked watching. But they both were products of their station in the realm, and they'd formed a bond of sorts. One based on necessity and mutual understanding rather than friendship, but sometimes, those were the ones that worked best.

Recently, Zadicus had approached Brecken, asking how much his silence would cost if he were to escape a few hours each week unaccompanied. Brecken had initially balked, knowing that letting Zadicus go anywhere in the realm without his protection was a violation of his contract with Raoul.

"We are both men who crave solace, Brecken," Zadicus said, determination in his ice-blue eyes. "If you give me a few hours a week to myself, I will pay your sister's tuition to the school for gifted students at Takelia."

Brecken had been floored by the offer. His youngest sister Rowena was the smartest of them all, and he hated she was relegated to the public school at Lynia. She had applied and been accepted to the school for the gifted and talented at Takelia, but their family couldn't afford it on the small stipend they received each month after their father was killed during an ambush on a Deamon-scouting mission over a decade ago. His mother worked as a seamstress, but that barely brought in enough for them to survive.

"If your father finds out, not only will I be fired, but I will be blacklisted as a bodyguard for eternity," Brecken replied. "I can't take the chance."

"We are not friends, but we both have a vested interest in keeping this from my father," Zadicus said, extending his hand. "Three hours per week in exchange for your sister's education."

Brecken stared at the man's hand for so long he thought he might retract it. Eventually, they shook, and the deal was made.

"Three hours per week. May the goddess keep you safe. I will set up comm devices with a secret channel for us to communicate and will be ready to answer your call at a moment's notice."

"I hope your sister takes this opportunity to lift herself out of poverty. An educated woman can go far in this realm thanks to Queen Miranda and Governor Evie."

"Yes," Brecken said, arching a brow. "Their decision to allow females to become combat soldiers has riled up some of the misogynists in our kingdom."

"Women should be protected by men," Zadicus said, dismissively waving his hand, "but it is their directive, so I'll choose to accept it."

Left unsaid between them was the blatant fact Zadicus himself needed the protection of a soldier, but Brecken decided to let it lie.

Now, several weeks into their deal, Rowena was thriving at her new school, and Zadicus seemed to be relishing his alone time. Brecken had no idea what he did during his excursions, but he always checked in over their secret channel and so far had returned home with Raoul none the wiser.

"For the goddess's sake, Brecken, are you listening?" Zadicus shouted, snapping his fingers as Brecken returned to the present moment. Straightening, his hands clenched on his belt from the man's irritable tone.

"Yes. What did you want to ask me?"

Eyes narrowing, Zadicus tilted his head, contemplating. "A while back, we were discussing our school days. I mentioned I hated schoolwork, and you said something about excelling at creative writing when you were a student. Do you remember?"

Brecken nodded, surprised the man recalled any of their prior conversations. "I loved school and honed my writing skills. I also figured it would help me pass the written army tests when I became a soldier."

Sighing, Zadicus ran a hand through his hair before trailing over to sit on the couch. "I always hated school. I paid one of our servants to do my homework for me. I found it exceedingly boring."

Brecken's lips twitched as he inwardly remarked he expected nothing less from the man who would inherit a fortune regardless of his performance in school.

"I'll pretend I don't see the smirk so we can continue our conversation," he said in a dry tone. "Since you excelled at creative writing, do you think you could possibly write love letters?'

Feeling his eyebrows draw together, he contemplated. "Love letters?"

"Yes," Zadicus said, slightly rolling his eyes. "As you know, I have set my sights on Callie. She is royalty and worthy of my hand and station. However, she is..."—he circled his hand, searching for the word—"high maintenance and requires extensive courting. I wrote her a poem, which she had the gall to snicker at several times before assuring me it was passable. I have a feeling she'd rather have love letters, but I have no idea where to start—which is where you come in."

Brecken studied the man who stared at him expectantly as disbelief coursed through his veins. "You want to hire me to write love letters to the woman you're courting?" he asked, slightly exasperated. "I understand you can afford anything you set your sights on, but isn't hiring another man to woo your girlfriend just a bit underhanded?"

"You don't have to make it seem nefarious," Zadicus said, standing. "Writing is something I'm terrible at, and apparently, it's a skill of yours. I'd actually be doing her a favor if you wrote to her instead of me."

Scoffing, Brecken shook his head. "No, thanks. I won't be any part of deceiving the woman you eventually plan to bond with."

"Goddess, you rural folk always see things with such rose-colored lenses."

Brecken's nostrils flared at the dismissive words, and he clenched his jaw to keep from telling the man to go to hell.

"I just want a bit of help. Like a wingman. You've told me you and Jack go out together and help each other flirt with women. I'm asking the same."

"Jack and I don't lie to the women we flirt with," Brecken said, holding up his hand when Zadicus opened his mouth to argue. "And even if I agreed, I'd be deceiving Jack since he's her adopted cousin. He's one of my best friends, and I have no desire to hurt him or Callie."

"How will she be hurt?" Zadicus asked, lifting his hands. "It will help move the process along, and she can finally bond with someone. It's common knowledge she isn't the most sought-after female in the realm. This will solidify her status as someone worthy so people don't focus on the prophecy."

Brecken took a moment to reflect on the Elven prophecy and the path the kingdom had followed since its discovery. When he was young, the realm had been embroiled in the vicious war with the Dark Lord Crimeous, Callie's grandfather, until Evie fulfilled the prophecy and saved them. The immortal world slipped into peaceful complacency, never realizing there were other threats on the horizon.

Bakari had appeared with a vengeance, determined to rule over the realm from which he felt ostracized when he was only a babe. Born between Latimus and Arderin, Bakari bore a mark on his inner thigh that the ancient soothsayers believed signified an evil hidden prophecy. Unbeknownst to his parents, Vampyre King Markdor and Queen Calla, the ancient soothsayers had transported him to the human world and left him to die. But Bakari survived and pieced together his past and was now determined to rule over the kingdom he believed was rightfully his.

Brecken thought it a sad tale, often wondering if the royal family would've welcomed and embraced Bakari if he'd returned to the kingdom with an open heart. Alas, it wasn't meant to be, and Bakari was intent upon destroying the Vampyre and Slayer royal families so he could rule in perpetuity. Another self-proclaimed demigod the immortals would have to vanquish before they could secure the peace they craved.

Added to the strife were the Elven scrolls Queen Miranda and Commander Kenden discovered several years ago in the long-forgotten soothsayer chamber at Restia. The scrolls held many prophecies, none more concerning than the one regarding Bakari and Callie:

Elven Prophecy #1

A lone Elf will survive our kingdom's destruction. He will evolve into a powerful being, castigated by the goddess Etherya. Embroiled in his hate, he will spawn children upon the Earth who will cause great devastation. The firstborn spawn of his firstborn spawn will align with the marked Vampyre prince to destroy Etherya's realm as we know it, and it will exist no more...

It was all a bit dramatic for Brecken, who favored practicality and succinctness, so he preferred the summarized version: Crimeous would spawn Darkrip, and Darkrip's firstborn child Callie would align with Bakari to pulverize the immortal realm. *Heavy.*

"If Callie is such an outcast, I'm surprised you decided to court her," Brecken said, resuming their conversation.

"Are you trying to piss me off?" Zadicus asked, scowling.

Brecken breathed a laugh. "No. It just seems as if your station is very important to you, and I'd think you'd want to solidify that with a bonded mate whose reputation is...unvarnished."

"Her reputation is fine," he muttered, beginning to pace. "She'll be a virgin on our wedding night thanks to a promise she made her mother, and I can work with the taint from the prophecy."

Brecken still thought it strange the man didn't care about his reputation since that was in direct opposition to everything he knew about Zadicus, but he remained silent.

"Regardless," Zadicus continued, "I would like your help. Agree to write some love letters to Callie, and I'll assure your mother gets the open seamstress position in the governor's mansion."

Feeling his eyes widen, Brecken pondered. The position paid five times what his mother made as a freelancer. "How soon could she start?"

"As soon as you write the first letter."

Inhaling a deep breath, Brecken let it churn in his gut, knowing what he was about to agree to was so very wrong. But he had his family to think about, and now that his father was gone, they were his responsibility.

"Okay," he said with a nod. "But I'll need to observe her to get an idea of what to write, and you'll need to give me feedback too."

"Yes, yes," Zadicus said dismissively. "She's planning on going to the street fair with Jack after she heals a horse at Restia tomorrow. Why don't you accompany them? You can take one of your sisters and act as if the meeting is a coincidence. As you know, we are having dinner with Aunt Melania and Uncle Cameron tomorrow night, and I will speak to them about hiring your mother."

Brecken had two days a week off from guarding Zadicus, and his ward always had dinner with his aunt and uncle on those occasions.

"All right. There's no need to manipulate the situation. I'll just call Jack and tell him I'd like to go with him. I'll take Rowena with me. She loves street fairs." Extending his hand, he enclosed it around Zadicus's and gave a resigned shake. Brecken knew Callie casually, having met her with Jack several times at Lynia and, more recently, when she began dating Zadicus. Frowning, he acknowledged his discontent at deceiving her.

She'd been nothing but gracious to him as he guarded them while Zadicus courted her. In fact, she treated him with a respect he wished his ward bestowed. Although Zadicus was cordial to him, he still treated him like a servant, often snapping his fingers or making underhanded remarks that would offend someone with a lesser temperament. Brecken was tough and usually brushed it off. After all, many aristocrats were raised to be dicks. It was just the way of the world.

Callie was different even though she was the daughter of royals. She had a generous heart and often spoke of the animals she healed throughout the kingdom. Feeling his lips twitch, Brecken recalled the last time she scolded Zadicus for his callous words. They'd been strolling in the garden, and Zadicus had summoned Brecken over from his spot several yards away where he'd been observing.

"Go inside and grab a wet cloth for us, will you, Brecken?" Zadicus asked. "I want to pick some flowers for Callie and wrap them in it so she can take them home."

"For the goddess's sake, Zadicus," Callie said, wrinkling her nose, "he's not your servant. If you want a cloth, go get it yourself. And honestly, you sent me a bouquet every day this week. I think I'm all flowered out."

"He doesn't mind—do you, Brecken?"

Brecken inwardly sighed, annoyed but used to the treatment. "It's fine—"

"No way," Callie interrupted, flashing him a brilliant smile. Goddess, but she was a looker, with a mass of black curls that fell down her back and stunning ocean-colored eyes. They were olive green in the center, like her father's, and sky blue on the rims like her mother's. "We're fine, Brecken. Feel free to go back to your corner in the shade. Thank you."

Her fingers encircled his wrist, and her soft skin grazed his, sending a jolt of arousal through his frame. Disengaging from her touch, he walked back to the house, standing in the shade as he observed them. Zadicus leaned down to kiss her forehead, and Brecken absently rubbed his wrist, still tingling from where she'd touched him. Closing his eyes for one brief second, he imagined pressing his lips to her forehead...to her full lips...to the curve of her neck...and then he promptly shut it down. Fantasizing about the girlfriend of his ward was a definite no-no.

And now, he'd signed up to deceive her. It certainly didn't sit well inside his core, but the income for his family was too valuable to deny. A governor's seamstress's salary could feed his entire family for decades, and their well-being was his priority. So, he would study Callie and write the letters for Zadicus.

"I think I'd like to head to the boxing club," Zadicus said, strolling toward the grand staircase. "Let me change, and I'll meet you back here."

With a brief nod, Brecken resumed his wide stance, hands clasped over his belt buckle, as he prayed to the goddess to forgive him for his future deception.

An excerpt from the diary of Calinda, daughter of Darkrip and Arderin

Dear Diary,

    I would like to officially report that being ten years old is the worst. We've been back in the realm for three years, and I still haven't made a lot of friends. It's hard when everyone looks at you like a freak and seems scared you're going to destroy the world. Daddy says they're dramatic and insignificant and they can go screw themselves (and then Mommy tells him not to use that word, although I'm obviously old enough to handle it. Sheesh!).

    But the truth is: I think I **am** a freak. Yesterday, I discovered something really cool and really scary about myself at the same time. We were having dinner at Aunt Lila's, and I went to the creek behind the house afterward to catch lightning bugs. As I was trying to catch one in my jar, I heard something wail and looked over to find a tiny chipmunk lying in the grass. After rushing over, I could tell he was hurt and picked him up to examine him. He had blood on his fur and looked like he'd been half-eaten by something with really sharp teeth. I have no idea why, but for some reason, I felt like I could fix him. Closing my eyes, I held my hand over his wound and summoned my powers.

    The little critter cried out, and I opened my eyes to see his wound healing. I was so excited—and so shocked—that I lost control of my power and felt it shoot through my arm into the chipmunk's body. He looked at me with his little beady eyes as his legs shook, and then he died in my hand.

"You ready for me to catch some lightning bugs with you?" Dad asked behind me.

Turning to him with tears streaming down my face, I lifted the animal. "I'm so sorry," I whispered. "I killed him. I didn't mean to. I was trying to heal him. It was working, and then...it wasn't."

He studied me before crouching down and examining the animal. Looking into my eyes, he stroked my hair. "It's okay, Callie." His voice was so soothing, and it made me feel a tiny bit better. "You tried your best."

"Does it mean I'm weird or...bad?"

"No," he said, shaking his head. "It makes sense you would inherit your mom's desire to heal and it would manifest through your powers. As long as you tried your best, that's all that matters."

"I think I can do it if I practice."

"Then we'll practice," he said, kissing my forehead.

After swiping my arm under my nose, I asked, "Can we bury him?"

"Absolutely. Let me get the shovel, and we'll have a proper funeral for him right here under the stars. Do you want your mom to help?"

I nodded before he went inside. I petted the chipmunk until he returned with Mom, and they helped me bury it. No one else came outside, and I knew Dad asked them to leave us alone. It was perfect because I decided I'm going to do my best to heal every animal I can in the future. Dad promised he'd help me learn to use my power, and I won't stop until I figure it out. Cross my heart.

Love, Callie

Chapter 2

Calinda, daughter of Darkrip and Arderin, kneeled beside the horse in the dim stable. Strained puffs of air exited the animal's wide nostrils, and its pain coursed through Callie as if it were her own.

"What do you think, Princess Calinda?" the horse's owner asked. "Will she be okay?"

"I told you to call me Callie, Shamus," she said, rising to look the man in the eye. "Tordor is the heir in this kingdom, and he can have all the fancy titles. I just want to be normal ol' me."

Shamus's lips twitched. "Sorry, princess, but I don't think you're like the rest of us. You're very special."

"Special," she muttered, striding to grab the bag she'd set by the barn door when she arrived. "People always call me that when they're afraid of me or want to avoid me."

"I assure you, ma'am, I don't want neither. I just want my horse to live. I need her for a whole heap of things at the farm and can't really afford another one right now."

"Yes," she said, crouching beside the horse and opening the bag. "The proclivity of Slayers and Vampyres to use horses on the rural compounds still baffles me. Aunt Miranda and Uncle Sathan built a magnificent railway connecting the compounds, which is a good start, but our people still haven't embraced driving cars—outside of battle, of course. The soldiers use four-wheelers quite frequently."

"They implemented a lot of fancy technology at Takelia since it's the newest compound, but I've never had much use for it, princess." He ran his fingers over the brown felt hat in his hands as she rummaged in the bag. "My wife, daughter and I do well here on the farm with what we have."

"Well, I guess that's all we can hope for," Callie said, pulling out the large plastic syringe and wiping it with an alcohol pad. "To be happy with what we've got."

"From your lips to the goddess's ears, ma'am."

"Callie," she corrected, resting her palm on the horse's side as the animal lay on the hay-covered ground. "All right, sweetie," she said, looking into the creature's dark eyes, "this will hurt for just a moment. We're going to withdraw some fluid so I can test it. And then I'm going to heal you. Okay?"

The horse nickered, and Callie smiled. Her abilities afforded her a connection with animals, and she could sense the creature's trust. Spreading her fingers wide, she inserted the needle, maintaining eye contact with the animal's deep brown orbs. The horse flinched slightly before Callie uttered a soft, "*Shhh...*" and she eventually relaxed on the ground.

Withdrawing the plunger, Callie extracted several milliliters of the dark red fluid from the abscess on the horse's stomach. Once finished, she placed the syringe in a plastic bag and deposited it in her medical bag.

Resting both palms on the horse's broad belly, she stared deeply into her eyes. "Okay, girl, you ready? This will be a bit uncomfortable for us both, but it will help. Close your eyes."

As if she understood the command, the creature closed her lids, the tiny black eyelashes stark against her brown mane.

Squeezing her eyes shut, Callie summoned the magic in her blood. It swam inside with dark and sticky remnants of her grandfather Crimeous's evil, alongside the reformed righteousness of her father, the regal valor of her grandmother Rina and great-grandfather Valktor and the feisty strength and self-healing properties inherited from her mother. The amalgamation of the powerful forces swirled and congealed in her veins, rushing toward the spot where her palms met the horse's skin. Letting it flow through, the energy enveloped the animal as it whimpered softly below.

Seconds later, Callie felt the horse release its pain. Sensing it was free from the sickness that had ailed it only moments earlier, Callie collapsed on the ground, pulling her hands from the animal and bringing her knees to her chest. Encircling them with her arms, she buried her face in her thighs and struggled to catch her breath.

"Princess?" Shamus asked, concern in his voice as her ears rang.

"Just need a minute," she said, holding up a hand, palm facing him. "It will pass. Just give me a sec..." Focusing on the yoga breathing techniques her mother taught her, Callie waited for the squeamish feeling inside her stomach to abate.

Moments later, the viscous energy left her body, and she lifted her head. Blinking rapidly, she stared up at Shamus. "Okay," she said, blowing out a breath. "I think we're both fine."

Proving her statement true, the horse whinnied before kicking its legs against the ground. After a few tries, she awkwardly rose, standing on strong legs, and elicited a joyful neigh before quickly trotting out the barn door to the attached fenced-in meadow.

"Wow, princess," Shamus said, bending and extending his hand to her. "That's something else. We Slayers always knew Vampyres had self-healing abilities, but you're the first person I know of who can heal others."

Grasping his hand, she let him pull her to her feet and swiped the hay off her jean-clad thighs. "Yes, it's a pretty cool party trick. All three of us—the grandkids of my woefully terrible Deamon King grandfather—inherited specific individualized traits, along with the ability to read others' thoughts and manipulate things with our minds. I got the ability to heal other living beings, my brother can walk through walls—which was super-creepy when I was a teenager, by the way—" she said, holding up a finger while Shamus chuckled, "and Rinada can render herself invisible. Much cooler in the whole 'things I inherited from creepy grandpa' scheme of things if you ask me," she teased, making quotation marks with her fingers.

"I think you all are amazing," he said, reverence in his tone. "You're hybrid children of some of the most powerful creatures on the planet. I told my wife she should come to the barn and meet you, but...well, she..."

"She's afraid," Callie said, giving a reassuring grin as she shrugged. "It's okay, Shamus. I'm used to it at this point."

"I don't mean no disrespect, ma'am—"

"It's totally fine," she said, waving a hand. "Call me if you need anything else for any of your animals."

Tilting his head, his eyes narrowed.

"What is it?"

Assessing her, he placed his hat on his head. "I just was wondering if it gets lonely sometimes. Being that different. There's comfort in blending in with the crowd sometimes."

"That there is," she said wistfully, lowering to close her bag. Grasping the handles, she straightened and extended her hand. "I'm happy I could help your horse, Shamus. I'll be handing over the sample to Nolan and Sadie to test. Bakari hasn't unleashed any new toxins that we know of in several months, but the threat is always there. Most likely, the abscess was caused by some bacteria she drank in the watering hole on the far side of the meadow. I would treat it before she drinks it again."

"Will do, princess," he said, shaking her hand. "Thank you so much for healing her."

"You're welcome." After a firm shake, she gave a salute and trailed out of the barn into the bright, sunny day.

Slinging her medical bag onto the passenger seat, she climbed into the four-wheeler and revved the engine. Putting the vehicle into gear, she pressed the pedal to the floor and began the drive to Takelia.

Shamus's farm at Restia was about a forty-five minute drive to Takelia, which would give her ample time to ponder the inner workings of her life as her hair blew in the wind and she soaked up the sun. She could've taken the train, since it connected all seven compounds of the immortal world, but she still would've had to find transportation from Restia's train station to the farm. No, it was better to drive through the open fields and enjoy the freedom she'd so deftly negotiated earlier.

Darkrip didn't like the idea of her driving to Restia alone. Bakari had amassed a powerful army, cloned from the Deamon inmates he'd sprung from Takelia's prison almost two decades ago. There was always a latent threat Bakari would launch a surprise attack or approach Callie and try to gain her alliance, especially since the prophecy declared they would align one day to destroy the world.

"Bakari hasn't ever approached me, Dad," she'd said to his reflection in the mirror of her vanity as she sat combing her hair earlier that morning. "I doubt he'll try today."

"If you recall, he did approach you," Darkrip said, crossing his arms over his chest as he loomed over her shoulder. "He took some of your hair from the playground swing when we lived in the human world."

"Yes, yes," she sighed, rolling her eyes as she dragged the brush through her long black curls. "And Tatiana used it to make the potion that allows Bakari to teleport like you and Aunt Evie. It's all my fault."

"It's not your fault," he said, cupping her shoulder. "I just don't want you to put yourself in harm's way."

Covering his hand, she smiled into his green eyes in the reflection. "What will you do if I bond with Zadicus and move in with him at Valeria? Will you come and check on me every day? Perhaps move into the room next door? Maybe you can listen while we—"

"Enough," he said, squeezing her shoulder. "I told you, if you ever mention having marital relations with anyone, I'll jump into the Purges of Methesda."

Snickering, she stood, shaking her head as she faced him. "Marital relations? Come on, Dad. You can say 'sex.'"

"Etherya help me," he muttered, glancing at the ceiling. Stepping back, he recrossed his arms and assessed her. "I won't let you go alone to heal the horse. Take a soldier with you."

"We both know I'm strong enough to overpower fifty soldiers," she said, lifting her hands in frustration. "I can read their thoughts, same as you, and although I can't transport, I did inherit the ability to crush things with my mind. I think I'll be fine."

"You're not a trained soldier—"

"I'm not a man," she said, thrusting up her chin. "Isn't that what you meant to say?"

"For god's sake," he said, rolling his eyes. "You and your mom play the sexism card anytime we have an argument. You know it's ridiculous considering I've never won an argument against either of you."

Callie smiled and squinted one eye. "You're right. I can't remember ever losing one..."

Chuckling, he stepped toward her and encircled her wrist. "You're my daughter, Callie. I love you. You and Creigen are proof I'm capable of doing good things in this wretched world. Let me keep you safe."

"Dad," she whispered, eyes welling as she cupped his cheeks. He'd always been such a strong, abiding constant in her life, and she loved him with every piece of her heart. "I'll be safe. Maybe you should say what you're really thinking. You're afraid Bakari is going to somehow contact me and manipulate me to his side. You're afraid I won't be able to deny the call of Grandfather's blood...of his evil."

Darkrip's eyes darted between hers. "You've never really had to fight the malevolence inside because your mother and I protected you." Palming her face, he ran his thumb over her cheek. "As you grow more independent, I worry I might have shielded you too much. I struggled with the darkness for centuries. I fear you haven't begun to comprehend how powerful it is."

Giving him a reassuring smile, she shook her head. "You and Mom did everything you could for us, but you can't keep me locked away forever. Hopefully, I'll be bonding soon, and there will be times you won't be there. You need to trust me. There's no way in hell I'd ever hurt anyone in our family. You know how important they are to me."

"You're telling that to the man who almost strangled me when I was pregnant with you," a sardonic voice chimed in from the doorway.

"Oh, brother," Darkrip muttered, glancing toward the door.

"Hey, Mom," Callie said, grinning as Arderin entered the room. "Dad was just worrying I'm going to turn into Grandfather and destroy the kingdom."

"Was he?" Arderin asked, standing on her toes and placing a peck on Darkrip's cheek. "How utterly fatalistic."

"Are you two really going to gang up on me when I was trying to protect our sweet, precious daughter?"

"The embellishment is a bit much," Arderin said, playfully rolling her eyes. "You heading out to Shamus's farm, sweetie?"

"Yes," Callie said, heading toward the bed and donning the light jacket that sat beside her medical bag. "Dad's worried."

"Fine—go on and get yourself abducted and murdered for all I care," he said, waving his hands in frustration as he turned to exit the room. "Goddess forbid I try to protect my own damn daughter—"

"Whoa, there," Arderin said, grabbing his wrist and drawing him to her side. "What your *sweet, loving* father meant to say is that we're going to settle on a compromise, right, darling?" She batted her eyelashes.

"I'm listening," he muttered.

"Callie, you'll carry the walkie on you at all times. If you see anything that's the least bit alarming, you'll radio Kenden and Latimus immediately and also send one of those weird telekinetic message thingies to your dad. Are we clear, young lady?"

"Mom, I'm almost twenty-five, for the goddess's sake—"

"Are we clear?" Arderin interrupted in the stern tone that implied she meant business.

"Yes, Mother," Callie said, contrite.

"Good. Darkrip, you'll have your spidey-sense all ready to go until she returns home, right?"

"Do I have a choice?"

"Stop it," she said, swatting his chest. "Agree with your wife, please."

"Yes, dear," he said, pecking her lips. "I'll be on alert. Callie, you have the walkie?"

"There's one in the four-wheeler. I'll radio Uncle Ken and Uncle Latimus before I head out."

"Fine," Darkrip said, rubbing the back of his neck. "I have a meeting with the compound governors today, but I can leave in a second if needed."

"My dad, the kingdom's ambassador. Who knew you'd be so great at instituting diplomacy between all the compounds?"

"Evie is a great governor, but that's too formal for me. I enjoy helping the seven governors run the realm. Ambassador was a good fit, and I need something to do while your mom floats around healing people at the clinics."

"Yes, it was world domination or ambassadorship. I'm so proud you chose the light," Arderin teased, sliding her arm around his waist. "Good luck with the horse, sweetheart. You're so wonderful to use your powers to help wounded animals. I'm so proud of you."

"Okay, no crying today, Mom," Callie said, noting the tears welling in her mother's eyes. "This is a happy day. We won another round against Dad."

Darkrip frowned as she stepped forward and gave them both a kiss.

"See you both when I get home. Love you!"

With that, she grabbed her bag and headed to Shamus's without so much as a blip from Bakari as she traversed the open fields between Takelia and Restia.

Now, on the way home, a slight melancholy settled in as she drove through the open air. She had no idea why—after all, she was *finally* being courted by a man who was well-respected and seemed determined to win her over. Zadicus romanced her with such zeal she sometimes marveled at how lucky she was to find him as her first love.

Callie had always been a romantic—a trait most likely inherited from her mother who was deeply in love with her father. Knowing her dad returned the sentiment gave Callie hope as she contemplated her own future. Zadicus was exceedingly handsome with his piercing blue eyes, austere features and jet-black hair. He embodied the regal appearance his aristocratic blood conveyed, and she enjoyed their passionate kisses when he visited Takelia to court her. Although she'd decided not to sleep with him until they bonded, it was nice to be desired by someone so handsome.

Arderin had always urged Callie to wait to make love until she bonded, and they had discussed it on several occasions as Callie grew into adulthood.

"Sweetie," Arderin had said during one of their discussions several years ago, "making love to someone is a big decision. I just want it to be as special as you deserve."

Callie had been moved by the words and the sentiment in her mother's voice. "I do like the idea of waiting until the time feels right. If it's the night of my bonding ceremony, so be it. It's not like anyone is beating my door down anyway."

"Someone will, and I can't wait for that day," Arderin said, running a soothing hand over Callie's curls.

She'd been right, as her mother often was. Two years later, she met Zadicus at a royal fundraiser at Valeria. The immortal royals were always holding fundraisers to encourage the wealthy aristocrats to fund the army, and this one had been particularly stuffy. Callie had exited onto the balcony of the castle at Valeria, and a smooth voice sounded in her ear.

"Are you as bored as I am?"

Glancing up at the handsome Vampyre, she grinned. "To death. These things suck. I attend because it makes my parents happy and shows my support of the cause, but, man, I hate them."

"They're not my cup of tea either." Warm breath caressed her ear as it blew the soft curls at her temple. "Want to take a walk by the river?"

She'd contemplated only a moment before giving a nod. "Sure. I can disappear for half an hour. Let's blow this joint."

They'd walked along the grassy riverbank, learning each other's stories as Callie's excitement grew at finally being pursued by a handsome, attentive suitor.

"So, you're Melania and Camron's nephew?" Callie asked. "I don't know them very well, but Lila is close with Camron."

"He's a great governor, and Melania is my father's sister."

Callie thoughtfully chewed her lip. "My dad mentioned a few times that Melania was once sympathetic to Bakari's cause. Aunt Lila always reminds him that she's chosen our side and that everyone deserves redemption."

"That's very kind of her. Melania has never spoken to me with anything other than support for the immortal royals."

"That's good. Perhaps she just made a mistake. None of us are perfect."

Zadicus halted, encircling her wrist and drawing her to his side. Blue eyes simmered in the moonlight as he stared down at her, desire swimming in the deep orbs.

"You seem pretty perfect to me, princess."

A laugh escaped her throat. "Then you really don't know me," she said, the words breathy and disjointed.

"That's something I would very much like to change."

"You would?" Her heart pounded as she stared up at his handsome features. No one had ever looked at her with such raw passion, and it was...exhilarating.

"Yes," he whispered, sliding a hand behind her neck and tilting her face. "Come here, princess. Let me taste you."

With that, Callie experienced the first truly passionate kiss of her life. She'd had a few others that were lackluster, but Zadicus embodied such zeal as he devoured her mouth. Afterward, she stared at him, attempting to catch her breath.

"I would like to court you, princess," he said, sliding his palm over her upper arm in warm, slow circles. "Should I ask your father? Forgive me, but growing up in an aristocratic family has made me quite formal."

Callie wrinkled her nose. "It's so different from the human world, but I think I quite like it. Yes, you can ask my dad to court me. If he doesn't disintegrate you on the spot, I'd very much like to be wooed."

Zadicus responded with a playful grimace but seemed undeterred. Days later, he embarked on a long discussion with Darkrip in their sitting room at Takelia. Darkrip had several reservations about Zadicus—the most glaring being that he was related to Melania. He also questioned why a high-ranking aristocrat would want to court someone as free-spirited as Callie. Although they were technically royals, their family unit was anything but traditional. But Zadicus had assured Darkrip his intentions were true, and Callie had all but begged him for his blessing. Finally, someone was eager to court her, and she was excited for the experience. Eventually, her father consented, and Zadicus began his courtship.

They'd now been dating for nine months, and Callie was all-consumed with zealous shows of affection from her handsome suitor. It was all quite overwhelming for Callie, who had struggled to find her place in the immortal world when they returned after Arderin completed her medical training. Being the focus of an evil prophecy wasn't the best way to fit in, and her teenage years had been tough. After going through her immortal change in her early twenties, she longed for affection and comradery with a partner. She and Zadicus certainly had mutual affection. Was she one hundred percent comfortable with him yet? Not really. But Callie figured those things took time, and she wasn't going to squander the chance to finally fall in love. They would eventually grow into a relationship similar to what her parents had, right? Gnawing her lip, Callie deliberated.

Zadicus had employed every tactic possible to win her love. Long walks by the river, moonlight picnics, flowers at every turn. Hell, he'd even written her poetry. Snickering as she drove the four-wheeler, she admitted his poetry was terrible. But the effort was sweet, and she hoped he didn't realize she thought it dreadful. There was no point in hurting his feelings after all.

Callie felt that within the next few months, Zadicus would ask her to bond. She would accept, although she would stick with her decision to wait until their wedding night to make love. The choice stemmed from a combination of several factors. Her promise to her mother she would wait until it felt right. Her desire to ensure Zadicus truly loved her with all his heart. And perhaps most important of all, the nagging feeling that her ardent suitor might be trying just a *bit* too hard.

The feeling swam in her gut, dark and heavy, and it created a secret doubt she hadn't expressed to anyone else. It was responsible for her slight melancholy and made her wonder if she was truly making the right decision. She considered herself a pretty chill person, and although the elaborate courting was nice, she didn't really need it. It was almost as if Zadicus had some strange ulterior motive to ensure she chose him.

Realizing she needed to express the feelings to someone she trusted, Callie slowed and parked in the open meadow. Pulling her phone from her bag, she called Jack.

"Hey," his deep voice said over the receiver. "You okay? I know you went to Shamus's farm today."

"Yeah," she said, picking at a frayed string hanging from one of the ripped holes in her jeans. "We're still on for the street fair tonight, right?"

"Yep. We'll be done at four. We're letting the soldiers go early so they can attend with their families. On that note, it's Brecken's night off, and he asked if he and Rowena can come with us. She's his youngest sister, if you remember."

"Oh, sure," she said as Brecken's face flashed through her mind. She was fond of Brecken and knew he was close with Jack. Now, she mostly saw him when he stood off in the distance protecting Zadicus. Callie always sensed his presence when he was near, which she attributed to her heightened senses from her Deamon blood.

Most wouldn't even sense the hulking bodyguard's presence—after all, it was his job to blend in and go unnoticed. But sometimes, she would catch him staring at her out of the corner of her eye and always felt a strange jolt of...*something*. Intensity? Awareness? She wasn't sure how to describe the feeling and usually wrote it off as a side effect of being observed. After all, it was a bit creepy to have another man watch you as you strolled with your suitor, even if he was a paid bodyguard.

The fact her suitor's protector was viscerally attractive was an entirely different rabbit hole Callie had no interest in chasing. Although, it was interesting to compare Brecken and Zadicus in those rare moments her mind went there. Zadicus was perfectly coiffed, attractive in a smooth, polished manner. Brecken was...*primal*. Sexy. Brooding. Sometimes, in those rare moments her eyes met his, golden flecks would flash in his deep brown eyes, and Callie would have to tamp down a shiver. Did they flash like that when he made love? Did the dark orbs simmer as he claimed his mate's body, marking her as *his*?

With a vicious shake of her head, Callie returned to reality. Why in the hell was she imagining Brecken having sex when she had a wonderful man expending excessive amounts of energy courting her? "Get it together, Callie," she muttered before resuming the call with Jack.

"Callie?"

"Sorry, I'm here. Should be fun. I like Brecken. I remember when we celebrated when you got him the bodyguard position. He paid for all my drinks, which wasn't necessary but was really nice. Obviously, I see him when I'm with Zadicus, but it's different. Anyway, it will be nice to hang with him outside of the whole bodyguard situation."

"I'm assuming Zadicus isn't coming?"

Callie chewed her lip. "No. I need a break from him. Please don't tell anyone else I said that. He's awesome, and I love hanging with him, but he's...*a lot* sometimes. I mean, sometimes, a girl just needs to Netflix and chill. He's kind of formal."

Jack's chuckle sounded in her ear. "He is, but I think you signed up for that. You *are* planning to bond with him, right?"

"Of course," she said, her tone cheerful, although the doubt lingered inside. "But I'm excited to hang with you guys. That's all."

"Sounds good. Want to meet me at my cabin at five? We can walk to town from there."

"Sure. I'll remind Dad I'll be home late so he won't have a heart attack. I'm in a four-wheeler, so I might get to you a bit early. Is that okay?"

"Yep. I'll leave the key in the lockbox hanging on the knob. Works out well since I don't have to reset the code considering you can unlock the thing with your powers."

"Perfect. I'll pick up some wine on the way. We can have a glass before we walk into town."

"Can't wait. See you in a bit."

The phone clicked, and Callie released a sigh. Spending time with Jack would clear her head, and she could always talk to him about Zadicus if she needed. Pressing her foot to the pedal, she told herself everything would be fine. Even people who loved each other needed a break sometimes. Zooming across the open field, she sped home to pick up the wine before driving to Lynia, excited for the evening ahead.

An excerpt from the diary of Calinda, daughter of Darkrip and Arderin

Dear Diary,

I would like to report that I am **not** enjoying sixth grade. At this point, I'd love to stay home and have Glarys homeschool me, but Mom says it's important I learn to handle adversity and make friends. We're royals and have a duty to uphold, but it's hard when everyone thinks you're a freak who's going to destroy the kingdom.

We started learning about the history of the immortal realm today, since that's part of the sixth-grade curriculum. After Miranda and Kenden discovered the hidden Elven scrolls, they wanted the contents to be taught across the realm. They're pretty vague, but they do give us glimpses of the extinct immortal species, and Miranda thinks it will help unite us. Now that Vampyres, Slayers and Deamons live on all the compounds, it's important we take lessons from the destruction of the Elves to help counteract and prevent our own mistakes.

Well, that's great and all, but when you're the subject of one of those deadly prophecies, leaning about it in a classroom of your peers kind of sucks. Today, as the teacher was explaining Bakari's history and his mention in the Elven prophecy, she also referenced my role in the prophecy. Several of my classmates shot me mean looks from their desks, and others looked at me as if they were terrified.

Afterward, when we went outside for lunch, no one would sit with me, so I sat alone like a super-dork. Some of the other kids snickered when I opened my soda and it sprayed all over my table. I shot them the bird, and my teacher sent me to the principal who said I had to go home for the day. You know what? That was just fine with me.

Mom picked me up, and we had a long talk when we got home. She says that one day, I'll find my people. People who accept me and love me just for me. I hope so because being an outcast really blows. At least I have Mom, Dad, Creigen, Jack and the rest of my family.

Love, Callie

Chapter 3

The day of the street fair, Brecken rose with the sun and went out for a run. He'd had a restless night tossing and turning as he envisioned Callie's reaction if she discovered his pact with Zadicus. Would those luminous eyes fill with tears? Or would she punch him in the nose and tell him to go to hell? Chuckling as he jogged, he realized he preferred the latter, if only so he could see her cheeks flush and observe the vibrant colors in her irises flare. For some reason, he imagined Callie angry would be fun. She was passionate and had a gregarious personality, which enthralled someone with his more stoic demeanor. What would she be like in bed? Would that passion translate between the sheets?

Swiping his damp forehead, Brecken told himself to shut it down and finish his jog. After a refreshing shower, he threw on jeans, a T-shirt and sneakers, happy to be free of his black tactical gear for the day. Raoul employed a floater security agent who observed Zadicus on his days off, and Brecken savored his free time. He did some chores around the cabin, prepared his Slayer blood weekly rations and washed the load of laundry that had been piling up for over a week. Eventually, the sun sat low in the afternoon sky, and he realized Rowena would be home from school. After running a comb through his thick, dark brown hair, he locked the door behind him and set off to his mother's house.

His cabin resided on a patch of land a few miles from the main square. His father had purchased the land centuries ago, and Brecken, being the oldest male, had inherited it. He thought the tradition antiquated and felt his mother should've inherited everything, but old Vampyre traditions took time to reform. Thankfully, Queen Miranda and Governor Evie were progressive and were slowly dragging the kingdom into modernity. Brecken had always believed in equality and supported the recent decision to allow females to become combat soldiers in the immortal army.

Some of his friends and fellow soldiers he'd trained with were resistant, but Brecken felt they would come around, especially with the focus on defeating Bakari. Why not employ every willing and able soldier they could to vanquish the threat forever?

When Brecken had completed his military training, he used his meager savings to build his own cabin on the opposite side of his father's land. It afforded him privacy as he moved into adulthood and allowed his mother to retain the home she'd lived in for centuries. He sold it to her for one lira, and the property was now evenly divided—his mother owning her home and land, and he his. It felt much more equitable and allowed him to get a break from his five sisters. Although he loved them dearly, they were a lot to deal with for a man who craved his space.

After walking through the thicket of trees and brush that separated his cabin from his mother's home, he approached the front porch and climbed the stairs. Reaching for the doorknob, he didn't have the chance to touch it before Rowena swung the door open.

"*Ohmygod*, get me out of here!" she said, rolling her eyes. "Jordana's boyfriend broke up with her, and I can't take the drama."

Laughing at his twelve-year-old sister, who was quite dramatic herself, he stepped inside. "I thought this one was a keeper. Jordana really liked Axe."

"He told her they both needed to date other people since they were eighteen and graduating soon. She might never recover," Rowena said, resting the back of her hand on her forehead and imitating a swoon.

"I'm sure she'll be fine," he muttered, strolling through the hallway to the living room where his mother sat sewing a shirt. "Hi, Mom." Leaning down, he kissed her light brown hair, which was pulled into a bun.

"Hi, dear," she said, gesturing with her head for him to sit in the chair beside her. "You heard Jordana's life is over?"

His lips curved. "How tragic."

Breathing a laugh, she shook her head. "I keep reminding myself the goddess blessed me with five daughters for a reason. And with one wonderful son." Leaning over, she patted his cheek.

"I do my best. Where is everyone?"

"Jordana is in her room railing at the universe, I'm sure. Betsy and Ludika are at soccer practice. Nala is out back wielding her sword if I had to guess. She's intent on becoming a soldier like you. I hope to introduce her to Queen Miranda one day. What a boon that will be for our little teenage warrior."

Brecken lifted his brows, wondering if it would ever happen. Queen Miranda was lauded as a champion of the people who loved all citizens regardless of their wealth or status, but the opportunity for a poor, rural teenager to cross her path was limited at best. Not wanting to dampen his mother's spirits, he nodded. "Perhaps it will happen."

"You could ask Calinda to set up a meeting…"

"I'm not allowed to speak to my wards or their companions without being asked first, Mom. You know that. Although, I'll actually be hanging with Callie at the street fair tonight. If it comes up naturally, I'll try to remember to mention it, but I doubt that will happen."

"It would make your sister's year," she said, smiling. "Do try to remember."

"On another note, I have some fantastic news."

His mother's eyebrow arched. "Do tell. Did you finally meet the woman of your dreams and fall madly in love so you can give me some grandbabies?"

"Um, no," he said, lips flattening. "You'll be receiving a call tomorrow from the house manager at Valeria's governor's mansion. They're going to offer you the open seamstress position."

Her hands dropped to her lap as she stared at him with a stunned expression. "How? I'm sure there are other qualified candidates at Valeria who won't have to ride the train from Lynia."

"They want *you*, Mom." Encircling her wrist, he squeezed. "The girls are all old enough to take the train to school, and you don't need to be at home every day. I figured you wouldn't mind commuting for the extra income. It could be a game changer for our family."

"Oh, my," she said, resting her hand over her heart. "I could finally add an addition onto the house so Ludika can have her own room. And I can actually buy all the girls dresses to wear to their dances instead of recycling the old ones. And don't even get me started on how the hot water never works in the second bathroom. I could finally hire a plumber. Heck, I could build a third bathroom."

Overcome with the joy in her deep brown eyes, he nodded. "There are so many possibilities, and it will allow Rowena to go to university at one of the aristocratic compounds if she chooses. I hope you'll take the position, Mom. It's a great opportunity."

"Of course I'm taking it, boy!" She playfully swatted his arm. "How magnificent. What did you have to do to secure this for me?" Her eyebrow arched, and he swallowed thickly, understanding his mother could read him well.

"Nothing. I'm doing a good job for Zadicus. He mentioned the open position, and we had a discussion about it."

Her eyes darted between his. "If there's one thing you should've learned by now, it's that you shouldn't lie to your mother, Brecken."

Giving her a droll look, he stood. "I'm not lying."

Narrowing her eyes, she studied him. "You are, but you must have your reasons. Just remember your father is watching us from the Passage. We must live up to our moral code and make him proud."

Guilt swirled within before he pushed it away. Seeing things in black-and-white was a privilege people on the rural compounds sometimes didn't enjoy. He wouldn't feel bad for securing a position for his mother that would help his family. Wishing for different circumstances was a waste of time, so he leaned down and kissed his mother before pivoting to find Rowena and head to the street fair.

"Everything will be fine, Mom," he said from the doorway, hand resting on the frame. "I love you. We're off to the fair. I'll make sure Rowena gets some Slayer blood and we're home by ten."

"Have fun," she said, blowing him a kiss. "And thank you for the opportunity. I love you too, son."

Sparing her one last smile, Brecken located his sister and began the twenty-minute walk into town, telling himself the entire time to let go of his trepidation because it wouldn't change a damn thing.

An excerpt from the diary of Calinda, daughter of Darkrip and Arderin

Dear Diary,

    Well, I'm officially a teenager, and I can say without a doubt, it sucks. We had our first school dance yesterday, and Mom said I should go because we're all intent on living our lives even though Bakari is trying to destroy the realm. If that wasn't heavy enough, I realized two weeks ago that no one was going to ask me to the dance. Mom says I'm pretty, and Dad always mutters he can't believe there's two of us since I look just like her. I think she's beautiful, but I'm not sure I'm as pretty as she is. My body looks weird lately, and I just feel awkward.

    Anyway, our family was over for dinner last week, and I overheard Mom and Dad telling everyone that no one had asked me to the dance. It was annoying, and I wish they would stay out of my business. I let it go because I didn't really want to talk about what a huge loser I was.

    Mom bought me a really pretty dress and did my hair, so I looked okay, I guess. I spent the first hour of the dance drinking about a thousand cups of punch, hoping someone would ask me to dance, but no one did. So I made up a boyfriend in my mind.

    His name is Henry (after Henry Cavill, of course. I might have left the human world, but that guy is hot no matter what realm you're in!), and he's everything I ever imagined. He smiles at me and tells me I'm pretty and thinks it's really cool I'm so smart and make straight As. He doesn't give a crap about the prophecy and wants to kiss me all the time. Yep, one day, I'll meet my Henry, and I can stop feeling like a freak.

Until then, I'll put up with the rejection and focus on the positives. I mean, life could be worse, right? I love my parents and my family, and my brother is okay too...most of the time. They've always accepted me, and that's what really matters. I can't wait for my Henry to meet them, whenever he shows up. I'll be waiting...

Love, Callie

Chapter 4

Callie arrived at Jack's cabin, teasing him when he opened the door with wet red hair spiked in a hundred different directions.

"Be careful going out in public like that, or Brienne won't ever take you back."

"Brienne and I are toast, I'm afraid," he said, stepping back and opening the door wider so she could step inside. "Apparently, I'm 'emotionally unavailable.'" He made quotation marks with his fingers. "Whatever that means."

"It just means you haven't met the right person yet. She's not your person, Jack."

His auburn eyebrows lifted. "And Zadicus is yours?"

"It seems so," she said, shrugging.

"I'm still not sure, but that's what courting is for, I guess." Closing the door, he gestured to the chairs in front of the fireplace. "Want to open the wine and have a glass before we walk to town?"

"Sure," she said, picking up one of the weapons that sat on the table by his front door.

"It's an improved TEC that Uncle Heden sent over. This is the prototype. I'm supposed to test it with Dad sometime over the next week."

She glanced up at him, concern in her eyes. "That means you'll have to encounter some Deamons."

"Yep," he said, smiling as if it were a normal occurrence to encounter vicious Deamon soldiers on a regular basis. Jack was extremely proud of his position as Chief Training Officer in the immortal army and his recent promotion to lieutenant. Callie knew he'd worked hard to attain it and didn't want anyone thinking he'd received special favors as the adopted son of Commander Latimus.

"General Garridan spotted a cluster of Deamons near the foothills of the Strok Mountains west of Uteria on their last scouting mission," he continued. "We'll probably launch a surprise attack and test the prototype. Not only does it kill a Deamon instantly like the old TECs, but it disintegrates them too, so there's nothing left behind to be cloned."

Her eyebrows lifted. "Go Uncle Heden...and Aunt Sofia. I'm sure she had just as much to do with it as he did."

"Most likely. They're both smart as hell."

Setting the weapon on the table, she turned and reached inside her bag. Lifting the bottle of wine, she shook it. "Cabernet. Your favorite."

"Sweet." Taking the bottle, Jack trailed to the kitchenette in the far corner and pulled two glasses from the cabinet. Callie walked over and opened the top drawer, locating the corkscrew. Setting the bottle on the counter, she screwed the cork free and poured them each a taste.

"It's good," Jack said after a hearty sip. "Fill me up."

"It's from Aunt Sofia's latest batch. I stopped home and grabbed it on the way here."

After filling their glasses, they clinked them together before drinking.

"Man, it is good."

"Almost as good as the first time you had wine," he teased.

"Oh, goddess," she said, heading toward the two chairs that flanked the tiny fireplace on the far side of the cabin. "Don't remind me." She fell into the chair.

"I don't think I've ever seen that much puke," Jack said, sliding into the vacant seat. "You were ripped."

Rolling her eyes, she rested her palm on her forehead. "I was so pissed Dad wouldn't let me drink and declared I'd drink every bottle in the cellar when he wasn't looking."

"Well, you were only sixteen. I think he was right."

"*Pfft.* Sixteen going on a hundred. Having extraordinary powers and being the subject of a dreadful prophecy ages a person."

"Does it?" he mused, glancing at the ceiling.

"Yes," she said, extending her leg to gently kick him. "Anyway, I didn't even have to read your thoughts to know how pissed you were at me."

Holding up a finger, he said, "Let's also not discount the fact reading people's thoughts violates the oath you gave your father."

Sighing, she lifted the glass and sipped before nodding. "Yes, I promised him I wouldn't use my powers to read others' thoughts unless I was in danger. How utterly boring."

Chuckling, he lifted a shoulder. "I think it's just the right thing to do. Although, knowing you, you've probably cheated a few hundred times over the years."

Her eyes lit with excitement as she straightened in the chair. "Oh my god, I have! Want to hear some of the best things I've discovered? You can't tell anyone because they would *kill* me, but it's so fun. I swear, it only happened when I didn't realize I was doing it. I'm much better at controlling the power now that I'm older." She made an "X" over her heart.

"Sure. Hit me with the scandalous details."

"So, I'm pretty sure your parents are into some kinky costume role-play when they're alone—"

"Ew," he interrupted, holding up a hand. "My parents are off-limits. Move on to someone else, please."

"Oh, fine," she said with a harrumph. "You're no fun. Let me see..." Tapping her finger on her lips, she contemplated. "Oh! I accidentally read Aunt Miranda's thoughts when we had family dinner at Uteria at few years ago. Your dad was talking about his resistance to having women join the combat troops, and she was *pissed*. I mean, she had some really vivid images of strangling him and then kicking him in the nuts. It was so funny I almost spit out my drink!"

"Miranda's tough as nails, for sure," Jack said, chuckling at the image. "Thank the goddess Dad came around on the subject so she won't need to render him inept with her knee."

"Seriously. I know Evie and Miranda were both thrilled with that decision." She imbibed the wine as her expression grew pensive. "I also see sad things sometimes."

"Like what?"

"Tordor," she said, eyes narrowing as she contemplated the ceiling. "He isn't sure of his place in the world. He feels a bit lost considering he's supposed to be the heir but Miranda and Sathan are immortal. It doesn't really offer an open position for him in the realm. And Rinada and Creigen both have their doubts about their place here, as do I. Being the grandchild of Crimeous and possessing powers no one else has is isolating. I guess the kids of the royal family are all fucked up in their own ways. Except for you," she said, tilting her head. "You seem relatively normal."

"I'm pretty sure you're really saying I'm boring, but I'll let it slide."

"Nah," she said, waving her hand, "You're the life of the party."

"Man, you're a terrible liar." Standing, he extended his hand to her. "Drink up so we can head into town. And before you make fun of me again, I'll also comb my hair."

She swallowed the last of her wine and handed him the glass. Striding to the sink, he rinsed them and placed them in the basin.

"This cabin is hella cute and all, but you're the son of wealthy royals. Have you ever considered living in a home where the kitchen isn't in the same room as your bed?" She gestured around the tiny space.

"Not really," he said, wiping his hands on the dishtowel. "The cabin is all I need, and it's close to home. If I ever need a bigger place to stay, I can always spend the night at Mom and Dad's. But I like it here. Must seem strange to someone who's seen as much of the world as you."

"No judgement at all," she said, standing. "It's just tiny. But, hey, whatever makes you happy. Ready to go?"

Nodding, he slipped on his socks and sneakers and headed to the bathroom. Returning with freshly combed hair, he turned off the lights, and they headed outside.

They began the trek to Lynia's main square, which was about a ten-minute walk. Callie debated whether she should bring up her doubts about Zadicus, not wanting to make a big deal out something she wasn't sure even required a conversation.

"Might as well spit it out," he said, breaking the silence. "I've already realized you have something on your mind. Give it to me."

Grinning up at him, she squinted in the late-day sun. "Maybe I'm not the only one who can read minds in this twosome?"

"Maybe not." He tapped his finger on his temple. "Go on. I'll try to help if I can."

"I appreciate you always letting me vent to you. It's been tough making true friends here since half the people think I'm a freak."

"No, they don't," he said, shaking his head. "We talked about this dramatic streak, right?" Rubbing his chin, he glanced at the sky. "I'm sure we did..."

"Stop teasing me," she said, swatting his arm. "Being the granddaughter of Crimeous *and* the subject of a doomsday prophecy isn't a bed of roses, Jack." She studied the dirt walking path, eyes downcast, as she continued. "People recoil from me sometimes, especially on the more rural compounds. It's gotten better as we've settled into the kingdom and the people realized Dad and Evie aren't going to pulverize them, but Crimeous tortured them for centuries. That fear doesn't dissipate overnight. A portion of my blood is inherently evil, as is Rinada's, Creigen's, Dad's and Evie's."

"You've never shown a hint of evil, Callie."

She shot him an acerbic glance. "You're placating me."

"Look, I know you accidentally hurt some birds and a few chipmunks when you were younger. But you were trying to heal them when they died. You just had to grow into your power."

"I still feel bad for every animal I hurt. But only through those experiences did I figure out how to heal other living beings."

"Learning new things takes time. The fact you feel remorse they perished is what matters."

"I guess," she said with a sigh. "Or maybe I'm just destined to be a freak. I think that's why I was so taken by Zadicus. He really expended some serious energy courting me—like he'd be extremely lucky to be my bonded."

Jack halted, turning to face her. "He would be the luckiest man in the world. Is that what's bothering you?"

"Yes," she said, hating that she was emotional over something so trite. An attractive, kind man was going out of his way to court her. She should be thrilled. But intuition was also important, and hers was telling her something wasn't quite right.

"Why is he trying so hard, Jack? At first, I was consumed by the flattery, but now that we're close to becoming engaged, I..." She ran her hand through her dark curls. "I don't know, I'm having doubts. It's almost as if he has an agenda for courting me that I just can't see."

"I think his agenda is to make you his wife. That's how courting works, Callie."

"Yeah," she said, absently gnawing her lip. "But it's so *much*. I like feeling special, but I also just want to feel...*normal*. I've rarely felt normal except with our family."

"It makes sense to feel comfortable with your family. These things take time to develop."

"But will I ever feel comfortable in my own skin with him? I feel as if he doesn't get me sometimes."

"I don't know. Do you love him? If not, then maybe you should take a break so you can figure this out. Bonding with someone is a huge commitment, Callie. If you have doubts, you need to address them."

She worked her jaw as her gaze fell to his shoulder. "I think I love him. I mean, my god, Jack, how do I know? He's literally the first person who's ever shown romantic interest in me. I feel all the butterflies and enjoy making out with him. I'm certainly excited to have sex with him when we bond. I want to know what all the fuss is about."

"Okay, that's probably TMI," he muttered, rubbing his forehead, "but only you can decide if this is just normal relationship jitters or something more."

"I just don't want to make a mistake." Slipping her arm into his, they resumed walking. "Maybe I'm overthinking it. Thanks for letting me vent. Perhaps I just needed to talk to someone."

"Life has a way of steering us where we need to go. You already know deep inside why you have doubts. Don't discount your intuition, Callie. It's usually a good barometer of things to come."

"Truth," she said with a nod. "Oh, is that Brecken?" she asked, spotting him and the girl by his side. Lifting her hand, she waved.

Brecken's full lips formed a smile before he leaned down, resting his hands on his knees. He smoothed a hand over his sister's hair, the sweet gesture sending a jolt of awareness down Callie's spine. She'd rarely observed emotion from the stoic man, and something about the gentle way he spoke to the girl called to her. His sister gave a wide grin before nodding up at him. Turning, she rushed toward them, stopping to stare up at Callie.

"My brother says I'm probably supposed to bow to you since you're a princess, but I don't know how," she said, lifting a shoulder.

"Oh, good heavens, no," Callie said, grimacing. Extending her hand, she asked, "How about a good ol'-fashioned handshake. I'm Callie."

"Rowena," she said, giving a firm shake. "I'm Brecken's youngest sister...and his favorite, but he'll never admit it."

"I don't have a favorite," he said, approaching and shooting her a playful glare. "But if I did, it *might* be you."

Biting her lip, Rowena smiled at Callie and held her hand to her face, mimicking telling a secret. "I'm totally his favorite," she whispered.

"Noted," Callie said, winking.

"Hey, man," Jack said, giving that weird high five thing men always did when they greeted. When they finished, Brecken faced her, his expression cordial as his eyes roved over her face. "Hey, Callie."

Callie suddenly wondered if she should've put on lip gloss after drinking wine. Did she have wine lips? Ew. Feeling a strange surge of heat on the back of her neck, she rubbed it as she smiled. "Hey, Brecken. Nice to see you outside of Zadicus's mansion. Glad you two could join us."

He gave a brief nod before directing his attention to his sister and asking her which booth she'd like to frequent first. Licking her lips, Callie rubbed her finger over them, hoping like hell she didn't look like a complete idiot. Reaching into her purse, she drew out her gloss and applied it before placing it back inside. Straightening her spine, she asked, "Where to first, guys?"

Brecken straightened, facing her and opening his mouth to answer. His gaze lowered to her lips, and Callie reflexively pressed them together.

"Rowena wants to start at the science booth," he finally said after an awkward silence. "She goes to Takelia's school for the gifted and talented, and they're studying physics right now."

"Oh, that's where I went," Callie said. "I loved the school even though I didn't have the greatest experience there."

"Why?" Rowena asked.

"Story for another time," she said, waving her hand and stepping forward. "Lead the way. I hear the Lynian museum curators who run the science booths have some awesome relics from our past. My grandmother, Queen Calla, used to collect meteorites that fell to Earth, and I think they have some pieces from her collection. Let's check them out." Extending her hand, she grasped Rowena's, and they began walking, Jack and Brecken falling into step behind them.

Callie could almost feel Brecken's gaze on her neck and told herself to get a grip. So what if he'd been looking at her lips before? He probably was just noticing her sparkly lip gloss. Pushing thoughts of the viscerally handsome man from her mind, she forged ahead with Rowena, excited to enjoy the street fair.

An excerpt from the diary of Calinda, daughter of Darkrip and Arderin

Well, Diary, today I turned eighteen. I'm pretty sure that means I'm too old to have a diary, so this will be my last entry (unless something really drastic happens and I need to vent. We all have our outlets!).

We had an awesome party at Takelia, and Mom even let me drink a beer. It tasted kind of gross and definitely wasn't as good as the wine I secretly drank with Jack a few years ago, but I didn't want to seem immature, so I sipped it until it was gone. Dad scolded her that she shouldn't give me any ideas about growing up too soon and muttered something about pulverizing any man who tried to touch me.

Well, he's in luck because no one's shown any interest. I swear, if a guy actually comes on to me one day, I'll probably say yes so fast his head will spin. Who doesn't want to be loved and desired? Now that I'm eighteen, I'd really like to see what all the fuss is about. Unfortunately, dating me seems to have about the same appeal as sticking a fork into a toaster. Good grief.

Of course, I'm still waiting for my Henry. Although I get discouraged sometimes, I'll never give up hope. I look at all the awesome women in my family and think about how long it took them to find love. I mean, it took Aunt Miranda a thousand years to find Uncle Sathan! Same for Mom, Lila and Evie, so I'm still a baby in this whole "find the love of your life" thing. I hope it doesn't take that long for me, but, hey, the journey only makes us stronger, right?

Anyway, it's been fun. Thanks for getting me through my awkward childhood. Hopefully, adulthood will be better. I'm going to try like hell not to destroy the world. We'll see how that goes. Wish me luck!
  Love, Callie

Chapter 5

Brecken trailed behind Callie and Rowena, barely able to focus on his conversation with Jack since he'd sprung a massive erection the second he saw Callie's lips slathered in the glittery lip gloss. How in the hell was a man supposed to think rationally when someone as gorgeous as Callie enhanced those luscious lips? Glancing at Jack, he hoped his friend didn't notice his body's reaction. So far, his attraction to Callie had been passing—something he noted but didn't dwell on. Would it magnify now he'd agreed to observe her in order to write the letters? Hoping that wasn't the case, he stared at her mass of dark curls as they bobbed. He could almost feel the soft tresses clenched in his hand as he directed her head toward his straining shaft, begging her to spread that sparkly gloss all over his cock...

"Earth to Brecken," Jack said, waving his hand in front of his face.

"Sorry," he muttered. "What were you saying?"

"Just asking how your day off was going. We miss you at the training sessions, and everyone said to tell you hi."

"I miss them too," Brecken said, thinking of the soldiers in his old battalion. "We need to plan a night out, hopefully once Bakari is vanquished. It would be an awesome celebration."

"Definitely," Jack said with a nod. "Siora speaks highly of you. She says you're friends from school."

"Yes. She was thrilled to be one of the first female recruits. It's a boon for rural Lynians like us who grew up poor. The army pays well and allows us to support our families in ways we never would have."

"Dad and Kenden will ensure the soldiers are taken care of even after we defeat Bakari. I know they plan to maintain an army considering there are always unknown threats that can emerge."

"Glad to hear it. If Zadicus ever fires me, I'll come back in a heartbeat."

Chuckling, Jack patted him on the back. "Don't think it will happen, buddy, but you're always welcome."

Crossing the main square, they approached the first row of tents that lined the street.

"Bella!" a jubilant voice called before a man with salt-and-pepper hair rushed over from his booth to hug Callie. "You grow more beautiful every day. The spitting image of your mother." He kissed both cheeks before turning to Jack and extending his hand. "Hello, Lieutenant Jack. So lovely to see you on this fine evening."

"Hey, Antonio," Jack said, shaking his hand. "How's it going?"

"My heart is still broken that your beautiful mother married the brave commander instead of me," he said, dramatically resting his hand over his heart, "but otherwise, I'm surviving, my young friend."

Chuckling, Jack placed his hands on his hips. "I know you were a very close second to Dad, Antonio. If she didn't love him so much, she definitely would've chosen you."

"The words ease my old heart, boy," he said, bowing. "And who do we have here?"

"I'm Rowena," she said, extending her hand.

"Well, hello, Rowena. It's lovely to meet you."

"This is my brother, Brecken. He's surly. That's what my mom says when he comes over and doesn't want to talk to us. 'Your brother is a bit surly today, Rowena. Best to leave him alone,'" she said, mimicking her mother's voice.

"There are four more just like her," Brecken said, his tone droll as he shook Antonio's hand. "You can understand my need for peace and quiet."

Chuckling, Antonio gave a nod. "Indeed." Beckoning them toward his tent, he stepped behind the table and gestured toward the gorgeous paintings. Landscapes, portraits and surreal masterpieces were all on display. "Would you like a painting for your mother, Callie? On the house for you, my dear."

"I'd never take one without paying you, Antonio," Callie said with a cheeky grin, "but I will be back to buy one sometime soon. Zadicus's parents love paintings, and I plan to buy them one of yours once I'm betrothed."

"Yes, I'm so happy to hear you have an ardent admirer, my dear," he said, clasping his hands in front of his chest. "I'm thrilled for you. Now, we have to find a nice young lady for our worthy lieutenant to bond with."

"The lieutenant is just fine flying solo right now, Antonio, but thanks," Jack said, his tone gently warning the man not to push it. "And I'll come back and check out the paintings one day soon. For now, we're heading into town to have a relaxing night off."

Antonio grinned as a woman approached his booth, appraising one of the paintings off to the side.

"Hello, ma'am," he said, pointing to the painting. "That one is on sale, and I've also reduced the price of this smaller print." He gestured toward the print that sat in a display holder on the table.

The woman craned her neck but didn't step closer. Tentatively, her gaze darted toward Callie before she shook her head. "I'll come back later. Thank you."

Callie's expression fell, and Brecken felt something well in his chest. As he observed the situation, he realized it was empathy. It was obvious the woman was wary of Callie, and Brecken felt the sudden need to protect her somehow.

"I'm Brecken," he said, extending his hand. "Son of Maddox and Wren. I live on the south side of the compound."

"I'm familiar with it," she said, unmoving as she assessed him. "I live on the north side near the cattle farms."

"I'm Jack, son of Latimus and Lila. I thought I'd met everyone who lived on Lynia at this point. Have we crossed paths before?"

"No," she said, not taking his hand either as her eyes darted to Callie. "I am thankful for your father and all he does to protect the kingdom. My husband was killed in the war against Crimeous. The Deamon Lord was an evil soul, and I fear there is more destruction to come."

"The future can be daunting," Callie said softly, taking a step forward. The woman recoiled and began to back away. Showing her palms, Callie shook her head. "I didn't mean to scare you."

"You are a vestige of Crimeous and a child of a terrible prophecy," the woman said, clutching her purse. "You should be locked away until Bakari is defeated."

"I have no desire to align with Bakari, ma'am—"

"Hateful creature!" the woman hissed before spitting on the ground. "Your existence denigrates my dear husband's soul." With an angry jerk of her head, she pivoted and walked away.

"My dear," Antonio said, his blue eyes filled with sympathy. "She doesn't know of what she speaks. Don't pay her any attention."

"It's okay," Callie said, her voice gravelly as her throat bobbed. "I'm used to it by now. Our people have been through a lot, and I'm a reminder of that pain. She has a right to her feelings."

"Fear leads to ignorance sometimes," Jack said, rubbing her shoulder. "Hopefully, once we defeat Bakari, this stuff won't happen."

"Yeah," she said, her lips forming a smile that didn't quite meet her eyes. "Well, let's see who else I can terrorize. As much as I hate scaring the living crap out of people, I'm starving, so we're heading into the street fair whether they like it or not."

"Go on, and have a good time, my friends," Antonio said, shooing them away. "And if anyone gives you trouble, you just let ol' Antonio know."

"Thank you," she whispered as her smile grew, and Brecken admired her strength. He'd always imagined Callie lived a charmed life since her parents were royals and hadn't considered what it must be like to live as the subject of a cataclysmic prophecy. Did people shun her often? She seemed resigned to the woman's treatment of her. Brecken admired her restraint. If anyone spoke to him like that, he'd certainly give them a piece of his mind. And if it were a man, he might subject his nose to a piece of his fist too.

"Oh, I see the science booth!" Rowena exclaimed before jogging ahead.

Jack smiled at Callie and jerked his head. "Come on. She's not worth it, Callie."

"I know. See you later, Antonio," she said, taking a step before staring at her shoe. "Go on. My sneaker is untied. I'll catch up."

Jack followed Rowena, but Brecken was frozen for some reason. Staring down at her as she tied her shoe, he had the sudden urge to stroke her hair. To soothe her and reassure her everything was going to be okay.

"All right," she said, rising and flashing him a brilliant smile. "Shoe is secured, and I'm ready to go."

Tilting his head, he studied her. "You handled that very well, princess."

"Ew. Don't call me that," she said, scrunching her nose. "I hate it, and also my dad calls my mom that, so it's really weird."

Breathing a laugh, he nodded. "Noted. I'm just impressed, that's all."

Shrugging, she turned and began walking while Brecken fell into step beside her. "It's happened all my life. Well, since we moved back here from L.A. People are scared of me, or think I'm a freak, or both. But my parents taught me that I can't control people's actions. I can only control my reaction, so that's what I do." She glanced up at him, and Brecken forced himself to focus on her sparkling eyes, which were almost as alluring as those sparkly lips. "Plus, we're royalty and have to set an example. So, I just deal with it."

"Like Jack said, hopefully, the burden will ease when we defeat Bakari. My father died in an ambush from one of his Deamon battalions when he was on a scouting mission over a decade ago. One of the slimy bastards shot him point-blank in the chest with an eight-shooter. He never stood a chance."

"Oh, Brecken, I'm so sorry," she said, her expression filled with such compassion he felt it wrap around his skin like a warm blanket. "And you have five sisters to look after. No wonder you put up with Zadicus. Now, I get it."

Lifting his eyebrows, he said, "I don't think you're supposed to speak about your future betrothed that way."

"Oh, I'm not saying it in a mean way," she said in a reassuring tone. "He knows he's stuffy and can be a bit dismissive sometimes. We've talked about it. He's working on it, but it takes time, especially when you're raised an aristocrat in the 'old world' mentality."

"I think your influence is good on him," Brecken said. "I'm happy you two found each other."

"Me too," she said wistfully. "I was sure I was going to die a washed-up spinster. Thank the goddess someone was willing to look past the prophecy and court me." Her tone was teasing, but Brecken understood the underlying context. Somewhere along the way, Callie had begun to believe she was unlovable. It nearly broke his usually impassive heart, considering she was kind and compassionate and one of the most gorgeous women he'd ever met.

Gazing down at her, Brecken felt a sudden sense of loss. What if they'd met under different circumstances? What if he'd been the first man to show interest in her? Would she have been open to dating a man far beneath her station who couldn't even fathom living the lavish lifestyle she was used to?

Deciding it never would've happened, Brecken pushed the thoughts away. Some things were just too far from reality. A royal princess didn't date blue-collar rural Vampyres from outlying compounds no matter how progressive their queen was. Brecken was a realist and understood his place in the world, and it was clear he and Callie didn't orbit the same circles.

Still, it was fun to imagine it for a moment. Holding her and being draped in all that long, silky hair while they were locked in a passionate embrace. Although he was pragmatic, he wouldn't lie to himself about wanting her. If he lived in a world where he had the chance to touch her, he'd latch on and never let go.

But he didn't live in that world, and neither did she, so he walked beside her, genuinely wishing she would find happiness with Zadicus. Perhaps writing the letters would help secure her happiness, and if they did, was it really such a terrible thing to do in the scheme of things?

Yes. The word floated through his brain, and his lips flattened. Yes, it was wrong. And Brecken had the strange feeling that the more he grew to know Callie, the worse he would feel about deceiving her. Feeling the aversion flow in his veins, he let it surge, understanding he deserved to feel like an ass because, well, he was one.

"Oh, she's so excited about the meteorites!" Callie called, pointing at Rowena as she stood in front of the science booth examining the rock. "Let me see." Approaching the booth, she smiled as Rowena held up the stone. Callie's excitement was as palpable as his sister's, and the weight of his deception sat on his shoulders, an unwanted but necessary burden.

"Well, they're excited about a bunch of rocks. Low bar, huh?" Jack teased, walking over.

"Yeah," Brecken said, rubbing his forehead.

"Come on. Let's check out the blacksmith's booth. He makes excellent swords and sparring weapons."

Nodding, Brecken followed his friend, pretending to examine the swords while watching Callie out of the corner of his eye the entire time.

Chapter 6

Bakari, son of Vampyre King Markdor and Queen Calla, sat at the desk in the cottage on the outskirts of the former Deamon caves. The cottage had been his home for years now and was protected by the invisibility shield Dr. Tyson concocted from a mix of chemicals and several hairs Bakari had collected from Evie's daughter, Rinada. The hybrid scientist was an expert at manipulating molecules to make various weapons and potions for Bakari, which added to his usefulness—for the time being anyway.

Bakari's ears pricked, and he straightened, head snapping toward the door. A moment later, he heard the crunch of leaves and branches outside. Rising, he stalked toward the door and pulled it open.

"Get in here before you're detected by one of Latimus's drones," Bakari ordered.

"Sorry," Zadicus said, frustration in his tone. "I can never find your house. The invisibility cloak is too good."

Closing the door, Bakari whirled around. "You're never to contact me unless I summon you. Showing up unannounced is dangerous and could ruin everything."

"I had no other way to contact you since we can't use phones or email as Heden and Sofia are so skilled at tracking devices. I'm sorry, but I felt the need to update you."

Worry began to spread in Bakari's chest. "Fine. We're shielded now that we're inside and the door is closed. Sit," he said, gesturing to the couch.

Once they were seated at each end, Zadicus cleared his throat.

"I am still on track to bond with Callie. I plan to propose to her on our eleven-month anniversary," he said, his tone devoid of passion. "I have devised a plan that will help move things along. She seemed enthralled by my gallant gestures when we began courting, but I fear the excitement is wearing off. Hopefully, this new tactic will help."

Bakari arched a brow. "You said wooing her would be easy."

Sighing, he rubbed his forehead. "I thought it would be, considering no one has ever courted her before. But we are very different people, and that is beginning to show."

"Well, then, I hope your new tactic works. I would ask you if you need help, but that wasn't part of our deal. You assured me you could win her over, Zadicus."

"Of course I can," Zadicus said, waving his hand. "I just felt you should know. I'll get her across the finish line. She's just so...*free-spirited.*" His features contorted. "It's unbecoming and not what I anticipated from a daughter of royals."

Laughing, Bakari ran a hand over his black hair. "She is a stubborn young woman whose veins pulse with Crimeous's blood. What did you expect?"

"I expected a boring, biddable woman," Zadicus said, crossing his ankle over his thigh, waggling his foot as he scowled. "Aristocrats of my stature at Valeria envision bonding with respectful, supplicant females."

"You knew what you were signing up for when we devised this plan, Zadicus. If you want to back out, tell me now. I've had enough dissenters over the years. The one thing I admire about your Aunt Melania is that she was forthright enough to leave the cause and admit she didn't have the constitution to carry out my plan. I prefer that to someone who can't get the job done."

"I'll get it done," Zadicus snapped, "and I would urge you—"

The man gasped before clutching his throat as Bakari assessed him, cold and unyielding.

"I am the son of King Markdor and Queen Calla and future ruler of this realm. I would caution you not to speak to me in that tone again."

Zadicus nodded furiously before Bakari released his telekinetic hold on the man's throat. Watching the Vampyre sputter as he strove to catch his breath brought Bakari great pleasure. Once his struggles abated, Bakari sighed.

"We must be aligned," he said, lifting his chin in the austere manner he'd acquired over the centuries. "For our plan to work, you must bond with Callie, impregnate her and bring the child to me. I will barter her child's safety for her alliance with our cause. A mother's bond is the strongest I've ever seen. It is the only thing I can fathom that would make her dissent from her family. Once we have her acquiescence, we will complete the prophecy, and I can finally kill the royals, cementing my place as ruler of the immortal realm."

"Every mother but your own," Zadicus murmured.

Bristling, Bakari inched closer and spoke through clenched teeth. "What did you say?"

"Your mother cast you out to the human world and resumed her life as if you never existed. Let's hope Callie has more care for her own child—"

Lurching from the couch, Bakari stood, backhanding Zadicus before he rose and pressed his hand to his rapidly self-healing bleeding lip.

"If you touch me again, our agreement is off," Zadicus declared.

"Don't forget what you have to gain here, Zadicus. I have promised you governorship over all the compounds once I defeat the royal family. Your lust for approval by the aristocrats of the kingdom makes no sense to me, but I care not what motivates you as long as you accomplish your mission."

"My family has been overlooked for years by the royal family. They should've made me governor instead of Camron all those years ago, when Sathan named him to the position. Aunt Melania did her best to cement her place as a respected member of the council when she married Camron, but that will never be enough. I have been shunned by the royal family for too long. We both have."

"Yes," Bakari said, stepping back to create space between them. "Our goals are aligned. It is why I approached you in the first place. Callie often feels isolated and misunderstood in this world, and you have done an excellent job seducing her. We're extremely close to accomplishing our mission. Have you slept with her yet?"

He huffed and rubbed the back of his neck. "She made some asinine pact with her mother she would wait until the night of her bonding ceremony."

Bakari's lips twitched, and he realized it was in admiration.

"You have affection for her," Zadicus said, eyes narrowing. "Perhaps it is *you* who won't be able to complete the mission."

"Don't be ridiculous. I've observed her since she was born. I feel a certain...fondness for her," he said, circling his hand, "because I sense her restlessness and feelings of not belonging. They are familiar to what I felt in my youth. But when the time comes, I will do what I must."

"Kill her," he said, his voice low. "You'll kill them all."

"It must be done," Bakari said with a nod. "They are a pestilence on this kingdom. Their fondness for humans and desire to breed hybrids..." He grimaced, wiping a hand over his face. "It is appalling. I cannot let it go on. My parents' legacy deserves better. Immortals deserve a leader who will uphold eons of tradition and return the kingdom to greatness."

"And a governor like me who shares those views," Zadicus said before striding to the door. "I'll get her across the finish line and give you the child you seek." He pulled open the door before Bakari called his name.

"Yes?"

"You're still willing to give up the child you conceive?"

He scoffed. "I want no child with Crimeous's blood. I want a purebred Vampyre, with the royal, aristocratic blood of a Valerian. Once Callie and the child are dead, I will marry someone with a pristine bloodline who is biddable and respectable."

"Good," Bakari said, giving a dismissive nod. "Remember that we need her alive to align with me and fulfill the prophecy. She must not be harmed as we carry out our plan."

"Understood." With a final salute, Zadicus exited the cottage.

Bakari took a moment to digest the conversation before striding from the cottage and approaching the nearby cave. Latimus and Kenden had attempted to destroy all the Deamon caves after Crimeous's defeat, but thankfully, some were left unscathed. The entrance to the cave where Commander Vadik lived with the Deamon troops was also masked by the invisibility cloak. Waving his hand, the cave's entrance appeared, and Bakari entered.

He trailed through the darkened walkway until he arrived at the expansive dwelling where the soldiers resided. His cloned Deamon army was now exceedingly strong and formidable. Approaching Vadik, the soldier stood and saluted.

"Hello, King Bakari."

"Commander Vadik," he said with a nod. "I trust the soldiers are doing well in their training exercises."

"Yes," he replied with a curt tilt of his head.

"Excellent," Bakari said, glancing over the troops who mulled about in the cave. "Calinda will have a child in less than two years' time if all goes according to plan. That is when we will strike. One final battle to end this conflict once and for all."

"You have been patient, Bakari," a female voice said over his shoulder. "I am impressed. I sometimes wondered if you would rush the outcome."

"Time has different meaning when one is immortal, Ananda," he said, turning to face the woman, her skin marred and wrinkled under white hair since she'd gone through her immortal change later in life. "I would rather do things right than quickly."

"Very wise indeed, although the immortals have been valiant foes. I am humble enough to admit I underestimated them. Every toxin you've created to kill the Slayers has been remedied with an antidote from Sadie and Nolan almost immediately. You've had many skirmishes but haven't been able to beat them by brute force."

"I realized years ago the only way we would prevail was to gain Calinda's alliance—whether it be by choice or by force. The Elven prophecy discovered in the hidden scrolls carries much significance. I have been preparing the Deamon troops and injecting them with Dr. Tyson's potions to increase their muscle tone and strength. When we have the final battle, all pieces will be in place, and we will emerge victorious."

Closing the distance, she regarded both men who towered above her. "I will be happy once the conflict is over. I only want to live in peace in a realm restored to its former glory. One without hybrids and impure bloodlines. My niece's children are a disgrace, as is her entire family."

"On that, we are all agreed," Bakari said, cupping her shoulder. Ananda had become a mother figure of sorts in the years he'd known her, although she was too coldhearted to ever inspire true deep affection. "I will be king, Vadik will be Commander, Zadicus will govern the compounds and you will finally be able to move back into your ancestral home at Astaria and live out the rest of your days in peace."

"May the goddess make it so," she said softly.

Solemn in their united goal, the three members of Bakari's alliance basked in the hope that the prophecy would come true and Etherya's Earth would flourish once again.

Chapter 7

A few days after the street fair, Callie took the train to Valeria to see Zadicus. He'd asked her to dinner and promised the servants would set up a lovely table in the garden so they could eat under the stars. Wrinkling her nose, Callie admitted she would've preferred he set up the dinner himself, but she wouldn't hold it against him. It was the thought that counted, and she was happy he wanted to give her a special evening.

When she arrived, a servant took her light jacket, offering to bring it to her if she got cold later on. Thanking him, she went in search of Zadicus, finding him in the garden leaning over and smelling one of the beautiful red roses.

"Look at you enjoying nature," she teased, approaching and glancing at the roses. "They're beautiful."

He plucked one, causing her to emit a huff. "Oh, no, don't—"

"For you," he said, handing it to her. "From one beautiful flower to another."

Callie had to legitimately contain her laugh at the cheesy words and lifted the rose to her nose to hide her lips. Someone cleared their throat in the distance, and she glanced over, noticing Brecken pressing his lips together, trying like hell not to laugh. Goddess, he must've heard Zadicus's terrible line too. Crinkling her features, she shot him a playful glare before focusing back on Zadicus.

"I didn't want you to pluck it, but now that you have, I'll say thank you."

"Why?" he asked, perplexed.

"Because once you pluck it, it dies, Zadicus. I wanted it to live with the rest of its friends in the garden."

"Only you would accuse a flower of having friends, Callie," he said, extending his hand. She took it, and he led her to the table that was set up along the row of neatly trimmed hedges. "It's a plant, for the goddess's sake."

He pulled out her chair, and she sat, resting the rose on the table as she settled into the seat. When he sat down across from her, she smiled.

"That's one more difference between us, Zadicus. You see a plant where I see a living thing. Each tree and bush and flower has their own energy signature if you look close enough."

Spreading his napkin over his lap, his eyes narrowed. "Whatever you say, sweetheart. I had the cook prepare a nice dinner for us. I'm starting to enjoy food very much. I only ever drank Slayer blood before you, although my mother has always enjoyed food even though we don't need it."

Realizing he was done with the plant discussion, she rested her elbows on the table. "Yes, us hybrids need food and Slayer blood for sustenance. I guess we're mutts, in a sense."

"Your mother's Vampyre blood is so pure," he said, rubbing his chin. "My aristocratic blood will help enhance it when we have children."

Swallowing thickly, Callie let the seriousness of the statement wash over her. "That would mean you're planning to ask me to bond with you."

"Well, yes, sweetheart," he said, lifting his shoulders. "What do you think we were doing here? We've almost been together for a year. That's certainly enough time to be sure we're right for each other."

Callie wasn't so sure, but her desire to be with someone...to be loved...was intense, and she truly did appreciate Zadicus's efforts. She enjoyed spending time with him, and her heart always thrummed during their passionate kisses. Betrothal and bonding were the next natural steps. She'd always known this and expected it. In fact, she'd looked forward to it when they first began courting. Now? Well, her excitement had waned immensely, which worried her.

He asked her about her day, and they slipped into conversation, although Callie's thoughts lingered on her hesitations. After her discussion with Jack at the street fair, she wondered if she was moving too quickly with Zadicus. Was a year too soon to get engaged?

After dinner, they conversed as they finished their bottle of wine. Callie relaxed as the wine coursed through her veins, reminding herself to enjoy the moment. She shortened the stem of the rose and stuck it behind her ear, pleased when Zadicus's eyes flared with appreciation. Settling into the moment, she told herself to calm her fears. Things would work out if she let them progress naturally. She'd always believed that, so why stop now?

When they finished, Zadicus took her for a stroll around the garden and drew her into a fervent kiss. Callie kissed him back, annoyed when her thoughts drifted to Brecken. Was he watching them? Somehow, the idea rankled her, and when she drew back, she glanced around, relieved she couldn't see him. He must've wanted to give them a bit of privacy and was probably flanked along the side of the mansion.

Eventually, Zadicus walked her to the train. Brecken trailed several paces behind, far enough away to go unnoticed, but she felt his presence anyway. It was that strange energy she always felt between them, and it registered in every pore of her skin as they strolled. When she turned to walk down the train platform stairs, Zadicus grabbed her hand and stuck an envelope in her palm.

"What's this?" she asked, grinning.

"A letter. Read it when you're home in your bedroom and think of me. Good night, sweetheart." Leaning down, he kissed her cheek.

"Good night. Thank you for a lovely dinner."

She followed his directive, not opening the letter until she was at home with her face washed, teeth brushed and in her comfy PJs. Sitting on the edge of her bed, she opened the envelope and pulled out the letter.

My Dearest Callie,

Since my first attempt at poetry was dreadful, I thought I'd try my hand at writing you love letters. It's something I've never done before, but you deserve nothing less than sweet words of devotion.

For this first letter, I wanted to remark on your beauty. Yes, there will be other letters where I will go deeper, but for now, I'll focus on how gorgeous you are inside and out. Sometimes, when you look at me with those stunning ocean-colored eyes, I struggle to breathe. They're always filled with kindness and a slight bit of mischief, which makes me wonder where you got your sense of humor. It's quite attractive, and I enjoy your playful self-deprecation and teasing. As you know, I'm quite stoic and appreciate having someone like you around to remind me life doesn't always have to be so serious.

And your lips. Sometimes, they shine under the late-afternoon sunlight after you've covered them in gloss, and my mind can't focus on anything else but kissing you. Perhaps you've employed your powers against me, for you've put me under a spell I never want to break.

And finally, there is your generous spirit, which is most beautiful of all. You're able to look upon those who castigate you with compassion and scold anyone who speaks to servants or soldiers without respect. It is a magnificent quality that many might not even know you possess. But I know, and it solidifies how lucky I am to be your suitor. Hopefully, one day, I will be your bonded. I will continue to write you these letters to ensure it happens.

Love,
Zadicus

Callie finished the letter and then read it again, impressed with Zadicus's soulful words. It was much better than the poem he'd written her and called to the teenage girl deep within who'd never been asked to dance.

"He thinks you're beautiful," she said, folding the letter and gently rubbing it with her fingers. "It's very sweet."

Trailing to her desk, she placed the letter on top of the folded poem he'd also written, heart full from his romantic gesture. She would certainly tell him how lovely it was next time they were together. It appeared he planned to write her more, which warmed her heart.

Sliding into bed, Callie turned off the lamp and snuggled under the covers. Settling into her dreams, she was too tired to question why it was Brecken's handsome face she saw admiring her sparkly lip gloss instead of the man to which she would soon become betrothed.

Chapter 8

Zadicus continued his courtship of Callie, and she focused on being open to his lavish gifts and fervent devotion. As the weeks wore on, she knew they were moving toward inevitable betrothal, and her concerns lingered. She couldn't decide if they stemmed from true misgivings or if they were just commitment jitters considering Zadicus was her first ever suitor. A part of her felt guilty for having doubts. After all, Zadicus was known as one of the greatest catches in the kingdom, and he'd set his sights on her. Even with the prophecy that loomed large, he wanted her. It was evidence of his genuineness, and she reminded herself of this when the reservations surfaced.

Of course, it didn't help that Callie had begun having highly sexualized dreams about a certain bodyguard whose presence she always felt even when he couldn't be seen. She had no idea why her mind wandered to Brecken in the dark of night considering the man barely acknowledged her.

She tried to speak to him on occasion, when he accompanied them into Valeria's main square or during other functions she attended with Zadicus. He would always look at her with those deep bronze eyes and remain silent until Zadicus urged her along. On the scant occasions he did reply, it was with one-word mumbles and grunts. He certainly was a man of few words, and Callie figured remaining silent was a requirement of his job, so she let it lie.

Zadicus continued to write her beautiful letters that certainly helped alleviate her fears they were moving too fast. The letters gave her a glimpse into his head and confirmed he was indeed getting to know her on a deeper level.

He also made an effort to attend some functions with her, although she suspected he didn't have the same desire to help the citizens of the kingdom as she did—especially the ones on the rural compounds. But his family always donated generously to the army, and she accepted there were many ways people could help their fellow immortals.

Zadicus did attend one of Lila's library functions with her, which warmed her heart. Her aunt ran literacy programs throughout the kingdom and was determined to teach every member of the realm to read. She often held events on the outlying compounds, and during one such event, Callie offered to help. Zadicus tagged along, although he sat in the corner most of the day, explaining he needed to help solidify the invite list for a lavish party his mother was planning to throw.

"You go on and help Lila, sweetheart," he said, urging her toward the center of the large room. "I'll be here if you need me."

Callie joined her aunt and proceeded to spend hours helping the laborers who'd shown up. They represented all age ranges, and she was thrilled at the turnout. Brecken stood off to the side, hands crossed over his belt as he observed. The only moment he broke rank was when Rowena showed up and ran to him, giving him a hug before jogging over to Callie.

"I brought some books to donate," she said excitedly, pulling them from her bag. "They're fifth-grade science books, and since I'm the youngest, we don't need them anymore. Mom says she's popped out her last kid."

Chuckling, Callie took the books, recognizing some of them as the old textbooks she'd used in school. "This is fantastic, Rowena. Thank you for donating. Do you want to help us teach the others?"

Her brown eyes widened, so similar to Brecken's, and she nodded. "I'd love that. I want to be a professor one day."

"Awesome. Come on—I'll get you set up." After she was situated with several citizens, Callie approached Brecken, flashing a brilliant smile. "Your sister's awesome. Guess it's possible for *some* people in your family to have an outgoing personality."

He gave her a droll look, causing her to snicker. "Sorry, I'm sure you're really exciting when you're off duty."

"Excitement's overrated," he muttered, returning his gaze to the center of the room.

"No way." She scrunched her features. "I crave excitement. I can't wait to get back to the human world and see all the places I haven't been yet. Zadicus says he's going to take me there on our honeymoon once we bond and once we've hopefully defeated Bakari."

His expression remained impassive. "That's nice. Congratulations."

Breathing a laugh, she shook her head. "Don't you want to see other things? There's so much out there to explore."

Rust-colored eyes drifted to hers, locking on as her breath caught in her throat. "Some don't have the luxury of traveling the world. I have to work, and I enjoy working. That's enough for me."

"Anyone can make something happen if they wish," she said, lifting a finger. "I'm sure it wouldn't kill you to take a few days off."

He remained silent, causing her to emit a huff. "Oh, fine. Stand here against the wall and frown all day. Sounds exhilarating."

His lips twitched, and she grinned, elated she'd gotten the small reaction out of him. Lila called her over to help, and she sauntered away, determined to continue to try and crack the serious soldier.

That evening, Callie rode the train home, and Zadicus pressed another letter into her palm. She read it on the train, her heart full as she cherished the romantic words.

My Dearest Callie,

I must remark on how gorgeous you were the night we had dinner in the garden. When you placed the rose behind your ear and smiled, I realized I'd never seen anything more beautiful. Sometimes, my eyes linger on your cute half-fangs and I imagine how they would feel against my vein. As you may have guessed, I am enamored with your mouth, your lips and all facets of your stunning beauty.

I was taken by your idea that plants are living beings with unique energy signatures, just as we are. Forgive me for first dismissing it. After some thought, it makes perfect sense and only highlights your compassion. The way you use your powers to heal animals speaks volumes about your character. You've told me how physically taxing it is, but you continue to help animals in need even if it causes you temporary pain. It is selfless, and I am honored to be with someone with such a benevolent heart.

I realize I will never be worthy of you, but I will try my best to be the man you inspire me to be. I am thankful for your affection, but perhaps even more grateful for your friendship.

Love,
Zadicus

Callie folded the letter, pleased at the tender words. She was slowly coming to see Zadicus in a new light with the missives and was glad he took the time to write them. She craved a lover who was also her best friend, which required cultivation considering they were quite different, and was happy to receive confirmation he felt the same. It went a long way toward squelching her doubts, and she settled into the plushy train seat, excited for the future with her surprisingly eloquent suitor.

※

Brecken arrived at Zadicus's home shortly after sunrise, admitting he was in a terrible mood. He'd been writing letters to Callie for weeks and was slowly realizing something quite disconcerting: he was falling under the spell of the woman his ward was going to marry.

Of course, he'd never meant it to happen. Attraction was one thing, and Brecken had always accepted his attraction to Callie. She was a beautiful, charming woman, and being drawn to that was natural for any man. But over these past weeks, as he'd observed her and truly gotten to know her, he'd seen past the attraction to the woman within. And what he observed was, in a word, *magnificent*.

Never had he met someone with her combination of humor, charisma and compassion. She devoted her time to healing animals and helping others learn to read, all while charming his sister, who claimed to be her best friend.

"I'm pretty sure Callie already has a best friend," he'd muttered to Rowena one night as they sat on the porch at his mother's house.

"Who?" she asked, shrugging. "Jack, maybe. They're really close. Not Zadicus though. He barely spoke to her at the library. She's really nice, but sometimes, people are mean to her. It's annoying because she's super-cool, so I've decided I'm going to be her best friend."

"You're not worried about the prophecy? That she'll destroy the world?" Lifting his hands, he playfully shook them, mocking being scared.

"No way," Rowena said, waving her hand. "When we learned about the prophecy in school, the teacher insisted it was very vague. I'm not scared of some old scrolls."

"Well, that's very progressive of you, but not everyone shares your view."

Huffing, she crossed her arms and sat back in the chair. "I'll change this kingdom one day. You mark my words. Queen Miranda is going to love me, and I'll help her and Evie bring equality and practicality to the kingdom."

Brecken smiled at his sister, knowing she would accomplish anything she set her mind to. Her words about Callie rang true: many people in the kingdom shunned her because they were worried about the prophecy. Even with that knowledge, she forged ahead, helping her people. She seemed guided by genuine purpose to help others and to help animals, and he admired her ability to help people who castigated her. Others might have railed at the world, but not Callie. She somehow brushed it off and carried on with her life, which impressed the hell out of Brecken.

As the letters increased in frequency and he got to know her better, he understood they were no longer a ruse. Instead, they were his small way of telling her how special she was, even if she would never know they came from him. Entering Zadicus's large sitting room, Brecken strode to his place in the corner, waiting for his ward to appear. They were going to town to pick up some flowers for his mother's dinner party later that evening. Brecken had no idea why they didn't just cut them from the multitudes of flowers in the garden, but who was he to question aristocrats' actions?

Silently waiting, he recalled the last letter he'd written to Callie. Closing his eyes, the words scrolled through his mind:

My Dearest Callie,

I find it hard to articulate just how seamlessly you've drawn me under your spell. Never did I expect it, but I find myself barely able to think of anything but you. So often, my thoughts will drift to your sparkling cobalt eyes or your mellifluous laugh, and before I know it, I'm lost in you once again.

Observing you teach the citizens to read warmed my heart, and I was especially taken with your interactions with the teenagers. Some of them have already dropped out of school to help their parents at home, and your determination to ensure they have access to education is admirable. Sometimes, you speak of the unknowns of having your own children since they will inevitably inherit some of your powers, but you don't need to worry, Callie-lily. Your gracious heart and natural intuition will serve them well, and they will be lucky to call you Mom.

I am excited to see what the future will hold. You deserve nothing but happiness, and I will do everything in my power to ensure you receive it.

Love,
Zadicus

Lifting his lids, Brecken smirked at the nickname he'd fashioned. His mother's favorite flower was the calla lily, and it seemed fitting for Callie. Of course, she thought Zadicus had penned the name, which rankled him, but he left it in the letter anyway. Perhaps as a small indication of his affection for her, even if she would never know.

"Good morning," Zadicus said, breezing into the room. "I'll be ready to head to town in five minutes."

Brecken gave a nod. "We're going to the florist on Main Street?"

"Actually, no." Rummaging around on the desk, he filtered through some papers. "We're going to buy Callie a betrothal ring. I made up the bit about the flowers so I don't ruin the surprise."

The words caused Brecken's heart to slam in his chest, and he resisted the urge to rub the sting. This was bound to happen eventually, and he'd thought himself prepared for their betrothal. Apparently, his heart had other ideas. Inwardly commanding the pounding to cease, he tilted his head.

"I thought you would give her one of the rings from the family's collection."

"No," he said, absently shaking his head. "I've decided to buy her something new. Something more fitting for her remarkable bloodline."

Although the sentiment seemed genuine, Brecken thought he heard a twinge of distain in his ward's voice at the word "remarkable."

"Your letters have helped immensely," Zadicus continued, stacking papers as he organized. "And she's none the wiser, thank the goddess. I wasn't sure if I should rewrite them, but when I compared our handwriting, it was almost identical. Perhaps one thing we actually have in common." Glancing his way, Zadicus arched an eyebrow.

"Perhaps," Brecken muttered, inwardly remarking they were indeed as different as two men could be. For starters, he'd never deceive his girlfriend the way Zadicus deceived Callie.

But you are deceiving her...

The words filtered through his brain, causing him to clench his jaw. Goddess, he hated the fact he had any hand in the ruse. At first, he'd justified it because it had secured his mother's job, which she was happily settled into and thriving. As the weeks progressed and the guilt began to gnaw at him, he continued to justify his actions by acknowledging he was doing what was best for Callie. After all, he wanted her to be happy. She seemed to genuinely care for Zadicus and often spoke of how wonderful it was to be courted. She was ready to settle down and bond, and Zadicus fit perfectly into her world.

Nowhere in their reality did there exist a possibility where Brecken could court her instead. They might as well have come from two different planets. Callie, with her royal heritage and wanderlust, who dreamed of traveling the world. Brecken from a modest, rural family with no path toward ever being anything but a working class soldier. He just couldn't imagine a scenario where it could happen.

So he wrote the letters, hoping it would push her toward happiness. Zadicus was wealthy and could offer her everything her heart desired. Although he was eccentric, he was kind to her, except for the deception with the letters, which irked Brecken. But Zadicus admitted he was terrible at writing and only wanted to woo Callie in every way she deserved. The justification was enough for Brecken, although it had recently begun to wear thin. Realizing this was an opportunity to end the uncomfortable arrangement, Brecken cleared his throat.

"Once she accepts your betrothal, I assume you won't need me to write the letters anymore."

Zadicus looked up from his missive. "No. I'll relieve you of the duty. Your mother's position is secure, and you've earned it. Callie adores the letters, and they've accomplished the task. I appreciate your efforts."

Brecken nodded, feeling the melancholy wash over him at the knowledge he'd never have the opportunity to pen more letters to the woman who now consumed his thoughts. Perhaps he would write her one more—a secret letter in which he'd finally tell her everything he wished to say. Yes, that would bring him some closure and be quite cathartic.

Grinning, he realized how much he'd changed in the span of a few weeks. Brecken had never needed closure or felt desire to write secret letters to any of the women he'd casually courted in the past. But Callie was different, and he wasn't too proud to admit she'd had a profound effect on him. Somehow, she'd tunneled her way into his heart and cracked open a door that had been firmly sealed. It was humbling for someone with his unemotional nature, and he admired the headstrong woman who'd elicited the change. Although he was ashamed of his deception, he was grateful for the opportunity to get to know her.

"Come," Zadicus said, dragging him from the thoughts as he padded across the room. "Let's head to town. Time to get this over with."

Brecken thought it strange he saw the task as a chore considering picking out a bonding ring for Callie would bring him great pleasure. But they were different men, and Zadicus had probably seen more fancy jewelry in his lifetime than Brecken could imagine. What was one more ring to add to the pile? Perhaps it was commonplace to someone as wealthy as Zadicus.

Following his ward, they headed into the bright, warm day and began the trek to Valeria's main square.

Chapter 9

Two months later

Callie gazed into the mirror as Glarys tugged and maneuvered the mass of dark curls upon her head. After one particularly hard tug, she uttered an *"ouch"* before Glarys's eyes grew wide.

"Oh, I'm sorry, dear," she said, concern in her ice-blue eyes. "Too rough?"

"Yeah," Callie said, grinning into the reflection. "I'd like to keep half of it attached to my scalp."

"Of course, dear. I'll be more careful. Your hair is so gorgeous, and I want it to be perfect for your wedding day."

Callie ruminated on the upcoming ceremony, now only hours away, and gulped the water in her slightly shaking hand. Everything had happened so fast over the past few weeks, and she'd been swept up in the excitement. Zadicus had bought her a lovely diamond ring and given her a sweet proposal where he'd lowered to one knee and asked her to bond.

She'd stared at him with equal parts excitement and trepidation as she contemplated her answer. In that moment, the memories of their courtship flashed through her mind, and she realized he'd given her everything she'd ever craved. Most importantly, she cherished his heartfelt letters, which showcased a window into his soul she didn't see when they were together. It showed his vulnerability, being able to open himself that way, and Callie found it so thoughtful. Pushing her reservations aside, she'd agreed to become his bonded mate.

Now, sitting in front of the mirror as Glarys styled her hair, the doubts were surfacing once more, causing little pricks of anxiety to pulse in her stomach.

"It's okay to be nervous, sweetie," Glarys said, hands fussing with her curls. "I remember how anxious Latimus was on the day of his bonding ceremony to Lila, although he'd never admit it. These big events can be intimidating."

"Were you nervous on either of your bonding ceremony days?"

Glarys's lips pursed. "No," she said, shaking her head, "but I felt so comfortable with Victor and Sam. I never believed in soul mates until I met them, but I'm extremely lucky to have had two."

"Sam's such a sweetheart, and he's pretty hot, Glarys," Callie said with a wink. "I love that you're the older woman. I need pointers from you."

"Oh, hush with that nonsense," she said, cheeks growing red under her snow white hair. "I still sometimes wonder why he wants me when he could have any woman he set his sights on."

"Because you're amazing."

"Well, thank you, sweetie," she said, palming Callie's shoulder. "I think I'm all finished. Do you like it?"

"I do," Callie said, turning her head to look at the half-updo. "I think the style will compliment my dress."

Squeezing her shoulder, Glarys gave her a knowing look. "If you want to take a few minutes to walk along the river, I could cover for you. It might be good to take some time alone with your thoughts."

Rotating on the stool, Callie gazed up at the sage woman. "Really? That would be awesome."

"Sure thing," was her kind reply as she stroked Callie's cheek. "Go on through the back door, and I'll tell everyone you're touching up your makeup one last time."

"Thank you, Glarys," she said, standing and placing a kiss on her cheek. "I love you so much."

"I love you, dear," she whispered, and Callie noticed the glimmer of tears in her eyes. "Now, go on."

Thankful for the reprieve, Callie dashed down the staircase and out the back entrance on the ground floor of the east wing of Astaria's castle. She and Zadicus had decided to have their bonding ceremony in the grand garden at Astaria since it was the official royal Vampyre compound—and since Bakari hadn't been able to penetrate Etherya's protective wall—thus making it the most secure place for a formal ceremony.

Inhaling the fresh late-morning air, Callie strode to the river, thankful she was still in her sweatpants and tank top and not yet clad in her fancy dress. Several minutes later, she approached the riverbank, observing the tall, willowy grass, and was soothed by the gurgle of the water.

Sitting on the soft bank, she stretched out her legs, mesmerized by the white bubbles in the water as they ran over the rocks.

"You are foolish to ignore your intuition, Calinda, daughter of Darkrip."

Flinching, Callie scrambled to her feet and stared at the woman who'd materialized from thin air. "Hello, Tatiana," she said, taken with the woman's deep amber gaze. "You scared the crap out of me." Realizing she was holding her hand over her pounding heart, she lowered it, resting it on her hip as curiosity swelled.

"I'm sorry," Tatiana said with a slow tilt of her head. "I thought you would be used to teleportation thanks to your father and Aunt Evie."

"I'm jumpy, I guess," she said, wondering why the strange woman felt the need to approach her during her moment of solitude. "Big day and all."

"Yes," Tatiana said, glancing at the ground before reclaiming Callie's gaze. "For more reasons than you can fathom."

Callie's eyes narrowed. "What's that supposed to mean? Look, I know you and Uncle Heden are friends and he likes your whole dramatic, creepy proselytizer routine, but I'm not really a fan."

Leaning down, Tatiana plucked a wildflower from the ground before straightening and slowly plucking away the petals as she spoke. "I don't mean to be obtuse, but I felt it necessary to give you a slight push in the right direction."

"And what direction is that?"

Long lashes blinked over the woman's luminous eyes. "Toward the prophecy."

Callie clenched her jaw. "Look, I get that the prophecy says I'm going to destroy the world, but I'm pretty chill just living my life, healing animals and trying to fit into a world that doesn't really get me half the time. I don't care about some faded scrolls that were written a million years before I was born."

"Fate cares not whether it is acknowledged as long as it is realized."

Emitting a frustrated groan, Callie sliced her hand through the air. "I have no stake in something that was predicted eons before I was born. Not interested."

"Your resistance is palpable, and that is understandable," she said, pulling the last petal from the flower before dropping the stem to the ground. "I believe it originates from fear, and there is no shame in that."

"Really?" She crossed her arms. "And what is it that I'm so afraid of?"

Running a hand over her long brown curls, Tatiana sighed. "That you are making a mistake marrying Zadicus."

Callie huffed. "I love him."

Shrugging, she smiled. "It's a believable lie to most, but not to you. You know deep within the words are false."

"You think I'm dumb enough to agree to marry a man I don't love?"

Her nostrils flared as she inhaled, gazing over the gurgling river before returning her attention to Callie. "I think you feel alone, as most descendants of Crimeous do. I believe you were taken by Zadicus's sweet words and gallant efforts, and you wished to make a bold choice."

Considering her words, Callie realized they weren't exactly *wrong*. In fact, they rang quite true. "Searching for yourself becomes demoralizing after a while. Sometimes, you have to make a decision even if you have reservations."

"True," Tatiana said with a nod, "and I appreciate your ability to make a firm choice...but it is the wrong choice."

"Excuse me, but you have some nerve to show up here and assert you know anything about my choices—"

"Have you read his thoughts?"

Callie bristled. "Of course not."

Tatiana nodded slowly, considering. "It is noble to honor the promise you made your father, but know that your powers are a great gift bestowed upon you by the goddess. Although you should not use them for nefarious purposes, there are times when they must be employed."

"Absolutely not," Callie said, lifting her chin.

Sighing, Tatiana inched closer, gently cupping Callie's jaw. Her skin was warm, creating a connection Callie couldn't deny, and she was helpless to pull away.

"The prophecy states you will align with Bakari and '*destroy Etherya's realm as we know it, and it will exist no more.*'"

"I'm familiar with the prophecy, thanks," she muttered.

"Have you truly dissected the words?" Amber eyes darted between her own. "The immortal world has existed in its current state for eons. Would it be such a tragedy for it to be destroyed?"

Callie's eyes narrowed. "I don't know what you mean."

"Yes, you do. Stop denying your heritage and your calling, daughter of Darkrip. You shy away from your power and your duty as if it were evil. I assure you, it is not. There is great salvation in following our true destiny if we only have the courage to choose the hard path."

Callie's chin quivered as she struggled with the raging emotions that swirled inside from the cryptic conversation. "Sometimes, I hate the prophecy and my powers so much I want to scream. They've always made me feel weird and unaccepted...and then Zadicus came along and was so into me." She stared at the ground before returning her gaze to Tatiana. "I just want to be loved for who I am. Is that so much to ask?"

"There are many who love you just as you are, my dear," she said, leaning forward and placing a soft peck on her forehead. "Do not ever forget that." Stepping back, she lowered her hand as her full lips curved. "You need me, Calinda, as much as I need you. You'll come to see that eventually. There is a connectedness we all share that cannot be denied."

"I have no idea what you're talking about," she said, exasperated at the woman's riddles.

"I know." Her lips twitched, and Callie would've been pissed, except the action seemed reverent instead of amused. "I will summon you again soon. Events have been set in motion that cannot be stopped. Follow your intuition until we meet again."

"Wait!" Callie called, the word floating across the river as the woman disappeared. Huffing in frustration, Callie collapsed on the grass, crossing her arms as she gazed upon the flowing water. "Well, *that* was confusing." she muttered, annoyed at the perplexing conversation. What events was she referring to? Whatever they were, it seemed the enigmatic woman was intent on contacting her again.

After replaying the disconcerting discussion in her mind no less than a zillion times—and tugging about a hundred blades of grass from the riverbank—Callie stood, wiping the dirt off her backside before trekking back to the castle. She was shaken by the encounter and realized she needed to speak to Zadicus before going forward with the ceremony. Heading inside, she set off in search of her betrothed, determined to have an open and honest conversation with him about her reservations. She owed him no less, and it would go a long way toward soothing the doubt that swirled deep within.

Callie traipsed through the large castle, eventually finding Zadicus in the foyer with his parents as they shrugged off their light jackets.

"Hi, sweetheart," he said when she breezed in the room.

"Hi. You're all right on time for the early prep. Raoul. Viessa," Callie said with a tilt of her head. With her own family, she would've probably greeted them with a peck on the cheek, but Zadicus's family was a bit more reserved. Still, she liked his parents and had always gotten along with them quite well. "It's great to see you both. If you don't mind, I'd like to steal Zadicus away for a private chat in the study. My parents are already in the garden, and I'm sure they'd love to share a glass of wine with you before the ceremony."

Surprise crossed Zadicus's face. "Sweetheart? Are you all right?"

"I'm fine. I just need to talk to you privately."

"Well, I think that's our cue, dear," Viessa said, waving Raoul toward the hallway. "We know the way. You two come meet us when you're done." Sparing a glance at her husband, she gave a small jerk of her head, and they disappeared down the hallway.

"Callie? What's gotten into you? That was extremely rude. You didn't even bother to greet them properly."

"I mean, they're going to be my in-laws, right?" she said, lifting her hands. "Do we really need to be formal?"

"They are two of the most revered aristocrats at Valeria. Yes, it would be nice if you would treat them with the respect they deserve."

"And I'm the granddaughter of Markdor, Calla and Rina, but I don't need a red carpet every time I enter the room."

He glanced toward the ceiling in frustration before rubbing his forehead. "Fine. Let's talk in the study."

They headed toward the room off the main hallway, Zadicus gesturing her inside before he followed behind.

"Close the door, please."

He arched a brow before slowly closing the door. "This sounds serious"

"It is." Assessing him, she tilted her head. "Are we making a mistake, Zadicus?"

His ice-blue eyes grew wide. "You're asking me this two hours before our bonding ceremony?"

"It would seem so." Sighing, she struggled to articulate the doubt and hesitation that churned within. She didn't want to hurt his feelings but was shaken by her conversation with Tatiana. "I'm sorry to spring this on you, but I wonder if we moved too quickly."

"We've been courting for a year, Callie," he said, palms showing as he widened them at his waist. "We share affection and have much in common—"

"Do we? I'm not sure that's true."

He swallowed. "We both come from two of the purest bred Vampyre lineages."

"That has nothing to do with *us*," she said, lifting her hands. "We're just products of our parents knocking boots."

Grimacing, he ran a hand over his face. "It means something in our world, Callie, and unites us as aristocrats."

Her foot tapped on the floor as she studied him. "That's kind of a weird thing to have in common. Why do you never ask to come with me when I heal wounded animals across the kingdom?"

"You know that isn't my thing, sweetheart. You enjoy it, so I let you help the commoners."

Her eyebrow arched. "You *let* me?"

"You know what I mean," he said, rolling his eyes. "Are you trying to start a fight? That seems counterproductive two hours before we're set to bond."

"Counterproductive," she murmured, inching closer. "Such a strange word, and one someone would use for a mission rather than a mate." Narrowing her eyes, she studied him. "Am I some sort of mission for you, Zadicus?"

Expelling a breath, he ran his hands through his hair. "I really wish I'd known about these trust issues before I proposed. We'll definitely need to work on that."

Callie gnawed her lip, contemplating. Finally, she lifted her chin as emotion swirled inside. "This is hard for me to say, but I think we moved too fast. You were my first suitor, and I was extremely honored with your efforts, but we should've taken more time to get to know each other.

Eternity is long freaking time, Zadicus. We have to call this off." She lifted her hands, giving a slight shrug. "I'm truly sorry and will publicly take full responsibility to mitigate any fallout."

"Sweetheart," he said, stepping forward, sliding his palms over her shoulders. "You're just having bonding jitters. It's completely normal."

Callie stared into his eyes, assessing the warmth from his hands, wondering why his touch didn't inspire passion. She'd always enjoyed their kisses but admitted they'd never set her body on fire. She'd always made the excuse that only happened in movies—and in the steamy romance novels Evie had supplied her with since she was a teenager. But perhaps she'd been wrong. Years ago, she'd imagined waiting for someone who inspired Henry Cavill-level passion. Why had she settled for less with Zadicus?

Narrowing her eyes, she struggled with the sudden urge to read his thoughts. Perhaps getting a glimpse into his mind would help her understand why she had such serious reservations. If she took a peek and found his motivations to be true, and his heart to be open, perhaps she could move forward with the ceremony. Knowing it was so very wrong but unable to stop herself after the disconcerting discussion with Tatiana, she focused her energy on crossing the barrier to his mind.

Something clanked in her brain as she attempted to extract his thoughts, preventing her from accessing what she sought. Realization entered his expression, and he drew back, dropping his hands as if she were on fire.

"What are you doing?" he hissed.

Craning her head, she studied him. "Why can't I read your thoughts?" she asked, the words slow and measured.

"Why are you *trying* to read my thoughts?" he demanded, frustration in his tone as he sliced a hand through the air. "Goddess, Callie! That's a huge violation of my privacy."

Frozen, ice circulated through her veins as comprehension washed over her. Clenching her fists, she said softly, "Someone has created a shield for you so I can't read your thoughts."

His throat bobbed as he swallowed, and silence spread thick and heavy between them.

"The only people capable of doing that are my father and Evie, neither of whom would, Tatiana whom you've never met and Bakari." Taking a measured step forward, she gazed up at his handsome, traitorous face, and whispered, "You bastard."

"Callie," he said, reaching for her before she recoiled, her stomach churning at his deception. "Sweetheart, I have no idea what you're talking about."

"Liar!" Holding up her hand, she used her powers to render him immobile. He stood before her, still as a stone except for his features, which were contorted into a mask of confusion, anger and fear.

"How dare you use your powers on me? I command you to let me go this instant—"

"Quiet!" she yelled, her outstretched hand shaking slightly as rage coursed through her body. "What did Bakari promise you? Good god, what did *you* promise him? What will he gain from your deception?"

"You're paranoid," he gritted. "Callie, this is absurd!"

"I wanted so badly to *loved*. Goddess, I was so stupid." Closing the distance between them, she gently placed the pad of her finger on his forehead, directly between his eyebrows. "If I want to rip away the barrier, I can, Zadicus. It will hurt—hell, it might kill you. Is that what you want? Is Bakari worth dying for?"

His eyes narrowed to angry slits, hatred whirling deep in the orbs, and Callie truly *saw* him for the first time: a vapid, petulant man consumed by his own demons and lust for power. "You make me sick," she spat.

A commotion sounded to her left, and she whirled, her finger still affixed to Zadicus's forehead. Bakari materialized into the room, causing her body to pulse with equal parts fear and apprehension.

"I'll kill him," she said, her tone ominous.

Sighing, he placed his hand on his hip, regarding her as if they were discussing where to have lunch rather than her betrothed's imminent death. "No, you won't, Calinda. You don't have it in you to hurt another living being. Not yet." His sky blue eyes roved over her. "Hopefully, one day, you will grow into your evil. If so, it will be truly magnificent."

Dropping her hand, she turned to face him. "I have no desire to embrace my grandfather's blood, nor do I care about the Elven prophecy."

"Your lie is easy to dismiss considering you approached Zadicus only minutes after Tatiana appeared to you. She is a nuisance I should've exterminated long ago."

"But you can't," Callie murmured, observing his reaction when he spoke her name. A reluctant reverence had flashed in his eyes. "You carry some sort of twisted affection for her."

"She was helpful in many ways when I realized who I truly am. I've always found the benefits of keeping her alive outweighed the consequences. Until now." Lifting his hand, he sliced it through the air, releasing Callie's spell. Zadicus sucked in a breath as he clutched his throat.

"Kill her," Zadicus demanded.

"So dramatic," Bakari said, rolling his eyes. "She's worth more than you can fathom." When the man opened his mouth to argue, Bakari shot him a look, causing Zadicus to cower. Slinking to the corner, he lowered into a chair to reclaim his breath.

"Calinda," Bakari said, holding up his hands. "You cannot fight the inevitable. I have powers that no other being on the planet possesses—thanks to Tatiana, Dr. Tyson and others. I've spent centuries plotting my revenge, and I *will* become ruler of this realm. I realize this can only be done after complete annihilation, followed by rebirth, and therefore, you must align with me to fulfill the prophecy."

"Never!" she vowed, spittle flying between her fangs as her body vibrated with emotion. "I love this kingdom and consider every person in this realm family. I would never harm them."

"But do they consider *you* family? An outcast raised in the human world who is a child of Crimeous and the subject of a deadly prophecy? Have you never questioned why you feel so alone here? Perhaps it is time to consider fulfilling the prophecy is the best course for the kingdom you profess to love."

The words were reminiscent of Tatiana's, causing her to bristle. A small tendril of acknowledgment blazed in her chest that the sentiment rang true. Was she supposed to bring about some sort of cataclysmic change for the immortal realm?

"Good," he said with a nod. "You're finally thinking like a child of Crimeous. Like a woman beginning to understand the gravity of the power she's been given. Embrace it, Calinda. It will bring your more happiness and more acceptance than you will ever find by denying your true heritage."

Suddenly, the door burst open, and Darkrip rushed inside. "Callie?" he asked, assessing the situation. His head snapped between her, Bakari and Zadicus. Lifting his hands, he spread his palms, attempting to freeze Bakari in place and telekinetically choke him.

"Oh, good, Daddy's here," Bakari mocked through clenched teeth, his fangs barely visible behind thinned lips. "If you want to do this now, I'm ready." Lifting his hands, he showed Darkrip his palms, which were visibly glowing.

Comprehension dawned as they slowly latched their gaze upon Bakari.

"How were you able to transport through Astaria's wall?" Darkrip almost whispered. "You haven't been able to get through for years."

"Dr. Tyson purchased some extremely powerful concoctions on his last visit to the human world. Years of experimentation finally paid off. As I informed Heden when we first met, I am a patient man. Every failure ultimately leads to success."

"How about this success, asshole?" a feminine voice asked behind Bakari before Evie materialized and punched him in the kidney. Sliding her arm around his neck, she choked him as he struggled to break free. Bakari landed a crushing blow to her side with his elbow, and she fell back, breathless. Rushing toward Zadicus, Bakari tugged him from the chair and began chanting unintelligible words in the cryptic language he used to render the dematerialization spell. In a flash, he disappeared, along with Zadicus.

"Fuck!" Evie yelled, rubbing her forehead. "I was so close to killing the bastard."

"I can't believe he figured out how to breach Astaria's protective wall," Darkrip said, approaching Callie and pulling her into his embrace. She shook in his arms as he soothed his hand over her hair. "Shh," he said, kissing her temple. "It's okay. I'm here."

"*Ohmygod*," she cried, burying her face in his neck and willing the tears away. "I'm so stupid, Dad."

"This is my fault," he said, his voice so comforting in her ear. "I had reservations about you bonding with Zadicus that I pushed away. This is the last time I listen to your mother."

"I won't even honor those words with a response," Arderin said, striding into the room and drawing them both into a firm hug. "Come here, baby." She rocked with them as Callie drew upon their strength. "You're okay now."

Lifting her head, she gazed back and forth between them. "I'm so sorry, guys," she whispered. Craning her neck, she glanced at Evie. "Really sorry."

"Listen, kid," Evie said, shrugging. "Shit happens, and people lie. Good thing you found out before you boned him because that would've been *really* awkward."

"Not helpful," Darkrip muttered.

"Well, it's true," she said, flipping her hair over her shoulder. "And you're welcome for saving your ass, dear brother." With a nod, she stalked from the room.

"How could I have been so stupid?" Callie asked, stepping from their embrace and rubbing her upper arms. "I thought he loved me. I should've known better."

"And what does that mean, young lady?" Arderin asked in her stern mom tone. "You're perfectly lovable."

"I'm a freak, Mom!" Callie said, all the swirling emotions twining into a mass of frustrated rage. "I've never fit in here. I've never fit in *anywhere*. All people see when they look at me is a vestige of Crimeous and someone who's the manifestation of a prophecy that will destroy them! It's awful." Lowering to the sofa, she buried her face in her hands, struggling to control the tears.

"Sweetie," Arderin said, sitting beside her and placing her arm over her shoulders. "We all have our crosses to bear. I know it's hard, but it makes us so much stronger in the end. You'll realize this one day."

"I just want to be a normal person who's not the subject of a cataclysmic prophecy," she said, lifting her face and swiping away the tears. "I'll never be normal, Mom."

"No, you won't," she said, soothing the hair at her temple. "And I, for one, am thankful for that. You and Creigen are special, and I love you just the way you are."

"Special," she sighed, blowing a breath over her bottom lip so it fanned her hair. "I'm so tired of hearing that." Lifting her gaze to Darkrip's, she noticed his crossed arms and furious expression. "I'm okay, Dad. You look like you're going to pulverize something."

"You're goddamned right I'm going to pulverize something," he muttered. "That bastard's face."

"Zadicus or Bakari?"

"Both."

Sighing, Arderin addressed Darkrip. "We need to inform everyone of what happened and call a council meeting. We'll need to piece everything together and try to figure out why Bakari was manipulating Zadicus into marrying Callie."

Silence blanketed the room as realization set in.

"He wanted leverage over me," Callie said softly. "It makes sense. If he controlled my bonded, he would have access to me...and to any children I would have. He most likely wanted to create some sort of bargaining chip."

"And he could ultimately blackmail you for your alliance in fulfilling the prophecy," Darkrip said.

"Yes," she whispered, twining her fingers in her lap. "And I almost let him. So fucking stupid."

"Okay, we're not going to beat ourselves up," Arderin said, rubbing Callie's arm. "The crisis was averted, and you figured it out before it got out of hand. How did you figure it out, by the way?"

"I went on a walk by the river earlier and Tatiana appeared." She stared into her mother's piercing blue eyes. "She indicated that fulfilling the prophecy is my destiny. She and Bakari seem to agree on that."

"I thought she was on our side?" Arderin asked Darkrip.

"She's wily," he said, shaking his head. "My assessment is that Tatiana has one side: her own. Forces like good and evil aren't differentiated for her as they are for us. Instead, they are both sides of the same coin and flow in tandem with one another."

"Well, I'll take your word for it since you're the only one who's ever gotten a glimpse into her mind," Arderin said.

"Yes, she let her defenses down for a scant moment that evening we had dinner together when we visited Heden years ago. Sofia's wine might be the most magical concoction of all since it led to Tatiana dropping her shield. I saw inside her head only briefly, but it was...intense. She's not like any other creature I've ever encountered—human, immortal or otherwise."

"Heden swears she'd never hurt us," Arderin said, concern in her tone.

"I think he's right," Darkrip said, tilting his head. "She's...it's hard to explain. She's striving toward something none of us can see in our limited world view. That's the only way I know how to articulate what I saw," he finished, shrugging.

"Well, we need to cancel the ceremony and send the guests home. Raoul and Viessa will need to be notified," Arderin said. "I'm pretty sure they had no idea Zadicus was working with Bakari."

"I'll speak to them and confirm they were unaware," Darkrip said.

"After that, we should probably convene a short council meeting and discuss today's events with everyone. Are you up to that?" she asked, tucking a dark curl behind Callie's ear.

"Yes," Callie said, standing and straightening her shoulders. "I want to record today's events and then purge them from my memory. *Forever.*"

"Pushing away anger and hurt is only a temporary solution, sweetie," Arderin said, standing.

"I know, but I've been made a fool of, and I need some time to assess why I didn't listen to my gut. You both should understand that."

"Of course we do."

"Thank the goddess I figured it out before it was too late. Fuck that jerk."

Arderin shot Darkrip an acerbic glare. "Well, she sounds like your daughter."

He smiled, closing the distance between them until he cupped Callie's cheeks. "Fuck him is right, honey. And I *will* kill him one day. He hurt you, and that's unacceptable."

"Aw," Callie teased, tilting her head. "It's what every girl wants her father to say. I hope you'll threaten to kill every man I ever date."

"Every fucking one," Darkrip said, an amused glint in his eye.

"Man, we're a really weird family," Arderin said, glancing at the ceiling. "I know I should be concerned, but I just find it adorable." Shrugging, she extended her hand. "Come on, baby. Let's get to it so you can lick your wounds and start to put this all behind you."

Clutching her mother's hand, Callie inhaled a breath, fortifying herself, and followed her parents from the room.

Chapter 10

Later that evening, Callie sat at the end of the large conference table in the council room at Astaria. The members of the council flanked her, all seated in the leather chairs that surrounded the table. Her father, Evie and Kenden sat to her left; Larkin, Aron, Lila and Latimus on her right. Miranda sat at the head of the table, Sathan planted in the foremost seat at the front corner, firm and attentive.

Miranda's face was a mask of frustrated anger as she gazed across the table at Callie. "Thank you for being so forthright, Callie," she said, resting her hands on the table as she leaned forward. "It takes a lot of strength to document what happened today with such candidness, especially since it was supposed to be a happy day of celebration. I'm so sorry."

Callie felt the sting of tears in her eyes and pushed them away, determined to embody the strength Miranda extolled. "I'm happy to help. What happened today signifies Bakari's determination to rule the kingdom, and we can't let that happen."

"We've given him ample chance to show a sliver of goodness," Latimus said. "I don't relish hurting my brother, but he must be vanquished. It's the only path forward for our people to live in peace." Sitting back in his chair, he laced his fingers atop the table. "I believe we've pieced together the story. After questioning Raoul and Viessa, I firmly believe they had no knowledge of Zadicus's alliance with Bakari. They seemed as sad and distraught as we all are before they left for Valeria. The good news is that Zadicus's failure ended up showing Bakari's hand. He's intent on aligning with Callie to fulfill the prophecy."

"Just a reminder that I am *not* on board with that plan," Callie said, raising a finger in the air as she tried to lift the heavy mood. The last thing she wanted was to be pitied. She might have made mistakes along the way, but she was no victim.

"We know you don't want to destroy the world, sweetie," Lila said in her gentle, supportive tone.

"Yes, I think we're all in agreement on that," Latimus said with a wink, instantly softening Callie. Gratefulness for her family and their unwavering support washed over her.

Gazing back at the group, he continued. "It is imperative we enter the final phase of our plan. We will draw Bakari, along with Commander Vadik and his troops, to a final battle on the field between Takelia and Uteria in one month's time. Bakari is dead set on fulfilling the Elven prophecy—which is never going to happen," he uttered, eying the council members, "but it makes Callie a target, and that's unacceptable."

"Agreed," Evie said with a nod. "And now that some of our more *hardheaded* members have agreed to let women become combat soldiers, I'm confident we can secure victory." She batted her eyelashes at Latimus as he frowned.

"It wasn't because I think women aren't capable, Evie—"

"*Misogynist*," she coughed loudly into her fist.

"That's incredibly unfair!"

"Okay, okay," Miranda said, standing and holding up her hands. "As much as I agree with Evie on this one, there's no need to rehash something that's been debated and decided. We're all happy women have joined the troops, and I think it will exponentially increase our chances of defeating Bakari."

"I only wanted to protect the women of our kingdom," Latimus murmured, dark eyebrows drawing together.

"Oh, I'm sorry," Evie said, reaching for her purse and pulling out her phone. Lifting it to her ear, she nodded. "Yes, he's right here." Extending it across the table to Latimus, she said, "It's the Middle Ages calling—"

"All right," Kenden interrupted, gently taking the phone from her hand. "My wife gets a kick out of torturing you, Latimus. You won, sweetheart. Let's move on."

"Fine," she said, rolling her eyes. "But if anyone in this room in possession of a penis ever utters the words '*women can't do*,' followed by literally anything, I have a mind to detach said penis from their body. Capisce?"

Callie observed several throats bob as the men remailed silent. Damn, her aunt was badass.

"Back to the business at hand," Miranda said, giving Evie a nod of solidarity. "I think we're all in agreement. The battle will commence one month from today, at sunrise. Ken and Latimus, are you confident you can draw Bakari's entire army to the field south of Takelia for the battle?"

"Yes," Kenden said with a nod. "Sadie has run extensive psychological profiles on Bakari. We believe he will respond to our call for an ultimate battle if we appeal to his ego and lust for power."

"And now, it seems he *wants* a battle in the hopes Callie will align with him," Latimus said. "We'll use his inflated sense of superiority against him and finally rid the planet of him and his supporters."

"Excellent," Miranda said. "I know we've tried many tactics over the years and were hesitant to enter into full-on war with Bakari after the War of the Species ended. Our people were tired, and we handled Bakari's attacks and poisons effectively but were never able to fully contain him. His Deamon army continues to grow, and it's time to put an end to this for good. Please let me know what you need to be fully prepared. I already approved the purchase order for the new TECs, but if we need more, just send a request my way."

"Will do," Kenden said. "Jack will continue training the new recruits, both *male* and *female*." He glanced at his wife before continuing. "Sadie and Nolan have also been testing antidote serums for every possible chemical combination of Dr. Tyson's we've discovered so far. If Bakari's army deploys chemicals on the battlefield, the docs will be stationed at infirmary tents nearby, ready to treat any Slayer soldiers affected. Thankfully, the Vampyre soldiers won't be affected due to their self-healing abilities."

"Arderin will be in the infirmary tents too," Darkrip said, resignation in his tone. "I tried to talk her out of it but stopped wasting my breath about five seconds in. Stubborn woman."

"I can volunteer too, Dad," Callie said. "I want to help."

"That's appreciated," Miranda said before Darkrip could speak, "but we want the kids as far away from the battle so you're safe. You're the future of our kingdom, and if something happens to the older generation, we'll need you to lead. Sathan and I will be with you, although I'd love to fight the bastards, but we trust the army to get the job done."

"Most of us aren't kids anymore, Aunt Miranda," she said, frustration lacing her tone, "and I think we all want to lead by helping with the battle."

"I know, and it means a lot." She smiled as she slid her hand over her husband's shoulder. "But Sathan and I have decided. Don't make us pull the 'king and queen' card. That would make us huge losers. Believe me, I want to kick Bakari's ass too, but we all have roles we need to play."

"Okay," Callie said softly, understanding the logic of remaining safe while the troops battled.

"Good." Straightening, Miranda assessed the room. "I think we're done then. Callie, thank you for helping us piece everything together. We love you very much, and that jerk will get what's coming to him."

"I called Camron and informed him Zadicus will be taken into custody if he's spotted on any of the compounds," Lila said. "Aligning with Bakari is unacceptable, and he will face consequences if he is apprehended."

"We should've known since Zadicus is related to Melania," Latimus muttered.

"Melania renounced Bakari years ago," Lila said, her tone firm. "If we don't embrace forgiveness and reformation, we're no better than our enemies."

"I'll let you do the embracing. I'm all set."

She glared at him before he scrunched his features, causing her to laugh. "My stern bonded. One day, I'll soften you up." She gave him a wink.

"Okay, get a room." Evie stood. "Come on," she said to Kenden. "I'm ready to hug our daughter, go home and put today behind us."

The meeting adjourned, everyone rushing to Callie to give her a warm hug. Overwhelmed by the love of her family, she accepted their embraces, reminding herself how lucky she was even if the day had royally sucked. Leaving the conference room, she trailed to the sitting room where her brother and cousins were waiting. They stood as she entered, their expressions lined with supportive concern.

"I'm okay, guys," she said, hugging Rinada, Adelyn and Symon before her brother pulled her into his side.

"Fuck that guy," Creigen said, rubbing her upper arm. "He wasn't good enough for you, sis."

"Thanks, Creig. Remember how awesome I am next time we argue about who's smarter."

"What's there to argue about? It's obviously me." He pointed his thumbs at his chest.

"As if," she responded, playfully shoving him.

"You ready, Rin?" Evie asked, craning her neck around the doorframe. "Dad and I want to head home."

"Ready," Rinada said, swiping her dark mahogany-colored hair over her shoulder before waving goodbye to everyone.

Her cousins and brother filtered out of the room until she was left alone with Jack, who slowly approached her.

"Callie," he said softly, his deep brown eyes laced with concern, "are you okay?"

"Yeah," she said, thankful for their close bond. "I mean, it sucks, but you knew my doubts about him. Guess I should've listened to my gut."

He smiled, the gesture filled with affection. "You deserve so much better. One day, you'll meet the person who's supposed to be your partner. I know it."

"Maybe we both will," she said, giving him a cheeky grin. "And we'll look back on today as a bad memory. Maybe we'll even laugh about it."

"I know we will." He cupped her arm, giving it a reassuring squeeze.

"In the meantime, I think I need a good cry alone while I inhale ice cream."

He breathed a laugh. "I'm sure Glarys can scrounge up ice cream in a snap."

"I'm sure she can." Grinning, she pulled him into a hug. "Thank you, Jack. I just need to process everything. I'm going to tell Mom and Dad I want to stay here tonight. I'll sleep in Heden's old room. It's still got the kick-ass flat-screen he set up years ago, along with his rom-com collection, which he always maintained was for 'research.'" Drawing back, she chuckled as she made quotation marks with her fingers. "I know he secretly loves *Pretty Woman*."

"I think he quotes *The Princess Bride* on an hourly basis," Jack affirmed.

"Exactly." Running her hand through her hair, she sighed. "I'll be fine,"—she held up a finger—"but I reserve the right to reach out if I need a shoulder to cry on."

"Always. You know you're my favorite cousin."

She squinted. "I'm pretty sure I heard you tell Rinada that last week."

"Me?" He pointed at his chest, his features a mask of mock innocence. "No way."

"Get out of here," she said, swatting his chest, already feeling better from his gentle teasing.

Glarys chose that moment to stride into the room. "There you are, dear. My goodness, what a crappy day. Would you like some ice cream? I have rocky road all ready to go in the freezer."

She and Jack shared a smile. "I'd love that, Glarys. Do you and Sam mind if I stay at Astaria? If I go home, Mom and Dad will hover. It's sweet but smothering."

"You're always welcome here, dear," she said, placing her arm over her shoulders. "Jack, do you want to stay too?"

"I've got an early training tomorrow," he said, leaning down to kiss the kind woman on the forehead, "but thanks. Take care of our girl."

"I will." Ice-blue eyes sparkled under Glarys's cap of white curls as she waved goodbye before he exited.

"Well, let's get you all set up. I have some of your mother's old clothes you can wear if you want to change out of those. She left them behind when she moved to the human world all those years ago. We'll get you all nice and comfy, sweetheart."

Enveloped in the caring mother figure's embrace, Callie followed her to the kitchen of the massive home, thankful for the support of every person in her extended family.

Darkrip was exhausted by the time the terrible day ended. After the council meeting, where Callie had informed everyone of the day's events and the subsequent ending of her betrothal, he'd longed to comfort her. She'd appeared both vulnerable and strong, reminding him how proud he was of his willful, headstrong daughter. As she recounted the details, he'd yearned to turn back time and prevent her pain.

Afterward, Darkrip had expected her to come home to Takelia but also understood her need for solitude.

"Glarys said I can stay in Heden's old room, Dad," she'd said, putting on a brave face even though hurt swam in her eyes. "I just want to be alone right now."

He'd studied her, tamping down the urge to pull her close and transport her home. Once she was there, she couldn't argue, and he'd be able to comfort her.

"I'm too powerful for you to transport," she said, giving a cheeky grin. "You won't be able to overpower me."

"Are you reading my thoughts?"

"No way. It's written all over your face that you want to whisk me home and comfort me. It's really sweet, but I need space."

Leaning down, he kissed her forehead. "I love you, Callie. Please call if you need me, no matter how late."

"Thanks, Dad," she whispered, the warble in her voice almost breaking his heart.

Now home, he slowly unbuttoned his starchy shirt as his mind wandered. He could disintegrate the damn thing off, but the slow, measured movements of his fingers offered a mundane task to occupy his thoughts. Once he'd shucked everything but his boxer briefs, he stared at his reflection in the mirror atop the dresser.

His ears had slight points, a vestige of his father's Deamon heritage. Of their *Elven* heritage. Miranda and Kenden had discovered the hidden Elven scrolls years ago, and they extolled some pretty outlandish stories. Some were prophecies, some were history, written down long ago and forgotten when the Elven world was destroyed. All were from a realm long assumed dead.

But Crimeous had survived, which meant others could have survived as well. Darkrip knew this to be true, and he'd stopped fighting the denial long ago. His father's blood gave him the ability to sense things others couldn't, and he would bet his life there were other Elven descendants that roamed Etherya's Earth. If not in the immortal world, then in the human world, where they could easily blend in with the oblivious species.

"Creigen is headphones-deep in his video game," Arderin said, entering the bedroom and trailing to his side. "I'd be worried that our eighteen-year-old son is so enamored with video games if I didn't know he used it to pick up girls. It's kind of geeky-sweet. Heden would be proud."

"How did they grow up so fast?" Darkrip asked, his gaze claiming hers in the reflection. "Yesterday, I was changing Callie's diaper, and now, they're both adults, falling in love and making adult mistakes."

"I don't know," she sighed, resting her chin on his shoulder. "I mean, we could have another one if you're missing the diaper phase."

Darkrip balked. "Uh, I'm all set, thanks. Two is enough, especially after the shit show we experienced today. I mean, I love them, but let's quit while we're ahead."

Chuckling, she nipped his shoulder. "Fine. But we'll keep practicing just in case."

His green eyes smoldered with desire in the reflection as his skin warmed. "Why are you wearing clothes?" he growled. Closing his eyes, he dematerialized her dress, leaving her in her bra and panties.

"I appreciate your desire, husband," she said in a sultry tone, touching her lips to his ear and setting his body on fire. "But we need to discuss something first."

Sliding against her smooth skin, he turned, drawing her close and aligning their bodies. "Dear wife, I can't think of anything to possibly talk about when you're pressed against me like this." Nudging her nose with his, he pushed his rapidly swelling erection between the juncture of her thighs.

"Darkrip," she whispered against his lips. "I need your word."

"I'll promise anything if you let me fuck you," he murmured, gliding his hand to her ass and squeezing the firm flesh.

"Obviously, I'm going to let you fuck me," she teased, rolling her eyes. "But I need your word you won't hunt him down. Latimus and Kenden have a plan for the final battle, and I don't want your vengeance getting in the way."

"As much as I want to murder that aristocratic bastard, I'll leave him be. Zadicus means nothing in the big scheme. I'm on board with the final battle. Evie and I are going to perfect a forcefield we can use against Bakari once he's drawn out on the battlefield. It will allow us to disintegrate every Deamon along with him so none can be cloned. We won't fuck it up this time. I'm over this fucking conflict."

"My husband, the noble warrior. I always knew you had it in you." She playfully bit his bottom lip.

"You saw the good in me before anyone else," he said, his tone reverent.

"Your mother saw it long before me. I just picked up where she left off."

Rina's face flashed in Darkrip's mind as he stroked Arderin's cheek with his thumb.

"Sweetheart?" she called softly.

"I wish she could meet Callie, Creigen and Rinada. Evie honored Mother when they named their daughter after her. I hope she'd be proud of the man I've become, even if I let Callie down today."

"You didn't let her down," Arderin said, sliding her arms around his neck. "You let her make her own mistakes. It's what we must do if she's going to learn to navigate the world. She has my wanderlust, and we can't keep her here forever. I'm surprised she's stayed with us this long and hasn't decided to get her own place."

"Today will always be a defining moment for her. I fear her innocence was shattered."

"Callie?" Arderin asked, scoffing. "She hasn't been innocent for a long time, dear. You choose to see her as your precocious little girl, but she's a woman who's slowly recognizing her own strength. I think today was exactly what she needed."

"But he hurt her," Darkrip said, feeling his heart rip open. "He hurt our little girl, Arderin."

"I know." The strokes of her fingers against the back of his neck were soothing. "It sucks. I'm hurting for her as much as you are."

Resting his forehead against hers, Darkrip held his wife, thankful for her stubborn strength and unwavering support. "I lived a solitary life for so long, swearing I didn't need anyone." He softly brushed her lips with his. "Now, I can't imagine surviving without the three of you. You're all I care about."

She stared into his eyes before cracking a smile. "Man, you've become really dramatic in your old age. Are you going for an Emmy there, old man?"

Growling, he crouched down, cupping her ass and lifting her. Squealing, she instinctively wrapped her legs around his waist, joyfully laughing as he carried her to the bed. Falling to the mattress, he cradled her, cushioning her fall before he loomed over her.

"You're going to pay for that smart mouth, princess."

Her tongue darted out, slow and deliberate, bathing her ruby red lips.

"Don't threaten me with a good time."

"You little bitch," he murmured, lowering to lick her wet lips. Extending his tongue, he ran it over the sensitive flesh, from corner to corner, as she shivered below him.

"I'd be pissed you call me that in bed, except it gets me really hot." Arousal flashed in her eyes.

"Good," he muttered, pecking her lips. "Now, open that smart mouth, sweetheart. We're going to put it to good use." Rising, he closed his eyes, dematerializing their remaining garments. Lifting his lids, he palmed his cock, beginning to stroke as he climbed over her and straddled her.

"You love my smart mouth."

Thrusting his fingers into her thick hair, he tugged, loving her arousal-laden gasp. Her eyes glazed with desire, and her lips hung open, wet and ready. Moving closer, he touched the tip of his aching shaft to her wet mouth. His wife smiled as he felt himself drowning in her piercing blue eyes. And then, she closed around him, and all he felt was pure, unadulterated bliss.

Chapter 11

Callie lay in bed watching the rom-com in Heden's old bedroom. She thought staying at Astaria would give her some much needed peace and quiet so she could digest her thoughts. Instead, she was restless. Throwing off the covers, she trailed to the dresser and rummaged in her bag. Locating the diary, she pulled it out, gently stroking the withered collection of musings from her younger self.

As she read the flowing scrawl, scattered with "i"s with heart-shaped dots, she tried like hell not to blame herself for being an idiot. The pages were filled with paragraphs upon paragraphs detailing her longing to be loved. Reading over the words, her loneliness was palpable on the slightly faded pages. No wonder she believed Zadicus when he'd courted her so zealously. She'd craved affection and had been ripe for a ruse. Her yearning to be loved had ultimately made her discount her gut feelings, and she vowed to never let that happen again. From this day forward, Callie would always trust her intuition and explore her doubts when something didn't feel right.

What baffled her most were the love letters Zadicus had written. They'd seemed so heartfelt and genuine, and she could barely believe he'd been able to pull it off. After all, he wasn't the most perceptive man, and she wondered how he'd noticed so many of the things he mentioned. Reaching into her bag, she pulled out the letters, which she'd packed along with her diary in a sentimental moment. The poem he'd originally written her was also in the pile, and she stacked the papers on the dresser. Reaching for one, she read it, and then another, noting the observant words.

Sometimes, your lips shine under the late-afternoon sunlight after you've covered them in gloss, and my mind can't focus on anything else but kissing you.

When you placed the rose behind your ear and smiled, I realized I'd never seen anything more beautiful.

Observing you teach the citizens to read warmed my heart, and I was especially taken with your interactions with the teenagers.

Sometimes, you speak of the unknowns of having your own children since they will inevitably inherit some of your powers, but you don't need to worry, Callie-lily.

Narrowing her eyes, Callie focused on the nickname. Now that she thought about it, Zadicus had never called her that except in his letters. How strange he would create a nickname for her and never use it.

It was also weird that he mentioned her volunteering at the literacy function since he'd sat in the corner the entire time working on the invite list for his mother's dinner party. In fact, she had no idea he'd even noticed she spent time with the teens who attended. The only person who'd seemed to notice was Brecken, considering Rowena had been in attendance. Callie remembered speaking to him as he stood against the wall, observing in his quiet, watchful manner.

Come to think of it, Brecken had been present during *all* of the moments mentioned in the letters. The literary function, the dinner where she stuck the rose in her hair...the street fair where she'd slathered on lip gloss. Searching her brain, Callie tried to remember if she'd worn lip gloss on her dates with Zadicus. She usually preferred to wear lipstick and only used lip gloss as a backup when she was in less formal situations. Like when she was worried she had wine lips and was accompanying a sexy bodyguard to a street fair...

Straightening in her seat, Callie's heart began to pound. As she pondered, she couldn't recall a time when she'd worn lip gloss instead of lipstick with Zadicus. Grasping the letters, she began to furiously read through them, quickly realizing every single occurrence happened under Brecken's watch. Glancing at the folded poem Zadicus originally penned for her when they first began courting, she reached for it with shaking fingers.

Lifting it, she opened it and read the prose. By the goddess, it was terrible, and so different from the flowing words that comprised the letters. Picking up the most recent letter, she held it beside the poem. At first glance, the writing looked identical. But as Callie narrowed her eyes and looked closer, the differences began to show. Tiny things she never would've noticed unless something drastic happened, causing her to look.

Something like her betrothed outing himself as a traitor who'd aligned with her nefarious uncle...

Swallowing thickly, Callie compared the writing, noting the inconsistencies. The slashes across the "t"s were different—the ones in the poem slanting upward while the ones in the letter were perfectly level. The "C" in her name also had a slight curl at the bottom in the letter but didn't in the poem. And the "Z" in Zadicus was quite large in the signature of the poem and rather small in the letter.

Lowering the missives, Callie pondered as blood thrummed through her veins. Glancing at the handwriting, there was only one conclusion she could draw: They were written by different people. Zadicus had written her the poem. *Brecken had written her the letters.*

Somehow, she knew it was inexorably true. Considering she'd just declared not to ignore her intuition, she let the realization sink in. For some reason, Brecken had aligned with Zadicus to deceive her. There was no other explanation, considering it was Zadicus who gave her each letter. Brecken wrote them and then passed them along to Zadicus to give to her.

A soft cry leaped from her throat as her eyes welled. What possible motive could Brecken have for agreeing to such a thing? Did he only do it to help his ward, or was he secretly aligned with Bakari too? Stacking the papers, she stared into the reflection as hurt and confusion swirled in her eyes.

"That son of a bitch," she murmured, rubbing her hand over her collarbone. "Why would he do this?"

Callie had no idea, but as the acknowledgment of his deception washed over her, fury swelled deep within. Her features grew more resolved in the reflection, and she knew what she had to do. Rising, she rested her palms on the vanity and stared into her furious eyes.

"You're going to confront him and figure out if he was also working with Bakari."

It was the right thing to do considering she would need to tell the council if Brecken was indeed aligned with her uncle. Even though she was pissed, something inside her railed against the notion Brecken would align with Bakari. He was a soldier and a protector, and so loving with Rowena. The idea that Zadicus was vulnerable to Bakari's machinations wasn't impossible to imagine. The notion that Brecken would align with him? It just didn't make sense at all. Knowing there was only one way to find out, she stuffed the letters into her bag and texted Jack.

Callie: Brecken lives on the south side of Lynia near Antonio's neighborhood, right?

A text bubble appeared, and she anxiously gnawed her lip.

Jack: Yep. His cabin is about a mile from Antonio's. Why?
Callie: No reason. Just wondering.

She could almost see her cousin's sardonic look flash through her mind.

Jack: Callie? What are you up to?

Callie: Nothing. I promise. You know I'd tell you if anything was wrong. For now, I'm crashing. Long day of being betrayed and all. Love you.

There was a pause before she noticed him typing.

Jack: I'm always here for you. Don't forget that. Love you too. Night.

Expelling a breath through puffed cheeks, she thanked the goddess he'd let it go.

Tossing the bag over her shoulder, she quietly walked through the house, toward the barracks, until she stepped into the expansive garage. Locating the keys to the nearby four-wheeler on the key rack that hung by the door, she threw her bag on the passenger seat. After backing out, she ensured the garage door was locked and secure.

And then, she set out into the night, under the silver moonlight, toward Brecken's cabin at Lynia.

Chapter 12

Brecken milled around his cabin, washing the cup from which he'd recently imbibed Slayer blood before depositing it in the rack. Drying his hands on the dish towel, he stared out the tiny window above the sink, his thoughts consumed with Callie as they had been since Jack called to tell him the news about Zadicus's alliance with Bakari and the canceled wedding. Raoul had also called to inform him they no longer needed his services. Brecken had heard Viessa crying in the background, and he clenched his teeth, frustrated at the pain Zadicus had caused everyone who loved him.

He hurt for everyone involved in the terrible situation and wished like hell he could smash Zadicus's nose about a zillion times with his fist. First on his list of grievances was the fact he'd hurt Callie. Guilt consumed him as he acknowledged he'd also had a hand in Zadicus's deception, even if only a small one. She deserved so much better, and he railed at himself for ever agreeing to Zadicus's stupid ruse. Gritting his teeth, he realized he was two seconds from ripping the dish towel in half and laid it over the counter to dry. Clad only in sweatpants, he strode over to the bed and sat on the edge, wondering what the hell to do.

He didn't think Callie would figure out he wrote the letters, but if she did, it would cause her yet another round of anguish. The woman who'd shown such kindness to him and his sister, and healed animals throughout the kingdom, would experience another crushing betrayal. Falling back on the bed, Brecken rubbed his hands over his face, furious at himself.

In truth, the guilt had already been too much to bear before he learned the wedding was called off. Brecken had already decided he was going to resign from his position as bodyguard and rejoin the army before Raoul had contacted him. Along with the guilt was the knowledge that somewhere along the way, he'd fallen for Callie. Hook, line and sinker, Brecken—who had never caught feelings for any of the women he'd casually courted in the past—was a goner.

The letters had become all too real, and he worried his affection for her would turn to obsession if he continued to see her every day. Plus, he couldn't stand the thought of her pregnant with Zadicus's child. Goddess, it made his stomach churn, causing him to realize she was the first woman he'd ever imagined pregnant with *his* child. Before Callie, Brecken had been perfectly happy being a bachelor. Now, all he wanted was to hold her...and soothe her...and care for her in all the ways she deserved.

"You really fucked up, man," he muttered, harshly rubbing his eyes. "And you helped that asshole betray her. You are some kind of jerk."

A loud banging sounded at his front door, and he lurched to a sitting position, feeling his eyes widen. Behind the pounding, he heard Callie's furious voice.

"I know you're in there, asshole!" *Thunk. Thunk. Thunk.* "And I know you wrote the letters!"

"Shit!" Brecken hissed, rising and running his hand through his hair. Callie was smart—hell, she'd gone to the special school Rowena attended. Of course she'd figured out he wrote the letters. Steeling himself, he strode to the door, preparing himself for her wrath. She deserved to rail at him, and he'd let her—although he wasn't going to grovel.

The intentions behind his actions had been pure, even if they were ultimately wrong, and the ruse had gotten him closer to Callie. It had allowed him to get to know her in a way he never would have otherwise. Considering his feelings for her, he was grateful for the opportunity to write the letters, although he knew she wouldn't see it that way.

Inhaling a deep breath, he gripped the handle and yanked the door open.

∞

Callie banged on the door, the letters clutched in her other hand as she fought the urge to scream. The excessive pounds echoed through the surrounding meadow before the door swung open. Brecken stared back at her, his expression impassive as his brown orbs simmered.

"I heard you the first time you knocked—"

Her palm crashed into his cheek so hard it stung. His nostrils flared as a muscle ticked in his jaw. Lifting her hand, she swung to strike him again. Brecken caught her wrist, quick as lightning, and squeezed.

"I'll give you one because you deserve it. But that's it, Callie."

Emitting a frustrated huff, she yanked her wrist from his grasp. "You bastard!"

His shoulders softened, and she swore she saw a flash of remorse in his eyes. Sighing, he stepped back and opened the door wider. "Come in. It looks like it's going to pour. And if we're going to have a screaming match, I'd rather do it inside."

Narrowing her eyes, she clenched her teeth so hard she wondered why they didn't disintegrate. "Why did you do it? I thought you hated Bakari. Why would you help Zadicus deceive me?"

Expelling a breath, he pinched the bridge of his nose and shook his head. "I didn't know he was working with Bakari, Callie." Reclaiming her gaze, he spoke with sincerity. "I know you have no reason to believe me, but it's the truth."

Her eyes fell to his bare chest as she pondered, and she told herself she didn't give a damn he had a perfect eight-pack under a smattering of tiny brown hairs. Nope. Not in the slightest.

"Please," he said, gesturing with his head. "Come in. I might even consider letting you slap me again if you come inside so we can argue in private." His lips curved, the tips of his fangs resting on his full lower lip. "Come on, Callie."

Lifting her chin, she breezed by him, striding into the center of the room before pivoting. The cabin was small, with one main room and what she guessed was a bathroom off to the side. The main room had a large bed against the far wall, a carpeted floor where she now stood, a fireplace to her left, a desk off to the side and a kitchenette to her right. It certainly wasn't fancy, but it was clean and well-kept.

"Not quite Zadicus's mansion," Brecken muttered, not meeting her eyes as he approached. Callie sensed resignation in his voice and realized he was embarrassed. As strange as it was, she wanted to comfort him. Before she could stop the words, they flew from her throat.

"It's nice," she said, shrugging. "Very organized and clean. It doesn't really matter how big your house is. The most important thing is that it feels like home."

His eyes latched onto hers, and she cleared her throat at the intense look.

"What?" she asked, exasperated.

"I just—" He broke off, rubbing the back of his neck. "I thought you'd prefer something fancy since you're a royal princess."

"Well, you thought wrong," she said, straightening her spine. "And since we're discussing things that are wrong, let's discuss the fact that you *wrote love letters for a man intent on deceiving me!*" Her voice rose with each word as she shook the papers in her hand.

"Do you want to sit—?"

"No, I don't want to sit down," she said, stomping her foot. "I want to know why you would do something so awful! What did I ever do to you?"

Heaving a sigh, he walked toward the desk and perched on the side, stretching his legs before him and crossing them at the ankles. He looked like a damn fitness model in his gray sweatpants and bare feet, and she crossed her arms as she waited.

"Zadicus asked me to write the letters to you the day before we went to the street fair. He said he was a terrible writer and remembered I'd mentioned excelling at creative writing in school."

"Impressive. Who knew you'd use your skills to make a fool out of me? Nice job."

He shot her a droll look. "I said no at first, but he offered to secure a seamstress position for my mother at the governor's mansion. It increased her salary exponentially, and I knew it would allow her to give my sisters things they could never have without it. So, I agreed. I knew it was wrong, but I agreed."

Callie thought of Rowena and the fantastic time they'd had at the street fair and the literacy function. She was a sweet, vivacious girl, and Callie wanted the best for her. Glancing at the carpet, she absently rubbed her arm, contemplating his motives. Although the action was terrible, at least the motive behind the action had been pure.

"I wish I could make it up to you, but I can't," he said, running his hand though his hair, resulting in wayward spiked tufts that looked so sexy Callie felt her skin flush. The scruff of his beard had grown in, and she quickly realized comfortable-at-home Brecken was just as hot as bodyguard-in-tactical-gear Brecken. Maybe even more so. Swiping a hand over her face, she pushed the thoughts away.

"I mean, you could say you're sorry. That might be one small step in trying to make it up to me." She held her thumb and index finger an inch apart.

Brecken just stared at her, arms crossed over his chest as he seemed to ponder.

"Um, hi," she said, waving her hand. "Did you hear me? You could apologize. It's really easy. You just move your lips and say the words 'I'm' and then 'sorry.'" Pointing to her mouth, she said it again slowly. "I...am...sorry...Callie. See? Piece of cake."

His lips twitched, causing fury to well in her gut. "Are you *laughing* at me?"

"Never," he said, pursing his lips to suppress an obvious laugh.

"You son of a bitch! I can't believe you. I want a fucking apology—"

"No," he interjected, rising and slowly stalking toward her. "I'll take responsibility for hurting you, but I won't apologize for writing the letters."

Feeling her throat bob, she tilted her head to stare at him, wondering why he was suddenly so close. The heat of his body seemed to meld with hers, and tiny flames of awareness flickered along her flushed skin. "You can't even bring yourself to apologize to me?" she asked softly, wondering why the sting of tears pulsed in tandem with her ragged heartbeat.

"No," he almost whispered, gently touching the skin of her upper arm, bare as she stood in her tank top and velour sweatpants. Gazing into her eyes, he slowly trailed his fingers down her arm, the caress so tender and arousing all at once. Reaching her hand, he grasped the letters and tugged them free.

"I won't apologize for doing something that brought me closer to you." Lifting the letters, he shook them. "Everything I wrote was true, Callie. Every. Single. Word."

She licked her suddenly parched lips, her body inflaming when desire sparked in his eyes. "But you called me your love," she said, noticing the rasp in her voice. "Your Callie-lily."

He grinned as his cheeks flushed. "Calla lilies are my mom's favorite flower. She talks about them all the time. How they're the most beautiful flower in every garden where they grow. It just sort of came to me and it seemed fitting for you."

"Because you think I'm beautiful?" she asked, feeling her brows draw together.

Amusement entered his expression. "Well, it seems we've gone from seeking an apology to fishing for compliments."

Scowling, she swatted his arm. "Screw you. For a second, I almost believed you. Damn it! Why am I so fucking gullible?" Uttering a frustrating groan, she pivoted, burying her face in her hand. "Screw the promise I made Dad. From now on, I'm reading everyone's fucking mind."

"Hey," he said, encircling her arm and gently turning her. "I'm joking with you, hon. Of course you're beautiful." He lifted the letters. "Maybe I'm a bit embarrassed because I poured my heart out to you. I know you're hurt, but this sucks for me too. I wrote sappy letters to someone who would never see me that way."

Callie's brow furrowed. "How do you know? You never gave me a choice. You just forged full steam ahead and deceived me. I'm having a really hard time seeing *you* as the victim here."

She sensed the wheels churning in his mind before he backed away and set the letters on the desk. Opening the top drawer, he reached inside and pulled out a folded piece of paper. Stepping toward her, he extended it.

"The damage is done, and you think I'm a huge jerk, so I might as well bare it all."

Callie stared at the paper, wondering if she should read it.

"Go on," he said, shaking it. "It will be highly embarrassing for me, but it will put us on more even ground. We can both feel like exposed idiots. It's the least I can do. Fair warning: It's a doozy. I have no idea how you'll react to it."

Curiosity swamped her as she reached for the letter. Unfolding it, she turned away and began to read, craving a small bit of privacy so she could truly digest whatever the missive held.

My Sweet Callie-lily,

Tomorrow, you'll bond with the man meant to be your mate. We live in a world where people choose who they love based on tradition and status, and I don't begrudge you for choosing Zadicus. It only makes sense based on your heritage, and I truly hope you find all the happiness you deserve.

There are so many things I want to tell you, but I understand it's better if I keep my secrets to ensure your happiness. So many times over these past few weeks, I wanted to tell you I wrote you the letters. That I was the one who longed for you from afar and was enthralled by your beauty, kindness and soulful laugh. But that would serve no purpose except to out me as a fool. Someone who decided to fall for a woman who could never be his.

Selfishly, a part of me kept the secret because I knew you'd be furious. It would create a rift between you and Zadicus and ruin the friendship we've started to build. I truly hope we can remain friends once you've bonded. I've decided that seeing you every day as you build your life with Zadicus would be too painful, so I will be resigning as his bodyguard and reapplying for the army. Still, I know I'll see you with Jack from time to time, and during those encounters, I hope our friendship will continue to grow. If you smile at me during those fleeting moments, that will be enough to fill my soul. It has to be, and I accept that.

Be happy, Callie-lily. Never stop grabbing the world by the horns and pushing through. I've never met someone as resilient as you, even though you've been faced with undeserved challenges. Others might crumble or curse the world, but you just forge ahead with grace and bravery. It is magnificent. **You** are magnificent. Thank you for letting me know you, if only just a little. You've opened my eyes to possibilities I never considered. I always relished being alone, but you've shown me there can be beauty in caring for someone else deep in your heart.

Love, Your Stoic Soldier, Brecken

Callie's chin trembled as she finished, and her hands shook as they held the letter. Struggling to catch her breath, she slowly rotated to gaze at Brecken. He stared back at her, resignation crossing his handsome features, along with something tender and...raw.

"Brecken," she whispered, slowly shaking her head. "I don't know what to say..."

He grinned and lifted his shoulder. "Not really sure there's much to say after that."

Folding the letter, she trailed over and gently placed it on the desk. Facing him, she tentatively stepped forward, heart lurching each time she took a step. When mere inches finally separated them, she lifted her hands, gently placing them over his pecs. He closed his eyes, appearing to cherish her touch, before slowly opening them and sliding his hands to cover hers.

"Callie," he whispered.

"I didn't know," she said, shaking her head, the movements almost imperceptible.

"I didn't know either." He squeezed her hands. "About Zadicus working with Bakari. I swear, if I'd known, I would've ripped the bastard's testicles off."

Breathing a laugh, she bit her lip. "You sound like my dad. He's first in line."

"Good. We'll murder both of them."

His thumbs smoothed the backs of her hands, caressing as she digested the letter.

"You still lied to me though. Why?"

"I'm a practical person, Callie. I saw an opportunity to help my family, and I took it. It was selfish and wrong, and I'm sorry for that. I never thought I'd develop feelings for you. It knocked me off my feet. You have a profound effect on people. I don't even think you realize it. You opened me up and made me feel all these uncomfortable emotions I had no idea how to handle. I should be pissed," he teased, his lips forming a tender smile.

Callie gazed at him, enthralled by the heat of his skin beneath her palms and the arousal that was rapidly increasing deep in her core. Letting it surge, she felt a twinge between her thighs and noticed his nostrils slightly flare.

"You smell so good," he murmured, his tone reverent as he stroked her cheek with the backs of his fingers.

"I think I'm aroused," she said, her voice gravelly.

"You're definitely aroused." Staring into her with desire-laden eyes, he inhaled a deep breath before slowly exhaling. "It smells amazing. I want to suck every fucking drop from between your pretty thighs."

The words slammed into her like a freight train, breaking the dam wide open. She shuddered and pressed her legs together as slickness coated the soft skin.

"I've never had sex. I was waiting for my bonding night."

"I know."

Rolling her tongue around her suddenly dry mouth, she pressed her fingernails into his chest, searching for a stronghold, elated when he uttered a soft hiss.

"I mean, it is still *technically* my bonding night."

His eyes darted between hers. "I don't want to be a replacement, Callie. I want it to mean something to you."

"Obviously, losing my virginity to you would mean something."

"You can lose your virginity to anyone. Maybe you should wait until you meet the man you'll actually bond with someday."

The statement elicited sadness and a bit of frustration. "Maybe I'll bond with you one day, Shakespeare. Have you considered that? Hmm?"

He bristled, causing her heart to fall to her knees.

"Wow. Okay, maybe I got the wrong impression here." Pulling away, she halted when he encircled her wrist.

"Wait," he said, drawing her close. "I just... This is a heavy discussion, Callie. You were engaged to another man hours ago. I think we just need to breathe a second."

"Breathe," she muttered, rolling her eyes. "I'm tired of breathing. Of always being altruistic and pragmatic. Where has that gotten me? To jilted bride status for the whole kingdom to see. Fuck that. I want to *live*. To throw caution to the wind and be selfish and needy for one damn night." Disengaging from him, she gripped the hem of her shirt and tugged it off, tossing it on the floor. His eyes widened as he stared at her breasts, encased in a lacy black bra.

"Callie," he whispered, hesitation marring his handsome features.

Sliding her arms around his neck, she rose to her toes. "I think it's time to stop talking, soldier."

"How the hell am I supposed to think when you're half-naked?" he asked, rubbing the tip of his nose against hers.

"You're not...and neither am I," she said, chucking her brows. Sliding her fingers into the thick hair at his nape, she squeezed, loving the slight growl he emitted as he tugged her tighter against his body. "Brecken?"

"Yes, honey," he whispered, barely grazing her lips with his.

"I want you to take my virginity."

His large frame shuddered in her arms, and she laughed with joy.

"Now, who's laughing at whom?" he teased.

Staring into his limitless eyes, Callie understood that every decision in her life thus far had been a step toward this very moment. She'd always held back with Zadicus, telling herself she would develop a burning passion for him. But deep in her heart, she acknowledged she'd never felt one ounce of the desire she now felt in Brecken's embrace. Never felt the thrumming arousal, or the wetness lining her inner thighs, or the tingle on every inch of her skin as she anticipated his touch.

Somehow, she'd waited for Brecken and ended up in his arms, exactly where she was supposed to be. Callie felt the sentiment deep in her bones and vowed to seize the moment. No more waiting for what felt right. It was time to just *feel*. To experience what she was destined to experience on her bonding night, with the man who'd written such beautiful words to her. Staring deep into his soul, she spoke with clarity and resolve.

"Make love to me, Brecken."

His eyes searched hers, hooded and filled with desire. "Are you sure? I don't want you to regret this—"

"I won't," she murmured, covering his lips with her fingers.

He placed a soft kiss against them before continuing. "Once I start loving you, I won't stop until I've kissed every inch of your body. Do you understand?"

"Yes, you daft man. That's what I'm asking you to do."

Chuckling, he rested his forehead against hers. He gazed into her eyes as his thumb caressed her heated cheek. "I'm terrified you'll regret this, hon. That you're angry and hurt, and that I don't deserve to touch you after the way I deceived you." Sliding his fingers into the hair at the nape of her neck, he almost growled. "And still, knowing all that, I'm not sure I can stop myself."

"Brecken?"

"Hmm?"

Nipping his bottom lip, she reveled in his soft moan. "Stop talking and fuck me—"

He all but sucked the words from her mouth, plunging his tongue deep inside as she mewled. Losing her grip on reality, she relaxed into his hard frame as he surged his straining erection into the juncture of her thighs. Praying to the goddess she would be good at sex, she held on for dear life, determined not to let go until they were both sated and replete—and she was no longer a virgin.

Chapter 13

Brecken swirled his tongue over Callie's, drawing her essence into his mouth as he struggled to breathe. She tasted like the honeysuckles he used to pluck and savor from the bushes that grew in his back yard, but so much sweeter since it was enhanced by the smell of her arousal. The aroma surrounded him, almost suffocating as he longed to tear off her clothes and plunge himself into the wet depths of her core. But this was her first time, and although he knew he didn't deserve to touch her, it was impossible to stop now. Knowing that, he was determined to focus on her pleasure and make her scream in ecstasy before he even thought of experiencing his own release.

Bending his knees, he palmed the luscious globes of her ass, lifting her as she yelped. Her legs instinctively wrapped around his waist, and he carried her to the desk, swiping the papers to the floor in one fell swoop.

"Hey!" she said, pouting as he set her atop the wooden surface. "I want to keep those. They're so romantic even if they were a bit underhanded."

Brecken glanced at the letters scattered on the floor. "I'm never going to live it down, am I?"

"Nope," she said, giving him an adorable grin. "I reserve the right to make you feel terrible about writing them forever."

Hooking his fingers in the waistband of her sweatpants, he began to tug. "I'm happy you want to keep them," he murmured against her lips, tugging her pants and underwear down her legs. "I think they're the only reason you're letting me touch you right now."

"Truth," she said, arching an eyebrow as he tossed her pants aside. "Thank the goddess I figured it out."

Reaching behind her, he unclasped her bra as he gazed into her eyes. "I was terrified you were going to." Pulling the lacy fabric from her body, he dropped it before sliding his palms over her abdomen, just below her breasts. Tenderly, he caressed as her skin trembled beneath. "And I thought you'd hate me forever."

Resting her hands on the desk, the little minx grinned and thrust her breasts high, making his mouth water as his erection strained inside his pants. "Well, then, make it up to me, soldier."

Sliding his hands behind her knees, he dragged her toward him, situating his straining cock between her thighs. He couldn't touch her there yet—one feel of that slick arousal, and he'd lose it. So he pressed against her and slid his hand into her hair, clenching her curls. After a soft tug, her head fell back, exposing the smooth skin of her neck. Lowering his lips, he pressed them to her pulsing vein.

She emitted a high-pitched moan that shot straight to his dick as he began to trail kisses over her neck, down to her collarbone and over the swell of her breast. Sighing his name, she locked her ankles behind his back and thrust her fingers into his thick hair.

Brecken trailed his tongue over her skin, wondering if he'd ever tasted anything so good. Circling her nipple and the darkened areola, he placed wet kisses as she whimpered beneath him.

"Look at me, Callie-lily," he rasped, needed to stare into her gorgeous eyes as he sucked that tight, puckered little nipple between his lips. Her eyes latched onto his, the ocean orbs swimming with desire, and his knees almost buckled at the sight of her swollen lips and flushed cheeks. Opening his lips, he gently placed them over her nipple, drawing the bud into his mouth and sucking it deep inside.

"*Ohmygod...*" she breathed, legs clenching his waist as she fisted his hair, sending jolts of pleasure through his frame. "Brecken..."

He moaned against her skin, sucking the taut bud as he gazed at her. Goddess, he could spend every moment for the rest of eternity right here, nestled against her body as she moaned above him. Popping her nipple from his mouth, he extended his tongue, flicking the nub in short strokes as her back arched.

"Do you like that, honey?"

"What do you think?" she rasped, her fingers so tight in his hair he wondered if she would rip it out. Hell, he didn't care as long as she stayed right here in his arms, squirming and pliant as he loved her. "Oh, *please*...do the other one."

Breathing a laugh against her warm skin, he trailed a row of kisses between her breasts until he reached the other nipple. Licking his lips, he formed a circle and blew a slow breath on the pebbled nub.

"Fuck!" she hissed, her heels digging into his buttocks as she clutched him. "Don't tease me."

"That's the best part, hon," he said, nudging her nipple with his nose. "I want to draw this out and make you feel good."

"I feel so good," she groaned, head falling back as he placed soft pecks on the underside of her breast. "Damn it. You're driving me crazy."

Deciding to end the delicious torture for them both, he closed his mouth over her breast, pulling her against his tongue. Her body trembled, mimicking his own tremors as he reveled in the pleasure of finally being in the arms of the woman he'd only dreamed of touching. It was humbling, the way she wrapped around him as if he were her guidepost, and he vowed to support her as he took her over the edge.

After sucking her nipple into a tight, straining point, he drew back, needing to gaze upon her naked beauty for one moment. Panting beneath him, she stared at him with hooded eyes as her pert nipples strained toward him, wet and glistening from his ministrations.

Placing his hand between her breasts, he slid his palm down her abdomen and across her navel. Tiny goose bumps sprang beneath his touch, her body quivering as he eventually reached her mound. Cupping her, he slid his finger between her drenched folds.

"I'm going to make you come over and over again, honey," he whispered, gliding his finger back and forth in a slow slide. "Let's make you come right here against my hand so we can take the edge off."

"Okay," she whispered, pushing against his hand. Chuckling, he searched, locating her opening and circling it with his finger.

"You're greedy," he teased, gathering her wetness as he prepared to plunge inside.

"I've only ever done this to myself," she whispered, the words breathy as she clung to him.

"Who do you think about when you play with yourself?"

Her half-fangs squished her lips as she grinned. "Henry Cavill."

"Superman?" He arched a brow. "Wow. That's a lot to live up to, hon."

"I have faith in you, soldier." Inching closer, her eyes narrowed as she seemed to contemplate. Finally, she said softly, "I thought about you too sometimes. I would dream about you and couldn't understand why. I mean, you're really hot, but I probably should've been dreaming about my betrothed."

"Fuck him," Brecken muttered.

"It seems I wanted to fuck you," was her sultry reply. "I'd wake up all sweaty after dreaming we were together, and I'd reach down and touch myself—"

Her words broke off with a gasp as he surged a finger inside her taut channel. "Like this?"

"Oh, yes..." she moaned, lips parted as she gazed at him while he slid his finger back and forth. "Like that. Just like that..."

"Fuck, you're so tight and wet," he rasped, adding another finger and pushing deep inside, trying to find the spot that would make her scream.

Rubbing her silken walls, he hooked his fingers, thrilled when a ragged moan leaped from her throat.

"Right there," he said, lowering his lips to her neck and kissing a path to her ear. Resting his lips on the shell of her ear, he murmured, "Fuck my hand, Callie. I'm going to make you explode."

She undulated her hips, thrusting against his fingers as he rimmed her ear with his wet tongue. Placing the heel of his hand against her clit, he pressed against it, stimulating the tiny bundle of nerves as his fingers milked the spot deep within. Her sweet, wet honey flowed over his hand and fingers, drenching him with her arousal. Closing his teeth around her earlobe, he lightly bit the tender flesh before drawing it between his lips.

"Oh, god," she moaned, head thrown back as her hips pushed against his hand. "I think I'm going to come."

"Yes, honey," he crooned in her ear, his hand working at a furious pace as he strove to give her pleasure. "You're going to come all over me, aren't you?"

Her spine snapped, body jerking as she cried his name, and joy swelled in his chest. Thrilled he could give her such pleasure, he whispered words of love and desire in her ear as the orgasm tore through her frame. Unabandoned, she opened for him, like the calla lilies that inspired her nickname, and he was overwhelmed by her acquiescence and trust. Goddess knew, he probably didn't deserve it, but he would drink it in, imbibing like a parched vagabond as she gave him everything. Her body. Her forgiveness. Her innocence.

Expelling a deep breath, Callie lifted her head, eyes sparkling as she struggled to catch her breath. Gazing deep into those cobalt orbs, his lips curved.

"Well, well, it seems that someone has put Henry to shame," she teased.

Chuckling, he drew his hand from her core and lifted his fingers to his mouth. They were coated with her essence and he began to lick it away. "I had the fleeting thought I was taking your innocence, but I quickly realized that's ridiculous." Sticking his finger between his lips, he sucked her honey before moving to the next. "You're not innocent at all, are you? Look at those fucking eyes and swollen lips. You ready to go again?"

Giving a sated sigh, she nodded, adorable as she bit her lip. "But I want to make you feel good too."

"I feel so good right now," he said, sliding his hands to cup her ass and lifting her. She held tight as he walked them to the bed, lowering her and stretching out above her lithe body. "You're naked in my bed," he murmured, caressing her cheek. "I'm in fucking heaven, honey."

Grinning, she encircled his neck and shimmied against him. "Take off your pants."

"Not yet. I'm going to make you come again. And then, if you still want to make love, we'll do that too."

Her fingers sifted through his hair, causing him to shiver. "I'm not changing my mind, Brecken. I want this. I want *you*."

His eyes darted over her face as he brushed away the hair at her temple. "I'm sorry for deceiving you, Callie. I just need to say that one more time. I'm so humbled you can forgive me."

"I understand your motives." Lifting her hand, she cupped his jaw. "But please don't lie to me again, okay? I mean, I could read your thoughts if I wanted to, but then I'd be violating your trust. Let's just be honest with each other from here."

"I can do that." Lowering, he placed a peck on her lips. "Now, I remember promising to lick every drop of your arousal. Let's get you nice and wet again so I can taste you."

Giggling, she gently pushed his head lower. "If you insist. And keep up the dirty talk. It's so freaking sexy."

His deep chuckle rumbled against her skin as he kissed his way down her stomach. His lips moved between her breasts and down to her navel. Staring into her eyes, his tongue dipped into the tiny indention before moving lower. Encircling her thighs with his broad hands, he dragged her toward the edge of the bed. Resting on his knees, he grinned at her from between her legs as she gazed at him, eyes simmering with lust.

"Look at you," he whispered, palming her inner thighs and spreading her legs. Her wet folds called to him, and he leaned in, gently smoothing his lips over the tender flesh. "Callie," he whispered, the words reverberating off her soft skin, "you're so pretty."

Her nose scrunched. "Can you be pretty down there?"

Laughing, he pushed her thighs wider and nodded. "Oh, yeah. You're a fucking goddess down here, honey." Placing his fingers on her folds, he pulled her open, feeling his cock jerk as he stared at her deepest place. Unable to hold back any longer, he buried his face in her center and began to feast.

She moaned above him as he licked a long trail over her opening, up to her clit, and flicked it with his tongue. Aiming to take her even higher than before, he closed his lips over the sensitive bud, sucking it in rhythmic movements as he circled her opening with his finger. Delving one finger into her channel, he slid it back and forth as his mouth worked her clit.

Callie writhed on the bed, fists clenching the comforter before she eventually reached down and thrust her fingers in his hair. Blood surged to Brecken's shaft when she drew him closer, rubbing her core against his face as he loved her. Goddess, she was so sexy like this, unencumbered as she pushed into his face, straining for release. Inserting another finger, he plunged them back and forth as his tongue flicked the engorged nub at the hood of her mound.

Finally, she screamed, losing control and wrapping her legs around his head. Brecken chuckled against her wet folds, accepting that if he suffocated with his face buried in her sweet pussy, it would be a magnificent way to enter the Passage. Eventually, she relaxed, her legs falling to the bed as her frame turned limp atop the comforter.

Rising, he shrugged off his pants, tossing them to the floor before crawling over her. Aligning his body with hers, he cupped her cheek, resting his weight on his other arm so he didn't crush her.

"Earth to Callie," he teased, kissing the tip of her nose. "Are you okay?"

"Sensory overload," she murmured, curls sliding over the bed as she shook her head. "My muscles melted."

His low-toned laugh surrounded them. "We don't have to do anything else, hon. I can just hold you and let you enjoy the high."

Squinting with one eye, she ran her calf over his. "No way, soldier. It's time. Make love to me."

His practical brain railed at him that he should give her more time. That losing her virginity was a huge decision that shouldn't be made after discovering a terrible betrayal. Sliding between her thighs, his body—and his cock—overrode his objections, pulverizing them to dust in his mind. Gripping her leg, he hooked it around his waist, elated when she used it to tug him closer.

"Do you want me to grab a condom?"

Although Vampyres couldn't transmit diseases due to their self-healing abilities, there was still a chance of pregnancy.

"No. Sadie gave me an IUD years ago to help regulate my periods. Go for it, soldier."

Wondering if he'd ever gazed upon anyone so simultaneously cute and sexy, he reached for his throbbing cock. Encircling the base, he aligned the sensitive head with her opening, closing his eyes in ecstasy when it dragged through her wet folds. She emitted a tiny mewl beneath him, and his lids flew open as his eyes latched onto hers.

Staring deep into those fathomless blue-green orbs, he began to push inside.

"Ohhhhh..." she whimpered as her arms and leg drew him closer. "Oh, yes...that feels...*Brecken*..."

"I'm right here, Callie-lily," he said, pushing into her tight channel inch by slow, excruciating inch. The plushy walls of her core squeezed him, pushing back at the invasion, and he gritted his teeth at the extreme pleasure.

"Relax, hon," he whispered, his heart slamming in his chest when she melted beneath him. The gesture showed such openness, and it moved something in his stoic soul. Driving deeper, he eventually reached the hilt. "You okay?"

She nodded and dug her nails into his shoulders. "Don't hold back."

Eliciting a feral growl, he began to move his hips, dragging his engorged cock through her swollen folds as she arched to meet him. Their bodies moved in tandem, learning each other's rhythm as he tried to hold off his release. He'd dreamed of fucking her for so long he was half-afraid he'd lose it before pleasing her.

"I feel you everywhere," she whispered, face contorting with pleasure as he moved deep within. "Holy shit, you're huge."

He froze, looming above her as he assessed. "Am I hurting you?"

"No way." Furiously shaking her head, she speared her nails into his skin. "Don't stop. It was just getting good."

Breathing a laugh, he resumed thrusting inside her warm body, lowering his head to capture her lips. He'd never really laughed while having sex, and it freed something, causing him to open himself to her. Together, they both bloomed into something more—two people who might never have connected except for the extraordinary circumstances that led them to this very night. Although he hated that Callie had experienced pain, he was exceedingly thankful for the opportunity to make love to her.

Cradling her head, he kissed her, thorough and deep, as he claimed her body. Her taut channel drenched him, enclosing him in a fist of silken pleasure, as he felt his muscles tighten. Sliding a hand under her body, he palmed her ass, lifting her to him each time he thrust inside. Striving to hit the inner spot he'd found with his fingers, he jutted against her swollen walls with the head of his cock.

"Right there," she whimpered, head tossing on the bed. "Oh, *god*, right there...keep hitting it..."

Gritting his teeth, he surged inside, ramming his cock against the tiny spot. Her nails speared his skin, most likely drawing blood, sending a surge of pleasure-pain through his entire body. Feeling his balls tighten, he buried his face in her neck and reached for the pinnacle.

She bowed beneath him, launching into an orgasm seconds before his own crashed down his spine, causing him to jerk his hips in a frenzied rush against her quaking body. Releasing a guttural groan into the sweat-soaked skin of her neck, he began shooting his release deep inside her body, coating her core...marking her as his.

"Mine," he gritted into her nape as she shuddered beneath him.

"Oh, god..." she moaned, lost in the climax as their bodies released and convulsed. Encircling her with his arms, he melded their bodies, admiring how perfectly they fit together. The thought was terribly sappy and quite unlike him, but the woman had turned everything else upside down. It was probably inevitable she'd turn him into a romantic dope.

His hips jerked as the last jets of release shot into her slick center. Relaxing against her, he cuddled her close, admitting he was a goner.

God, he'd never craved cuddling in his entire life. Now, all he wanted was to hold her tight and never let go.

Lifting a shaking hand, she sifted her fingers through his hair. "Are you laughing?"

He nodded against her neck. "You've turned me into a pansy."

Her joyful chuckle enveloped them, and she kissed his ear. "How so?"

Raising his head, which now seemed to weigh more than a four-wheeler, he stared into her sated eyes. "I've turned into a letter-writing dope. Let's leave it there."

Snickering, she scrunched her features. "It's sweet. I want you to write me more."

"Shit." Pecking her lips, he shook his head. "I've created a monster."

They exchanged lazy smiles, stroking each other's heated skin as their gazes mingled. Finally, he asked softly, "Are you okay?"

Nodding, she cupped his jaw. "That was amazing." His cock twitched inside her, causing her to gasp. "I still feel you."

"I wish I could stay here forever," he murmured.

A loud clap of thunder sounded outside, jolting them, and Brecken felt himself slipping. Hating to leave her gorgeous body, he kissed her cheek before slowly rising. "Stay here."

"I'm not going anywhere," she said, lifting her arms over her head as she stretched over the bed. "Best workout *ever*."

He strode to the bathroom and wet a cloth before returning to her. Lifting her leg, he placed her ankle on his shoulder, opening her so he could clean away the evidence of their loving. She gazed at him, curls strewn over the bed, looking like a sated queen.

When he was done, he wiped his cock, mourning the loss of her essence spread over the sensitive skin. Once he recovered, he'd take her again—slower this time—and treasure that wet warmth spread around him.

"Can I ask you something weird?"

"Sure." He walked to the bed, sitting on the edge.

Rising to her knees, she tilted her head. "Have you ever danced in the rain? It's one of my favorite things. I used to do it with my mom when I had a bad day at school. She said it cleansed everything away so we could start the next day fresh."

"That's pretty cool. I've never tried it."

"Well, I had a pretty shitty day—except for the past hour, of course." She winked, sending his heart right back into overdrive. "So I'd really like to wash it away. Any chance you'd want to do it with me? I'm pretty sure it's pouring from the sound of the thunder." She pointed to the ceiling.

"Sure, I'm game." Standing, he extended his hand.

Taking it, she leaped from the bed, throwing on her clothes while he tugged on his sweatpants. Grabbing his hand, she dragged him outside until they stood in the wet grass while large droplets fell from above. Extending her arms, she began to twirl, mouth open as she tried to drink the drops. Brecken thought she looked like a regal imp, intent on showing the world it wouldn't get the best of her. In a word, she was glorious.

"Isn't it fun?" she asked, halting mid-twirl. "Come on, you have to twirl!"

Feeling like an idiot, he extended his arms and began to turn, overjoyed by the sound of her effervescent laughter. "See?"

"It feels good!" he said, excited most of all by her gregarious smile.

"I'm not a virgin anymore!" she yelled, and he froze, his features drawing together.

"Jeez, Callie, my mom's cabin is just across that meadow." He pointed toward the deep thicket of trees and brush that sat at the far side of his lawn. "Keep it down."

"Not on your life, buster. I've waited too long to find my Henry."

He scowled. "Should I be worried about this Henry Cavill obsession you have?"

Tossing her head back, her neck glistened from the dewy rain. "No way. You're my new Henry, and you're so damn sexy, Brecken."

Approaching her, he decided he'd gone long enough without touching her. Tugging her close, he drew her into a passionate kiss as droplets coated their sated bodies. Pulling back, she laced her arms around his neck. "I know you don't want to be sappy, but I'd really like to cuddle with you...and then I want to bone again, obviously."

"I've never cuddled before, so I might be bad at it."

"Well, I'm no expert either, but we could figure it out together. I mean, if you want to. I think I'd like snuggling with you while it storms outside. Sounds pretty romantic." She waggled her eyebrows.

Crouching down, he lifted her as she squealed. Placing a firm kiss on her lips, he strode across the yard. "Dancing in the rain and cuddling. Damn, woman. At this rate, you're going to get another letter out of me before sunrise."

"*My hero*," she sighed, holding onto him as he walked up the porch steps.

Carrying her inside, he shut the door behind them and located some towels so they could dry off. And then, Brecken cuddled with a woman for the first time in his life, noting it was nothing short of magnificent since it was his gorgeous Callie in his arms.

Eventually, the cuddling turned to another round of hot sex, which almost blew his mind.

And then, at his woman's request, he wrote her another damn love letter, pretending he hated it but secretly enamored with her smile as he read it to her before sunrise in his deep, reverent tone.

Chapter 14

Bakari paced inside the cave, furious and fierce.

"You had one job, Zadicus," he said, jutting his finger in the man's face as he sat on the nearby rock. "Goddess, I never should've recruited you in the first place. I knew you didn't have the temerity to see this through. You're no better than your aunt."

"Callie is powerful," Zadicus said, standing and lifting his arms. "The shield you placed was imperceptible until she decided to look for it. You can't blame me for her discovery."

"Said like the victim you are," Bakari spat, turning to face Commander Vadik. "Has Dr. Tyson returned from the human world?"

"Yes," Vadik said with a nod. "He's in the lab working on various potions." Gesturing toward the tunnel, he asked, "Would you like me to summon him?"

"No need," Dr. Tyson answered, appearing from the mouth of the tunnel. "I'm here. What do you require of me, Bakari?"

Bakari studied the hybrid, who professed to be half-Slayer and half-Vampyre, although Bakari knew the truth. The slight points of his ears would be imperceptible to most, but Bakari had met other Elven-Vampyre hybrids over his long life, all of them in the human world, passing as the inferior species.

"You procured the elements needed to create the new potion, Quaygon?"

"Yes," he said, holding up a small vial. "And I've asked you to call me by my human name rather than my immortal one."

"Yes, yes," Bakari said, waving a dismissive hand. "The concoction is as potent as promised?"

"We will need to test it on a live subject, but I am confident in its potency."

"Good. I have just the subject we need." Extending his hand toward Zadicus, Bakari narrowed his eyes, summoning the powers that swirled in his blood as a result of all the concoctions Dr. Tyson had formulated thus far. After a moment, he froze Zadicus in place.

"What are you doing?" the man asked, eyes widening in fear. "Bakari...please. I'm sorry I failed with Callie. I can fix it, I swear."

"Stop groveling," Bakari gritted through clenched teeth. "Your life as you knew it is over. You've been outed as a traitor and can never return to immortal society. It is time for you to embrace your true purpose."

Glancing at the doctor, he urged him over by hooking the fingers of his free hand. "Come, Dr. Tyson. It is time to test the new potion."

"I can give him two CCs to start. Otherwise, it will be too much."

"How many CCs will turn him into the soldier we need?"

Dr. Tyson's eyebrows drew together as he studied the vial. "Five or six, but that's too much for a first dose."

"Give him six CCs," Bakari commanded.

"You don't understand. That dose will effectively kill him. All that will remain is brute strength and the ability to follow orders."

"Good. Perhaps I should've transformed him from the beginning. Inject the potion, Dr. Tyson."

"Please, no..." Zadicus pleaded, chin trembling as he stood frozen.

"I'm sorry, my friend. You'll have better use to me this way. Failure must be punished at all costs. I hope your soul finds its way to the Passage." Glaring at Dr. Tyson, he commanded in a low tone, "Inject the potion."

Dr. Tyson's throat bobbed before he stepped forward, pulling a syringe from the pocket of the white lab coat he wore. Inserting it in the vial, he withdrew six CCs and approached Zadicus. Lifting the man's sleeve, he thrust the needle into his arm.

Zadicus gasped, ice-blue eyes laced with fear as Dr. Tyson injected the potion into his body. For a moment, all was silent...and then, the vein in Zadicus's neck began to pulse wildly. The man screamed, his fangs glistening in the dim light of the torches that lined the cave walls as his skin began to bulge and transform. Bakari observed with labored breaths, power surging through his frame at the creation before him.

"He might not be able to withstand the transformation," Dr. Tyson murmured.

"He will," Bakari said, willing it to happen.

Zadicus's gaze locked with his, filled with terror and confusion, before the light inside suddenly dimmed. Any last vestige of the Vampyre's soul left his body, leaving a robotic warrior in its place. Releasing the freezing spell, Bakari spoke.

"Step forward, warrior."

The creature followed the command, stoic and steady. "I am at your command, Bakari." His voice was lower, less filled with nuance and life, and Bakari was pleased.

"Excellent job, Dr. Tyson. His self-healing abilities will be magnified?"

"Yes," the man said softly, seemingly overcome with the gravity of the transformation. "He's essentially been transformed into a super soldier. As long as you give him Slayer blood every few days, he will remain a powerful asset. He now possesses the strength of twenty Vampyre soldiers."

"Good. That will come in handy during our final skirmish. The immortals are intent on one ultimate battle to end this war, and I aim to give them one. Commander Vadik, you will instill Zadicus into your lineup immediately and train him to fight alongside the Deamon troops."

"Yes, sir."

Bakari thought he noticed a hint of annoyance in the man's expression.

"Do you want to voice a concern?"

"No," Vadik said, shaking his head. "I'm just ready to end this conflict. It has raged for too long. I want to end the war and instill Deamon supremacy over the caves once again. We will create our utopia there in Crimeous's name while you rule the immortal world. It is time for the species to be separate once again, as the goddess intended. I don't relish the idea of having a genetically modified Vampyre on my squad, but I see the advantage."

"Good," Bakari said. "You will have your utopia soon enough, Vadik. We all will. For now, I require some rest."

The men gave a respectful bow before Bakari exited and returned to his cottage. Now that his plan to blackmail Callie through Zadicus had backfired, he was determined to find another way to secure her alliance.

Entering his cabin, he stripped down to his underwear, noting the slight throbbing on his inner thigh where his mark was branded. After pouring a decanter of Slayer blood, he sat in the broad-backed chair beside the fireplace, tracing his finger over the pentagram that had been embedded on his pale skin since birth. The symbol signified the hidden Elven prophecy that was discovered when Miranda and Kenden found the secret scrolls at Restia. It was the reason he had been exiled from the realm by the soothsayers, and he felt a deep calling to fulfill it. When he'd learned of Callie's role in the prophecy, he knew it was only a matter of time before he secured her alliance. Patience had always been his virtue, and reimagining the world took time and careful effort.

Sipping the thick liquid, he wondered if perhaps he'd approached the situation from the wrong perspective. Callie often felt ostracized due to her powers and lack of acceptance in the realm. Perhaps he could approach her himself. If anyone understood being cast out from the very people who were supposed to accept you, it was Bakari. Did they possess enough common ground for her to consider listening to him?

Thinking back on their conversation at Astaria, Bakari remembered the jolt that flashed in her eyes when he'd mentioned the prophecy. Was it possible she saw a miniscule advantage to destroying the immortal world as it existed now?

Understanding there was only one way to find out, Bakari mulled different scenarios in which he could approach her until he crawled into bed, still mindful of the pulsing black mark upon his thigh.

Callie's eyes fluttered open, and she assessed the darkened surroundings. A steady cadence sounded to her right, and she turned to find Brecken softly snoring as his head rested upon the pillow. Smiling, she reached for him, aching to swipe the tuft of hair from his forehead. Halting, she decided to study him a bit longer as he slept.

For the love of the goddess, she'd lost her virginity last night. Not to the man she'd promised herself to for the better part of a year, but to Brecken, the sexy bodyguard who'd been in the background the entire time. Callie had always enjoyed their playful banter and gentle ribbing. She thought him quite serious and loved teasing him, especially when those full lips quirked at her chiding. He would feign indifference, but she usually caught the amusement in his eyes. But somehow, she'd missed the affection lurking just beneath the mirth. Why hadn't she seen it?

For someone who could read minds, she was seriously daft. Settling on her back, she glared at the ceiling, trying like hell not to beat herself up for missing so many things. Zadicus's betrayal, the letters, and Brecken's affection for her. By the goddess, she'd missed them all. Callie considered herself a pretty intelligent person and wondered why she'd been so oblivious.

Pondering, she thought back to the way she was raised. Her parents were always so careful to support and encourage her since she'd been bestowed with her father's powers. They'd done an excellent job, and she loved them dearly, but their encouragement probably created a false sense of complacency for her. She trusted others because her world was safe. What would've happened if circumstances were different? If her grandfather's evil blood had been set free and allowed to dictate her actions without her parents' intervention?

Shivering, Callie realized she didn't relish that thought. She was determined to live a life of honor, worthy of her station. She looked up to her parents, Miranda, Evie and everyone in her family and wanted so badly to be a force for good in the kingdom. Lost in thought, she didn't hear Brecken rouse beside her until his finger gently grazed her arm.

"Hey," she said softly, turning to face him.

"Hey." His raspy voice rolled over her, sending a rush of arousal to her core. By the goddess, he was so fucking sexy. Now the door had been opened, Callie was pretty sure she wanted to bang him at every opportunity. "It was hard to sleep with the excessive teeth grinding."

Breathing a laugh, she bit her lip. "Sorry. I was just thinking about my childhood and what made me so fucking gullible. And I was also thinking we should probably just bang every day for eternity."

Lazy brown eyes assessed her as he rubbed her arm. "You're not gullible, hon. Zadicus worked hard to deceive you, and he fooled me too. I'm pissed I didn't discover his alliance with Bakari. He negotiated several hours a week away from my watch, and that's probably when he met with him. I'm furious I let him manipulate me too."

"I guess no one's perfect," she said, wrinkling her nose. "But we have to be smarter from now on."

"Definitely."

"Miranda's probably going to want to question you in front of the council too."

As if on cue, Callie's phone dinged. Reaching for it, she picked it up from the bedside table and scrolled through the texts.

"Everything okay?" he asked.

"Yeah," she said, her finger moving over the screen. "Miranda and Sathan have called an emergency council meeting and she wants the rest of my family to attend as well. Apparently, Tatiana contacted Uncle Heden last night, and I'm somehow involved. She also wants to question you afterward." Gazing at him, she smiled. "You'll get to meet my family. How sweet."

His expression was impassive, causing her to wonder if her playful teasing crossed a line. After all, they'd had sex, but what did that mean? Did they start courting now? The jilted bride and the out-of-work bodyguard. What a pair.

Callie had no idea, but one thing was certain: she liked Brecken. The sex had been amazing, but beyond that, she actually enjoyed his company. He was a good man who'd handled Zadicus's arrogant commands with grace and treated his sister like gold. Callie longed to dig deeper. To see him with his mother and other sisters and grow their connection. They already had explosive chemistry and affection. What if it could grow into love?

"Did I scare you away?" she asked, heart thrumming as she awaited his answer.

"No." Inching closer, he rested his head on his palm, elbow firm on the mattress as his other hand caressed her collarbone. "I just have no idea how to navigate this. You were betrothed to someone else yesterday, and we come from different worlds, Callie. You haven't even had time to process things."

"Well, I *did* give you my virginity. I think that counts for something."

A breathy laugh escaped his lips before he leaned down to give her a soft kiss. "It means so much, hon. Honestly, I'm overwhelmed. Part of me thinks I'm dreaming."

"Wait till you meet my dad. More like a nightmare. He's a bit overprotective." She held her finger and thumb an inch apart.

"How pissed is he at Zadicus?"

Shrugging, she considered. "Somewhere between crushing his balls and murder."

Pursing his lips, he nodded. "Same here."

"You two can align in your hatred of my ex-betrothed. It's what every girl dreams of."

Grinning, his eyes darted over her face, and she could see the wheels churning in his mind. "Let's not decide anything now. I want to make love to you one more time, to convince myself this is real."

Sliding her hand between their bodies, she encircled his cock, thick and turgid as it nudged against her thigh. "Oh, I think it's pretty real," she said in a sultry voice.

Uttering a soft moan, he jutted into her hand. "From virgin to sex goddess in one night."

"Sex goddess?" she asked, eyes widening. "Oh, I like that."

"I like it too, you little tease." Sliding over her, he wedged himself between her legs. "We'll talk after the council meeting today, okay, hon?"

Sliding her arms around his neck, she nodded. "Okay. Get to work, soldier."

Gazing into her eyes, he drew her close, aligning their bodies. Callie spread her legs wide, inviting him to ravish her. Gripping her shoulder, he anchored her and surged inside. No foreplay this time. Just raw, passionate connection with her lover. Clutching him, she rode the wave, allowing him to take her to the peak as she shuddered in his arms.

Chapter 15

After her passionate morning tryst with Brecken, Callie headed home in the four-wheeler. She felt a bit guilty lying to her parents—after all, they believed she'd spent the night at Astaria. But she was an adult, for the goddess's sake, and had every right to spend the night wherever she damn well pleased. Once home, she took a long, warm shower, touching herself between her thighs and remarking on the slight soreness. Her Vampyre blood had self-healing properties, but Brecken was *huge*. In her opinion, at least, which probably didn't amount to much since his was the only erect cock she'd ever seen. Still, she decided he was the most studly, prolific lover ever and snickered under the spray at her silly musings.

Refreshed, she threw on her sandals, jeans and tank top and headed to Uteria. Her parents had texted her to meet them there since they'd already headed over. Darkrip was meeting Evie to practice their combined forefield, and Arderin had promised to help Lila prepare some lunch for the council members.

On the drive to Uteria, Callie's thoughts drifted to Brecken. She would certainly see him since he was slated to meet with the council directly after their meeting to discuss Tatiana's contact with Heden. Would he remain stoic and give her that sexy smirk when they saw each other? Or would he allow the lust in those deep bronze eyes to simmer?

She wasn't sure, but she realized she wanted their relationship to remain secret for a little while longer. Not because she was ashamed or embarrassed. Brecken was a kind, thoughtful man, and any woman would be lucky to have him as her partner. Instead, she was still angry and a bit embarrassed at her own predicament and the fact that by now, the entire kingdom must know of her canceled nuptials. It would be nice to develop a relationship with Brecken outside of the watchful eye of others.

Although she loved her parents and her family with her whole heart, they were a *lot* sometimes, and she knew they would meddle if they found out.

Arriving at Uteria, Callie parked beside the barracks and headed into the castle. Entering the conference room, she noticed the council members floating about. Her father, Latimus and Jack were already seated, and others milled around, sliding into open seats. Callie slid in between Larkin and Aron, flashing them both a smile.

"How are you today, Callie?" Larkin asked with a gentle smile. He was a valiant Slayer soldier who'd fought to protect his people for centuries. Callie thought him so brave and liked him immensely. He was a bit of a loner, which called to her since she often found it easier to spend time alone rather than attempt to hang with people who didn't understand her.

"I'm fine," she said, reaching over to squeeze his hand. "Thank you for asking. I'm navigating through the embarrassment phase and will soon enter the *'thank the goddess I dodged a bullet'* phase, hopefully." She made quotation marks with her fingers.

Chuckling, he winked. "I'm sure you will. You're pretty amazing and quite beautiful. I know you'll find someone who fits you better than Zadicus. You deserve that."

"Maybe one day." Studying him, she asked, "Have you ever found anyone who fit? The idea seems so faraway at the moment, but maybe you can give me hope."

His expression turned wistful, and a hint of sadness entered his brown eyes. "I found someone once...but he..." Glancing down, he twirled his thumbs together atop the table. "He died."

Callie's eyebrows lifted, and she tamped down her surprise. She didn't realize Larkin was attracted to men and certainly didn't realize he'd once been in love and lost his lover. "I'm so sorry," she whispered, encircling his wrist. "I'd love to hear your story one day. I know our kingdom is super-stuffy and still somewhat antiquated, but I spent the first seven years of my life in L.A. It was a beautiful place filled with acceptance of who people were no matter who they loved."

"I'd like to tell you one day. It's not something I talk about very much—I'm a pretty private person. You know, stoic soldier and all." His lips curved into a sweet smile. "But I think talking to you about it would be nice. I haven't talked about him for a long time."

"Then we'll do that one day. My only request is that we have lots of wine present so you can relax and tell me every last detail."

"I'd like that, princess. Thank you." He squeezed her hand atop his wrist with his free one before Miranda strode into the room, effectively ending their conversation.

"Thank you all for showing up this morning for another meeting. As you know, Heden and Sofia received a transmission from Tatiana, and we wanted to address it expeditiously."

"I can take it from here, Miranda," Heden's voice boomed as his face appeared on the screen of the large TV mounted on the conference room wall. "Can you all hear me?"

"Loud and clear," Miranda said, sliding into her chair. "You've done a great job with the newest communication updates, Heden."

"Piece of cake. We needed to upgrade everything so we could video chat with you all yesterday since we couldn't attend the bonding ceremony. Sorry to hear about Zadicus, baby toad. Want me to smash his face in?"

Callie's heart swelled at the nickname, used only by Heden. "I'm okay, Uncle Heden. Thank you."

"Of course. I've always got your back. Once Sofia stopped flirting with me long enough to let me work, I really enjoyed upgrading the systems last week. Although the wedding didn't happen, the upgrade was timely and will only improve our communications between the human and immortal realms."

Sofia appeared, palming Heden's face and pushing him out of the way to face the camera. "What my husband is *trying* to say is that I did *all* the work and he now wants to take all the credit. I wrote the entire front end code of the most recent upgrade, and he figured out a teeny, tiny part of the back end."

"I like your back end a lot better," Heden teased, smacking her butt. "Guys, I think I might need to take five—"

"I'm leaving," Sofia said, rolling her eyes as she gave him a playful scowl. "As you know, the twins are leaving for their high-school field trip to Paris tomorrow, and I'm a nervous wreck, which is why we couldn't come to the bonding ceremony. We love you very much, Callie, and I'm making an extra special batch of wine to drink with you one day while we imagine punching that bastard right in his nose."

"Can't wait, Aunt Sofia. I appreciate your support, and you know I love your wine."

Sofia smoothed her fingers over Heden's thick hair. "I'll be helping the kids pack while Heden updates you. He's got all the info, but please text me if he carries on." She pulled her phone from her back pocket and wiggled it. "I'll be happy to save you."

"Thank you, Sofia," Miranda said, chuckling.

Sofia waved, smiling under her springy black hair, now with tiny white streaks that coursed through the strands, and smacked a kiss on Heden's lips before exiting the frame.

"She's obviously obsessed with me," Heden said, shrugging. "Can't say I blame her. Look at this handsome mug." He pointed to himself as everyone laughed around the table.

Callie noticed the hair at his temples had started to turn gray ever so slightly, but he still was as handsome as he'd been all those years ago when he chose to become human so he could be with Sofia. Emitting an inner sigh, Callie wondered if she'd ever find someone who would make such a valiant choice for her. Her thoughts drifted to Brecken, and she shut them down immediately. Plenty of time to digest that later.

"As you know, Tatiana hasn't appeared to us in years," Heden said, holding up a finger. "Until yesterday when she appeared to Callie. Now, she seems ready for another chat, but she's summoning us to her this time."

"How so?" Miranda asked.

"Last night, we received an email from an encrypted address. It simply read, '*Calinda can find me here.*'"

Heden's face disappeared from the screen, and a picture of a rock appeared, surrounded by dirt and a few sparse cacti.

"A rock?" Callie asked, squinting to see the images carved across it. "Are those Native American drawings?"

"That they are, baby toad," he said, zooming in on the stone. "This rock sits in the Arizona desert in a national forest called the Sierra Ancha Wilderness Area. It has a rich history from being colonized by American Indigenous People over a thousand years ago who are now called the Hohokam."

"And she wants *me* to find her there?" Callie asked, pointing at herself.

"Yes," Heden said with a nod. "I'm not quite sure what's going on, but she's suddenly all up in your grill, Callie. I'm certainly not psychic, but I have a feeling this is all tied into the prophecy."

"She did say yesterday that she has more she wants to discuss with me," Callie said, chewing her lip. "I thought she'd appear to me again, but if she wants me to come to her, there must be a reason."

"From my conversations with Tatiana over the years, she has the blood of many human ancestors flowing through her veins from several different cultures. Sofia and I believe one of those cultures are the Hokokam. They have long disbanded and descended into other tribes, but it's possible Tatiana has ties to the area. Perhaps she's staying in the ruins there or working on one of her weird concoctions that require ingredients only found in the desert. I'm not sure, but she's requesting your presence, Callie."

"Absolutely not," Darkrip said, shaking his head. "No way in hell is Callie going to the human world to rendezvous with some witch whose motives we can't fathom. End of discussion."

"Ahem," Callie said, clearing her throat. "While I appreciate your concern, Dad, I'll remind you that I'm a grown woman and can make my own decisions, thank you very much."

"Not in this instance. I can't protect you since I'm needed here to work with Evie to fortify and practice our skills for the final battle with Bakari."

"I wasn't asking you to go with me," Callie said, feeling her nostrils flare. "In case you've forgotten, I have powers of my own and am extremely capable of defending myself."

"No," Darkrip said, crossing his arms over his chest. "Not happening."

"Not that I want to argue with the man who can pulverize my head into a million pieces," Heden chimed in, "but having Callie approach Tatiana if she is in fact summoning her could actually increase our chances against Bakari. Although Tatiana has remained neutral up to this point, her appearance and interference yesterday opened a door. I think she might be ready to choose a side. To choose *our* side."

"She could supply us with information on every potion she's ever designed for Bakari and inform us of any plans he might have divulged," Callie murmured, eyes narrowing as she debated the advantage of following the lead.

"Absolutely. The thing is, I think Tatiana *wants* to talk. Call it some sort of weird intuition, but I think she's extremely invested in our conflict. For whatever reason, she's chosen Callie as the person to communicate with."

"I think she wants me to fulfill the prophecy," Callie said, leaning forward and resting her forearms on the table. "I don't think she sees the prophecy as something evil, but instead as something..."—she circled her hand, searching for the word—"necessary."

"I'm not letting my daughter travel to the human world alone. I don't care that she grew up there, that she has powers, nor how old she is. It's not fucking happening." Darkrip's tone was firm.

Callie clenched her jaw, ready to give him a piece of her mind, before Jack interjected.

"So, I have an idea," he said, leaning forward and resting his palms on the table. "Brecken is outside waiting to be deposed about Zadicus. He's trained in private security and is unemployed at the moment."

"He should've figured out that Zadicus was working with Bakari," Darkrip muttered. "I'm looking forward to debriefing him."

"So am I," Jack said with a nod. "Brecken is a good friend, and I trust him implicitly. After we question him, I'm sure you'll find he knew nothing of Zadicus's deception. I think he should accompany Callie to the human world. He's a trained soldier and will keep her safe."

Callie's heart slammed at the suggestion. It made perfect sense and would allow her to spend some time with the man who now consumed her thoughts. "I think it's a great idea. I consider Brecken a friend and would feel comfortable with him as my companion."

Darkrip's lips thinned as he considered. "Maybe I should just go with you. If you all are intent on Callie chasing this lead, I want to ensure her safety."

"We need to practice the forcefield, Darkrip," Evie said. "This is different than the shield we created to kill father thanks to all the dark potions running through Bakari's blood. I don't want to lose time practicing with you, especially since the final battle is only weeks away."

Sighing, Darkrip nodded. "Fine. Jack, you trust Brecken with Callie's safety?"

"I do," Jack said with a nod.

"All right. I'm open to agreeing to it once we question Brecken and confirm he had nothing to do with Zadicus's deception. I could always read his thoughts if I have concerns."

Callie's eyes widened, and she straightened in her chair. No way in hell did she want her father reading Brecken's thoughts. He'd discover she'd slept with him, and that would open a can of worms she wasn't ready to discuss with anyone.

"You made an oath not to read people's thoughts, Dad. It's a violation of his privacy."

Darkrip scowled. "I want to be sure his intentions are true."

"I think he'll alleviate any concerns during his questioning," Jack said. "We spoke this morning, and he informed me he intends to rejoin the army now that he's no longer employed as a bodyguard. He's a good man, Uncle Darkrip, and wants to protect our people."

"Fine," Darkrip said, running a hand over his face. "I won't read his thoughts unless I sense something dire. I look forward to the debriefing."

"Then it's settled," Callie said, thankful for one small crisis averted. "Uncle Heden, you'll prepare supplies for us for the mission?"

"Got you covered," Heden said. "You'll need fake IDs to rent a car, credit cards for lodging and supplies, an untraceable prepaid phone that works on their grid and everything else a trip to the human world requires. I'm going to overnight everything to a parcel delivery locker in Phoenix for you. Once you retrieve the package, you can rent a car and drive to the site. It's about a hundred miles east of Phoenix."

"Perfect. Thank you."

"Sure thing. You both stay safe, okay? I don't think Tatiana has any ill intentions, but keep your guard up."

They discussed for a while longer before Miranda ended the meeting. Afterward, Callie beelined toward the hallway, smiling at Brecken who stood as she approached.

"Hi," she said, feeling awkward since she wanted to hug him but also not wanting to incite any curiosity from her family. "So, a lot of stuff just happened in the meeting. They're going to question you in a few minutes. Heads-up: They want you to accompany me on a mission to the human world."

Surprise laced his expression. "What?"

"They'll explain it to you in the meeting. I'll be there too and will interject if needed. Whatever you do, look 'trustworthy,' okay?" She made quotation marks with her fingers. "The last thing I need is Dad reading your thoughts and knowing we boned our brains out last night."

Arderin chose that moment to appear at her side. "How are you doing today, baby? Can your ol' mom give you a hug?"

"Hey, Mom," she said, embracing her as she shot Brecken a gaze over her shoulder, silently telling him to remain cool. He just smirked at her, and she tamped down a laugh. Of course he would remain stoic and calm. It was Brecken after all. If anyone needed to remember to be chill in their twosome, it was Callie. Drawing back, she smiled at her mother.

"I'm doing okay. Thanks for checking on me."

"Of course, sweetie." Facing Brecken, she extended her hand. "I'm Arderin, and you must be Brecken. So nice to meet you."

Callie smiled at the sight of her mother shaking hands with the man who'd written her such beautiful letters. One day, she would tell Arderin about his sweet words, knowing she would adore them as much as Callie did.

"Nice to meet you, uh…"

"You don't have to address me formally," Arderin said, shaking her head. "Just Arderin is fine."

"I'm honored to meet you, Arderin," he said with a reverent tilt of his head. "I haven't met many royals in my life."

"Well, get ready, because you're about to meet them all." She gave a cheeky grin. "Oh, and don't mind my husband. He's a surly grump and will most likely interrogate the hell out of you."

"I'm ready, ma'am. Bring it on."

"Oh, I like him," Arderin said, smiling at Callie. "He'll be a good companion on your trip, sweetie."

"I think you're right," Callie said, giving him a tender smile. "Can't wait."

"Okay, let's get this show on the road. Come on. You can sit beside me, Brecken," Arderin said, gesturing with her hand. "I'll try to save you from my husband."

Brecken fell into step beside her, and Callie followed them to the conference room, grinning from ear to ear at the natural comradery between her mother and her secret lover.

The meeting with Brecken went well, and the council members all recognized fairly quickly that he hadn't known about Zadicus's deception.

"I made an error in judgement, agreeing to Zadicus's request to have a few hours alone each week," Brecken admitted, lacing his fingers atop the table as he sat beside Arderin. "He bribed me by agreeing to pay my sister's tuition to Takelia's school for the gifted and talented. There was no way we could afford to send her without his help, but I should've declined."

"I think we can all understand that motivation," Arderin said, placing a supportive hand over his arm. "We're a close family and would move mountains to help those we love. Right, guys?"

"It should've occurred to you he was doing something nefarious if he sought to be free from your watch," Darkrip muttered, arms crossed as he assessed Brecken. "The lack of perception is completely unacceptable for a trained private security agent."

"That's a bit harsh, dear," Arderin said.

"He's right," Brecken said, shrugging. "It was a severe lapse in judgement and all I can do is learn from it. Unfortunately, I can't change the past. It led to him deceiving Callie, and I'm extremely remorseful and frustrated at that."

Darkrip studied him through slitted lids. Eventually, he sighed and ran a hand through his dark hair. "Fine. I don't sense any deception in your demeanor. It was an honest mistake, but we can't afford mistakes from this point forward. Especially if you're going to accompany my daughter to the human world."

"I will protect her with my life," Brecken said, straightening and lifting his chin. "You have my word."

The council members exchanged glances before Miranda cleared her throat at the head of the table. "Okay, I think we've gotten what we needed. Let's take a vote on moving forward with Callie approaching Tatiana in the human world and Brecken accompanying her."

After a unanimous vote, Miranda addressed Brecken. "I understand you wish to reapply for the army now that you no longer have a bodyguard post."

"Yes, ma'am."

"Good. We'll go ahead and recommission you so you will be paid for protecting Callie."

Lifting his hands, he shook his head. "I'm happy to accompany Callie without pay. It's the least I can do to atone for not discovering Zadicus's deception."

"It's a noble offer, but I insist," Miranda said. "We pay our soldiers around here. You all are appreciated and deserve every penny."

Brecken swallowed, causing Callie to wonder if he felt uncomfortable accepting pay since they were now sexually involved. Deciding she'd question him about it on their trip, she spoke up. "Please accept the commission, Brecken. I'm a *lot* to deal with. Jack says I'm exceptionally dramatic." She swiped her hair over her shoulder, causing several of the council members to chuckle.

"Okay," he said, giving her a smile that sent tingles to every cell in her skin. Did anyone else notice how sexy he was? Feeling flushed, she squelched the urge to fan herself. "Thank you, Queen Miranda. I look forward to protecting Callie and to a successful mission."

Murmurs of agreement and encouragement filtered through the room, and Callie prepared herself for task ahead. She had no idea why Tatiana was summoning her, but she was determined to find out and help her people.

Chapter 16

Tordor, son of King Sathan and Queen Miranda, wiped his hands together, displacing the dirt from the wooden stake he'd just shoved into the ground. Turning toward the woman who stood with arms crossed over her chest in an angry stance, he said, "I think you're all set, Luna."

"*Pfft*," she hissed, glaring at the man who stood on the other side of the fence. "I'm sure his vicious little spawns can still find a way to cross onto my property if they try."

"I'm sorry the kids came onto your property and that Scooter dug the hole in your yard," the man said, glancing down at the dog panting beside him. "I'll do a better job of keeping an eye on them."

"You do that," Luna said with a tilt of her head, "or next time, I'm filing trespassing charges."

"I think Kildor has learned his lesson, right?" Tordor asked the Deamon who'd recently purchased the property next to the aristocratic woman.

"I definitely have. I'm very sorry, Luna."

"The fact that your parents are now letting Deamons move to Astaria is appalling enough, but I won't let them on my property."

Tordor assessed her, feeling she was mere seconds away from spitting on Kildor's shoes. "There are many Deamons who were unwilling participants in Crimeous's plans, Luna. Those that renounced him and embraced the kingdom are free to live on any of the compounds. It's important to my parents—and to me—that we are united as one kingdom of immortals."

"A kingdom of criminals—"

"The goddess teaches repentance and forgiveness," Tordor interrupted, cupping her shoulder. "It's time you get on board. I wouldn't want to have to tell my parents you're unsupportive of their policies."

"Of course, I respect our king and queen," she said, appearing slightly chagrined. "As a Vampyre, I was supportive of aligning with the Slayers. I guess I have a harder time with the Deamons. I've never understood their purpose on Etherya's Earth."

"Crimeous created us to be an army for his vengeance against Etherya, but all I've ever wanted is to live in peace, Luna. My wife was tortured by him for centuries, and I was forced to fight in an army I never supported. Now, we just want to live a quiet life with our children...and Scooter," Kildor said, leaning down to pet the pooch on the head.

"Fine, but don't come on my property again. Prince Tordor, thank you for replacing the fence post. I wasn't strong enough to do it myself after the little critter dug around it."

"You're welcome, Luna. Anytime."

With a dismissive nod, she turned to walk back to her home, situated in the distance across the sprawling yard.

"Whew, that was close. I thought she was going to report me to your father." Kildor swiped his arm across his forehead, wiping away the sweat. "Thank you for intervening."

"Of course," Tordor said. "I know she says she wants to be left alone, but my dad has known Luna for centuries. He has it on good authority she loves the fancy teas the vendors sell in Astaria's main square. Maybe pick her up a box next time you're in town."

"I sure will. Thanks for the suggestion. You're quite exceptional at diplomacy, my prince." He gave a bow. "I wish I could find a way to properly thank you."

"Just keep Scooter off her lawn," Tordor said, craning his neck to look at the pup. He whimpered as if he knew he was in hot water. "He's a cute little thing, but I don't think Luna's a fan."

Laughing, Kildor shook his head. "Got that message loud and clear. Thank you. See you around Astaria."

"See you." With a salute, Tordor headed back to his four-wheeler and revved the engine, setting off toward his home. Uteria's castle had been his home for his twenty-six years on the planet, along with the castle at Astaria. His parents had split time between the two compounds as they worked to reunite the Slayer and Vampyre kingdoms. They both had their appeal, but he found the castle at Uteria more welcoming, whereas the castle at Astaria was more austere. Still, both housed some wonderful childhood memories, and he cherished them all.

When he finally pulled up to Uteria's wall and drove through, he noticed several of the council members exiting in their various vehicles. Thankful he'd missed yet another stuffy council meeting, he parked his four-wheeler behind the barracks and spoke to a few of the soldiers milling about before heading inside the castle. It seemed quiet, and he searched for signs of life, finally finding his mother in the sitting room, examining what looked to be knitting loops and yarn.

"Uh, Mom?" he asked, assessing her as she sat on the couch. "Are you...knitting?"

Miranda expelled a breath through her lips as they flapped together, making an exasperated sound. "Lila gave me this starter kit before she left. She says kitting is relaxing and reduces stress." Lifting the sticks, she shrugged. "All I see when I look at these things are weapons. Like, really cool knitting nunchucks." Rising, she swiped them through the air. "See? I feel like fighting with these bad boys would be much more relaxing than knitting."

Chuckling, Tordor held up his hands. "Don't shoot...or, uh, stab, I guess? I *do* need both my eyes if I'm going to inherit the kingdom one day."

Laughing, she tossed the loops toward the couch and approached him with open arms. "Come here, sweetie. I missed you at the meeting." They embraced, Tordor rubbing his chin on her silky black hair.

"I'm sure you and Dad had everything covered. You always do."

Drawing back, she cupped his cheeks. "Do you have a few minutes to sit and chat with your mom? I'd love to hear how it went with Luna. Man, she's a See You Next Tuesday if I ever met one."

Unable to control his laugh, Tordor nodded as they sat on the couch. "She's not so bad. All bluster and no bite if you ask me. But no one said uniting the species would be easy. You and Dad knew that from the beginning. There's still a lot of distrust and misconception out there, and these things take time."

Smiling, Miranda squeezed his hand. "My son, the peacemaker. You possess a diplomatic quality I've rarely seen in others. You're like the hate whisperer or something."

"Well, I'm the child of two people hell-bent on peace. It was probably embedded in my DNA from the start."

She studied him, smiling as love shone in her eyes. "Our baby who isn't a baby anymore. Man, I still remember when you were born. Your dad doted over you like nothing I'd ever seen. Our perfect little heir."

"I'm pretty sure I'm far from perfect, but okay," he said, leaning back and resting his arm over the back of the couch.

Sighing, she settled into the couch before speaking. "Your father wishes you would attend the council meetings—"

"Are we really going to have this discussion again, Mom?"

"Don't interrupt me, young man," she said, holding up a finger. "I don't care how old you are, I'm still your mother."

"Yes, ma'am," he said, feeling his lips form a pout.

"The frown is cute though. You look just like your father."

Grinning, he squeezed her hand. "Go on. Tell me what a disappointment I am. I'm ready for the lecture."

"You're not a disappointment," she said, scooting closer and palming his cheek. "I hate it when you say that."

"I'm the heir to a kingdom with two immortal rulers who were born for the roles. It's a job I don't want, nor one I deserve. I love having you two rule while I implement diplomacy for our people. It's what makes me happy."

"I was so proud when you set up the Office of Official Complaints for the realm. Not only did it save me a ton of paperwork, but it freed up so much time for me and your father when you began addressing the complaints."

"I enjoy it, Mom. As I've told you a thousand times, I don't enjoy the council meetings or strategizing for war. It's not my strength. My strength is figuring out how to bring people together on a personal basis. I think there's nobility in that, even if I'm not fulfilling the role I was born for."

"Look," she said, swiping her fingers through her hair, "I can give you a million speeches about how your grandfather lectured me on my duties as heir. They were all antiquated and went against everything I wanted for my life. All I ever wanted to was to instill peace for our people and maybe to kick a little ass along the way." She winked. "So if you've found something that makes you happy, I'm all for it. Your dad's a bit less progressive, so we'll have to push him along."

"I know how much he wanted a male heir, and I want to make him proud. I just need to do it in my own way."

"I know, sweetie. It does break my heart a tiny bit that you don't want to attend the council meetings,"—she held her thumb and index finger an inch apart—"but I'm not going to force you. I always promised I wouldn't make my father's mistakes when I had kids. Hopefully, I'm fulfilling that oath with you."

"Have you and Dad talked about having another baby? I know you've discussed it over the years, but it's never been the right time. It would give you someone else to fixate over." He gave a cheeky grin, indicating his teasing.

"I would like to have a little girl one day," she said wistfully, glancing toward the ceiling. "But then I remember being pregnant with you and how I literally emptied my guts into the toilet every day, and I always decide to push it off."

He took her hand, lacing their fingers. "I'm sorry your pregnancy with me was so rough, and I know the birth wasn't a bed of roses either. You're amazing, Mom. It's one of the reasons I don't want to let you down."

"You've never let me down and never will." Clutching his hand, she arched a brow. "And you can blame your blood-sucking father for the tough pregnancy. It's all his fault."

Tordor breathed a laugh. "Well, I can't really disparage his Vampyre lineage since it's half of my DNA too."

"I guess not." Sighing, she shook her head. "I don't know. I do want to have another baby one day. Maybe once we beat Bakari and the kingdom is at peace, I'll pop out another one."

"Well, you know I'd love to have a baby sister or brother, and I'd help in any way I can."

Eyes sparkling, she leaned closer. "Or you could have a baby of your own. You're certainly old enough to find a nice young lady to settle down with."

Sighing, he shook his head. "I'm not ready. It took you a thousand years to find Dad. Give me some time."

Deep green eyes darted between his. "I know it's hard to find someone who gets you when you're the heir, but you'll never meet anyone if you don't put yourself out there. I don't think it would kill you to go on a date here and there. I'm sure there are so many women who would love to spend time with you."

Tordor struggled with his response, not understanding how to explain his feelings to her. For whatever reason, he didn't feel a pressing need to date or to settle down. Although he loved helping the people of the kingdom and was very sociable, he also had a hard time connecting with people on an intimate level. The idea of baring himself to someone—of literally stripping bare and allowing them to see into his soul—was foreign to him. Instead, he actually preferred flying solo. It gave him independence and the freedom to chart his own path.

Tordor could only see himself experiencing sexual attraction for a woman after making a strong emotional connection with her. He had no interest in casual dating or hooking up. Many aristocratic women of the realm would love to snag the kingdom's prince, and he had no interest in being anyone's prize. No, he'd rather wait until it felt right—until he met someone he clicked with. For some reason, he felt as if he would just *know* when that person came along.

And it was why he was still, in his mid-twenties, a virgin.

Whereas other men might have felt shame or embarrassment at that fact, Tordor didn't at all. He was a confident man and intrinsically knew he wanted to share his first time with someone he cared deeply for. Hopefully, with someone he *loved*. There was no shame in that aspiration, and he refused to settle for less than what he truly wanted.

Of course, explaining this to his mom was difficult and slightly awkward, so he fidgeted on the couch, attempting to come up with some way to discuss it with her.

"It's okay," she said, her features filled with compassion. "You don't have to explain. Sorry for being a nosy mom. I just want you to be happy."

"I'm perfectly happy with my life, Mom. I promise."

"Then we'll leave it at that. If you ever want to talk to me, I'm always here."

"I don't want to take time away from your knitting," he teased, gazing at the discarded knitting kit.

"Um, yeah, don't tell Lila, but there's no way I'm taking up knitting. I'd rather spar with the troops. I appreciate her efforts, but we'll just put this one down as a loss."

Standing, he tugged her to her feet and encircled her in his arms. He towered over her, but her embrace was as comforting to him as it had been when he was small. "I love you, Mom."

"I love you so much, sweetheart. Keep up the good work. You're sowing peace in our little kingdom one conflict at a time."

"Happy to do it." Drawing back, he smoothed her hair. "I'm going to grab a workout before I head to Takelia later today. One of the street vendors filed a complaint against another who sells a similar product. I'm going to try and get them to work together. I think if they join forces, they could actually sell more than they sell individually. We'll see if it works."

"If anyone can make it happen, you can. Have a good day, sweetie."

Placing a kiss on her silken head, Tordor exited the room to change into his workout clothes. Reminiscing on the conversation, he was glad his mom understood him well enough to let him chart his own course. For now, he was happy, although he would like to experience love one day. Would it take centuries, as it had for his parents? Or would he meet someone in the near future while he was still relatively young in the scheme of immortals? Tordor wasn't sure, but he was excited to find out whenever his life turned in that direction. For now, he was content implementing diplomacy in the realm his parents ruled, and for their people, whom he cherished deep in his heart.

∞

After the meeting, Callie was whisked away by her parents and returned to Takelia. It made sense to Brecken they would want to comfort her after yesterday's events, but he still felt the loss of her presence. After one night with her, he wanted more...everything she could give him, so he could see her cheeky grin and chide him with her playful teasing. The good news was that he would get to spend a lot of time with her on their mission. It was as if the goddess had answered his request to be near her, and he would take full advantage. Striding down the front stairs of Uteria's castle, he headed toward the train station so he could head back to Lynia.

"Hey, man," Jack called, pulling up in a four-wheeler. "You survived the meeting."

"Yeah," Brecken said, sliding his hands in his pockets. "Thank the goddess. Ambassador Darkrip is tough."

"That he is. I'm heading to a training at Lynia. Want a ride?"

"You don't mind?"

"Nope. Come to think of it, you should attend if you can. I know your mission with Callie starts tomorrow morning, but you're officially a soldier again, and I'm sure everyone would love to see you. Might as well get back on the horse."

Brecken pondered, admitting it was a good idea. Packing wouldn't take much time, since he could only carry a small bag through the ether, and he might as well use his spare time to entrench himself back in the battalion.

"Let's do it," he said, climbing in the passenger seat. "I just need to stop at home and change into my training gear. I want to look presentable for the council."

"No prob, man."

They set off through the open fields, chatting about the events of the past few days, their families and other topics. After changing in his cabin, Brecken climbed back into the vehicle, and Jack drove them to the sparring field.

Pulling up to the open meadow, Brecken realized how much he'd missed being a soldier. The smell of the dirt and grass that composed the training field called to him, and his fellow soldiers greeted him with firm handshakes and pats on the back.

"Well, well, look what the cat dragged in," a gruff female voice chimed. "The fancy bodyguard has decided to grace us with his presence yet again."

"Hey, Siora," he said, grinning at his lifelong friend. She'd grown up on a farm not too far from his home, and they'd attended school together. He'd always appreciated her frank nature and forthright attitude. In a nutshell, she was badass, and he felt she embodied the characteristics Miranda and Evie were intent on implementing in the kingdom.

"You're finally a soldier," he said, giving her a salute. "I'm proud of you. Have you kicked everyone's ass yet?"

Scoffing, she narrowed her eyes. "I'm close. Radomir and Cian are ranked higher in our training class, but I'm a close third. By the time the final battle with Bakari arrives, I'm determined to become co-leader of one of the battalions. And soon thereafter, I'll become the first female battalion leader in the immortal army. Mark my words."

"I have no doubt. If anyone can do it, you can."

Tilting her head, she studied him. "So, you're accompanying the fancy princess with the cryptic prophecy hanging over her head to the human world. Interesting."

"Wow," he muttered, rubbing his neck. "Word travels fast around here."

"She's beautiful like her mother. Careful you don't decide to do more than protect her, if you catch my drift. It's not a good idea to get googly eyes for someone who couldn't fathom falling for peasants like us."

"And how would you know?" he asked, arching a brow. "How many aristocrats have you fallen for?"

Emitting a *"pfft,"* she waved her hand. "As if. The only aristocrats I know are Jack, Commander Latimus and General Garridan. Jack and the commander are okay, but Garridan is another story."

"Do tell," he said, sensing there was more to the story considering her cheeks flushed ever so slightly at the mention of General Garridan.

"He's a misogynist pig," she said. "Doesn't think women should be in the army no matter what he says out loud. Thinks we all should be prissy and do as we're told." She bowed in a dramatic curtsy before batting her eyelashes. "Oh, my," she said, placing the back of her hand on her forehead, "I feel so faint. I hope a big, strong man will come along and save me."

Snickering, Brecken assessed her. Not only did she possess a wicked dry sense of humor, but she was a natural soldier. No one would ever describe her as demure or prissy. No—Siora was a warrior and an asset to the army. She had a muscular build and was physically stronger than half their male soldiers, although she would probably spit at that statement and pronounce she was stronger than *all* of them.

"I think asking you to do anyone's bidding is a ship that sailed long ago. You're a powerhouse, Siora. Whoever bonds with you is going to be a very lucky man."

"I have no desire to bond with anyone," she said, sparing him a droll glare. "Flying solo is where it's at. And you don't have to placate me. I know I'm not pretty like the fancy princess and all the other aristocratic women. Garridan's all but betrothed to Celine. Hope he has enough patience to find her lady parts under the formal gowns she still insists on wearing. Waste of good fabric if you ask me."

Brecken studied her short hair, sky blue eyes and tan skin, darker than most Vampyres since she'd been training outside. She was quite stunning, with long, thick eyelashes that surrounded her almond-shaped eyes and full red lips. Aristocrats might prefer smaller, willowy woman—hell, who was he to know?—but the right man would find Siora's tall, voluptuous build sexy. He hoped she would find a mate one day who could navigate through her tough exterior because she was extremely deserving of love.

"Why are you smiling at me weird?" she muttered.

"No reason. I just think you're pretty amazing, and I know there's someone out there who'll think you're as beautiful as I do."

A dash of red scarred her cheeks before her eyes narrowed. "Okay, this conversation took a turn. I'll say 'thank you' because my father taught me to accept compliments when given. And then I'll get back to training, because all I've ever wanted to be is a soldier and don't give a damn about anyone's opinion of my appearance."

Brecken smiled, understanding she was mostly bark with little bite.

"Don't get yourself killed in the human world, okay? I kind of like you. Now, leave me alone so I can get back to work." With a wink, she trailed over to join the troops at the obstacle course.

Jack appeared at his side, giving him orders to join the troops, and just like that, Brecken was one of the crew again. He threw himself into the training, excelling at the obstacle course before sparring with several of the soldiers. It felt amazing to work his muscles, and he knew he'd sleep like the dead when he finally made it home.

Sure enough, he wandered into his house long after the sun set, exhausted but elated from the day's events. After packing a small bag, he lifted his phone to text Callie.

Brecken: You didn't text me even though I gave you my number, so I hope you're not reconsidering your vow to sleep with me for eternity. I'm counting on limitless sex until my ultimate demise.

He smiled, hoping she would laugh at his teasing words.

Callie: OMG. I wanted to text you about a zillion times today but didn't want to be *that* girl.

Brecken: What girl?

Callie: You know, needy, you-took-my-virginity-so-now-I'm-obsessed-with-you girl. I'm sure you've met your fair share of those. Wait, don't tell me. Ew. I don't want to hear about you with any other girls. Okay, wait, now I'm being that girl again. Help.

Chuckling, he reveled in how damn funny she was.

Brecken: Don't worry. You're cool. I won't mistake you for someone needy. I mean, you chose an aristocratic douche over me while I wrote you sappy love letters. Maybe I'm the needy one.

Callie: No way. Let's just agree we're both awesome and not needy at all.

Brecken: Done.

Chewing his inner lip, he debated telling her how much he missed her. Were they there yet? Everything had happened so fast. Maybe she was at home mourning the loss of her relationship with Zadicus.

Callie: I miss you. I'm so excited to spend some time with you on our mission. Hope that's not too much. Just tell me if it's too much and I'll chill.

Thrilled at the words, his thumbs moved across the keypad.

Brecken: I miss you too, hon. I promise I'll keep you safe. Can't wait to see you.

Callie: Safe is good, but you're going to bone me too, right? I can't stop thinking about being with you again.

Although her sentiments thrilled him, he also didn't relish being a rebound. He wanted to make sure they didn't move too fast so she could adequately process what happened with Zadicus.

Brecken: We'll see. It's hard for me to keep my hands off you, especially now that I've touched you, but I don't want to be a consolation prize, Callie.

Callie: YOU'RE NOT! But I understand your concerns. Let's get to the human world and have a nice, long talk at the hotel. I think we need to do that to set some expectations. I'm determined to be honest and clear about what I want moving forward. No more mistakes. Deal?

Brecken: Deal. Sleep tight, hon. I'll see you at 9:00 a.m. at the ether.

Callie: See you then.

She sent him a kiss emoji, and he grinned before setting his phone on the nightstand. After prepping for bed, he slipped between the covers and placed his hands under his head. Staring at the ceiling, he let her scent wash over him, still fresh upon the sheets from their lovemaking. Closing his eyes, he gave over to exhaustion and joined her in his dreams.

Chapter 17

Brecken drove to the ether the next morning ready to tackle the mission head-on. He'd never been to the human world, and the excitement of the new experience thrummed in his veins, along with the anticipation of spending time with Callie. Last night's dreams of her had been vivid, and he'd woken up in a pool of sweat with a raging hard-on. Brecken couldn't remember ever being more viscerally attracted to a woman, and he couldn't wait to taste her again.

When he pulled up to the ether, he noticed Darkrip embrace Callie as he cut the engine. Squelching the lascivious thoughts, he grabbed his small backpack from the bed of the vehicle and slung it on. Although Callie's father had taken a vow not to read others' thoughts, Brecken didn't want them front of mind, just in case the Slayer-Deamon's resolve slipped.

"Hello, Ambassador Darkrip," he said, approaching. "It's nice to see you again."

He gave a curt nod, and Brecken was reminded of Arderin's assessment that he was a grump. "Callie has a phone that can communicate with me through the ether," Darkrip said, his tone crisp and businesslike. "If you need me, please don't hesitate to call."

"We will, sir. I promise to protect her with my life." He extended his hand, and Darkrip stared at it before he gave it a firm shake.

"Um, hi," Callie said, raising her hand. "I'm capable of strangling multiple attackers with my mind and all, but, hey, if you two want to commiserate about protecting me, go ahead and waste your breath."

"I just want you to be safe, sweetheart," Darkrip said, drawing her into a hug and kissing her temple. "Please stay in contact with us."

"I will, Dad, but Heden warned us there won't be cell service at Tatiana's location in the desert."

"Then call me as soon as you reach an area with service."

"I will." Facing Brecken, she smiled, jump-starting his pulse as her eyes sparkled in the morning sun. "Ready?"

"Ready."

Darkrip stood firm as they walked to the ether, and Brecken urged her to enter first. She stepped through the viscous, cloudy substance, and he followed close behind.

After wading through the dense barrier, they exited onto soft ground covered with dirt. Struggling to catch his breath, Brecken searched for Callie.

"Whew," she said from a few feet away, hands resting above her knees as she bent over. "I've waded through that stuff a hundred times, but I still feel like I'm going to pass out when I reach the other side. You okay? The first time is always a doozy."

"It's no picnic, but I'll survive." Approaching, he smoothed her hair away from her shoulder. "Are you okay?"

"Yeah." Straightening, she flashed him a dazzling smile that damn near buckled his knees. "Welcome to the human world. It's so exciting here—in my opinion at least. I can't wait for you to see it."

At the moment, all he cared to see was her gorgeous face as her palpable excitement at being in the human world surrounded them. Inching closer, he slid his palm over the back of her neck.

"Did you miss me?"

Chuckling, she nodded. "Yeah. Did you miss me?"

Sliding his arm around her waist, her drew her into his body. "I dreamed of you," he murmured, nudging her nose with his.

"Oh, how exciting. What were we doing—?"

Inhaling the words from her lips, he drew her into a sizzling kiss, unable to exist for one moment longer without tasting her. Her high-pitched mewl shot down his throat, causing his dick to jerk in his pants as he surged against her. Their tongues warred and mated, fighting in a battle where both ultimately won. Finally, he retreated, placing soft kisses on her swollen lips as her lids slowly lifted.

"Wow," she whispered, shaking her head. "You almost let me marry Zadicus when you kiss like that? I should be pissed."

"Don't remind me," he said, scowling.

She exhaled a soft breath. "Don't remind me either. I feel like such an idiot."

Smoothing his hand over her curls, he searched her ocean-colored eyes. "Are you okay, hon? You must be hurting from everything that's happened over the past few days."

Sighing, she lifted a shoulder. "I am. It's so hard for me to understand why one person would viciously deceive another. I know some in the kingdom think my dad and Evie are inherently evil, but they're just my family. I've never seen anything from them as remotely awful as what Zadicus did to me."

"He's a small-minded man who couldn't get out of his own way," Brecken soothed, stroking her hair. "He's not worth your tears."

Her features scrunched. "Tears? No fucking way. I want to interrogate him. Tie him to a chair and backhand his perfect aristocratic nose until he explains his motives and begs for my forgiveness."

Laughing, Brecken nodded. "It's a nice fantasy." His brows drew together before continuing. "Bakari will most likely kill him, Callie. Now that he's been banished from the realm, he'll be useless to him."

"I know." Swallowing thickly, her gaze fell to his chest. "That's why I'm not railing at the universe. Zadicus sealed his own fate, and I'm truly sad he chose the wrong path. Raoul and Viessa were always very nice to me. They were a bit cold and formal, as some aristocrats are, but they're good people. I hate what he did to all of us, but he'll get his comeuppance. Of course, I'm angry, but mostly, I'm just sad."

"That says a lot about you," he murmured, lowering his hand to squeeze hers. "Your compassion is one of the things I admire most about you."

"Thank you," she said, her soft smile inciting relief deep within. The last thing he wanted was to enter into a tense discussion, but he also wanted to check in and make sure she was okay. "I'm taking it day by day, and I think that's all I can do. It certainly helps that a sexy, kind soldier is helping me pick up the pieces. I didn't expect it, but I'm grateful."

Emotion overwhelmed him as he stared at her, longing to tell her *he* was the grateful one. For her forgiveness, her understanding, her affection and the amazing gift she'd given him when she'd opened herself during their lovemaking. Of course, that would make him sound like a bigger sap than he already was, so he gave his signature smirk before winking. "I'll try and stick around, since I've promised to protect you and all. You're okay."

Giggling, she swatted his chest. "Jerk."

Stealing a swift kiss, he straightened and searched the surroundings. "We're in the woods adjacent to the park with the ballfield as planned. According to the email your Uncle Heden sent us last night, the locker where he shipped our supplies is across the street."

Drawing back, she extended her hand. "Lead the way, soldier."

Lacing his fingers with hers, they trekked across the street and entered the facility with the lockers. After punching in the six-digit code Heden had sent them, Brecken swung open the locker door to find a cardboard box wrapped in cellophane.

"I'd bet anything this cellophane was specially fashioned by Heden and Sofia so the detectors couldn't pick up the weapons inside," Callie said, removing the box and closing the locker.

"Agreed. We should find a secure place to open it. I don't want to incite suspicion in any humans who might be nearby, and I'm sure this place has cameras."

"I saw a fast-food restaurant down the road. Let's go there. One of us can open it in a bathroom stall and hide the weapons so they're imperceptible."

They trailed to the restaurant and decided Brecken should assemble the contents in the men's bathroom. Once equipped, he returned to Callie, who was slurping a milkshake at one of the booths.

"How did you get a milkshake?" he asked, sliding into the seat across from her. "I have all the money."

"I kept a stash from my allowance when I was a kid. Brought ten whole dollars with me." Lifting some bills from her back pocket, she shrugged. "Well, eight dollars now." Taking another slurp of the milkshake, she grinned. "So worth it. This is awesome. I miss human comfort food. It's so good."

Glancing around, he took in the surroundings. "So, this is a human restaurant. It seems more...*plastic* than I imagined."

Chuckling, she circled her hand. "This is a fast-food restaurant, so it's not fancy. There are definitely other places that aren't as bright and sterile-looking."

His eyes darted over her face as the newness of his surroundings set in. "There's so much to see. It's daunting for a soldier's kid from Lynia who never expected to see anything beyond the borders of the compound. If we weren't on a mission, I'd ask you to show me your favorite places."

Her lips closed around the straw, sucking the milkshake as he imagined her performing the act on the now rapidly swelling flesh between his legs. Popping her lips from the straw, she said, "Maybe we can come back one day and I can show you around. I do have a canceled honeymoon trip I need to make up for."

Brecken gave her a soft smile, not wanting to ruin the moment by bringing up the obvious point that an excursion to the human world was a luxury he couldn't afford. Not only could he literally not afford it on his military salary, but soldiers didn't take time off from the army, apart from a predetermined day or two that was pre-negotiated with their commanding officer. It was a reminder they were worlds apart, and he could never give her the things Zadicus had promised her.

"Wow, did I lose you?" she asked, waving her hand. "Bueller?"

His eyebrows drew together. "What's Bueller?"

Breathing a laugh, she shook her head. "One of Uncle Heden's favorite movies. I'll show you sometime. Anyway, you zoned out for a moment there."

"I'm here," he said, tabling the morose thoughts. Reaching for the supplies, he slid an ID and a folded wad of cash toward her. "Here are your credentials."

Lifting the ID, she studied it. "Calinda Marie Jones. It was the surname we used all those years ago when we lived here. I always thought Mom and Dad could've come up with something a *bit* more creative, but whatever."

Brecken laughed as she picked up the prepaid phone Heden sent them. Once it was up and running, Callie used the credit card to purchase internet browsing and rented a car from the dealer a few blocks away. After finishing her milkshake, they walked to the rental car dealer and then drove to the hotel, where they rented two rooms side by side.

Entering the elevator, she grinned up at him when the doors closed. "So, I didn't want to make it weird, but I'm a bit put out you didn't want to share a room."

Sparing her a glance, he said, "I figured you'd like your own space. Didn't want to assume anything."

"Space is good, but don't be surprised if I come knocking on your door, soldier."

Arching a brow, he reveled in her sultry grin. "I won't mind at all." Lowering, he rested his lips on the shell of her ear. "I like what happens when you knock on my door unannounced."

She bit her lip, giving him an adorable smile as the elevator dinged. Exiting on the third floor, they located their rooms, and Callie called his name before heading inside.

"Yeah?" Brecken asked softly.

"I'm going to need to eat eventually. It's warm here, and I saw an Italian place a few blocks away. Want me to pick up pizza and we can eat by the pool?"

"That sounds nice."

"I'll pick up wine too," she said, giving a cheeky grin. "In the hopes of getting you tipsy and possibly taking advantage of you."

A laugh escaped his lips. "Okay, but not too much. We need to leave around sunrise in the morning. We'll stop at a store along the way to buy a tent and some supplies before heading to the desert. Your Uncle Heden thinks Tatiana might be residing in the ruins, so we might need to camp there several days. He also indicated she does things on her own timeline and in her own way, and it's impractical for us to drive back to Phoenix every night."

"Ten-four," she said, giving a salute. "I'll be ready to rough it."

Chuckling, he inserted the plastic key in the door. "Call me when you're ready to go get the food so I can walk with you."

After entering the room, Brecken tossed his bag on the table and fell onto the bed, rubbing his face as he imagined Callie in a bikini by the pool. Judging by the size of her bag, it would be small, most likely only covering small swaths of her smooth skin. Eagerness for the night ahead curled in his gut, and he grinned like a lovesick teenager, anticipating their evening together.

Chapter 18

Callie spent the day catching up on all things human, realizing how much she'd missed the world she grew up in all those years ago. She also watched four *Saved by the Bell* reruns before the sun began to set, indicating it was time to order dinner. She'd loved the show as a kid, although Zack Morris was a bit more of a dick than she remembered. Still, it brought back memories, and she enjoyed the nostalgia.

After placing the dinner order, she searched through her bag to find something to wear to the pool. Figuring she might like to swim after they ate, she threw on her bikini under some cutoff shorts and a loose tank top. Tugging on her sandals, she headed to Brecken's room.

He opened the door after her swift knock, and she almost balked at how viscerally sexy her handsome soldier was. How in the hell had she ever even looked at Zadicus when Brecken was nearby? She'd always thought Zadicus quite handsome in a coiffed sort of way, but Brecken's raw sexuality was engrossing. In reality, she'd seen what she wanted to see. A man who was bestowing the love she craved, even if he was wrong for her. Determined to be wiser in the future, she straightened her shoulders.

"Ready?"

"Ready," Brecken said, stepping out and closing the door behind him. He was wearing shorts, a black T-shirt and athletic slip-ons perfectly situated for their pool excursion. Callie's eyes drifted over his biceps, muscled and tanned under his shirt sleeves, and her mouth turned dry as sandpaper. Arousal slammed through her as she tamped down the urge to climb him like a tree. A very tall, hard, sexy-as-hell tree.

"Callie?"

"Oh, sorry," she said, turning to follow him to the elevator. "Got lost in a daydream." *A super-hot, erotic daydream.*

Resisting the urge to fan herself, she entered the elevator and took her place at his side. His scent washed over her—picked up by her Vampyre senses—and she closed her eyes, inhaling the musky sandalwood aroma. She'd woken up covered in his scent after they made love and longed to have it envelop every inch of her body again.

The elevator chimed, indicating they'd reached the lobby, and Callie's eyes flew open. Exiting, they traveled through the whooshing automatic doors of the hotel and started down the sidewalk toward the Italian restaurant, making sure to pick up a bottle of wine along the way.

They chatted about the new female recruits and the pet guinea pig Callie had healed for a little boy at Naria a few days ago. The conversation flowed, and she was enamored by how comfortable she felt with him. She never felt the need to be anyone other than herself with Brecken, even when they'd had playful conversations when he was guarding Zadicus. It was refreshing to be in the presence of someone with whom she didn't have to hold pretenses, and she realized how precious it was. Zadicus had always been quite formal, and it had sometimes rankled her.

After picking up the pizza, they headed to the pool located behind the hotel. Sitting in two long plastic chairs, they munched on the food as they stared up at the star-filled sky.

"It looks the same as it does in the immortal world," Callie said, head resting on the tall chair as she ate the remaining crust. "That's one of the things I always liked about the nighttime sky."

"Although they're two different worlds, everyone sees the same sky when they look up," he remarked in his smooth baritone.

"Mm-hmm," she said, swallowing the last of her pizza before wiping off the crumbs. "It was comforting for someone like me who had trouble fitting in sometimes."

Brecken finished his slice and wiped his hands on a napkin before setting it aside. Tilting his head against the chair, he looked at her with compassion in his eyes. "I'd love to hear your stories, if you want to tell me."

It was such a sweet offer, said in his soothing voice, and Callie couldn't resist. Relaxing in her chair, she opened up to him, telling him about her awkward experiences and all the things she'd written in her diary. He listened intently, asking intermittent questions throughout, sometimes stroking her arm when she recalled a particularly painful moment.

"I'm sorry you felt lost, Callie-lily," he said, the nickname causing her to shiver. "You returned to a world you didn't know with a prophecy over your head, and you still managed to become a kind, caring person. Many people wouldn't be so strong. It's really admirable."

"Well, it also led me to latching onto the first guy who showed any interest in me, and look where that led me." She rolled her eyes. "So I didn't handle it *that* well."

"You did the best you could. We all want to be loved, Callie. That's just natural."

Blood thrummed through her veins as she assessed him. "Do you want to be loved?"

"Of course," he said, eyebrows drawing together. "And I want to make my father proud. My mom and sisters are my responsibility now, and I do my best to ensure their happiness."

"That's so sweet," she said, squeezing his hand as she held it between the chairs. "Rowena is awesome. I'd love to meet your mom and your other sisters."

"They're a handful," he said, giving her a sardonic glare. "Careful what you ask for."

Laughing, she swung his hand, thoroughly enjoying the conversation. "Well, I'm a handful, so we'll definitely get along."

"I love that about you," he said, waggling his brows. "Your personality is so vivacious, hon. It moves something in me since I'm a bit reserved."

"You?" she asked, feigning surprise. "I hadn't noticed."

"Imp," he muttered, lifting her hand and nipping her fingers. "You deserve someone who can give you everything you want. I hate that the prophecy made you feel like you weren't worthy of love or affection. That's not even close to true. You're amazing, Callie."

"You're pretty amazing too, you know?"

Exhaling a soft breath, he shrugged. "The thing is, I'm not, hon. I'm not rich or aristocratic or any of the things you deserve. I'm just a poor guy from Lynia who wants to protect our people."

"Brecken," she said, leaning closer to accentuate her point. "Protecting our people is extremely admirable. And there are so many qualities you're not giving yourself credit for. Look at the beautiful letters you wrote me. They're Shakespeare-level good."

"Uh, yeah, I briefly remember learning about him in school, although we didn't focus on him since he was human. I remember him being wordy." He gazed at the sky and rubbed his chin.

"Well, you're rather wordy in your letters,"—she lifted a finger when he shot her a glare—"but I really like it."

"If you say so," he muttered. "I'm terrified you're going to tell my army buddies I wrote them. I'll never live it down."

"I'll keep them secret if you like." She swung their hands between the chairs. "Something just for us."

Emotion laced his bronze orbs. "I like the sound of that."

"When I think of the letters, and the way you are with Rowena, and the steps you take to ensure your family is secure...Brecken, those are wonderful qualities that are so much more important than money."

His thumb traced the skin of her hand as he pondered. "You should be with someone who can take you places, Callie. Who can show you the world and take the time to enjoy it with you."

"And why can't you do those things?"

He scoffed. "Because I have to work, hon. Soldiers don't just traipse off to the human world and take vacations. That's a luxury we don't have. And my cabin is the only home I'll ever be able to afford. That, along with helping my family, takes up most of my salary, especially now that I'm not in private security."

"So, um, a few things," she said, releasing his hand and sitting up in her chair. Ticking her fingers, she said, "First, I'm a royal, which means I have money even though I didn't do anything to earn it."

"I wouldn't dream of touching your money, Callie—"

"Hey," she said, glowering. "I let you talk, and now it's my turn."

Grinning, he nodded. "Go on. Sorry."

Tilting her head, she continued. "I enjoy healing animals and am basically the kingdom's veterinarian. Self-proclaimed, of course." She rubbed her fingernails over her chest before blowing on them while Brecken chuckled. "I do it for free because I want to help our people and it's the right thing to do. I've always seen bonding with someone as a partnership. When I do marry one day, what's mine will be his, and vice versa."

"That was easy to say when you were bonding with Zadicus."

"It would be easy to say if I were bonding with *anyone*," she said, exasperated. "I don't care about material things. I never have. Now, do I want to travel the human world and see places I've never seen? Of course. But not all the time. I enjoy healing animals in the immortal world, and my family is there, which is very important to me. But I can certainly take a vacation here and there."

"That's great, but—"

"But nothing," she interjected, arching a brow. "I happen to know the commander of the immortal army." Lifting her hand to her mouth, she whispered, "He's my uncle."

Tossing back his head, Brecken gave a laugh as his Adam's apple shone in the moonlight. Drawn to him, she imagined leaning over and plunging her fangs into the vein that pulsed at his neck.

"I know he's your uncle," he finally said, mirth in his eyes. "But asking for special favors is not my style, hon."

"Oh, fine. I know for a fact Jack takes days off from training, and a few days off won't kill you. That's all I'm saying."

"You can be with anyone, Callie," he said, his expression reverent under the silver moonlight. "So much has happened over the past few days, and I want you to remember that."

Her teeth gnawed her lip as she pondered. "Maybe, but I also have peculiarities a partner would need to accept. First, there's the prophecy, which scares the crap out of most people."

"People are scared of things they don't understand. That has nothing to do with you."

Smiling, she let the sentiment sink in. "You're one of the few people who don't see it as weird. I don't know why, but it's pretty awesome." Sighing, she waved her hand. "Anyway, besides the prophecy, there's the fact that any kids I have will inevitably inherit some of my powers. I don't know which ones, and it's a lot to ask a partner to accept. Zadicus and I spoke about it, and he assured me it didn't matter, which I now know was just a line of crap to placate me and send me on my way."

"Asshole," Brecken muttered, swiping a hand over his face. "Anyone who truly loves you will embrace your children's powers, Callie."

"I hope so," she said wistfully.

"I mean, I'm no expert. There's nothing remarkable or special about my blood. I'm just a seamstress's kid from a rural compound who finished high school and joined the army the next day. It's why I bent over backward to send Rowena to her special school. I want more for her."

Emotion flooded her heart at the soulful words. His devotion to his family was so attractive to her, and she marveled at his dedication to their well-being. Clenching his hand, she felt the sting of tears as she gazed upon his handsome features.

"You're a good man," she whispered.

They gazed into each other for a long, solemn moment before Callie scrunched her nose. "Okay, soldier, I think we've completed the serious discussion portion of the evening. You're convinced you're unremarkable, and I'm a jilted bride with strange powers. Maybe we're, like, some weird superhero duo or something."

A hearty laugh bounded from his throat. "Maybe so."

"No matter what, you're smokin' hot, and I aim to take advantage of it." Scooching off the chair, she shrugged off her shorts and tank top, tossing them aside before extending her hand. "Since we seem to have this area to ourselves, I'd very much like to play with you in the pool."

His eyes raked over her frame clad in her skimpy white bikini, and Callie swore she saw a tenting in his shorts. "Define play," he said, his tone sexy and gravelly.

"I'd rather show you," was her sultry reply as she waggled her brows.

Chuckling, he grasped her hand and rose before tugging off his shirt and tossing it aside. "I play dirty sometimes, hon. Careful."

"Ohhhh..." Her eyes grew wide as anticipation hummed in her veins. "Should I be worried?"

Fast as lightning, his hand snaked around her wrist, drawing her into his body. Crouching down, he lifted her over his shoulder and carried her to the pool. Eliciting a squeal, she held on for dear life, hoping like hell he wouldn't drop her.

Brecken stopped at the edge of the deep end and swung her around, holding her above the pool as she giggled.

"You wouldn't," she said, noting the mischief in his eyes.

"You said you wanted to play, honey," he said, his tone both menacing and teasing as he held her above the pool.

"I take it back—"

Gasping, the words were cut off when he tossed her into the air. Closing her eyes, Callie inhaled a huge breath…before crashing into the warm water as Brecken's deep laugh echoed above her.

∞

Brecken observed Callie surface, gasping for air as her arms flailed.

"You son of a bitch!" Her tone was filled with laughter rather than anger, causing him to smile.

Wading in the deep water, she jerked her head. "Come on in. It feels great, actually."

Throwing caution to the wind, he sucked in a breath and cannonballed into the water. Bobbing above the surface, he swam toward her, scowling when she splashed him.

"Hey!"

"That's for throwing me in," she said, sliding her arms around his neck.

His arm snaked around her waist, and he guided them to the wall, swimming to a point where his feet touched the bottom. Callie wrapped around him, her legs slick in the wetness as his back rested against the wall.

"We probably shouldn't make out in the hotel pool," he said, gripping her butt to hold her in place. "I'm supposed to be protecting you. Hell, Bakari could be watching at this very moment."

"I can protect myself," she said, her tone regal and confident. "And besides, I think Bakari has a lot of other shit to deal with, including the fact he's training an army in the immortal world and dealing with my shithead ex-betrothed."

"True," he said, gently squeezing the globes of her ass as they settled in the water.

Ever so slowly, she trailed her hand over the curve of his neck, down the scratchy hairs of his chest and eventually, to the waistband of his shorts. "Ooohhh," she said, hooking a finger inside the elastic. "What do we have here?"

Brecken had been hard as a rock since she'd first bared all that smooth, luscious skin in the skimpy bikini. Now, with her hand inches from his cock, he thought he might combust into a pile of unsated lust at any second.

"Is it really a good idea to do this in a public hotel pool, Callie?"

Mischief flashed in her blue-green eyes as she slowly slid her hand under the fabric, gliding it to his massive erection. Her fingers encircled him, and he sucked in a sharp breath.

"Do what?" she asked seductively.

Unable to utter a response, Brecken heaved air into his lungs, praying to the goddess he wouldn't pass out and drown in the damn pool.

"Do you like it when I move my hand like this?" Gripping him in a firm vise, she began stroking him from base to tip, and he closed his eyes in ecstasy.

"Someone might see..." he gritted through clenched teeth.

"The hotel is a freaking ghost town, Brecken. I want to make you feel good."

Lifting his lids, he stared into her limitless eyes. They blazed with desire, her lips still swollen from their recent kiss. Lifting his hand, he smoothed his thumb over her lip. "You're so beautiful," he whispered, cupping her jaw.

She smiled, the gesture transforming her features into something so breathtaking Brecken knew he'd see the image in every future dream. Her hand worked along his cock, smooth and steady in the warm water, and he felt like a fool for already feeling his climax on the horizon.

"That feels so good, hon," he murmured, sliding his hand to clench the hair at her nape. "When you touch me, I want to fucking explode."

"Good," she replied, slowly licking her lips. "Don't forget, I'm the virgin here. Well, until recently."

"Now, you're a sex queen," he teased, nipping her lips.

"You're goddamned right I am." Gliding her other hand under his shorts, she cupped his balls, massaging them as she stroked his cock. He squeezed the flesh of her ass, holding her so she didn't fall.

"Do you like that?"

"Yes," he rasped. "I'm going to come in the fucking pool. Shit. I'm pretty sure that's going to get us an extra cleaning charge on the bill."

Throwing back her head, she laughed, the skin of her neck glistening in the moonlight. "I'll work it off," she said, reclaiming his gaze as she arched a brow. "I want you to come. I love touching you this way."

"Callie..." he groaned, gripping her ass and her hair, feeling his balls tighten as she maneuvered them in her hand.

"I can talk dirty too, you know?" Leaning forward, she touched her lips to his ear and spoke with a gravel-laden voice. "Come while I stroke your cock, soldier," she commanded, causing him to moan with pleasure. "And then take me inside and fuck me."

Giving into the pleasure, Brecken closed his eyes, pulling her close and burying his face in her neck. His hips pumped into her hand, mindless and jerking, as he scraped his fangs over her nape.

"*Oh, god,*" she moaned, pressing the flesh against his lips. "Bite me."

"Not yet, honey," he groaned, sucking the sweet skin of her neck between his lips. Drinking blood was considered sacred in Vampyre culture, and was usually only done between bonded mates. Brecken had never drunk from a woman during sex, and he felt it too intimate since their relationship was so new. Still, he longed to taste her that way, and now that the door had been opened, it would most likely become one more thing to dream about when he thought of Callie.

"One day," she whispered in his ear, her hands moving with ardent fervor. "One day, you'll taste me that way too."

"Oh, *fuck...*" he groaned, pressing his face into her neck before mumbling unintelligible words as his body shook with pleasure. Gasping her name, he embraced the orgasm, letting it claim his body as he clutched her.

"*Yesss,*" she hissed in his ear, sending him into overdrive as he jerked and sputtered in her hand. Jets of release shot from his cock as she continued to stroke him, driving him insane with lust.

"No more," he cried, lowering his hand to stop the maddening, pleasurable strokes. "Oh...*god...*"

His large frame shuddered and quaked in her arms as she lifted her hand to stroke his scalp, the points of her nails digging deep and adding to the bliss. Brecken encircled her with his arms, drawing her into every nook of his body as he emptied himself against her. Sighing as his muscles quivered, he nuzzled her nape with his nose.

"Damn, that was really hot," she said, chuckling. "You're so fucking sexy, Brecken."

"Right now, I think I'm just dead," he mumbled into her neck. "You decimated me."

Her fingers caressed his scalp as they lounged in the water, replete and sated. "I'm glad I made you feel good. I had weird hang-ups that I was going to be bad at sex."

Lifting his head, which felt like it weighed a hundred pounds, he stared into her eyes. "Why in the world would you think that?"

Shrugging, her gaze lowered to his chest. "I just told you what happened in middle and high school. I was a pariah who didn't get asked to one dance."

Placing his fingers under her chin, he tilted her face to reclaim her gaze. "If I could go back in time, I'd beat up all those middle school losers for you. And then I'd dance with you, even though I hate to dance."

Her brilliant smile buckled his knees. "My hero."

Running his hand over her wet curls, he longed to return the favor. "Let's go inside so I can taste you again."

"Ohhhhh, are we going to have a sleepover?"

"Fuck yes, we are."

Constricting his fingers on the swell of her ass, he straightened, reveling in her laugh as she wrapped her legs tighter around his waist. Wading through the pool, he lifted them both out, strong and secure, and walked them to the chairs.

After cleaning up the remnants of their dinner, they headed inside to his room, where Brecken took his time removing the scraps of her bikini before submerging himself in her gorgeous body.

Chapter 19

Callie slept more soundly than she had in ages. The hollow in Brecken's chest was perfectly tailored for her cheek, and his deep breaths soothed her as they lay entwined in the hotel bed. After making love, they'd showered and fallen asleep, exhausted by their travels and sexy trysts. When they awoke, he loved her once more, slow and thorough as he stared into her with those deep bronze eyes.

As he loomed above her, his strong hips undulating into hers, she felt a deep connection, as if their energies were entwined along with their bodies. Never had she felt so cherished as when he surged inside and whispered, "Take me deep, Callie-lily. Open for me, honey."

She pressed her legs against the bed, offering herself to him as they reached for ultimate pleasure. In those moments, her mind drifted to the future, and she began to allow herself to dream. What if he was her mate? The one she was meant to be with this whole time? Perhaps Zadicus was just a blip in the road that led her to her strong, thoughtful soldier.

After they recovered from their lovemaking, they prepared for the day and gathered their belongings before heading to the lobby and paying the bill. Once situated in the rental car, they drove to the recreational equipment store to purchase a tent, sleeping bags and the other essentials they would need to survive in the desert for several days.

After stocking up on nonperishable food and water at the grocery store, Brecken secured the stash in the trunk before closing it and wiping his hands.

"Well, I think we've got everything we need. Ready to head to the desert?"

"Ready," she said, sliding into the passenger seat as he sat behind the wheel. "I have a million questions buzzing in my brain."

They discussed her questions as they drove. What did Tatiana want to say to her? Was she ready to choose a side? Was she even in the desert, or was she screwing with them? She was known to be fickle and flighty at times, and Callie hoped she wasn't leading them on a wild-goose chase.

Two hours later, they drove past a sign labeled "Sierra Ancha Wilderness Area" and pulled into one of the open spaces in the sparsely populated parking lot. Glancing around, Callie noticed the rugged terrain swathed by cacti and brush. In the distance, she spotted red rocks and jagged mountains and thanked the goddess Brecken was with her. She was an adventurous person, but hanging out by herself in an arid desert didn't really hold much appeal.

"Well, we made it," he said, opening his door and heading to the trunk. "We'll take as much as we can carry in our packs with the assumption it might be several days until we get back to the car."

Nodding, Callie began packing her backpack, making sure to include a blanket, sleeping bag and as much of the packaged food as she could carry without collapsing. Being half-Vampyre made her strong, and being Crimeous's granddaughter gave her the ability to hover the pack above the ground, although that took energy. Wrinkling her nose, she decided she'd keep it as light as possible. Fainting in the desert wasn't really high on her agenda, thank you very much.

"Y'all heading out for a hike?" a genial deep voice asked behind them.

Whirling, Callie looked to see a gray-haired man approaching with a woman who looked to be similar in age beside him. Covering her heart with her hand, she nodded. "Yep. Sorry, you scared me."

"Sorry, ma'am," he said with a sheepish grin. "I'm Vernon, and this is my wife Katherine. We didn't mean to scare the bejesus out of you. We both retired last year and are traveling across the country in that RV over there." He pointed to a large vehicle, and his wife extended her hand.

"Katherine Grant," she said, shaking Callie's hand and then Brecken's. "Sorry we scared you. Vernon and I just spent two nights camping by the ruins. We figured we'd warn you about the drifters living out there."

"Drifters?" Callie asked.

"They seemed to be of Native American descent, but I can't be sure," Vernon replied. "We saw at least four of them and figure they're living in the ruins. Doesn't bother me since they're not bothering anyone, but they didn't seem too friendly. We tried to approach them and offer some food, and they declined. Probably just want to be left alone. Hell, I can understand that, I guess. Kat here hasn't left my side for a year, and I've forgotten what it's like to read the paper in silence." He slipped his arm across her shoulders, smiling as he teased her.

"Oh, he's just being mean," she said, swatting his chest, "and no one reads the paper anymore, dear." Facing Callie, she said, "He loves spending time with me and won't let me have a damn minute to myself. It's been that way ever since we got married over forty years ago. Perhaps you two can understand. You have the look of young lovers."

"Do we now?" Callie asked, smiling up at Brecken. "Did you hear that, darling?"

"Yes, dear, loud and clear," he teased, winking at Callie before facing Vernon and Kat. "I appreciate the warning. We'll stay alert. Are you going to stay another night here in the park?"

"We're on our way to Cabo San Lucas. Vernon promised me a week in paradise. We're getting on the road in a bit and will head to the next park along the way to camp for a few days. Eventually, we'll make it to the Baja Peninsula."

"How lovely," Callie said wistfully. "There's a species of jackrabbit found only on the island of Espiritu Santo near Cabo San Lucas. One of my bucket list goals is to see one of them someday."

"Well, we'll have to check out Espiritu Santo as well," Kat said, looking at Vernon. "Add it to the list, dear."

"Already added," he said, tapping his temple.

"We wish you luck on your camping excursion," Kat said with a nod. "The terrain isn't too rough, and you seem well-stocked. Good luck and stay well."

"Nice to meet you both," Callie called as she and Brecken waved goodbye. Strapping her pack on her back, she beamed up at Brecken. "Ready to eat my dust?"

Arching a brow, his expression turned droll. "Actually, I was already debating how much you'll slow me down."

With a *"pfft,"* Callie pivoted and began walking to the trail, leaving him behind to lock up the car.

"Head starts don't count!" he called behind her.

"See you at the ruins." She held up her hand and gave a wave.

He eventually caught up to her, and they hiked under the blazing sun, stopping several times along the way to drink water and Slayer blood.

"How much longer, do you think?" she asked, sitting on one of the large stones beside the trail.

"An hour at most until we get to the ruins. Interesting about the people living there. It's possible they're armed, so I want you to stay alert. I've got the gun strapped to my belt and a knife in my boot, just in case."

Nodding, Callie screwed the top back on her canister and fell into step beside him, reaching over to grab his hand before lacing their fingers. He grinned down at her, squeezing her hand as they plodded along the trail.

Rewarding him with a blazing smile, they trekked deep into the desert, clutching each other's hand every step of the way.

As the sun hung low in the afternoon sky, Brecken and Callie approached the rocky cliffs. They stood tall, surrounded by green and brown brush, creating a natural open cavern with a dry creek bed that ran down the middle. As they entered the cavern, hiking between two high cliff walls, Callie noticed the first opening in the red rock about fifty feet ahead.

"See that?" she asked softly, pointing. "It looks like a man-made doorway fashioned into the rock of the cliff. The edges are too precise to be natural."

"Yep," Brecken said, pulling up the images of the maps he'd stored on his phone. "This is where Heden said we'd find Tatiana."

They continued forward, rocks crunching beneath their sneakers on the dusty path, until they stopped before a stone that jutted in the middle of the trail. Crouching down, Callie ran her fingers over the drawings etched on the rock.

"The trail that leads to those ruins with the door has been recently used," Brecken said, eyes narrowed as he stared at them in the distance. "This is most likely where the drifters are staying."

Standing, Callie wiped her hands on the thighs of the thin cargo pants she'd packed for hiking in the desert. "I don't see anyone—"

A bristling sounded behind them, and they both whirled around, noticing the rock that fell from several feet above the grassy embankment. It clanked down the hill and landed with a soft thud on the dirt ground.

"Stay close," he said, encircling her wrist and drawing her behind his body. "Let's see if there are any other ruins built into the cliffs."

He led them forward, and they walked several yards, passing the man-made opening before easing around the side of the embankment to find an enclave of ancient ruins. Red and brown stones were stacked to form small shelters, each with openings set several feet apart. The dwellings were set into the cliffside, offering them natural protection and privacy.

"Whoa," Callie breathed, taking in the site as the gravity of the moment set in. An ancient culture of humans had lived here, each with their own family, history and story. Awed by the energy of the place, which seeped deep into her bones, she barely heard the soft giggle behind her.

Turning, her gaze fell on a little boy who crouched behind a nearby rock wall. It was part of the ruins, and several rocks at the top had seen better days, which allowed her to see the boy's full head of black hair.

"It seems like we have a hiking buddy, Brecken," she said, placing her finger over her lips as she stepped toward the rock.

His hand snaked out, grasping her arm to halt her. "It might not be safe," he murmured.

"It's fine," she said softly, her expression urging him to let her go. When he released her arm, she tentatively approached the rock. "I love meeting new hiking buddies, but I walk really fast. Do you think you can keep up with me?"

The boy's head raised above the rock, his gaze locking with hers. He whispered something, but it was carried away by the wind, and she stepped closer.

"I didn't catch that. I *think* you said you were too slow to keep up with my pace."

"I hike fast too," he said, slowly sliding out from behind the wall. His fingers twisted together as he studied her, looking both curious and anxious.

"Well, that's great to hear. We'll have to become friends then. My name is Callie. What's yours?"

Curious eyes observed her as he stood silent.

"No name?" she asked, grinning over her shoulder at Brecken. "Okay then, I'll just have to make one up for you."

He gnawed his lip, visibly debating if he should divulge the information. Finally, he tilted his head and whispered, "Ho'ok."

Callie's eyes narrowed. "That's your name?"

Lifting his hand, he pointed at her. "Ho'ok," he repeated.

Callie looked at Brecken, who had slowly inched up beside her. "I don't understand."

"It's the name of a powerful witch in his people's folklore," a woman's voice called behind them. "He senses your powers and thinks you're a witch."

Turning to face her, Callie said, "No more a witch than you are, Tatiana."

Tatiana smiled and gave a gentle nod. "Agreed. Come here, Adriel." Extending her hand, she gestured to the boy. "Come now, Callie is not a witch, although she is very powerful. She is my friend, and I would like you to meet her."

Adriel tentatively approached, taking Tatiana's hand before gazing up at Callie. "Hello," he said softly.

"Hello, Adriel. Nice to meet you. This is my friend, Brecken."

Brecken bent down, resting his hands above his knees so he was on eye level with the boy. "Hello, Adriel. That's a super-cool name."

"It means 'symbol of skill,'" he said, lifting his arms and flexing his biceps.

Brecken and Callie laughed as Tatiana ruffled his hair. "As you can see, he wants to be a warrior one day like you, son of Maddox and Wren. With his tenacious nature, I have no doubt he will succeed." Leaning down, she kissed his head. "Go on inside and find your mother. I smell dinner, and you must be hungry."

Giving a short wave, he ran off toward one of the structures built into the cliffs and bounded inside.

"I'm a bit overwhelmed to finally get to meet the mysterious Tatiana in person," Brecken said, placing his hands on his hips. "I'm not sure whether to be terrified or elated."

"Perhaps you should just be," Tatiana said with a shrug.

"She likes to speak in riddles," Callie muttered.

"I sense your disapproval, Calinda, and I am sorry you experienced hurt after I approached you by the river. I haven't felt emotion in so long I sometimes forget how crushing it can be."

The words spurred sadness in Callie's heart. "That sounds lonely. We all crave emotion and affection, don't we?"

Her full lips formed a smile, although it held no joy. "I had affection once, and the loss of it almost killed me. But that is a story for another time." Glancing around the ruins, her expression was thoughtful. "A family lives here, as the human couple already informed you in the parking lot. They are descended from the tribes of people who thrived here centuries ago."

"Do they need something from me?" Callie asked, lifting her hands. "Is that why you summoned me here?"

"Yes," she said, gesturing to the nearby rocks. "Please, these are flat enough for us to sit on while we speak. The sun will set soon, and you will need to set up camp. There is a clearing just over there that will allow the early morning sun to heat your tent before you rise. You will be safe here, I assure you."

They sat on the rocks assessing each other as Tatiana gathered her thoughts. "Long ago, I traveled through this area when the people who are now known as the Hohokam lived here. I made many friends, one of whom became like a sister to me."

Callie remained silent, interested in the story Tatiana would surely weave.

"Eventually, the woman became sick, and the time of her death drew near. The moment before she passed, she asked me to keep watch over her children. All of her children, for however many generations they would roam the Earth."

"Okay," Callie said. "I'm pretty lost, but keep going."

Chuckling, Tatiana smoothed her hand over the rock. "You are quite funny, daughter of Darkrip. I appreciate your sense of humor."

"Uh, thanks, I guess. So, you were telling me about the deathbed promise to your friend," she said, circling her hand in a gesture to continue.

"Yes. Elu was her name. It means 'beautiful' in Zuni, which was spoken here at the time. For centuries, I have kept my promise to her. I was able to see—in the way I see things others cannot—that one of her descendants would become very important to the future of the planet."

"*Heavy*," Brecken murmured.

"I often deal in heavy," she said with a dismissive shrug. "Elu's descendants are members of the family that now inhabits these ruins. One of her lineage is a woman named Kasa, who has two boys of her own. One of them is Adriel, whom you just met." Rising, she stared up at the rapidly darkening sky, gray now that the sun had set behind the cliffs. "The other is named Nuka, which aptly means 'younger brother.'"

Urging them to stand, she began walking toward the dwellings. Callie and Brecken rose and followed her until they stopped at the door of one of the structures. "You may want to cover your nose. The smell can be quite pungent. I have been mixing various potions to no avail."

She stepped inside, and Callie looked at Brecken before following her, comforted by the fact he was behind her. After her eyes adjusted to the dimness, her gaze fell to the boy lying on the bed of furs in the corner. His skin was drenched with sweat, and his eyes were glassy. They approached, and Callie covered her nose and mouth with her hand. The odor of herbs and medicine was potent but not overwhelming. No, the scent she smelled was from the boy himself. Stopping beside the bed, she acknowledged the gut-churning aroma.

The little boy who lay in the furs was surrounded by the stench of death.

Training her gaze on Tatiana, she felt the urge to weep. The boy was suffering from intense pain, and she longed to free him from it.

"Yes, Calinda," Tatiana said, gently cupping her shoulder. "That is why I've brought you here. I need you to heal the child."

Staring down at the boy, Callie shook her head. "I don't use my healing powers on humans or Slayers. Dad was always clear they could only be used on animals. The energy transfer between evolved beings is too unstable. It could kill us both."

Tatiana's features remained impassive. "The risk is high, but you are both children of great importance in this world. Heal the boy, and I will align with your cause to defeat Bakari."

Sucking in a breath, Callie deliberated.

"The boy's life for my alliance," Tatiana said, piercing the silence. "He has only days left, so I will give you until morning to decide. Choose wisely, Calinda, as I am to play a role in the final battle that you cannot foresee. I am encouraged by the choice you made after we spoke by the River Thayne. Hopefully, you will continue to make choices worthy of your station. I will return when the sun has risen above the southwest cliff." She gestured toward the far-off cliffs. "Until then, take solace in Brecken's embrace and let him be a sounding board for your fears."

Glancing at Brecken, Callie muttered, "Well, I guess she knows we're together."

"He is a worthy match for you, Calinda," she said, backing toward the entrance of the dwelling. "Draw on his strength to help make your choice." Closing her eyes, the rocky walls rumbled slightly before she vanished into thin air.

Callie stared down at the boy, overcome by his short, labored breaths and the way his small fingers clutched the furs. Resigned, she looked at Brecken. Concern swam in his eyes as she opened her mouth to speak.

"If I can save his life, I have to do it," she whispered.

A muscle ticked in his jaw. "I know."

Swallowing thickly, Callie prepared herself for a night of deep deliberation, already acknowledging she was going to risk her life to save the child.

Chapter 20

U pon exiting the dwelling, Callie observed the woman who stood outside. She had long, silky black hair, spun into a braid that snaked down her side and almost reached her waist. She wore faded jeans, sneakers and a sweatshirt that read, "Arizona Diamondbacks." Glancing toward Nuka's dwelling, her features contorted in anguish.

"It is hard for me to visit him when he is in so much pain," she said, her throat bobbing as she swallowed. "Tatiana has been helping me, and we are eternally grateful. She has kept the promise she made to my ancestor for centuries."

"You must be Kasa," Callie said.

The woman nodded and gestured toward a nearby doorway built into the cliff. "You met my son, Adriel, and my husband, Lonan, is inside as well. We would like to offer you food and answer any questions about Nuka. Please." She gestured toward the dwelling.

"We met some people in the parking lot who warned us you weren't too friendly," Brecken said, his tone slightly hesitant.

"That is my husband's fault," she said, a look of annoyance crossing her face. "He's wary of strangers and was quite rude to them when they offered us some food."

"I can provide for our family," a man said, exiting the dwelling. "We don't need charity."

"They were just being nice, dear." Pointing at Brecken, she asked, "Is he stubborn as a mule too?"

Callie grinned. "Eh, he's okay. I think I'm probably the stubborn one between the two of us."

"Probably?" Brecken teased, and she punched his arm.

"I am on edge from our son's sickness," Lonan said, trailing toward his wife and placing his arm across her shoulders. "I'm sorry." He placed a firm kiss on her lips.

Sighing, she shrugged. "It's hard to stay mad when he apologizes with the sad face. Come on inside. We are about to sit down for dinner."

Callie and Brecken followed them inside, and she inwardly remarked how nice their home was for a dwelling built into a cliffside. Beautiful tapestries lined the rocky walls and the floor was covered in soft-woven carpets. A cauldron hung above a fire in the corner, and Callie noticed Adriel sitting beside it playing a handheld video game.

"Although we've decided to live separate from modern society for the time being, little boys still crave their video games," Kasa said. "We let him play an hour per day until the batteries die and Lonan can hike to the nearest town to buy more."

"Yes!" Adriel said, pumping his fist. "I beat level fifty-three."

"That's wonderful, but it's time to put it away and eat dinner, Adriel."

Sighing, he nodded and clicked off the game. Setting it aside, he beamed at Brecken and Callie. "We never get any visitors here except some random hikers and Tatiana. You can sit beside me if you like," he said, waving his hand over the carpet.

"I'd love to," Callie said, striding toward him and sitting down. "Thank you."

"You're welcome." He was adorable as he gave her a gap-toothed grin.

Eventually, they all sat near the cauldron, and Kasa began filling bowls with the stew that marinated inside. "It's coyote stew," she said, handing a bowl to Callie. "Lonan hunts them, and we eat what he brings home."

Lifting the bowl to her nose, Callie inhaled, noting it smelled delicious. She wasn't sure about the ingredients but figured it wouldn't kill her if everyone else was eating it. Taking the spoon Kasa handed her, she took a tentative taste.

"Wow, this is fantastic," she said, consuming another spoonful. "Thank you, Kasa."

"You're welcome. Brecken?" Kasa asked, handing him a bowl.

"I hope you don't think it's rude of me to decline," he said, holding up his hand. "I don't eat food all that much."

She nodded and handed the bowl to Adriel before preparing one for herself and Lonan. They sipped the stew, the wooden spoons clanking against the brown clay bowls, as Kasa studied Brecken.

"Is this because you drink blood to survive?"

"Yes," he said with a nod. "It's something humans wouldn't usually know, but I'm guessing Tatiana already told you I'm a Vampyre."

"She did." Kasa took another bite before continuing. "And she also told us of your unique heritage, Callie."

"Unique is one way to put it," she mumbled.

"Callie is magnificent, and some people in our realm aren't wise enough to realize it quite yet," Brecken said, placing his hand on her back and slowly rubbing.

Callie's heart melted at the beautiful words, and she gave him a wink. "It's been hard living between two worlds and not quite fitting in, but I'm not going to whine about it. I've had it a lot better than most, and I'm thankful for that."

"I appreciate your gratitude. It is an important quality to possess."

Nodding, Callie gave her a sympathetic smile. "I'm so sorry about Nuka. When did he become sick?"

"It's been two months now," she said, eyes welling with tears as she set down the bowl. "He complained of a stomach ache at first, and I thought it was something he ate. But then he began having chills and developed a fever. I sent a prayer to the universe, hoping Tatiana would hear the call, and she appeared. She takes her oath to my ancestor very seriously and has tried to help."

"It seemed she made a lot of potions from what I saw in Nuka's dwelling. I can't believe none of them helped. Her concoctions are extremely powerful and have given a Vampyre in our realm the ability to transport."

"She does not understand why they are ineffective," Kasa said, running her fingers over the rug. "Lonan took Nuka to see a doctor in Phoenix who performed a multitude of tests, and the results showed no disease. It is baffling. We cannot treat a problem we cannot diagnose."

"That's strange," Callie said, feeling her eyebrows draw together. "He's obviously very sick."

"Would it help if you put him in a hospital?" Brecken asked. "I don't want to pry about why you're living out here, but it might help."

"I lost my job over a year ago, and we couldn't afford rent anymore," Lonan said. "This was our ancestors' home, and Kasa and I felt a calling to live here for a while and try to connect with our heritage. It might seem strange to some, but we've been happy out here…until Nuka became sick."

"The doctors wouldn't admit him because he doesn't have a diagnosable condition for them to treat—"

"And because we don't have health insurance," Lonan mumbled.

"That too," Kasa sighed. "Regardless, Tatiana sees much more with her mind than we do with our eyes. She believes Nuka possesses special abilities and must be healed by someone who does as well. Although Tatiana is powerful, her spells and potions are external. You were born with the ability to heal, so she believes you can help him. She also believes there is a greater purpose connecting you to Nuka."

"What purpose?"

"She has latched onto the belief that you are meant to heal our son in exchange for her alliance in your cause to defeat Bakari."

Callie finished her stew, sipping from the bowl before placing it on the ground. Contemplating, she gnawed her lip as she debated the repercussions of healing the boy. "So far, I've only used my power to heal animals. There is an energy transfer that happens during the healing process that we've never been able to understand. My father and aunt Evie tried to study it, but we've never figured out how to collect any of the energy. I'm telling you this so you understand what you're asking. The outcome could be disastrous."

"I understand he could die, but he will die without your help, so I am willing to take the chance."

Callie rubbed her arm. "It's possible I could die too. It's a huge risk for both of us."

"I'm so sorry to ask you to put your life in danger," Kasa said, reaching over to grasp her husband's hand. "We are strangers, and you owe us nothing. If you decide not to heal our son, we will accept that choice. What we are asking of you is extremely unfair, and we would not ask if we had another option."

Blowing out a breath as her lips fluttered, Callie contemplated. "I'm pretty sure I've already decided to do it." She gave a slight shrug, feeling her lips curve into a compassionate smile. "But I need to spend some time contemplating the repercussions. We have no way to reach my family since there's no cell service or internet access here. A part of me wants to go home and discuss with them before I heal Nuka."

"We don't have time for you to travel home," Kasa pleaded. "Tatiana said Nuka only has a days to live. Oh, god," she cried, burying her face in her hands. "I can't lose him, Lonan."

Her husband slid closer, embracing her as she cried on his shoulder. "I know, sweetheart. It's okay."

"She cries a lot," Adriel said, staring up at Callie. "It makes my chest hurt right here." He rubbed his hand over his heart, the gesture calling to Callie as she sifted her fingers through his thick hair.

"I get that, kid. I bet your heart hurts for your brother too."

He nodded. "Really bad. I miss playing with him. He's my best friend."

Callie looked over at Brecken, and he gave her a sympathetic smile. "Hard to say no to that."

"It sure is."

Kasa's tears abated, and she lifted her head, wiping the wetness from her cheeks. "I'm sorry. The pain and sadness are overwhelming sometimes. Please take the night to contemplate. Do you want to sleep in the dwelling next door?"

"We'll set up our tent outside in the spot Tatiana suggested," Brecken said. "But thank you."

"Of course." Sliding toward the cauldron, she scooped some stew into a clean bowl. "I need to take this to Nuka and sit with him while Lonan gets Adriel to bed. If you need anything during the night, please let us know."

"We will," Callie said, rising as Brecken stood beside her. "Have a good visit with Nuka, and thanks for the stew. It was really good."

After saying good night, Brecken and Callie headed to the cliffside clearing about fifty feet away, and he set up the tent while Callie tried like hell to find a cell signal. Holding up the phone, she trailed around, frustrated, and eventually gave up.

"No service?" Brecken asked as he popped the last part of the tent in place.

"Nope, but we knew that. I really want to talk to my parents right now. The two of them always have such great perspectives on things. They're usually different perspectives, which helps me come to a logical conclusion based on their combined advice."

"Well," he said, holding out his hand, "I'm not as powerful as Darkrip, nor as educated as Arderin, but I have two good ears and would love to listen to you try to talk yourself out of healing a sick child."

Her cheeks puffed as she took his hand. "Yeah, you already know I'm going to do it. But I'd like to talk about it anyway."

Nodding, he led her into the tent, zipping it once they were inside. They changed into shorts, and Callie threw on a soft tank top before Brecken zipped their sleeping bags together. Callie lay down beside him, comforted by his soft caresses as he held her inside the plushy fabric. Resting her head on his chest, she began to relay her fears, thankful for her strong soldier who listened intently and offered her solace.

Brecken's fingers sifted through Callie's curls as she nuzzled into his body. She spoke about her fears of healing Nuka, the musings sometimes drifting to philosophical questions about suffering and death. Lifting her head, she cradled her face as her elbow rested on his chest.

"You must think about death since you're a soldier. What do you think happens when we die?"

"I believe in the Passage and hope I go there," he said, smoothing the hair at her temple.

"Not *after* we die," she said, holding up a finger, "but *when* we die. That moment it all begins to slip away."

"Well, hopefully, I'll never have to find out," he teased, "but if I do, I imagine it will be peaceful. You know, like whatever pain you're experiencing just melts away and your soul is free."

"That's beautiful," she said with a soft smile. "I should've expected it from all the poetic letters you wrote."

They stared into each other's eyes, silently communicating until he spoke. "I think you have to do it," he said, acceptance lacing his expression. "If you're looking for my opinion, there it is."

"I agree. Securing Tatiana's alliance is key. With her help, we can hopefully end this conflict once and for all."

"And you'll be free of the prophecy," he murmured.

"Unless I destroy the world," she muttered.

"Never gonna happen," he said, sifting his fingers through her hair. "You're too pretty to cause the apocalypse."

Breathing a laugh, she dramatically swiped a curl over her shoulder. "I guess I'm okay."

Their chuckles mingled as she slithered atop his body. Lowering her lips, she pressed them to Brecken's, drawing him into a slow, languid kiss as she reached between their bodies. Reaching into his boxer briefs, she pulled his aching shaft through the slit and pushed the fabric of her tiny shorts aside. Grasping him, she ran the head of his cock through her slick essence as he palmed her hips. As their lips consumed each other, she slowly slid over his straining shaft, enveloping him in her wetness.

"Goddess, you feel so good," he murmured, using his hands to guide her as she writhed atop his body. The slick inner walls of her channel gripped him, so snug he never wanted to let go.

Resting her palms flat on either side of his head, she anchored above, undulating back and forth in a rhythm that drove him wild. Every time her drenched folds ran along his sensitive flesh was more pleasurable than the last. Digging his fingers into the swells of her ass, he increased the pace, bucking his hips to push himself deep inside her quaking body.

"I feel so connected to you," she whispered, her dark curls tickling his chest as she loved him. "How is that possible?"

"Come here," he whispered, threading his fingers in her hair and drawing her into a blazing kiss. Their tongues mated, breath mingling as they slid over each other...into each other.

Lowering his hand, his finger delved between her folds as she rode him, locating the sensitive bud under the hood of her mound. Pressing the pad of his finger to the engorged nub, he stimulated it, groaning when she mewled and increased the gyration of her hips. Determined to let her remain in control, he surged inside, their bodies working in tandem to reach their peak.

"Let go, Callie," he rasped against her lips, his finger circling her clit in firm, rapid strokes as she trembled. "Let me see you come, honey."

Her spine snapped, head tossing back as she flew over the edge. The rapid movements drew him deeper into her body, and he thrust, surging as far as he could go as the base of his spine began to tingle. Gritting his teeth, he pummeled her quivering frame, feeling her pulse around his turgid cock. Unable to hold back the release, a growl escaped the back of his throat as he began to come, coating her core with the evidence of his desire.

She collapsed against him, squeezing him with her thighs as she straddled him, gripping him with her tight channel as he emptied everything inside her. Scrambling to catch his breath, he buried his face in her soft curls, drowning in the scent of his gorgeous Callie. His frame jerked as he expelled the last of his release, and she clung to him, arms and legs wrapped around him until he didn't know where he ended and where she began. Awash with contentment, he stroked her hair as their bodies cooled.

"Brecken?" she mumbled into his chest.

"Hmm?"

"I don't want to fight what's happening between us," she said, the words lazy and sated as her fingers softly caressed his neck.

Joy coursed through him even though he had reservations. The nagging notion that she would be wrapped in another man's arms if certain circumstances hadn't occurred lingered in his mind as well as the discussion they'd had at the pool. He loved being with her, but it didn't change the fact he would never be wealthy or revered.

"Neither do I. Let's focus on you healing Nuka and gaining Tatiana's alliance while we let what's between us breathe."

"Okay." She snuggled into him, sending sated jolts of bliss through his body. "I feel like healing Nuka and gaining Tatiana's alliance is part of something bigger. If it helps us defeat Bakari and leave the prophecy behind, I'm all in."

"That's really brave," he said, kissing her hair. "I'll be there the whole time while you heal him, honey. You're not alone."

"I know. Thank you, Brecken. Night."

Tucking the sleeping bag around them, he encircled her in his arms, content to have her sprawled against him for eternity. "Night."

Closing his eyes, he fell asleep as he so often dreamed, with Callie in his embrace.

Bakari stood under the night sky, observing the troops as they sparred. Zadicus in his new form was magnificent, and Bakari felt the warrior increased the probability of destroying the royal family. As he stood atop the hill, he heard a rustling to his side and turned to observe Tatiana appear.

"Hello," he said with a brisk nod. "I wondered when you would appear to me again. As you can see, the potion Dr. Tyson created has transformed Zadicus into a formidable weapon."

Tatiana's eyes narrowed as she watched Zadicus spar with the Deamon soldiers. He plowed through them one by one, as if they were feathers he was plucking from a down pillow. Sucking in a breath, she slowly shook her head. "You killed him."

"He is still alive."

"His soul is dead," she snapped, her gaze angry as she stared up at him. "Have you learned nothing in all your centuries on the planet? Death is not for you to wield like a god. You assign yourself too much importance."

"You're the one who aligned with me, Tatiana."

"I *helped* you," she said, lifting a finger, "but you've never had my allegiance."

"Semantics," he said, giving a frustrated wave. "Why are you here? Did you come to lecture me?"

Lifting her chin, she spoke into the gentle breeze. "I have come to inform you I have decided to align with the immortal royals."

Anger swelled deep in Bakari's gut, causing him to face her and lift his hands. "Why would you align with them? I thought you saw the purpose of my cause."

"I saw the purpose of pushing you toward the moment when you will fulfill the prophecy with Calinda. We are close to the conclusion of this woeful story, and I, for one, am glad." Lifting a shoulder, her lips formed a crooked smile. "In all honesty, I am tired, Bakari. Once the prophecy is fulfilled, I will have a nice long sleep. Until then, I have finally chosen a side."

"Why are you telling me this?" he asked, crossing his arms over his chest. "It would make more sense for you to keep it secret."

"No, it wouldn't. You need to know your weaknesses so you can prepare for the final battle. Losing me is a weakness. I have supplied you with many powerful concoctions and spells for quite some time."

Something burned in Bakari's chest, and he uncrossed his arms to rub the spot above his heart before realizing it was sadness. "I'm not sure what to say. Thanks for telling me, I guess. I should probably murder you but don't want to expend the energy."

Her lips formed a wistful smile. "I have been drawn to you, Bakari. To your pain and feelings of not belonging. Most see you as evil, but I see you as damaged."

"Well, you're no bed of roses either, Tatiana."

"No," she said, gaze falling to the grass before reclaiming his. "Fear and pain guide me, as they do you. I don't see happiness in either of our futures, and for that, I am quite sad."

Bakari studied her as curiosity snaked down his spine. "You have seen my death? When will it happen?"

"You know I will not answer that." Stepping closer, her expression turned serious. "But I do want to help you one last time."

"How?"

"The battle between you and the immortal army needs to happen in the field to the south of Restia, near the ether. Therein lies your only chance of fulfilling the prophecy."

"You're sure?"

"I'm sure," she said with a nod. "Draw the immortal troops there in two weeks' time and commence the final battle on the open field. Callie will be there. I have seen it."

"She will align with me?"

"Yes."

"But you still choose to side with the immortal army?"

"Yes," she said with a nod.

Frustrated, he swiped a hand over his face. If she wanted to choose the losing side, who was he to argue? Perhaps she would survive. If anyone could, it was Tatiana. She always had indiscernible motives at best, and he didn't have the will to figure out her riddles any longer.

"All right." Clearing his throat, he wondered how to say goodbye. Tatiana had been a fixture in his life for many decades, and he was embarrassed to realize he would miss her.

"You don't have to say anything, son of Markdor. I'm sorry your life has taken the path it did. You deserved better before you gave into your hate. Ultimately, that choice will be your undoing."

"My hate makes me powerful, Tatiana. I will restore balance to Etherya's realm and rule over the kingdom I was denied so long ago."

Sighing, she shook her head. "You are blinded by your pain. I hope you are freed from it someday. Until we meet again, goodbye, Bakari." With a nod, she disappeared.

"Frustrating creature," he muttered, kicking the ground before turning to face the troops. Clutching onto her assurance that Callie would align with him and fulfill the prophecy, he pushed the soldiers well into the night, ensuring they were prepared for the final battle.

Chapter 21

In the morning, Callie and Brecken rose to find warm sunlight surrounding their tent. Stretching her sore muscles, she yawned and felt him stir next to her.

"Rise and shine," she said, sitting up and swiping the hair from her forehead. "It's a great day to heal a sick kid. Let's do this."

Sitting up, he rested his forearms on his knees as he grinned. "Someone's in a good mood."

"I want heal him, Brecken, and it will cement Tatiana's alliance. If I can pull it off, this will be a pretty fucking awesome day."

"I know you'll do it," he said softly as he pushed the sleeping bag aside. "Let's get to it."

They dressed before stepping outside the tent to breathe in the fresh air. Tatiana appeared at Callie's side, and she turned to face her.

"I'm going to heal Nuka."

"I know. I have already informed Bakari I will be aligning with you."

Callie scowled. "Why would you do that? Now, we've lost the element of surprise."

Tatiana breathed a laugh. "He asked me the same thing. I have my reasons. Now, it is time to heal the boy. I must admit, I am disappointed in my failure to remedy his illness. I do not like feeling helpless. My potions and knowledge are the core of my identity."

"How long has it been since someone just saw you as *you*?" Callie asked, head tilting as she studied her.

Tatiana's eyebrows lifted. "Now, it is you who speaks in riddles."

"I'm not trying to be obtuse," she said, lifting her hands. "I just...I sense an emptiness in your words, and it makes me sad. Although you're a tough nut to crack and quite meddlesome, you deserve love like everyone else, Tatiana."

Her lips twitched, and she gazed at the ground before lifting her eyes back to Callie's. "Thank you for the kind words. I do not often receive sympathy or comfort. Your empathy is one of your greatest strengths, Callie."

Callie smiled. "I think it comes with the territory. You know, healer and all." Lifting her hands, she shook them.

Giving a nod, Tatiana gestured toward the dwelling. "I have carried on too long. Come. It is time to heal Nuka."

They followed her, waving hello to Kasa, Lonan and Adriel as they stood outside. Kasa stepped forward and pulled Callie into a firm embrace.

"Thank you," she whispered, hugging her so tightly Callie struggled to breathe. "I can never repay you for your sacrifice."

"It's not a sacrifice to heal someone in pain." Drawing back, she squeezed Kasa's shoulders. "I'll do my best."

The woman nodded, tears streaming down her face, as Tatiana urged Callie to enter Nuka's dwelling. "You all will stay out here while Callie uses her magic. Brecken and I will observe inside. It is possible the ground will shake and rocks will be displaced. Stay alert."

The family nodded, and Callie ducked slightly to enter the dim room. Nuka lay in the furs as the stench of death and illness permeated every corner of the space. Covering her mouth and nose, she closed her eyes.

"I just need a minute. The sickness is overwhelming to me. I feel it and his suffering as if it were my own."

Tatiana and Brecken stood firm, giving her the time she needed. Crouching next to Nuka, she gently touched her fingers to his burning skin.

"Hello, Nuka," she said, smiling as the boy wheezed, terror swimming in his deep brown eyes. "My name is Callie, and I have special powers." Holding up her hands, she rotated them as the boy looked on. "There is magic that seeps from my hands, and it will lock onto your sickness and pull it from your body. Do you understand?"

Short breaths exited from his lungs as he stared up at her in fear.

"*Shhh...*" she said, placing her palm on his damp forehead. "Do you feel me? I want you to try to breathe just a bit slower, okay?"

His eyes darted back and forth between hers before his chest began to rise and fall in longer breaths.

"Great job," she said, smiling as she caressed his cheek. "I've got you, sweetheart."

She stayed like that for several seconds, allowing him to feel her touch. Eventually, she pulled off the fur and pinched the fabric of his sweat-soaked T-shirt.

"I'm going to take this off, okay? I need to touch your skin with my hands. Are you okay with that?"

He gave an almost imperceptible nod, and she smiled. She tugged the fabric off his body and sat firmly on the rug, wanting to feel as grounded as possible to the earth below. Holding up her hands, she explained, "I'm going to place both hands on your body. One over your heart, and one over your belly, okay?"

He answered with labored breaths, but Callie saw the acceptance in his eyes. "When I touch you, I want you to think of your favorite thing in the whole world. It can be a toy, or the beach, or hugging your mama. Anything that makes you happy, Nuka." Lowering her hands, she placed them on his body, closing her eyes to cement the connection.

Illness swirled beneath her palms, sticky and corrosive, and she concentrated on the darkness behind her eyelids so she wouldn't become overwhelmed with nausea. Inhaling and exhaling, she used her mother's yoga breathing techniques to remain calm. Summoning her powers, she began to extract the illness from his body.

The sickness choked her, robbing air from her lungs as she struggled to maintain control. It held a power she'd never felt before, and Callie understood it was generated by someone or *something* wicked and inhuman. There would be time to analyze that later, but for now, she concentrated on dragging it from Nuka's body so she could destroy it.

Suddenly, her brain was flooded with images, and Callie's eyes snapped open to focus on Nuka. The boy stared back at her, shaking and terrified, and she longed to soothe him but was frozen by the pictures that flashed through her mind. Images from long ago of a peaceful species who inhabited a small corner of Etherya's realm. A simple species with loving families and gentle laughter that filled their pointed ears until they were all washed away in a great flood.

One of them remained and evolved into a hateful creature who would come to be known as Crimeous, King of the Deamons. But there were others who'd been washed away and survived. The destruction of their kingdom led them to the human world, where they began anew, blending in with the species and sometimes procreating with them to create hybrids. Elu, Nuka's ancestor, was one of those hybrids, and she learned the ways of witchcraft so she could cast spells to diminish the Elven genes in her descendants. She felt they would thrive in the human realm if they did not possess immortal qualities.

But the spell did not work for all of her progeny, and some retained the immortal attributes. Nuka was one of those creatures. Pressing her palms into his skin, Callie focused on the task at hand. Closing her eyes, she clenched her teeth, trying like hell to draw the sickness from his body.

"Hello, Callie," a voice called, and she turned to look at Nuka, who now stood beside her. Confused, she held up her hands, glancing at the dark dome that surrounded them.

"Hello, Nuka."

"We are in your subconscious now," he said, smiling to reveal two missing front teeth. "You are still healing me in the physical realm, but our powers allow us to speak here."

Squinting one eye, she placed her hands on her hips. "You certainly don't talk like a little boy. How old are you?"

"In the physical world, I'm five, but in the scheme of things, my soul is already wise, as Tatiana's is. It is hard to explain, but it stems from our Elven heritage. The destruction of our people was traumatic—both the Elves and our Native American ancestors—and our blood is fortified to ensure future generations survive."

Callie's eyebrows drew together. "I don't sense any special elements in your family's blood."

"No. The Elven gene lies dormant in some, and many would say they are lucky to only be human. They will never know the fear the Elven hybrids feel. The Elven council only hunts those who express the traits of our ancestors."

"I'm not familiar with the Elven council, but they sound like some pretty bad eggs."

Laughter bounded from his throat. "Your intuition is correct. They do not embrace human-Elven hybrids who exhibit Elven traits and have decreed to destroy us one by one. This is where my sickness stems from. One of the purebred Elves poisoned our stew without my knowledge. Since the Elven gene is suppressed in my mother and brother, they were not affected."

"I didn't realize there were still purebred Elves on the planet."

"It is a discovery that could only be realized once the War of the Species ended and the immortals were reunited. The Elves are an entirely different breed of immortal from Slayers and Vampyres and much more highly evolved than Deamons. There will be a reckoning in the future, where several of the species collide, but other things must happen first. There is an order to the chaos of the immortals."

"I'm guessing one of those things is that I need to fulfill the old Elven prophecy?" Callie muttered, crossing her arms over her chest.

Nuka smiled. "Yes, but you do not understand the prophecy as Tatiana and I do. You see it as evil, but I assure you, it is not. Change often arises from things we don't understand."

"Was this meant to happen? You falling ill so I would need to heal you?"

"Yes. Tatiana eventually realized this, which helped close the loop. Now, you have her alliance and can move forward."

"And you'll stay here with your family?"

He nodded. "I will experience my childhood with my family until I grow old enough to accept my position as a crusader in the human-Elven conflict. Then, I will fulfill my prophecy, as you will yours."

"You have a prophecy too?" she asked, eyebrows arching.

"We all have a prophecy, Calinda. The question is: Are we brave enough to execute it?"

Her lips twitched as she bent down, resting her palms on her thighs so she could look him in the eyes. "You're a basket of riddles, kid. I think I like it."

"Remember these words at the moment you fulfill the prophecy," he said, lifting a finger. *"May the world begin anew as the prophecy is fulfilled."*

"May the world begin anew as the prophecy is fulfilled," she repeated. "Got it. Not really with you on the whole 'I'm going to actually fulfill the prophecy' thing, but I'll remember just in case," she said, making quotation marks with her fingers.

Stepping forward, he extended his arms, and she crouched down to give him a tight hug.

"Thank you for healing me, Calinda. The transfer is almost complete. You need to return to the physical world now."

Drawing back, she searched the darkened surroundings. "How do I do that? I have no idea how I got here."

Lifting his hand, he extended his finger. "You already know." Ever so gently, he tapped his finger between her eyes, causing her to gasp. Suddenly, her lids flew open, and she was back in the dwelling, above Nuka's body, hands melded to his skin as she drew the sickness out. Gritting her teeth, she gave a harsh groan and extricated the last of the murky energy from the boy's body.

Nuka cried out atop the furs, and Callie drew her hands away, unable to touch him any longer. They burned with the buzzing dark energy of the sickness, and she curled into a ball on the rug, gagging as she pulled her knees to her chest.

"Callie?" Brecken called, his voice so faraway as she drowned in the sticky energy.

"No!" Tatiana yelled, and Callie knew she was holding him back. "You cannot touch her. She must eradicate the sickness with her powers."

Tears flooded Callie's eyes as she gasped for air, face buried against her knees as she wept.

"I'm here, Callie," Brecken's deep voice called behind her, soothing her as she shuddered and quaked. "I'm not leaving your side no matter how long it takes. Listen to my voice. I'm here."

She nodded, unsure if the movement was visible, and clutched her sides as pain vibrated in every cell of her body. Nuka cried next to her, his weeping a song of fear and relief weaved into the high-pitched noises, and she knew he was going to live. By the goddess, she'd healed him, and he was going to be okay. The knowledge gave her strength, and she blew out huge breaths of relief before slowly lifting her head.

"Hey, buddy," she said, smiling at Nuka. "You okay?"

His shallow breaths echoed hers as his gaze latched onto hers. Giving a nod, he slowly wiped the tears from his cheeks.

"Good. I need a minute. You were pretty sick there, kid. Holy crap." Collapsing back into the fetal position, she allowed herself to relax and regulate her breathing.

Minutes later, Tatiana spoke behind her. "You can go to her now, but be gentle."

Brecken rushed to her side, tenderly cupping her arm and turning her on the ground. "Callie? Are you okay?"

Tears welled in her eyes again as she observed the concern and sentiment that laced his handsome features. Reaching for him, she clutched on tight as he drew her into his lap, cradling her as he rocked back and forth.

"That was amazing," he rasped, holding her as he kissed her temple. "I've got you."

They swayed back and forth, enveloped in each other's embrace, as Kasa rushed into the dwelling.

"Nuka? Are you okay, my love?"

"Mama?" he called softly.

Kasa rushed over, dragging him into her embrace as she wept. "My baby. Oh, god, your fever has broken. Do you feel better?" Lifting her head, she cupped his cheeks as he nodded.

"I feel better, Mama."

"My sweetheart," she whispered, kissing his forehead. Turning to Callie, she swiped the wetness from her cheeks. "Thank you."

"You're welcome," Callie said, clutching onto Brecken as he soothed her. There, between the old rock walls, they comforted each other, grateful for Nuka's recovery.

Chapter 22

Eventually, the excitement of the morning abated, and Callie and Nuka stepped outside to breathe the fresh desert air. Grasping his hand, she smiled into his eyes.

"Do you remember the conversation we had while I was healing you?"

His small features scrunched together as he contemplated. Tilting his face, he shook his head.

"That's okay. Maybe it was a dream, or maybe we're meant to reconnect in the future when you've grown big enough to remember it. I can't wait to see you again, Nuka."

He squeezed her hand, showcasing the same crooked grin he'd flashed during their cryptic interaction.

"Be good for your mom and dad, okay?"

Brown hair swished as he gave an excited nod before he ran back to join his family. Callie and Brecken trailed back to their tent, Tatiana strolling beside them.

"Thank you, Calinda," she said, facing her when they approached the tent. "I will visit Sadie and Nolan at Uteria and supply them with information on the chemicals Bakari uses in his poisons and potions. They should be able to create antidotes that will heal any Slayer affected by them, and any on the battlefield if he chooses to use them in the final skirmish."

"And you will fight alongside us during the battle?" Brecken asked.

"Yes," she said, lifting her chin. "Not only will it add a formidable ally to your regime, but it will allow me to ensure things go as planned. As I informed Calinda, there is a role in the final battle I must play. I saw it in a vision, and I take my premonitions very seriously."

"Do you want to train with us? I can set it up with Jack."

"No," she said with a soft smile. "I'll let you focus on training with the soldiers and will appear when the battle is upon us. Don't worry. I will be ready to fight when the moment arrives."

"I had an encounter with Nuka during the healing," Callie said. "Or a version of Nuka who seemed to exist in my subconscious. It didn't make a ton of sense."

"Nuka is like me," Tatiana said, gazing off in the distance. "We are remnants of mysterious creatures whose secrets have been scattered by the winds of time. He will eventually grow into the soul whom you had the encounter with. Our souls experience the world differently than others."

"He said there are still purebred Elves on the planet."

Sighing, Tatiana nodded. "Yes. That is a matter for another time. First, we must defeat Bakari. His story is tragic but necessary for all the pieces to fall into place. Now, it is time for him to leave the Earth. I look forward to our alliance and to finalizing this part of the immortals' history."

"Goodbye, Tatiana," Callie said, feeling the urge to hug her. There was a loneliness in the slight hunch of the woman's shoulders, and she took a step forward to embrace her.

"Goodbye, Calinda," she said, holding up a hand to halt her. "I must go. I will see you both in due time." Closing her eyes, she lifted her face to the sky and disappeared.

"She's so sad," Callie whispered, turning to face Brecken. "I've formed some sort of connection to her, and I can *feel* it, Brecken."

"I hope she finds happiness one day," he said, encircling her wrist and tugging her close. "For now, I just want to hold you and bask in how fucking awesome you are. Holy shit, Callie. I've never seen your powers close up like that. I'm pretty overwhelmed."

Wrinkling her nose, she shrugged. "Yeah, I'm pretty badass," she teased before giving him a wink. "I'm dying to call Mom and Dad. I can't wait to tell them everything."

"Let's pack up the tent and our bags, and we'll hike back to the car."

As they were packing, Callie thought of the days ahead. Once they returned to the immortal world, their days would be filled with preparing for the final battle. Brecken would dedicate his time toward training with the troops, and she would need to record everything that happened on their trip so she could debrief the council and arm them with as much knowledge as possible for the final battle. Of course, she was eager to help, but she wondered what it meant for her and Brecken. Would she even see him when they returned, or would they both get bogged down by real life? What would that mean for their fledgling romantic relationship?

"Brecken?" she called softly as he packed the last of the tent in the felt bag.

"Hmm?"

"I want to propose something."

Glancing up at her from his crouching position, he nodded. "Okay."

Reaching down, she offered her hand, tugging him to stand before placing her palms on his chest.

"I need one more night with you before we go home."

His lips curved as his gaze roved over her face. "I want that too, but we've got a lot of information to relay to the council."

"I know." Swallowing thickly, she felt her heartbeat thrum, most likely from fear they would lose what they'd so recently found. "But we can take one more night, right? We can go back to the hotel and rent a room. I can video chat Mom and Dad, relay the important details, and tell them we're exhausted and need to crash overnight before returning home."

Sighing, he palmed her cheek, gently rubbing his thumb over the tiny freckles that lined her skin. "Delaying one day won't push away the inevitable. We have to return to real life eventually, hon."

Callie imagined telling her family her relationship with Brecken had turned romantic. It was slightly terrifying since she'd recently been publicly betrayed and had already dragged them through that embarrassing charade. Was she ready to set herself up for that again?

"What are you thinking?"

"That I wish we could just date in secret," she said, lifting a shoulder. "Without anyone else involved. I just want it to be you and me—for a while anyway."

He dropped his hand, his expression resigned. "I don't blame you. You need time to process what happened with Zadicus and decide if you even want to be with anyone. Maybe you need to be alone for a while."

Her eyes narrowed. "You think you're some sort of consolation prize, and it's just not true, Brecken."

Lifting a hand, he showed her his palm. "I just think we need to be thoughtful as we navigate this, Callie, and you have a right to be cautious."

Sighing, she tapped her foot. "I guess so. I'm usually a person who just forges ahead. It's probably good you're making me stop and think for a bit."

Grinning, he tilted his head. "Your fortitude is one of the things I admire most about you. I think I'm just a bit more reserved. It probably balances us out."

"That makes sense considering the responsibility you inherited when your father died. You have to look out for your entire family." Stepping forward, she placed her fingers over his jaw. "For one night, I think you should choose to do something just for you. And for me, since I plan to ravish you." Biting her lip, she waited expectantly for his answer.

Chuckling, he drew her close and placed a soft kiss on her lips. "Goddess, you're adorable. I think Adriel was right. You are a little witch."

She waggled her brows. "I'll work some magic in the hotel for you."

Their laughter mingled with passionate kisses before he agreed to spend one more night in the human world. With that settled, they packed their remaining belongings and hiked back to the car. Callie clutched Brecken's hand the entire way, determined to stay in the moment and enjoy the evening before returning to the stark reality that awaited them at home.

***

They drove back to the hotel, securing a room before initiating the video call with Darkrip and Arderin. Callie updated them on the events of the past few days, and Brecken noticed the wonder and surprise in their reaction.

"Wow, sweetie," Arderin said, her face appearing on the screen as they chatted. "I'm so glad you were able to heal the boy. It sounds like we'll have to go back and wade through all the hidden scrolls when you get home. The fact he and Tatiana are Elven hybrids is extraordinary."

"Yes," Callie said, nodding as she sat on the hotel bed. "I'm happy to spend some time cataloging things and looking for clues that could help in the final battle. And Tatiana should be visiting Sadie and Nolan soon to turn over any additional info they need for their antidotes."

"It's interesting that she wants to be present at the final battle," Darkrip said over Arderin's shoulder. "I'm not quite sure how I feel about that."

"At this point, I think it can only help. She says there's a role she's meant to play in the final battle. I've formed a connection with her, Dad. She reminds me of us a little bit. Existing in a world where we don't have a place."

"You and your father both have a place, young lady," Arderin said, kissing Darkrip on the cheek. "I can't wait for you to come home so I can hug you."

"We'll be home tomorrow morning," Callie said, grinning at her parents' obvious affection. "Probably sometime around ten. I'm just so drained from the healing and don't want to travel through the ether tonight."

"We understand," Darkrip said. "Thanks for protecting her, Brecken. I'm glad everything worked out so you could accompany her."

"Yes, sir," he said with a nod. "I'm happy to do it."

After they said their goodbyes, the screen went dark, and Callie grinned up at him. "Well, I'm starving. Can we go find something to eat before we bang?"

Laughing, he sat beside her on the bed and tucked a curl behind her ear. "I was planning on drinking the Slayer blood in the fridge, but I don't want you to starve to death." She playfully scrunched her features before he continued. "Honestly, I'd really like to take you on a date. You deserve that, Callie. How about the Italian place?"

"Aw," she crooned, her cheeks flushing in a way that made her whole face glow. "I'd love that. Let me shower and throw on a dress so I look presentable."

"You always look gorgeous, but I could definitely use a shower too."

She showered first, and then Brecken took his turn, washing away the dirt and dust from the desert. Emerging from the bathroom with a towel wrapped around his waist, he found her dressed in a simple wrap dress that had easily fit in her small bag. She looked so pretty with her long black curls covering her shoulders, and he was honored to be her date for the evening.

They strolled to the Italian place hand in hand and had a lovely pasta dinner and bottle of red wine. On the way back to the hotel, he noticed her hiccups and teased her for being tipsy.

"I feel so good," she said, lifting her arms in the air and twirling. "Nuka is healed, I didn't croak, Tatiana's on our team, and I get to spend tonight with you. I think I'm just punch-drunk or something."

"Well, it looks good on you," he said, placing the tip of his finger in the center of her head so she could twirl beneath it on the sidewalk.

"You're getting really good at this twirling thing, soldier."

"Goddess forbid," he teased softly, taken by her beaming smile and glowing energy. When they reached the hotel, they were silent entering the room as the sexual tension began to claw at them. Kicking off his shoes, he turned to face her.

She slipped off her sandals and padded over to him in bare feet as he stood frozen by her beauty. Drawn to her, he eventually found the strength to move and slowly closed the remaining distance between them.

Her chest rose and fell with soft breaths as he lifted his hand, pressing the pad of his finger to the silken skin above the valley between her breasts. Gliding it down, he pushed the fabric aside, baring one breast and then the other as they trembled beneath the cups of her black bra.

Guiding her toward the bed, he sat, drawing her between his legs. Untying the knot at her waist, he freed the material, gliding the dress off her body until it pooled on the floor. Tracing his finger over the lace of her black panties, he hummed in approval when she clutched his shoulders.

Brecken slid his palms up her sides, reveling in the way her body trembled beneath his touch. Cupping her breasts in his hands, he ran his thumbs over her nipples, still covered in the black, silky material.

She reached behind her back, unclasping the bra and tossing it to the floor. Brecken slowly massaged her breasts as she trembled. "My greedy little sex imp," he whispered.

"Please, Brecken..." she whimpered, sending shards of pleasure through his frame when her nails speared into his shoulders.

Drawing her closer, he gazed into her eyes and rained kisses over the swell of her breast. Overcome with her tiny mewls of pleasure, he extended his tongue, licking the tight nipple as her back arched in pleasure.

"Oh, god..." she moaned, pressing the eager flesh farther into his mouth.

Brecken sucked her deep, flicking the bud with his tongue while he massaged her other breast. Popping her from his mouth, he trailed kisses across her chest and asked, "Do you like it when I suck your pretty breasts, hon?"

"Yes..." she cried, head lolling back when he sucked her other nipple into his mouth. Swirling his tongue over the sensitive bud, he reveled in her shivers as she clutched onto him for dear life.

After thoroughly flicking her nipple with the tip of his tongue, he drew back and cupped her breasts. Pushing them together, he extended his tongue, swiping it from one bud to the other as she mewled above.

"It feels so good," she said, sliding one leg onto the bed, and then the other, to straddle him. "Sorry, I was about to collapse."

"Hold on tight," he said, sliding one hand to palm her back before thrusting the other one into her thick curls. "I'm not done with these sexy nipples." Gently tugging her hair, he urged her to arch her back as he lowered his mouth to her breast again. "I need more," he rasped, flicking her nipple before sucking it between his lips. "Goddess, you taste so good."

She arched into his body, taking everything he gave her as he devoured her breasts. The points of her nipples were red and swollen, and Brecken could smell the arousal gushing between her thighs. Unable to control his desire, he slid his hand from her hair, down the side of her quaking body, and between her thighs. Pushing the slip of fabric aside, he found her slick opening and jutted two fingers inside as she writhed atop his thighs.

"Mmm..." she moaned, her hips gyrating as she pushed into his fingers. She pumped against him, reaching for the pleasure, as he closed his mouth over her breast. Inflamed with lust, he thrust his fingers inside her deepest place as his tongue licked and lathered her nipple.

"Brecken!" she cried, head snapping as her gaze locked with his. He nipped her breast as she pumped her hips into his hand.

"Right there," he said, hooking his fingers as her eyes closed with ecstasy. "There's the spot I remember."

"*Mm-hmm,*" she whimpered, nodding as she moved above him. "Suck my nipple while your fingers are inside me."

Brecken followed her command, closing over the ruddy bud as he hooked his fingers against the tiny speck filled with nerve endings. She pressed into his body, free and open, and he knew he'd never experience anything more gratifying than making love to her. Their connection was palpable, and having his fingers inside her while sucking her into his own body consumed him.

Her spine bowed, and she cried his name as she exploded into the orgasm. Her hips jerked with wild movements as she pushed into his fingers, and Brecken stimulated the spot even more as she screamed with pleasure. His lips sucked her turgid nipple until she tugged him away, burying her face in his neck and murmuring, "Too much. Oh, god, too much."

Closing his eyes, he inhaled her scent, stroking her hair as his fingers slowed inside her body. Sighing, she shuddered against him before lifting her head and swiping the hair from her face.

"Um, hi," she said, pecking him on the lips. "You're *really* good at that. Holy shit."

Giving her a sultry grin, he withdrew his fingers, lifting them to his mouth and closing his lips over them, determined to drink every part of her essence. Staring deep into her blue-green eyes, he drank her honey from his fingers as she watched, mesmerized. Eventually, he licked himself clean, and she shook her head in wonder.

"Brecken," she whispered, sliding her hand over his jaw. "I'm so hot for you."

Chuckling, he nudged her nose. "I'm hot for you too, hon. Sometimes, when you walked with Zadicus in the garden, the sunlight would shine on you in just the right way..." Sighing, he caressed her cheek. "It made my heart splinter."

"There's my Shakespeare," she said, flashing him her half-fanged grin. "Now that we've crossed the chasm, I want to bang you all the time. Like, once an hour, every day, until I drown in orgasms."

Throwing back his head, he broke into a joyful laugh. "Wow, that's a lofty goal. Can someone actually drown in orgasms?" He rubbed his chin. "I think you might be setting me up for failure."

"I believe in you...and your cock." She waggled her eyebrows. "Speaking of, I think I need to play with him now."

Brecken's shaft jerked in his pants, affirming her statement. "I think he'd like that very much," he said, nipping her nose. He was thoroughly enjoying their banter, reminding him how much he adored her sense of humor.

Gliding off his lap, she helped him undress until they both were naked in the soft light of the bedside lamp. Urging him toward the bed, she pressed him down to lie on his back, his head resting on the pillows as she slithered atop the bed. Kneeling beside his waist, she placed both hands on his upper thighs, gliding them over the hairy skin as his cock sat proud and erect atop his abdomen.

"Is it bigger than most?" she asked, gently palming his cock with both hands.

"Never ask a man that," he gritted, drowning with desire at the sight of her clutching his cock while she sat naked upon the bed. "They'll always tell you theirs is the biggest that ever existed."

Snickering, her hands traveled up and down his shaft. "I'm just asking because it's the first one I've seen up close like this," she said, studying his dick as she slowly pumped her fists. "I mean, I saw Creigen's when I helped Mom change his diaper when he was a baby, but that doesn't really count."

"Uh, yeah, not really the same thing," Brecken teased as she giggled.

"Nope." She worked her hands over him as she gave him a curious look. "Does it feel good? Tell me what to do. I've watched porn before because I was hella curious, but I don't think that's true to life."

"Having your hands anywhere near my cock is heaven, honey," he said, reaching down to run his fingers over her arm. "But it feels better when it's wet so you can glide over the skin."

Her eyebrows drew together before she nodded. "Okay," she said softly, seeming to assess his dick. And then, she lifted him high and lowered her head, licking her lips before touching them to the tip. Staring into his eyes, she glided her mouth over his cock, from tip to base, causing Brecken to emit a loud curse.

"What?" she asked, drawing away. "Did it not feel good?"

"Goddess, Callie, it felt so good," he said, shaking his head on the pillow. "It was just intense."

Her gaze traveled from his shaft to his eyes and back to his shaft before she asked, "So, I should do it again?"

"Yes, you little tease," he rasped, clenching the covers. "Please do it again."

Smiling, she lowered her head, surrounding him with her lips and slowly sliding over every inch of his cock. Brecken clenched his jaw, unable to focus on anything but her wet mouth lathering his sensitive skin. Eventually, she picked up the pace, sucking him deep, then shallow, as he writhed with pleasure.

"Grip the base and jerk it while you suck me, honey," he commanded, possession swelling deep within when she complied. Lost in her, he realized he wanted her like this forever, bent over his cock as he gazed into her stunning eyes. Emotion swamped every cell in his body, and he had to restrain himself from blurting out words he knew it was too soon to say. Craving a deeper connection, he sat up and slid his hands under her arms.

"Hey," she cried as he lifted her across the bed, black curls splaying over the white pillowcase. "I was just getting good at that—"

Brecken sucked the words straight from her lips, devouring her in an ardent kiss as he gripped her behind the knees. Lifting her legs high, he aligned the tip of his cock with her opening, still wet with arousal. Breaking the kiss, he loomed over her as she panted.

"Tell me to fuck you," he commanded, needing her permission before he ravaged her body.

"Yes," she cried, reaching for him as he groaned. "Please, Brecken—"

He plunged inside her slick, tight channel, still wet with arousal.

She gasped below him, taking him deep as desire overrode any other thought. Releasing her legs, he balanced on his palms as he pistoned into her lithe body. "Wrap your legs around my back, honey."

Her long legs snaked around him, drawing him further inside her deepest place, and explosions of pleasure ignited in his brain. He fucked her, hard and deep, until his cock felt ready to explode. Lowering over her, he aligned their bodies, creating a more intimate angle as the sweaty skin of his chest moved over her taut nipples while his hips worked in a frenzied pace.

"Callie-lily," he breathed, locked onto her eyes as her hips rose and fell, their sweaty bodies crashing together in an intimate moment.

"*Brecken...*" She shook her head on the pillow as her nails dug into his shoulders.

"I love being inside you like this," he rasped, feeling his climax on the horizon.

She tugged his head down, drawing him into a kiss, ending all conversation as they gave into the raw desire. The slick walls of her channel choked his cock, tugging and gripping until he could take no more. He surged the head of his shaft against her inner bundle of nerves, hoping like hell it would send her over the edge with him.

Screaming her name, he began to come, shooting thick pulses of release into her deepest place as she quivered below. Her head fell back on the pillow as she broke into a blissful laugh, and Brecken knew she'd reached her peak as well. Jerking inside her body, he emptied himself, every last drop of his burning desire for his magnificent Callie. Collapsing against her, he wrapped himself around every part of her skin, craving the connection as they fell back to reality. She cinched her legs tighter around his waist, drawing him against her, and he sighed with sated joy.

"Mmmm..." he murmured against her neck, kissing the pulsing vein that was pumping double time due to their sexy shenanigans.

"You can still bite me, you know. I don't mind."

"Too soon," he mumbled, licking the salt from her skin, knowing he couldn't handle drinking from her yet. One taste of her blood on his tongue, and he'd never be able to let her go. Until they figured out what the hell they were doing, he would deny himself that which he craved so vehemently.

Sighing, she ran her fingers through his hair. "We'll figure this out, soldier. Mark my words."

Lifting his head, he rested his cheek on his hand, balancing on his elbow as he brushed the hair away from her eyes. Unable to resist her swollen lips, he drew her into a proper kiss as they clutched each other, sated and replete.

"Don't move yet," she said, sliding her calf over the back of his thigh. "Let's stay like this for a while."

Nodding, he lowered to draw her against his body, partially resting on his side so he didn't crush her but allowing himself to remain inside her sweet body. Nuzzling into her, he felt sleep tug at his consciousness.

Warm breaths feathered the hair across his forehead as she lazily stroked his back. Vowing to only lie there a few minutes, he was lulled by her scent and soft caresses. And then, in only a matter of minutes, slumber claimed him as he held his woman cradled in his arms.

Chapter 23

They awoke in the morning, the mood slightly somber as they dressed and packed their bags. Once they were ready, they checked out of the hotel, returned the rental car and headed back to the park where they'd crossed through the ether.

"Ready to walk through?" Brecken asked, smoothing her hair as they stood in the wooded area near the ballfield and playground.

She nodded, smiling although it didn't reach her eyes.

"Hey," he said, sliding his hand down her arm. "Don't worry, hon. We'll find some time to see each other. Now that I've kissed you, I'm kind of addicted."

"Me too." She gazed at him with those luminous eyes. "I'm fine with taking some time to digest things, but I want to date you, Brecken. I want to meet your family."

"It means so much to hear you say that," he said, rubbing her arm. "I just want to make sure you've really processed what happened with Zadicus. I also want you to really think about what being with someone like me will look like. Will you be happy in a meager home at Lynia? I'd love to tell you I'm open to moving to Takelia, but I need to be close to my family."

"Honestly, I'm ready to move out of my parents' house, and I love Lynia. Lila and Latimus live there with my cousins, and Jack's there. I think I'd really like it."

"It wouldn't be fancy. I'm a pretty simple person."

Biting her lip, she shook her head. "I'm not buying it, Shakespeare. Your letters are far from simple. There are a lot of layers I'm dying to peel away."

"I want to get to know you better too," he said, tugging one of her curls. "I want to know your fears and your dreams and learn about your powers." Shaking his head, he marveled at how special she was. "If we do end up going for this and we figure it out, I'll do everything in my power to make you happy, Callie."

Her wistful sigh sent shivers through his frame. "God, you're so sweet. I never would've known if you hadn't written the letters. I was so pissed when I found out, but now, I'm so thankful." Lifting to her toes, she kissed him. "I already miss you."

Leaning down, he gave her one last kiss. "Ready?" he asked, gesturing her toward the ether.

Inhaling a deep breath, she closed her eyes and began walking through with Brecken close behind. The thick, murky substance was choking as he followed her, and he emerged on the other side to see her leaning over, hands on her knees, as she caught her breath. Approaching, he rubbed her shoulder as he gulped air into his lungs.

Glancing around, he noticed the four-wheeler, left where they'd parked it days ago. Smoothing his hand over her hair, he waited for her to straighten.

"I'll drive you to Takelia before heading home." His phone buzzed, and he pulled it from his bag, scowling at the screen. "It's Jack." Lifting the phone to his ear, he answered. "Hey, buddy. We just got back a few minutes ago."

"Bakari is on the move," Jack said, urgency in his tone. "He's suddenly taking the offensive and attacking outlying areas of Restia and Uteria."

Bristling, Brecken's eyes narrowed. "It's probably because he knows Tatiana aligned with us."

"Yes, Darkrip and Arderin updated the council on the information you sent back. I know you just got home, but we need you at Restia if you're able to get here, Brecken. There are several attacks happening at the moment, and we need all hands on deck. Garridan is already at the south side of the compound with Siora. She's a smart soldier, and they work well together on the field, although I'm worried they might kill each other the rest of the time."

"I'm happy to report for duty. I've got a four-wheeler, but Callie is with me, and I need to ensure she's secure before I head over."

"Darkrip should be free to transport her if you call him. I don't think the attacks are serious enough to require his help...not yet anyway."

"Okay," Brecken said, rubbing his forehead. "Let me update Callie. Give me a second." Lowering the phone, he detailed her.

"I'll call Dad to come and get me." Dialing the number, she lifted the phone to her ear. A moment later, Darkrip appeared, pulling her into his embrace as he eyed Brecken.

"Thanks for coming to get me, Dad. Brecken needs to head to Restia."

"I'm going to take the four-wheeler. You all will be okay?"

"Yes," she said, eyes brimming with concern. "Keep me updated."

"Will do." He had to squelch the urge to kiss her as her father stood at her side. "Goodbye, sir."

Darkrip's olive green eyes narrowed as he mumbled a goodbye, and Brecken had the uncomfortable feeling he knew he'd had his hands on his daughter only hours ago. Considering he was a powerful Slayer-Deamon who had once been aligned with Crimeous, concern swirled in his gut.

Realizing now wasn't the time for suspicion and doubt, Brecken hopped into the four-wheeler, ready to kick some ass and help his fellow soldiers. There would be time to assess his relationship with Callie, and he understood he needed to figure it out sooner rather than later considering her father could literally read minds. Carrying on a secret love affair with the powerful ambassador's daughter was definitely not the smartest idea. Resolved to tackle one crisis at a time, he drove under the bright sun as fast as the vehicle would carry him.

Brecken arrived at Restia, parking in the barracks behind the main castle. Spotting Commander Latimus, Brecken waved before heading into the barracks to stock up on weaponry. Once he was ready, he stalked toward Latimus and saluted.

"Ready to fight, sir. Where do you need me?"

"Jack is commanding a battalion over there," Latimus said, gesturing toward the field.

Brecken spotted his fellow soldiers and nodded. "I'll join them now. Thank you, sir."

Rushing to fill his post, he saluted Jack when he appeared. Jack tilted his head in acknowledgment before he addressed the battalion.

"This will be a test of our fortitude, soldiers," Jack's deep voice boomed. "Garridan and Siora are on the south side of the compound with the rest of the Lynian soldiers. They're holding off the Deamons, although Vadik is there. Hopefully, the new TECs work their magic."

"So, we'll flank the north side?" one of the men asked.

"Yes. Larkin spotted another cluster of Deamon soldiers in the woods outside the wall. We think it's only a matter of time before they attack. He's already there with two battalions. Commander Kenden is at Uteria, warding off an attack there. Bakari's faction is smaller there for some reason, but Kenden's troops are on it."

"Head out with your battalion, son," Latimus commanded from several feet away. "I'm staying here to wait for the last soldiers we summoned, and then I'll meet you at the north side."

"Ten-four." Turning to the troops who were now lined in formation, Jack walked over to address Brecken. "Thank you for arriving so quickly. We have no idea why he suddenly decided to attack today."

"Well," Brecken said, "let's show him he's going to fucking lose."

Jack flashed a confident grin before patting him on the shoulder. "Good to have you back, man." Placing two fingers in his mouth, he gave a loud whistle. "Load into the utility vehicles, troops, and we'll deploy to the north side of the compound."

The soldiers gave a, "Ten-four," and began loading into the vehicles. Brecken jumped in behind Jack, and his friend directed the driver toward the northern quadrant of Restia.

When they arrived, Jack jumped out, and the soldiers fell in line behind him, Brecken close at his back. Surveying the area, he double-checked the TECs on his belt and swung the rifle around his shoulder, prepared for battle.

They slowly approached the stone wall that protected the compound, and Jack lifted his walkie-talkie from his belt. "Larkin?" he asked into the device. "Do you copy?"

"I'm outside the wall." Larkin's voice crackled over the receiver. "The Deamon troops are visible in the woods. It's like they're trying to draw us toward them."

"We'll scale the wall and join your troops. Give us two minutes."

Jack directed the soldiers to climb the wall since the only opening was at Restia's main entrance miles away. They'd all completed a multitude of similar wall-climbing drills in the obstacle courses Jack ran during training sessions and were extremely capable. Grabbing onto the rock wall, Brecken began to climb, dropping to the soft grass on the other side once he breached it.

Surveying the woods, he saw the Deamon soldiers who lined the woods, their beady eyes staring back as if they were waiting for something.

"How long have they been there?" Jack asked Larkin, who approached on his right, two battalions of men falling in line behind him.

"Half an hour at least. I have no idea what they're waiting for."

They stood, alert, as the soft breeze whipped the trees. Something crunched to Brecken's left, and his head snapped toward the sound. A Deamon soldier stepped from the woods and lifted his hand high, holding a gun. He fired a shot, and chaos ensued as the Deamon soldiers yelled and began to charge.

The immortal troops rushed to meet them, rifles firing as they clashed. Several of the skirmishes became one-on-one battles, each soldier sliding the rifle behind their back to draw their swords. The immortal army was unique in that it trained its troops on modern warfare such as TECs and firearms, but also on hand-to-hand combat with swords and fists so they would be prepared for individual battles. Immortals were hard to kill, so every form of battle was taught and practiced.

Whirling, Brecken began sparring with a Deamon who rushed his side. Lifting the butt of his rifle, he whacked the creature in the face before pulling the TEC from his belt and disintegrating him into thin air. Pivoting, he clutched the TEC, ready to find another Deamon to decimate.

Feeling his eyes grow wide, Brecken froze, unable to believe the image in front of him. A huge soldier loomed several feet away, who appeared to be...Zadicus? Brecken had seen enough in his time on the planet to realize the creature before him was no longer the Vampyre who'd been his ward for several years.

The hulking soldier's skin was pale and pasty—even more so than a Vampyre's ever should be now that they walked in the sun. Blue veins showed under his skin, popping from the bulging muscles that comprised his frame. The soldier began to walk forward, his gaze cemented to Brecken's, causing him to sling his rifle around and fire at the creature.

Zadicus continued to approach, the bullets skidding off his skin as if it were made of Teflon. Eventually, he neared Brecken and thrust out his hand, surrounding Brecken's throat as he squeezed.

"What did he do to you, Zadicus?" Brecken gritted through clenched teeth as he gripped Zadicus's hands, attempting to drag them from his neck. "You don't have to fight for Bakari. We can help you."

"Zadicus is dead," the creature spoke. "You may call me Baal."

Sputtering, Brecken kicked the giant's shins, trying to break free.

"Baal is a devil in human religious mythology," a deep voice said above the sounds of swords clashing and gunfire. "I thought it a fitting name for my new weapon."

Brecken twisted to see Bakari standing several feet away, his face impassive, as if he didn't care there was a major battle ensuing around them. "My, my. What do we have here?" Bakari asked, stepping forward. Narrowing his eyes, he assessed Brecken as Baal held him by the throat. "You've been touching things that don't belong to you, haven't you, boy?"

"Release him, now!" Jack's voice boomed in the distance.

Bakari gazed at him through narrowed lids before lifting his hand. "Cease!" he yelled, and the Deamons froze. Baal released Brecken's neck, and he backed away, coughing as he neared Jack. Latimus appeared at their side, his battalion flanking them, and he called to Bakari.

"I'm sorry it has to be this way, brother. I wish you would've strived for peace, but I realize you will never choose that path."

"I have grown more powerful than you can imagine, Latimus," Bakari said, lifting his hands. "It is futile to fight the inevitable. Surrender now, and I'll spare your soldiers' lives."

"We've been at this too long for me to believe your lies, Bakari." Stepping in front of the troops, Latimus held up an eight-shooter.

"You don't have the courage to shoot me—"

The blast from the eight-shooter drowned out Bakari's words as Latimus fired. Eight silver bullets rushed forward, each directed toward one chamber of Bakari's heart. Lifting his hand, Bakari caught the bullets in one swift motion.

"Impossible," Latimus breathed, lowering the eight-shooter. "No one can stop bullets in midair."

Closing his eyes, Bakari looked toward the sky, basking in his assumed glory. "I will be more powerful than Etherya soon," he said, reclaiming Latimus's gaze before dropping the bullets to the ground. They scattered like dandelion seeds over the grass, inept and useless. "You are already doomed."

Brecken saw the confusion in the commander's eyes and for the first time wondered if they might be vulnerable to Bakari.

"The prophecy is almost ready to be fulfilled," Bakari declared. "You understand my strengths and have seen my new weapon," he said, gesturing to Baal. "I will be on the field south of Restia by the ether at sunrise in two weeks' time, ready for the final battle. Bring *all* your men. I want to eradicate them so I can easily assume the throne."

"Never going to happen—" Latimus shouted but abruptly stopped speaking when Bakari closed his eyes and began to chant. Seconds later, he disappeared...along with each and every one of his soldiers.

"What the hell?" Larkin asked from a few feet away.

"He just transported the entire army," Jack said, wonder in his voice as he gazed around the field on the immortal soldiers left behind. The walkie buzzed at his belt, and he lifted it to his ear.

"General Garridan reporting," a voice said over the device. "I'm not sure how to explain this, but the Deamon soldiers attacking the south side of Restia all just disappeared."

"Same on the north side," Jack said into the receiver. "Bakari was here, and it seems he transported them all."

Silence blanketed them before Garridan's voice crackled, "Holy shit."

Lifting his own walkie, Latimus spoke. "Get the soldiers back to the barracks. We'll regroup and strategize before sending everyone home. Looks like the final battle will take place by the ether south of Restia."

"The ether?"

"We'll explain when at the barracks, General. See you there."

Addressing the soldiers, Latimus ordered them to return to the barracks so they could debrief. Brecken followed the order, understanding time was running out and the final battle loomed large.

Arderin observed her husband stalk in their bedroom as she was adding the finishing touches to her makeup to head out to the clinic at Lynia. Alarm shot down her spine when she spied his angry expression.

"Where's Callie?"

"She hightailed it to her bedroom when we got home."

Eyes narrowing, she stood from the vanity and trailed over to him. "Okaaaaay. Want to tell me why you look like you want to murder someone?"

"No," he snapped.

Arderin bristled. "Um, excuse me. I don't know what crawled up your ass, but I don't appreciate the tone."

"I'm not using a tone," he muttered, heading to the dresser and opening the drawer, angrily shifting the clothes inside.

"Wow," she said, approaching him. "You have two point three seconds to tell me why you're being an ass, or I'm never touching you below the waist again, buddy."

Lips thinning, he glanced at her from the corner of his eye. "Sorry," he murmured, his hands stilling as he sighed.

"I think you need to do a *tad* better than that," she said, encircling his arm and turning him to face her. "Sweetheart, what's wrong? Is Callie okay?"

"She's fine."

Arderin stared at him, exasperated when he remained silent. "I'm going to need a bit more of an explanation why you're mad as a hornet." She lightly rapped her knuckles on his forehead.

Quick as lightening, he snatched her wrist and drew her hand away. Arderin frowned, and his shoulders deflated into a defeated stance. "Sorry." Kissing her inner wrist, he gave her a look so solemn she wondered what could've happened. Her husband was stoic—and a bit grumpy—but he was rarely angry at her or their children.

"Did something happen?" she asked, eyes darting between his. "Sathan texted me that Bakari and his army are attacking the Slayer compounds, although he said Latimus and Kenden have it under control."

"I told Latimus to call me if he needs me, but it's not that." Releasing her wrist, he swiped a hand through his hair before beginning to pace. Finally, he turned to her, resting a hand on his hip. "They're fucking, Arderin."

Confusion swamped her. "Who?"

"Callie and Brecken."

Arderin straightened as understanding washed over her. Tilting her head, she stared deep into his forest green eyes. "Darkrip, tell me you didn't."

"I didn't mean to," he said, lifting his hands as he paced. "But there was this weird energy between them, and before I knew it, I was reading his thoughts."

Crossing her arms, she began to tap her foot. "Darkrip, I can't believe you! You sat our children down when they were young and took an oath that none of you would read other people's thoughts."

"It was an accident," he said, halting and angrily jabbing his hand at the floor. "Do you think I *want* to see images of my daughter fucking someone? Oh, god. Kill me. Just fucking shove me in the ground and get it over with." Collapsing on the bed, he covered his face with his hands and groaned.

Arderin would've laughed at his dramatic reaction if the situation wasn't so tense. Approaching the bed, she sat beside him. "For the love of the goddess, sit up so we can talk about this."

Rising, he gave her an acerbic glare. "I have no desire to discuss this. We sent him on a mission to protect her, and he seduced her while she was weak and vulnerable after Zadicus's betrayal."

Laughter bounded from her throat as he glowered. "Callie? Weak and vulnerable? Try again, dear. Have you met our daughter?"

"Well, there's no way in hell she initiated anything."

Snickering, Arderin covered her mouth as her husband fumed beside her.

"Stop laughing," he gritted.

Facing him, she palmed his cheeks. "Darling, you're being obtuse, and it's not a good look on you."

His lips formed a pout. "Don't say it—"

"It's very possible *she* seduced *him*," Arderin interrupted, breaking into a grin. "Perhaps she sought comfort from him after Zadicus's betrayal. I mean, he's extremely hot, and they were already friends. It's not the craziest scenario I could imagine."

Sticking his fingers in his ears, he pulled away and began pacing again. "No more."

"Oh, for the goddess's sake," she said, drawing his hands from his ears. "You're being ridiculous. This hang-up you have about Callie having sex is understandable since you're her father, but it's enough already. She's a grown woman, Darkrip."

"She'll always be my little girl," he said, shaking his head. "Don't you understand she was the first thing I ever did right?"

Compassion filled her heart as she inched closer to him. "I understand. But she's her own woman, sweetheart. She's going to make mistakes and keep secrets and have sex. I'm pretty sure all of that is inevitable."

Huffing, he rubbed his forehead. "It took me a long time to get used to the idea of her with Zadicus. I had reservations, but I wanted her to be happy. I've had no time to digest this. I don't even know this guy. What if he's a jerk? What if he hurts her? I need to vet him." Standing, he began to pace again.

"You will do no such thing," she said in the firm mom tone she'd used with her children when they were young. Rising, she closed the distance between them. Grabbing his wrist, she forced him to stop pacing. "She has to make her own mistakes, Darkrip. We talked about this. She just went through a very public betrayal and canceled wedding. Can you really blame her for keeping this secret? Do I need to remind you that we kept our relationship secret from my brothers for months?"

"This is different."

Laughing, she shook her head. "No, it's not. You need to chill the fuck out and let her tell us in her own time. And once she does, you're going to apologize to both of them for reading Brecken's thoughts." Lifting a finger, she arched a brow. "Do you hear me?"

Darkrip nipped at her finger, sparking tiny flames of desire throughout her body. Biting her lip, she shook her head. "Nope. I can't bone you right now. I have to be at Lynia in thirty minutes."

Inching closer, he slid an arm around her waist, aligning their bodies and resting his forehead on hers. "I only need ten minutes."

Tossing back her head, she gave a joyful laugh. "No, Darkrip, I have to go."

Pressing his lips to hers, he spoke against them. "I'll let the situation develop with Callie, and I'll try my best not to hover. It's hard for me, Arderin. I want to protect her."

"I know," she whispered, sliding her arms around his neck. "From what I saw of Brecken in the hour we questioned him, he's a good man who has chosen to fight for our people. And he doesn't deserve to have his privacy invaded." She gave him a stern look.

"Fine." Closing his eyes, Arderin heard a *whoosh* before a rush of air covered her skin. Emitting a surprised yelp, she realized her husband had just disintegrated their clothes. Arousal surged deep within as he picked her up and carried her to the dresser. Placing her on the cool wood, he spread her legs and walked between her thighs.

"Damn it, Darkrip. I have to go—"

His fingers clenched her hair, tugging her head back as she gasped. Staring deep into her eyes, his erection rubbed against her rapidly slickening folds. And then, her husband diminished any lingering objection when he rested his forehead against hers and said softly, "I love you so much, princess. Thank you for being my partner. I'm honored to be your mate."

Sighing at the romantic words, her body relaxed as she hooked a leg around his waist. "You win," she whispered. "Make it fast—"

Her husband surged inside, capturing her lips as their bodies moved in tandem. Clutching on for dear life, Arderin reveled in the life they'd built together, thankful he cared so deeply about her and their children.

Eventually, she made it to Lynia...and was exceedingly proud of herself for only arriving five minutes late.

Chapter 24

Callie returned to real life, although the events that transpired in the desert were ever-present in her thoughts. The day after her return, she met with the council to detail the events. Miranda had asked the entire family to attend, even though some weren't officially on the council, so everyone was on the same page. Callie told them about her cryptic conversation in the dreamlike state when she was healing Nuka.

"Nuka is special, like me," Callie said as she sat at the head of the conference room table. The council members all listened thoughtfully as she relayed the information. "I mean, not exactly like me, because he's not a Deamon, but Deamons were spawned from Elves if the soothsayers' stories are true. This means they could hold powers we haven't even begun to fathom."

"Tatiana does have strange abilities we've never understood," Darkrip said, rubbing his chin. "I've always attributed them to her study of voodoo and dark magic, and the rituals she conducts that were passed from her ancestors. If she is a human-Elven hybrid, her power could be unimaginable."

"Well, I guess it's a good thing I healed Nuka and cemented her alliance," Callie said, lifting a shoulder.

"You did a great job, Callie," Miranda said from the head of the room. "And you saved a little boy, which is awesome. We're all so proud of you."

"Thank you, Aunt Miranda," she said softly, glowing from her praise.

"We'll wait for Tatiana to contact us and go from there," Miranda continued. "From what we know, she's always lurking, even if she's unseen. In the meantime, how are you, Callie? I'm sure hearing the news about Zadicus was hard."

Callie's gaze lowered as she thought about the man she'd been betrothed to. According to Jack and Latimus, he'd now been transformed into a soulless warrior named Baal and would fight by Bakari's side at the final battle.

"I'm just sad," she said, gaze dropping to her fingers as they fidgeted atop the table. "Although he was a jerk and chose the wrong side, I didn't want him to die. I feel bad for Raoul and Viessa. They loved him very much."

"It's a woeful tale and proves the lengths Bakari will go to defeat us," Latimus said. "We must prevail."

"So, the plan is for us to meet Bakari and his army in the field by the ether at sunrise in two weeks' time." Evie said. "I'm fine with that, but Darkrip and I still haven't worked out all the kinks on the forcefield we need to generate to keep Bakari from transporting so we can kill the bastard once and for all. Now that it seems like he can stop an eight-shooter with his bare hands, we need it to be perfect."

"You need more power," Rinada chimed in, causing heads to swivel toward her. Callie's cousin was reserved, with a personality more like Kenden's than Evie's, so it was a bit shocking to see her speak up in such a large meeting. "Let Callie, Creigen and me help you. I'm tired of being sidelined. We all have powers that are curses most of the time. Let's make them a blessing for once."

"You want to join all of our powers to make the forcefield stronger," Evie mused, sitting back in her chair and tapping her chin. "It could work—"

"No," Darkrip said, straightening in his chair. "It puts them at too much risk. I can't believe you're considering this, Evie."

"When did you become such a stick in the mud?" she asked, eyebrows drawing together. "Rinada has a point. If we're going to beat the bastard, we'll need all the power we can get. Great job, kid," she said, winking. "I knew there was a reason I loved you so much."

"Thanks, Mom," Rinada said, scrunching her nose. "But I'm serious. I want to help. Bakari has imperiled the kingdom my entire life. I'm over it. I want to live in a world that isn't under constant threat."

"I agree," Creigen said. "I'm in. Plus, it will make me look hella cool with the chicks."

"Not sure that's a reason to risk sudden, torturous death, but who am I to judge?" Callie murmured, giving her brother a droll glare. "I'm in too."

"Absolutely not," Darkrip said, slicing his hand through the air. "There are too many unknowns. Even if you don't die, you could be severely injured or injected with some potion like Zadicus."

"Or I could give in to the evil of Grandfather's blood and align with Bakari," Callie said, lifting her chin. "It's what everyone is thinking, so let's just say it out loud. Prophecies carry a lot of weight in this realm, and I know you all have your concerns."

"There are so many possibilities, sweetheart," Arderin chimed in. "I think that's what your dad is saying. What if Bakari somehow concocts a potion that exacerbates the evil in your blood? What if he casts some sort of spell that urges you to follow some inner calling that's lain dormant for all these years? I know it sounds crazy, but we have to at least consider every possibility surrounding the prophecy."

"This is absurd. I'm pretty pissed my own family would doubt me. You all have to see the logic of us all combining our powers."

"Let's table this for another time when we can discuss it," Miranda said, holding up her hands. "It requires a lot of consideration, and the council needs to vote on it."

"We want to help, Miranda," Callie said as her temper flared. "This is our kingdom, and we love the people too."

"I know," Miranda said with a firm nod, her tone indicating the subject was closed. "We'll discuss it at the next meeting, Callie. Thank you, and Rinada and Creigen, for offering to help." She made eye contact with each of them. "It's appreciated and noted."

Callie fumed for the rest of the meeting before heading outside to clear her head. Stalking to the River Thayne, she hiked to one of the old forts the army had used during the War of the Species. It was built into a hill and had lain dormant for decades, but the history of the forts had always called to her. They were relics of a terrible conflict and proof that peace could be secured.

Sighing, she flopped down on the grass by the fort, listening to the river gurgle. Her phone dinged, and she lifted it to her ear.

"Hey," Brecken's baritone chimed, and she closed her eyes, relishing the sound. "We have five minutes, so I snuck away to call you."

"Aw, does that mean you miss me?"

Chuckling, she could almost see the mirth that must be swimming in his brown eyes. "Always."

Plucking at the grass, she said, "I want to see you. Can we try to find a time to get together?"

"Yes. I'll talk to my mom and see when she's available. I'd love to have you over to meet her and my sisters. If you want to."

"I want to." Her lips curved into a sappy smile. "I should have you over to formally introduce you to my parents too, although I'm kind of annoyed at them at the moment."

"We can move at whatever pace you want, hon. Our situation is certainly unconventional to say the least."

Chuckling, she nodded. "It is, but I'm kind of digging it. Being with you feels good, Brecken. That's what I'm focusing on right now."

"I'm glad." A moment passed before he asked, "Why are you annoyed at your parents?"

She told him about the council meeting, frustrated when he agreed with the consensus. "I don't want to piss you off, but, selfishly, I don't want you anywhere near that field, honey."

"I'm the granddaughter of the most powerful Deamon who ever lived, Brecken. It gives me immense power—probably more than I even realize. I'm fine with that, because I don't want any part of Grandfather's evil tendencies, but it makes me extremely capable of fighting against Bakari."

"I know, hon, but I still worry. I just found you and don't want to lose you."

Melting at the sweet words, she sighed. "Okay, I forgive you for being a misogynistic ass."

His laugh traveled through the phone. "Thank you, I think? Where are you right now?"

She told him about the old forts and how they were one of her treasured spots in the immortal world. "I used to play here when I was young and we visited Miranda and Sathan. There's something peaceful and reverential about them, and they're great hiding spots when you want to get away from your little brother."

"I'd love for you to show me one day," he said. "I want to see all the places you cherish, Callie."

"Then I'll show you."

A voice boomed in the background, and he cleared his throat. "Okay, I've got to run. I'll reach out about getting together soon. I can't wait to kiss you again."

Biting her lip, she fought the urge to giggle like a teenager with a terrible crush. "Can't wait either. Bye."

Lowering the phone, Callie took some time to digest everything that had happened over the past few weeks. She thought of Zadicus, allowing herself to mourn the loss of that relationship and trying not to blame herself for being naïve. Eventually, her thoughts turned to Brecken, and she closed her eyes, thanking Etherya for her romantic, soulful soldier.

Before everything fell apart, she never would've imagined a life with Brecken. Not because he wasn't worthy or sexy—because he definitely was—but because it just hadn't occurred to her to look. Muttering to herself that she was an absolute dolt for her obliviousness, she vowed to foster their connection. After everything that had transpired in their growing courtship, Callie could easily envision a future with him. One full of laughter and love and his strong, unwavering support. Squeezing her lids together, she could almost imagine their children. Little girls with his deep brown eyes, and little boys with the cute, wayward tufts of hair that always spiked when he dislodged it with a swipe of his hand.

They would be adorable, and Callie knew a relationship with Brecken would be built on affection, loyalty and the laughter they always seemed to inspire in each other. It gave her hope after the disaster with Zadicus, and she felt the yearning deep within. Although their bond was still new, Callie could imagine it growing into something far better than she'd ever dreamed, all those years ago, as a lonely teenager in a world that didn't accept her.

Realizing her anger had abated, Callie rose, wiping the dirt off her backside and inhaling the damp, lush air. Yes, the future was bright, and she only had to seize it. She would learn from her mistakes and build something even better in the wake of adversity.

And she sure as hell wasn't going to align with Bakari. No matter what happened, and no matter what the prophecy said, she would never choose that path. Resolved, she strode back to the castle to find her family and head home.

Chapter 25

Brecken threw himself into preparing for the final battle, knowing it was imperative they defeat Bakari. Seeing the power he wielded, along with the creature he'd transformed Zadicus into, left no doubt he must be vanquished. Otherwise, the kingdom would never attain the peace it ultimately sought.

Brecken agreed to help Jack with the new recruit trainings, which doubled his workload and led to exhaustion each night when he fell to sleep. It also prevented him from spending time with Callie, and he began to long for her during the lonely nights when she wasn't nestled against his side. He'd gotten used to her honeysuckle scent and brilliant smile when they'd been alone in the desert, and he missed her terribly. They texted often, and he was enamored by her gentle teasing and sexy flirting.

Finally, a week and a half after returning from the desert, Jack urged Brecken to take a day off.

"You can't keep up this pace, man," his friend said, patting his shoulder as they stood on the training field. "I need you to take a day off so you can breathe before the last push. We've got less than a week until the final battle."

Brecken mulled, wanting to make sure he did his part to help the kingdom. "Only if you're sure—"

"I'm sure," Jack said with a firm nod. "Go home and spend some time with your family. We'll be here when you get back."

With his friend's blessing, Brecken returned home that night, excited to invite Callie to spend the next day with him.

Brecken: Hey. Good news. Jack gave me tomorrow off. I already talked to my mom, and we'd like to have you over for dinner.

The text bubble appeared right away, causing Brecken to grin.

Callie: Yes, yes and yes. Do I seem too eager? You know what? I don't care. What time?

Narrowing his eyes, he pondered.

Brecken: She said to come over at three so we can chat and you can hang with everyone before dinner. Why don't you come to my house at two? That way, I can kiss you a little while before we walk over.

Callie: Perfect. Do you want me to stay over? I can tell my parents I'm hanging with Jack. I'm just not quite ready to tell them about us yet. It will lead to an intense discussion I need time to prepare for. Hope that's okay.

Scowling at the deception, he typed his reply.

Brecken: I'd love for you to stay, but I don't want to lie to your parents. Honestly, you dad scares the crap out of me. I'm terrified he's going to find out we're having sex.

Callie: I get it. We can discuss when we're together. They'll want to meet you as soon as I tell them, so you'll need to be prepared. You think my dad grilled you at the council meeting? Wait till he finds out we're banging.

Brecken: This is *not* making me feel better.

She sent him a geek face emoji, causing him to laugh.

Callie: I've got your back, soldier. We'll figure it out. Can't wait to see you.

Brecken: See you tomorrow, hon. Good night.

The next day, she arrived in a four-wheeler, gorgeous as she leaped from the vehicle in a pretty blouse, jeans and sandals. Brecken rushed down the porch steps as she ran to him, catching her when she vaulted into his arms and wrapped her legs around his waist.

"I missed you so much," she said, peppering his face with kisses as he relished being back in her arms. "Oh my god, Brecken. I don't ever want to go that long without seeing you again. It felt like forever."

Laughing, he kissed her, slow and thorough, before drawing back to gaze into her stunning ocean-colored eyes. "Forever is a bit dramatic, but I definitely missed you too, hon."

Sticking out her tongue, she swatted his shoulder. "Don't make fun of me."

"Never." Setting her on her feet, he took her hand and laced their fingers. "You didn't really get to see the property last time. Want me to give you a quick tour? It's small, so there's not a ton to show, but Jordana planted some flowers in the back, and they spruce the place up."

"Sure," she said, flashing the smile he'd craved since he last saw her.

He showed her around, a bit worried she'd think his home provincial considering her lavish upbringing, but she was extremely gracious as he showed her his back yard and the tiny creek that ran behind it.

"This reminds me of the creek behind Aunt Lila's house," she said wistfully, gazing toward it. "It's where I first discovered my power to heal animals, and I have lots of fond memories there."

They trailed around the yard as she recounted stories of working with her father to harness her powers. Eventually, they ended up inside, where he opened the refrigerator and pointed at the contents inside. "I stocked it with some food too, in case you're hungry in the morning."

Her full lips curved, warming every cell in his body. "That's so thoughtful. Thank you. What time do you have to report to the field tomorrow?"

"Eight a.m."

"Got it. I'll make sure I wake up at dawn and bang you one last time before you go so you can have something to remember me by." She chucked her brows.

Laughing, he drew her into a passionate kiss. "I'm definitely taking you up on that, hon."

After a thorough session of heavy petting, they headed to his mother's house. Brecken had prepared his sisters to be on their best behavior since they were hosting royalty, but, of course, it all flew out the window when his sisters bounded from the house, running toward them and introducing themselves to Callie.

"Okay, okay," Brecken said, holding up his hands. "One at a time. Jeez, guys. I thought we'd decided to be proper in front of Callie."

"Proper?" Callie asked, grimacing. "Gross." Facing his sisters, she lifted her chin. "Please don't ever act proper in front of me."

Rowena snickered before glancing at her sisters. "See? I told you she was cool."

"You've already met Rowena," Brecken said, giving her a good-natured glare. "This is Nala, who's fourteen and already a better warrior than I'll ever be."

"Hi," Nala said, stepping forward and extending her hand. "I've heard so much about you from Rowena. I hope to meet Queen Miranda one day, and Betsy says you can make that happen."

"Nala," Brecken said with a warning.

"Of course I can make it happen," Callie said, shaking her hand. "Aunt Miranda is hella awesome, and she'd love to meet you. And you must be Jordana," she said, releasing Nala's hand before facing her.

"Yes," she said, shaking. "Pleasure to meet you. These are my twin sisters, Ludika and Betsy."

"Lovely to meet you all," Callie said after she'd shaken everyone's hands. "Brecken has told me about you, but I want to know more. Don't hold back, okay?"

"Can you come to the back yard?" Nala said, grasping her hand. "I want to show you my training spot."

Callie grinned at Brecken. "Well?"

Wren chose that moment to appear, striding toward them with a gleam in her eye. "Hello, Callie. I'm Wren, Brecken's mother. I hope you don't mind if our girls whisk you away. It's probably easier to just get the obligatory tours of training spots and gardens over with now. Make sure you show her the calla lilies, Nala. They're blooming and are absolutely gorgeous."

"Lead the way," Callie said, sparing Brecken a grin before Nala dragged her away, the rest of his sisters following close behind.

"Well, you've finally brought a girl home," Wren said, sliding her arm around Brecken's waist and leaning her head on his shoulder. "And a kind, beautiful princess at that. How lovely."

"I'm crazy about her, Mom," he said, watching them disappear around the side of the house. "What the hell am I supposed to do? She's a wealthy princess who has extraordinary powers and is used to a royal lifestyle."

Facing him, she cupped his cheeks. "I think the answer is obvious, son. You tell her you love her, and you give me some grandbabies."

Chuckling, he shook his head. "I don't think it's that easy."

"Take it from your highly intelligent, centuries-old mother: It will always be easy if you choose love. Will you face challenges? Yes. Will there be strife? Of course. There were times I thought I might strangle your father when we were embroiled in an argument. But I loved him to the depths of my soul, and we never went to bed angry. I was his princess no matter how poor we were, and he gave me my beautiful children."

"Don't cry, Mom," he said, swiping the tear that trailed down her cheek. "I know you miss him. We all do."

"He would be so proud of you, Brecken," she said, squeezing his upper arms. "You're such a good man. Don't ever doubt that. If Callie chooses you, and you choose her, it's because of who you are, not what you possess."

"Good advice," he said, kissing her forehead. "Should we check on them? I might need to save her."

Chuckling, she patted his arm. "Yes, you do that. I'm going to finish dinner. It's exciting to cook food, and I want to make it extra special for Callie. Go on now."

Brecken trailed around the side of the house to find Callie with a sword in her hand as Nala gave her pointers on how to wield it.

"Just let me know if you need to escape!" he called, eliciting a glower from Nala.

"It's fun!" Callie replied, laughing as she swung the sword through the air. They practiced for a while, his other sisters cheering them on, before Rowena asked if she could show them her powers.

"You don't have to entertain them," Brecken said, sidling up to her. "Just say the word, and we'll tell them to scram."

"Stop it," Callie said, shooing him away. "Okay, let me see…oh, here we go. See this dying plant? I can definitely use my powers to heal it. Come on, ladies. I'll show you."

She proceeded to kneel beside the plant his mother always complained never thrived no matter how much she watered it. His sisters "*ooohhhed*" and "*aaahhhed*" as Callie showed her palms, the centers glowing red as she summoned her powers. Concentrating, with her tongue between her teeth, she cupped her hands over the plant, shooting the energy into it. The broad leaves began to turn from brown to green, stiffening and regaining their form as they reached for the afternoon sun. Eventually, the plant stood tall, and Callie fell to her butt, clutching her legs as she caught her breath.

"Are you okay?" Rowena asked, concerned.

"Yeah," Callie said, flashing a smile. "The energy transfer always zaps me for a second. With plants, it's not so bad, so I just need to breathe for a minute."

"That was so cool," Ludika breathed. "Wow."

"Thanks," Callie said, extending her hand. "Someone want to help me up?"

They collectively helped her stand and continued on, giving her a tour of their small plot of land before taking her inside and showing her the three-bedroom home. Afterward, they had a lovely dinner of Slayer blood and the food Wren prepared, Callie happily chatting along with his sisters as they got to know each other.

Finally, the night wound down, and they prepared to head home.

"Thank you so much for your lovely hospitality, Wren," Callie said, giving his mother a tight hug. "I can't wait to come over again soon. We'll need to make sure that plant keeps thriving."

"Thank you, dear," Wren said, locking eyes with Brecken over her shoulder and mouthing, "*I love her!*"

Thrilled at his mother's acceptance of the woman whom he was enamored with, Brecken gave her a hug, said goodbye to his sisters, and they set out across the field toward his home. After trailing through the brush that separated the two properties, they headed up the porch stairs. Callie pointed to her left and grinned.

"Right there."

"Right there what?"

"That's where we're going to put a swing. It will be a nice place to relax and make out."

"I can get down with that," he said, unlocking the door and gesturing her inside.

"And if things work out and we decide I should move in, we could always add on some extra rooms."

"If *we* decide?" he asked, arching a brow as she sauntered toward the bed.

"*Mm-hmm.*" Kicking off her sandals, she spread across the comforter, giving him a sultry look. "I'll pay you in sexy times for any renovations that are needed, soldier." Lifting her hand, she hooked her fingers, and Brecken toed off his shoes before rushing the bed.

Their laughter mingled as they tore away their clothes before Brecken set about kissing every inch of her silken skin. After he'd tasted every crevice of her gorgeous body, he crawled over her, overcome by her beauty as her curls spread across his pillow.

"*Brecken,*" she whispered, opening herself to him as he slowly nudged his cock inside her body. "God, I missed this."

"I missed you too, hon," he said, working his hips as he undulated inside her taut channel. "I hated washing the sheets because I missed your scent."

"Aw," she said, wrapping her leg around his waist, drawing him deeper. "I think I'm supposed to make a sexy joke about being dirty, but—" Breaking off, she gasped when he began jutting against the spot that drove her wild. "Oh, yes...no jokes now...oh, *god...*"

Breaking into joyful laughter, he surged inside her, acknowledging that she was the one. Never had he craved someone's smile...or presence...or *love* as much as he craved Callie's. In that moment, he knew he would never love another. Vowing to figure out how to make her happy, he pressed his lips to hers.

"Callie-lily," he breathed, reveling in her shiver at his sappy nickname. "I want to give you the world, honey..."

Tightening around him, she undulated her hips against his. "I only need you," she whispered, clutching him as they approached their peak. He took them both high before the inevitable crash, their bodies exploding in flames of pleasure before they collapsed against each other, sweaty and replete.

Afterward, he stared down at her flushed face and half-lidded eyes, gently running a finger over the soft skin between her breasts.

"Write me another love letter," she murmured, her lips forming a shy grin.

Glancing at his desk, he pondered. "I think the two pens I have are both out of ink."

Snickering, she shook her head on the pillow. "You're a terrible liar. Write me one here, on the fly. But just say it out loud instead of writing it down. Come on. You can do it, soldier."

Playfully rolling his eyes, Brecken admitted he was officially a lovesick sap. Denying her request was as impossible as denying himself oxygen. Sighing, he continued the lazy strokes across her skin as he began to speak, softly and tenderly.

"My beautiful Callie-lily."

"Good start," she said, adorable as she bit her lip.

Gazing down at her, he decided there was no point in holding back. Releasing every reservation and doubt, he gave her everything left to give.

"I have no idea why a gorgeous, brilliant princess ever looked my way, but when you did, my life changed for the better. Somehow, you took my impassive heart and made it beat in ways I never imagined. Many will probably say I don't deserve you, and I sometimes worry they might be right. But I'm a determined man, and I know that even if I can't give you riches, I can give you love and support and amazing orgasms."

He waggled his eyebrows as she giggled against the pillow.

"Small-minded people will always judge and fear what they don't understand. I'm sorry you had to deal with that in the years before I knew you. The fact you still thrived and developed the generous spirit you have today only proves your resilience. Those same people somehow made you feel that you didn't belong...that you were unlovable. But my sweet Callie-lily, I assure you that isn't true. There are so many out there who love you exactly for who you are, and we are all awed by you."

Tears welled in her eyes as he continued, lifting his hand to swipe away the errant drop that slid down her cheek. "You're not unlovable, Callie," he whispered, gazing deep into her eyes. "Because I love you."

A sob exited her throat, and he encircled her with his arms, aching to hold her. "Shhh..." he soothed against her temple. "It's okay, hon."

"Brecken..."

"I know, sweetheart," he murmured, kissing her hair.

As her sobs abated, he slid against her, repositioning their bodies so they lay on their sides. Gazing into each other as their cheeks rested on the pillow, their legs entwined as their lids grew heavy. Eventually, she fell asleep, her long, dark lashes stark against her pale cheeks. Brecken stroked her hair, inhaling the aroma of her skin as sleep tugged him closer to its wake. When they woke in the morning, they made love once more before they rose.

"I'm going to tell my parents about us," she said, slipping on her sandals.

"You don't sound thrilled," he murmured, as he laced his boots.

"I just..." Sighing, she shook her head. "It's going to be a lot to hit them with after the shit show with Zadicus. I wonder if they'll question if I'm moving too fast."

Standing, he approached her, placing supportive hands on her shoulders. "If you want to wait, that's fine, honey."

She trailed her fingers over his jaw. "I want to tell them before the final battle. Of course, I'm terrified something will happen to you...or Jack, or my uncles, or anyone I love for that matter. But I know you all are trained and ready, and I have faith you'll prevail." She absently stared at his shoulder, contemplating. "I just need to figure out the right time to discuss our relationship with my parents. Once I do, and the final battle is over and we've defeated Bakari, I'll have you over to formally meet them."

"I'd like that," he said, tucking a curl behind her ear. "Should I start preparing for your dad's interrogation now?"

"Oh, definitely, buddy," she said, chuckling.

"Honestly, it's worth it if it ensures I get to keep kissing you."

Expelling a long breath, she said softly, "My hero."

After a sizzling goodbye kiss, Brecken watched her drive away and prepared for the day ahead. It was only as he walked across the long meadow to the sparring field that he realized she hadn't repeated his words of love. Frowning at the recognition, Brecken forged ahead, telling himself not to create an issue that didn't exist. Callie had melted in his arms when he'd loved her and cried when he spoke the words. That in itself was all he needed.

Throwing himself into his work, he prepared himself for the battle ahead, pretending he didn't notice the seed of doubt that lingered deep inside from the unspoken words he longed to hear.

∞

Callie entered her home, still glowing from her night with Brecken. After hanging up her jacket in the foyer, she turned and gasped, spotting her father in the far corner, arms crossed over his chest.

"How was your night with Jack? Did you enjoy the street fair?" Darkrip asked, his tone laced with an angry annoyance that caused her to bristle.

"It was fine," she said, lifting her chin. "I'm going to make some breakfast. Want some?" She began to breeze by him, but he stepped into her path, ire flashing in his olive green eyes, causing her to bristle. "What the hell, Dad?"

"Is this what we do now, Callie? Lie to each other? I thought your mother and I taught you better than that."

The wheels in Callie's mind began to churn as she realized he knew about her relationship with Brecken. How much did he know? *How* did he know? Eyes narrowing, she began to feel her own anger well deep inside.

"Did you read my thoughts?" she whispered.

"Of course not," he snapped.

Lowering her gaze, she mulled before emitting a soft cry. Staring deep into his eyes, she was overcome by yet another sense of betrayal. Hell, she should've been used to it at this point, after so many instances in the recent past, but betrayal by her father, whom she loved deeply, was almost too much to bear.

"You read Brecken's thoughts when we returned from the human world. Dad! I can't believe you!" She jutted her finger in his face.

Grabbing it, he furiously shook her hand. "I have every right to protect you, Callie! After everything that's happened, I'm extremely disappointed you would sneak around in secret with someone I barely know. It's dangerous and detracts from our mission to defeat Bakari."

"*You're* disappointed?" she exclaimed, yanking her finger from his grasp. "You read someone else's thoughts. Someone I care about! That's an extreme violation of his privacy."

"He should never have touched you," Darkrip muttered, crossing his arms.

"Well, I didn't give him a choice." Resting her hand on her hips, she shrugged. "I went to his house the night of my bonding ceremony and tore my clothes off until we had sex. There, you want the truth? There's the truth."

"Spare me the details," he muttered. "I can't believe you would be so reckless. People are bending over backward to protect you from your supposed role in this prophecy. Do you understand? What if Brecken is also a spy? You should've been more careful."

"Brecken loves me and would never betray my trust the way you have!" Furious tears burned her eyes before she began stomping toward her bedroom. Once there, she located her duffle bag and began stuffing clothes inside.

"What are you doing?" Darkrip asked from the doorway.

"I'm going to stay with Evie until the final battle is over. She's the only one who seems to honor promises in this family, and she supports the idea of us fighting alongside you in the final battle."

"We don't want you, Creigen or Rinada harmed, Callie," Darkrip said, slowly approaching her. "That's why the council voted to not have you fight with us."

"Well, the council can stuff it," she said, zipping her bag. "And you can stuff it too." Tossing the bag over her shoulder, she straightened, heart pounding from their terrible argument. "I should've moved out a long time ago. I love you and Mom, and it was always comfortable for me here. Safe, even. But you've ruined that by reading the mind of someone I cherish, Dad. I never thought you'd do that." Willing the tears away, she began to stride from the room.

"You kept a relationship with a man I don't know from me, putting yourself in danger," he said, grasping her arm. "That is *not* okay, Callie."

Shaking her head, she tried not to drown in the pain caused by someone she thought would never betray her. "I haven't needed your permission for a long time, Dad. I let you and Mom tether me to you because I love you, and honestly, I've had a pretty lonely life. You two were my rocks, and now you've broken that. Don't you see?" Disengaging, she gave him one last sorrowful glare. "Don't contact me. I need some time. I'll be at Evie's, and I'll be safe. Goodbye."

Pivoting, she strode through the hallway, head held high, and back into the bright sun. She trekked down the sidewalk, walking several blocks to the governor's mansion. When she reached it, she hiked up the stairs and pounded on the door.

The house manager urged her inside, and she trailed to Evie's office, finding her sitting behind her desk. Callie knocked on her open door, and Evie glanced up, smiling before her expression turned inquisitive. Rising, she slowly walked toward Callie as she struggled to keep it together.

"Well, shit," Evie said, approaching. "What did my bonehead brother do this time?"

Laughing, Callie swiped at her nose. "You're not reading my thoughts are you? Because I just had a screaming match with Dad about that very issue."

"No," she said, eyes narrowed. "I've been around long enough to know there's tension between you two, and he's been extra grumpy lately."

"He broke his promise, Evie, and I'm just so fucking pissed."

Sighing, Evie drew her into a comforting embrace. "That sucks, but I'm sure he had a good reason. He loves you, Callie."

"He didn't read my thoughts. He read Brecken's." Drawing back, she stared at Evie with wet eyes. "I'm with him, Evie. I...I'm crazy about him. It happened so fast, and I didn't want to tell my parents because I knew they would hover and question everything. Dad especially," she muttered.

"Oh, my," she said, smoothing Callie's hair. "That is big news. Well, you can stay here until the dust settles. Ken is rarely home since he's preparing for the final battle, and Rin would love to have you. You can take some time to gather your thoughts and get some much needed space from your dad. Come on. You can put your bag in the guest bedroom."

Evie led her through the hallway, and they began trekking up the expansive staircase.

"So," Evie said, grasping Callie's hand, "you finally boned someone. I don't know Brecken well, but he's very handsome." Grinning, she asked, "Did he take care of you? It was time for you to get some nookie in my opinion."

Breathing a laugh, she grinned at her aunt. "He wrote me love letters, Evie. Beautiful, heartfelt love letters. And he definitely takes care of me. He's...amazing," she finished with a sigh.

"Ah, young love," she teased, rolling her eyes. "I can't wait to hear more about it. I've got some paperwork to finish, and then we'll have lunch together. I'll ask Rinada to join us too—if you're okay with her knowing."

Entering the guest bedroom, Callie placed her bag on the bed. "I guess everyone's going to know at this point, so why not? If this relationship doesn't work out and ends in public tragedy, I'm going to throw in the towel on love, Evie."

"Well, then, we'll just have to make sure it thrives," she said with a wink. "Make yourself at home, kid. See ya at lunch." Closing the door behind her, she headed back downstairs.

Callie fell to the bed, grabbing the pillow, determined to have a good cry before letting the angst of the morning go. She hated fighting with her father, but it would probably lead to better boundaries between them, and that was definitely a positive. And this was the push she needed to announce her relationship with Brecken to the world.

After last night, there was no doubt he was the man she wanted to build a future with. When he'd looked at her with those gorgeous bronze eyes and spoken such reverent words, she'd melted into a pile of mush. And when he'd told her he loved her...

Sighing, Callie clutched the pillow, remembering the sweet moment. She hadn't said the words back for two reasons. One, she'd been a sniveling mess, almost unable to control her emotional reaction at the magnificent show of affection. But more importantly, she wanted to wait to tell Brecken she loved him until after she'd told her parents about their relationship. She didn't want to utter the words in a world where her two favorite people hadn't spent time with Brecken or given their approval.

She knew they would, of course, since he was amazing, but it hadn't felt right to speak the words until everything was out in the open. Callie felt she owed that to her parents after the disaster with Zadicus.

Of course, now, she wished she'd just said them back to Brecken since her father was a complete jerk who'd read her lover's thoughts. Frustrated at his betrayal, Callie settled into the bed, digesting the events of the morning, wishing the confrontation with Darkrip had gone differently.

Knowing she couldn't change the past, she decided she would stay with Evie until after the final battle. Once that was complete and they'd hopefully defeated Bakari, she would speak with Brecken about moving in with him. Biting her lip, Callie hoped he would be open to cohabitation. After all, he *had* said he loved her, so this was the next natural step, right?

Praying things would work out, Callie clutched onto her remaining positivity and her hope of a happy future once the final battle was over.

Chapter 26

Callie settled into Evie's home, allowing the hurt and anger at her father to slowly abate. Arderin called her to check in, and Callie relished her support.

"Your dad should've never read Brecken's thoughts, sweetie," Arderin said, "and I understand why you're upset. But I'm also really hurt you didn't tell me. I would've really liked to hear about Brecken and his courtship of you. I like him very much."

"I'm sorry, Mom," she said, picking at a wayward string on the comforter in Evie's guest bedroom. "I think I was scared it happened so fast, and I thought you all might think I was rushing into a rebound or something."

"Well, we might have, but I would've listened with an open mind. I can't speak for your father. His hang-ups about your dating life are as annoying to me as they are to you."

Laughing, she snuggled into the soft mattress. "I feel bad we argued. I love you guys so much, Mom. I'm sorry I kept my relationship with Brecken secret. I just wanted something that was mine after what happened with Zadicus."

"I understand. We'll talk after the final battle. Your dad is a wreck. He feels terrible, although he probably won't admit it."

"Good. He should. I can't believe he violated my trust that way, or Brecken's."

"You're right. As upset as you are, I hope you'll consider coming home before the final battle. I don't like the idea of your dad walking onto that battlefield while there are unspoken things between you."

Sighing, Callie pondered. "Okay. I probably will. You're very wise, Mom. Thank you for being my stable parent."

Her chuckle drifted over the phone. "Let's not tell your father that. He would probably die of exertion from the resulting eye roll."

Callie giggled. "Seriously. I love you, Mom."

"Love you too, sweetie. Text me when you decide to come home."

Callie digested the conversation, admitting she didn't want her father to enter the final battle when things weren't settled between them. Deciding she would indeed return home the next evening, she settled in for bed and texted Brecken.

Callie: I wish I could see you before the battle.

Brecken: I know, hon. I'm consumed by the training. It will be worth it once we win, but I miss you.

Callie: Miss you too. I think I'm going to go back home tomorrow night.

Brecken: Good. You need to make up with your dad before the battle. Also, I'm afraid he wants to crush my testicles. How much does he hate me?

Laughing, her thumbs darted over the keyboard.

Callie: He's going to love you once I have the chance to properly introduce you to him. I promise. Stay safe. I can't lose you, Brecken.

Brecken: I will. I have so much to fight for—the most important thing being you, honey. I want you to be free from the prophecy for good. I promise, I'll do my best to secure peace.

Callie typed back the two words that represented her strong, loving soldier.

Callie: My hero.

The next morning, Callie awoke to a call from the animal shelter at Naria. One of the puppies that was set to be adopted was sick, and the owner wondered if she could heal it. It was a welcome distraction from the drama in her life, and she immediately agreed to help. After dressing in comfortable jeans, a tank top and sandals, she stopped by the kitchen to grab an apple before heading out.

"Morning, guys," she said to Evie and Rinada, who were sitting at the large kitchen island of the Takelia governor's mansion eating breakfast. "I'm heading to Naria to heal a puppy. Do you mind if I take one of the four-wheelers?"

"No problem," Evie said, spreading butter over a muffin. "You'll have the radio with you, right? Your father and I are going to be perfecting the forcefield all day, which could interfere with any telekinetic messages you try to send us."

"I'll have the radio by my side," Callie confirmed. "Let me know how Dad's disposition is today. I think I'm going to head back home tonight."

"I think he's still stewing, but who knows with my brother?" she asked, taking a bite of the muffin. "It's kind of entertaining."

"For you, maybe," Callie muttered. "I hate that this happened right before the battle where I'm supposed to destroy the world. Yay," she finished weakly, lifting her hands and shaking them in a mock cheer.

"There's no way that will happen, Callie," Rinada said with a reassuring smile.

"Thanks," Callie said with a wink. "I hope you're right." Selecting an apple, Callie slung her bag over her shoulder. "Thanks for the apple and for letting me borrow the four-wheeler. See you guys later."

"I'll walk with you to the garage," Rinada said, rising and falling into step beside her as they trailed down the hallway.

"Creigen and I spoke yesterday, and I wanted to update you," Rinada said. "We want to help with the battle and don't want to be sidelined."

They stepped into the garage, halting on the concrete as Callie faced her. "I'm willing to help too. If Evie and Dad can't generate a forcefield strong enough to contain Bakari, the chances of victory are diminished."

"Agreed," Rinada said with a nod. "The fact Bakari can transport the entire Deamon army means his power has grown exponentially. Creigen and I have decided to meet in the forest adjacent to the field where the battle will take place before sunrise. I thought you might like to join us."

"I would," Callie said, feeling her eyebrows draw together. "We'll be violating the council's directive."

"Honestly, I don't give a damn. I'm so tired of this conflict, and it's got to end. Your brother feels the same, and Tordor does as well."

"You spoke to Tordor too?"

"Yes." She gnawed her lip. "Although he doesn't possess our powers, he agrees with our decision to defy the council's orders. He thinks it's a good idea to be present in case Latimus or my dad order us off the field. Tordor's words carry weight in the kingdom, and he's assured me he will support our efforts to join our powers with Mom and Darkrip's. As the royal heir, Latimus and Dad won't openly defy his orders, and his diplomatic skills will come in handy if he needs to explain the benefits of us being there."

"Okay," Callie said, contemplating the risks and benefits. "We'll have to make sure to keep him safe and make sure your mom and my dad don't read our thoughts."

"I don't think they would considering the pact we've all made to respect each other's privacy, but we need to remain alert."

Callie gave her a sardonic look. "My dad isn't really the best example of following that pact right now."

"True," Rinada said, arching a brow. "But Mom says he feels terrible about what happened between you two. Anyway, I agree with you about protecting Tordor. I mean, what are cousins for if not to use their powers from their evil grandfather to safeguard each other?"

Grinning, Callie cupped her arm. "It's not easy, is it? I don't want to complain, because we have so much, but it just fucking sucks to be so different sometimes."

"It does," Rinada said, shrugging. "And in my case, not only am I different, but I'm the daughter of the most beautiful woman in the kingdom. It's a lot to live up to."

Callie's gaze roved over Rinada's long, dark reddish-brown hair, the color more muted than Evie's, and her eyes, which were a deep shade of brown with dark green flecks. Tiny freckles covered her nose and cheeks, and Callie thought her exceptionally pretty.

"And now you're almost nineteen, which is a scary time in one's life. I remember not knowing what I wanted to do. Eventually, I settled on healing animals, and it's so rewarding, but it's hard to find a purpose since we don't really need jobs in the kingdom."

"Right?" Rinada said, lifting her hands. "I don't want to complain about the fact we're princesses with royal parents since that would be super-lame. But I have no idea what I'm supposed to do with my life now that I'm done with school. After I graduated earlier this year, I told my parents I needed some time to figure it out."

"That's perfectly understandable."

Excitement flashed in Rinada's eyes. "I know this sounds strange, but I find myself wondering what it would be like to go to college in the human world. Uncle Heden found a way to stream the Science and History Channels to the TV in my bedroom years ago, and I'm so enamored with the documentaries there. I'd love to train in archeology or history even though it's the history of a different species. Is that weird?"

"Nope," Callie said with a smile. "It's actually hella cool. And you could train there and eventually bring your knowledge back to our world too. I mean, we have some insane history here that needs scientific evaluation. The Elven scrolls are a great place to start."

"Definitely. After the battle, I'm going to talk to my parents and contemplate it more. I've never lived in the human world though. Do you think I'd do okay there?"

"It's a different place, for sure, but you'd do great. You're a bit more soft-spoken than your awesome older cousin,"—Callie pointed at herself as Rinada snickered—"but I know you'd charm anyone you meet. And Rin?"

"Yeah?"

"You're really pretty, inside and out. Take it from someone with a drop-dead gorgeous mother: Comparisons will get you nowhere. Beauty is in the eye of the beholder, and when it's time, you'll find someone who adores you. I have no doubt."

"Like you found Brecken?"

"Yes," Callie said, breaking into a wide grin. "It's so strange to find someone who was there all along but who you didn't really *see*. I'm thankful for Zadicus, if only because he was the catalyst for me and Brecken."

"That's amazing. I'm so happy for you, Callie."

Arching a brow, she said, "Well, I've got a lot of shit to figure out before we get to happily ever after, but I'm determined to get there." Lifting her phone, she checked the time. "Okay, I'm a go for our plan. I'll meet you guys before the battle in the surrounding woods. Thanks for running point."

"Sure. It's time to set the realm free. I'm ready."

"Me too."

After a warm embrace, Callie located the four-wheeler she would drive to Naria and headed off toward the compound under the morning sun. Deciding to compartmentalize, she pushed away thoughts of the impending discussion with her father until after she healed the puppy. Healing the animal would bring her peace, and afterward, she could sit down and prepare what she wanted to say before heading home. Concentrating on the task at hand, she never realized she was being observed as she drove through the open fields of the kingdom.

~

Dr. Tyson sat in the lab he'd built in the squalid Deamon cave. He'd designed it with care, and Bakari had supplied him with labor and materials to create the various chemical formulas he'd concocted over the years. Bakari had asked him to create one more batch of the super-strength formula to inject into his Deamon soldiers. It wouldn't make them as formidable as Baal, since he'd been injected with an experimental formula filled with poisonous herbs that had been perfected over several years.

After spinning the various vials in a centrifuge, he needed some fresh air and decided to head outside while the concoction congealed. Stepping through the mouth of the cave, he walked around, inhaling the warm air as he contemplated the final battle. He'd been useful to Bakari thus far, which had many advantages. It kept him alive and off the radar of the Elven council that existed undetected in the human world. Bakari had assumed Dr. Tyson was half-Slayer, half-Vampyre when they first met, but he suspected his leader now realized he was actually an Elven-Vampyre hybrid. His kind was hunted by the council, and Dr. Tyson relished the protection he received as part of Bakari's team.

But what would happen after the war was over? Bakari was no fan of hybrids no matter their makeup. Would he cast Dr. Tyson out, or worse, murder him once his mission was complete? And what if Bakari lost? Surely, the royal family wouldn't accept the scientist who'd aligned with their enemy into the realm. He would be banished back to the human world with no protection whatsoever, increasing his chances of discovery by the Elven council. Concerned for his well-being in either scenario, he pondered his future as he paced.

"You are right to fear for your safety, Quaygon," a voice called to his left. "Allegiance to Bakari no longer serves you."

Facing her, he shrugged. "I believe you are correct, Tatiana, but I have nowhere else to go."

"The threat from the Elven council will need to be addressed after Bakari and Callie fulfill the prophecy. That will be my next endeavor once I get some much needed rest." Lifting her arms, she smiled. "Even one such as I need a small respite now and then."

Studying her, he placed his hands in his pockets as the questions swirled in his mind. Eventually, he asked, "You are a human-Elven hybrid, yes?"

Dark eyebrows drew together as she gazed into the distance. Nodding, she shifted her amber eyes to his, the orbs seeming to glow in the midday sun. "Humans and immortals were never meant to procreate. This is why the Elven council wants us eradicated. Some of us are more powerful than others, and I've tried to protect the ones who are vulnerable."

"That's a big job for one woman, depending on how many hybrids there are scattered across the human world."

"It's exhausting," she said, flashing a grin, "but worth it. I care deeply for all creatures, human or immortal."

"And yet you've supplied me with enough toxins to kill many Slayers over the past two decades."

"Yes," she sighed, kicking the ground with the toe of her shoe. "It was imperative I push Bakari toward the prophecy so Callie could align with him. It is finally time, and I am glad it is almost over."

"How will the fulfillment of the prophecy help immortals or hybrids living in the human world?" he asked, lifting his hands. "I don't understand."

"You will after the prophecy is fulfilled. My advice is to return to the human world before the battle begins. Otherwise, you might perish."

Swallowing thickly, he contemplated that option. "I lived in the human world for centuries, passing as a physician and chemist. I worry for my safety now that I have aligned with Bakari as I'm sure it put me on the council's radar. They most likely want to eradicate Vampyre-Elven hybrids as much as human-Elven hybrids."

"That is correct," she confirmed. "The purebred Elves believe in an angry god who punished them for wanting more than he provided. When he washed away their world, the few Elves who remained vowed to live a simple life in the human world, secluded so they could rebuild in peace. Eventually, some of the inhabitants grew restless with that life and wanted to explore the new world they inhabited. These original dissenters are our ancestors."

"My mother told me the story many centuries ago, before she died," he said softly. "My father was an Elf who believed there was value in surveilling the immortal world to see if there was a possibility of building a new Elven colony in a place undetectable by Vampyres, Slayers or Deamons. He was captured by a Vampyre soldier and imprisoned because the Vampyre thought him a Slayer."

"The Vampyre would not have known he was an Elf," she said, compassion in her tone. "The immortals only became aware of the Elves' existence again once the War of the Species ended and they realized Crimeous's true heritage."

"Yes. They banked my father's blood along with the Slayers, although it held no nutrition for them. My mother was a laborer employed by the prison. She took him food and water, learning his story before they fell in love. Eventually, he fell ill and passed, but not before I was conceived. My mother fled to the human world, knowing she would be castigated if anyone knew of her hybrid child."

Tatiana's eyes narrowed. "It is possible your father had royal Elven blood. Otherwise, the chances of creating a hybrid are small."

"Mother never told me his name. She said it would jeopardize my safety."

"Then he must have been a powerful Elf indeed." Taking a step forward, she assessed him. "It is an interesting story, and one I would like to pursue. I hope you will take my advice and return to the human world before the prophecy is fulfilled."

"My mother passed centuries ago, and I have no idea where to go."

Tatiana closed her eyes, the pupils moving under her lids as she concentrated. "She is in the Passage," she said, lifting her lids. "How did she pass?"

"She was poisoned, most likely by the Elven council. They were probably after me, but she always tasted our food first since she was a Vampyre and had self-healing abilities. But there are poisons that can render those abilities inert if one has the knowledge. We know this all too well."

"I'm very sorry for your loss," she said with a tilt of her head. "I have also lost loved ones, and it is devastating."

Perking his ears, Dr. Tyson noted the sound in the distance. "Bakari will be returning with his troops soon, and I must head inside. Thank you, Tatiana. I will consider your words."

"You are welcome, Quaygon," she said with a gentle smile. "I hope we see each other again after the prophecy is fulfilled. Goodbye."

Closing her eyes, she dematerialized. Processing her words, Dr. Tyson headed back into the cave to finish the last formulas he would ever create for Bakari.

Chapter 27

After healing the puppy, Callie felt too restless to head straight back to Takelia. There was a small creek that ran on the outskirts of Naria, and she drove there, hoping the fresh air and gurgling water would bring her some peace as she contemplated her future. Sitting on the damp ground, she drew her knees to her chest, surrounding them with her arms as she stared at the water that sluiced over the rocks in the creek bed.

Something rustled to her right, and her heart lurched in her chest when Bakari appeared. Pushing from the ground, she eyed the four-wheeler, calculating how long it would take to sprint and grab the walkie-talkie to radio Latimus.

"There's no need to panic, Callie," he said in his deep voice. "I only want to talk. You're too important for me to harm. I'm sure you've realized that by now."

"Because I'm going to align with you and fulfill the prophecy? I don't think so." Crossing her arms, she stood firm, hoping he couldn't read how terrified she was.

Holding up his hands, he said, "I'll admit I made a lot of mistakes along the way. Once Miranda and Kenden discovered the Elven scrolls, everything suddenly made sense. I knew I'd have to find a way to secure your alliance and fulfill the prophecy once you grew into your power."

"Well, that didn't really work out for you, did it? Zadicus did a good job of seducing me, I'll give him that, but I always knew in my gut it was wrong. It was only a matter of time until I discovered his deception."

"I agree," he said, taking a step closer.

Callie bristled. "Don't come any closer, or I'm going to use some of my powers you seem so vested in."

Dropping his hand, he studied her. "I was wrong to use Zadicus as a means to gain your alliance. I realize that now. I should've just approached you directly, and this is why I am here now."

"And what makes you think I would've even contemplate listening to you?"

His lips twitched. "You're listening now, my dear. I think a part of you has always been curious about the true essence of your grandfather's blood."

"What essence?"

"The evil, Callie. Your feigned indifference doesn't fool me. I understand everything you went through as a child in this world, feeling lost and outcast. Don't tell me you never had the urge to embrace your evil and destroy those who maligned you."

"Never," she said, lifting her chin. "My parents taught me forgiveness and acceptance even for those who didn't accept me."

"Your parents taught you to deny your true heritage. Your father embraced his evil for the first two centuries of his life. He won't admit it to you, but it brought him great satisfaction."

"My father has spoken to me extensively about his past. He regrets his transgressions and is committed to embracing his Slayer heritage—to embracing his goodness. You could learn something from his transformation. I'm extremely proud of him."

"Your father knows the power of the evil in your blood because he listened to its call for centuries." Bakari took another step forward, and Callie lifted her hand, palm facing him as she prepared to freeze him in place. "Don't be scared," he said, inching closer. "I only want to show you the truth."

Quick as lightning, Bakari swung his arm, revealing a vial in his hand. Thrusting it into her arm, he emptied the contents as she struggled to push him away.

"There, there," he said, removing the needle and backing away. Placing the empty vial in his pocket, he waited as shock coursed through her body. Furious, she lifted her hand and began to choke him with her mind.

"Yes!" he gasped, clutching his throat, although his expression was delighted. "Do you feel the serum beginning to take hold? It will exacerbate the evil in your blood. Embrace it, Callie. It will make you so much more than what you are."

Callie wanted to tell him that she was already enough—that his urging would accomplish nothing. But there, by the babbling creek, something shifted inside as the serum coursed through her veins. Closing her eyes, she tried to ward off the effects, but it was too late. Lifting her lids, she tightened her invisible hold on Bakari's throat.

"You can kill me now, or you can achieve true power," he rasped, falling to his knees on the ground. "Join with me during the final battle. It is time to fulfill your destiny, Calinda."

Dark, sticky pulses jolted into every cell of her body as the potion exacerbated her grandfather's evil blood. In a few scant moments, Callie understood her father's concerns about embracing Crimeous's malevolence. It was sickening on one level, and her stomach rolled with nausea. But on another level, it was...*magnificent*.

Releasing her hold on Bakari, Callie's head tilted back, and she closed her eyes, embracing the all-encompassing feelings of supremacy and maliciousness. With this amount of power, there was nothing she couldn't accomplish. No one would cast her out or disparage her. If they did, she could disintegrate them with a snap of her fingers.

"Your parents have held you back your entire life, Callie," Bakari said, rising. "Let the evil flow. There are so many possibilities you've never even considered. You could inject your brother and Rinada with the serum, and we could all rule with dominion over the kingdom. Miranda and Sathan are false rulers who disparage Etherya. Align with me, and we will rebuild the kingdom."

Quaking with the splendor of her newfound strength, she shook her head, confusion twining in her gut. Although the evil was overwhelming due to the serum's effects, her mother's goodness and father's Slayer heritage still beckoned deep within. Callie felt the tug, and it created a dichotomy that made her want to retch.

"I don't want these powers," she cried, opening her hands and trying to expel them from her body. "I'm not evil. I want to choose the light."

"Evil is in the eye of the beholder, Calinda," Bakari said, inching forward.

"No! Don't come any closer. I can't control it."

"Good. Loss of control is a part of chaos. Align with me, Callie." He extended his hand.

"No!"

"You have felt the malevolence of your blood now. There is no turning back. Join me, and we will rule Etherya's realm and restore order."

Callie had never been able to transport like her father and Evie. Although she'd inherited the ability to read thoughts and manipulate objects with her mind, dematerialization wasn't something any of Crimeous's grandchildren had inherited. And yet, as she felt the firm ground below her feet, she knew the heightened effects of her grandfather's blood would allow her greater authority. Would she possibly be able to transport away from Bakari?

Gritting her teeth, Callie reached deep inside, combining all her fear, knowledge and confusion, and imagined transporting to the woods beside the River Thayne at Astaria. Emitting a loud cry, she fisted her hands and visualized materializing there.

"You can't escape your destiny, Callie!"

Bakari's words trailed off as she flew through time and space before crashing on a spot of soft ground. Landing with a thud, she gripped the grass, lifting her head to survey her surroundings. The banks of the River Thayne sat in the distance, surrounded by tall trees and green grass. Glancing toward the far riverbank, Callie thanked the goddess she'd transported to one of the forts she knew well. It offered her a natural shelter so she could try and figure out how to combat the serum.

Unable to gain full control of her body with the enhanced malevolence swimming through her veins, she crawled toward the fort and shuffled inside, thankful for the safe space. It offered latent comfort in a world that had suddenly turned chaotic. Curling into a ball, she lay on the soft ground, willing the serum from her body...and hoping with all her might it hadn't inexorably changed her into the person so many across the kingdom feared she would ultimately become.

Brecken spent the day with the troops, performing a multitude of drills to ensure they were ready for the impending battle. Callie was ever-present in his thoughts, but he tucked them away so he could focus on the task at hand.

By the time the sun set, Brecken lifted his phone from his belt, expecting to see a text from Callie, perhaps telling him she'd returned home to speak with her father. Checking their text chain, he frowned when he realized she hadn't texted him since arriving at Naria to heal the puppy.

A small tendril of worry curled deep within since it wasn't like her to go several hours without texting him. After changing from his training gear, Brecken stepped on his porch, inhaling the warm air as he dialed her number. Lifting the phone to his ear, he scowled when it went straight to voicemail.

"Hey, Callie-lily. Just wondering if you're okay. I haven't heard from you all day. Please shoot me a text and let me know you're all right. Thanks, hon."

Clicking off the phone, Brecken stared over the horizon, unable to shake the feeling something was wrong. After an hour with no return text, he understood what he had to do. Throwing on his light jacket, he locked up the house and hightailed it to the train platform.

Entering the high-speed train car that would take him to Takelia, he was filled with a sense of foreboding. Showing up on Darkrip's doorstep wasn't his style, especially since the man knew he'd been sleeping with his daughter. But he had the nagging feeling Callie was in trouble, and her safety was more important than any wrath he would incur from her father. Arriving at Takelia, he all but jogged to her parents' home, concern growing with each moment.

When he arrived, he knocked on the door, straightening when a surprised Arderin opened it.

"Well, hello, Brecken. Nice to see you. I...uh...Callie's not here."

Brecken frowned. "I'm sorry to show up unannounced, ma'am. She hasn't texted me since this morning, and that's not like her."

Arderin's eyebrows drew together. "She's staying with her Aunt Evie. I assumed she was there."

"I'd feel better if we could confirm, ma'am."

"Right," she said, opening the door wider. "Come in. Let me grab my phone and call Evie."

She led him into the sitting room, locating her phone and selecting the speaker option. "Evie? Callie is with you, right?"

"Nope. She never came home after healing the puppy at Naria today. Figured she headed back to your place to finally talk to Darkrip."

Terror shot down Brecken's spine as fear entered Arderin's expression. "She's not here, Evie. Brecken just showed up worried because she hasn't texted him all day."

Silence stretched over the line. "Do you think Bakari got to her?"

Darkrip chose that moment to stride into the room. Focusing on Brecken, he asked, "What the hell is he doing here?"

"Darkrip just walked in. I'll call you back, Evie."

"Callie hasn't texted me all day, sir," Brecken said, lifting his hands. "I'm worried she's in danger. No one has heard from her since she healed the puppy at Naria this morning."

Darkrip scowled. "Did you try to text her?"

"I left her a voicemail and sent several texts," he said with a nod. "She's never gone radio-silent like this before."

Huffing a breath, Darkrip closed his eyes. "Let me try to locate her." His eyelids fluttered as he concentrated. Finally, he lifted his lids and shook his head. "I can't see anything. Something is blocking my powers."

"Darkrip," Arderin called, shaking her head. "What if Bakari has her? What if he hurt her? Oh, god." Lowering her head, she palmed her face and began to cry.

"Crying won't solve anything, sweetheart," Darkrip said, approaching her and pulling her into an embrace. "Shh... Let me think."

"What's going on in here?" Creigen asked, strolling into the room. "Mom? Why are you crying."

"Your sister is missing," Brecken said, observing his shocked expression. "We fear Bakari might have her."

"Well, let's go find her," he said, lifting his hands. "Dad? I'll go with you. Let's figure this out. We can look for clues at Naria and check her favorite spots, just in case she's just taking some time to think."

"We should check the forts at Astaria by the River Thayne," Brecken said. "They're a safe space for her."

"She told you that?" Darkrip asked.

"Yes, sir."

"She doesn't tell anyone about the forts," Creigen said, lifting his eyebrows. "Take it from her little brother who desperately wanted to play there with her when we were young. She always told me to get lost. Typical older sister." He lifted a sardonic brow. "I'm impressed she told you."

"So I'm assuming you know about their relationship too?" Darkrip asked, his expression acerbic.

"Rinada told me," Creigen said with a shrug. "I think it's great. Zadicus was a dick. Hopefully, you'll treat her better."

"Her happiness is my number one concern," Brecken said, pleased at his acceptance. "Callie has told me a lot of things in our short time together. I know you weren't happy about our relationship or that it formed in secret, and I'm sorry about that, sir."

"I was upset that she lied to me instead of just telling me you'd formed a bond. After what happened with Zadicus, you can understand my reservations."

"I can," Brecken said, clutching his hands over his belt. "This may not mean much to you since I'm just a common soldier from Lynia, but I love her, sir. Very much. I want to spend my life giving her everything she deserves, no matter how hard I have to work to make it happen."

Lifting her head, Arderin smiled at him through her tears. "Oh my god, that's so romantic. We just want her to be happy, Brecken, and if you're able to make her smile, that's all I really care about."

"And I don't give a damn about your heritage," Darkrip said, releasing Arderin to stalk toward one of the side tables. Yanking open the drawer, he located some flashlights. "I just care about your intentions with my daughter."

"My intention is to love her, sir. That's as honest as I can be."

Stalking over, Darkrip thrust the black object at him. Brecken eyed it before Darkrip sighed. "It's a flashlight, not a bomb," he said, shaking it until Brecken grasped it. "Unless you have X-ray vision, we'll need it to find her. I assume you want to come with us on our search?"

"Yes, sir."

"Fine," he said, rubbing his neck. "And stop calling me 'sir.' It's annoying and makes me feel like I'm a million years old."

Feeling his lips twitch, Brecken gave a nod.

"Once we find her, I want your word that you will spend some time letting me question you about your intentions."

"Darkrip!" Arderin hissed.

"I'm fine with that, sir—er, um, Ambassador. I'm happy to answer anything you want to know."

"Just call me Darkrip," he muttered before Arderin cleared her throat quite loudly. Glaring at her, he rolled his eyes. "And I'm sorry for reading your thoughts. It won't happen again."

"Thank you," Brecken said.

Darkrip's gaze held acknowledgment before he turned to speak to Arderin. "Call Evie back and ask her to help us. We can transport Creigen and Brecken around the kingdom as we look for Callie."

Lifting the phone to her ear, Arderin made the call as Brecken prepared himself for the search ahead.

Chapter 28

Brecken, Darkrip, Creigen and Evie searched the entire premises of the animal shelter at Naria, finding nothing that led them to Callie. Afterward, Darkrip and Evie transported them to the River Thayne at Astaria. Darkrip faced Brecken, and his green eyes flashed in the darkness.

"Lead the way."

Brecken understood that allowing him to lead the search was Darkrip's way of showing his acceptance. Thankful Callie's father wasn't holding a grudge, they began their trek. Trailing along the riverbank, they called Callie's name, hoping to find her near one of the forts where she sought solace.

They covered several miles as Brecken struggled to control his fear she was hurt. As they neared a clearing by a bend in the river, Brecken saw something sparkle in the beam of his flashlight. Nearing the glow, he bent down and picked up the tiny stone to examine it.

"This fort has been recently disturbed," Evie said, shining her light around the inside of the embankment through the open door. "There are flattened leaves, as if someone lay down, but no one's here."

"It's an earring," Brecken said, holding up the stone.

Inching closer, Darkrip examined it. "It's is one of the opal earrings I gave her on her eighteenth birthday."

Evie and Darkrip studied the earring, silent as the gravity of the discovery set in. Callie had been here and left her earring behind, and now she was gone.

"Damn it," Darkrip said, running his hand over his face. "She loves those earrings."

"What do you want to do?" Evie asked. "We've searched extensively along the river. Should we try a new location?"

"Give me a minute," Darkrip said, backing away and holding up his hand. Closing his eyes, the ground slightly shook, and leaves rustled on the nearby trees as he attempted to track her with his mind. "She's alive," he murmured, eyes cinched tight. "I can't locate her, but I feel her presence. Something is wrong but also...*inevitable*...if that makes any sense. I don't know how else to describe it."

Evie lifted her chin. "Perhaps she is meant to fulfill the prophecy after all. As the subject of an age-old prophecy myself, I recall the trepidation and anticipation as the battle with Father grew closer. Although we all disparage Callie's role in the prophecy, it might be unavoidable."

"She won't align with him," Brecken said, firm in his belief.

"I don't believe she will either," Darkrip said. "She's too much her mother's daughter." Sighing, he hung his head. "We've searched for hours at this point. I'm willing to continue, but I think we should regroup first." Lifting his head, he eyed Brecken. "You should come to our house. I have maps of the entire realm on my laptop, and we can comb through them to theorize possible places we can look for her. It will make our efforts more efficient."

"That's an excellent idea," Evie said. "Do you want me to come over?"

Darkrip shook his head. "Go home to Rinada and Ken, and I'll let you know when we're ready to go back out. We'll search the places we come up with through mid-morning, and then you and I can take a break to practice the forcefield. I'm still not one hundred percent confident in it."

"Okay." Cupping his shoulder, she squeezed. "We all love her, Darkrip. Have faith. Summon me when you're ready." Closing her eyes, she disappeared.

"Come on," Darkrip said, gesturing to Brecken. "I'll transport us home."

Brecken held on tight before being *whooshed* to Takelia. When they arrived in the living room, Arderin rose from the couch, her expression morose.

"Anything?" she asked, cheeks ruddy under long tear streaks.

"Nothing yet, princess," Darkrip said, opening his arms so she could rush into his embrace. "Shh..." he soothed, stroking her hair. "It's going to be okay."

Brecken placed his hand on Creigen's shoulder. "We'll find her. I won't rest until I do."

"I know," he said softly, eyes so much like Callie's filled with concern. "I just hope she's okay."

"She's one of the most resilient people I've ever met," Brecken said, his heart warming at how strong she was.

"I believe that too," he said with a soft grin. "I mean, she's my older sister, and I've always looked up to her. Even when she accused me of being annoying, which was most of the time."

Brecken breathed a laugh.

"Thanks for helping us search," he said, cupping his arm. "I'm happy she's found real love this time. Don't mess it up, okay? She deserves to be happy."

"Never. She's too important to me."

Giving him a nod, Creigen walked over to hug Arderin as Brecken reminded himself to stay calm. He had faith in Callie and wouldn't rest until they found her.

After a cat nap on Darkrip's living room couch, Brecken awoke, determined to resume the search. After looking over the maps, they decided to scour the area where the Deamon caves had been destroyed after the war against Crimeous. Evie and Darkrip believed Bakari had a stronghold there, although none had ever been found. Still, with his spells and potions created by Dr. Tyson, they knew anything was possible. Perhaps he had created a cloaking spell or some other magic to shield them from the immortal army.

They looked for hours, even nearing the Purges of Methesda at one point, but came up dry. Eventually, they decided to return home. Darkrip and Evie headed to their practice session, and Brecken returned to Lynia to join the troops.

When he arrived at the sparring field, Latimus and Garridan approached, concern in their expressions as they regarded him.

"You didn't find her," Latimus said softly.

Brecken shook his head. "Darkrip swears she's alive. That he can feel her presence, but he can't track her. We're going to look again tonight, but I'll make sure to get some rest before tomorrow's battle."

"It's possible she has been kidnapped by Bakari and he will show up with her at the battle," Latimus said.

"Yes." Feeling his throat bob, Brecken fisted his hands on his hips. "I know she won't align with Bakari to fulfill the prophecy. It's not even a possibility in my mind." He tamped down the ragged emotion flooding his chest.

"I know, son," Latimus said, cupping Brecken's shoulder. "None of us believe it. Callie is too good."

"Thank you for letting me have time off to search. I guess the entire family knows about us at this point. She wanted to wait to tell everyone after what happened with Zadicus."

"Just make her happy, Brecken. That's all that matters."

"I'll try my best, sir." Gazing across the field, he noticed Siora and several of the other soldiers glancing his way, concerned. "I'm going to go do some exercises with the troops. I need the distraction."

Latimus gave a nod, and he tracked across the meadow, ready to work off some of the heavy energy that pervaded his bones. Picking up a sword from the nearby rack on the training field, he faced Siora.

"You look like you're ready for a fight, soldier," she said, marching over to pick out her own sword.

"Don't go easy on me," Brecken said, lifting his weapon as she faced him and did the same.

"Got it," she said, a challenge in her eyes along with the empathy that resided there.

Raising his sword high, he sliced it through the air, reveling in the crash of metal upon metal when it collided with Siora's weapon.

"Is that all you've got?" she asked, pivoting and setting her stance. "Come on, fancy bodyguard. I'm ready to break a sweat."

Thankful for her gentle chiding, they sparred for several minutes before the other soldiers joined in. Eventually, the entire battalion entered the fray, preparing their bodies and minds for the imminent fight yet to come. After the sun set and they'd trained long into the night, Brecken headed home and changed before Darkrip showed up to whisk him away for another search.

Hours later, Brecken returned to his cottage, despondent they hadn't located Callie. He didn't want to sleep knowing she was out there, possibly alone and afraid. But when he dragged off his clothes and showered, he fell onto the bed, murmuring her name before he crossed over to unconsciousness.

Callie huddled in the cave by the river for hours, attempting to ward off the nausea brought about by the enhanced evil coursing through her body. When she realized the serum had taken hold and she had no ability to control it, she decided to take action. Rising from the damp ground, she exited the fort and looked to the rapidly darkening sky, wondering what the hell to do.

Massaging her arm, which felt hot to the touch, Callie pondered for what seemed like hours, although it was likely only minutes. As her hand rubbed her heated skin, she realized she wasn't as afraid as she'd been when Bakari first injected her. Now that the enhanced blood had coursed through her for hours, it felt almost...normal. Lifting her arm, she studied the skin, turning it in the shafts of moonlight from the newly risen orb.

"Is this all part of the prophecy?" she muttered, studying the pale skin of her forearm. Lifting her eyes to the sky, she stared up at the stars—the same here as they were in the human world. "Was this meant to happen all along?"

Closing her eyes, Callie concentrated her energy, clenching her jaw as she attempted to transport again. Feeling her muscles contract and expand, she was suddenly conveyed through time and space. Lifting her lids, she stared down at the Purges of Methesda. It was where her grandfather's body had been disintegrated all those years ago when Evie finally fulfilled the prophecy. Staring at the swirling lava, Callie was drawn to it and extended her hand.

"Not too close, daughter of Darkrip," a voice called beside her. "It wouldn't be prudent for you to fall in."

Turning her head, she stared wide-eyed at the goddess Etherya. She'd almost become a fairy tale at this point, rarely appearing to Vampyres or Slayers after Crimeous's death. The one exception had been her appearance to Heden, which had reminded everyone of her vast power. Facing her, Arderin was awed by her ethereal form, which floated above the ground, draped in long white robes.

"I'm honored by your presence, Etherya," she said, dropping to one knee in reverence.

"Stand, my child."

Rising, she studied the goddess's long red hair, stark as it trailed over the pristine robe. "I must be in deep if you're appearing to me."

The goddess might have smiled, although Callie wasn't sure. She gazed over the Purges before focusing on Callie, her eyes dark and beady as they bore into her.

"You are now on a journey, which I knew would happen long ago. I am sad for the destruction of my world, but the Universe is fickle. It sees things I cannot, and I have learned to live with its decisions."

Tears flooded Callie's eyes as she felt the insane urge to fall to the ground and weep. "I don't want to destroy anything. I don't believe in the prophecy."

A wispy laugh escaped her throat. "That matters naught."

Staring at the ground, Callie ran her hand through her hair, realizing her earring was missing when it didn't scratch the skin of her hand. Sadness coursed through her, exacerbated by the serum in her blood.

"Do not cry, Calinda." Her airy fingers reached over to lift Callie's chin. "If I can accept the inevitable, you must as well."

"So, it's a foregone conclusion I'll align with Bakari and destroy the realm."

"Yes," she said, dropping her hand. "But destruction does not always mean death. Tatiana and her kind know this. You have always been scared for no reason, my child. Great change can only come from great destruction. You are the catalyst for this."

"I don't want to hurt anyone." Lifting her hands, she slowly rotated them. "Bakari injected me with something that enhances my grandfather's blood. Enhances my *evil*. What if I hurt someone I love?"

"Dear child, you have never been evil. Even your father, who insisted he was evil for centuries, was never truly wicked. Valktor's blood was too prevalent in his soul, as it is in yours. You will choose the light."

"I finally have something to live for," Callie said, lifting her hands. "I'm in love with Brecken, and I didn't tell him because I was waiting to tell my parents about us." Sighing, she shook her head. "Am I just destined to be an idiot when it comes to love? Good grief, I'm terrible at it."

"You are not so bad," Etherya said, tilting her head. "You and your soldier will find your way. Love is a mysterious force, but your love with Brecken is true and earnest."

"Will it go away?" Callie rubbed her forearm, the skin still warm to the touch. "The enhancement of grandfather's blood from the serum?"

"The serum has opened something inside your cells that will never truly fade. It will diminish over time, but you need the enhancement to fulfill your destiny. You've already gained the ability to transport. Embracing your newfound power will only enhance your potency."

"And that's a good thing?"

"I believe so," she said with a tilt of her head. "If you were inherently evil, I would be more concerned, but there is no need."

"So, what do I do now? Half of me is terrified to go back to the realm with my enhanced blood. It's almost like I don't trust myself. What if I somehow can't control it and align with Bakari—?"

"I will make the decision for you, Calinda," Etherya interjected, closing the distance between them and placing the tip of her wispy finger on her forehead. "You are too close to fulfilling the prophecy to detract from the mission."

Callie tried to move, but her muscles lost the ability to function as soon as Etherya touched her.

"I have placed you in a trance, my child. Dream of the prophecy and what you must do. You will wake an hour before sunset and meet your loved ones on the battlefield. Follow your intuition, and all will be well."

A cloud of deep, curling exhaustion spread through Callie's body, and she lowered onto the soft grass that lined the hill above the Purges. Closing her eyes, she felt something cover her skin and tugged it under her chin. Forcing her lids open, she realized it was a layer of Etherya's robe, placed over her by the goddess.

"You will be safe here," Etherya whispered in her ear, her breath cold against Callie's skin. "When you wake, you will be ready to fulfill your destiny. I am with you and all my beloved children, always."

Huddling under the robe, Callie felt the goddess's presence wane. Unable to fight the spell, she yielded to the visions that formed in her mind. Visions of the battle to come and what she must do to ensure Bakari's threat was halted once and for all.

Chapter 29

Brecken awoke three hours before sunrise, ready to face the most important battle of his life. Worry for Callie loomed large in his heart, and he thought of her as he dressed in his tactical gear, wondering where she was. Sending silent thoughts of love to her, he hoped she received them and knew he was waiting for her return.

Throughout the night, his belief she would appear at the battle had solidified. Still, he was confident she would never align with Bakari and was thankful he would be on the battlefield by her side.

Approaching the darkened training field at Lynia, he met up with Latimus and several battalions of soldiers. They loaded into the large tanks and headed to Restia, where they convened with Kenden's troops. Latimus and Kenden addressed the soldiers as the sky against the horizon turned from black to pale gray. After a raucous cheer from the immortal troops, they were ready to seize the day and defeat Bakari.

Latimus, Jack and their Lynian battalions would line up on the south side of the field, backed by the ether, giving them a natural fortress to launch their attack. Kenden's soldiers would wait in the nearby forest and attack from the flank once the battle had initiated. Latimus and Kenden felt this would generate an element of surprise that would allow them to employ the TECs on many unwitting Deamon soldiers, lessening the amount of Deamons Evie and Darkrip would have to destroy along with Bakari when joining their powers.

Armed with their plan, the troops departed Restia. When they arrived at the open battlefield, Brecken noticed the realm's physicians, Sadie and Nolan, had already set up medical triage tents on the east side of the meadow.

"Come over with me to check on the infirmary tents," Jack said, waving his hand at Brecken. Jumping out of the army vehicle, they strode to greet them.

"Hi, Jack," Sadie said, giving him a glowing smile. "We've set up a hundred stretchers and can nurse any soldiers who are wounded. Oh, hello, I'm Sadie," she said, extending her hand.

"Brecken," he said, shaking.

"This is the man I was telling you about, Sadie," Arderin chimed, approaching. Drawing him into a hug, she whispered, "I'm so worried."

"I know," Brecken said, squeezing her back. "I have faith in her, Arderin. I know she's going to be okay."

Arderin smiled before turning to give Jack a hug. "Me too. With you two on our side, how can we fail?"

"Hello, Jack," Nolan said, trailing over. "And hi, Brecken. Nice to see you outside of our regular army physicals."

"Hey, Nolan," he said with a nod.

"Tatiana gave us an extensive list of the chemicals and herbs she supplied to Bakari over the years," Nolan said, sidling up beside Sadie and placing his arm around her shoulders. "If the Deamon soldiers use chemical warfare or poison-tipped weapons, we'll be ready with antidotes."

"My baby's out there, and I feel helpless, so I'm going to help in every way I can." Arderin said, straightening her spine. "I don't relish the opportunity to kill my own brother, but this has got to end."

After wishes of good fortune all around, Brecken and Jack headed to the field where the troops were assembling.

"There are twenty TECs on this belt," Latimus said, handing the soldiers large leather belts strapped with the tiny weapons. Brecken fastened it over his shoulder so it hung across his torso.

"Is Arderin in the triage tent?" Latimus asked Jack, his expression sour.

"Yes. I know you're worried for her, but she wants to help."

Sighing, he placed his hands on his hips. "I don't love the idea, but I see the merits of having another medic. Miranda and Sathan are at Uteria, but I half-expected her to show up too. We've got some kick-ass female warriors in this family, huh?"

"For sure," Jack said. "Mom's with Miranda and Sathan?"

"Yes," Latimus nodded. "And the kids are there too. They'll all be safe."

The walkie-talkie at Latimus's belt emitted a low beep, and he lifted it to his lips. "Repeat?"

"Rinada and Creigen aren't here," Miranda's voice called over the device. "They were supposed to show up fifteen minutes ago. Should I be worried?"

Latimus's eyebrows drew together. "They didn't answer their phones?"

"No. And we can't find Tordor anywhere either. He usually jogs early in the morning, but I didn't expect he would *this* morning. Shit, now I'm worried. They wouldn't show up at the battle, would they?"

"The council forbade it, but has that ever stopped anyone in our family, Miranda?"

Silence crackled over the devices before she sighed. "Damn it. What can I do?"

"Keep an eye on the rest of our family and keep them safe. You and Sathan must stay far from the battle. If something happens, and goddess forbid we lose, you know where the safehouses are."

"You're not going to lose, Latimus. No fucking way. I'll keep everybody safe and calm. Now, go kick that bastard's ass. I'm ready to rule a kingdom that isn't embroiled in war for once in my damn life, you hear me?"

"Loud and clear. We're taking back our realm. I'll check in after the battle. Stay safe, Miranda."

Placing the walkie back on his belt, Latimus eyed Jack and Brecken. "Ready to kick some ass?"

"Ready," they said in unison.

Pivoting, they joined the battalion and prepared for battle.

Callie's visions throughout the night were filled with cryptic images she didn't understand. Visions of humans mingling with immortals and of purebred Elves sitting at an expansive circular table, discussing topics she couldn't quite discern. It all seemed rather confusing, and when she awoke, Etherya's spell was broken and she regained control of her body. Standing to gaze across the burning lava, she focused on the most intense vision from her reverie.

In the vision, she stood tall and unafraid, approaching Bakari as he held out his hand. He seemed sure of her alliance, although she knew deep within she had chosen the light. Slowly, she slipped her hand into his...and the sky burst into flames. Consumed in a flash of brilliant, blinding light, the entire world faded away.

And that was where the vision ended.

"Well, it's dramatic, at least," she mumbled as the molten rock simmered below.

Inhaling a deep breath, Callie embraced the moment. She was meant to appear on the battlefield today and align with Bakari. She always had been. But she no longer feared the outcome. Her role in the prophecy was embraced by Tatiana, Nuka, and Etherya. How could she be afraid when so many assured her of her destiny?

Straightening her shoulders, she accepted the enhanced blood running through her veins. It would only make her stronger, and although it was dark and murky, it gave her immense power. She knew without a doubt Bakari would perish today, which sent a jolt of sadness through her heart. Even though he'd wrought so much pain across the kingdom, he was still her blood. But he'd made his choices, and he would pay the ultimate price.

Would the rest of the world perish alongside him? Callie hoped not, considering she was only in her mid-twenties and had a lot of life left to live—hopefully with Brecken by her side. In order to make that wish come true, she needed to seize her fate.

Steeling herself, she lifted her face to the rapidly brightening sky and transported to the woods near the battlefield where she knew Rinada and Creigen would be waiting.

***

Brecken stood behind Latimus on the broad field as the immortal battalions loomed behind them. The first shafts of sunlight were now rising over the far-off hills, and a nervous excitement coursed through his frame.

Bakari appeared in the distance, flanked by his entire battalion of Deamon soldiers, and Brecken noted the vastness of the army. They would be formidable, but he was determined not to fail. Bakari marched closer until he was separated from them by approximately forty yards. Holding up his hand, he halted the march. Baal stood behind him, large and menacing, along with Deamon Commander Vadik and the two allies Brecken recognized as Ananda and Dr. Tyson. Ananda appeared nonplussed while the doctor seemed trepidatious, eyes wide behind the glasses he wore and hands clenching in nervous motions in front of his waist.

"Ananda and Dr. Tyson are not warriors, Bakari," Latimus called. "Although they must pay their debt to our kingdom for aligning with you, it is not fair to pit them against our immortal soldiers. Our physicians have set up a triage center to the east." He gestured toward the triage, barely visible from the battlefield. "Let us take them into custody until the battle is over. We will give them a fair trial afterward."

"They are prepared to fight!" Bakari called. "We all believe in the cause. Etherya's kingdom, rebuilt in the image she initially created."

A rustle sounded to Brecken's right, and Tatiana appeared dressed in combat gear and ready for battle. "You did not heed my words, Quaygon," she shouted, her tone angry. "It was unwise not to flee before the battle."

"I'm sorry," Dr. Tyson called, a slight waver in his voice. "I have nowhere to go."

Sighing, she closed her eyes and flicked her hand. Dr. Tyson and Ananda vanished, and Bakari cried out in frustration.

"Where did you transport them?"

"I placed a freezing spell on them and transported them to the infirmary tent." Looking toward Latimus, she asked, "Your sister will understand she needs to bind them and hold them until after the battle?"

Lifting his walkie, Latimus said, "Nolan, did you receive the two prisoners?"

"We've got them," Arderin's voice chimed over the device. "I've already slapped handcuffs on both of them, although they're frozen like a pair of rocks. We'll keep them sequestered until you give us orders."

"Ten-four." Placing the device on his belt, he looked toward Tatiana and gave a nod. Facing Bakari, he yelled, "The sun is now fully risen. It is time, brother."

Bakari held his hands high and exclaimed, "It is time to reclaim my heritage, *brother!*"

Drawing the sword from the sheath on his back, Latimus held it high and yelled, "Charge!"

The immortal troops gave a valiant cry that mingled with the yells of Bakari's army. Draped in the rays of the newly risen sun, the armies surged toward one another, determined to eradicate the other.

Chapter 30

Callie felt the soft ground of the forest beneath her and opened her eyes, searching the surroundings. Gathering her bearings, she looked for Creigen, Rinada and Tordor at the agreed-upon site.

"Whoa," her brother's voice said behind her. "When in the hell did you learn to transport?"

Turning, she smiled. "You probably could too if Bakari injected you with whatever the hell he stuck in my arm."

Tentatively approaching, he gently cupped her arms. "Are you okay? We looked for you everywhere. Dad and Evie even took us near the Purges, but we didn't see you."

"Strange," she said, eyebrows drawing together. "I was there, and Etherya appeared. Maybe she cloaked me in some invisibility shield or something. Guys, I have a lot to tell you."

Rinada rushed her, embracing her in a warm hug before Creigen and Tordor did the same.

"I don't want to be the pragmatic ruler, but there's a huge battle going on out there," Tordor said, pointing through the trees toward the field. "I want to hear everything, Callie, but we need to implement our plan."

"Agreed," she said with a nod. "Tordor, you have the earpieces, right?"

"Uncle Heden sent them by way of Tatiana, who showed up here before you all arrived," he said, handing them all the tiny earbuds. "I get the feeling he thinks it's badass we want to fight. We'll be able to communicate this way, and I'll stay in the forest as we discussed. If I sense any danger, I'll let you guys know."

"And if you need to intervene, we'll inform you," Callie said.

Tordor nodded. "Mom and Dad are at Uteria, which means I'm technically the ruling royal at this battle. Latimus and Kenden are bound by duty to follow any directives I give—well, I think they are, at least. Hopefully, they'll accept you on the field. If not, I'll order them to let you fight."

"Good," Creigen said, placing the headset in his ear. After testing them, Callie, Rinada and Creigen began trailing toward the edge of the forest. Before they entered the clearing, they turned and waved to Tordor.

"May the goddess be with you," Tordor called.

Resolved, the grandchildren of Crimeous stepped onto the battlefield.

Brecken sparred with the Deamon soldiers, preferring to use his sword so he could get close enough to deploy the TECs. Every time he latched the weapon onto one of the creatures' foreheads and disintegrated them to dust, a thrill shot down his spine. Glancing around, he noticed Latimus, Garridan, Siora and the rest of the troops fighting with valor and grit. It was too early to tell if they were winning, but Brecken liked their chances.

A sudden cry erupted at his side, and Brecken turned to see Baal ripping a Slayer soldier nearly in half as the soldier screamed in pain. Dropping the man on the ground, Baal stepped forward, approaching Brecken.

"Get him to the infirmary tent," Brecken called to the soldier nearest the injured Slayer, but he already knew it was too late. Sheathing his sword in the holster on his back, he swung his rifle around and began firing at Baal.

The bullets bounced off the creature's skin as if they were made of rubber, and the metallic taste of fear flooded Brecken's tongue. But he'd felt fear before and knew it meant the stakes were high and he must not fail. Slinging the rifle behind his back as it sat strapped over his shoulder, he reached for the blades fastened to his thighs. Gripping the handles, one in each hand, he drew them, ready to fight the massive creature.

Baal closed the distance, throwing a firm punch with his thick arm that Brecken blocked before slicing his skin with the blade. It healed immediately, and they began dueling in a blade-to-hand combat Brecken knew he must win. His skill with the blades was impressive due to many years of drills and sparring sessions, and he moved with sure strokes as he fought the beast.

Suddenly, Baal lifted his arms high, emitting a roar as a sword appeared in his hands. Brecken understood Bakari had most likely materialized it in the creature's grasp from across the field, and that it was probably poison-tipped, meaning his self-healing body would succumb to its blow. Knowing he only had moments to act, Brecken threw one of his blades to the ground. Thrusting the other into Baal's exposed chest, since the creature's arms were still in descent, he twisted the weapon, opening a large wound above his heart. Grabbing a TEC from his belt, Brecken retracted the blade and shoved the device inside Baal's chest where the open wound bled.

The detonation should've blown him to bits, but Baal puffed his chest, and Brecken watched in awe as his body absorbed the weapon. *Shit.* Realizing he was out of options, Brecken tugged the knife from his boot, ready to fight the creature to the death.

"You cannot beat him, Brecken," Tatiana said, appearing at his side. Lifting her hands, her palms began to glow. "I saw this in one of my visions. It is one of the reasons I aligned with you."

Baal marched forward, knocking Brecken out of the way as he approached Tatiana. She lifted her hands and closed her eyes as she began to chant in a language Brecken had never heard.

"Witch!" Baal cried, lurching toward her before she caught his arm. Her glowing palms must've burned his skin because he began to scream as he slowly lowered to the ground.

"*Dan de lum nan da lokiam...*" Tatiana chanted, and Brecken swore her eyes glowed. "Your soul is not wanted here."

Baal fell onto his back, and she leaned over, placing her hand over his heart. As her chants grew louder, she clenched her teeth before plunging her hand into Baal's chest cavity. Brecken observed, shocked, as she pulled the beating organ from the creature's chest and held it high.

"May the winds of change absorb this darkened soul as the prophecy is fulfilled!" Lifting Baal's bleeding heart, she clenched her fingers together, and the organ disintegrated, scattering across the field as the warriors fought. Rushing to her side, Brecken bent down to assess her.

"Are you okay?" he asked as she heaved deep breaths, hands resting on her knees. "Holy shit, that was badass. You saved my life, Tatiana. Thank you."

Baal's body lay lifeless on the ground as she nodded. "I foresaw his preeminence and had a vision he would kill you if I did not intervene. He was a formidable creature."

A bright light burst onto the field, and Brecken whipped his head toward the commotion. Evie and Darkrip materialized several feet from the main skirmish, ready to combine their powers to defeat Bakari. Lifting their hands, they created a joint energy forcefield and surrounded an entire battalion of Deamon soldiers on the west flank. A loud boom sounded before every soldier inside the energy field was pulverized to dust.

Some of the Deamons nearby saw the destruction and began to run toward the forest. Kenden's troops emerged, fighting them valiantly and pushing them back toward the main fray. Evie and Darkrip generated the forcefield again, expanding it to surround more Deamon soldiers.

"Your powers mean nothing!" Bakari cried, thrusting his hand into the air and emitting a ball of fire from his palm. It crashed into the forcefield, disintegrating it before their eyes.

"Damn it. He's full of potions that are giving him exponential powers," Evie yelled to Darkrip. "We need more energy."

"Here," Tatiana said, transporting to Darkrip's side. "Let me try."

The three of them created a new forcefield that glowed a brighter red as Bakari began chanting one of his spells. With a flick of his wrist, he eradicated the barrier in seconds.

"We're here to help!" Rinada said, approaching Evie and Darkrip with Creigen and Callie by her side.

"Get off the field!" Darkrip yelled. "The council forbade you to fight—"

"We want to help, Dad," Callie said, lifting her arms. "Let us generate the forcefield with you."

"Calinda!" Bakari called, causing Callie to whip her head toward him. "Did you embrace your newfound powers?"

"End this now, Bakari," Callie pleaded, taking several steps toward him as the soldiers surrounding them fought. "We could still try to save you. This doesn't have to be the end. You must surrender."

"Never!"

Determined to help, Brecken grabbed his blades and began running toward the skirmish.

Bakari lifted his face to the sky, dematerializing before reappearing in Brecken's path. "I understand what I need to do to gain your alliance, Calinda."

Brecken stopped short, tossing his weapons to the ground and slinging his rifle from behind his shoulder. "These might not kill you, but they're going to hurt pretty fucking bad, Bakari." Gritting his teeth, he began emptying the magazine of bullets into Bakari.

The powerful foe held up his hand, freezing the bullets as Brecken lost control of his muscles. Locked in place, he stared into Bakari's ice-blue eyes, unable to do anything but watch as he slowly approached.

Bakari drew a strange-looking gun from his belt and discharged a small pellet into Brecken's chest. Gasping at the invasion, Brecken saw Callie appear out of the corner of his eye. She flicked her hand, and he regained control of his muscles. Stepping back, he clutched the area where the pellet now sat, directly above his heart.

"I've injected your soldier with a tranquilizer capsule containing a thousand poisons his self-healing body can't combat, Callie." Lifting a tiny vial from his pocket, he shook it. "This is the only antidote. Align with me, and I will let him live."

Callie rushed to Brecken's side as he crumpled on the ground, struggling to breathe. The tranquilizer pellet pulsed in his chest, and he clutched the skin, trying to force it out although it was impossible.

"Brecken," she said, falling to her knees and running her hands over his face, neck and chest. "I can remove the pellet with my powers."

"Do it, and he dies," Bakari said, shaking his head from several feet away. "I will destroy the antidote now if you wish."

"I know you won't align with him, Callie," Brecken rasped, his voice low so Bakari wouldn't hear. "But maybe he needs to think you will."

Tears glistened in her eyes as she gave him a warbled smile. "How did you know?" she whispered, clenching his hand as it sat over his heart. "That's exactly what I saw in my vision when Etherya approached me last night."

Brecken swallowed, tamping down the pain that pulsed through his body. "Because I love you, Callie-lily." Turning his hand beneath hers, he squeezed her fingers. "Go fulfill the prophecy...and maybe grab the antidote while you're at it."

"It is time, Calinda," Bakari called, a warning in his tone.

"I'll heal you even if he destroys the antidote," she said to Brecken in a rushed whisper. "Long story, but I'm hella powerful now. Can't wait to tell you. I have so many things to tell you, Brecken."

Lifting their joined hands, he kissed her knuckles. "When it's over," he said.

"Yes," she said, covering his lips with her fingers. "We'll say everything when I've destroyed the world." Leaning close, she placed her lips on the shell of his ear. "Destruction isn't a bad thing, according to Etherya. Let's hope she's right."

Rising, Callie faced the field and held up both hands, reaching toward the sky. Clouds rushed in to cover the bright sun, and thunder boomed over the wide meadow. Closing her eyes, she yelled, "Halt!" as bolts of lightning jolted from the rapidly darkening clouds into her outstretched hands, causing her body to emit a yellow glow. The sounds of war immediately ceased, and Bakari seemed stunned.

"Yes, Calinda," he said, extending his hand. "Your grandfather's blood runs so powerfully through your veins. Join me, and I will give you the antidote to save Brecken after we fulfill the prophecy."

She slowly walked toward him as Darkrip yelled for her to stop in the background. Clutching his chest, Brecken observed her, regal and brave as she approached Bakari. Pain sliced through his body, and he clenched his teeth, determined to hold on and watch her prevail.

Dr. Tyson listened to the hurried sounds of the three physicians rushing around the infirmary tents, healing the wounded soldiers as they were brought in. Although his muscles were frozen, his mind worked furiously to find an escape as he sat against the far tent wall, hands bound behind his back. Glancing at Ananda, he noticed her stiff expression, which was generally her *usual* expression, so he couldn't credit it to Tatiana's freezing spell.

"Hey," he whispered, causing her to turn and glare at him. "We have to get out of here."

"I agree, but we seem to have lost our ability to move any muscles below our neck," was her sardonic reply.

"There has to be a way—"

Suddenly, his muscles snapped to attention, and he regained control. Realization entered Ananda's expression, and she shuffled from her sitting position to her feet—difficult since her hands were bound behind her back. Dr. Tyson eventually found his footing as well, and they listened to the sounds outside the tent.

"Callie seems to have frozen everyone on the field except Bakari, including Darkrip, Evie and Tatiana," a deep voice with a British accent said outside the tent, and Dr. Tyson knew it was the human physician the immortals employed. Armed with the new information, Dr. Tyson looked at Ananda.

"If Tatiana is under a freezing spell herself, this must be why our spells were broken. We have to make a run for it."

"Agreed," Ananda said. "I'll run to the east, and you run along the ether toward the western woods. We'll have a better chance if we split up."

Nodding, he courteously tilted his head since his hands were bound. "I wish you luck, Ananda. May you find happiness wherever you go."

"Will you still pursue Bakari's cause if he loses?"

"I no longer believe in the cause," he said, shaking his head. "I wish to live far from danger after being surrounded by it for so long."

"I will always believe in the cause, but I cannot fight it alone," she said through her thin lips. "Good luck, Quaygon."

With one last tilt of the gray bun on her head, she inhaled a deep breath and ran from the tent. Steeling himself, Dr. Tyson sent a prayer to every god he'd ever known and sprinted from the tent. He ran along the wall of ether, feeling as if his lungs might burst, noticing bright flashes of light on the far-off battlefield. Too concerned for his own safety to care, he finally reached the woods, halting beside a large tree in a dense thicket of forest to catch his breath. Leaning over, he almost didn't hear the stick crack behind him. Jolting upright with fear, he turned to find a Slayer soldier.

"Whoa," the man said, holding up a rifle with one hand and showing the palm of his free hand. "You are Bakari's doctor who makes the potions?"

"Yes," Dr. Tyson said, swallowing the lump of terror in his throat. "I no longer believe in Bakari's cause and should've defected before the battle.

If you shoot me, I will bleed for days but most likely heal. I am a Vampyre hybrid."

The soldier's eyebrows lifted under his thick brown hair. "Vampyre-Slayer?"

Studying his deep brown eyes, Dr. Tyson shook his head. "Vampyre-Elf."

The Slayer considered him before slowly dropping his weapon. "What is your name?"

"Dr. Tyson."

"Your *real* name?"

Licking his lips, he softly uttered, "Quaygon."

A huge boom sounded from the battlefield, causing them both to turn their heads before their gazes locked back on each other. The Slayer's piercing eyes bore into his before he expelled a large breath.

"Go, Quaygon, before I change my mind. I don't want to see you anywhere near the immortal kingdom in the future, understood? If I do, it will be your last day in our realm. Are we clear?"

"Crystal," he said with a hurried nod. "Thank you."

"Go on," he said, jerking his head.

Quaygon turned to run, but curiosity won out. Rotating back, he asked, "What is your name?"

"Larkin," the man said, lifting his gun again. "And you have five seconds to run before I use this."

Taking the cue, Quaygon began sprinting through the forest toward the wall of ether that ran along the far side. Although he had nowhere to go in the human world and would certainly be hunted by the Elven council, it was better than death in the immortal world. Thankful for the kind Slayer soldier, he knew he would always remember Larkin, the man who spared his life.

Chapter 31

Callie walked toward Bakari's outstretched hand, veins thrumming with the gravity of the moment. Resolved to fulfill her destiny, she placed her hand in his, their touch emitting a spark as her skin glowed a soft yellow from the magnitude of her newfound power. Stepping closer, she held up her palm.

"Give me the antidote first," she said, her tone unwavering.

"It won't matter once we combine our powers and destroy the immortal army—"

"Give it to me," she interrupted, teeth clenched. "Now."

Bakari handed it to her, and she placed the vial in her back pocket. Staring deep into his ice-blue eyes, she tilted her head and slowly regarded him.

"I'm sorry it's come to this," she whispered, squeezing his hand. "You deserved better when you were born. Your later choices require retribution, but you were dealt a terrible hand. I hope you find peace wherever your soul lands."

"We will destroy the immortal army and rule the kingdom, Callie," Bakari said, although his tone lacked the confidence she'd heard in their previous interactions. "I am willing to rule with you if you pledge your allegiance to me."

Shaking her head, she felt the sting of tears. "May the goddess be with you."

Closing her eyes, she focused on the touch of his hand as she centered every speck of her power deep within her core. Bakari began chanting unintelligible words of an immortal language long since extinct, and she clutched onto the low-toned mantra as feelings of both terror and euphoria coated her skin. Sounds of thunder echoed above from the darkened sky, and the ground began to rumble.

Both armies surrounded them, still frozen by Callie's spell, and she hoped like hell her intuition was correct. If she hurt her parents, or Brecken, or any other immortal on the field, she would never forgive herself. Gripping Bakari's hand, she chanted the words Nuka had given her in the vision.

"May the world begin anew as the prophecy is fulfilled..."

She repeated the phrase over and over, her words mingling with Bakari's. Suddenly, a massive bolt of lightning blazed from the sky, reaching the ground and igniting an explosion. A red cloud of fire burst from the meadow and began to grow, enveloping the soldiers, and then the meadow, and the forest beyond. Fiery red turned to blazing white light, and all were blinded by the magnificence of the glow as one final *boom!* clapped from every possible direction.

The ground shook with the force of a thousand earthquakes, and Callie cried out, losing her grip on Bakari's hand and falling to the ground. Clutching the earth as she balanced on her knees, she struggled to inhale oxygen from the void of light that surrounded her. Lifting her head, she saw Bakari collapse, clutching his throat as he gasped. Callie's ears rang with the high-pitched sound of destruction as the blinding light faded to pitch-black darkness.

Suddenly, the ground ceased its quaking, and she lifted her head to stare into the void. Small shafts of light began to ease through the murkiness, and Callie blinked rapidly, trying to gain her bearings. Coughing, she rose and trailed over to Bakari's body. It lay still atop the ground, and she wondered if he was dead.

Surveying the surrounding meadow, she noticed immortal soldiers scattered about, sitting up and shaking off the freezing spell as they patted their extremities searching for injuries. Callie scanned as far as she could see but didn't see any Deamon soldiers.

"They have been purged," Tatiana said, appearing at her side. "All of them, including Baal and Commander Vadik. Bakari's corporeal form is all that remains." Placing her hand on the small of Callie's back, she urged her forward. "Go. Ease him into the great beyond. His tragic story deserves to end with the niece he's come to revere by his side."

Stepping forward, Callie crouched beside Bakari and took his hand. Lifting it, she held it to her cheek. "I'm so sorry," she whispered as he stared up at her with her mother's eyes. "Even I can't heal you now. Imminent death from the prophecy is too strong even with the new powers you instilled in me."

"Please," he pleaded, coughing as he sputtered the words. "My hate will make me clutch onto this world forever even though I know I've lost." Eyes darting between hers, he whispered, "Please, Calinda."

Inhaling a breath, she nodded before placing her hand over his heart. "I've only ever used my power to draw sickness from others, but I will use it to end your suffering. Close your eyes, Bakari."

Sliding his hand over hers, he cinched them together over his heart, the poignant gesture spurring a lone tear to trail down her cheek. Closing his eyes, he waited for the inevitable. Sucking in a breath, Callie centered her power into her hand, surging it into his body and stopping his heart. His large frame shook as he expelled one last slow breath before relaxing into the ground. A strong wind blew from the east, and she observed his body shrivel and turn to dust before scattering across the battlefield in one final goodbye.

After taking a moment to center herself, Callie stood and searched for Brecken. Jogging toward him, she fell onto her knees beside him.

"I need to extract the capsule," she said, tugging off his layers of weapons and helping him remove his shirt as he struggled to breathe. "If it deploys, I have the antidote and can still probably heal you, but if I extract it, that saves us the trouble. It will probably hurt."

"That's okay," he gritted, heaving labored breaths. "I trust you."

Sitting on the ground and stretching one leg over Brecken's thighs, Callie placed her hand over the entrance wound on his chest. Closing her eyes, she focused her powers, directing them toward her palm against his warm skin. Suddenly, she was flooded with a thousand heartrending images—snapshots from when Brecken had longed for her when he guarded Zadicus, and his shoulders hunched over his desk as he wrote the letters to her. Joy surged deep within, and she smiled.

"Your thoughts are coming through from the energy transfer. I can't control it."

Giving a strangled laugh, he nodded. "That's fine, hon. I think the whole world understands I'm crazy about you. I don't have anything to hide."

Smiling deep into his eyes, she concentrated, surrounding the pellet with her healing energy and slowly drawing it back through the entry wound. Removing her hand from his chest, she opened her palm, showcasing the capsule. Closing her fist, she used her powers to pulverize it before wiping away the dust on the soft grass. Releasing a breath, she drew her knees to her chest and rested her forehead against them.

"Callie is freaking tired," she mumbled into her legs, trembling as the effects of using so much of her power in such a short span began to take its toll.

Sliding behind her, Brecken encircled her with his long legs, and then his arms, burying his face against her nape as he stroked her hair. "I've got you, Callie-lily," he said, cradling her as they slowly rocked back and forth, his front bracketing her back. "I'm never letting you go."

Snuggling against him, she took comfort as she recovered. Finally, she lifted her head, her gaze landing on Tatiana, Evie and Darkrip before scanning the field. "Did I destroy the world?" she asked, staring up at Tatiana.

"You destroyed Bakari and his army. And yes, you destroyed the realm as we know it, and it exists no more," Tatiana said, quoting the prophecy.

Gently disengaging from Brecken, she craned her neck to look across the field. "It doesn't *seem* destroyed...unless this is all some really vivid dream we're sharing."

"Stand, Calinda, and observe the destruction you wrought," she said, pointing toward the ether.

Callie stood, Brecken helping her to her feet as he rose, the gash over his heart almost completely vanished due to his self-healing abilities. Turning, she gazed toward the ether and gasped.

"It's gone," she whispered.

Beyond where the ether used to exist were expansive hills lined with trees and forest as far as the eye could see. Confused, she faced Tatiana.

"Did I destroy the ether?"

"Yes," Tatiana replied, a sparkle in her amber gaze. "You obliterated the ether that separates the immortal and human worlds. It is gone forever and will now only be remembered as a relic of a long-lost realm."

Callie's eyebrows drew together as she struggled to understand.

"Your destiny all along was to destroy the ether, Calinda. Now that you have fulfilled the prophecy, you have *destroyed the realm as we know it, and it exists no more*. Now, you are one realm, coexisting with the human world, and the immortals must chart a new path to create one united kingdom upon the Earth."

"All this time, I thought 'destroying the realm' meant I'd annihilate everyone in our kingdom."

"You've finally caught up," Tatiana said with a tilt of her head. "Prophecies are murky and best not taken literally. When you've lived as long as I, you understand this."

Lifting her hands, Callie said, "I mean, you could've just told me that from the beginning, Tatiana," her tone slightly exasperated. "This prophecy hasn't been a bed of roses, you know."

Breathing a laugh, Tatiana shrugged. "I am sorry, my dear, but everything had to occur as it was meant to be. You will understand this in time. Bakari's journey upon the Earth, from the tragic events of his birth to his conflict with the immortals and his imminent demise, were all imperative to guide you to this very point. We all are products of our own destinies, whether we believe in them or not."

"We'll see about that," Callie muttered before turning to glance across the spot where the ether used to be. "What do we do now? Surely, the humans will investigate the huge hole that has opened up in the side of their world."

"Your first interaction with those on the other side will happen shortly." Taking a step back, she lifted her hands. "I will leave you to deal with those who arrive. The new era of the immortals has begun, and your history henceforward will be entwined with humans as well as other species you don't yet know or understand. Tread carefully but hopefully into the future. I will see you all again soon. Goodbye, my friends." With one last reverential gaze, she closed her eyes and disappeared.

They all stood, stunned, as she vanished under the sky, which was once again sunny and bright. Darkrip rushed toward Callie, drawing her into his arms and clutching her so tight she could barely breathe.

"I'm okay, Dad," she soothed, rubbing his back as he held her, swaying back and forth. "Everything's going to be okay."

Drawing back, he gazed into her eyes, his own brilliant green orbs glassy and filled with emotion. "I'm supposed to say that to you," he whispered, cupping her cheeks. "I was so worried. You're my heart, Callie. You know that, right? You, your mom and your brother make me who I am."

"I know," she said, unable to stop the tears streaming down her cheeks. "I love you so much. I'm sorry about everything."

"I'm sorry too," he said, kissing her forehead. "I was never supposed to be a parent. I'm fucking terrible at it. I just want to keep you from making my mistakes."

"Eh, you're not so bad," she teased, swiping her tears. "And I'm really good at making mistakes, so we're going to have to figure out how to coexist with that knowledge."

"As long as you're safe, I don't care."

"Callie!" Arderin cried, darting across the field and rushing into their shared embrace. Callie squeezed her parents tight, so thankful for them, before Creigen joined the bear hug.

"You're in big trouble for appearing on this field today, young man," Darkrip warned, ruffling Creigen's hair to soften his words. "Are you two *trying* to give your father a heart attack?"

Craning her neck to look at Arderin, Callie asked, "Has he always been this dramatic?"

"Every damn day since I met him," Arderin said, her tone filled with mirth.

Chuckles filtered over the field as the reunions continued, Rinada running into Evie's arms before Latimus and Kenden appeared. The family members embraced, so thankful to be safe and alive, and Callie tugged Tordor into her arms. "Well, I guess we didn't need you after all. Still pretty badass of you to show up. I'm proud of you, Tor."

"I'm in awe of you, Callie," he said, wonder in his expression. "Man, there's a lot to process. I can't believe the ether is eradicated. We have no separation from the human world. The prospects are daunting."

Someone loudly cleared their throat, and heads swiveled to gaze upon the woman who stood several feet away where the ether once resided. Straight blond hair fell in a short style that landed just above her shoulders, and she wore a black jacket with the initials "ITU" and black cargo pants above dark boots.

"Hi," she said, eyebrows arching as she gave a wave. "Sorry to bust up the family reunion, but we need to contain this situation, stat."

Chapter 32

Tordor disengaged from Callie's embrace and slowly approached the woman who now stood in front of where the ether used to reside. "I am Tordor, son of King Sathan and Queen Miranda, and the ranking royal on the field—"

"Yep, you can save the introductions," she said, cutting him off and giving a nod. Lifting a badge that read "ITU," she gave a cheeky, almost sardonic grin. "We've been waiting for Callie to fulfill the prophecy and eradicate the ether so we can implement our plan. Guys!" she yelled before placing her thumb and forefinger in her mouth and emitting a loud whistle. "Roll out the barrier."

A team of twenty soldiers, all dressed in black gear, rushed over the nearby hill and thrust tall rods into the ground, each about ten feet apart. Latimus and Kenden exchanged looks before Latimus jerked his head. "Go round up the troops and prepare them for more combat. I'll stay here until they're in formation."

"Ten-four," Kenden confirmed.

"Whoa, whoa," the blond woman said, placing the badge in her pocket before holding up her hands. "No one needs to prepare any troops. We're here to help."

"Help, how?" Latimus asked.

"Uh, someone's got to put up a temporary barrier to keep your realm shielded until we can approach the human leaders and explain they've got a bunch of immortal creatures joining their world. Did you think you could just hop on over and have brunch at Chili's with the humans while sharing your mango margaritas?"

"What's Chili's?" Rinada asked softly in the background.

"Human restaurant chain," Evie murmured, her arm around her daughter's shoulders. "Not nearly as good as Chipotle—"

"Enough!" Latimus called, swiping his hand through the air. "I want to know right now who you are and what your purpose is in our world."

"Wow, let's lower the temperature," the woman said, features contorting into an exaggerated grimace. "And I hate to break it to you, but it's not *your* world anymore, Latimus, son of Markdor. It's *one* world now—thanks to your magnificently powerful niece—and a proper transition needs to occur."

"I want answers now!"

"That's enough, Uncle Latimus," Tordor said, holding up his hand as Latimus glowered. Turning toward the woman, he extended his hand. "Let's start over. I'm Tordor, which you already know. And you are?"

"Nice to finally get a proper greeting," she said, slipping her hand into his and shaking. "Esmerelda, daughter of Dakath. You can call me Esme."

"Nice to meet you, Esme. Forgive me, but I don't know who Dakath is."

"Oh, yes, that would help. He's the king of the Elves, of course. Maybe you didn't see my ears." She pointed to them, noting the slightly tipped edges. "Inherited these from good ol' dad."

"Unfortunately, the history of the Elves was lost to us centuries ago," Tordor said. "My mother and uncle discovered some ancient Elven scrolls, which added to our knowledge, but we are still vastly undereducated about their species."

"You'll find out soon enough, believe me," she said flippantly, arching a brow.

"Uh, I'm not sure how to interpret that."

"We'll get around to interpretations later," she said, waving her hand. "For now, I'm here as the commanding officer of the ITU to erect a makeshift barrier so we can keep the immortals hidden from the humans for a bit longer."

"And your father sent you?"

"Good lord, no," she said, features scrunching. "My father detests me."

"Oh, I'm sorry," Tordor said, slightly taken aback. "I don't understand."

"I'm the unfortunate result of my dad's indiscretion with a human eons ago. It's a nasty little stain on his stance to only support the existence of purebred Elves. But that has nothing to do with the ITU."

"Which stands for?"

"Immortals Transition Unit. We're an underground society comprised of hybrids and humans who never quite fit in with our own kind. We make it our business to understand the history of all our ancestors, their various prophecies, and help ease the way when they are fulfilled."

"And you wish to help us transition our realm to amalgamate with the human world now that the ether is gone?"

"Yes," she said with a nod. "This will allow you to approach the humans on your own terms without them discovering you, which they will do eventually. You were already cutting it close with how much you all travel back and forth to the human world. Nice jaunt in the hotel pool, by the way, guys," she said, craning her neck to wink at Brecken.

Brecken's eyes widened as he searched for Darkrip.

"Don't say a word," Callie muttered, sidling up beside him. "Nothing to see here, guys," she said cheerfully, batting her eyelashes.

Darkrip gave a loud cough, and Callie shot him a good-natured glare.

"I like you guys together," Esme said, pointing between Callie and Brecken. "Way better than Zadicus if you ask me. Now, I'd like to get back to the issue at hand, even though I'm glad you found true love and all that jazz."

"Thank you," Callie said, grinning as she squeezed Brecken's side.

"*Anyway*," Esme continued, "humans have this propensity to declare war, use nuclear weapons and employ all sorts of nefarious methods when they're taken by surprise. Therefore, my team is erecting a temporary barrier where the ether used to be so we can approach the humans on our terms before they blow up Uteria or something." Wrinkling her nose, she said, "That would just be messy, wouldn't it? Are you catching my drift, Tordor, son of King Sathan and Queen Miranda?"

Breathing a laugh, he nodded. "Why don't you just call me Tordor? Or Tor is fine too."

"Tor it is," she said, grinning. "The barrier will take my men a few hours, and then we'd love some food and shelter at one of your fancy royal compounds if you're amenable to that."

"I don't think it's a good idea to let strangers onto our royal compounds," Latimus said.

Tordor contemplated Esme. "You must understand our concerns. We've had no time to vet you."

"I know," she said, lifting a jump drive from her pocket. "Which is why I sent an identical drive to this one to your Uncle Heden by special messenger. It should've been delivered at sunrise in Italy, and he's most likely scrutinizing it now. It has all the information he'll need to vet us, and I also sent a sample of my blood in the package so he can analyze it. It will show my immortal Elven lineage as well as my human DNA. You can have this one and study it to your heart's content."

Turning toward Latimus, Tordor asked, "What do you think?"

A muscled clenched in Latimus's jaw as he contemplated. "I'd be open to sheltering Esme and her team if Heden says it's safe. Kenden?"

"I agree," Kenden said.

"Great," Esme said, flashing a smile and depositing the jump drive in Tordor's hand. "In the meantime, I'm going to help the team erect the barrier. Nice to meet you all. Hope you're ready to charm some humans while evading my father's council of Elves intent on eradicating hybrids. Fun times all around, hey?" With a jaunty wave, she pivoted and headed toward her team.

"Wow," Callie said, staring wide-eyed at her family. "Talk about surreal."

"You're not kidding," Kenden said before approaching Latimus. "We need to regroup with the troops, assess the injured soldiers, and have a final meeting before we send everyone home for some much needed rest."

"Agreed. Let's get to it."

"I want to talk to you, but I need a huge nap first," Callie whispered to Brecken as he held her against his side.

"You can crash at my cabin if you want," he said, gently rubbing her back. "I'm going to help Jack and Latimus, and then I'll head home."

"Perfect." Facing her family, she said, "Guys, I'm going to crash at Brecken's cabin, but I promise I'll come home tomorrow after he and I have had a chance to talk. I can't wait to tell you everything."

"Sounds great, baby," Arderin said, sandwiched in between Darkrip and Creigen, her dad slightly scowling as her brother smiled. "And I'm dying to hear the story about the pool—"

"No stories about the pool," Darkrip interrupted. "Do you hear me, young lady?"

Callie playfully rolled her eyes. "Fine, Dad. I'll just tell Mom."

Darkrip muttered an annoyed, "*Bollocks*," before the family said their goodbyes. Tordor decided to remain behind and help Esme and her team, and Larkin offered to join him so he could ensure his safety. As Latimus and Kenden prepared to address the troops, Brecken turned to Callie.

"Be safe, hon. I just got you back and am terrified to let you go."

"I will be," she said, giving him a wistful smile. "I'm going to transport home, grab some clothes and then shower at your place. I'll probably be asleep when you get home," she said, placing her hands under her cheeks to mimic sleeping. "I'm freaking exhausted."

"I can't believe you can transport," he said, wonder etched across his handsome features. "I want to hear everything, Callie."

She lifted to her toes and kissed him softly on the lips. "I have an eternity to tell you everything, and I can't wait, Brecken."

"Neither can I," he whispered back.

After one last sweet kiss, Callie called upon her newfound powers and transported away from the battlefield, thankful to close the chapter of her life consumed by the prophecy, and hopeful for the next phase to begin.

Bakari felt his soul reform in a void of darkness. One moment, he was gone. The next, he was conscious again. Lifting his lids, he tentatively searched his surroundings. A large fountain sat to his right, streaming long trails of water from the mouth of the statue that sat in the center. The trickling sound of the water hitting the stone was soothing, and he rose, although his body didn't feel quite solid.

"My son," a female voice whispered, and Bakari turned toward the sound. Several feet away stood a tall woman with long, curly dark hair that resembled Arderin and Callie's. Behind her stood a hulking Vampyre who looked very much like King Sathan.

"Mother?" Bakari called, his voice cracking as he stood frozen.

"Bakari," she said, seeming to float toward him across the ground that wasn't quite solid. Gently cupping his cheeks, she shook her head as tears swam in her ice-blue eyes. "How could you think I didn't want you?"

Swallowing the emotion that clogged his throat, he worked his jaw, trying to form words. "You let them take me," he rasped, angry and heartbroken all at once.

"I did not know, son," she said, running her thumbs over his face. "If I had known, I would've searched the ends of Etherya's Earth for you. Don't you understand?"

"You and Father were so powerful. Surely, you came to know of my existence at some point."

"We were slain only years after you were born, Bakari," Markdor said, approaching and gently cupping his arm. "Calla and I might have learned of your existence if we'd survived, but sadly, we did not have the chance."

"It's my fault," Slayer King Valktor said behind them, floating over to glance at Bakari with his deep green gaze. "I slayed them in an effort to save Rina, and now, my daughter is as lost to me as you were to Markdor and Calla. Our souls now reside here in the Passage as we watch over our remaining children, hoping they will correct our mistakes."

"We have forgiven you, Valktor," Calla said with a reverent nod. "And we are happy to see our kingdoms united through our children."

"But the kingdoms were meant to be separate," Bakari said, confused. "The species were never meant to procreate and form hybrids. It goes against everything Etherya originally fashioned."

"It is true that I created the species to remain separate but equal," the goddess said, floating over to address them, her long, blood-red hair stark against her white robes. "But the Universe ultimately controls all. It was a hard lesson to learn for one as powerful as me."

Regarding them, Bakari contemplated. "What was my purpose, then? I do not understand."

"It was always your destiny to be taken to the human world, discover your past, and embrace your hatred of the immortals who you believe cast you out. The Universe did not like having a hidden realm on my Earth, and now it is hidden no more. Your conflict with my species resulted in Callie destroying the ether, and the realm is now reborn anew."

As he digested the information, Bakari's skin began to tingle, and he rubbed his arm, although it felt odd in the ethereal form his body now inhabited. "I feel strange," he said as the tingles began to grow into slight points of pain, flickering over his entire body.

"You will be transported to the Land of Lost Souls now, Bakari," Calla said, her tone sad. "You have hurt too many to remain here."

Gazing at the ground, he nodded. "I knew if I lost, that would be the inevitable outcome. I was determined not to fail but will accept my fate."

"That is very brave, son of Markdor," Etherya said. "And since you were denied your birthright, I have an offer for you."

Bakari tilted his head, indicating she should continue.

"Our beloved Rina requested an audience with Darkrip centuries ago. The Universe would only allow me to grant the request if I exacted something of great value from her. She was adamant and valiantly chose to visit her son in exchange for spending eternity in the Land of Lost Souls."

"A courageous choice indeed," Bakari said.

"Yes," Etherya said, clasping her airy hands as she floated above the ground. "You will be relegated to the Land of Lost Souls instead of with us here in the Passage due to your actions upon the Earth. However, I have made a deal with the Universe that will hopefully ensure your redemption and help Rina."

"What must I do?" Bakari asked.

"Rina's mind and spirit were broken by Crimeous. She suffers greatly in the Land of Lost Souls and has fallen into a pit of darkness she cannot escape from. If you can locate her and pull her from the darkness, I will consider it an act of salvation and bring you both to the Passage, along with Marsias, who suffers there with her."

"I have taught myself to hate the Slayer and Vampyre royals for so long," he murmured, "and now, you want me to save one of them."

"That I do," Etherya said, her thin lips forming the barest hint of a smile. "And I believe you will choose to take up the mantle."

"Please, son," Calla pleaded. "Our time with you was stolen, and I would like to rectify that. I hope you will accept Etherya's mission."

Bakari stared at his parents, their expressions so genuine, and felt the tug of longing he'd suppressed so many centuries ago. Letting it reemerge, he inwardly clutched it, admitting he would like to at least try to save his soul. Straightening, he said in a clear voice, "I accept your mission, Etherya. I will do my best."

"Very well," the goddess said as his skin began to burn with the heat of a thousand suns. Closing his eyes to ward off the pain, he clenched his teeth as the visions before him began to fade. "Go now, into the Land of Lost Souls, and remember to seize the vestiges of goodness that always lingered in your heart. Your fondness for Calinda and Tatiana and your desire to know your parents. May you one day be reunited in the Passage."

"Goodbye, son," Calla's voice warbled as he fell deeper into the void. "We can't wait to see you when you return."

"Goodbye, Mother," he called, extending his hands toward the light before it dimmed into a point of nothingness. Succumbing to the void, Bakari accepted his fate as the vestiges of his spirit hurtled through space and time before entering the Land of Lost Souls.

Chapter 33

Brecken returned home just as the sun set behind the far-off hills. It had taken some time to wrangle up the troops, assure everything was in order, and send them home. Latimus and Kenden directed them to take a two-week break to spend time with their loved ones before returning to duty. The army would need to be refashioned to comport with the new circumstances of not actively being involved in conflict but living in a world that was no longer separated from humans by the ether. There would be time to reconfigure, but for now, everyone deserved a respite to rest and recharge.

Brecken cut the engine on the four-wheeler Jack had lent him and quietly entered his cottage in case Callie was sleeping. Sure enough, she lay in the center of his large bed, black curls spread across the pillow as she slept peacefully. Carefully approaching, he gently ran a finger over her cheek, overcome with the sight of her in his bed. It was as if she belonged there, and his heart swelled. She smacked her lips and muttered something unintelligible, causing him to snicker, before he left her to shower and wash away the grime from the long day.

After showering, exhaustion slammed into his bones, and he flipped off the beside lamp she'd thoughtfully left on for him. Sliding under the soft sheets, he drew her close, spooning her as she instinctively nuzzled into his body.

"Brecken," she murmured, wriggling her butt into his rapidly growing erection. Although he was beat, it was impossible to tamp down his body's response to her silken skin.

"You're naked," he murmured into her neck, sliding his arm between her breasts and drawing her close.

"Mm-hmm. I'm still so sleepy, but you can try to bang me if you want."

Chuckling, he kissed her nape. "I'm beat too, hon. We'll bang tomorrow. I liked coming home to you naked in bed though."

"I like it too," she whispered.

Inhaling her scent, he snuggled into her. "Good. We'll talk in the morning, okay?"

"Okay. Brecken?"

"Hmm..."

"I love you. I'm sorry I didn't say it back before. That was really dumb of me. I hope you can put up with someone like me who sucks at love."

Closing his eyes, Brecken relished the words. "You don't suck, honey. We're still figuring this out, that's all."

"Night," she said, yawning before nestling deeper into his body.

"Night," he whispered. "I love you so much, Callie-lily."

His thumb gently caressed the skin below her neck as he slipped into slumber, so thankful she was safe. Vowing to hold her like this every night for eternity, he succumbed to his dreams.

∞

Callie awoke to the sound of bacon sizzling and inhaled the mouthwatering aroma. Glancing over toward the tiny kitchen, she observed Brecken standing over the stove, shirtless in gray sweatpants as he scrambled eggs with a spatula.

"*Ohmygod*, that smells good," she groaned, sitting up and pushing her hair out of her face.

Gazing over his shoulder, he grinned, and Callie's heart flip-flopped in her chest. The sight of him broad-shouldered and cooking breakfast for her was pretty much a wet dream come true. "I figured you'd be starving. I have some Slayer blood in the fridge too."

"Starving because I destroyed the world yesterday?" she teased, sliding out of bed and approaching to peer over his shoulder. "Look at my Vampyre lover cooking breakfast. It's so sweet."

After kissing her forehead, his eyes roved over her frame, filled with desire. Leaning down, he rested his lips against her ear. "I think you should put on some clothes before I abandon cooking completely."

Giggling, she nodded and trailed to the bag she'd packed. "I'm only getting dressed because I'm *starving*," she said, pulling on sweatpants before donning a tank top. "After we eat, we're totally going to have awesome, sweaty sex."

"You don't have to ask me twice," he chuckled, scooping the eggs and bacon onto a plate.

Grinning, she fell into one of the chairs by his small fireplace. He brought the plate over, and she thanked him before digging in. After pouring two decanters of Slayer blood, he trailed over and sat in the seat across from her.

"So," he said after taking a sip, "tell me everything."

Between bites, she explained the strange events that occurred. Brecken listened with rapt attention, entranced by her story. When she was finished, she sat back and took a sip of Slayer blood.

"So, there you have it," she said, lifting her shoulders. "I can still feel the enhancement of Crimeous's blood, but it's slight, like a light pulsing or something. It's hard to explain, but it's just *there*, and it's a part of me I'm not sure will ever truly diminish."

"Do you feel any urgings from it?"

"No," she said, narrowing her eyes. "It just feels like a part of me I never knew is now awake, if that makes any sense. In a way, I feel more whole. Maybe this will make me finally embrace who I really am—who I've been afraid to be sometimes with others."

"I hope so, because you're magnificent, Callie."

Reveling in his words, she stood. "Okay, let's do this right." Walking to the kitchen, she deposited her plate and cup in the sink. Brecken followed her and did the same before she took his hand and dragged him outside to stand on the soft grass.

"Wow, you look ready for some big revelations," he teased, tugging one of her curls.

"I'm so ready," she said, unable to control her wide grin.

"Me too, honey."

Inhaling deeply, she straightened her shoulders. "I know this is still new and that we need to grow into our relationship, but my feelings for you are so pure, Brecken. I assure you, this is not a rebound for me, and I know exactly what I'm asking of you. I love you, and I want to build something with you."

"I love you too," he said softly. "I fell in love with you all those months ago when I started writing the letters and convinced myself I could never have you." Closing the distance between them, he gently rubbed her arms. "And now, you're here, and I'm almost afraid to believe this is happening."

"Oh, it's happening, soldier," she said, waggling her brows. "And I don't care if you have two lira to your name. You're a good man who writes me beautiful letters and supports me in every way possible. You love your mother and sisters to distraction, which embodies such loyalty. I hope I can learn to make you half as happy as you make me, Brecken. I really want to make this work."

"Then we'll learn together," he said, slipping his hand into hers and twining their fingers. "I'm certainly no relationship expert, but I like our chances, Callie. I realized a while ago you're the only woman I'm ever going to love."

Sighing at the romantic words, she squeezed his hand. "I would love it if you would agree to take a *few* days off to travel with me sometimes," she said, lifting a finger, "and the cabin is perfect, but my Uncle Kenden loves building things. I know he would help us add on a few rooms, and it never hurts to have extra space."

Brecken glanced at the cottage, squinting as he contemplated. "I'm pretty handy and could help him. It would lower the cost significantly."

"If you don't mind doing some manual labor, I'll get Kenden to help, and maybe my dad will help too. He's not very handy, but he'll never be able to resist the one-on-one time with you so he can size you up. I'll pay for the materials as my contribution. That's the least I can do in exchange for you allowing me to move in."

His eyebrow arched as he gave her that signature smirk, almost causing her knees to buckle. Clenching her thighs together, she awaited his answer.

"Are you asking to move in with me? That's a big step."

"Um, yeah, what do you think we're doing here?" She waved her hand in front of his face. "You're stuck with me now, Shakespeare."

Chuckling, he gnawed his inner lip as he considered. "I don't like the thought of taking your money."

"*Our* money," she said, squeezing his fingers. "That's how this partner thing works, Brecken. I need you to accept that."

He smoothed a hand over her hair. "I'll try, but I want to provide for you, hon. I want to make you proud. You deserve things I'll probably never be able to give you, and I hate that."

"Give me kisses," she said, rising to her toes and pecking him on the lips. "And make me breakfast and write me love letters. That's all I need."

Breathing a laugh, he nodded. "I can do that."

"Honestly, you're getting a handful here," she said, lifting a shoulder. "If we go full steam ahead with this and eventually bond, you need to understand that having kids with me won't be easy. I have no idea what powers they'll inherit. It's a huge risk for you when you could be with someone normal."

"You're normal," he murmured.

Giving him a sardonic look, she asked, "Were you on the same battlefield as me yesterday? I'm definitely not normal, Brecken."

"Well, you're pretty perfect to me."

Grinning, she stared deep into his bronze orbs. "I'm not, but I'm so happy you see me that way. I'm happy you see me for who I am. I've never had to hold any pretenses with you. You'll never know how much that means to me."

"Well," he said, inching closer and resting his forehead against hers. "I guess we should make it formal then." Resting his palms on her cheeks, he caressed the smooth skin with his thumbs. "Calinda, daughter of Darkrip and Arderin, will you move in with me?"

"Finally! How many times does a girl have to invite herself to move in before her man gets the hint? Of course I will."

Chuckling at her teasing, he slid his arm around her waist and devoured her lips. Callie encircled his neck, squeezing him tight as her tongue roved over his, her body inflamed with love and desire as he moaned into her mouth.

"Brecken..." she moaned, sliding her leg around his thigh, entwining their bodies as he devoured her mouth. "I need you—"

The words were cut off as he gripped the mounds of her butt, lifting her as she squealed. Instinctively wrapping her legs around his waist, she held on tight as he carried them up the stairs, his lips continuing to steal kisses from hers as he shut the door behind them. Trailing across the room, he bypassed the bed and set her on the counter. Thrusting his fingers into her thick curls, he drew her head back and began kissing a path down her neck.

"I want to drink from you while I fuck you, Callie," he breathed in her ear, undulating his hips into hers as she writhed on the counter. "I'm dying to taste you, honey. But if you want me to wait, I will. It's a big step for both of us."

"Oh, god, yes...and I want to drink from you too."

Reaching for the waistband of her sweatpants, she struggled to remove them. Growling with lust, Brecken drew back, tugging them off her legs before shucking his own pants and returning to the spot between her legs. Gripping the base of his shaft, he ran the smooth head over her wet folds.

"Damn it, I should give you some foreplay, hon—"

"Screw foreplay," she groaned, gripping his hips. "Get inside me *now*."

Emitting a strangled laugh, he slid his hand to cup her thigh. "Wrap those pretty legs around me and hold on tight."

Callie complied, opening herself to him as she clung to his broad body. Gliding his fingers into her hair, he fisted the silken tresses as he surged into her slick channel. She groaned, staring deep into his gorgeous eyes as he claimed her.

"*You feel so good*," he growled, undulating back and forth as he fucked her in a maddening rhythm that was too fast and too slow all at once. "There's that sweet, tight little spot no one else will ever touch. It's mine, Callie."

"Only yours," she whispered, spearing her nails into his shoulders, causing him to groan.

"Oh, *god*, that feels amazing," he rasped, increasing the pace of his hips. "Do you how beautiful you are when we make love? Your lips get so full and red." He traced them with his finger before dipping it inside her mouth. She sucked the tip, elated when he moaned in ecstasy. "Goddess, you're so sexy."

Throwing her head back, she opened her body, wanting to feel every inch as he slammed inside her. Need curled deep in her gut as she imagined drinking from him as he claimed her.

"It will probably hurt if I bite you," she rasped, lifting her head to stare into his hooded eyes. "I only have half-fangs, so they're not as sharp as yours."

"I don't care," he gritted, palming her ass and lifting her to walk the small distance to the bed. Tossing her on top of the covers, she giggled as he crawled over her body.

"I like this rough side of you, soldier," she said in a sultry voice as he slid his hand behind her knee, lifting her leg high. Looming over her, he aligned the head of his cock with her opening and surged into her again. "Remember, I've got some enhanced blood now. It might make me even better in bed."

"You're already amazing," he whispered, drawing her into a deep, thorough kiss as his hips undulated into hers. "You ready?" he asked, breaking the kiss to stare into her eyes.

"Yes," she whispered, clutching her hands behind his neck. The smile he gave her was so adoring, his fangs white against his full lips, before he trailed a row of kisses across her jaw and over the pulsing vein at her neck. His tongue darted out to lick the soft skin, his self-healing saliva preparing it for his invasion. When the tips of his fangs scraped her, she closed her eyes in anticipation, overwhelmed with the sensation. Brecken's fingers clenched her hair, and he pierced the skin, groaning as he impaled her and began imbibing her essence.

Callie gasped at the immeasurable pleasure of having her lover inside her, both at her core and at the sensitive skin of her nape. Burying her face in his neck, she licked him, tasting his musky essence before aligning her fangs with the rapidly pulsing vein. Spearing her nails into the skin of his upper back, she thrust her fangs into his neck, joy flooding every part of her soul as his essence surged against her tongue. Pressing her lips to his sweaty skin, she drank, rocking her body against his as he loved her.

His thick cock pulsed inside her quivering core, the blunt head stimulating the tiny spot deep within that held a thousand nerve endings, and her body inflamed with the desire. Brecken's small groans vibrated through her as he drank, and she wrapped her legs around his waist, wanting to pull him inside and never let go.

"Come with me," he gritted against her neck, his hips now furiously hammering into her as beads of sweat dripped from his body, mingling with hers. "I'm so close..."

Callie surged against him, pushing the pleasure-filled spot against his shaft, causing stars to explode behind her eyelids as she crashed into a dizzying orgasm. Clutching him for dear life, she rode the wave, imbibing the metallic taste of his blood until she broke the connection, throwing her head back on the bed as his body rammed into hers.

Dragging his fangs from her neck, he pressed his face into the drenched skin, rasping her name as his body devolved into a quivering mass of jerks and spasms. Joy-filled laughter exited her throat as he shuddered against her, expelling jets of sticky release inside her deepest place. Feeling more connected to him than ever before, she welcomed the invasion, already anticipating the eternity they would spend loving each other so intimately.

Ragged breaths exited his lungs as he slowly relaxed above her, his shaft still deep inside her body as it pulsed the last bursts into her tight channel. Running her nails over the wet skin of his back, she reveled in the small tremors that still shook his frame.

"Am I crushing you?" he mumbled into her neck.

"Yeah, but I can take it."

"Tough cookie," he said, extending his tongue to lick the wounds at her neck, his self-healing saliva aiding in the healing. Callie licked his punctures, sending him into a new round of shivers.

"Goddess, that was...I don't even know how to describe it."

Chuckling, she trailed her fingers over his back. "Was it everything you'd hoped for? I know you were waiting for the right person."

Slowly lifting his head, he stared into her eyes as he gave her a slow, poignant kiss. "I was waiting for *you*."

"Brecken," she whispered, sliding her fingers over his jaw as a single tear slipped from the corner of her eye. "Thank you for loving me. I was so sure I was broken, but you never saw me that way. I'm so grateful for you."

"Loving you is the easiest thing I've ever done, Callie-lily." Resting his lips on her cheek, he sipped away the tear. "I can't wait to build our life together."

Tightening her arms around his neck, she grinned. "Once we recover, we need to go over so I can formally introduce you to my family."

Puffing out a breath, he nodded. "Your dad didn't murder me when we searched for you, so I'm seeing that as a positive."

Laughing, she shook her head, her curls bobbing against the comforter. "I'll remind him to chill and tell him to be on his best behavior. But let's lie here a little while longer. I like having you inside me, all sweaty and hot."

"I love it too, hon." Relaxing against her, he trailed soft kisses across her temple as their bodies cooled upon the bed. Free from the shackles of the prophecy and ready to exclaim her love for Brecken to the world, she held him close as their hearts beat together in one rhythm, steady and connected.

Chapter 34

Two weeks later

Miranda stood beside her husband, hating that she was suddenly an emotional wreck. Throwing her arms around her son's neck, she squeezed, causing him to laugh.

"I'll be fine, Mom," Tordor said, drawing back and smoothing her hair from her face. "I'm thrilled to join Esme's team and feel like I'm a perfect fit to represent the immortal realm as we approach the humans. I've never wanted to rule, and you two are so good at it anyway. I love diplomacy and am dedicated to ensuring a smooth transition between our worlds."

"I know," she said, swiping her nose with her arm as Sathan edged up behind her. Encircling her waist, he rested his chin on her shoulder to smile at their son. "I'm just going to miss you," she continued. "You're my baby no matter how old you are. I love you so much."

"I love you," he said, kissing her before grasping them both in one last bear hug. "I'll report back as often as I can. We'll be doing some reconnaissance, so I'll be off the grid for weeks at a time. If you don't hear from me consistently, I don't want you to worry."

"Just stay safe, son," Sathan said, his deep baritone vibrating in her ear. "We'll keep the kingdom secure for when you're ready to return."

"The kingdom is yours, guys," he said, backing toward the invisible wall Esme's team had erected the day of the battle. "It always has been. But keep our family safe, okay? I'll see you guys soon."

"Bye, super-awesome immortals," Esme called, waving as Tordor approached her in front of the wall. "Thanks for your hospitality. The team thinks you're rad."

"Bye, Esme," Miranda called. "Take care of him."

"He's a foot taller than me and has self-healing properties, but sure, whatever you say!"

Pulling a small device from her pocket, she depressed the button, opening a section of the wall. They stepped through, following the rest of her team who'd departed minutes before, and the barrier closed behind them.

Blowing a breath through her lips, it fanned the hair at Miranda's forehead as Sathan held her tight. "What if something happens to him?"

"He's resilient, little Slayer," he said, kissing her temple. "And he seems happy to have found a purpose. It's what we always wanted for him."

"Yeah," she warbled, feeling the tears form again. "But I already miss him."

Gently placing his fingers over her jaw, he tilted her head to look into her eyes. "He'll always be our son, but he's a man now, Miranda. A virtuous man who's ready to make a life for himself. We did a good job, and we must have faith in him."

"We did do a good job, didn't we?"

Chuckling, he nodded. "We sure did. And I'll save you from making some flippant comment about my inflated ego by saying I'll give you most of the credit."

She pursed her lips. "Like, eighty percent, right?"

Squinting, he contemplated. "Sixty-five."

"Whatever, blood-sucker," she teased, rolling her eyes.

Gently rocking together, they searched each other's gazes, so in tune after several decades together. Finally, he said, "It's time, Miranda."

Nodding, she slowly turned and slid her arms around his neck. "I'm ready, but it has to be a girl this time."

Arching a brow, he grinned, flashing his fangs. "And if we have a boy, what will you do then? I think we'll have to keep him."

Wrinkling her nose, she said, "Leave the jokes to me, mister. You're terrible at them."

"Arderin says I've gotten funnier in my old age." His lips formed a slight pout.

"Arderin loves you and is a very nice younger sister."

"Fine. I'll leave the jokes to Heden...and to you," he finished when she opened her mouth to argue.

Smiling, she lifted to her toes and kissed him as the gentle breeze surrounded them. "I think it's settled then. Put another baby in my belly, Vampyre. I'm ready."

"That is the least sexy thing you've ever said to me, and yet I still want you. How strange."

Throwing her head back, she broke into a joyous laugh. "I take it back. You are pretty funny. Come on—let's go home. We've got a lot of sexy shenanigans to accomplish."

Straightening, he took her hand and led her to the four-wheeler. "I can't wait, little Slayer," he said, revving the engine after he sat behind the wheel.

Miranda smiled from the passenger side and slid her hand over his thigh, the need to touch him as voracious as the day they met even after all this time. Lifting her face to the sky, she inhaled the fresh air, hair whipping in the wind as her husband drove them home.

Epilogue

Several months later

Callie watered the plants that hung next to the swing Brecken had installed for her. He'd recently renovated and expanded the home with the help of Kenden and Darkrip, although her father had griped about how terrible he was at performing the work. He certainly wasn't a master home-builder, but Callie appreciated his efforts. It allowed him to spend time with Brecken, and Callie was pretty sure they were becoming friends, which warmed her heart.

"Dad acts grumpy, but he likes our handsome soldier, doesn't he, Bertha?"

The plant's leaves blew in the breeze, and Callie took that as a "yes."

"And how are you today, Laverne?" She watered the fern as she spoke. "Oh, things are lovely here, thank you for asking. Mom called me with an update on Tordor and Esme's efforts in the human world today. Tor is doing a great job keeping the peace, but what I really wanted to know was if he's banged Esme yet." Leaning down, she whispered, "I saw how he looked at her before they left for the human world. I'm obviously no love expert, but mark my words, he wants to bone her." Snickering, she continued watering Laverne until her gaze lifted to the horizon.

Brecken appeared in the distance, walking across the meadow after a day spent helping with new recruits at Lynia's training base. Overcome with the sight of his broad shoulders and muscular body, Callie grinned and waved.

Approaching the cottage, he marched up the wooden steps and tilted his head. "Did I see your lips moving?" he asked, arching a brow. "Are you talking to the plants again?"

"Yes," she said, sticking out her tongue. "Bertha has been thriving since we started having our little talks, and Laverne's leaves are so much greener," she said, pointing to the plants. "Make fun of me all you want, but they love it."

Chuckling, he drew her close and planted a sweet kiss on her lips. "I think it's cute. I fell half in love with you when you took pity on the flower in Zadicus's garden. You tried to convince him to let it live with its friends. Remember?"

"Yep. You weren't supposed to be spying on us."

"Couldn't help it. You're too pretty."

"Aw," she said, setting down the canister and sliding her arms around his neck. "Okay, you're forgiven for teasing me about talking to Bertha and Laverne." Her eyebrows drew together. "I thought you'd be home earlier. Did the training run late?"

"No. I had an errand to do on the way home."

"Oh? Do tell."

Stepping back, he took her hand. "Come on."

Curious, Callie followed him toward the soft grass in front of the cottage. He drew them to a halt and faced her, his features so handsome under the late-afternoon sun.

"I'm in suspense here," she said, eyes widening.

Clearing his throat, she noticed his Adam's apple bob. "I stopped by Takelia to speak to your dad."

Callie's heart slammed in her chest. "You did?" she asked softly.

"Yes." Reaching into the pocket of his black pants, he pulled out a velvet box and lowered to one knee.

Emitting a sob, Callie covered her lips with her fingers. "*Ohmygod.*"

His teeth flashed, fangs resting atop his lips as he gave her a brilliant smile. "Your dad gave his blessing, thank the goddess." Opening the box, Callie gazed at the ring—a small diamond encircled by tiny blue-green stones in a silver band.

"My amazing Callie-lily," he said, love shining in his deep brown eyes. "It's not the biggest ring in the world, but I designed it myself, and it was fashioned with love. I even had Antonio help me when I was sketching it out. I wanted it to be beautiful for you."

"It's gorgeous," she whispered.

"Opals on the edges—blue and green like your eyes. And a diamond in the center to signify my love for you. It's pure and rare like this diamond, and I'm so lucky to have found it with you. I want to take every breath on this earth knowing you're my wife, Callie. Please say you'll bond with me."

Falling to her knees, she rained jubilant kisses over his face as he laughed. "I think that's a 'yes'?"

"Yes!" she cried, throwing her arms around him. "This is so romantic! Did you write me another letter too?"

"Maybe," he said, squinting one eye. "I'd like to read it to you after I shower...and once we're both naked."

"Ohhhhh," she said, waggling her brows. "I love that idea."

Taking her hand, he slid the ring on her finger, and Callie wiggled it under the rays of the sun. "It's perfect. Thank you, Brecken." Palming his cheeks, she pressed her lips to his. "And thank you for talking to Dad. You're brave."

Placing the box back in his pocket, he encircled her and lifted them both as she gave a yelp. Wrapping her legs around his waist, she clung to him as he began to slowly circle.

"What are you doing?" she asked, laughter bubbling from her throat.

"I'm twirling you, honey." Resting his forehead against hers, he twirled them over the grass as Callie's heart almost shattered from the poignant gesture.

"You hate twirling," she said, nipping his lips.

"Not anymore. I love anything that makes you smile, Callie." Cementing his lips to hers, he drew her into a deep kiss, solidifying their promise to love each other for eternity.

Desire skated through her veins when he finally drew back. Sighing, she stroked the back of his neck, feeling his body harden against hers, magnifying her arousal. "My hero," she called softly.

After one last tender kiss, he carried her up the porch steps as Callie held tight.

"I think your dad kind of likes me now," Brecken said, opening the door and stepping inside. "We've both got the stone-faced stoic thing going on."

"You're a teddy bear inside," she said as he set her on her feet in their newly added bedroom.

"You haven't told anyone besides your mom and Evie about the letters, right?" he asked, tugging off his shirt.

"Nope." She made an "X" over her heart.

Kicking off his shoes, his eyes narrowed as he shrugged off his pants. "I'm pretty sure you're lying to me, honey."

Biting her lip, she tugged off her dress. "I mean, I had to tell Lila, obviously. And Jack because he's, like, my best friend...and also *your* best friend. Oh, and Rinada. She thought it was so sweet."

Naked, he trailed toward her, hooking a finger in her panties. "Anyone else?"

She wrinkled her nose. "Maybe?"

Brecken grabbed the silk covering her mound and ripped it with both hands before tossing it to the floor. Callie's body inflamed as she giggled.

"If I admit to telling more people, will you punish me?"

Bending down, he lifted her in his arms and carried her to the bathroom. "I'm going to punish you all night long. We're going to put this fancy new tub to good use."

"Well, we *are* pretty hot when water is involved. I mean, we lit up that hotel pool."

Tossing back his head, he laughed before setting her down and turning the faucet over the tub. The water began to rush into the white marble before he faced her. "That was just the beginning, hon. Let's christen this sucker."

"I'm so ready. Do you think betrothed sex will be hotter than courting sex?" Lifting her hand, she wiggled her fingers as the ring sparkled.

"I think any sex with you is my ultimate fantasy, honey." Leaning down, he brushed her lips with his. "Now, be a good fiancée and get in the tub."

Biting her lip at the sexy command, Callie shivered with excitement before lowering into the rapidly filling warm water. Gazing at her betrothed, she watched him stroke his hardening length. Mouth watering in anticipation of their sexy times, she sighed.

Approaching, he gave her a sultry grin. "Look at you. I swear, sometimes, I feel like this is still a dream. I promise I'm going to give you everything, Callie-lily."

Extending her arms, she beamed, beckoning him toward her and toward their future together. Happiness washed over her, as encompassing as the warm water heating her skin. The lonely girl who'd written woeful tales in her diary would always be a part of her, but Callie had finally grown into herself—a woman worthy of love who'd shed the cryptic prophecy.

With Brecken by her side, she had no doubt eternity would be far brighter than she'd ever imagined. Callie couldn't wait to create their infinity together, one day at a time, in their small corner of Etherya's Earth.

Before You Go

Want to find out what happened in that bathtub between Callie and Brecken? I wrote a bonus extended epilogue scene exclusively for my newsletter subscribers. Follow this link to sign up, and you'll be able to read it right away: https://BookHip.com/MLFVGTC.

∞

Well, dear readers, thank you for reading Callie and Brecken's story! I hope you enjoyed the first of many books about the next generation of immortals in Etherya's Earth. I love stories where the hero writes the heroine love letters and hope you were as enamored with sexy Brecken and sassy, kindhearted Callie as I was. As you probably expect, *Etherya's Earth, Book 7*, **The Diplomatic Heir**, is about Tordor and Esme, and I assure you, Tordor is definitely going to lose his virginity.

In the meantime, did you enjoy meeting our awesome female warrior Siora in The Cryptic Prophecy? You can read her story in **Garridan's Mate**, *Etherya's Earth #6.5*. She swears she's not interested in love but sexy Vampyre General Garridan is ready to prove her wrong!

As always, thank you from the bottom of my heart for reading my books. The End of Hatred was the first book I ever published almost three years ago, and the characters who inhabit Etherya's Earth will always be so special to me. I'm so very glad they're special to you too, and that so many of you think of them as friends. See you in the next book, and thank you for supporting indie authors!

Acknowledgments

I am eternally thankful for you, dear readers. Thank you for continuing on this journey with me.

As always, thanks to Megan, Bryony and Anthony for being part of my team and for making my books better!

About the Author

Rebecca Hefner grew up in Western NC and now calls the Hudson River of NYC home. In her youth, she would sneak into her mother's bedroom and read the romance novels stashed on the bookshelf, cementing her love of HEAs. A huge Buffy and Star Wars fan, she loves an epic fantasy and a surprise twist (Luke, he IS your father).

Before becoming an author, Rebecca had a successful twelve-year medical device sales career. After launching her own indie publishing company, she is now a full-time author who loves writing strong, complex characters who find their HEAs.

Rebecca can usually be found making dorky and/or embarrassing posts on TikTok and Instagram. Please join her so you can laugh along with her!

ALSO BY REBECCA HEFNER

Etherya's Earth Series
Prequel: The Dawn of Peace
Book 1: The End of Hatred
Book 2: The Elusive Sun
Book 3: The Darkness Within
Book 4: The Reluctant Savior
Book 4.5: Immortal Beginnings
Book 5: The Impassioned Choice
Book 5.5: Two Souls United
Book 6: The Cryptic Prophecy
Book 6.5: Garridan's Mate
Book 7: The Diplomatic Heir
Book 7.5: Sebastian's Fate
Book 8: Coming Soon!

Prevent the Past Trilogy
Book 1: A Paradox of Fates
Book 2: A Destiny Reborn
Book 3: A Timeline Restored

Made in United States
Troutdale, OR
03/28/2025